FORGOTTEN REALMS®

R.A. Salvatore's
WAR OF THE SPIDER QUEEN BOOK V

Annihilation

PHILIP ATHANS

WIZARDS
OF THE COAST®

R. A. SALVATORE'S

War of the Spider Queen Book V: Annihilation

Published by Wizards of the Coast, Inc.

FORGOTTEN REALMS, WIZARDS OF THE COAST, and their respective logos are trademarks of Wizards of the Coast, Inc., in the U.S.A. and other countries.

All Wizards of the Coast characters, character names, and the distinctive likenesses thereof are property of Wizards of the Coast, Inc.

Printed in the U.S.A.

Cover art by Brom
Map by Todd Gamble
First Paperback Printing: August 2005
Original Hardcover Edition: July 2004
Library of Congress Catalog Card Number: 2004116878

9 8 7 6 5 4

ISBN: 978-0-7869-3752-3
620-96703000-001-EN

U.S., CANADA,
ASIA, PACIFIC, & LATIN AMERICA
Wizards of the Coast, Inc.
P.O. Box 707
Renton, WA 98057-0707
+1-800-324-6496

EUROPEAN HEADQUARTERS
Hasbro UK Ltd
Caswell Way
Newport, Gwent NP90YH
Great Britain
+322 467 3360
Please keep this address for your records

Visit our web site at **www.wizards.com**

FORGOTTEN REALMS®

R.A. Salvatore's
WAR OF THE SPIDER QUEEN

BOOK I
Dissolution
RICHARD LEE BYERS

BOOK II
Insurrection
THOMAS M. REID

BOOK III
Condemnation
RICHARD BAKER

BOOK IV
Extinction
LISA SMEDMAN

BOOK V
Annihilation
PHILIP ATHANS

BOOK VI
Resurrection
PAUL S. KEMP

For Deanne

Acknowledgements

The people who made this book and the others in this series possible are: Peter Archer, Mary Kirchoff, Matt Adelsperger, Liz Schuh, Mary-Elizabeth Allen, Rachel Kirkman, Angie Lokotz and her outstanding team, and the workflow masters Marty Durham and Josh Fischer.

Needless to say there would be no Book V without Books I, II, III, IV, and VI so I owe a huge debt of gratitude to the other Spider Queen authors: Richard Lee Byers, Thomas M. Reid, Richard Baker, Lisa Smedman, and Paul S. Kemp. Thanks to Elaine Cunningham for helping us with a particular continuity problem and Ed Greenwood for Creating the World in the first place. Brom, thank you for the cover paintings; masterpieces all. Thanks also to game designers Eric L. Boyd, Bruce R. Cordell, Gwendolyn F.M. Kestrel, and Jeff Quick for lots of fun new Underdark toys.

But most of all I have to thank R.A. Salvatore, who gave so much more than just his name to this series. He gave his limitless creativity, energy, and generosity of spirit in portions larger than any of us had a right to expect. If any of these six books are good at all, it's because of him.

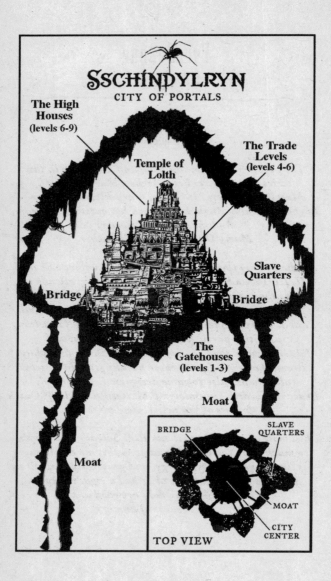

SSCHINDYLRYN
CITY OF PORTALS

The High Houses
(levels 6-9)

Temple of Lolth

The Trade Levels
(levels 4-6)

Slave Quarters

Bridge

Bridge

The Gatehouses
(levels 1-3)

Moat

Moat

BRIDGE

SLAVE QUARTERS

MOAT

CITY CENTER

TOP VIEW

She was the strongest. She had feasted on more than any still alive. She had killed more than any still alive. She had killed all those around her and hadn't even bothered to devour their carcasses before moving on to those outside the zone of the dead.

She was the strongest. She knew she was the strongest as yet another fell before her snapping mandibles. She was the one who would rise through the carnage and rule.

She was the strongest.

The others soon knew this as well.

So she was dead.

Within the chaos, there was intelligence and purpose. Within the hunger and the slaughter, there was common cause. She was the strongest and would kill them all or rule them all, so they bonded together and tore her eight legs from her, devouring her fully before turning again upon each other.

Another rose to prominence through deed and fearsome assault.

That one, too, fell to the common cause.

The mortal test continued. The strongest died, but the smartest remained. The manipulative remained—those who hid their strengths beyond what was necessary to kill the present opponent.

Those who stepped forward, who rose above the tumult, died.

Through all the millennia, she had recognized those who were stronger than she, and she had persuaded them to do her bidding or be killed. Strength came not from the size of her muscles but from the power of her cunning.

In the frenzy of the birthing, in the contest of the slaughter, these traits paved the road to victory.

To find the moment when individual strength was beyond the collective power to defeat it.

To intrigue amidst battle to destroy any who were stronger.

And for some, to admit defeat before oblivion's descent, to escape and survive, new demons of chaos to run wild about the planes and in the end to serve the winner.

The numbers dwindled. Those left grew in power and size.

Each waited and watched, deciding who must die before she could reign supreme, sorting through the tumult to facilitate that desired end.

Those driven by uncontrollable hunger were dead now.

Those driven by simple self-defense were dead now.

Those driven by foolish pride were dead now.

Those driven by instinctual survival were dead or were fleeing.

Those driven by cunning remained, knowing only one could emerge in the end.

For all the others, it would be servitude or oblivion. There were no other choices.

As she had manipulated the mortals who served her and the mortals who feared her, as she had maneuvered even other gods through the centuries, so she controlled her offspring. This was the test of her decree.

There were no other choices.

Gromph found himself growing accustomed to seeing the world through his familiar's eyes. It was that feeling that prompted him to do something about it. Gromph Baenre, brother of the Matron Mother of the First House of the City of Spiders, Archmage of Menzoberranzan, would not look through the eyes of a rat any longer than he had to.

Kyorli's head bobbed from side to side and up and down as she sniffed the air. The rat was bound to look where Gromph willed her to, but she was easily distracted. She didn't see as well in the dark, either, which in the Underdark meant she didn't ever see well, and there were no colors. Gromph perceived the casting chamber, like the rest of the world, in dull hues of gray and black.

Gromph knew the chamber well enough, though, that he didn't need the rat's vision to reveal its limits. The fuzzy blurs at the edge of Kyorli's vision were the great columns that rose to a series of flying buttresses, eighty feet into the gloom overhead. The carvings on the columns were sparse, and what they lacked in beauty they made up for in magical utility. The chamber, deep in the maze of Sorcere, was there for a purpose and not to impress. Spells were cast there in the course of training the students, testing the masters, in researching new spells, straining the limits of their powers, and for the odd summoning or scrying.

Gromph stepped into the center of the room, and from the corner of Kyorli's eyes he saw the two drow waiting for him. They bowed. The rat was sniffing the air, her nose angled up in the direction of the circle of giant mushroom stems that had been secured to the floor in the center of the cavernous chamber. There were ten of them, and to each was bound a single drow male.

"Archmage," one of the two wizards in attendance whispered reverently, his voice hissing off the distant walls in a thousand echoes that Gromph doubted he would have heard if he still had his eyesight.

The archmage willed Kyorli to turn her head to face the wizards, and he was satisfied to see that they were dressed and equipped as he had commanded.

During his time away from Menzoberranzan, thanks to the traitorous lichdrow Dyrr, certain elements within the Academy had revealed themselves. It had taken Gromph less time that he feared but more time than he'd wished to reassert himself at Sorcere. Triel had, to Gromph's surprise, actually done well in maintaining the House's hold over the school of wizards, but still there were traitors to kill and conspirators to bring back into the fold. All that had delayed his efforts to regain his eyesight. No more.

"All is prepared," the whispering mage—his own distant nephew, Prath Baenre—said.

Prath was young, still barely an apprentice, and though Gromph couldn't see the two dark elves' faces since Kyorli insisted on occasionally scratching her own hindquarters with her sharp front teeth, he was sure that the other—a Master of Sorcere named Jaemas Xorlarrin—was looking at the younger drow with impatience. Baenre or no, Sorcere had its hierarchies.

"Master Xorlarrin," Gromph said, making his own feelings on the necessity of that hierarchy clear, "as is obvious, I have some trouble seeing. I will require simple answers to some simple questions. You will stand at my left. The boy will step aside until called."

"As you wish," the Xorlarrin mage replied.

The rat left off her scratching when Gromph snapped his fingers. He watched through the rat's eyes as Kyorli scampered up his leg, to his hand, up his arm, and sat, twitching and sniffing, on the archmage's shoulder. Seeing himself through the rat's eyes unsettled Gromph, and feeling the rat's feet on him—both senses detached from each other—was something the archmage was determined not to experience again.

Gromph stepped toward the bound dark elves, sharply aware of the Xorlarrin mage following close behind him. As they came closer, a shadowy form revealed itself—another drow standing inside the circle of captives. It was Zillak, one of the archmage's most trusted assassins.

"Is the boy prepared with the sigils?" Gromph asked.

He was answered by a faint clang of metal and the sound of scurrying steps that finally slid to a halt.

"Yes, Archmage," Jaemas Xorlarrin replied.

Gromph stepped close to one of the bound dark elves. All ten of them were cousins—the wicked sons of House Agrach Dyrr and traitors to Menzoberranzan every last one. Gromph had asked for the youngest, the strongest, the ablest of them to be spared.

"Dyrr," the archmage said, doing his best to fix his sightless eyes on the captive's face.

The prisoner squirmed a little at the sound of his family's name. Gromph wondered if the boy felt the shame his traitorous House had inflicted on every last one of his kin.

"I . . ." the prisoner muttered. "I know why I'm here, Baenre. You can do your worst to me, and I will not betray my House."

Gromph laughed. It felt good. He hadn't had a good laugh in a long time, and with the siege of Menzoberranzan only digging in, with no word of Lolth or break in her Silence, he didn't think he'd be laughing much in the days, tendays, months, or even years ahead.

"Thank you," the archmage said to the boy. He caught the edge of the captive's confused, surprised expression as Kyorli began again to worry at her itchy hip. "I don't care what you might have to say about your doomed House. You will answer only one question . . . what is that sigil?"

There was a silence Gromph took as confusion.

"The sign," the archmage said, letting impatience sound in his voice. "The sigil my young nephew is holding up in front of you."

As ordered, Prath had taken up a position some yards away, against the wall of the giant chamber, and was holding up a small placard maybe six inches on each side. Painted onto its surface was a simple, easily recognizable rune—one any drow would recognize as marking a way to shelter, a place of safety in the wilds of the Underdark.

"I could compel you to read it, fool," the archmage drawled into the prisoner's hesitation. "Tell me what it is, and let us move on."

"It's . . ." the captive said, squinting. "Is it the symbol of Lolth?"

Gromph sighed and said, "Almost."

The archmage mentally nudged the rat on his shoulder and turned her head to see Zillak wrap a thin wire garrote around the prisoner's neck. When blood began to ooze from under the wire and spittle sprinkled from his mouth, Kyorli paid closer attention. Gromph waited for the prisoner to stop struggling, then die, before he stepped to the next traitor.

"I won't read it!" that one barked, the fear coming off him in waves. "What is this?"

Gromph, aggravated at the waste of time a spell of compulsion would take, tipped his head to the Xorlarrin mage who still stood right behind him and asked, "What color?"

"A garish magenta, Archmage," Jaemas answered.

"Well," Gromph replied, "that won't do at all, will it?"

That was enough for Zillak, who slipped the garrote, still dripping with the first Dyrr cousin's blood, around the second's neck. Gromph didn't bother waiting for the prisoner to die before stepping to the third in the circle.

There was a sharp stench of urine that almost made Gromph step back, and a spattering of droplets echoed on the hard stone floor. The archmage blew air out his nostrils to clear the smell.

"Read it," he said to the terrified captive.

"It's a way shelter rune," the terrified Dyrr cousin almost barked. "A way shelter."

Gromph could tell by the feminine timbre in his voice that he was a younger cousin. That was positive in itself. Kyorli, perhaps sensing the boy's fear or drawn to the stench of piss, looked the prisoner in the face and Gromph did his best to keep the rat's gaze fixed on the boy's eyes.

Jaemas Xorlarrin leaned in from behind and said quietly, "A pleasing blood red, Archmage."

Gromph smiled, and the bound prisoner did his best to look away.

"The smaller," Gromph said then listened to the sounds of Prath's robes rustling behind him. "Read it," he said to the prisoner.

The boy looked up, tears streaming down his cheeks, and blinked at the young Baenre, who Gromph knew was holding up the other side of the placard upon which was drawn, half again smaller than the way shelter rune, the number . . .

"Five," the prisoner said, his voice squeaking in a most unseemly way.

Gromph smiled and stepped back, Jaemas moving smoothly to get out of his way.

"Yes," the archmage said, "this one."

Jaemas snapped his fingers and Prath came quickly back to attend his superiors. The sound of a dark elf being strangled again echoed through the chamber, then again, and seven more times as Zillak executed the rest of the captives, save the one with the sensitive, blood-crimson eyes.

As Zillak went methodically about his bloody work, Gromph, Jaemas, and Prath stripped off their robes to stand barefoot, naked from the waist up, covered only by simple breeches. Gromph concentrated on the sounds of the executions, keeping his mind as clear as he could.

In his rise through a demanding House, then through the ranks of Sorcere, Gromph had seen and done much. He was no stranger to pain and sacrifice and was able to withstand much that would break even other noble drow. He told himself that he would bear the proceedings that day as well, for his own good and for the sake of Menzoberranzan.

He kept mental note of the number of strangulations he heard, and when Zillak was squeezing the last of the life out of the last of the Dyrr captives, he said, "Bring in the table when you're through there, Zillak. Then leave us."

"Yes . . ." the assassin grunted as he strained through the last execution, "Archmage."

When that last life was spent, Gromph caught a glimpse through Kyorli's eyes of Zillak walking quickly out of the circle of dead, wiping his hands dry on a rag. The surviving Dyrr was crying, and by the sound of it Gromph thought the boy was more ashamed than afraid. He had broken, after all. He had behaved like some . . . goblin—certainly not a drow. Dark elves didn't wet themselves at the prospect of death or torture. Dark elves didn't cry in the face of their enemies—didn't cry at all. If the boy hadn't proved his keen darkvision, Gromph might have thought him half human.

An example, he thought, for us all.

Zillak wheeled in a table upon which were secured four sturdy rothé leather straps. At one end was a drain that emptied into a big glass bottle hanging from the bottom of the table. Zillak left the table where Jaemas Xorlarrin indicated and quickly left the room.

Gromph took hold of Kyorli and cradled the rat in his arms as he sat on the table. Holding the rat, he found he could turn the beast physically to keep her eyes focused where he wished. Gromph chuckled at the odd timing of that revelation and turned the rat's face to Jaemas. The Xorlarrin mage was making a point of not acknowledging Gromph's sign of humor. Young Prath just looked nervous.

"This is something," Gromph said to his nephew, "that few masters have seen in a centuries-long lifetime, young nephew. You will be able to tell your grandchildren that you were here to witness it."

The apprentice mage nodded, obviously unsure how to respond, and Gromph laughed at him even as he lay down on the table. The steel was cold against his back, and Gromph broke out in gooseflesh. He let out a long sigh to keep from shivering and held Kyorli to his bare chest. The rat's claws pricked him, but Gromph didn't mind. There would be greater pain soon, and not only for the archmage.

Reeling at first from the dizzying perspective, Gromph held the rat aloft and turned it to face the Master of Sorcere. From the bowl that Prath was holding Jaemas had taken a polished silver spoon. No ordinary eating utensil, the edges of the spoon were sharpened to a razor's keenness. Jaemas gestured for Prath to step closer to the prisoner, and Jaemas began to chant a spell.

The words of power were like music, and the sound of them sent a shiver through Gromph's already freezing spine. It was a good spell, a hard spell, a rare spell, and one that only a handful of drow knew. Jaemas had been chosen carefully, after all.

As the cadence rose and fell, the words repeating then turning upon themselves, the Xorlarrin mage stepped closer still to the shaking, terrified captive. He held the spoon in a delicate grip, like an artist holds his brush. With his other hand, Jaemas held the prisoner's left eye open wide. It wasn't until the shining silver spoon was an inch from the boy's eye that the captive seemed to understand what was about to happen.

He screamed.

When the sharp edge of the spoon slipped up under his eyelid, he screamed louder.

When Jaemas, in one deft, fluid motion, scooped the eye from its socket, he screamed louder still.

When the eye fell with a soft, wet sound into the bowl that Prath held under the prisoner's chin, he shrieked.

Seen through the rat's eyes, the blood that poured from the empty socket looked black. Jaemas held open the prisoner's right eye and the young drow started to beg. All the while, the Master of Sorcere continued his incantation, not missing a beat, not missing a syllable. When he slid the spoon under the right eyelid, the boy began to pray. When the eye came out, all the traitor could do was shake, mouth open wide, cords showing in his neck, blood flooding over his face.

Gromph had a fleeting thought of telling the prisoner, paralyzed with agony and horror, that at least the last thing he saw was a drow face and the simple line of a silver spoon. The next thing Gromph would see might drive even the archmage mad.

Gromph, of course, said nothing.

Through Kyorli's eyes, Gromph saw Jaemas slip the silver spoon into the bowl, careful not to cut either of the fragile orbs. The Xorlarrin mage, still incanting, took the rat from his master's hands, and Gromph's vision reeled. He heard Prath set the bowl gently on the floor, and Jaemas turned the rat so that Gromph could see himself lying on his back on the cold steel table. He could see Prath's hands shaking as he gently, almost reluctantly, folded the leather straps around Gromph's right wrist. He fastened the strap, but not nearly tight enough.

"Tighter, boy," the archmage growled. "Don't be squeamish, and don't be afraid you're going to hurt me."

Gromph allowed himself a laugh as his nephew tightened the strap then moved on to his right ankle. Jaemas continued to chant the words of the spell as Prath finished strapping his uncle to the table at both wrists and both ankles. When Gromph was satisfied that he was properly secured, he nodded to the Xorlarrin mage.

Odd, the Archmage of Menzoberranzan thought as Jaemas set Kyorli down on his bare chest. If Lolth wished it, none of this would have been necessary, but whether she answers her priestesses' prayers or not, all of it would still be possible.

That thought brought a tentative peace to Gromph. The

knowledge—no, the certainty—of his power had always reassured him, and it did still. It was that certainty that helped him breathe normally and remain still as he watched, from the rat's own eyes, Kyorli's meandering, reluctant march up his chest and onto his chin. The rat paused and Gromph saw black fingertips—Jaemas's—descend over his left eye with a twisted bit of wire. The Xorlarrin's touch was cool and dry on Gromph's eyelids. The archmage held still while the Xorlarrin mage set the wires gently, carefully, to hold his eyelid open. That was repeated on his right eye while Jaemas continued to chant, and Kyorli looked on with uncharacteristic patience. The rat was slowly coming under the influence of the spell, and it was that magic that was focusing the rodent's attention on Gromph's eyes.

Though he could feel the wires holding his eyes open, Gromph, when he let his concentration fall away from his familiar, could see nothing. There was not a hint of light or shadow, not a sliver of reflection.

Gromph took a deep, steadying breath and said, "Proceed."

His concentration off the rat and onto himself, Gromph couldn't see Kyorli crawl over his face, but he could feel every needle prick of her claws, could smell her musk, and could hear her sniffing. A whisker slipped across one of Gromph's open eyes, and he flinched. It stung. His eyes might have been useless, but they could still register pain.

Well, thought Gromph, too bad for me.

The first bite sent a wave of burning agony blasting through the archmage's head. Gromph's entire body tensed, and his teeth ground together. He could feel the rat back off and could feel the blood slowly drip down the side of his face. Jaemas continued to chant. The pain didn't stop either.

"Kyorli," the archmage grunted.

The rat was hesitating. Even under the influence of the spell, even offered the tasty morsel of a living—if sightless—eye, the rat knew that she was mutilating her own master, a master who had proven in the past to be anything but forgiving.

Gromph slipped his consciousness into his familiar's, and despite the one already ruined eye sending blood dripping down the side of his head, Gromph could see. It was the same colorless, dull rat's vision, though. He could see the bite the rat had already taken out of his right eye, could see the blood, could see himself shaking, could see the grim set of his jaw, and the open, helpless orb of his other blind eye awaiting the rodent's reluctant ministrations.

Gromph compelled the rat to finish her work.

Kyorli might have hesitated at the orders of Jaemas, but she responded to her master's invitation to feed without a second's pause. For at least three bites, Gromph watched his own eye being chewed out of his head, then Kyorli's vision blurred as she plunged her head into the ruined orb to tear at the tender, blood-soaked bits inside.

The pain was unlike anything Gromph had ever imagined, and in his long, uneasy life, the Archmage of Menzoberranzan had imagined a lot.

"Scream if you have to, Archmage," his nephew whispered into his ear, barely audible over the sound of the feeding rat. "There is no shame in it."

Gromph grunted, trying to speak, but kept his jaw clamped shut. The young apprentice had no idea what shame was, but even in his maddening agony, Gromph promised himself that his nephew would learn and that would be the last time Prath Baenre offered his uncle advice.

Gromph didn't scream, even when the rat moved on to the other eye.

TWO

The demon steered them to the darkest part of the lake, and not one of the drow thought anything of it. Bobbing at anchor in the deep gloom of the Lake of Shadows, the ship of chaos—*Raashub's* ship of chaos—stood out stark white against the inky darkness. The water itself was a black matched only by the deep ebony of his drow master's skin. The wizard, the one they called Pharaun, had found him, bound him, chained him to his own deck, and had done so with no humility, no respect, and no fear. The thought of it made the wiry black hairs that dotted the demon's wrinkled gray flesh stand on end. For a few moments, the demon stood reveling in the hatred he felt for that drow and his haughty kin.

The drow had been gating in one servile, simpering, weak-willed mane after another. The damned souls of petty sinners were food in the Abyss, and they were food for the ship of chaos. The uridezu took note of the number of manes the drow wizard brought in at any given time in hopes of gauging the dark elf's power. If it was an exact science, the gating in of lesser demons, Raashub didn't know its finer points, but so many of them were coming through there could be no doubt that the drow was skilled. Raashub wasn't helping the drow and was happy to let them not only feed his ship but exhaust their spells, efforts, and attention in the process. The presence of all those wailing, miserable demons must have clouded the drow priestess's senses enough that at times Raashub could push the boundaries of his captivity.

A rat's primitive consciousness intruded on his own, and Raashub sent only the tiniest hint of a glance its way. He'd been calling them, subtly, for two days—ever since the drow had first come aboard. The rodents swam the surface of the Lake of Shadows, and they inhabited the spaces between decks and under steps on the ship of chaos the same way rats everywhere swam, hid, and survived. Raashub, an uridezu, was as much rat as anything else a mundane prime could understand, and he knew the rats of the Underdark as he knew rats in every corner of the endless planes.

The rodent responded to Raashub's glance with a silent twitch of its whiskers, a gesture the uridezu felt more than saw. It scurried behind the thick base of the main mast and crept cautiously toward the draegloth.

They called the half-breed Jeggred. As draegloths went he was an average specimen. If Raashub were stupid enough to engage him, the draegloth would win a one-on-one fight, but the uridezu would never be that stupid. He would never be as stupid as the draegloth.

The rat didn't want to bite the half-demon, and Raashub had to silently insist. It was a gamble, but the uridezu didn't mind the odd risk for the odder reward. His psychic urging drew the attention of one of the female drow again, though, and the uridezu backed off, looking away before they made eye contact. All of the drow deferred, if grudgingly, to the female named Quenthel, who was apparently some high priestess of the drow spider-bitch Lolth. That one was as conceited and as unworthy of that conceit as the rest of them, but she was sensitive. Raashub worried that she could actually hear him when he didn't want her to.

Darting in fast, the rat nipped at the draegloth's ankle. The half-demon swatted it away with a grunt, and the tiny rodent flew through the air, out into the darkness. The splash was almost too far away to hear. The draegloth, whose skin was unmarred by the puny creature's teeth, locked his eyes on Raashub's and glared at him.

The draegloth had been doing little the past two days but glare at him.

Annoying little vermin, Raashub sent into the draegloth's mind, *aren't they, Jeggred?*

The draegloth blew a short, vile-smelling breath out of his nostrils and his lips peeled slowly back to reveal fangs—rows of dagger blades as sharp as razors and as piercing as needles. The half-demon hissed his anger, and boiling spittle sizzled on his lips.

Pretty, Raashub taunted.

The draegloth's eyes narrowed in confusion. Raashub allowed himself to laugh.

The high priestess turned and looked at them both. Again, Raashub avoided eye contact. He moved his foot enough to let the chain that bound him rattle against the single dragon bone that comprised most of the deck of his ship. Above him, the tattered sails of human skin hung limp in the still air. The demon heard Jeggred turn. Raashub liked the game—they were both caught by a sternly disapproving mother in their boyish mischief.

Quenthel looked away, and Jeggred locked his eyes on Raashub again. The uridezu didn't bother taunting him anymore that day. It was becoming boring. Instead, the demon contented himself with standing quietly, occasionally nudging the ship a little closer to the deeper gloom along the cavern wall.

Patience was not normally a quality enjoyed by his kind, but Raashub had been trapped in the Lake of Shadows for a long time. The appearance of the drow had been something of a godsend—though by the tone of their conversations and the snippets of facts regarding their mission the drow had let slip, Raashub knew it was hardly a god or goddess who'd sent them. They had managed to release his ship and release him. If he was anything but an uridezu, a demon born in the whirling chaos of Mother Abyss, he might have been . . . ah, what was the word? Grateful? Instead, he was patient, a little patient for a little longer.

Soon the drow would slip into their Reverie, their meditative trance so like sleep, and the high priestess would look inward. When that time came and she couldn't sense what he was doing, Raashub would bring another of his kind across the limitless infinity between planes. He had already called one of them the day before. The drow, over-confident in their measure of control over him, hadn't sensed him calling, failed to notice his cousin Jaershed cross from the Abyss, and still didn't realize that the other uridezu was even then clinging to the keel, wrapped in conjured darkness, waiting.

Jaershed hadn't learned patience the way Raashub had, and the lust for blood and chaos sometimes came out of him in waves. When it did the damnable high priestess would look around as if she'd heard something, as if she thought she were being watched. Raashub would silently wail, then, adding his mental voice to the anguished moans of the parade of manes they brought in and led into the hold one by one. Quenthel would be curious, disturbed even, but she would ultimately believe.

15

The dark elves had bested Raashub after all. Their powerful mage had trapped him on that miserable plane, chained him to his own deck, cowed him, enslaved him . . . and none of them could imagine that as true as that was, nothing—not in the Abyss, the Underdark, the Lake of Shadows, or aboard a ship of bone and chaos—lasted forever.

Raashub closed his eyes, suppressed his anticipation, and smiled.

Ryld Argith peered into the darkness of the Velarswood night and sighed. In the places where the trees were tall enough and close enough together to block out the star-spattered sky, it almost felt comfortable for him, but those times were few and far between in what the weapons master had come to learn was a relatively small forest. The sounds didn't help—whistles and rustling all the time from every direction, often not echoing at all. His hearing, sensitized by decades of training at Melee-Magthere, was tuned to the peculiarities of the Underdark, but in the World Above, it was making him a nervous wreck. The forest seemed always alive with enemies.

He turned to scan the darkness for the source of some random twittering—something he'd been told was a "night bird"—and instead he caught Halisstra's eye. She knew what he was doing—startling at every sound—and she smiled at him in a way that only days before Ryld would have taken as a sign that she'd identified a weakness in him, one that she'd surely exploit later. The twinkle in her crimson eyes seemed to imply the opposite.

Halisstra Melarn had confused Ryld from the beginning of their acquaintance. The First Daughter of a noble House from Ched Nasad, at first she had been every inch the haughty, self-possessed priestess she'd been raised to be, but as her goddess turned her back on her, her House fell, then her city crumbled around it, Halisstra had changed. Ryld abandoned his long-time ally Pharaun and the rest of the Menzoberranyr to go with her, and he didn't regret that, but he wasn't sure he could turn his back forever on the Underdark the way she so obviously had. Ryld still had a home in Menzoberranzan—at least he assumed he did, absent any news from the city that was already feeling the effects of Lolth's Silence when they'd left. When he thought about it, he felt certain that someday he would return there. When he looked at Halisstra he saw a dark elf like him but also unlike him. He knew that she would never be able to go back, even if she had a House to go back to. She was different, and Ryld knew that eventually he would have to change too or go home without her.

"Are you all right?" she asked him, her voice a welcome respite from the cacophony of the forest.

He met her eyes but wasn't sure how to answer. Thanks to the Eilistraeen priestesses Uluyara and Feliane, he was not only alive but unwounded. The poison that had nearly claimed him had been pulled from his blood by their magic, and his wounds and Halisstra's had been healed, leaving not even scars to mark their passage. The alien goddess of the surface drow had granted him his life, and Ryld was still waiting for her or her followers to present a bill.

"Ryld?" Halisstra prompted.

"I'm—"

He stopped, turned his head, and when he heard Halisstra inhale to speak again, he held up a warning hand to silence her.

Something was moving, and it was close. It was on the ground, and it was moving toward them. He knew that Feliane had gone ahead of them—the Eilistraeeans were always sensitive about giving the two newcomers time alone—but she was farther away and in a different direction.

Behind you, he signaled to Halisstra, *and to the left.*

Halisstra nodded, and her right hand moved to the enchanted blade at her hip. Ryld watched her turn, slowly, and as he drew his own mighty greatsword from his back, he took the briefest moment to admire the curve of Halisstra's hip, her mail glittering in the starlight against the dark background of the forest. Her feet whispered in the snow, and Ryld tracked the sounds. Whatever it was wasn't moving in a very deliberate way, and it sounded as if there was more than one, though the lack of echoes still made it hard for him to be sure. He didn't detect any change in the way it was moving when either of them drew their swords, so Ryld thought it unlikely the trespasser had heard them.

A spindly plant devoid of green—the Eilistraeeans had called one like it a "bush"—quivered, but not from the wind. Halisstra stepped back and held the Crescent Blade in the guard position in front of her. She had her back to him, so Ryld couldn't communicate with her in sign language. He wanted to tell her to step back farther, to let him take care of whatever it was, but he didn't want to speak.

When the thing rolled out from behind the bush, Halisstra hopped back three fast steps, keeping her sword at the ready. Ryld rushed at the bundle of bristly brown fur assuming Halisstra would clear the rest of the space for him. When she didn't he was forced to stop, and it looked up at him. The closest thing to the creature Ryld had ever seen was a rothé, but it was no rothé. The creature was small, the size and weight of Ryld's torso, and its wide eyes were wet and innocent, weak and—

"Young," Halisstra whispered, as if she was finishing his thought.

Ryld didn't let down his guard, though the beast sat calmly on the ground, looking at him.

"It's a baby," Halisstra said, and slipped the Crescent Blade back into her scabbard.

"What is it?" Ryld asked, still not ready to let down his guard, much less sheathe his sword.

"I have no idea," Halisstra answered, but still she crouched in front of it.

"Halisstra," Ryld hissed, "for Lolth's—"

He stopped himself before he finished that thought. It was another habit he would have to change or take home with him.

"It's not going to eat us, Ryld," she whispered, looking the little creature in the eyes.

Its nose twitched at her, and its eyes held hers. It seemed curious, with a face vaguely elflike, but its gaze betrayed an animal's intelligence and no more.

"What are you going to do with it?" he asked.

Halisstra shrugged.

Before Ryld could say anything else, two more of the little animals wandered out of the bushes to regard their comrade and the two dark elves with a meek curiosity.

"Feliane will know what to do with them," Halisstra said, "or at least be able to tell us what they are."

It was Ryld's turn to shrug. One of the creatures was licking itself, and even Ryld wasn't wrapped so tight that he could still see them as a threat. Halisstra sent out a call the Eilistraeeans had taught them—the sound of some bird—and Ryld slipped his greatsword back into its scabbard.

Feliane would hear the call and come to them. Ryld cringed when he realized that when she got there and saw the two of them dumbfounded by what looked like harmless prey animals . . . they would both look foolish again. At least, Ryld would.

Feliane came stomping through the underbrush. Ryld was surprised by not only how fast the Eilistraeen was moving but by how loud she was. He'd come to respect their ability to slip through the forest un—

He realized at that moment that what he heard crashing at them through the pitch-black forest wasn't Feliane. It wasn't a drow, or a surface elf, or even a human. It was something else—something big.

The thing burst out of the thick tangle of underbrush like an advancing wall of matted brown fur. Ryld managed to get his hand on Splitter's pommel but couldn't draw it before the beast rolled over him. The weapons master tried to tuck his body to protect his belly from the monster's trampling claws, but he didn't have the time.

The creature stomped on him, tripped on him, rolled on him, then stepped on him. All Ryld could do was keep his eyes pressed closed and grunt. It was heavy, and when it first punched him into the ground Ryld heard then felt at least one of his ribs snap under its weight. It finally came off him, and Ryld rolled off to one side—any side—ending up curled under a spindly "bush" with thorns that harried at his armor and *piwafwi*. Snow packed into the spaces between his armor's plates and chilled his neck and hands.

The creature stopped, rolling all the way over in the end and coming back onto its feet still facing away from Ryld. The weapons master looked up and blinked at it. It looked like a bigger—much bigger—version of the little animals that had wandered up to twitch their noses at the drow. It was a clever ruse and surely a successful hunting strategy: Disarm and distract your prey with your curious young, then trample it into the ground when it isn't looking.

Still, the Master of Melee-Magthere grimaced at his having fallen for it, however clever it was.

I'm getting slow, he thought. All this open air, all this talk of goddesses and redemption . . .

Shaking the distracting thoughts from his mind, Ryld spun to his feet at the same time he drew Splitter and whirled it in front of him. The lumbering animal turned to face him, and Ryld was ready for it.

The beast looked him in the eye and Ryld winked at it over the razor edge of his greatsword.

Steam puffed from its nostrils as it coughed out a series of loud grunts. It scratched at the snow with one of its front paws, and Ryld saw its black claws, the size of hunting knives, at the end of surprisingly well articulated hands. The look in the creature's eyes was a mix of slow-wittedness and feral anger—a look Ryld had seen before and had learned to respect. Stupid foes were easy to defeat and angry foes even easier. Mix the two together, though, and you're in for a fight.

The beast charged, and Ryld obliged it by meeting it in the middle. When it reared up at the end of its charge, the animal was nearly three times the drow's height. That display would likely frighten lesser opponents, but for Ryld all it did was open the thing's belly. The weapons master brought his greatsword in fast at shoulder height in a hard slash meant to open the animal's gut and end it quickly. The beast was faster than it looked, though, and it fell backward, rolling onto its back as the edge of Ryld's sword flashed past it, missing by a foot or more. Ryld had no choice but to follow through with the swing, but he managed to make use of the inertia to send him dodging off to the left when the creature slashed at him with its hind claws.

Ryld spun to a halt, blade up high, while the animal continued its roll and flipped back onto its feet. Both of them blew steam into the frigid air, but only Ryld smiled.

They went at each other again, and Ryld was ready for it to try to either trample him or rear up again. The animal did neither. It reached out for the drow warrior with both hands, obviously trying to grab him by the shoulders—or by the head. Ryld slid toward it at the end of his run, stabbing up with his greatsword as he passed under the animal's chin. He intended to impale it, maybe even behead it, but his opponent proved still more surprisingly agile. It ducked its head to one side, and all Ryld managed to do was nick one of its ears.

The weapons master continued his slide, bringing his arms in so he could stab again and at least get the creature in the gut, but the animal jumped to one side and rolled off, again managing to elude the drow's attack.

Ryld hopped to his feet, and the two opponents faced each other again. Ryld heard a voice to his left and glanced over to see Halisstra, bent in an attitude of prayer, mumbling her way through some kind of chant. The animal took advantage of Ryld's momentary attention gap and leaped at him, clearing easily eight feet before crashing to the ground in front of the drow. The creature had to dodge back, unbalancing itself, to avoid another slash from Splitter. It opened its jaws wide, revealing nasty fangs, and let loose another series of angry, frustrated grunts.

It swiped at Ryld with one set of claws. Ryld was ready to meet it, fully engaged to sever the animal's front leg at the elbow—when both of them jerked backward to avoid something that whizzed through the air between them in a flurry of feathers, talons, and turbulent air.

Ryld followed the animal's eyes as it followed the new player's mad course through the air. It was some kind of bird, but with four wings. Its multicolored feathers blended well into the dark background of the forest, and Ryld actually lost sight of it for a second. The huge furry beast stepped back, trying to look at Ryld and look out for the bird-thing at the same time.

Even Ryld wasn't able to do that, and since the furry animal was in front of him and at least a little off its guard, the weapons master stepped in to attack again—and again the bird-thing flashed between them, raking the air with its needle-like talons.

Ryld barely twitched away, but the big animal all but fell onto its back to avoid the newcomer. Ryld, already in mid-slash, quickly changed the direction of his attack and was half an inch from cutting the fast-flying bird-thing in half when Halisstra called out from behind him.

"Wait!" she shouted, and Ryld tipped the point of his blade down barely enough to let the bird fly past. "It's mine. I summoned it."

Ryld didn't have time to ask her how she'd managed to do that. Instead he stepped back three long strides, keeping his eyes on the beast, which was already back on its feet. The bird-thing slashed in from the darkness behind the animal and dragged its talons across the beast's head. The creature howled in pain and surprise and snapped its jaws at the passing bird-thing, missing it by a yard or more.

"What is that?" Ryld asked, not looking at Halisstra but keeping his eyes on the furious forest animal.

"It's an arrowhawk," Halisstra answered.

Ryld could hear the pride and surprise in her voice, and something about that sent a chill down his spine.

The animal looked at him, grunted, and came on. Either it had forgotten about the arrowhawk or had given up trying to see it coming. Ryld crouched, Splitter out in front of him, awaiting the beast's charge. He kept his shoulders loose and told himself that the fight had gone on long enough. He was not going to be made a fool of by—

—and the arrowhawk swished over his head, missing the top of his close-cropped white hair by a finger's width.

Ryld tucked his head down as it shot over him. The bird flew as fast as an arrow shot from a longbow, and it was easy for Ryld to understand how the creature had received its name. It looked as if the hawk was flying straight for the furry creature's eyes. Half of Ryld wanted the arrowhawk to kill it, the other half didn't want to be shown up by some conjured bird. At least not in front of—

That thought too went unfinished when Ryld heard himself gasp at the sight of the huge ground animal grabbing the arrowhawk right out of the air with one huge, clawed hand.

The bird let out an ear-rattling squawk, and the creature looked it in the eyes as it started to squeeze. Ryld didn't doubt for a moment that the big animal could break the long, slender arrowhawk in two with one hand. It was half a second away from doing just that when the arrowhawk flipped its long, feathered tail up and pointed it at the animal's face. An eye-searing flash of blinding light arced from the arrowhawk's tail to the tip of the animal's nose. Ryld snapped his eyes shut and gritted his teeth against the pain. There was a loud rustle of feathers, another angry squawk, and a high-pitched wail that could only have come from the big ground animal.

Ryld opened his eyes and had to blink away an afterimage of the graceful purple spark that had shot from the arrowhawk's tail. The animal had let go of the bird, which was nowhere to be seen. A tendril of smoke rose from its burned nose, and the stench of singed hair quickly filled the still night air.

Halisstra stepped up to Ryld, and they shared a glance and a smile as the big animal writhed in pain.

"Not bad," the weapons master joked, and Halisstra responded with a pleased smile.

"Praise Eilistraee," she said.

As if it understood her and had no love for her goddess, the big animal looked up, coughed out two more feral grunts, and started at them. Ryld put out one hand to push Halisstra behind him, but she had already skipped back into the darkness. He set his feet, ready for the charge, and saw the arrowhawk shoot out of the darkness again. The arrowhawk whipped its tail forward, and Ryld, knowing what was coming, closed his eyes and lifted one arm—both hands on Splitter's pommel—to shield his sensitive eyes.

There was a sizzle of electricity, the faint smell of ozone, and the none-too-faint stench of burned hair again. The furred creature growled in agony, and Ryld opened his eyes. Again, the arrowhawk was nowhere to be seen, likely whirling through the forest dodging tree trunks, circling back for another pass.

"Wait!" a woman's voice called. Ryld thought at first that it was Halisstra.

"No, Feliane," Halisstra called back. "It's all right. Between Ryld and the—"

"No!" the surface drow cut in.

Ryld would have turned to watch Feliane approach, but the animal had decided to charge him again. Not sure what Feliane was trying to stop, exactly, Ryld stepped in toward the big animal. He saw the arrowhawk coming, though and slid to a stop in the snow. The animal must have realized why the drow came to such a sudden halt, and when the arrowhawk came in low for another slash with its talons, the creature saw it as well.

Jaws snapped over the arrowhawk. There was a loud confusion of fluttering wings, screaming, growling, snapping, and popping—and the arrowhawk fell to the snow in two twitching, bleeding pieces.

"What's going on here?" Feliane called, her voice much closer. "What in the goddess's name are you doing?"

Its long, fang-lined jaws dripping with the arrowhawk's blood, the animal looked fiercer, more dangerous, and angrier than ever. Ryld smiled, spun his massive enchanted greatsword in front of him, and ran at the thing head on.

Behind him and off in the underbrush, Halisstra and Feliane were talking in urgent tones, but Ryld's trained senses put that aside. They were allies, and the only opponent of note was the furious beast. Whatever they were discussing, they could tell him about it later, after he had dispatched the vicious, cunning predator.

The creature reared up again as Ryld came in, and the drow slipped Splitter in low in front of him, slicing a deep furrow in the beast's exposed underbelly. Blood oozed from the wound, and quickly soaked the matted, dirty brown fur around it. Ryld spun his greatsword back around and pointed it forward, held in both hands above his head, for a final impaling stab.

The forest predator again proved it wouldn't go down easily. Before Ryld could plunge Splitter home, the thing's huge, hand-like claw wrapped around his right arm, digging into the space between his pauldron and vambrace to puncture the skin of his underarm.

Ryld tucked his right arm down, pressing the claw against his armored side to keep the beast from tearing away his paul-dron—and a good portion of skin and muscle with it. That had the unfortunate effect of tipping the point of his greatsword up. The animal pushed down, and its weight was enough to send Ryld sinking, slipping, then falling onto his back. Splitter's tip passed harmlessly past the animal's shoulder. When he felt the other claw clamp onto his left pauldron, Ryld knew he was pinned.

The beast snapped at his face, but Ryld still had enough room to jerk his head out of the way. With all his considerable strength, the weapons master pushed up, but with his arms trapped over his head and his sword all but immobile next to the animal's ear, he had to use his back and shoulders to try to lift himself off the ground—carrying the fifteen-foot animal that must have weighed a ton at least with him. He didn't move it far, but when the animal felt him trying to push up, it pushed down, extending its arms the fraction of an inch Ryld needed to muscle his sword down and under. Twisting his wrists painfully, Ryld managed to get the greatsword's tip up under the beast's chin.

The animal rolled its dark, dull eyes down and stretched its neck up and away from the sword. The two of them were stuck that way, and Ryld feared that that was how they were going to remain for a very long time: it pushing him away, he trying to stab it through the throat.

"Halisstra!" Feliane screamed. "No!"

The sound was shrill, panicked, and close enough that it finally registered on Ryld that the two females were still there. He wasn't alone. As females were wont to do, they were letting him take the brunt of the punishment, but they wouldn't leave him like that—or would they? From the sound of Feliane's voice, it was exactly what she intended to do.

Ryld redoubled his efforts, but so did the beast and they got no closer to a resolution—until Ryld heard a woman growl in an odd way, realizing it was Halisstra. The thing dipped that fraction of an inch forward that Ryld was hoping for.

The tip of the greatsword bit into the animal's throat, and blood poured down the blade. The animal grunted, opening its mouth a quarter of an inch—and allowing the blade to slip that much farther in. Hot red blood exploded from the wound, then pumped out of the monstrosity's neck in rhythm to its speeding heart—Ryld had found the artery he'd been hoping for.

He saw Halisstra's boot to his right and heard a sword come out of its sheath. She had jumped onto the animal's back and was straddling it, drawing the Crescent Blade to deliver the killing blow.

Ryld celebrated that realization by twisting Splitter's tip into the creature's throat, bringing more blood and sending a shiver rippling through the creature's fur.

Feliane ran up next to them and must have hit the side of the animal hard. Halisstra grunted, and the hulk started to topple sideways. Ryld sawed into its neck for good measure, not sure it was actually dead.

Feliane's boot scuffled in the snow next to him, and she said, "Stop it. For Eilistraee's sake, that's not what the Crescent Blade was meant for."

Ryld let the quivering carcass roll off him and fall into a dead sprawl in the underbrush. Wincing from the pain in his shoulder and underarm, he slid his blade out of the dead animal's neck and got to his feet, stepping back a few steps before he had his legs under him.

Halisstra and Feliane were standing next to the fallen animal, and Feliane's hand was wrapped tightly around Halisstra's sword arm.

"I couldn't . . ." Halisstra said, her voice quavering, each word punctuated by a puff of steam that rolled into the frigid air. "I couldn't let it kill him."

Both of the women turned to look at Ryld, who could only shrug.

"She was only protecting her young," Feliane said.

She was looking at Ryld, but the weapons master got the distinct impression she was talking to Halisstra. Ryld didn't understand. Who was protecting . . . ?

"The animal?" he asked.

"She's a giant land sloth," the Eilistraeen said, releasing Halisstra's arm and stepping away from her. "She *was* a giant land sloth. They're rare, especially this far north."

"Good," Ryld said. "It was tougher than it looks."

"Damn it!" Feliane cursed. "She was only protecting her young. You didn't have to kill her."

Halisstra was looking at her sword, the blade glowing in the darkness.

"Why," Ryld asked, "would it attack an armed drow to protect its young? It could have lived to birth more."

Feliane opened her mouth to answer but said nothing. A strange look came over her, one that Ryld couldn't remember ever seeing on the face of a drow.

Halisstra looked down at the dead sloth and whispered, "She. . . ."

Ryld shook his head. He didn't understand and was beginning to think he never would.

THREE

It had been two days since Pharaun had contacted his master, and the news that sending had brought still sat heavily on the wizard's shoulders. The spell allowed only a short message to travel through the Weave from the Lake of Shadows into Menzoberranzan and an equally short message back.

Ship of chaos is ours, Pharaun had sent, careful to use no unnecessary words though that was against his natural tendencies. *Advise on proper diet. Don't trust captain. Any word of Ryld Argith or Halisstra Melarn? Sent home to report details.*

He'd waited the interminable seconds for a reply, all the time wondering if the time he had been waiting for had come—the moment when Gromph Baenre, Archmage of Menzoberranzan, would fail to answer. That would be the moment Pharaun would know that they had failed, that they had no city to return to, no civilization to protect.

That time had not yet come.

Feed it manes, the archmage had replied. *As many as you can. Captain will serve power. Master Argith and Mistress Melarn not here. Stop your squabbling and get moving.*

Pharaun didn't stop to wonder how Gromph had known that the tenuous alliances within the expedition were fraying. Gromph was a drow himself, after all, and probably assumed it. If he thought he'd had the time, Pharaun might have studied that point much more closely, tried to determine the degree to which Gromph was aware of their actions, but there was work to do.

A manes demon was hardly the most daunting creature to either summon or control, but it was a demon nonetheless. He would have to use powerful spells to summon and bind them, all the while maintaining some measure of control over the uridezu captain who gave his name as Raashub. It had been two long, difficult, and tiring days for Pharaun. He had taken only enough Reverie to replenish his spells and was doing everything his considerable training allowed him to push his casting to its limit. The parade of hideous, groveling, snapping sub-demons he brought to the ship's deck began to amaze even himself, and Pharaun hoped that Quenthel and the others were taking note. Those among them capable of gauging such abilities would have to be impressed, and if they were impressed they would be scared. So long as they were scared, he would be safe.

As he led a string of the vile-smelling fiends into the gnashing jaws of the demonic ship's hold, Pharaun let his mind wander back to the rest of that sending. Ryld hadn't made it to Menzoberranzan, but that could mean anything. He could be dead anywhere between that cave on the World Above and the City of Spiders, or he could still be on his way. There was no straight line between any two points in the Underdark, and he could be only a few miles as the worm bored from Menzoberranzan and still have a tenday's travel ahead of him.

Ryld might still hold a grudge for Pharaun's having abandoned him all those days before, back in the city, but Pharaun knew he still had a powerful ally in the Master of Melee-Magthere. The warrior might have fallen under the spell of the First Daughter of House Melarn, but if Halisstra herself still lived, surely she would be on her way to Menzoberranzan herself. Pharaun couldn't imagine the homeless priestess had anywhere else to go.

Without Ryld at his side, Pharaun had given Quenthel and her draegloth nephew Jeggred as much room as the cramped deck allowed. They hadn't appreciated Pharaun leaving them to spin while he'd gone to pick up Valas and Danifae first. Even Valas and Danifae had been surprised by that one, but Pharaun had long ago learned that whenever possible a cautious drow lets his enemies twist for a while, if only to remind them that he can.

Still, the Mistress of Arach-Tinilith had been more than a little displeased, and Jeggred had made another serious attempt at a physical assault. Quenthel had held him back, if reluctantly, and charged the draegloth with guarding the uridezu. They were two of the same: demons on the wrong plane, pressed into the service of drow who were ready to take them back to the Abyss that spawned them. Pharaun let himself sigh at that thought. He knew it was a bad idea on its surface, going to the Abyss, but they had passed up the acceptable a long time before. They were in new territory. They were headed for the Spider Queen herself, and right when Lolth seemed least inclined to greet them.

Pharaun was sure he wasn't the only one who had second thoughts about the expedition, even as strenuously as he'd argued for their going forward. For a Master of Sorcere, it was a mission that could make him Archmage of Menzoberranzan. For her part, Quenthel had already achieved the highest post she could hope for.

As Mistress of Arach-Tinilith, Quenthel was the spiritual leader of all Menzoberranzan and the second most powerful female in the city. Some would argue that she was indeed more powerful than her sister Triel.

Of all drow under Faerûn, she would surely be welcomed into Lolth's domain—assuming there was either a Lolth or a Demonweb Pits at all anymore—but still the high priestess was on edge. Her normally stern countenance had gone nearly rigid, and her movements were jerky and twitching. Any talk of the journey ahead made her pace around the deck, all but oblivious to the lesser demons that often snapped at her or reached out to grab her.

Even Pharaun, cynical as he was, didn't want to believe that the Mistress of Arach-Tinilith might be losing her faith.

The fact that Jeggred also noticed Quenthel's unease didn't make the wizard feel any better. The draegloth's expressions weren't always easy to read, though the half-demon was the least intellectually capable of the party, but since coming to the Lake of Shadows—perhaps even before—Jeggred had looked at his aunt quite differently. He could see her agitation, though he might have thought it fear, and he didn't like it. He didn't like it at all.

Pharaun closed his eyes and took a deep breath as the last of the day's manes went down the ship's gullet. He felt tired enough to sleep like a human. Without even bothering to cross the deck to the place where he'd set his pack, Pharaun sank to the fleshy planks and sat.

"Before you slip into Reverie," Valas Hune said from behind him, "we should discuss practical concerns."

Pharaun turned to look at the Bregan D'aerthe scout and offered him a twisted smile.

"Practical concerns?" the wizard asked. "At this point I'm too tired for any kind of concerns . . . other than . . . the . . . ones that are . . ."

Pharaun closed his eyes and shook his head.

"Are you all right?" the scout asked, his tone comfortably devoid of real concern.

"My wit has failed me," Pharaun replied. "I must be tired indeed."

The scout nodded.

"We'll need supplies," he said, addressing all four of them.

Quenthel didn't look up, and Jeggred only glanced away from the chained demon for a second.

The draegloth shrugged and said, "I can eat the captain."

Pharaun didn't bother to look at the uridezu for a response, and the demon, sensibly, didn't offer one.

"Well, I can't," Valas replied. "Neither can the rest of us."

"There will be no opportunity to stop along the way?" Danifae asked.

Pharaun regarded the beautiful, enigmatic battle-captive with a smile and said, "We'll travel from this lake across the Fringe and into the Shadow Deep. From there to the endless Astral. From there to the Abyss. Any roadhouses along the way will be . . . unreliable to say the least."

"Which is to say," Valas cut in, "that there won't be any."

"What did you have in mind, Valas?" Pharaun asked. "How much are we talking about?"

The scout made a show of shrugging and turned to Quenthel to ask, "How long will we be away?"

Quenthel almost recoiled from the question, and Jeggred turned to stare daggers at her back for a heartbeat or two before returning his attention to the captured uridezu.

"One month," Pharaun answered for her, "sixteen days, three hours, and forty-four minutes . . . give or take sixteen days, three hours, and forty-four minutes."

Quenthel stared hard at Pharaun, her face blank.

"I thought your wit had abandoned you, Master of Sorcere," Danifae said. She turned to Quenthel. "An impossible question to answer precisely, I understand, Mistress, but I assume an educated guess will do?"

She looked at Valas, her white eyebrows arched high on her smooth black forehead. Valas nodded, still looking at Quenthel.

"The simple fact is that I have no idea," the Mistress of Arach-Tinilith said finally.

The rest of the drow raised eyebrows. Jeggred's eyes narrowed. It wasn't what any of them expected her to say.

"None of us do," she went on, ignoring the reaction, "which is precisely why we're going in the first place. Lolth will do with us as she pleases once we are in the Demonweb Pits. If we must be supplied, then we will need supplies for the length of our journey there and perhaps our journey back. If Lolth chooses to provide for us while we're there, so be it. If not, we will need no sustenance, at least none that can be had in this world."

The high priestess wrapped her hands around her arms and hugged herself close. All of them saw her shiver with undisguised dread. Pharaun was too taken aback to see the further reactions of the others. A low, rumbling growl from Jeggred finally drew his attention, and he looked over to see the draegloth's eyes locked on Quenthel, who was successfully ignoring her Abyssal nephew.

"You talk like humans," the draegloth growled. "You speak of the Abyss as if it was some feral dog you think might nip at your rumps, so you never rise from your chairs. You forget that for you, the Abyss has been a hunting ground, though you do most of your hunting from across the planes. Are you drow? Masters of this world and the next? Or are you . . ."

Jeggred stopped, his jaw and throat tight, and returned his steely gaze to the uridezu. The demon captain looked away.

"You assume much, honored draegloth," Danifae said, her clear voice echoing across the still water. "It is not fear that prepares us for our journey, I'm sure, but necessity."

Jeggred turned slowly but didn't look at Danifae. Instead, his eyes once more found the Mistress of Arach-Tinilith. Quenthel appeared, to Pharaun's eyes at least, to have succumbed to the Reverie. Jeggred blew a short, sharp breath through his wide nostrils and turned a fang-lined smile on Danifae.

"Fear," the draegloth said, "has a smell."

Danifae returned the half-demon's smile and said, "Fear of the Spider Queen surely smells the sweetest."

"Yes," Valas broke in, though Danifae and the draegloth continued to stare at each other with expressions impossible to read. "Well, that's all well and good, but surely someone knows how long it will take us to get there and how long to get back."

"A tenday," Pharaun said, guessing for no other reason than to get on with it so he could rest and replenish his magic. "Each way."

The scout nodded, and no one else offered any argument. Jeggred went back to staring at the captain, and Danifae drew out a whetstone to sharpen a dagger. The vipers of Quenthel's scourge wrapped themselves lovingly around her and began, one by one, to sink into slumber.

"I'll be off then," Valas said.

"Off?" Pharaun asked. "To where?"

"Sshamath, I think," the scout replied. "It's reasonably close, and I have contacts there. If I go alone, I can be there and back quickly, and no one who doesn't fear Bregan D'aerthe will even know I was there."

"No," Danifae said, startling both Valas and Pharaun.

"The young mistress has a better suggestion?" Pharaun asked.

"Sschindylryn," she said.

"What of it?" asked Pharaun.

"It's closer," Danifae replied, "and it's not ruled by Vhaeraunites."

She sent a pointed look Valas's way, and Pharaun allowed himself a smirk.

"I'm tired," the Master of Sorcere said, "so I will weaken enough to speak on Valas's behalf. He is Bregan D'aerthe, young mistress, and his loyalty goes to she who is paying. I don't believe we'll have trouble with our guide jumping deities on us. If he can get to, through, and out of Sshamath faster, then let him do what he's been hired to do."

"He will go to Sschindylryn," Quenthel said, her voice so flat and quiet that Pharaun wasn't certain he'd heard correctly.

"Mistress?" he prompted.

"You heard me," she said, finally looking up at him. She let her cold gaze linger for a moment, and Pharaun held it. She turned to Valas. "Sschindylryn."

If the scout had any thought of arguing, he suppressed it quickly.

"As you wish, Mistress," Valas replied.

"I will accompany you," Danifae said, speaking to Valas but looking at Quenthel.

"I can move faster on my own," the scout argued.

"We have time," said the battle-captive, still looking at Quenthel.

The high priestess turned to Danifae slowly. Her frigid red eyes warmed as they played across the girl's curves. Danifae leaned in ever so slightly, eliciting a smile from Pharaun that was as impressed as it was amused.

"Sschindylryn. . . ." the wizard said. "I've passed through it a time or two. Portals, yes? A city crowded with portals that could slip you in an instant from one end of the Underdark to another . . . or elsewhere."

Danifae turned to Pharaun and returned his smile—impressed and amused.

"How much time do we have?" Valas asked, still ignoring the more subtle, silent conversation-within-a-conversation.

Pharaun shrugged and said, "Five days . . . perhaps as many as seven. I should have provided the ship with adequate sustenance by then."

"I can do it," Valas replied. "Barely."

The scout looked to Quenthel for an answer, and Pharaun sighed, pushing back his frustration. He too looked at Quenthel, who was gently stroking the head of one of her whip vipers. The snake swayed in the air next to her smooth ebon cheek while the other vipers slept. Pharaun got the distinct impression that the snake was speaking to her.

A sound caught Pharaun's attention, and he saw Jeggred shifting uncomfortably. The draegloth's eyes twitched back and forth between his aunt and the viper. Pharaun wondered if the draegloth could hear some silent, mental exchange between the high priestess and her whip. If he could, what he heard was making him angry.

"You will take Danifae with you," Quenthel said, her eyes never leaving the viper.

If Valas was disappointed, he didn't let it show. Instead, he simply nodded.

"Leave when you're ready," the high priestess said.

"I'm ready now," the scout replied, perhaps a second too quickly.

The viper turned to look at the scout, who met its black eyes with a furrowed brow. Pharaun was fascinated by the exchange, but exhaustion was claiming him all the more quickly as the discussion wore on.

Quenthel slid back to rest against the bone rail of the undead ship. The last viper rested its head on her thigh.

"We will take Reverie, then, Pharaun and I," the Mistress of the Academy said. "Jeggred will stand watch, and the two of you will be on your way."

Danifae stood and said quietly, "Thank you, M—"

Quenthel stopped her with an abrupt wave of her hand, then the high priestess closed her eyes and sat very still. Jeggred growled again, low and rumbling. Pharaun prepared himself for Reverie as well but couldn't help feeling uneasy at the way the draegloth was looking at his mistress.

Danifae slipped on her pack as Valas gathered his own gear. The battle-captive walked to Jeggred and put a hand lightly on the draegloth's bristling white mane.

"All is well, Jeggred," she whispered. "We are all tired."

Jeggred leaned in to her touch ever so slightly, and Pharaun looked away. The draegloth stopped his growling, but Pharaun could feel the half-demon watch Danifae's every move until she finally followed Valas through a dimensional portal of the scout's making and was gone.

Why Sschindylryn? Pharaun asked himself.

It was the battle-captive's calming touch with the draegloth that accounted for the wizard's uneasy Reverie.

A little more than half a mile under the ruins of the surface city of Tilverton, two dark elves ran.

Danifae breathed hard trying to keep up with Valas, but she stayed only a few strides behind him. The scout moved in something between a walk and run, his feet sometimes appearing not even to touch the slick flowstone of the tunnel floor. As they'd emerged from the last in a rapid, head-spinning series of gates, Valas had told her they were more than halfway to Sschindylryn, and it had been only a single day. Danifae admired the mercenary's skill in navigating the Underdark, even as she dismissed his obvious lack of ambition and drive. He seemed content in his position as a hired hand—scout and errand boy for Quenthel Baenre—and the idea of that sort of contentment was utterly alien to Danifae.

After all, she thought in time, Valas is only a male.

The scout came to an abrupt halt, so abrupt in fact that Danifae had to stumble to an undignified stop to avoid running into him. Happy for the chance to pause and rest, though, she didn't bother to complain.

"Where—?" she started, but Valas held up a hand to silence her.

Even after all her years as a battle-captive, a servant to the foolish and slow-witted Halisstra Melarn, Danifae hadn't grown accustomed to shutting up when told to. She bristled at the scout's dismissive gesture but calmed herself quickly. Valas was in his element, and if he wanted silence, both their lives might well depend on it.

He turned to her, and Danifae was surprised to see no hint of annoyance or irritation on his face, even as her one word still echoed faintly in the cool, still air of the cavern.

Another portal up ahead, he told her with his fingers. *It will take us to Sschindylryn, but it's not one I've used in a very long time.*

But you've used it before, she replied silently.

Portals, especially portals like this one, Valas explained, *are like waterholes. They attract attention.*

You sense something? she asked.

Danifae's own sensitive hearing detected no noise, her equally sensitive nose no smell but her own and the scout's. That didn't mean they were alone.

As if he'd read her mind, Valas replied, *You're never alone in the Underdark.*

So what is it? she asked. *Can we avoid it? Kill it?*

Maybe nothing, he answered in turn, *probably not, and I hope so.*

Danifae smiled at him. Valas tipped his head to one side, surprised and confused by the smile.

Stay here, he signed, *and keep still. I'll go on ahead.*

Danifae looked back along the way they'd come then forward in the direction they were going. The tunnel—twenty-five or thirty feet wide and about as tall—stretched into darkness in both directions.

If you leave me behind. . . . Danifae threatened with her fingers and with her cold, hard eyes.

Valas didn't react at all. He seemed to be waiting for her to finish.

Danifae again glanced to the seemingly endless tunnel ahead, only for half a heartbeat. When she turned back, Valas was gone.

❦   ❦   ❦

Ryld drew the whetstone slowly along Splitter's razor edge. The enchanted sword hardly needed sharpening, but Ryld found he was always better able to think when he was performing the simple tasks of a soldier. The sword had no outward signs of an intelligence of its own, but Ryld had convinced himself some years before that Splitter enjoyed the attention he gave it.

He was alone in the crumbling, weed-choked hovel he shared with Halisstra. The sounds and smells of the forest all around him managed to invade even that personal time with his sword and his thoughts. He knew he was as relaxed as he would ever be on the surface in the daylight under the endless sky—at least, when Halisstra wasn't with him.

The Master of Melee-Magthere was alone because he hadn't been invited to the circle that Halisstra had gone to join. The curious, heretical surface drow were planning something, and Halisstra and her newfound toy—the Crescent Blade—were obviously a big part of it. He had killed the raging animal that attacked him, and as many times as Feliane had tried to explain it to him, he couldn't imagine why that made him an outcast. Still, Ryld knew he had been left out for more than that one reason.

He sat alone also because, unlike Halisstra, he had not openly rejected the Spider Queen nor openly embraced her sun-ravaged rival, the Lady of the Dance. Ryld didn't understand that frivolous goddess of theirs. The Lady of the *Dance?* Were they to set their lives along a path defined by *dancing?* What sort of a bizarre goddess could draw, much less mete out, power from something so pointless as dancing? Lolth was a cruel and capricious mistress, and her priestesses held her power close, but she was the Queen of Spiders. Spiders were strong, resourceful predators—survivors. Ryld could see himself as a spider. Spiders knew no mercy and never asked for forgiveness. They spun their webs, caught their prey, and lived. Spiders made sense, spiders had power, and power was all any drow needed.

Apparently not every drow.

Still, Ryld knew that there was a third reason why he sat sharpening his sword while the females plotted and planned, and that was precisely because he wasn't a female. In Menzoberranzan, Ryld Argith was a highly regarded and well-respected warrior, a soldier with powerful friends and much to recommend him to his superiors. He led a comfortable life, wielded some items imbued with powerful magic—the greatsword not the least of them—and was even trusted to be a principal member of the vital expedition in search of their silent goddess. Despite all that, Ryld Argith was a male. As such he would never be anything but second, and he well knew likely not even that. He would lead other males, other warriors, but would never command a female. He would be asked his opinion, and that opinion would occasionally even be considered, but he would never make decisions. He would be a soldier—a tool, a weapon—but never a leader. Not in Menzoberranzan among the daughters of Lolth and not in the sun-baked forest among the dancing priestesses.

Three reasons for being left out, Ryld thought, while at home there is only the third. Three reasons to go home to Menzoberranzan.

One reason to stay.

In the past lingering hours of solitude Ryld had thought often of returning to the Underdark. Pharaun and the others would have moved on, continued their quest. Likely they'd all forgotten about the Master of Melee-Magthere who had left the City of Spiders with them. Ryld held no illusions about his worth to the likes of Quenthel Baenre, and Pharaun had at least once proved that Ryld's life was less important than the wizard's convenience, let alone the Master of Sorcere's own well-being.

Pharaun, however, was predictable. Ryld knew the mage and knew what to expect—even if that meant expecting betrayal. Pharaun was a dark elf, not only well tuned to, but prone to revel in, his drow nature. Quenthel Baenre was the same, which was why they so irritated one another. Those two and the others—even the laconic Valas Hune—were like spiders too: predictable, efficient survivors. Ryld saw himself in the same terms, and being in like company had a compelling draw.

Until he thought of Halisstra.

In his years in Menzoberranzan, Ryld had enjoyed the company of more than a handful of females, but like any male in the City of Spiders he knew well enough not to allow attachments to run too deep. He had known from time to time that he was a plaything, a tool, a dalliance, a performer—but never one of those surface elf words, those oddities such as lover, companion, friend, husband. Those words had no meaning until Halisstra.

Ryld tried and tried, but he couldn't understand the hold the First Daughter of House Melarn had on him. He had even drawn upon the unique power of Splitter to dispel whatever magic she had cast on him to draw him along with her—but there was no magic. She had cast no spell, sang no *bae'qeshel* ballad, slipped him no potion to wrap herself around him so tightly. She hadn't, Ryld mused, even done or said anything too different than things he'd heard before, though in the past such things were said in tones of mockery or even cold, bitter irony by those dozen or more drow females who had had him.

Halisstra had simply smiled at him, held his gaze with hers, touched him, kissed him, looked at him with fear, longing, regret, pain, anger, desperation . . . looked at him with honesty. Ryld had never seen any of it before, not on the black face of a dark elf, not in the cool gloom of the Underdark. He could feel her when she was close, as if she gave off some ripple that tuned his senses to her. She was simply Halisstra, and the Master of Melee-Magthere was dumbfounded to find that was enough. Her mere presence was sufficient to drag him away from a life that was, and would continue to be, as rewarding as a drow male could expect.

There he was, putting up with the same things, still the male whose strong sword arm would be called into service on a second's notice but who would not dine at the same table.

The fourth reason that he was alone that day and had been alone for much of the day before roared into Ryld's mind then, and he let it come, but only for a moment.

They mean to kill her, he thought as a chill raced down his spine and the whetstone that had so slowly and so carefully and so rhythmically been drawn along his blade came to a sudden stop. They mean to kill Lolth.

Ryld closed his eyes and drew in a long breath, calming his suddenly racing heart.

It was, after all, why Halisstra had been sent to retrieve the Crescent Blade. It was why the Eilistraeen priestesses put up with the obviously unpleasant presence of the Master of Melee-Magthere—at Halisstra's demand. It was why Halisstra stayed and why she carried herself with a confidence and composure he hadn't seen . . . well, never in the outcast from the ruins of Ched Nasad. It was why Halisstra no longer trembled in fear. It was why she woke in the morning and why she drew breath during the day.

In Eilistraee's name, Halisstra Melarn meant to murder the Queen of the Demonweb Pits in her sleep.

Ryld set the whetstone in motion again and smiled.

Maybe, he thought, she's more like a spider than she wants to admit.

Valas held the crystal to his left eye and scanned the chamber. He stood in the deep shadows at the edge of where the tunnel—a very old lava tube—emptied into the pyramidal cavern. The ancient monastery was obvious to even his unaided darkvision. Set against the northern wall of the cathedral-like space off to Valas's right was a half circle of stone, perhaps seventy-five feet in radius. The curved wall rose as tall as two hundred feet before rounding to a domed roof, with the apex about thirty or forty feet above that. Two huge slit windows, not much wider than Valas was tall but eighty feet in length, were set high on the walls. A thief might have to climb the brick wall for a dangerous hundred feet before being able to slip inside. Between the two tall windows and a few feet below their bottom edges loomed a pair of small, dark holes tall enough that Valas might be able to step through them without dipping his head. Below those round holes a drooping oblong opening led into the pitch-black interior of the ruin.

The windows, the two round holes, and the oblong opening

gave the ruined monastery the look—obviously intentional—of a frowning face.

Stalactites had formed along the upper edge of the mouth and hung down to form ragged fangs, and dripping water had carried centuries of sediment onto the dome so that a wide patch of smooth white flowstone capped the far end of the great head like some gaily off-kilter hat. What grim ceremonies might have been held before that giant face Valas didn't bother to imagine. The centuries that had passed since his ancient ancestors had abandoned it had been unkind to the building, but Valas knew that the ravages of dripping water, mold, and earthquakes hadn't touched the gate that rested inside it. Twice before, though many years gone by, Valas had climbed into that drooping, melancholy mouth and passed between two rune-carved pillars to step two hundred miles to the northwest shore of Lake Thalmiir, an easy walk to Sschindylryn.

Valas knew he wasn't the only one who'd used it.

A crystal normally hung on his vest—an enchanted garment that gave Valas much of his nimble footing and lightning reaction—with many other magical trinkets he'd picked up over a lifetime in the wilds of the Underdark. Through that crystal the scout could see that which others couldn't—most things rendered invisible by magic either sorcerous or innate.

Valas slowly and carefully scanned the base of the great face, then to the left along the still pool of black water that bisected the round floor of the cavern. There was a cave low in the sloping wall across from him and a smaller one—another lava tube of similar dimensions to the one Valas had come through—higher up and to the right. The scout began to scan the roof of the ruined monastery when he heard Danifae all but stomping through the tunnel behind him.

Valas didn't stop his slow, methodical examination of the

structure. He knew that Danifae would walk past him, their shoulders close to touching, and she would never see him. He had told her to wait, and if she disregarded his warning it was her choice.

Let her stomp on in, he thought. Let her—

Valas froze when the crystal revealed the tip of what could only be a talon resting on the top of the monastery. Holding his breath, the Bregan D'aerthe scout drew his head back half an inch and played the crystal, still held close to his left eye, along the domed roof of the ancient face.

The creature that rested atop the ruin wasn't too big, at least not as far as dragons go. No taller than Valas himself, with a wingspan maybe twice that, the beast was coiled comfortably but alert atop the dome. Though the crystal tended to bleed any color from the scene, Valas knew the monster was as gray in color as it appeared to him through the magic item. Even through the crystal it seemed undefined, blurred as if it had been painted onto the giant face in watercolors.

That's how you hide, Valas thought. You blend into the darkness.

Danifae passed him and strode uncaring to the mouth of the lava tube. She stood for a moment, one hand resting casually on the rock wall, gazing out into the cavern. Valas could tell she hadn't seen the dragon on the top of the face, but a last quick glimpse through the crystal showed him that the dragon had seen her. It slowly uncoiled itself, drawing up its wings.

Valas slipped into the cavern, relying in no small part on his own training and experience but not too proud to call on the power of an enchanted ring to speed his way. Mithral chain mail hushed any sound he might make as he moved, and it helped his toes find safe, quiet footing. Keeping always in shadow, always without the slightest scrape of sole on stone, without the faintest reflection of stray light on metal, Valas came down the incline from the mouth of the lava tube and along the bowl-shaped edge of the huge space to the yawning black cave across.

He risked the occasional glance up at the creature, whose outline he could only barely discern in the gloom high up in the cavern—and only then because he knew it was there. Valas also risked a glance or two back at Danifae, who was slowly, and with surprising grace, making her way down into the bowl of the cavern. She looked all around but not up. Her eyes never rested on either Valas or the stone-gray dragon.

Danifae walked slowly toward the edge of the pool as Valas drew the shortbow from his back. He nocked an arrow and drew back the string.

The female was all but offering herself on a silver platter to the beast, and though Valas ached to allow her to see her folly through, he worried about Quenthel. The high priestess seemed to have taken a liking to the Melarn battle-captive, stealing her away without a thought from the female from Ched Nasad. Valas didn't want to find out the hard way that he'd let the battle-captive die when Quenthel had plans for Danifae beyond their occasional loveplay.

"Valas?" the female called into the dark, still cavern.

Her voice echoed, Valas cringed, and the dragon took wing.

🕷 🕷 🕷

Nimor Imphraezl watched from above as the duergar engaged the spiders. Drow warriors—all male—rode the enormous arachnids into battle. The spiders skittered and whirled around them while the riders sat stiff and straight in their saddles. The mounted drow carried long pikes—weapons the duergar were unaccustomed to, as rare as the long weapons were in the confines

49

of the Underdark—and they skewered one after another before the gray dwarves drew any dark elf blood.

The spider riders were hopelessly outnumbered by the horde of duergar who continued to lay siege to the slowly crumbling city of Menzoberranzan, and Nimor was content to lose a few gray dwarves for the chance to watch the drow fight. They were good, he would grant them that. The spiders killed as many duergar as the pikes did, but the beasts were never out of their riders' control. All in all it was a beautiful, bloody dance.

In the center of the spider riders a mounted drow male wearing armor of the finest mithral positively glowed with magic. He carried a pike like the others but hadn't brought his to bear. He held it up, and from it a long, thin banner wafted in the cool Underdark air. It took Nimor a minute or so to recognize the sigil emblazoned on the banner. The riders represented House Shobalar—a lesser House, but one loyal to the Baenres and known throughout the drow-settled Underdark for their effective and impeccably trained cavalry. The dark elf with the banner must be their leader.

One of the riders took two duergar at once, pinning them together then using their weight at the end of his pike to topple three more of their companions onto the flowstone floor. Nimor smiled.

He had come to that particular tunnel after hearing three separate times of unusual activity there. The duergar had managed to kill a Menzoberranyr scout only a day before, and even the gruff gray dwarves had admitted that other drow had been there and gotten away. It wasn't the most well defended approach, and Nimor had been keeping an eye on it, certain the Menzoberranyr would be testing it.

When the scout was killed, Nimor had Crown Prince Horgar send reinforcements, but only a few. Enough, Nimor hoped, to satisfy the drow but not enough to close the approach. Nimor wanted to draw them out, and like the arrogant aristocrats they were, they'd taken the bait.

Nimor hung upside down, hidden by a spell of invisibility, his *piwafwi*, another spell that prevented anyone using similar magic from finding him, and another that would draw enemies' attention away even if they thought to look up at him. Those things and the immediate threat of the duergar soldiers were enough that he could wait and watch in peace—wait and watch for the spider rider captain to send his arachnid mount scurrying into the fray, scurrying right under Nimor.

With a touch to a brooch that bore the sign of the Jaezred Chaulssin, Nimor dropped slowly, still hidden from sight by magic. As he descended, Nimor drew his dagger—a very special dagger—and when he came to rest on the spider, inches behind the cavalry leader, he flicked the blade across the back of the drow warrior's neck. There was a perfect space there between his helm and his pauldron.

The spider rider flinched and turned in his saddle. Nimor, still invisible, grabbed the drow around his neck and held the poisoned blade to his throat.

The spider rider couldn't see him, but he could hear Nimor whisper in his ear, "What is your name, Shobalar?"

"Who are you?" the warrior asked, and Nimor cut him again—not too deeply—in response.

The drow grunted, and Nimor could feel his body stiffen, jerk, and quiver.

"Yes," Nimor hissed into the slowly dying officer's ear, "it is poison. Very, very elegant poison. It will paralyze you, twist your throat closed, squeeze the last gasp of air from your lungs, and keep you from screaming while you suffocate."

The drow growled and said, his voice already quiet and tight, "My House will avenge me."

"Your House will burn, Captain . . . ?"

"Vilto'sat Shobalar," the drow answered even as his throat squeezed shut, "of the Spider Riders of House Sh—"

Smiling all the while, Nimor held the dying drow upright in his saddle as he suffocated. The Anointed Blade of the Jaezred Chaulssin waited until Captain Vilto'sat Shobalar quivered through his last attempt at a breath and his magenta eyes glazed over. Then Nimor levitated up and away from the suddenly uncontrolled, feral war-spider.

The arachnid went berserk, chewing through duergar after duergar then turning on another of its kind. The rider of that spider turned his attention to protecting his mount from the wild arachnid—just long enough for a particularly enthusiastic duergar footman to take his head with a poleaxe.

Nimor killed eight more drow himself over the next ten minutes or so, while the duergar claimed three. The rest finally turned and ran back through the tunnel, past the outer siege line and back into Menzoberranzan. They had taken back nothing, and Nimor had four of their spiders and the dead drow.

Nimor ordered up more duergar to resecure the position, had the spiders bound and made ready for travel, and went back to his command post with the corpse of Captain Vilto'sat Shobalar.

Spoils of war.

Valas could tell that Danifae didn't know the drake was behind her until the second his arrow sliced through the fine membrane of its wing, surprising it. It made a noise deep in its throat, the arrow made a wet ripping sound as it entered, and the drake's smooth motion ended in a jerk. All that was enough for anyone to sense some disturbance behind her and turn—and it was that simple reflex that saved Danifae's life.

Though the drake forgot its intended target, it landed hard in a skidding roll and would have bowled her over if she hadn't jumped clear—and she barely managed that.

The portal drake whirled in the direction from which Valas's arrow had come. Saliva dripped from its open mouth, curling around jagged teeth and collecting on the cave floor in steaming pools. Valas saw the intelligence in the thing's eyes, the great age—centuries spent stalking the alluring magical portals of the Underdark—and the cold, hard anger.

The drake searched the darkness for him, but Valas knew it wouldn't see him. Valas didn't want to be seen; it was that simple.

Behind the creature, Danifae scrambled to her feet, drawing her morningstar at the same time. Valas already had another arrow in his hand, and as he slipped sideways along the edge of a deep shadow he set it to his bow and drew back the string. The drake mirrored that expansive movement by drawing air into its lungs. It couldn't see Valas, but it had apparently concluded that all it had to do was get close. It was a conclusion with which Valas could—unfortunately—find no fault.

After taking a heartbeat to aim, Valas let the arrow fly. The drake exhaled, releasing a billowing cloud of greasy green vapor into the air. It rolled and expanded as it left the dragon's mouth. The drake began to strain to get it all out.

Danifae struck with her morningstar—a weapon enchanted with the power of lightning—from behind, and the portal drake jerked forward. Valas's arrow bit deeply into its chest, finding the half inch it needed between two hard scales. The thing's armored skin quivered, and muscles rippled and jerked. The breath caught in its throat, and its cloud was cut short. Still the gas rolled in Valas's direction.

The scout could see it coming. It was aimed toward rather than at him, so he flipped backward away from it. He had no way to protect himself from poison gas. It was a weakness in that situation that Valas found frustrating. All he could do was avoid the gas, and avoidance, at least, was something he was well versed in.

"Hide in the dark there if you wish, drow," the portal drake hissed in Undercommon. Its voice was cold and sharp, almost mechanical, and it echoed in the high-ceilinged chamber with a sound like glass breaking. "I can't see you."

The creature turned to face Danifae, who was whirling her morningstar, looking him in the eye. She was backing up.

"But I can see her," the drake said.

Danifae smiled, and the expression sent a chill down Valas's spine. He stopped, noting the sensation but utterly confused by it.

When the battle-captive lashed out with the enchanted morningstar again, the drake dodged it easily.

"What are you expecting, lizard?" Danifae asked the drake. "Do you think he'll reveal himself to save me? Have you never met a dark elf before?"

Valas, about to draw another arrow, let it drop silently back into his quiver. He slipped the bow over his shoulder and made his way around the back of the drake, skirting the edge of the cavern wall toward the giant face. He quickly estimated the number of steps, the number of seconds, and gauged the background noise for sound cover.

"Dark elves?" the drake said. "I've eaten one or two in my years."

Danifae tried to hit him again, and the drake tried to bite her. They dodged at the same time, which ruined both their attacks.

"Let us pass," Danifae said, and her voice had an air of command to it that got Valas's attention as well as the drake's.

"No," the drake answered, and Danifae stepped in faster than Valas would have thought her capable of.

The morningstar came down on the portal drake's left side, and Valas blinked at the painfully bright flash of blue-white light. The burning illumination traced patterns in the air like glowing spiderwebs. The creature flinched and growled again, its anger and pain showing in the way its lips pulled back from its teeth.

Danifae stepped back, setting her morningstar spinning again. The drake crouched, and Valas stopped and stiffened. The drake didn't lunge at her—it burst into the air with the deafening beat of wings. In less than a second it was high enough to disappear into the gloom up in the cathedral-like space.

Valas stepped forward and let his toes scrape loose gravel on the floor. Danifae looked up at him.

Run back to the tunnel, Valas traced in sign language. *Go!*

Danifae saw him, didn't bother to nod, and turned to run. Valas slipped back into the darkness, drew his *piwafwi* up over his head, and rolled on the floor until he knew he was back in a place where no one would be able to see him.

Valas watched the battle-captive run, knowing she wouldn't be able to see the portal drake. He drew another arrow slowly so that it wouldn't make a sound as it came free of the quiver. He turned and twisted a fraction of an inch here, a hair's breadth there, so the steel tip would reflect no light. Breathing slowly through his mouth, the Bregan D'aerthe scout waited—but didn't have to wait for long.

The sound of the portal drake's wings echoed from above, doubled, then doubled again, and more—not just echoes.

Five, Valas counted.

Still cloaked in auras of invisibility and the gloom of the long-abandoned cavern, Valas started forward.

Five portal drakes swooped out of the shadows in formation. The two at the far ends swept inward, and two others shifted out. They changed positions as they flew, but their target was the same.

Danifae hesitated. Valas could see it in her step. She heard them and knew they could fly faster—many times faster—than she'd ever be able to run. To her credit, though, she didn't look back.

The five portal drakes were identical in every detail, and no one who had traveled as extensively as Valas had could have been fooled for long. Only three wing-beats into it, Valas knew what they were.

Not all of the trinkets the scout wore were enchanted, but the little brass ovoid was, and Valas touched it as he ran. The warmth of his fingers brought the magic to life, and only a thought was needed to wake it fully. It happened without a sound, and Valas never missed a beat or revealed himself at all.

Danifae stopped running anyway, leaving Valas to wonder why.

Similarly confused, the portal drakes drew up short, fluttering to a halt, crossing each others' paths and coming within fractions of an inch from collision.

Danifae smiled at the dragons—all five of them rearing up to shred her with claws like filet knives—and she said, "Careful now. Look behind you."

The toothy sneer that was the drake's reply played out simultaneously on all five sets of jaws.

Valas let his arrow fly, and all four of his own conjured images did the same. The little brass ovoid—a container for a spell that had been very specially crafted by an ancient mage whose secrets had long ago been lost—had done its work, and for each of the five portal drakes, there was a Valas.

For each of the five portal drakes there was an arrow.

The dragon might have heard them or sensed them in some other way, or maybe its curiosity had gotten the better of it. The creature whirled around and met the arrows with its right eye. Four of the arrows blinked out of existence the instant they met with the false drakes, and those illusionary dragons disappeared as well. The barrage left only one real arrow, one real portal drake, and one real eye.

The force of the impact made the creature twitch then stagger back a step.

Valas could tell that the dragon could see him—all five of him—with its one good eye.

"I'll eat you alive : . ." the portal drake rasped, "for that."

Valas drew his kukris, and his images did the same. The dragon, blood pouring from its ruined eye, didn't bother to pull out the arrow that still protruded from its eye socket. Instead it charged, wings up, claws out, jaws open.

Valas stepped to the side, into the drake's blind spot. The creature had obviously never fought with only one eye before, and it fell for the feint. Valas got two quick cuts in—cuts each answered with a deep, rumbling growl.

The drake lashed out, and Valas stepped in and to the side, letting one of his images cross in front of the attack. The portal drake's claw touched the image's shoulder, and by the time the talon passed through the false scout's abdomen the illusion was gone.

The dragon grumbled its frustration, and Valas attacked again. The creature twisted out of reach and snapped its jaws at Valas—coming dangerously close to the real dark elf. When the dragon's single eye narrowed and smoldered, the scout knew the dragon had pegged him.

Valas danced into the drake's blind spot, stepping backward and spinning to keep the dragon off balance and to keep his own mirror images moving frenetically around him. The drake clawed another one into thin air then bit the third out of existence.

Valas watched the image disappear and followed the portal drake's neck with his eyes as it passed half an arm's length in front of him. He looked for cracks, creases, for any sign of weakness in the monster's thick, scaly hide.

He found one and sank a kukri between scales, through skin, into flesh, artery, and bone beneath it. Blood pumped from the creature in torrents. The dragon flailed at Valas, though it couldn't quite see the scout. As the creature died, it managed to brush a claw against the last false drow. The drake started to fall, and Valas skipped out of the way. The narrow head whipped around on its long, supple neck, and the jaws came down on Valas's shoulder, crinkling his armor and bruising the black skin underneath.

The scout pulled away, rolled, and came to his feet with his kukris in front of him.

No attack came. The portal drake splayed across the floor of the cavern. Blood came less frequently and with less urgency with every fading heartbeat.

"Always knew . . ." the dying dragon sighed, "it would be . . . a drow."

The portal drake died with that word on its tongue, and Valas lifted an eyebrow at the thought.

He stepped away from the poisonous corpse and sheathed his kukris. There was no sign of Danifae. Valas didn't know if she'd kept running back the way they'd come or if she was hiding somewhere in the shadows.

With a shrug and a last glance at the portal drake, Valas turned and went to the abandoned monastery. Assuming that the Melarn battle-captive would eventually return to the cavern and the portal that was their goal there, Valas climbed into the great downturned mouth.

Inside the semicircular structure were two tall, freestanding pillars. Between them was nothing but dead air and the side of the tall cavern wall. The interior was shrouded in darkness, and from it came the sharp smell of the portal drake's filth.

Danifae stood between the pillars, her weight on one foot, her hand on her hip.

"Is it dead?" she asked.

Valas stopped several strides from her and nodded.

Danifae looked up and around at the dead stone pillars and the featureless interior of the huge face.

"Good," the battle-captive said. "Is this the portal?"

When she looked back at Valas, he nodded again.

"You know how to open it," she said, with no hint that it might be a question.

Valas nodded a third time, and Danifae smiled.

"Before we go," she said as she pulled a dagger from her shapely hip, "I want to harvest some poison."

Valas blinked and said, "From the portal drake?"

Danifae walked past him, smiling, spinning her dagger between her fingers.

"I'll wait here," he told her.

She kept going without bothering to answer.

If she survives that, Valas thought, she might just be worth traveling with.

🕷 🕷 🕷

Pharaun traced a fingertip along the line of something that hadn't been there the day before: a vein. The blood vessel followed a meandering path along the length of the bone rail of the ship of chaos. At random intervals it branched into thinner capillaries. The whole thing slowly, almost imperceptibly, pulsed with life—warm with the flow of blood. When they'd first come aboard the demonic ship, the railing was solid, dead bone. Half a tenday spent gating in minor demons and feeding it to the ship was changing it. It was coming to life.

"Will it eventually grow skin?" Quenthel asked from behind him.

Pharaun turned and saw the high priestess crouching, examining the deck the same way he was examining the rail.

"Skin?" the wizard asked.

"These veins it's growing seem so fragile," she said. Her voice sounded bored, distant. "If we step on them won't we cut them?"

"I don't know," Pharaun said. What he meant was that he didn't care. "What difference could it possibly make?"

"It could bleed," she said, still looking down at the deck. "If it can bleed, it can die. If it dies when we're . . ."

Pharaun could tell she didn't finish that thought because she was afraid to. He hated it when a high priestess was afraid. Things rarely went well if they started with that.

"Not everything that bleeds dies," he said with a forced smile.

She looked up at him, and their eyes met. He expected her to be angry at least, maybe offended, but she was neither. Pharaun couldn't tell what she was thinking.

"It troubles me," she said after a pause, "that we know so little. A ship like this . . . you should have studied it in the lore, shouldn't you? At Sorcere?"

"I did," Pharaun said. "I've been feeding it a steady diet, I've cowed its captain, and we're nearly ready for our little interplanar jaunt. I know what it is and how it works, which means I know enough. For a priestess you can be overly analytical. Will it grow skin? If it wants to. Will it bleed to death if your spike heels slice a vein? I doubt it. Will it behave exactly the same way every time for everyone? Well, if it did, it wouldn't be very chaotic, now would it?"

"Some day," Quenthel said without a pause, "I will sew your mouth shut so you'll stop talking long enough for me to kill you in peace."

Pharaun chuckled and rubbed cool sweat from his forehead.

"Why, Mistress," the mage replied with a smile, "whatever for?"

"Because I hate you," she replied.

Pharaun said nothing. They gazed at each other for a few moments more then Quenthel stood and looked around.

"I'm getting bored," she said to no one in particular.

You're getting scared, Pharaun thought.

"I'm getting angry," Jeggred cut in.

Both Pharaun and Quenthel looked over to where the draegloth sat. The half-demon was slowly, methodically, skinning a rat. The rodent was still alive.

"No one asked, nephew," Quenthel said with a sneer.

"My apologies, honored aunt," the draegloth said, his voice dripping with icy sarcasm.

"Valas and Danifae will be back soon," Pharaun said, "and we will have the ship ready when they get back. We will be on our way presently, but in the meantime we mustn't let the tedium of this cursed lake get the better of us. It wouldn't do to have a party of dark elves fighting among themselves."

"It's not the lake I find tedious, mage," Jeggred shot back.

Pharaun rejected his first half-dozen retorts before speaking, but his face must have revealed something. He could see it reflected back at him in the draegloth's amused sneer.

"Yes," the wizard said finally, "well, I will accept that gracious threat in the spirit in which it was offered, Jeggred Baenre. Nonetheless, I—"

"Will shut up," the draegloth interrupted. "You will shut your damned mouth."

Jeggred licked the dying, squealing, flayed rat, leaving blood dribbling from his cracked gray lips.

"I don't like this," the half-demon said. "This one—" he tipped his chin to indicate the captive uridezu—"is planning something. It will betray us."

"It's a demon," Quenthel replied quietly.

"Meaning?" the draegloth asked, almost shouting.

"Meaning," Pharaun answered for her, "that of course it will betray us—or try to. The only thing you can trust about a demon is that it will be untrustworthy. It might cheer you to know we feel the same way about you, my draegloth friend."

Pharaun had expected some reaction to that comment but not the one he got. Jeggred and Quenthel locked stares, their eyes boring into each other's. There was a long silence. It was Quenthel who looked away first.

Jeggred actually seemed disappointed.

Aliisza nuzzled close to Kaanyr Vhok, her long ebony tresses mingling with the cambion's silver hair.

"Have you been entertaining ladies while I was away?" the alu-fiend cooed into her lover's neck.

The cambion let out a slow breath through his nose and slid a hand onto Aliisza's back. He drew her closer to him, so their sides were pressed together. Aliisza could feel his blazing body heat, so much hotter than a dark elf's. So comfortable and reassuring. So powerful.

"Jealous?" Kaanyr Vhok whispered.

Aliisza thrilled that he was playing along. It was a rare reaction from the half-demon, who normally kept his feelings so carefully guarded.

"Never," she whispered back, pausing to let her hot, moist lips brush along his skin. "I just wish I could have joined you."

She hoped for further playfulness but instead got a dismissive chuckle. Kaanyr Vhok withdrew from her, and she plastered a coy pout on her face, narrowing her deep green eyes in a scowl.

Vhok flashed her a rare grin and put a finger gently to her lips.

"Don't cry, my dear," he said. "When this mad war is over, we'll have time for dalliances to thrill the likes of even you."

"Until then?"

He took his hand away and stepped to a small table on which was set a tray, a crystal decanter of fine brandy stolen for sport from a shop in Skullport, and a single glass.

"Until then," Vhok said, pouring a splash of the rust-colored liquid into the glass, "we'll have to occasionally break for business."

"How goes that business?"

"Menzoberranzan is under siege," the cambion answered, making a sweeping gesture to indicate their surroundings, "and will be for a very long time, unless someone manages to inject some intelligence—or dare we hope, imagination—into our gray dwarf allies."

"You don't sound hopeful," she said.

"They're as dull witted as they are ill tempered," Vhok replied, "but we make do."

He turned to look at her, and Aliisza smiled, shrugged, and sat. More accurately, she let her body pour onto a richly upholstered sofa, her lithe body draping seductively across it and her eyes playing over his body. Her leather bodice looked stiff and restraining, but it flowed over her the same way she flowed over the sofa, shifting to her will like her own skin. The sheathed long sword at her hip tucked under one leg.

Vhok's own costume was typically opulent, a tunic embroidered in a military style. A long sword of his own hung at his hip, and Aliisza knew he wore any number of magical bits and pieces, even in the privacy of his own temporary quarters.

The tent they inhabited at the rear of the siege lines was cloaked in enchantments that would prevent anyone from overhearing, peeking in, or spying on them in any conceivable way, but still Aliisza felt exposed.

"That lake," she said, her eyes drifting around the silk-draped confines of the tent, "is the dullest place I've ever been, and I've spent time in duergar cities."

Vhok took a small sip of the brandy and closed his eyes, savoring it. Aliisza had long ago gotten over not being offered any.

"It's a dreary, gray cave," she added. "I mean, the air is actually gray. It's awful."

Vhok opened his eyes and shrugged, waiting for more.

"They captured the captain," she continued.

"An uridezu?" the cambion asked.

Aliisza nodded, lifting an eyebrow at the oddly accurate guess.

"Sometimes," Vhok said, "I think you forget what I am."

"I remember," she said hastily.

Kaanyr Vhok was a cambion, the son of a human father and a demon mother. He shared the most dangerous qualities of both those chaotic animals.

Aliisza reached out a hand and shifted on the sofa.

"Come," she said. "Sit with me, and I'll tell you everything I saw. Every last detail. For the war effort."

Vhok downed the rest of the brandy in one gulp, set the glass down, and took Aliisza's hand. His olive skin looked dark and rich against her own pale flesh. Not as dark as Pharaun's of course, but . . .

"Sounds to me," the cambion said as he slid onto the sofa next to his demon lover, "as if these drow are planning a trip."

"They are past planning," she said.

"They are past foolishness," replied Vhok. "Typical drow, serving a chaotic mistress with such strident lawfulness. Always marching in lockstep, with their Houses and their laws and their infantile traditions. No wonder the spider bitch turned her back on them. I'm surprised she suffered their nonsense this long."

Aliisza smiled, showing perfect teeth—human teeth she chose for intimate occasions. She'd found over the decades that even Vhok could be put off by her jagged fangs. Aliisza smiled often and nearly as often changed the size and shape of her teeth to fit her mood.

"You think too little of them," she cautioned. "One or two drow have proven interesting. One or two of the interesting ones, together, can prove dangerous."

Vhok answered with a noncommittal grunt then said, "I suppose I should apologize for calling you back from the Lake of Shadows before you could make contact with this wizard of yours. It was unforgivably officious of me."

The alu-demon leaned in closer and let the tip of her tongue play along the edge of Vhok's pointed ear. He sat still, responding in ways more than simply physical. Aliisza could feel herself flush.

"You will get us both in trouble," the cambion whispered to her, "with the wrong dalliances."

"Or make us both triumphant," she replied, "with the right ones."

Vhok didn't bother answering, and Aliisza moved to whisper very close, very quietly into his ear, "They could do it. The ship of chaos could get them there."

Vhok nodded, and Aliisza tried to read that response. She thought he was happy with her at least for being as discreet as she was with that opinion, even in the spell-warded tent.

She began to unbutton his tunic, teasing him with each slow twist of her fingers, each incremental loosening of his clothing. Aliisza knew what to expect of Kaanyr Vhok without his clothes. Though from all appearances the marquis cambion was an aging half-elf from the World Above, his chest, arms, and legs were covered in green scales. That demon's flesh was a sight few had ever lived to see twice.

"They go in search of the spider bitch," Vhok said, twisting to help her more easily slide his tunic off.

"They mean to wake her?" Aliisza asked, turning her attention to the glistening scales on Vhok's broad chest.

"They mean to take their quest for her favor to her sticky little throne," the cambion replied, "or her sticky little bed . . . or her sticky little tomb, and wake her from her sleep. You say they've been feeding the ship?"

"A constant diet of manes," she whispered into his ear.

Vhok nodded as he began to undress her.

"The wizard?" he asked.

"Pharaun," she answered.

"He can do it, then," Vhok decided. "A Master of Sorcere no less, with the captain enthralled."

"They can get to the Demonweb Pits," she said, "but do you think they can wake her?"

"No," came a startling third voice in what Aliisza was sure was a tent occupied by only two.

Both of them stood and in a thought had their swords in their hands. The blades, identical to the finest detail, practically hummed with magical energy. They stood back-to-back, a defensive stance born of instinct more than practice.

Aliisza could see no one but could feel Vhok tense behind her. She had come to know his moods well, and what she sensed from him was anger, not fear. Aliisza continued to scan the room until a figure presented itself.

"Nimor," Aliisza breathed.

"A dangerous decision," Vhok said to the shadowy figure of the drow assassin, "walking in here unannounced."

"Believe me," Nimor replied, stepping into the warm torchlight nearer the center of the tent, "voyeurism was the last thing on my mind. As you said, Lord Vhok, there is business to be handled. Besides, I didn't 'walk' in."

Vhok slipped his sword, a blade he called "Burnblood," back into its sheath and stepped away from Aliisza. With slow, deliberate motions, he picked up his tunic and slipped it back on, covering the scaly flesh he so seldom exposed.

The edge of Nimor's thin lips slipped up in wry amusement. Something about that reaction made Aliisza uneasy—more so than normal when in the assassin's presence.

"What business brings you here now, Anointed Blade?" asked Vhok.

"That drow expedition, of course," the assassin replied. "They have found a ship of chaos, and they mean to pay their sleeping goddess a visit?"

The assassin was looking at Aliisza, expecting an answer. She sheathed her own sword and slipped back down to the sofa, never taking her eyes off the dark elf. The alu-fiend didn't bother refastening the clasps Vhok had undone on her bodice.

"There's very little reason to suspect they'll succeed," said Vhok.

"Would you agree, Aliisza?" Nimor asked.

Aliisza shrugged and said, "They have a wizard with them who could likely handle the ship. I became acquainted with him in Ched Nasad just before the end, and I found him quite capable."

"Ah, yes," Nimor said, "Pharaun Mizzrym. He could be the next archmage, or so I hear. If his name were Baenre, that is."

"They could do it," Vhok said.

Nimor took a deep breath and said, "There are a thousand things that could go wrong between the Lake of Shadows and the Abyss, and a thousand thousand things could go wrong between the edge of the Abyss and the sixty-sixth layer."

"What will they find there, Nimor?" Aliisza asked, genuinely curious.

Nimor smiled, and Aliisza momentarily thrilled at his feral expression.

"I haven't the vaguest notion," he answered.

"If they find Lolth?" asked Vhok.

"If they find Lolth," said Nimor, "and she's dead, then we can settle in for as long a siege as necessary. Menzoberranzan is doomed. If she sleeps and they can't wake her or if she has simply decided to abandon her faithful on this world, the same is true. If she sleeps and they do wake her or she is ignoring them and they regain her favor, well, that would pose a difficulty for us."

"How do we know what they'll find?" asked the cambion.

"We don't," Nimor answered.

The dark elf folded his arms across his chest and tipped his head down. His features grew tighter, darker as he wrapped himself in thought.

"Let them go, but . . ." Aliisza suggested, the words tripping over her tongue before she'd thought them through.

"Send someone with them," Nimor finished for her.

The alu-fiend smiled, showing a row of yellow-white fangs.

"Agrach Dyrr is alone," Triel Baenre said. "Alone and under siege."

Gromph nodded but didn't look at his sister. He was captivated by the sight of Menzoberranzan. The City of Spiders stretched out before him, ablaze in faerie fire, magnificent in its chaos, in its perversion of nature—a cave made into a home.

"Good," Gromph replied, "but don't assume they'll give up easily. They have loyal servants of their own and allies who make up for what they lack in intelligence with superiority of numbers."

From where they stood on a high belvedere on the outside edge of one of the westernmost spires of the House Baenre complex, Gromph had a largely unobstructed view of the subterranean city. The Baenre palace stood against the southern wall of the huge cavern, atop the second tier of a wide rock shelf. It was the First House, and its position above the rest of the city was more than symbolic.

"They may have thrown in with the gray dwarves," Andzrel Baenre said, "but no dark elf in Menzoberranzan fights on their behalf."

Gromph turned to his left and looked west across the high ground of Qu'ellarz'orl. Before him was the high stalagmite tower of House Xorlarrin and beyond that the cluster of stalactites and stalagmites that housed the treasonous Agrach Dyrr. Flashes of fire and lightning—the work of Xorlarrin's formidable and plentiful mages—flickered across the ground and in the air around Dyrr's. The lichdrow who was the rebel House's master was holed up inside there somewhere, and his own mages answered back with fire and thunder of their own. Gromph could feel his sister Triel and the weapons master Andzrel behind him, waiting for him to speak.

"It seems as if I've been gone a very, very long time," Gromph said, his voice subdued but carefully modulated to covey to his sister his grave disappointment at the state of the war.

He could sense Triel stiffen behind him then shake his words off.

"You have been," she said, letting no small amount of acid into her own voice, "but let us not dwell on failures in the face of such grave danger to all we hold dear."

Gromph allowed himself a smile and glanced back over his shoulder at his sister. She was staring at him, her arms folded in front of her, cradling them as if she were cold. He turned back to the ongoing stalemate around the foot of Agrach Dyrr and noted with some satisfaction how well his new eyes were seeing. The blurring and the pain were mostly gone, leaving Gromph to enjoy the irony of watching House Agrach Dyrr fall with a set of Agrach Dyrr eyes.

"Not all the Houses are at our beck and call, though, are they?" he asked.

Triel sighed and said, "It is still Menzoberranzan, and we are still dark elves. Houses Xorlarrin and Faen Tlabbar are firmly with us. Faen Tlabbar brings with it House Srune'lett, who's strongly allied with House Duskryn. Of the lesser Houses we can rely on Symryvvin, Hunzrin, Vandree, and Mizzrym to serve us."

"That's all?" Gromph asked after a pause.

"Barrison Del'Armgo perhaps still stings over Oblodra," Triel replied. "They remain loyal to Menzoberranzan, and they fight, but they keep their own council."

"And carry their own allies," Gromph added.

"Thankfully, no," Triel corrected, obviously pleased with proving her brother wrong at the same time she was pleased that that powerful House was on its own. "The other lesser Houses remain neutral but offer their assets in defense of the city. Better a dark elf neighbor you hate than a duergar in any capacity."

"Or a tanarukk," Gromph added.

"Or a tanarukk," his sister agreed.

Gromph turned his attention back to the city at large. There were very few drow in the streets and the archmage could see columns of troops moving, some at double time, through the winding thoroughfares.

"The city is quiet," he commented.

"The city," Andzrel cut in, "is hard under siege."

Gromph bristled at that but knew better than to kill the messenger, at least in that case.

"We are surrounded on all sides, but we're fighting," the weapons master continued, "and will continue to fight. Our own forces hold Qu'ellarz'orl and are moving to support House Hunzrin in Donigarten north."

"The siege of Agrach Dyrr," Triel offered, "is largely House Xorlarrin's, and they seem to have it well in hand."

"Is the lichdrow dead?" asked Gromph.

There was a pause, during which neither the matron mother nor the weapons master bothered to answer.

"Then they could have a firmer hand," the archmage concluded.

Andzrel cleared his throat and continued, "Faen Tlabbar, aside from blocking Agrach Dyrr's retreat west, guards the southwest approaches to the Dark Dominion from the Web to the western tip of Qu'ellarz'orl. They face the largest concentration of gray dwarves, assisted by House Srune'lett. Faen Tlabbar also supports House Duskryn's efforts to hold the caves north of the Westrift."

"Well," said Gromph with a wry edge to his voice, "isn't Faen Tlabbar impressive."

"They are," Triel agreed, "and Srune'lett and Duskryn require no more proof. If Faen Tlabbar were to betray us, they would take those two Houses with them at least."

"Why in all the Underdark might they do that?" Gromph joked.

Triel laughed, and the weapons master cleared his throat.

"What of the lesser Houses?" Gromph asked.

"Symryvvin assists Duskryn above the Westrift," Andzrel said.

"Another probably in Ghenni's pocket, should it come to that," Triel commented.

Gromph shrugged and said, "If they defend Menzoberranzan now, let them make plans for afterward. If we survive, we survive as First House."

"I agree, Archmage," said Andzrel.

Gromph turned to look at the warrior, letting a cold gaze linger over the drow's rough features and battle-scarred armor.

"Of course you do," the archmage said, his voice barely above a whisper.

Andzrel looked down then looked at Triel, who only smiled at him.

"House . . ." the weapons master began, obviously thinking it safer to continue his debriefing than further patronize the powerful archmage with his support. He cleared his throat and continued, "House Hunzrin is hard pressed against forces of the Scoured Legion in Donigarten north. Vandree holds well against duergar south of the Westrift. Mizzrym lends what it can to Xorlarrin's efforts against Agrach Dyrr, and they also send patrols into the mushroom forest where they've encountered the odd spy."

"The tanarukks are mostly in the east, then?" Gromph asked.

"As one would expect, Archmage," the weapons master risked. "They marched from below Hellgate Keep, which lies to our east. The duergar are from Gracklstugh."

Gromph let a breath out slowly through his nose.

"I never thought I'd live to see the day," Triel murmured. "Gracklstugh . . ."

"The tanarukks are more formidable foes," Gromph went on, ignoring his sister. "Tell me that more than House Hunzrin are holding against them."

"Barrison Del'Armgo fights well in the south of Donigarten," Andzrel replied, "against the largest concentration of the Scoured Legion."

"Mez'Barris will have her heroes," Triel sighed.

"North?" Gromph asked.

"Barrison Del'Armgo again, with help from the Academy, holds the Clawrift," replied the weapons master, "mostly east into Eastmyr. The duergar are thin there. There have been reports of illithid incursions—mostly one or two at a time—in the east, from beyond the Wanderways."

"The flayers sense weakness," Gromph said. "They're scavengers. They'll harry us when they can and disappear entirely when they can't. Some of them can prove . . . irritating, but they'll wait till we're weaker—if we let ourselves get weaker—before they appear in force."

Neither Triel nor Andzrel risked comment on that.

"And the other Houses?" asked Gromph.

"They protect themselves," Triel answered. "They patrol the immediate surrounds of their manors, assist in keeping the peace in the streets, and I'd prefer to believe, they await command."

"Well," said Gromph, "I'm sure we'll find out soon enough. Still, I'd have liked more allies within our own damned city."

"Tier Breche is with us," Triel said, "though I doubt I have to tell you that. In Quenthel's absence, Arach-Tinilith answers only to me. I know you have done well in your return to power at Sorcere, and Melee-Magthere will always fight should one raise a blade against the City of Spiders."

"Your gold has paid for the mercenaries, I assume," Gromph said.

Triel shrugged and replied, "Bregan D'aerthe is on extended contract, though the Abyss knows where Jarlaxle's been. It'll take every dead duergar's gold teeth to replenish our coffers in the end, but in the meantime, Bregan D'aerthe act as infiltrators and scouts and are moving forces throughout the city to monitor and support the lesser Houses."

"Much of what we've told you today, Archmage," Andzrel offered, "came from Bregan D'aerthe reports."

"Good for them," Gromph lied.

"Menzoberranzan will stand," Andzrel declared.

"But not forever," Triel added.

"Not for long," said Gromph.

There was a long silence. Gromph spent the time watching the flickering of valuable battle magic being spent against House Agrach Dyrr.

"What will be left?" asked Triel after a time.

"Matron Mother," Andzrel said, "Archmage, in my opinion the greatest threat from within the city is no longer Agrach Dyrr but Barrison Del'Armgo."

Gromph lifted an eyebrow and turned to look at the weapons master.

"Even without any of the lesser Houses at their side," the warrior went on, "they are the greatest threat to the First House's power. Matron Mother Armgo is already making overtures to many of the lesser Houses, especially Hunzrin and Kenafin."

"And?" Triel prompted.

"And," Gromph broke in, finishing on Andzrel's behalf, "they could bite off Donigarten."

"Our food supply," Andzrel added.

Gromph smiled when Triel's face turned almost gray.

"Yes, well," the archmage said, "all things in their turn. Barrison Del'Armgo will answer for their ambitions only after I've cleaned up a more open insurrection."

"Dyrr?" Triel didn't have to ask.

"It's time for our old friend the lichdrow to die again," Gromph replied. "This time, permanently."

SEVEN

Danifae counted the warriors in front of her—eight armed with spears, and a row of a dozen crossbowmen behind them—and waited.

"Welcome to the City of Portals," one of the spearmen said, his blood-red eyes darting quickly, alertly, between Danifae and Valas. "If you reach for a weapon or begin to cast a spell, we'll kill you before you get a single breath out."

Danifae flashed the male a smile and was gratified to see his gaze linger on her. If Valas were going to attack, he would have at that moment. He didn't, so Danifae found herself in the position of having to trust him again.

"Who are you, where are you from," the guard asked, "and what is your business in Sschindylryn?"

"I am Valas Hune," the scout answered. He paused and reached up slowly to the neck of his *piwafwi*. When he drew his cloak aside, the guard's eyes fixed on something. Danifae was sure it had to be the insignia of the mercenary company to which Valas was attached. "My business here is to resupply. Give us a day or so to gather what we need, and we'll be on our way."

The guard nodded and looked at Danifae.

"And you?" he asked. "You don't look Bregan D'aerthe."

Danifae chuckled playfully and replied, "I am Danifae Yauntyrr. And you?"

The guard was puzzled by the question.

"She is a battle-captive in the service of the First Daughter of House Melarn," Valas answered for her.

Danifae felt her skin tingle with suppressed rage. What kind of scout volunteered such information? Or did he mean to put her in her place by reminding her that while he was free, she was not?

The guard smiled—leered almost—and looked Danifae briefly up and down.

"Melarn?" he said. "Never heard of it."

"A lesser House," Valas answered again before Danifae could speak up. "It was destroyed with the others in the fall of Ched Nasad."

The guard looked at her again and said, "That means you're free, eh?"

Danifae shrugged, saying nothing. She, unlike Valas, wasn't about to give away information. The last thing she needed was for anyone to know that she'd come to Sschindylryn to address that very question once and for all.

"We want no trouble with Bregan D'aerthe," the guard said to Valas. "Get your supplies, then get out. Menzoberranyr are less than popular here."

"Why would that be?" asked Valas.

The guards visibly relaxed, and half the crossbowmen slipped the bolts off their weapons and stepped back from the firing line. The spearmen put their weapons up but still stood ready.

"It's your fault," the guard replied, "or so they say."

"What is our fault?" Danifae asked, not certain why she identified herself as Menzoberranyr, having never even been there.

"They say," the guard said, "that it was a Menzoberranyr who killed Lolth."

Valas laughed, letting a generous portion of contempt coat the sound.

"Yes, well . . ." the guard finished. "That's what they say."

"This way," Valas said over his shoulder to Danifae.

The battle-captive nodded, took stock of her belongings, and followed the scout past the guards and toward the wide, open gate into the city proper. As she passed him, Danifae gave the guard captain a playful wink. The male's jaw opened, but he managed to catch it before it dropped.

When she was certain they were out of earshot of the guards, Danifae drew closer to the Bregan D'aerthe scout. Valas flinched away from her touch then seemed to force himself to relax. Danifae, making careful note of his reaction to her, leaned in very close. With a greater than necessary exhalation of hot air from her husky, hushed voice, Danifae whispered into his ear.

"I'm not going with you," she told Valas.

"Why not?" he answered, matching her discreet volume but not her flirtatiousness.

"I never enjoyed shopping," Danifae replied, "and I have errands of my own."

For a moment it looked to Danifae as if Valas were actually going to argue or at least press her for more information.

"Very well," he said after a few seconds. "I have a way of calling you when it's time to go."

"I have a way of ignoring you if I'm not ready," she replied.

Valas didn't respond, though that time Danifae was sure she'd broken through his impenetrable armor. She turned away and stepped into the crowd that was flowing past the columned, temple-like structure that surrounded the gate. Within seconds she had effectively lost herself in the strange city, leaving the scout behind.

The city of Sschindylryn was contained in a single pyramid-shaped void in the solid rock some unfathomable distance below the surface of Faerûn. The pyramid had three sides, each more than two miles long, and the apex was two miles above. Bioluminescent fungus grew in patches all around the smooth outer walls, giving the whole city an eerie, dim yellow ambient light. The drow who called the city home lived in houses constructed of stone and brick—unusual in a dark elf city—that were built on stepped tiers. The outer edges of the city were actually trenches carved into the stone floor of the pyramid. In the center, a sort of huge ziggurat rose up into the cool, still air. There was no physical way in or out of the city. No tunnel connected the cavern to the rest of the Underdark. Sschindylryn was sealed. Locked away.

Except for the gates, and there were thousands of those.

They were everywhere. In only the first few blocks Danifae saw a dozen of them. They led to every corner of the Underdark, onto the World Above, perhaps beyond to the planes and elsewhere. Some were open to the public, left there by no one remembered whom. Others were commercial ventures, offering transport to some other drow city or trade site of the lesser races for a fee. Still others were kept secret, used only by a chosen few. Gangs controlled some, merchant costers controlled more, while the clergy maintained hundreds.

On the narrow streets Danifae passed mostly other dark elves, and all of them seemed, like her, concerned entirely with their own business. They ignored her, and she did likewise. As she walked, she became increasingly aware that she was in a strange city, alone, looking for a single drow who was very likely still making every effort to hide.

❈   ❈   ❈

House Agrach Dyrr had been part of the political landscape of Menzoberranzan for more than five thousand years. Only House Baenre was older.

For most of that time, Houses Baenre and Agrach Dyrr had maintained a close relationship. Of course there was never trust, that wasn't something that existed in any but the must tenuous and rudimentary form in the City of Spiders, but they had had certain arrangements. They shared common interests and common goals. Agrach Dyrr had fulfilled its role in the city's hierarchy. It went to war with the city, defended itself against rival Houses, destroyed a few from time to time as necessity dictated, and in all things followed the teachings and the whims of the Queen of the Demonweb Pits.

Matron Mother Yasraena Dyrr enjoyed pain. She enjoyed chaos, and she enjoyed the blessings of Lolth. When that last bit went away, things changed.

From their palace on the wide shelf of Qu'ellarz'orl, the Lichdrow Dyrr had stood with his much younger granddaughter and watched the city turn against them. Well, that wasn't entirely accurate, the lichdrow knew. He had turned against the city, and he had done it with precise and careful timing. He had made the final decision, as he always had in times of greatest peril and greatest opportunity. Yasraena did what she was told, occasionally being made to feel as if it was her idea in the first place, sometimes merely given an order.

Most days, the youthful matron mother was as much in

command of the House as any of the city's matrons. When it truly counted, though, the lichdrow stepped in.

The palace of House Agrach Dyrr was a ring of nine giant stalagmites that rose from the rocky floor of Qu'ellarz'orl, surrounded by a dry moat crossed at only one point by a wide, defensible bridge. In the center of the ring of stalagmites, behind a square wall of spell-crafted stone, was the House temple. That massive cathedral was more than a symbol to the drow of House Agrach Dyrr—it was a sincere and passionate proclamation of their faith in the Spider Queen.

In the past months, though, the temple had grown as quiet as the goddess it was built to honor.

"Lolth has abandoned us," the lichdrow said.

He stood at the entrance to the temple. A hundred yards in front of him, his granddaughter kneeled before the black altar and stared silently up at an enormous, stylized representation of the goddess. The idol weighed several tons and had been shaped by divine magic out of a thousand of the most precious materials the Underdark had to offer.

"We have abandoned her," Yasraena replied.

Their voices carried through the huge chamber.

The lichdrow floated toward her, his toes almost touching the marble floor. She didn't turn around.

"Well," he said, "what could she expect?"

The matron mother let the joke hang there without comment.

"The bridge holds," Dyrr reported, sounding almost bored. "Word from agents within Sorcere is that Vorion was captured but was later killed. I'm still finding out if he broke."

"Vorion . . ." the matron mother breathed.

She had taken Vorion as her consort only a few years before.

"My condolences," the lichdrow said.

"He had a few admirable qualities," the matron mother replied.

"Ah well, at least he died in defense of the House."

Dyrr tired of the subject, so he changed it.

"Gromph has regained his sight."

Yasraena nodded and said, "He'll be coming for us."

"He'll be coming for *me*," the lichdrow corrected.

The matron mother sighed. She must have known he was right. The priestess, bereft of her connection to Lolth, was still a force to be reckoned with. She was experienced, cruel, strong, and she had access to the House's stores of magical items, artifacts, and scrolls, but against the Archmage of Menzoberranzan, she would be little more than a nuisance. If Gromph was coming, he was coming for the lichdrow, and if Agrach Dyrr was to survive, it would be the lichdrow who would have to save it.

"I don't suppose you can count on your new friends," the matron mother said.

"My 'new friends' have problems of their own," Dyrr replied. "They lay siege to the city, but Baenre and the others Houses have done a surprisingly good job of holding the entrances to the Dark Dominion."

"They have us bottled in our palace like rats in a trap," said the matron mother.

Dyrr laughed, the sound muffled and strained from under his mask. The lichdrow almost never allowed anyone to see his face. Yasraena was one of the few to whom he would reveal himself, but even then, not often. Though she wasn't looking at him, he maintained the affectation of leaning on his staff. The outward illusion of advanced age and physical weakness had become second nature to him, and he'd begun to maintain that attitude even when no one was looking. His body, free of the demands of life for a millennia, was as responsive as it had been the day he died and was resurrected.

"Don't begin to believe our own ruse, granddaughter," Dyrr

said. "Not everything has gone strictly to plan, but all is far from lost, and we are far from trapped. We were meant to be in the city, and here we are. The two of us are in our own temple, unmolested. We have lost troops and the odd consort and cousin, but we live, and our assets are largely intact. Our 'new friends' as you call them, have the city hard under siege, and many of the Houses refuse to join the fight—join it in any real way, at least. All we have to do is keep pressing, keep pressing, keep pressing, and we will win the day. I grant you that it is an inconvenience that Gromph escaped my little snare. I do wonder how he managed it. But I assure you it will be the last time I underestimate the Archmage of Menzoberranzan."

"Did you underestimate him," she asked, "or did he beat you?"

There was a moment of silence between them as Yasraena stared up at the idol of Lolth, and Dyrr waited in mute protest.

"This assassin. . . ." she said at last.

"Nimor," Dyrr provided.

"I know you don't trust him," she said.

"Of course not," the lichdrow replied with a dry chuckle. "He is committed to his cause, though."

"And that cause?" asked the matron mother. "The downfall of Menzoberranzan? The destruction of the matriarchy? The wholesale abandonment of the worship of Lolth?"

"Lolth is gone, Yasraena," Dyrr said. "The matriarchy has functioned, but as with all things past it too may not survive the Spider Queen's demise. The city, of course, will endure. It will endure under my steady, immortal hand."

"Yours," she asked, "or Nimor's?"

"Mine," the lichdrow replied with perfect finality.

"He should be in the city," Yasraena added before there could be too significant a pause. "Nimor and his duergar friends should be here. Every day that goes by, Baenre and Xorlarrin wear us down. Little by little, granted, but little by little for long enough and . . ."

She let the thought hang there, and Dyrr only shrugged in response.

"If you expected to do this without Gromph on their side," Yasraena asked, "what now that he's back?"

"As I said," the lichdrow replied, "I will kill him. He will come for me, and I will be ready. When the time comes, I will meet him."

"Alone?" she asked, concern plain in her voice.

The lichdrow didn't answer. Neither of them moved, and the temple was silent for a long time.

❦ ❦ ❦

He had come for a little food and a few minor incidentals. They could drink the water from the Lake of Shadows but could use a few more skins to carry it in. Under normal circumstances nothing could be easier for someone as well traveled as Valas Hune.

Normal circumstances.

The words had lost all meaning.

"Hey," the gnoll grumbled, hefting its heavy war-axe so Valas could see it. "You wait line, drow."

Valas looked the gnoll in the eyes, but it didn't back down.

"Everybody wait line," the guard growled.

Valas took a deep breath, left his hands at his side, and said, "Is Firritz here?"

The gnoll blinked at him, surprised.

Valas could feel other eyes on him. Drow, duergar, and representatives of a few more lesser races looked his way. Though they would be angry, impatient at having to wait in line while Valas presumed to bypass it, none of them spoke.

"Firritz," Valas repeated. "Is he here?"

"How you . . . ?" the gnoll muttered, eyes like slits. "How you know Firritz?"

Valas waited for the gnoll to understand that he wasn't going to say any more. It took seven heartbeats.

With a glance at the increasingly restless line, the gnoll said, "Follow."

Valas didn't smile, speak, or look at the others. He followed the gnoll in silence the full length of the line then through a mildewed curtain into a very large room with an uncomfortably low ceiling. The space was so crowded with sacks and crates and barrels that in the first few seconds after entering, Valas saw at least one of everything he'd come for.

A single, stooped old drow sat at a table in the center of the storehouse. A dozen different types of coins were arranged in neat stacks on the table in front of him. The gnoll nodded toward him, and Valas stepped closer to the merchant.

"Firritz," the scout said, his voice echoing.

The old drow didn't turn to look at him. Instead, he slowly counted a stack of gold coins then wrote the total on a piece of parchment on the table in front of him. Valas waited.

Perhaps ten minutes went by, and in that time the gnoll left the room and came back three times. Each time he came back, he seemed a bit more perplexed. Valas hadn't moved a muscle.

Finally, when the gnoll had left the room again, Firritz looked up from his counting and glanced at Valas.

"That's about how long you would have waited in line," the old drow said, his voice reedy and forced. "Now, what can I do for you?"

"Remember that you kept Bregan D'aerthe waiting," Valas said.

"Don't threaten me, Valas Hune," Firritz said. "Menzo's reputation has become a bit less impressive of late. Gray dwarves, I heard. Why aren't you there to defend the motherland?"

"I go where the coin leads me," said the scout. "Just like you."

"The coin doesn't lead to Menzoberranzan anymore, does it?"

"Bregan D'aerthe's credit is still good here," Valas said. "I need supplies."

"Credit?" said Firritz. "That word implies that your master at some point intends to pay his debt. I run up a tab, more and more, year after year, and see nothing for it. Maybe things have changed enough that that isn't necessary anymore, eh?"

"Take a deep breath," Valas said.

The old drow looked up at him. They stayed like that for a bit, but finally Firritz drew in a deep breath then exhaled slowly.

"That's what you see for it," Valas finished, "and it's necessary I get a few supplies."

Firritz frowned and said, "Nothing magical. Everyone's been buying up the magic bits—and for twice, even thrice the market value."

"I need food," the scout replied, "waterskins, a few odds and ends."

"You have a pack lizard?"

"No," Valas said with a smile and a tip of his head, "so I'll need something to carry it in. Something magical."

Firritz swept his arm across the table, scattering the coins onto the floor with a thousand echoing clatters.

"Food, Firritz," Valas said. "Time has become an issue for me."

Chapter

EIGHT

Danifae could feel the Binding, and she could feel Halisstra. No matter how many thousands of feet of rock separated them, they were connected.

Danifae's skin crawled.

The farther from the center of the city she walked, the higher the mix of non-drow she passed on the streets. It was with no little relief, and after enduring lewd remarks from a trio of hobgoblins that she came to her destination.

She had never been to Sschindylryn before and had never seen that one particular structure, but she had gone straight to it. She'd made no wrong turns and asked for no directions.

Danifae stood in front of a complex jumble of mud bricks and flagstones arranged into what looked like some kind of hive or termite hill. Over the wide door—wide enough to accommodate a pack lizard and a decent-sized wagon—hung a slab of black stone into which was carved an elaborate sigil. The symbol contained unmistakable traces of the Yauntyrr crest but somehow turned in on itself, imploded, perverted.

Danifae reminded herself that no matter what happened, House Yauntyrr was gone. The integrity of its heraldry was of no concern to her, nor, she was sure, to anyone else.

She stepped inside.

Zinnirit's gatehouse, not unlike the larger gatehouse they'd entered the city through, was mostly open space on the street level. There looked to be room for another floor or even two above—likely Zinnirit's private residence—but the heart of the establishment was in that single cavernous chamber.

There were three gates, each a circle of elaborately interconnected stones easily thirty feet in diameter. No seething magical light pulsed through them. All three were inactive, dark.

"Zinnirit!" Danifae called.

Her voice echoed in the empty space. There was no immediate reply. Danifae had lost track of time quite a while before, and as she called the former House Mage's name again, she realized she might have dropped in on the wizard in the middle of his Reverie.

She didn't care.

"Zinnirit!"

A quiet, slow shuffling of feet answered Danifae's third entreaty. The sound was unmistakable but difficult to trace in the huge, echoing space. Despite the echoes, Danifae got the distinct impression that there was more than one set of feet. She couldn't count exactly how many—maybe half a dozen—and they were getting closer.

Danifae drew her morningstar and set it swinging at her right side.

"Zinnirit," she called. "Show yourself, you old fool."

Again, the only answer was that same echoing set of shuffling footsteps.

A shadow bobbed back and forth at the edge of her peripheral vision from deeper into the gatehouse. Danifae reacted with a thought, calling without question or hesitation on an ability bred into all highborn drow.

Five figures blazed to life with shimmering purple light. The faerie fire ringed their bodies and outlined them against the dull gloom behind them. The figures slowly shambled toward her and took no notice of the faerie fire.

The realization of what they were hit her half a second after the foul smell did.

They were zombies: walking dead of what looked to be mostly humans, though Danifae wasn't interested in conducting a thorough physical examination.

"Zinnirit . . ." she breathed, irritated.

One of the zombies reached out for her, and a quiet, painful-sounding groan escaped its rotting, tattered lips.

In answer, Danifae stood straight, arched one delicate eyebrow, held out one slim-fingered hand, and said, "Stop."

The zombies stopped.

"That will be all," she said, her voice a perfect, level calm.

The zombies, all still aglow in purple, turned clumsily, bumping into each other, and shambled away from the battle-captive. They were moving a bit faster away from her than they had come at her.

"Well," a firm male voice said, the single word echoing a thousandfold in the gatehouse chamber.

Danifae put her hand down, let it rest on her hip.

"You shouldn't have been able to do that," the voice said, quieter but closer.

Danifae followed that echo back to its source and saw another drow-shaped shadow at the edge of the gloom.

"No need for faerie fire," he said and stepped close enough for Danifae to see him.

"Zinnirit," she said, pasting a broad grin on her face. "How lovely it is to see you, my old friend."

The aged drow moved a few steps closer to her but still kept a respectful—no, suspicious—distance from Danifae.

"You were taken to Ched Nasad," the wizard said. "I heard that Ched Nasad fell apart."

"It did," Danifae answered.

"I honor Lolth as much as any drow," the wizard said, "but you can keep buildings made of web, thank you very much."

"That wasn't the problem," Danifae replied. "Of course, you don't give the south end of a northbound rothé what happened to Ched Nasad."

"You know me too well still," he said.

"As you know me."

"It isn't easy, you know," the old wizard said, taking a few steps closer. "What you want done. It's not something you simply . . . dispel."

Zinnirit looked different. Danifae was amazed at how stooped he was, how thin, how wizened. He looked like a human, or a goblin. He looked bad.

"You've adopted the fashions of your new home, I see," Danifae remarked, nodding at the wizard's outlandish dress.

"Yes, I have," he replied. "Good for business, you know. Doesn't frighten the neighbors as much as the old spiky armor."

"You know why I'm here," said Danifae, "and I know you knew I was coming. Were the zombies meant to scare me?"

"Another bit of showmanship, actually," the mage explained. "Drow and lesser races alike are attracted to the odd bit of necromancy. Makes me seem more serious, I suppose."

"You knew I was in Sschindylryn the second I stepped through the gate," she said.

"I did, yes."

"Then let's get on with it."

"Things have changed, my dear Danifae," Zinnirit said. "I am no longer your mother's House mage, subject to the whims of her spoiled daughters."

"You expect me to pay?" she asked.

"You expect something for nothing?"

Danifae let one of her eyebrows twitch in response. That barely perceptible gesture made the old wizard look away. She took a deep breath and concentrated on that corner of her mind in which the Binding hid.

"I know why you've come," Zinnirit pressed. "It's always there, isn't it?"

Seeing no reason to lie, Danifae said, "It is. It's been there every second since I fell into the hands of House Melarn."

"It's an insidious enchantment that binds you . . ." said the old drow, "binds you in a way that only a drow could imagine. While the Binding is in effect, you will never be free. If your mistress . . . ?"

"Halisstra Melarn."

"If Halisstra Melarn dies, so goes Danifae," he continued. "If she calls for you, you'll go to her. No question, no hesitation, no choice. You can never—much as you might like to, even as a method of suicide—raise your hand to her. The Binding won't let your body move in a way that would result in your mistress's death."

"You understand well," she whispered, "but not completely. In many ways, it's the Binding that fuels me. That spell keeps me alive, keeps me vital, keeps me listening, watching, and learning. That spell, and my desire to break its hold, is what I live for."

Danifae saw fear flash across the old wizard's eyes.

"You weren't the only member of our House to be brought to Ched Nasad," he said. "After that last raid—the one that destroyed the redoubt, that destroyed the family—others were taken by Ched Nasad's Houses, and the rest were scattered over a wide swath of the Underdark. Those who lived, anyway, and that was precious few."

"Zinnirit Yauntyrr made it to Sschindylryn," she continued for him, "and did quite well here. That never surprised me. You were a talented spellcaster. No one could teleport like you. You were the master. And teleporting isn't all you're good at.

"You're ready," she said. "I know you."

"What will you do when you're free?" he asked.

Danifae smiled at him and stepped closer. They could touch each other if either lifted an arm.

"All right," the old mage breathed. "I don't need to know, do I?"

Danifae offered no response. She stood waiting.

"I will have to touch you," the wizard said.

Danifae nodded and stepped closer still—close enough that she could smell the old man's breath: cinnamon and pipeweed.

"It will hurt," he said even as his hand was reaching up to her. He placed the tips of his first and second fingers on her forehead. His touch was dry and cool. Strange words poured from his mouth. It might have been Draconic he was speaking but a dialect she couldn't quite pin down. After a full minute he stopped and lowered his hand. His red-orange eyes locked on hers. Danifae did not pull away, much as she wanted to.

"Tell me," he whispered, "that you want to be through with it.""I want it gone," she said. Her voice seemed too loud, too sharp to her own ears. "I want to be free of the Binding."

No sooner had that last syllable left her lips than her chest tightened, then her legs, her arms, her feet, her hands, her neck, her jaw, her fingers and toes—each one. Every muscle in her body cramped and seemed to rip into shreds under her skin. She might have screamed, but her throat was clamped shut. Her lungs tried to force what air was left in them up and out through her closed throat, past her clenched jaws, between her grinding teeth. She went blind with pain.

It was over.

Her body loosened so quickly and so completely that she collapsed. Vomit poured from her, and her vision was a swirling blur. Her eyes watered, her nose ran, and she came within half a second of wetting herself.

That was over too.

Danifae was shaking as she stood. She mastered the barrage of emotions that assaulted her—everything from humiliation to homicidal rage—with a single thought:

I'm free.

She wiped her mouth on her sleeve and stepped away from her own sick. Zinnirit followed, reaching out to steady her in case she fell again, but she avoided his touch, and he seemed as reluctant to touch her.

"I can't feel her," Danifae said even as she realized that the connection was truly gone.

"She won't feel you either," said the mage. "She'll probably think you died . . . wherever she is."

Danifae nodded and collected herself. Part of her wanted to shriek with delight, to dance and sing like some sun-cursed surface elf, but she did not. There was still one more thing she needed. The battle-captive turned free drow blinked the tears from her eyes and looked at the old mage's hands.

Zinnirit wore many rings, but Danifae was looking for one in particular, and she recognized it immediately. On the second finger of Zinnirit's left hand was a band of intertwined platinum and copper traced with delicate Draconic script.

"You kept it," she said.

He looked at her with narrowed eyes and shook his head.

"That ring," she explained. "My mother's ring."

Zinnirit nodded, unsure.

"You enchanted that for her yourself, didn't you?" she asked.

Zinnirit nodded again.

"Wherever she might go," Danifae mused, "that ring would return her home to her private chamber in House Yauntyrr in far Eryndlyn. I remember she used it once when we were in Llacerellyn. The ring took us both home when an idle threat turned into an assassination attempt and someone sent an elemental after her.

"You've never used it? You've never tried to go back?"

"There's nothing there," the mage answered too quickly. "Nothing to return to. I retuned the ring years ago to bring me back here."

"Still, have you ever had necessity to use it?" she asked. "Has it ever brought you back here from some distant cave?"

Zinnirit shook his head.

"Never stepped through your own gates?"

The old drow shook his head again and said, "I have nowhere to go."

Danifae tipped her head to one side and let the tiniest smile of appreciation slide across her lips.

"You poor thing," she whispered. "All these years . . . so lonely. Waiting for one last chance to serve a daughter of House Yauntyrr."

Danifae reached out and took Zinnirit's hand. The mage flinched at her touch but didn't pull away.

She lifted his hand to her lips and kissed it. Considering she'd just thrown up all over his floor, Zinnirit winced at the gesture, but still allowed it. Danifae pressed the old drow's hand to her cheek. It felt warmer, less dry.

"Dear Zinnirit," she whispered, looking the old mage in the eye, "what has become of you?"

"I'm a thousand years old," the mage replied. "At least, I think I am. I have no House, just these three gates and whatever meager tolls I can charge. I'm a stranger in a strange city, with no House to protect me, no matron mother to serve. What has become of me? I can barely remember 'me'."

Danifae kissed his hand again and whispered, "You remember me, don't you, House Mage?"

He didn't reply but didn't take his hand away.

"You remember our lessons," she said, punctuating her words with the gentle brush of her lips against his hand. "Our special lessons?"

She took his finger into her mouth and let her tongue play over it. The old drow's skin was dry and tasteless then there was the tang of metal against her lips.

"I didn't . . ." the mage mumbled. "I don't . . ."

Danifae slipped the ring off his finger, slowly teasing his flesh with her lips all the way. She tucked the ring under her tongue before kissing the back of his hand again.

"I do," she said.

Danifae twisted the old drow's arm down and around hard and fast enough that more than one bone snapped in more than one place. Zinnirit gasped in pain and surprise and didn't even try to stop Danifae from turning him around. She brought her other hand up and cupped his chin. She was standing behind him, his broken arm twisted painfully behind his back.

"I remember," she whispered into his ear. Then she broke his neck.

For any mage, the preparation of a day's spells was part experience, part intuition, and part inspiration. Pharaun Mizzrym was no different.

From time to time he looked up from his spellbook to refresh his eyes and let a particularly complex incantation sink into his memory. What he saw when he looked up was the still, quiet deck of the ship of chaos. Larger patches of sinew and cartilage and ever more complex traceries of veins and arteries embellished the bone ship. It lived—a simple, pain-ravaged, tortured, insensible life—and when it was quiet and the others were still in Reverie, Pharaun imagined he felt the thing breathing.

The uridezu captain lay in his place, visited only by the occasional rat. He was curled into a tight ball, his body wrapped into itself in a way that made Pharaun's back ache to look at it. His breathing was deep and regular, punctuated by the odd snore.

Jeggred sat opposite the captured demon, his knees drawn up to his chest and his head down. Unlike Pharaun and his fellow dark elves, the draegloth slept. Obviously that was a trait carried over from his father, Belshazu.

Well, the Master of Sorcere thought, you can't chose your parents.

Quenthel sat as far away from the rest of them as she could, at the very tip of the demon ship's pointed bow. Her back was turned to Pharaun, and she sat straight and stiff, meditating.

Can you talk? a voice echoed at the edge of his consciousness—a voice he recognized.

Aliisza? he thought back.

You remember me, the alu-demon's voice echoed more loudly in his head—or was it more clearly? *I will consider that a supreme honor.*

As well you should, Pharaun sent back, instinctively attaching light, playful emotions to the thought. *Where are you?*

On the ceiling, she replied, *right above you.*

Pharaun couldn't help but look up, but even with his fine darkvision, the gloom of the Lake of Shadows hid the ceiling from his sight.

How did you find me? he asked.

I'm a resourceful, intelligent, and talented woman.

That you are, he replied.

If you levitate straight up, she sent, *you'll come right to me.*

Well, Pharaun returned, *in that case . . .*

The wizard closed the book he was working on, the spell still not fully prepared, and tucked the volume back into his pack. He stood and touched the brooch that held his *piwafwi* on his shoulders.

Straight up? he sent.

I'll catch you, came the alu-demon's playful reply.

Pharaun's feet left the deck, and he accelerated, the ship falling rapidly away beneath him. When it was lost—or more properly when *he* was lost—in the pitch-dark shadows of the ominous cavern, he slowed.

"A little more," Aliisza whispered to him, her voice barely audible.

Pharaun came to a stop slowly, a defensive spell hanging on his lips in case the alu-demon turned on him—she was a demon after all, so there was always some possibility of that.

There was a surprisingly loud rustle, and Pharaun looked up. Aliisza, her batlike wings spread out behind her, was slowly sinking toward him. He turned so they were facing each other.

They were almost together when Aliisza asked, "Can your levitation hold me up?"

Pharaun almost had a chance to answer before her arms folded around his neck and her full—though not substantial—weight fell on him all at once. He concentrated hard on the brooch, almost losing his defensive spell in the process, and managed to hold them both aloft. They bobbed a bit at first, but ultimately managed a tight embrace in the gloomy air near the ceiling of the Lake of Shadows.

They were face-to-face, less than an inch apart. Pharaun could smell the beautiful alu-demon's breath. The touch of her skin against him, the curves of her body in his arms again, and the soft caress of her fleshy wings folding around him, enclosing him, made his body react of its own accord.

A playful smile crossed Aliisza's full lips, and she showed a set of perfect white teeth with the exaggerated canines of a vampire. Pharaun remembered her habit of playing with her teeth. He didn't bother wondering why he liked that about her so much.

"Yes," she whispered, "I remember you."

Pharaun returned her smile and asked, "So, what brings a bad girl like you to an evil place like this?"

That made her laugh.

"The Lake of Shadows?" she replied playfully. "Oh, I try to get here a couple times a year, if I can. To take the waters."

Pharaun nodded, smiled, but didn't bother extending the banter. Kaanyr Vhok's consort had come there for a reason, and he wasn't quite smitten, or egomaniacal enough to think it was only to see him.

"You're spying on us again," he accused.

"No," Aliisza replied with a pout, "I'm spying on you *still*. Doesn't that make you feel important, having someone like me spying on you all the time?"

"Yes," he said, "and that's precisely the problem."

"What do you hope to find in the Abyss?" she asked abruptly. Pharaun had to blink a few times to get his head wrapped around the question. "That is where you're going in that wonderful old ship of chaos you've salvaged, isn't it?"

"What would Kaanyr Vhok care what we do," he asked, "or where we go?"

"Can't a girl be curious?"

"No," he replied with some finality. "In this case, no, she can't."

"You can be quite the rodent when you want to be, Pharaun," she said, and she smiled again.

"Shall I take that as a compliment?"

Aliisza looked him in the eyes. Drow and demon were both smart and pragmatic enough to know they weren't some pair of star-crossed human lovers. They might even be combatants on opposite sides of a war that could ruin both their civilizations—if Kaanyr Vhok's ragged Scoured Legion could be called a civilization.

"Can I come too?" she asked, tipping her head, and looking almost as if she were trying to read an answer written across his brow.

"With us?" he asked. "On the ship?"

She nodded.

"I'll have to check with the purser to see if there's a cabin available, but at first glance I'd have to say no way in all Nine Hells and the Barrens of Doom and Despair besides."

"Pity," she said. "I've been there before, you know."

"Where else have you been?" Pharaun asked, intentionally jarring the subject away from her joining their expedition. "Have you visited the City of Spiders lately?"

"Menzoberranzan?" she replied. "Why do you ask?"

"News of home and all that," said the wizard.

Her wings tightened around him, and Pharaun liked the sensation. It was similar to the warmed blankets his favorite masseuse used to drape on him in Menzoberranzan. He'd been traveling too long.

"You're missing some of your comrades," the alu-demon

noted. "The big fighter with the greatsword and the other one. The scout."

"You *have* been spying on us," Pharaun replied.

He couldn't imagine why she'd want to know that unless she was testing their strength, or . . .

"Reporting back to Kaanyr Vhok?" he asked.

She pretended to blush and batted her eyelashes at him.

"Menzoberranzan is under siege," he said. "I suppose you know that."

She nodded and asked, "You've sent your warriors back to aid in the defense of the city?"

Pharaun laughed, and Aliisza looked put out. He didn't care.

"Tell me they didn't run afoul of some less civilized denizen of the Underdark between Ched Nasad and here," she said. "It would break my heart."

"Your heart will remain intact then," he replied. "I don't suppose it would hurt you to tell me who lays siege to my home."

"It might just," she replied with a wink. "Let's not risk it. Of course, if I knew what you know about the fate of your Spider Queen, that might cushion the blow."

"Ah," he said, "I tell you the big secret, and you tell me the little one."

"There are no little secrets," the alu-demon replied, "if you're the one in the dark."

"You know, Aliisza," Pharaun said. "We should get together and tell each other nothing more often. It beats preparing spells or getting on with my life."

"You're a sarcastic little devil, Pharaun. You know, that's just what I love about you."

"Please assume I feel the same," was the mage's reply. "So if we're done not speaking to each other, can I go?"

"We've spoken to each other, Pharaun," said Aliisza, "I'm sure of it. For instance, until now I hadn't imagined you didn't know who was laying siege to your City of Spiders. Oh, and you told me you were going to the Abyss."

"Yes, well," Pharaun said, unconcerned that she'd drawn those obvious conclusions. "Good for you. Do run along and change the course of life in the Underdark."

"You're playing games with me," the alu-demon said, ice in her voice and in her eyes like Pharaun had never seen. "I like that but not forever."

"You're withholding information from me," he retorted. "I never like that."

They floated in midair, wrapped in a tight, familiar embrace, staring into each other's cold, uninviting eyes for a long time.

"I could be your friend still, Pharaun," Aliisza said quietly, her voice barely above a whisper.

The Master of Sorcere found himself struggling for something to say. He knew they were finished, feared they were finished forever, and found himself wishing that weren't true.

Longing, Pharaun silently mused.

Yes, Aliisza replied directly into his mind, *longing*.

Pharaun pushed her away. Aliisza hung in the air for half a second before she started to fall. She stared daggers at him even as her wings opened to slow her descent. Pharaun thought she looked more hurt than angry.

"We'll talk again," she said, then she was gone with a flash of dull purple light, and Pharaun was alone in the impenetrable shadows.

I hope so, he found himself thinking. I really do.

Chapter

NINE

Something was missing.

Halisstra could feel it—or rather, she *couldn't* feel it. She couldn't feel the Binding. She couldn't feel Danifae.

Having a captive bound to her by that obscure drow magic was a strange and subtle experience. It wasn't something she was conscious of really, not on a moment-by-moment basis. Rather it was always there, in the background, like the sound of her own breathing, the feeling of her own pulse.

She was dancing when it stopped. The priestesses who had welcomed her into their circle danced often. They danced in different combinations of certain females and danced in different places both sacred and mundane. They danced naked most of the time, clothed some of the time. They danced wearing armor and weapons and danced with offerings of fruit or works of art. They danced around fires or in the cold. They danced at night—in the dark that Halisstra still found comforting—or in the day. She was still learning the significance of each of those different venues, every subtle shift in components and approach, rhythm and movement.

When the feeling came upon her, Halisstra stopped dancing. The other priestesses took no notice of her. They didn't even pause, let alone stop their joyous ritual.

Halisstra stumbled out of the circle and made her way quickly and with a sense of impending doom back to where she had left Ryld. The weapons master wasn't included in the circles of priestesses, and she could tell that was wearing on him. Halisstra was gone hours at a time, and returned to questions she couldn't always answer. She had no way to be sure Ryld loved her—she wasn't entirely certain yet what "love" was, though she thought she was learning, but the warrior stayed. He stayed there in the cold, light-ravaged forest with her, surrounded by worshipers of what to him must have still felt like a traitor goddess.

She staggered into the cool, dark chamber they shared, interrupting him in a meditative exercise she'd seen him do before. He was standing on his hands, eyes closed, toes pointed, legs bent back at the knee. The weapons master held that position for hours sometimes. Halisstra couldn't do it for more than a second or two.

He opened his eyes when she came in and must have seen something in her expression. He rolled forward in a single, smooth motion and was on his feet. There was no sign he was dizzy or disoriented.

"Halisstra," he said, "what happened?"

She opened her mouth to reply, but no words would come.

"Something happened," he said, and he looked around the room.

"Ryld, I . . ." she started to say, then watched as he began to arm himself.

He grabbed Splitter—his enormous greatsword—first then quickly buckled his sheathed short sword to his belt. He had his armor in his hands when she touched his arm to stop him. His skin felt warm, almost hot, but there was no sweat. Deep black skin was stretched over muscles so hard he felt as if he were chiseled from stone.

"No," she said, shaking the cobwebs from her head finally, "stop it."

He stopped, and looked at her, waiting. She could see the impatience in his eyes, impatience mixed with frustration.

"What is it?" he asked, and she could see him comprehending even as he spoke.

She smiled and he sighed.

"It's Danifae," she said finally. "I can't feel her anymore. The Binding has been broken."

His eyes widened, and she could tell he was surprised. Not surprised, necessarily, that the Binding had been broken, but it was as if he were expecting to hear something else.

"What does that mean, exactly?" he asked, leaning his breast-plate against the wall next to the bed they shared.

Halisstra shook her head.

"She died?" he asked with no trace of emotion.

"Yes," Halisstra replied. "Maybe."

"Why does that frighten you?"

Halisstra stepped back—was literally taken aback by that question, though it was a logical one.

"Why does that frighten me?" she repeated. "It frightens me . . . concerns me, that she's free of me. One way or the other, I'm no longer her mistress, and she's no longer my battle-captive."

Ryld frowned, shrugged, and asked, "Why does that matter to you?"

She opened her mouth to respond and again could form no words.

"I mean," the weapons master went on, "I'm not sure your new friends would approve anyway, would they? Do these trait—I mean, other . . . these priestesses even take battle-captives?"

She smiled, and he turned away, pretending to be deeply involved in returning Splitter to its ready position under their bed.

"They aren't *traitor* priestesses, Ryld," she said.

He hung his head briefly in response then sat down on the bed and looked at her.

"Yes they are," he said, his voice as flat and as beaten as his eyes. "They're traitors to their race, as surely as we are. The question I keep asking myself now is, is it so bad to be a traitor?"

Halisstra stepped to him and knelt. Draping her hands on his knees. He put out a hand and brushed her long white hair from her black cheek—the gesture seemed almost instinctive.

"It's not," she said, her voice barely audible even in the quiet of their little room. "It's not so bad. We can really only be traitors to ourselves anyway, and I think we're both finally being true to ourselves . . . and each other."

Halisstra's heart sank when she saw the look on his face, his only response to those words. He didn't believe her, but she couldn't help thinking he wanted to.

"How does it feel?" he asked her.

She didn't understand and told him so with a twitch of her head.

"Not being able to feel the Binding?" he said.

She shifted her weight onto her hip, sitting on the floor, and leaned her head against his strong leg.

"I can feel everything about my old life being replaced piece by piece with something new."

He touched her again, one finger gently tracing the line of her shoulder. Her flesh thrilled at his touch.

"Lolth has been replaced by Eilistraee," she said. "Dark has been replaced by light. Suspicion has been replaced by acceptance. Hate has been replaced by love."

An unfamiliar warmth and wetness filled her eyes. She was crying.

"Are you all right?" he asked, his voice a concerned whisper.

Halisstra wiped the tears from her eyes and nodded.

"Hate," she repeated, "has been replaced by love, and apparently slavery has been replaced by freedom."

"Or was it that life was replaced by death?" Ryld asked.

Halisstra sighed.

"Maybe it was," she answered, "but either way, she's free. She's gone to whatever afterlife awaits her. For her sake, I hope it's not that empty, ruined shell of the Demonweb Pits. Maybe she still wanders the Underdark, alive and strong. Alive and free, or dead and free, she's free just the same."

"Free. . . ." Ryld repeated, as if he'd never spoken the word before and needed practice at it.

They sat like that for a long time until Halisstra's legs started to grow stiff and Ryld sensed her discomfort. He lifted her into the bed and drew her close to him as if she weighed nothing at all. His embrace was like a shell around her, a life-sustaining cocoon.

"We have to go back," she whispered.

His embrace tightened.

"It's not what you're thinking," she whispered because she knew he wanted to go back underground and never come back. "The time has finally come to find Quenthel and her expedition."

"And stop them?" he asked, the words touching her neck with each exhalation of his hot breath.

"No," she whispered.

"Follow them?" he said into her hair, his hand pressed into the small of her back.

Halisstra moved into the warrior until she felt as if she were flattening herself against him, disappearing into his night-black skin.

"Yes," she said. "They'll take us with them, whether they want to or not. They'll take us to Lolth, and we can end it."

Halisstra knew that he began to make love to her then because he didn't want to think about it, and she let him because she didn't want to think about it either.

🕷   🕷   🕷

Pharaun stood at the rail of the ship of chaos, staring into the empty darkness of the Lake of Shadows, because he couldn't think of anything else to do. Valas and Danifae hadn't returned from their supply mission, he had fed the ship enough petty demons to satisfy it, the uridezu captain was cowed and quiet, and there was no sign of Aliisza.

The Master of Sorcere went over their conversation again in his mind and was still convinced that the alu-fiend had managed to tell him nothing but had gone away having learned nothing from him. Still, she'd found him and had seen the ship. She knew where they were going and what they hoped to accomplish there—but anyone who'd been at the fall of Ched Nasad could figure that out easily enough.

He put the alu-fiend out of his mind and peered deeper into the darkness, though there was still nothing to see. Pharaun didn't have to turn around to know that Quenthel was sitting against the rail, absently chatting in some kind of silent telepathy with the bound imps that gave her venomous whip its evil intelligence. He couldn't imagine the substance of a conversation someone might have with a demon trapped in the body of a snake that was stuck to the end of a whip.

Whatever they talked about, it didn't seem to be helping Quenthel. The high priestess, as far as Pharaun could tell, was going quietly mad. She had always been sullen and temperamental, but recently she had become . . . twitchy.

Her half-demon nephew grew angrier and angrier the more bored he became. Jeggred sent a large portion of his hatred out through his eyes and into the uridezu. Raashub did an admirable job of ignoring him.

Something caught Pharaun's attention, movement out of the corner of his eye, and he stepped back from the rail as an emaciated, soaking-wet rat scurried along the bone-and-cartilage rail in front of him.

Pharaun watched the rat run, absently wondering where it thought it was going.

Anywhere dry, he thought.

Noises echoed from behind him—Jeggred fidgeting.

Pharaun stepped back to the rail and was about to let his eyes wander through the impenetrable darkness again when another rat crawled quickly past.

"Damn it," the Master of Sorcere whispered to himself.

He turned to voice some impotent complaint to Jeggred, but the words stuck in his throat.

There were more than the two rats that ran past him. There were dozens of them, hundreds perhaps, and they swarmed over Jeggred.

Something's wrong, thought Pharaun, marveling even as the words formed in his head at how slowly his mind was working after days of tedium aboard the anchored ship.

The draegloth looked more annoyed than anything else. The rats were crawling over him, tangling themselves in his hair, nibbling at any loose fold of skin, but they could not pierce the half-demon's hide. More of them were climbing onto the deck. Pharaun could hear splashing in the water on the other side of the demonic vessel. It sounded as if dozens, even hundreds more rats were swimming up to the ship.

Pharaun started casting defensive spells on himself, watching as Quenthel finally looked up and over at her nephew.

The Mistress of the Academy's eyes widened, then narrowed as she watched Jeggred smash one rat after another in his bigger set of hands, while his smaller hands brushed others off his face. Quenthel slowly rose to her feet, the vipers tangling loosely, affectionately around her legs.

"Jeggred?" she asked.

"Rats," was the draegloth's grunted reply.

Pharaun layered more magical protections over himself as Quenthel started toward the draegloth.

"Raashub," Pharaun said, keeping his voice steely and cold.

The demon flinched at the sound of his name but didn't look up.

"What are you doing, Raashub?" Pharaun asked between two more spells of protection. "Stop it. Stop it now."

The demon looked up at him with smoldering eyes and hissed, "It's not me. They're not my rats."

Pharaun couldn't shake the feeling that the uridezu was telling the truth—at least, a version of the truth.

"Pharaun?" Quenthel said, and the mage detected a trace—more than a trace—of panic creeping into her voice. "What are all these rats . . . ?"

"Pay close attention, both of you," Pharaun said, at the same time readying a more offensive spell. "There's ano—"

A globe of darkness enveloped Quenthel.

Any drow could have done it but not only a drow.

The unmistakable sounds of a physical struggle resounded from inside the slowly undulating cloud of blackness. Something hit the deck, and something cracked.

Pharaun changed direction before he'd actually begun casting the spell he'd had in mind. Instead, he formed the words and gestures to a spell he hoped would eliminate the darkness.

From inside the gloom, Pharaun could hear the shriek of metal being dragged across metal—or was it bone against bone?

His spell went off, and the darkness blew into nothingness.

Suddenly visible, Quenthel lay on her stomach on the deck. She was patting the carved bone surface in front of her, reaching for her scourge, which lay just out of her reach. Her nose was bleeding, and she winced every time she bent her back.

Standing over her was another uridezu.

The demon was, like Raashub, a humanoid rat. Smaller than Raashub, thinner, it wore tattered rags that left little of its mottled gray body to the imagination. Its long, pink tail was spattered with pustules. Cold black eyes stared down at the high priestess with murderous intent. Foam gathered at the corners of its fang-lined mouth, and angry yellow claws curved at the ends of its spindly, arthritic fingers.

"Jeggred . . ." Pharaun said, glancing over at the draegloth.

The half-demon was covered head to foot with rats of every size and description. It was as if all the vermin in the Lake of Shadows had staged some sort of family reunion—one that took place on, under, and all around the draegloth. They swarmed onto him faster than he could kill them, though he was dispatching the rodents four at a time.

Pharaun ran quickly through possible spells, stepping forward a few paces toward Quenthel.

The uridezu smashed her on the back with its tail. The high priestess's face was forced into the bone-hard deck. Blood sprayed, but not much, and she took the strong hit with a grunt.

Pharaun was impressed. Something made him set aside his first choice of spell.

Too much, he thought, for only one . . .

The Master of Sorcere looked over at Raashub. The demon captain's eyes were darting rapidly between Quenthel and the newcomer.

He's testing us, Pharaun thought. The wily bastard gated in one of his kind and is setting it against us so we can show off, reveal our strengths and weaknesses.

Raashub might have been bound, but he was a demon still, and there was always fight left in a demon—it always had a way out.

The other uridezu clawed at Quenthel's legs, opening deep gashes, and she kicked back at it. The demon danced out of reach of her boots. The high priestess extended a hand back over her head, but she still couldn't reach her whip. The vipers seemed panicked and weren't able to coordinate their movements well enough to crawl to her.

Pharaun pronounced a quick set of rhyming syllables and made a fast motion with his right hand. Pushed by his magic, the viper whip slid along the deck a few inches, well within Quenthel's reach.

As the high priestess's fingers closed around the handle of the scourge, Pharaun laughed inwardly. The spell he'd used was no more than a cantrip, a transmutation so simple any first year student at Sorcere could master it. It would tell Raashub nothing about the limits of his power.

The uridezu hissed at Quenthel, backing farther away from her, his tail twitching behind him, and his claws flickering in anticipation. The demon obviously thought he was well out of reach of the whip. He was wrong.

The five vipers that comprised Quenthel's scourge were five feet long, giving the weapon considerable reach. The high priestess was still on the deck and didn't bother to stand. She lashed the whip behind her, her jaw set tightly and her eyes wild with rage. When she brought the weapon forward, the snakes whipped outward to their full length. The uridezu flinched, though he seemed confident enough that he was still out of the weapon's range. The vipers extended farther, though, drawing themselves out, stretching thinner and thinner, farther and farther, adding another few feet to their length.

The uridezu didn't register what was happening nearly fast enough to avoid the vipers. All but one of them sank needle-sharp fangs into the rat-demon's flesh. As the whip lashed back, they dug long, bleeding furrows in the uridezu's leathery hide.

The demon screamed, high-pitched and loud enough to rattle Pharaun's eardrums.

Anything else would have been dead. Each viper possessed a deadly venom, wickedly potent. Quenthel, wild with a battle-frenzy Pharaun had never imagined, much less seen from her, wouldn't have let the snakes hold a drop of venom back. It would have been enough to drop a rothé.

The victim of that venomous lash wasn't a dumb food beast; it was an uridezu, and Pharaun had studied demons long enough to know the traits that all of them shared. Poison would never affect one. The whip had wounded the captain but hadn't killed him. Pharaun knew he could take more than that. Even a demon as relatively weak as an uridezu—and the rat-creatures were hardly the sturdiest of their kind—could withstand extremes of cold and heat and muster innate magical abilities such as the darkness he had used to ambush Quenthel. Uridezu could call on their rodent cousins, as the one Pharaun faced had set them against Jeggred. There was something about the bite of the uridezu that Pharaun knew he should remember, but that wasn't coming to him. Of course, like all tanar'ri, lightning only passed through them.

Even as that thought crossed his mind Pharaun had a hand on a wand that would have unleashed lightning bolts. Knowing that was useless, the Master of Sorcere shifted his hand an inch over and drew a different wand.

Pharaun hesitated and watched Quenthel hop nimbly to her feet and face the uridezu. The demon hissed at her, but Quenthel made no sound or sign she'd heard it. The high priestess cracked her whip at the demon again, and three of the five snakes bit deeply into the rat-demon's chest. The creature lashed out at the snakes with one set of razor-sharp claws, but the vipers withdrew in time, and the talons slashed through empty air.

Ignoring that failure, the uridezu whirled, whipping at the drow priestess with its heavy, fast-moving tail. Quenthel brought the buckler in her left hand up to meet the tail. The appendage hit her with enough force that Pharaun was sure her arm would snap, but instead she managed to bat the tail away.

The uridezu recovered more quickly than Quenthel, though, and the tail reversed and dropped lower, clipping the priestess in the ribs. Pharaun could hear the breath driven from her lungs. She stepped to the side, almost staggering. The demon, a feral smile spread across its face, stepped in. It meant to bite her and rake her with its claws at the same time.

Pharaun drew a breath to pronounce the command word for his wand even as the demon attacked—and took Quenthel's buckler full in the face. There was a loud, wet *crack!* and blood splashed out from between the buckler and the uridezu's nose. The demon's hands flailed harmlessly in front of Quenthel and each of the five vipers took their pick of the demon's most sensitive spots in which to sink their fangs. The uridezu howled in agony.

Well, Pharaun thought, not bothering to activate the magic in his wand, looks like she's got this well in—

His eyes settled on Raashub, and Pharaun stopped. The bound uridezu was looking at him, his eyes running down the length of the wand. Anticipation was plain on the demon captain's face.

Pharaun looked at his wand then back at Raashub. Their eyes locked, and Raashub smiled at him.

With a smile of his own, Pharaun slid the wand back into his pack where it belonged. Raashub hid his disappointment well, turning his attention back to Quenthel and his fellow uridezu.

Pharaun made the decision to help Jeggred. Raashub would know what the draegloth was capable of, and if Pharaun could deal with the swarming rats and allow Jeggred to help Quenthel, the unbound uridezu could be dispatched quickly and without Pharaun having to take a more active—and more revealing—role in the fight.

As Pharaun came to that decision, a loud series of cracking and popping noises drew his attention back to Quenthel. The Mistress of Arach-Tinilith pulled up a whole section of railing. Bone and cartilage separated from the deck, snapping off like dried mushroom stems. Her whip was in her belt, the uridezu was staggering in front of her with blood pouring from its ruined snout, and she lifted the ten-foot length of railing over her head.

Pharaun quickly prepared a spell to aid Jeggred, and Quenthel attacked. The high priestess brought the section of railing down on the uridezu fast and hard. The demon, not quite blinded by its bleeding nose, skittered away from the attack and managed to leap out of range at the last second. The railing crashed onto the deck and shattered, sending bone fragments whirling through the air. Several of them bounced off Pharaun's spell-wards and shields, and he watched a couple of them slice into two of the rats that covered Jeggred.

Quenthel growled in nearly incoherent rage, and Pharaun found the noise unsettling—unbecoming to the Mistress of the Academy.

Pools of blood were collecting where the railing had smashed into the deck. The ship of chaos itself was bleeding. The wizard wasn't sure if he'd be able to repair it, and any further damage might delay or even prevent their voyage. However, Pharaun didn't want to say anything out loud, and Quenthel wasn't looking at him so he couldn't sign to her to stop damaging the ship.

Pharaun cast a spell at the rats on Jeggred. It was a simple spell, one that conjured a cone of flickering, multicolored Weave energy. Pharaun was careful in his placement of the spell so that the effect brushed along the side of the rat-encrusted draegloth. The magic didn't affect Jeggred in the least, but a goodly portion of the swarming rodents fell off him and onto the deck, where they lay twitching and writhing in a pile of wet, furry bodies.

Jeggred roared as he shook himself, sending his wild mane of snow-white hair whipping rats, blood, and water across the deck. The draegloth smashed four more of the filthy creatures—one in each hand—and stepped on three others.

Pharaun sneaked a glance at Raashub and was rewarded by a look of disappointed frustration on the uridezu captain's face. It was another easy spell the Master of Sorcere cast, one he'd learned while still a child, and Raashub knew it.

Pharaun turned his attention back to Jeggred and called, "Leave the rats, Jeggred. Your mistress is having demon troubles."

With another roar, Jeggred threw more dead or unconscious rats off him and leaped at Raashub, bringing all four of his hands up, ready to shred the uridezu captain. Raashub shrank away from the draegloth, holding up his hands and straining against his bonds.

"No!" Quenthel shouted, her voice hoarse and feral. "Not that one, damn it! Kill *this* one!"

Jeggred whirled, his eyes flashing across the scene of the ongoing struggle between Quenthel and the second uridezu.

The rat-demon, taking full advantage of Quenthel's momentary lapse in attention, slipped in and raked claws across her midsection, digging deep furrows across her armor and drawing blood. Quenthel grimaced and gritted her teeth against the pain but answered in kind with her scourge. Both of them staggered a bit, their footing treacherous amidst a pile of bone fragments from the shattered railing and pools of blood from the wounded ship.

Jeggred's lips curled back to reveal a monstrous row of vicious fangs, and the draegloth entered the fray.

C h a p t e r

T E N

Danifae sat on the floor of the gatehouse for what felt like a very long time. She hadn't allowed herself to think too much about her life before her captivity. There were only a few ways to survive as a battle-captive, including convincing yourself that you've always been one.

Before the raid that put her in the hands of House Melarn, Danifae had been taking lessons from the Yauntyrr House Mage. Zinnirit was a capable and detail-oriented teacher, and Danifae had learned much from him, especially in the fields of teleportation, translocation, and dimensional travel. They hadn't actually begun her study of the arcane Art before her House was overwhelmed, but Zinnirit had familiarized the young daughter of House Yauntyrr with a variety of enchanted items.

Danifae touched her mother's ring, feeling the cold metal

warming against her skin. The ring could bounce her across the Underdark—but just her and one other. Danifae had plans that required more than that.

Her eyes settled on the still hand of the dead wizard.

"More rings," Danifae whispered, a smile playing at the corners of her mouth.

All she had to do was remember how to work them.

❧   ❧   ❧

Even as the uridezu was bringing his tail around for another hard slap at Quenthel, Jeggred pounced on him. The draegloth caught the heavy appendage in his larger set of hands. The tail's momentum, stopped so abruptly by the draegloth's grip, staggered the uridezu and it toppled in a heap onto the ruined rail. Jagged bits of bone cut deeply into the demon's already bleeding body. At the same time, all five of the vipers from Quenthel's scourge bit into sensitive areas, released, then bit again. Waves of agony pulsed through the demon's body, and it coughed out phlegm and blood.

"We . . ." the demon gasped. "We will see you in the Abyss . . . drow bitch!"

We? Pharaun thought, stealing a glance at Raashub, who was watching with keen interest.

"Kill it now, Jeggred," Quenthel commanded, her voice still husky and mingled with deep, panting breaths. "Kill it before it goes home."

Feral light flashed in the draegloth's eyes and he brought a single claw across the uridezu's midsection. The daggerlike talon disappeared into the demon's flesh, burying itself six inches deep. Jeggred cut the thing's belly open wide enough to spill a pile of ropy yellow intestines, steaming with the demon's hot blood, onto the deck of the ship of chaos.

The demon screamed, the sound echoing unnaturally then fading even as the uridezu itself began to evaporate into nothingness. It was returning to the Abyss while it still lived.

Pharaun had to admit that he wasn't sure how long a demon might live after it had been disemboweled, but more than one breed of them could regenerate completely from even so grievous a wound.

As the demon began to fade, though, Jeggred quickly withdrew his claw and grabbed the uridezu's head in both his larger, stronger hands. The draegloth twisted and pulled, hard enough that Pharaun could see veins protrude against his straining muscles.

There was a sickly wet cracking sound and a sicker wet *pop!* and the uridezu's head came off in Jeggred's hands.

The rest of the demon's body disappeared, but the head and entrails remained. The black eyes stared, dead, at nothing. The demon's guts slowly sizzled away, being absorbed, Pharaun noted, by the ship itself. The wizard realized that most of the fragments of bone from the shattered rail had gone as well. The ship was feeding on itself, repairing the damage bone by bone.

Jeggred, obviously taking no notice of the ship of chaos's convenient regenerative capacities, tossed the uridezu's head overboard as he turned to face the captain.

Raashub, already backed away as far as his bonds would allow, put his hands up in supplication and looked away.

Jeggred, a low growl rumbling in his throat, started forward, stalking the bound uridezu with unveiled intent.

"I don't know, nephew," Quenthel said, her voice and breathing slowly returning to normal. She was bleeding but paid her injuries no heed. "I have yet to make up my mind."

The vipers seethed at the end of her whip, and Quenthel glanced at one of them as if she'd heard it speak—and certainly she had, though Pharaun was still not privy to that communication.

"Wait," the wizard said, stepping closer but not foolish enough to move between Jeggred and the uridezu. "I'm afraid we still need him."

Jeggred growled, not looking at Pharaun, but he did hesitate.

"It was to be expected," Pharaun said. "You've both worked with demons before, haven't you? So he tried to kill us and failed."

Quenthel's head snapped to look at him. The abrupt motion caused the vipers in her whip to shudder and turn on the wizard as well.

"You can't control him," she said to Pharaun. "How can you stop him from doing that again?"

"It wasn't me, Mistress," Raashub pleaded, his voice reedy and dripping with false humility. "The Lake of Shadows is home to many of my kind."

Pharaun lifted an eyebrow at that obvious lie then began to cast a spell.

"Let me eat his kidneys," Jeggred growled, his eyes still locked on the uridezu. "Maybe just one kidney."

Pharaun, ignoring the draegloth, finished his spell.

Raashub screamed.

The sound was so sudden and so loud that even Jeggred stepped back from it. Wild horror passed through the captive uridezu in visible waves. Raashub threw up his hands and clawed at the air in front of him, whimpering, sobbing, and shrieking in different combinations as Pharaun, Quenthel, and Jeggred looked on.

"What are you doing to him?" Jeggred asked, confused.

"Showing him things," Pharaun replied.

He looked at Quenthel, who obviously wanted a more detailed explanation.

"Even demons have nightmares, Mistress," the Master of Sorcere explained. "My spell is letting a few of those play out for him. I assure you both, it is an experience our dear friend Raashub will not soon forget, and he knows I can do it again."

Jeggred sighed so heavily Pharaun could smell his rancid breath. The draegloth moved toward Raashub.

"Hold, Jeggred," Quenthel ordered.

The draegloth hesitated before doing so, but he did stop.

"Raashub still serves a purpose," the high priestess said as she began to assess her injuries.

Jeggred turned to look at her, but she ignored him.

"Who told you that?" the draegloth asked in a low growl. "The dandy?"—he nodded at Pharaun—"or the snakes?"

Quenthel ignored the question, but Pharaun thought long and hard about it.

      🕷   🕷   🕷

It took Danifae somewhat longer than she'd intended to remember Zinnirit's favorite command words and determine which of them powered which of the rings. Then she turned her attention to studying the finer points of the portals she had "inherited" from the late Yauntyrr House mage. Not only had she lost all track of time as she studied Zinnirit's collection of scrolls and tomes on the subject, made a few exploratory scans through open portals, and ignored a summons from Valas, but she had exhausted the limits of her own familiarity with the arcane Art. Danifae was no wizard, but fortunately she didn't have to be to use many of the features of Zinnirit's gatehouse.

The gates were used primarily for transportation—whisking someone or something hundreds, even thousands of miles in the blink of an eye—but they could also be used to *find* someone. Though the strong psychic link that the Binding had provided was gone, Danifae still had some connection to her former mistress. She knew Halisstra better than anyone ever had, even ranking members of House Melarn. Halisstra's sister had tried to kill her, and her mother had always been the model of the aloof, controlling matron mother. Danifae, though always seething with hate, had served Halisstra loyally and well every minute of every day.

Ultimately all Danifae really had to do was remember her. All she had to do was imagine what Halisstra looked like, visualize her, and activate one of the portals in precisely the right way. At least, she thought that was all she needed to do.

After several false starts and failed attempts, Danifae stepped away from the gate and began pacing. As she did she fiddled with a ring on her finger, then another ring on her other hand, and—

She stopped and looked at her hands. Danifae had taken three rings from the dead wizard. Two of them were tucked safely in a pocket. She wore the ring that Zinnirit had created for her mother, the one that would bring her back to the gatehouse from anywhere, but she wore another ring as well—one she'd almost forgotten about. It belonged to Ryld Argith, the Menzoberranyr weapons master who, like Danifae's former mistress, had abandoned the expedition.

They had been spending some time with each other, Ryld and Halisstra. Even in the cave where Pharaun had summoned the demon Belshazu, Danifae had suspected that Ryld was sneaking off to join Halisstra. If he had, she could use his ring as a focus.

It was only after several more false starts that Danifae finally found her mistress. The former battle-captive had been, like the Menzoberranyr, under the impression that Halisstra had gone to the City of Spiders to report on their progress (or lack thereof), and much of Danifae's time had been spent searching for her there. Hours later, Danifae realized that Halisstra wasn't even in the Underdark but in the bizarre landscape of the World Above.

Danifae had suspected that Halisstra was in the process of

turning entirely from the worship of Lolth. They had all seen her reaction to the chaotic, empty Demonweb Pits.

Even having seen that ruined plane herself, though, Danifae had been a priestess of Lolth when she was free and living in Eryndlyn, and she had served the goddess more faithfully and more sincerely than she served House Melarn ever since, so her faith remained strong. Guarded, perhaps, more curious, but strong. Danifae wouldn't presume to question the goddess's will, and Halisstra's commitment to the Spider Queen was none of Danifae's concern. Danifae could easily enough set aside her religion if necessary, but she would never set aside her vengeance. Halisstra Melarn had to die, and not on Lolth's behalf. For Danifae it was a simple imperative.

As certain as she could be that the portal was properly tuned to the place on the World Above where Halisstra and Ryld were, Danifae stepped through. She felt as if she were being turned upside down and inside out at the same time, though there was no pain—only a dull, throbbing vertigo—then she was there.

It was night, and Danifae thanked Lolth for that. Her eyes still had to adjust to the bright glare of the starlight against the white snow, but she wasn't totally blinded. She had appeared, apparently silently and without the sort of fanfare—flashing lights and thunderclaps—that often accompanied arcane magic, in front of a ruined building. The structure was overgrown with vegetation. No light or fire glowed from inside.

Danifae drew her *piwafwi* close around her shoulders against the biting cold in the air. She stepped as quietly as she could to the entrance. Her eyes adjusted little by little, and by the time Danifae reached the ruin, she could see fairly well. Inside, Halisstra sat back to back with Ryld. The two of them were deep in Reverie and in a position that told Danifae everything she needed to know about their relationship.

The former battle-captive felt a growing respect for Halisstra, as well as a growing contempt. Halisstra had managed to outwit Quenthel and the others, seduce the steadfast weapons master—admirable, even for someone schooled her entire life in manipulation and deceit—and had set up a sweet little household for them in the freezing, animal-infested forest—a bizarre and unseemly act of betrayal against her essential nature as a dark elf.

Danifae took a deep breath and let it out in a thin, reedy whistle. Halisstra came out of Reverie without a blink and looked at her. The First Daughter of House Melarn had established that sound as their signal years before, and they had both had occasion to use it more than once.

Halisstra let one side of her mouth draw up into half a smile. She indicated Ryld with a slow movement of her eyes, and Danifae shook her head.

Halisstra stood slowly and carefully, making sure not to disturb Ryld.

"Are you all right?" the weapons master whispered, his eyes still closed.

Halisstra replied, also in a whisper, "I'm fine. I'll be right back."

Ryld nodded and returned to his meditation as Halisstra slipped out of the ruined structure. Certain that Ryld hadn't seen her, Danifae led her former mistress a good distance from the ruin, waiting for Halisstra to indicate they'd gone far enough. They stopped and faced each other for the first time as two free drow.

The Binding? Halisstra signed.

Danifae replied, *Removed by Quenthel . . . Pharaun, really, but on Quenthel's orders. We have found a ship of chaos to take us back to the Abyss.*

Halisstra visibly withdrew and signed, *I can see why you escaped.*

I didn't, really, replied Danifae. *I was sent with Master Hune to gather supplies for our doomed little voyage.*

How long before they leave? Halisstra asked.

Days still, answered Danifae.

Why are you telling me this? Halisstra asked. *You're free now. Go back to Eryndlyn if you dare, or go on with the Menzoberranyr until you all inevitably die. Do as you wish, but you no longer need seek my permission.*

I served you, Danifae replied, *and now I serve Quenthel. I'm not as free as you might think, Binding or no Binding.*

There was a short silence as the two of them studied each other in the darkness. Danifae could somehow feel how far Halisstra had strayed from the path of Lolth, but it was confirmed seconds later by Halisstra herself.

I serve Eilistraee now, Danifae. There will be no more slaves for me.

Danifae pretended to consider that last statement for a while. Internally she tried to get her head to stop spinning. The depth of her former mistress's betrayal was worse than she'd imagined. Danifae couldn't believe she'd ever allowed herself to be taken captive by so weak a mistress—one who would turn her back on her entire culture at the slightest provocation, at the first sign of weakness. It was that thought that snapped Danifae out of her confusion. Halisstra must have seen Lolth's Silence as a sign of weakness and used that opportunity to escape, just as Danifae had seen Halisstra's doubt as a sign of weakness and used that opportunity to escape herself. But would any priestess seek to *escape* the service of Lolth?

I like the sound of that, Danifae signed, *but we are all slaves sooner or later.*

We don't have to be, Halisstra was quick to reply.

Danifae blinked at how strident, how obvious, and how careless her former mistress had become.

Lolth isn't coming back, is she? Danifae asked.

I don't know, replied Halisstra, *but it doesn't look good.*

If I die still serving her, Danifae asked, *where will my soul go? There were no drow souls in the Demonweb Pits, and no entrance past the sealed doors. Where are all those souls?*

Halisstra looked at her former servant with a wounded, open look that made Danifae's skin crawl.

What, Danifae asked, *are your intentions here?*

You found me, her former mistress replied. *Tell me, what are your intentions? Spying on me for that Baenre bureaucrat?*

No, Danifae replied sharply. *I sneaked away from Valas in Sschindylryn. It was the only place to find a portal and to find you. I don't trust the Menzoberranyr.*

Why would you? Halisstra replied, eyeing her former servant carefully.

What is the weapons master doing here? asked Danifae.

She could see by Halisstra's reaction that things between she and the weapons master had gone a considerable distance toward the bizarre. The light and air of the World Above must have affected Halisstra in unpredictable ways. Danifae marveled at how such a thing might be possible.

You sit in Reverie against his back? Danifae asked,

Halisstra drew herself to her full height and tried to recapture the manner of a slaveholder. Danifae was unwilling to play the part of the battle-captive.

Instead of flying into a rage, Halisstra simply relaxed.

Do you sit the same way with Quenthel? Halisstra signed.

Danifae made a convincing show of being uncomfortable with that question. She was intimate with Quenthel not out of some alien emotion like love or compassion but because Quenthel could help her. Quenthel, in turn, used Danifae for physical pleasure and to gain a toady. It was all perfectly natural. Halisstra, however, seemed to have turned a corner with Ryld Argith, and that was something Danifae knew she could exploit.

You said that Quenthel is taking the expedition back to the Abyss, Halisstra signed, changing the subject. *Why? Why that way? Why all that?*

Danifae could have given her some of the reasons, but some were still not clear to her.

I can explain all, Danifae lied, *but I must return to Sschindylryn. Valas will grow suspicious, then he'll leave without me. I have to go back to the Underdark then back to the Lake of Shadows. I will contact you again.*

Halisstra looked her up and down, appraising her.

"I'll be waiting," Halisstra whispered in Danifae's ear.

Danifae nodded, gave Halisstra a slight bow, and did her best to look at the First Daughter of House Melarn with a face full of sisterhood and friendliness.

When Halisstra disappeared into the dark forest, Danifae signed after her, *We'll meet again very soon, Halisstra Melarn. Sooner than you think.*

Danifae touched the ring she'd taken from the dying Zinnirit, and a second or two of bizarre sensation later and she was back at the gatehouse.

Perfect, thought Danifae. It worked perfectly.

Chapter

E L E V E N

Valas purchased more supplies than he probably should have—three large bags that carried more than would seem possible from their size or weight—but he couldn't help thinking they'd be gone longer than Pharaun had estimated. Already their journey had lasted longer than any of them had assumed when they'd left Menzoberranzan.

He sat at a small table in an open café high up and in the center of the ziggurat-city, waiting for Danifae. The battle-captive hadn't been joking, obviously, when she'd told him that she would ignore his summons. Valas wasn't necessarily anxious to return to the Lake of Shadows, but he did want to leave the city. Dark elves throughout Sschindylryn were looking over their shoulders. Tempers were short, and the lesser races had a dangerous gleam in their eyes. The city wasn't quite as bad off as Ched Nasad, but the scout could see it was headed in that direction and sooner rather than later.

"Waiting for me?" Danifae asked.

Valas turned, surprised, to see her standing behind him. He hadn't noticed her.

"Cities. . . ." the scout sighed.

He stood, quickly gathering up his bags.

"Are we really in such a hurry?" Danifae asked as she slid into the chair across the table from him.

She looked up at him with one arm raised and a wide, bright grin on her face. She looked different. Valas couldn't help but stare.

"In the Surface Realms," Danifae said, "it's customary for a gentleman to buy a lady a drink. Well, so I hear."

Valas shook his head but found it difficult to take his eyes off the female.

The chair he had been sitting in slowly slid toward him. She pushed it with her foot from under the table.

"Order us a bottle of algae wine," she purred.

Valas turned to order the wine but stopped himself.

"We should get back," he said. "The others will be waiting for us."

"Let them wait."

Valas took a deep breath and shifted the bags onto his shoulders.

"Mistress Quenthel will be displeased," he said, not caring but wanting to be on his way.

"Let her be displeased," Danifae shot back, still smiling, but her eyes grew colder. "I feel a bit like taking a holiday."

"Her House is paying," the mercenary said, still not sitting down.

Danifae looked at him, and Valas felt his skin crawl. It was as if she was peeling off his flesh with her eyes and looking inside him.

She stood slowly, unfolding herself from the chair piece by piece, and Valas watched every subtle movement that made up the whole. She held out a hand.

"I'll carry one," she said.

Valas didn't move to hand her a bag.

Whatever it was about Danifae that had changed, Valas was trying desperately not to like it.

❀   ❀   ❀

For the drow, as with other sentient races above and below the surface of Faerûn, each individual had his own set of skills and talents, his own individual use that served the whole in some way, even if only as an irritant. In Menzoberranzan talent was something that was identified early, and skills were a commodity traded on the open market and imparted on the young only with great care and economy. Individuality was accepted only within certain limits and rarely if at all for males of the species.

"He is a lich," the Master of Sorcere said, "so his touch will paralyze."

There were a few places where male drow had some advantage, and one of those places was the halls of Sorcere. It was the females who held the power, and when things were as they should be, the ear of Lolth, but it was the males who were attuned to the Weave. Of course, not all wizards were male . . . only the best were, and Gromph Baenre, the Archmage of Menzoberranzan, had more than a little to do with that. It was his responsibility, after all, to identify talent for the Art in young drow from every House in the city, and it was his right to choose those who would go to Sorcere to study. It was his whim that decided whether or not they would ever finish their course of study. The fact that the majority of wizards in Menzoberranzan were male was no coincidence, no

132

accident of birth or statistics, but a carefully and often less than subtly played turn in the great *sava* game of the City of Spiders. That most females preferred serving Lolth anyway only made that bit of manipulation easier.

"He will radiate an aura of fear," the Master of Sorcere continued, "but you probably won't be affected by that."

While there was no question that the priestesses had and would always have dominion over the city, his dominion over the Art was simply a small consolation—something that would warm Gromph's heart in his private moments. With Lolth silent, withdrawn, and the priestesses scrambling for answers, thrown into the sort of chaos only a demon goddess could conjure . . . well, things had changed.

"Once in each twenty-four hour cycle," said the Master of Sorcere, "he can kill with a touch."

The strangest thing, for Gromph, about the shift in power was how little he liked it. He had, after all, spent a lifetime manipulating the system to best serve his House and himself. When the system faltered, he might have been in a position to unseat his sister and the rest of the matron mothers and take control of Menzoberranzan himself—but why? What would he hope to gain? How could his position be any better? He enjoyed all the benefits of House Baenre's position and Sorcere's, but there was always someone else onto whom he could deflect responsibility, always someone who could be manipulated.

"There are a number of spell effects that will be of no concern to the lich," said the master. "These include cold, lightning, poison, paralysis, disease, necromancy, polymorph, and spells that affect or influence the mind. Best not even to bother preparing such enchantments."

Gromph was the third most powerful dark elf in Menzoberranzan, and Lolth be damned, he liked it that way.

"He will likely be wearing a robe of black silk," the Master of Sorcere continued, "that will allow him to conjure a barrier of whirling blades."

Well, he might like to be second, but still . . .

"The crown," the Master of Sorcere finished, "is more than simply a crass affectation. It can store and reflect back offensive spells."

So it was that Gromph Baenre sat on the floor of a very small, very dark, and very secret room in the deepest heart of Sorcere, surrounded by a circle of mages who were the most powerful in the city—among the most powerful spellcasters in all the Underdark. The other mages, Masters of Sorcere all, whispered or chanted and waved or gesticulated, and tossed into the air or pinched between fingers all manner of tokens, totems, focuses, and components. They showered the archmage with protective magic, doing it at so fast a pace they'd stopped even bothering to tell him what they were casting on him. Gromph had few doubts that by the time they were done, he'd be immune to everything. Surely no one would be able to harm him—no one but a spellcaster of greater power than the Masters.

And it was precisely such an opponent that Gromph meant to face.

"I should go with you, Archmage," Nauzhror Baenre said, his voice conveying a lack of real desire in that regard.

"If any of you say anything like that," Gromph replied, "even once more, I will . . ."

He let the threat go unfinished. He wouldn't do anything, and they all knew it, but out of respect for the archmage, none of them suggested going with him again. They were all smart enough to know that Gromph meant to face an enemy who, all things being equal, was the most dangerous being in Menzoberranzan. The lichdrow was a spellcaster of extraordinary, sometimes almost godlike, power. Of course they didn't really want to face him in the way that Gromph meant to: toe to toe in a spell duel that would surely find its place in drow history.

That duel was something only the archmage could fight. In Menzoberranzan, it had come down to that: male against male, wizard against wizard, First House against Second, establishment against revolutionary, stability against change, civilization against . . . chaos?

Exactly, Gromph thought—though he would never say it out loud. Order against chaos, and it was Gromph who fought for order, for law, in the name of one of the purest embodiments of chaos in the multiverse: Lolth, a goddess with the heart of a demon.

"Strange," the archmage murmured aloud, "how things work out."

"Indeed, Archmage," Nauzhror answered as if he was reading Gromph's mind—and perhaps he was. "It is strange indeed."

The two Baenre wizards shared a smile, then Gromph closed his eyes and let the others continue their casting. The protective and contingency spells were draped over him one after the other. Sometimes Gromph could feel an itching, warmth, a cool breeze, or a vibration, and sometimes he would feel nothing at all.

"Have you decided where to face him?" Grendan asked, pausing briefly between defensive spells,

Gromph shook his head.

"Somewhere out of the city?" Nauzhror suggested. "Behind the duergar lines?"

Gromph shook his head again.

"At the very least," said Nauzhror, "let us send guards to secure the arena . . . wherever it might be . . . before you arrive. They could remain hidden and come into play against the lichdrow only if necessary."

"No," said Gromph. "I said I will go alone, and I will go alone."

"But Archmage—" Nauzhror started to protest.

"What, precisely, do you think a House guard could do for me against the lichdrow Dyrr?" Gromph asked. "He would dry them up and smoke them in his pipe—precisely as I will do to any soldier Dyrr decides to bring with him. Dyrr will face me on my terms because he has to. He has to beat me, and he has to do it in front of all Menzoberranzan. If not, he will always be second, even if he manages to defeat House Baenre."

The masters continued with their spells, leaving only Nauzhror and Grendan still considering more than the magical practicalities of the duel at hand.

"Donigarten, then," suggested Grendan.

"No," Gromph said, then paused while another spell made him shudder briefly. "No."

He looked up at Nauzhror, who raised an eyebrow, waiting.

"The Clawrift, I think," Gromph said—deciding the second before he actually said it.

"An excellent choice, Archmage," Nauzhror said. "Away from any property of value and away from most of the finer drow of Menzoberranzan, of whom we have so few to spare on the best day."

A younger student entered and quickly set a small crystal ball on a short golden stand on the floor in front of the archmage. Gromph made no effort to acknowledge the student who was even then racing from the room.

He looked deeply into the crystal ball, holding up a hand to still the barrage of protective castings. The crystal grew cloudy, then flashes of light flickered in the roiling clouds inside the once perfectly clear globe.

Gromph brought a memory-image of the lichdrow into his

mind's eye and held it there then did his best to convey that image into the globe. It would find the lichdrow, unless Dyrr expended some energy in avoiding it.

Gromph put his hand down, and several of the more ambitious masters started casting again—muttering incantations and tracing invisible patterns in the air—as if they'd been sitting there holding the thought.

There, Gromph thought as an image coalesced in the crystal ball of the lichdrow striding confidently across a reception hall in House Agrach Dyrr. There you are.

Gromph recognized the hall. He had been there himself on several occasions, back before things started to dissolve and Houses Agrach Dyrr and Baenre were close allies and business associates. He kept his attention on Dyrr. As he watched the lichdrow barking orders to his House guards and other armed drow, Gromph cast a spell of his own.

"Good afternoon, Dyrr," Gromph told the image in the crystal ball. "It will be the Clawrift. I know I don't have to tell you to come alone. I know you're always ready."

Gromph didn't wait for a response. He nodded to his masters and closed his eyes.

"We will be watching, Archmage," said Grendan, "and we'll be in constant contact."

"It would be irresponsible of me," Nauzhror said, "not to ask one more time if I might take your place in—"

"It would be irresponsible of me to hide behind my students," Gromph said. "Besides, Cousin, you were archmage for a little while, and by all accounts you liked it."

"I did, Archmage," Nauzhror admitted, "very much so."

"Well, if you hope to live long enough to be archmage again, you will await me here."

The lichdrow Dyrr dismissed his guards and proceeded via dimension door to the sitting room. There he found Yasraena and Nimor, who were occupied with trying not to speak to each other. Both seemed relieved when the lich stepped from the transdimensional doorway and into the room.

"It is time then?" Nimor asked.

Yasraena drew in a deep breath and held it, her eyes fixed on the lich.

"He awaits me at the Clawrift," Dyrr replied.

The matron mother exhaled slowly, and Nimor nodded.

"As good a place as any," the assassin said. "A hole in the ground . . . no sense damaging the merchandise we're paying so dearly to acquire."

"If by 'merchandise,' " Yasraena hissed, "you mean Menzoberranzan the Mighty, you—"

"Yasraena," Dyrr interrupted, his voice like ice.

The matron mother pressed her teeth together and turned away from Nimor, who stifled a laugh.

"I am prepared, as always," Dyrr said to them both, "and I will leave at once."

Yasraena turned to Nimor and said, "Go with him."

The assassin raised an eyebrow, and Dyrr—if he had any blood he would have felt it boil.

"Surely," the lichdrow said to Yasraena, "you don't mean to imply that I might not achieve the necessary victory on my own. Surely you don't . . . worry over my safety."

He locked his gaze on the young matron mother's eyes and held her there until she went gray, blinked, and turned away.

"You know that all of House Agrach Dyrr has the utmost confidence in you," she said, her voice low, stretched thin. She turned to look Nimor up and down. "But this is no time for personal vendettas. We have aligned ourselves with this . . . whatever he is. Why not use him?"

Nimor smiled, and Dyrr was reminded of the carnivorous lizards that inhabited the wilds of the Underdark.

"You wouldn't know where to begin to use me," the assassin said.

Dyrr simply shrugged off the meaningless exchange. He began to cast a series of protective spells on himself, ignoring a few more tiresome minutes of Yasraena and Nimor's verbal scuffling. Dyrr blinked after having cast on himself a spell that would make unseen things visible to him. Nimor looked different but in ways that seemed incongruous, even impossible. The drow assassin was no drow, as Dyrr had know for some time, but for the first time Dyrr could see something that might have been wings.

The lichdrow let that matter fall to the side in favor of a series of carefully crafted contingencies. After all, Dyrr himself wasn't exactly a drow anymore either. If Nimor was something else than a drow, so be it—as long as the dark assassin remained useful.

Something that Yasraena said made Dyrr stop in the middle of an incantation.

"Will House Agrach Dyrr be evacuated from Menzoberranzan," she asked Nimor, "should things not go the lichdrow's way?"

Dyrr struck her. The slap echoed in the Spartan sitting room, and Yasraena fell in an undignified heap onto the worg-carpeted floor. The lich took some of her life-force with the slap—only a taste, but enough to turn her gray and leave her gasping for breath. She looked up at him from the floor with wide, terrified eyes.

Matron mother indeed, Dyrr thought.

Nimor made no move and barely even seemed to take notice. Finally, he looked down at Yasraena as she began to struggle to her feet.

"If the lichdrow gives his leave," said the assassin, "I would like to answer that question."

The cold gleam in Nimor's eyes was enough to convince Dyrr that the assassin would give the right answer. The lichdrow nodded.

"House Agrach Dyrr," Nimor said to Yasraena, who had managed to get to her feet though her knees shook, "lives or dies in Menzoberranzan."

Yasraena nodded, rubbing her face with trembling hands, and Dyrr caught Nimor's attention.

"Precisely, my friend," the lichdrow said, "as do you."

Nimor stepped toward him, squaring his shoulders. It could never have crossed the lichdrow's mind for a second to back down, and he didn't.

"If I believe you are soon to fall," Nimor said to Dyrr, "I will rescue you."

Dyrr wanted in that moment to kill Nimor Imphraezl, but he didn't. Instead, he laughed. He was still laughing as he teleported away.

🕷   🕷   🕷

The Clawrift, a natural rent in the bedrock, cut into the northern sections of Menzoberranzan east of Tier Breche. Gromph stood at the very edge of it, looking down into the blackness. Even his newly acquired, much younger eyes were incapable of seeing the bottom. Sorcere was behind him. In front of him, across the wide chasm, was the City of Spiders. The stalagmites and stalactites that had been carved into homes and places of business for the drow were aglow with faerie fire. He could see House Baenre all the way on the other side of the cavern and the odd flash of light that marked the continuing siege of House Agrach Dyrr.

The lichdrow appeared in midair over the mile-deep chasm and hung there, a dozen yards away or more. He appeared facing Gromph as if he knew exactly where the archmage would be.

"Ah, my young friend," the lichdrow called, his voice floating over the space between them and echoing into the Clawrift itself, "there you are."

"As promised," Gromph replied, bringing a string of spells to mind.

"So it has come to this, then?" Dyrr asked.

"The two of us," replied Gromph, "fighting to the death?"

The lich laughed, and Gromph knew the sound would have sent lesser drow running.

"Why, Dyrr?" the archmage asked, not really expecting an answer.

The lichdrow turned his palms up and lifted his arms to his sides, looking around, gesturing toward the city.

"What better reason," asked Dyrr, "than the City of Spiders herself? From here, the Underdark, and from there, the World Above."

It was Gromph's turn to laugh.

"That's it then?" the archmage asked. "Mastery of all the world? Isn't that a bit of a cliché, lich? Even for you?"

The lichdrow shrugged and replied, "My existence knows no bounds, Gromph, so why should my ambition?"

"A simple enough answer, I suppose," Gromph said, "to a simple question."

"Shall we get on with it, then?"

"Yes," Gromph replied, "I suppose we had better."

They began slowly, both feeling each other out with minor divinations. Gromph could feel himself being explored even as he explored the lich. Nauzhror's voice, and Grendan and Prath's, whispered in his mind. Defenses were noted, items and clothing assessed for enchantment, notes compared. Gromph had brought a staff with him and was surprised to see that Dyrr had one too. He hadn't expected Dyrr to bring a staff.

Fire, Nauzhror told him after a tense few minutes of study. *The most effective weapon against the undead wizard from the traitor House will be fire.*

That's it, Gromph thought. Dyrr had made his one mistake.

"You're going to surprise me today," the lich called to Gromph, "aren't you, my dear archmage?"

"The only two things I'm completely sure of, Dyrr," Gromph replied, "is that we will surprise each other today and I will destroy you."

They started casting at the same time. Gromph was an experienced enough diviner to know that like himself, the lichdrow had cast his last defensive incantation.

The spells burst into being from the Weave at the same instant. A freezing wind blew from the lichdrow, carrying with it thousands of razor-sharp splinters of ice. That shredding storm met Gromph's fireball over the black depths of the Clawrift. The fire blew out even as it melted the ice. The two effects ate each other before either came close to touching their intended targets.

Well, Gromph told himself with a sigh, this is going to take a while.

Things were quiet but tense on the ship of chaos. Pharaun tried not to look at Quenthel. He couldn't help but notice that she seemed unable to take Reverie. Her shoulders were stiff, and her viper-headed scourge never left her hand. The snakes writhed constantly, sliding the sides of their arrowlike heads against the priestess's warm black skin. The uridezu was surreptitiously eyeing her.

Pharaun found that curious. He was the one who had bound the demon, yet Raashub was more concerned with Quenthel. True, the Baenre priestess was still nominally "in charge" of the expedition, but her leadership had always been more ceremonial—at least in Pharaun's mind.

The Master of Sorcere couldn't quite organize his thoughts on the matter—not just then anyway—but the demon was looking at her oddly.

He sighed and stared out across the black water of the Lake of Shadows again. He placed his hand on the rail then removed it when he felt the warm pulse of blood running through it. The ship barely moved in the dead calm of the black lake, but still Pharaun felt as if he needed to hold onto something. His hand found the twisted gray-yellow rigging—looking for all the world like a length of intestine—but he couldn't hold that much longer either.

The demonic ship didn't quite figure into Pharaun's esthetic. The wizard brushed the hair from his eyes and tried not to think about what he must look like. He hadn't bathed in far too long—hygiene had become secondary for them all, and they were rapidly beginning to stink. Jeggred was the worst of them all on a good day, but the wizard found himself avoiding Quenthel as well. Still, the thought of bathing in the cold, dark waters of the Lake of Shadows held no appeal. Pharaun could well imagine what might be living in that lake's depths, and he didn't want to offer himself up like a worm on a hook.

The ship creaked and groaned but not too much. Only rarely did there come the echo of a splash or drip or other small disturbance from the water. Pharaun was beginning to think it was the silence itself that he found so unnerving.

Something hit him in the back of the head hard enough to drive him facefirst into the bonework deck.

Surprised as much by the fact that he'd been taken by surprise, Pharaun lay blinking for a few seconds—enough time for whatever had hit him to grab him by the ankle. His foot instantly went numb, then whatever it was lifted him bodily off the deck. Still not quite having regained his wits—Pharaun hadn't realized at first that he'd been hit that hard—the Master of Sorcere found himself being spun in the air by the ankle. As he was whirled through the air, he caught glimpses of what was happening.

A party of uridezu were boarding the ship, crawling over the rail dripping with lake water and maggots. Their gray skin glistening and their pink tails twitching, the rat demons attacked in force, though Pharaun couldn't get an accurate count of them while being spun around by the ankle by another uridezu.

The wizard knew that he'd been right, that the first uridezu Raashub had gated in was meant to test them.

The demon let go, and Pharaun was sent pinwheeling through the air. He watched the rail pass beneath him, and when he was over open water he cast a spell while still in midair. By the time he hit the surface in a sprawling, stinging splash, Pharaun could breathe water.

The wizard didn't waste any time. Swimming and using the levitating powers of his brooch to help pull him downward, Pharaun dived deeper and deeper into the pitch-black water. The lake was cold enough to make him tense and stiff, but he still swam as fast as he could. All around him were the shadows of living things. There were fish, he hoped, and snakes, he feared, and other things—things crawling on the bottom.

The lakebed was covered in a fine silt that felt oddly alluring to the touch. Pharaun let himself sink into it up to his neck and closed his eyes to mere slits so that all anyone might be able to see would be his black face against the uniformly black silt.

Something brushed past his leg, but Pharaun didn't move.

The deep water and the stirred-up silt taxed Pharaun's dark-vision to its limits, but he saw two uridezu dive into the water above him. Secure in his hiding place, ignoring another . . . something . . . slipping past his side, Pharaun watched the rat-demons swim with surprising agility, their heads waving back and forth as they searched the lake bed for the drow wizard. Pharaun waited for them to draw closer . . . closer . . . close enough. He threw an aura of faerie fire around them both.

The demons reacted to the magic with twitching confusion.

The purple light not only outlined their silhouettes in the dark water, making them painfully obvious, it also picked out details of the folds of their skin, their whiskers, and the knitting of their worried brows.

Pharaun kicked once and rose slowly from the silt, already casting a spell. The uridezu looked over at him and swished their tails in the water. They swam quickly away from each other, smart enough not to both be caught in the same spell. Pharaun picked one at random and froze the water around it.

The Master of Sorcere knew that the ice would have no wounding effect on the demon, but it was thick enough to stop it. Pharaun smiled briefly at his handiwork. The uridezu, frozen solid in a thick block of ice, slowly sank to the lakebed, leaving a trail of bubbles in its path.

The second uridezu swam in fast, a stream of glowing purple maggots fanning out behind it. The tiny worms came from its ruined left eye, an old wound that had evidently festered for a very long time.

Pharaun tried to swim away from it, but the rat-demon was faster. It whirled in the water and brought its leathery pink tail to bear on the wizard. Pharaun took the hit with a grimace. It hurt.

As the uridezu twisted around, obviously meaning to shred Pharaun with its ragged claws, the Master of Sorcere touched his steel ring. The rapier appeared before him, and Pharaun set it against the demon with a thought. The dancing sword scored a deep slash, and the uridezu's attention—as Pharaun had planned—was drawn entirely to defending itself against the magically animated blade.

Content to let the rapier keep the demon busy, Pharaun kicked away from the duel, pulling his hand crossbow and a quarrel from his belt at the same time. When the bolt was set and cocked,

Pharaun called on the power of his brooch to levitate quickly up and out of the lake. The second his face broke the surface he coughed out lungfuls of fluid. He shot into the air a dozen feet above the water and hung there, black droplets pattering off him to rain back down onto the rippling surface of the Lake of Shadows.

The wizard turned his attention to the ship of chaos. Never had the vessel seemed so aptly named. Quenthel and the draegloth fought for their lives against the rat-demon boarding party. Before Pharaun could get the whole situation sorted, Jeggred ripped a gash in the belly of one uridezu that was deep enough to spill its bowels onto the deck. It crumpled in a heap of steaming entrails at the blood-soaked draegloth's feet.

Pharaun counted four more of the demons, in addition to Raashub. The captain had gathered seven of his kind.

The wizard looked down, checking on the progress of the dancing rapier. The animated blade slit the swimming uridezu's throat. The demon shivered then went limp in the water, slowly floating to the surface. Its scalding blood sent coppery-smelling steam rising into the air below the hovering mage.

Pharaun recalled his rapier. Leveling his hand crossbow, he looked back at the ship of chaos. Quenthel held one uridezu at bay with her whip while another rushed her from behind. Pharaun couldn't get a clear shot, so he paused, and that was all the time it took for the uridezu behind her to bite Quenthel in the neck.

Blood welled up around the deep wound, and the high priestess gnashed her teeth in pain. With a hard, sharp jerk of her shoulder, Quenthel knocked the demon away. From a distance it was difficult for Pharaun to see, but he was sure the uridezu left a few teeth in the mistress's neck.

Movement from Jeggred caught Pharaun's eye. The draegloth advanced on Raashub. A wave of panic coursed through the Master of Sorcere. Attack or no attack, they needed Raashub to pilot the ship. Jeggred had been itching to kill the captain since they'd first claimed the vessel, and the boarding action was excuse enough for him to finally make good on his many threats.

Pharaun, fully aware of the irony of the situation, threw a spell that set a wall of invisible force between the uridezu captain and the advancing draegloth. Jeggred hit the wall hard, setting him back on his heels for a moment. Raashub cowered away from the draegloth then started to sniff the air in front of him, as puzzled by his unexplained, last-second reprieve as was Jeggred.

Quenthel threw an elbow at the uridezu that had bitten her, but the demon was able to avoid the blow. Quenthel's attacks were spasmodic and haphazard, and Pharaun knew it was only a matter of time before the two uridezu she faced managed to kill her.

The Master of Sorcere made his way quickly through a spell and sent its energy flowing out from him to the uridezu that had bitten Quenthel.

An enormous, disembodied black hand faded into existence from the thin air, and Pharaun took control over it with a thought. The uridezu that were harrying Quenthel stepped back from the hand but too slowly for the demon that had bitten her. The hand closed around the creature and began to squeeze.

Taking stock of the situation again, Pharaun saw that Jeggred had moved on to another uridezu, leaving Raashub to grovel behind the wall of force.

The wizard had only to will the spell-hand to squeeze as hard as it could and he could leave it to its own devices. As the uridezu trapped in the hand started gasping for air, Pharaun tightened his finger around the trigger of his hand crossbow and sent the bolt whizzing through the air. The missile slammed into the other demon's chest. It paused and turned to look at the source of the projectile.

The uridezu in the hand had its mouth wide open, but no sound came out. All the air had been squeezed from its lungs. Pharaun reloaded his hand crossbow, and the conjured hand squeezed even tighter. The demon's eyes bulged, and Pharaun couldn't help but watch.

The wizard launched another bolt at the demon that was still managing to dodge the high priestess's whip. The missile slammed home, pushing the uridezu toward Quenthel. The rat-man was staggered but far from dead—which was more than Pharaun could say for the creature in the hand. Its body bulged past the breaking point then burst in a torrent of blood and tissue. A few agonizing seconds later and it was dead.

Pharaun reloaded his hand crossbow again and watched the uridezu his last bolt had pushed toward Quenthel. The high priestess advanced quickly, scourge in one hand, the other wrapped into a tight fist.

The Mistress of the Academy hit the uridezu that faced her so hard its head burst into several large pieces that fell completely away from its shoulders. The rat-demon's glistening gray-and-yellow brain came free and went skipping out across the still surface of the lake. Pharaun knew that her strength was coming from a magic item, and he made a mental note to stop being surprised by feats of strength from the priestess.

Movement and light from below him caught Pharaun's attention. The uridezu he'd frozen in place had finally managed to break free, and it was moving with great whips of its ratlike tail. It swam up and toward Pharaun, who was still hovering and dripping above the water.

Pharaun cast a spell that let him push the advancing demon back down into the water. The Master of Sorcere continued pushing until the uridezu slipped beneath the layer of silt. He pushed harder until the creature finally hit the rocky lake bed, four feet under the drifting sediment. He pressed, crushing the monster into the lake bed. He could feel the thing's back break but kept pressing still.

❀ ❀ ❀

Aliisza held her breath watching the drow fight off the uridezu. The rat-demons weren't necessarily the most impressive foes, but all things considered the dark elves made a fine show of it. Pharaun was especially alluring, hanging in midair over the water, so wet and intense. It made Aliisza all tingly.

The invisible alu-fiend drifted in the air over the regal female drow, who had been paralyzed by the bite of the uridezu she'd dispatched in a messy and uncreative way.

Another of the rat-demons swayed before the paralyzed priestess, its fangs bared and dripping with toxic spittle. It giggled in a shrill, excited way as it inched ever closer to the helpless drow female.

A low rumble drew Aliisza's attention to the draegloth. The half-demon growled in the face of another rat-demon then slashed the thing across the midsection with the razor claws of one hand. The demon bounced back on its heels only barely far enough to avoid having its guts opened onto the deck. A hiss exploded from the uridezu's quivering lips, and its tail lashed around at the draegloth. The half-drow, half-demon behemoth avoided the appendage with surprising agility.

The captain of the ship of chaos rattled his chain but remained bound to the deck. Aliisza sensed the presence of an invisible wall separating the captain from the rest of them. It was as if the air had turned solid there. She could see the magic shimmering in her Weave-sensitive eyesight.

Aliisza didn't particularly care what became of the uridezu

captain or the uncouth, unappealing draegloth, but she couldn't stand the thought of the attractive, impressive drow priestess being eaten alive while paralyzed by a creature as lowly as an uridezu. The alu-fiend began to drain the life-force from that particular rat-creature while still hanging invisible in the air.

The uridezu looked around. It could feel that something bad was happening to it. Maybe it felt cold, or weak, dizzy, sick. Aliisza was killing it, and it had to know it was dying. The rat-demon drew its arms around itself, and Aliisza sensed that it was on its way back to the Abyss—but something kept it there on the ship. Aliisza could see that magic too, binding it to the very air around them. Only Pharaun could have been responsible for that.

The fact that the dark elf wizard had that power made Aliisza uneasy.

She wondered where the invisible wall had come from when she heard a horrid ripping sound and had to dodge an arc of dark-red blood. The draegloth ripped the arm off the uridezu that was stupid enough to stand up to him. Aliisza didn't like the smell of the rat-demon's blood . . . at least not as much as the draegloth seemed to.

The half-demon picked up the uridezu's arm and lifted it behind him until it bounced off the invisible wall. That startled the draegloth—no, not startled, *annoyed* him. Aliisza realized someone was trying to separate the uridezu captain and the draegloth.

That had to be Pharaun's handiwork. As the draegloth beat the rat-demon to death with its own arm, Aliisza sorted out why the wizard might be trying to protect the captain.

She whispered a quick spell and rose higher into the air so that no one but Pharaun would be able to hear her. She had to stop draining the life-force from the last survivor of the demonic boarding party, but the draegloth had already begun stalking toward it.

"Pharaun," she whispered over the intervening yards, her voice coming to the drow wizard as a whisper in his ear.

She saw the mage react and continued, "Yes, it's me. You're protecting the captain from your own draegloth?"

"What of it?" the wizard asked, his voice sounding as a whisper in her ear too.

"You don't need him," she said.

"Yes, I do," replied the mage. "It's a ship of chaos, Aliisza, and I'm a drow who isn't much for boats. I've never piloted one of these things before. Probably no drow in history ever has."

"It's not that hard," she explained. "The ship is alive. You simply *will* it to go where you want."

"It's that easy?" Pharaun asked, skeptical.

Aliisza watched the draegloth shred the weakened uridezu with a flurry of claws and fangs and said, "After a fashion, yes."

Barely missing a beat, the half-demon turned on the invisible wall and went at it with claw and fang, wild and feral. The sight made Aliisza's heart race.

The uridezu captain was cowering behind the wall. He didn't bother trying to pretend he didn't know what the draegloth was going to do to him if he got through the invisible barrier.

"Let the draegloth have him, darling," Aliisza said as her spell began to fade. "We can pilot the ship together."

Pharaun opened a dimensional rift and stepped through. In an instant he was standing on the deck of the ship of chaos next to the paralyzed priestess and directly under the hovering, unseen alu-fiend. She began to sink toward him.

"Jeggred," the drow wizard said to the draegloth, "stop it. Stop it, now. We need him."

The wizard turned to the high priestess, who stood, her hand dripping with uridezu gore. The snakes at the end of her whip hissed at Pharaun, warning him away.

"Mistress," he said to her, "tell him to stop it."

"She's paralyzed," Aliisza whispered in his ear, close enough then to do it without a spell.

Pharaun didn't flinch but smiled and said, "He won't listen to me."

"I told you it's all right, Pharaun," whispered the alu-fiend, "we don't need him."

"We?" he asked.

Aliisza blushed, though Pharaun still couldn't see her.

"If Raashub can pilot this vessel," she asked, "why can't we? Could it be that hard?"

Pharaun drew in a deep breath and let it out in a sigh.

"He's only going to keep defying me anyway, isn't he?" Pharaun asked.

"Who are you . . ." Quenthel said, her joints jerking as she recovered from the uridezu's paralyzing bite, ". . . talking to?"

"Wouldn't you, in his place?" Aliisza whispered, ignoring the high priestess.

Pharaun turned to her and looked her in the eyes, though she was sure he wasn't able to see her. He winked at her then turned back to the priestess.

"Jeggred means to kill the captain," he said.

"Let him," the priestess replied as she scanned the deck apparently looking for something with which to clean the blood off her.

"Well," Aliisza whispered into the wizard's ear, "it's her idea now, isn't it?"

Pharaun waved a hand and dropped the wall.

The draegloth leaped onto the uridezu captain. They both went over the rail. The chain that bound the uridezu to the deck—and to the material plane—snapped as if it were made of mushroom stem. There was a huge, echoing splash that sent lake water rolling onto the deck to mingle with the spilled demon blood.

Aliisza hovered over them as Pharaun and Quenthel ran to the rail and looked over into the black water. Bubbles peppered the surface, and there were ripples that made it obvious that some violence was occurring below the surface.

Then the bubbles stopped. The ripples played themselves out, and there was nothing.

"Go after them," the priestess said to Pharaun.

Aliisza caught herself before she laughed out loud.

Pharaun raised an eyebrow, looked at the priestess, and said, "I'm afraid I had to cancel the spell that allowed me to breathe underwater."

The priestess turned on him angrily, but any further discussion was stopped by the sound of another splash. Something arced out of the water and thumped onto the deck. The uridezu captain's head rolled to the other side of the ship and came to rest looking blankly up at nothing.

"Well," Quenthel breathed, glancing at Pharaun, "never mind."

The draegloth climbed slowly onto the deck behind the two dark elves. The half-demon shook himself hard, spraying water all over Pharaun and Quenthel. The two dark elves turned to regard the draegloth.

"That," the half-demon rumbled, "was almost worth the wait."

Chapter

THIRTEEN

Danifae wanted them to meet her in a ruined temple on the edge of a swamp, on the east bank of which a wide river emptied into a sea. Halisstra spent the first night's walk explaining to Ryld what most of those words meant. By sunrise the first day, they had made the coast. The sight of the seemingly endless expanse of cold gray water took Halisstra's breath away. Like most of the rest of the World Above, it had made Ryld uncomfortable, even nervous. Halisstra was confident that he'd eventually get used to it, even grow to like it. He had to.

They followed the western shore of what the surface dwellers called the Dragon Reach for two long nights' march, using Ryld's keen senses, Halisstra's *bae'qeshel,* and Eilistraeen magic to avoid fellow travelers and unexpected dangers. In the hours before sunrise of the third day they stood at the bank of the wide Lis river delta, the Dragon Reach spreading out in angry, windswept white and gray to their right. To their left—north—was the river and intermittent woods and rolling, snowy hills. The weather was dark and bitterly cold, and Halisstra had to use spells to keep them from losing fingers and toes.

"We have to cross that?" Ryld asked, though he knew the answer.

They were concealed in a copse of sparse, leafless trees. The river delta crawled with boats of all sizes. Halisstra had never seen such vessels. Most bobbed on the angry waves, lanterns on their decks swaying in the chill wind. The drow caught the occasional glimpse of an armed human pacing the decks, wary of what, Halisstra couldn't imagine.

"It's an abandoned temple," Halisstra told him again. "An old temple to the filthy orc god Gruumsh. Danifae said it sits at the western edge of a vast swamp . . . a flooded place where water covers the vegetation, and many dangerous things hunt. The swamp is on the other side of the river."

Ryld nodded and continued to study the water as the sun's glow began to kiss the horizon.

"Would you know how to work one of those boats?" Halisstra asked.

The weapons master shook his head.

"Then we'll need help getting across," said the priestess. "It's too far and too cold to swim, and we'll attract too much attention using spells. If we keep our *piwafwis* up and over our heads, a less observant ferryman might not mark us as dark elves."

Ryld let out a sigh that told her he doubted that was possible but that he would try anyway.

They set out along the river's edge, working their way slowly northward in the pre-dawn gloom. Ryld stopped her occasionally to look around or study a boat that was either sitting on or adrift close to the riverbank. He never bothered to explain why he rejected first one then another and another, and Halisstra didn't ask.

Finally, they came upon a wide, square-keeled boat with a single long oar attached to a tall pole. The vessel had been pulled up on the riverbank, and a few feet away there was the indistinct lump of some humanoid creature asleep on the coarse sand. He'd built a fire before he drifted off to unconsciousness, and it sat next to him, the last of the embers quickly fading.

Ryld moved to within a few inches of the ferryman without making a sound. The weapons master slowly, silently drew his short sword and held it in a loose, easy grip. He crouched next to the humanoid, and the sleeper let out an odd sort of sustained, rumbling cough. Ryld half stood, looked at Halisstra, and shrugged. Halisstra returned the gesture. She had no idea what the sound could signify except that maybe the man—if it was a man—was choking.

Ryld rolled him over with a purposely harsh, violent push. The sleeper had the gruff grayish-yellow features of an orc, but not entirely. His eyes bulged, and he took a deep breath, his heavy brow wrinkled in anger. Ryld dropped the blade of his short sword to the boatman's neck, and the angry man stopped very suddenly. Halisstra stepped in. When she looked more closely at him, she saw that the ferryman was a half-orc. That was good luck for them. Half-orcs tended to be as despised on the World Above as they were in the Underdark, so he would be easier to manipulate into keeping their presence secret.

"Silence," Ryld whispered in the guttural trade tongue of the surface races.

The half-orc glanced once at Halisstra, then met Ryld's eyes and made a show of relaxing. He said nothing.

"We require a boat," the weapons master said quietly. "You will take us east across the river, and you will tell no one of it."

The half-orc looked at him, considering it.

Ryld nicked the man's neck with his short sword, barely enough to draw a half-inch sliver of blood.

"I wasn't asking," the weapons master added, and the half-orc nodded.

Within minutes they were on the boat. The horizon in front of them turned from black to a deep indigo. Halisstra had begun to grow accustomed to the sun, but Ryld still hated it, so they had been traveling at night. In order to make their arranged rendezvous with Danifae, they might have to continue through the morning, but Halisstra knew Ryld wouldn't complain.

"I think the ferryman expects us to pay him when we get to the other side," Ryld said in Low Drow, glancing at the half-orc who was pretending not to be staring at them. "Or do they breed half-orcs as slaves here too?"

At first Halisstra thought he was joking. It was hard to see his eyes with the cowl of his *piwafwi* pulled over his head. Halisstra wore her own hood the same way, but by the time they got to the midpoint in the wide river delta, the priestess realized that no one on any of the other boats was bothering to look at them and night-blind humans wouldn't be able to see them in the dark—not from a distance anyway. She slipped the hood off her head, eliciting an irritated scowl from Ryld, who kept his own cowl up.

"Why don't you ask him?" Halisstra said, nodding at the boatman.

Ryld shook his head.

"Danifae is going to kill you," he said, his voice flat.

"Is she?"

"I would," the weapons master replied. "She was your battle-captive for a long time, and now she isn't. Of course she will seek revenge for her years of bondage."

"Maybe," Halisstra had to admit, "but I don't think so."

"We don't get your kind around here much," the boatman blurted suddenly in heavily accented Low Drow.

The sound of the half-human, half-orc thing speaking the language of the dark elves made Halisstra's skin crawl. Ryld drew his short sword.

The boatman put up a hand, shaking, and said, "I mean no disrespect or anything. I was just saying . . ."

"You've seen drow before?" Halisstra asked then flashed a quick sentence in sign language: *An extra hundred gold pieces if you forget all about us.*

The half-orc had no reaction to the signed question. He didn't even seem to notice that she'd been trying to communicate.

"Sure," the boatman replied, "I've seen a drow or two. Not recently, but . . ."

Halisstra shrugged off the boatman's answer and signed to Ryld, *I think he wanted us to know he understood us, so we wouldn't say something that would make us want to kill him for hearing it.*

That drew a smile from Ryld.

You can put your sword away, she added.

The weapons master sheathed his blade and said, "If he understands the sign, he should say so now or I will kill him."

The half-orc waved a hand and said, "No, no, sir. I swear to you. I didn't even know what you were doing. I just paddle, yes? Paddle? You don't even have to pay me."

"Pay you?" Ryld asked.

The half-orc looked away.

He heard us mention the temple, Ryld signed. *It goes without saying that he can't be trusted.*

Who can? Halisstra answered.

Not Danifae, the weapons master signed.

Eilistraee will guide us, she replied. *Danifae has no goddess to guide her.*

Ryld nodded, though he made his continued skepticism plain.

They rode the rest of the way in silence, and soon they were at the other side of the river. Halisstra stepped off the boat, wading in inches deep water to the rocky riverbank. She looked back for Ryld, who was stepping toward the half-orc. The weapons master reached behind the ferryman, unsheathed Splitter, took off the half-orc's head, and resheathed his weapon in precisely the space of one of Halisstra's heartbeats. The head splashed into the water, and the weapons master kicked the body in after it.

Ryld turned to wade ashore, and Halisstra looked away into the blue-gray light of the dawn. She could hear his footsteps in the water then on the rocks behind her, but she didn't want to look at his face just then.

Danifae materialized on the deck of the ship of chaos and was instantly struck by how much had changed. Valas appeared next to her, and she watched his expression change from his normal stoic, blank pragmatism to an uneasy curiosity—he'd noticed it too.

Pharaun and Quenthel both looked bad and smelled bad. The ship itself looked different. The deck, which had been a dull white expanse of stark bone, was covered in spots with pink tissue and crossed with gently throbbing arteries. Sinew and what might have been ligaments stretched between gaps in the bone. The ship felt alive.

Pharaun and Jeggred both looked up at them when they appeared, but only Pharaun stood. The draegloth looked to one side, and Danifae followed his gaze to Quenthel. Jeggred's eyes burned when he looked at the high priestess, who sat on the deck with her back to the others, one hand absently caressing one of the vipers that made up her whip.

"Welcome back to the Underdark's dull wet arse," the Master of Sorcere said. He only glanced at Danifae but approached Valas with his hand out. "You have what we need?"

The Bregan D'aerthe scout nodded and handed the wizard one of the magical sacks that held their supplies.

Danifae kept her attention on Jeggred, who made eye contact with her finally and nodded. The former battle-captive gave the draegloth a smile and a slight bow—then she noticed that the bound uridezu was missing.

"What happened here?" she asked Pharaun.

The wizard began to laugh, and at first it seemed as if he would be laughing for a long time. When no one joined him, he calmed himself and took a deep breath.

"Mistress?" Danifae called to Quenthel.

Nothing.

Jeggred stared at the high priestess's back, saying nothing as well.

"Are we . . . ?" the scout asked Pharaun.

"Oh, yes," the wizard replied, "we'll be setting sail as planned. It turns out that we didn't need the captain's services after all. Jeggred was kind enough to retire his commission for us. I will be piloting the ship to the Abyss and back."

Valas nodded, sat, and began to sort through their supplies. Pharaun stood over him, occasionally commenting on what the scout had purchased. Quenthel continued to sit with her back to the rest of them, saying nothing. Danifae approached Jeggred, gauging his mood as she moved closer. He seemed to want to speak to her, so she sat down next to him.

"Reverie?" she asked, nodding at Quenthel.

"No," said the draegloth, making no effort to lower his voice. "She has been unable to take the Reverie. The mistress is weakening."

Danifae took a deep breath, searching the draegloth's eyes

for some hint that he was anything but genuinely angry with Quenthel. It didn't seem possible that Jeggred had come that far in the relatively short time that she and Valas had been gone, but obviously things had progressed much more swiftly than she'd hoped.

"The 'captain'," Jeggred grumbled, "gated in some of his kind. They attacked us, and we prevailed."

"Quenthel didn't fight?" Danifae guessed.

Jeggred looked at the silent high priestess and thought about that for a while.

"She fought," the draegloth said finally, "but she . . ."

Danifae waited a few heartbeats for him to finish then prodded, "We all serve greater mistresses, Jeggred. The Matron Mother of House Baenre, in your case, and in mine, Lolth herself—both greater mistresses than Quenthel. If you have something that either your matron mother or your goddess need to know, you must speak. Duty demands it."

Jeggred looked deep into her eyes, and she let him. She held the half-demon's gaze for a long time, never permitting herself the slightest twitch, the most miniscule sign of weakness or indecision.

"She's . . . sensitive," the draegloth said.

"Sensitive?" Danifae pressed.

"The Mistress of Arach-Tinilith has a sensitivity to beings from the outer planes," he said. "She can sense the presence of demons and communicate with them. It's not something that everyone knows about her, but I do."

"Then why didn't she know that Raashub was gating in . . . ?" She let the question fade away.

The look in Jeggred's eyes as he stared at Quenthel's still back told her all she needed to know.

"I am a priestess of Lolth," she told the draegloth. "I serve the

Queen of the Demonweb Pits, and on this ship that means I serve Quenthel Baenre."

Jeggred tipped his huge head to one side, his wild mane of white hair spilling over his muscular, gray-furred shoulders.

"I serve her," Danifae went on, "whether she knows it or not, whether she appreciates it or not, and whether she desires it or not. Something is . . ."

Danifae wasn't sure how to finish that thought.

"She has succumbed," the draegloth said.

"Succumbed?" asked Danifae.

"To fear."

Danifae let that settle in then said, "She requires our services more than ever now. Lolth's servant demands our service, and we both live to serve, do we not?"

Jeggred nodded slowly, making it plain he was waiting to hear more.

The former battle-captive reached into her pouch and drew out one of the rings she'd taken from the cold, dead hand of her former House mage. She held it up so that only Jeggred could see it, sliding it between her fingertips so that it reflected the feeble illumination—enough for the draegloth's dark-sensitive eyes to see it. Jeggred opened one hand, and Danifae let the ring fall onto the half-demon's palm.

I need you to go somewhere with me, Danifae signed, her hands close to her stomach so none of the others could see, *and do something for me.*

Ask, he replied, also careful to keep his hands where only she could see them. *I live to serve, Mistress.*

C h a p t e r

F O U R T E E N

They hadn't managed to kill each other yet.

Gromph floated in the still darkness above the Clawrift surrounded by a globe of magical energy. He'd conjured it from his staff, draining some of the item's magical essence in the process. The cost was worth it to keep out even the rudimentary spells the globe protected him from. Gromph knew the lich was capable of much more powerful castings—spells that would pass through the globe without the slightest degradation in power—but at least it would limit Dyrr's options.

Regardless of the globe, no matter what he tried, Gromph couldn't get within sixty yards of the lich.

The repulsion effect is coming from Dyrr's staff, Nauzhror whispered into Gromph's mind. *We are studying possible solutions.*

The repulsion was another petty defense, another meager

drain on a powerful item, and in that way Gromph and Dyrr were even—again.

"What are you afraid of, lich?" the archmage called to his opponent. "I won't try to kiss you."

Dyrr, who was also floating above the black depths of the Clawrift, actually laughed.

"We could simply float here," Dyrr replied, "waiting for one of the defenses to go down—your globe, my repulsion . . . but where's the sport in that?"

"Good question," Gromph whispered, not caring if the lich could hear him or not.

The archmage began to cast a spell, and the lich pressed his fingertips together, waiting to defend against it. Gromph set himself moving through the air toward the lich the second he finished his incantation and knew it was successful when the distance between them abruptly closed. The repulsion effect successfully dispelled, Gromph swooped in quickly to get into range for a more damaging spell.

Dyrr, who didn't seem the least bit surprised, dropped out of the air. Gromph knew he'd dispelled the repulsion effect, not Dyrr's ability to fly. The lich was trying to escape into the black abyss of the Clawrift.

Gromph dropped after him. The air, moving fast over the surface of the magical globe that still surrounded him, made a curious humming sound that Gromph found distracting. Still, he managed to cast another spell as he flew and succeeded in closing the distance between them even more.

A bead of pulsing orange light appeared in Gromph's right hand. He looked up at Dyrr, brought his arm back to throw the bead, and hesitated. Dyrr, a cold light in his dead eyes, was coming at him. The distance between the two mages was closing faster and faster—and the lichdrow was casting a spell.

The words of Dyrr's spell—a series of almost nonsensical quatrains in an obscure dialect of Draconic—echoed around them both. Gromph drew his right arm back farther still, aiming the bead at his opponent's face while holding his staff in his left hand. Dyrr had something cupped in his own left hand and his own staff in his right. It was as if they were both looking in a mirror.

Dyrr threw his first. A cloud of sparkling red dust—*Crushed rubies,* Grendan reported—burst into the air around the lich. The dust swirled on some twist of wind for half a heartbeat then was gone. As the last grain of the powdered gemstone disappeared, Gromph threw the bead.

The archmage came to a sudden stop in the air. The breath was forced from his lungs, and he grunted loudly. His own staff hit him in the face, numbing his bottom lip and making his eyes water. His joints went limp for a few seconds, and his arms and legs flapped out of control.

The bead of compressed fire should have hit the lich in the face and exploded in a ball of flame six paces wide. It should have burned the lich's face off—but it didn't.

Gromph, as he finally gained control of his body and came to rest once again hovering in midair, could see the tiny speck of orange light fly true toward the lich's face then curve in the air and dive into the garish crown the Agrach Dyrr wizard had the audacity to wear. The bead blazed briefly to life in a splash of orange and yellow luminescence that lit the lichdrow's face but didn't come close to burning it off.

The crown, Gromph thought. I should have remembered.

The fireball has been absorbed by the crown, Nauzhror hissed into Gromph's mind.

Gromph was certain he'd see it again.

The item will allow him to redirect the fireball at you, Grendan warned.

Yes, gentlemen, Gromph replied. *Thank you.*

Dyrr drew to an abrupt stop and hung in the air, bouncing ever so slightly. He looked like a mushroom cap bobbing on the surface of Donigarten Lake. Gromph, on the other hand, was frozen in air, standing on what felt like a solid surface but looked like a dim, phosphorescent glow.

Gromph's globe was still up, but it wasn't the only thing that surrounded him.

An impressive spell, Nauzhror said. *Difficult to cast and expensive what with the ruby dust and all. It's nothing you can't handle, Archmage.*

"A forcecage?" Gromph asked.

The lichdrow didn't bother answering. Instead, he began to cast another spell. Clearly he thought he had Gromph trapped, so of course he would take advantage of the situation. The archmage brought a spell to mind and rushed through the casting of it, racing the lich, though he would likely still have to suffer through whatever Dyrr was throwing at him. He needed to get the forcecage off him. Being trapped in a magical box was hardly convenient at that moment.

Dyrr's spell took effect half a heartbeat before Gromph's. As the lich finished the last gestures and the final complex verbalization and crunched a lodestone and a pinch of dust in his right hand, something opened under the archmage's feet.

Gromph's spell went off, and his own globe fell victim to it—but so did the forcecage—and Gromph was falling into whatever it was Dyrr had conjured underneath him.

The archmage touched his brooch and made himself stop quickly, well before he contacted Dyrr's dramatic magical effect. As he drew himself up, moving farther and farther away from it, Gromph looked down—and into a whole other universe. The lichdrow had opened a gate beneath him, and a blinding, eye-searing light poured out of it. Gromph had seen light like it only a few times in his long life. It was sunlight, and the Archmage of Menzoberranzan didn't like it at all.

"Where are you trying to send me?" Gromph asked his opponent.

The World Above? Prath mused, though only Gromph could hear him.

Dyrr didn't answer but busied himself gathering some spell component or perhaps another magic item.

"You've imprisoned me more than once already," Gromph went on, "though they seem to hold me less time each attempt. Now you want to send me away? For pity's sake, Dyrr, why not simply kill me and get it over with? Or is it that you *can't* kill me?"

Gromph certainly wished that were the case—and maybe by some bizarre twist of fate it was—but Dyrr seemed to have something else in mind. The lich finished casting his spell. The immediate effect was that Gromph's stomach lifted in his gut. He caught his breath in a hissing gasp and started to fall.

He couldn't levitate—Dyrr had dispelled the magic that was keeping him aloft—and Gromph fell toward the rotating pool of daylight beneath him. Knowing Dyrr, it would be a worse fate than simply splattering at the bottom of the Clawrift. It was a fate Gromph would do anything to avoid.

The archmage extended himself, wiping more stored energy, more access to the Weave from his mind than he normally would have had to, but he needed the spell to take effect faster and couldn't spare the time for complicated incantations. The effect felt the same as Dyrr's dispelling of his levitation, but instead of falling down, Gromph drifted to a stop then started falling upward. The source of gravity, with enough magic, could be moved.

Gromph twisted in the air as he accelerated toward the roof

of the cavern that housed Menzoberranzan. As the lich crossed his field of vision, Gromph could see him grimace in frustration. The archmage didn't waste time gloating. His brooch was useless to him—at least for the time being—Gromph would continue to fall upward toward the new source of gravity until he was dashed against the ceiling. He would have to stop himself.

The command word, Gromph sent to the masters of Sorcere. *Quickly.*

The staff that he'd used to surround himself in the globe of protective magic had been charged with more than one effect. He'd never used it, but the staff would grant him the same power of levitation as his brooch.

Sshivex, Nauzhror provided.

"*Sshivex,*" Gromph repeated and immediately began to levitate "up" and away from the ceiling.

In a fraction of a second—before he "landed" on the ceiling—Gromph once again drew to a halt in midair. The pool of blinding sunlight was far below him. The light made it difficult, but Gromph finally managed to spot the lichdrow, who was flying slowly, well away from the gate, and casting another spell.

"That was close, Dyrr," Gromph called out. "You almost—"

The words caught in Gromph's throat. His vision blurred. For a few seconds he couldn't breathe.

"You al—" Gromph started again, but the words were pinched off when his throat clamped shut.

Tears welled up in the archmage's eyes, and a wave of over-whelming despair passed through him, leaving his skin clammy, and his head spinning.

It's an enchantment, Grendan told him.

He was going to die. Gromph knew that with absolute certainty, but what was worse, Menzoberranzan would die soon after him. Everything he'd built over a life spent in the corridors of power had come to nothing. Menzoberranzan was eating itself alive. Everything Gromph had considered a strength—in himself, and in his race—had proven a weakness.

A compulsion, added Prath.

The hate and mistrust, the vendettas and animosities, had finally come home to roost. The once great City of Spiders had been reduced to a besieged, ragged, self-destructing ruin of its former glory—glory that was proving with every dead drow to have been a lie all along.

Fight it, Archmage, Nauzhror urged.

Lolth was dead, and Gromph would be dead soon too. Lolth was dead, and so was House Baenre. So was Sorcere. So was Menzoberranzan. It had all come to nothing, as he himself had come to nothing.

Archmage . . . Nauzhror prodded.

Gromph's body shuddered through an alien sensation: a sob. He wiped at his eyes with the back of his hand and tried to blink away the tears, but more came. Through the tears he saw that Dyrr had moved and was floating above him.

"That's it, young Baenre," the lichdrow said. "Lament. Cry for fallen Menzoberranzan. Cry for House Baenre."

Cry? Gromph thought. Am I crying?

"Slow," Dyrr said, his voice like a gentle caress against Gromph's pain-ravaged brow. "Stop, young mage."

No, a voice in Gromph's mind all but shouted.

Gromph hadn't realized he was moving—levitating slowly "down" toward the ceiling, moving away from the blinding light pouring from Dyrr's gate. The archmage slowed his descent and came to a stop, hanging only a few yards from the jagged stalactites that hung from the ceiling like fangs ready to puncture the neck of Menzoberranzan the Mighty, ready to punish them all for their weakness.

"There . . ." the lichdrow murmured, his voice sending a quivering chill down Gromph's spine. "There . . ."

The lich was holding something.

How did he get so close?

Archmage, the voice in his head asked, *shall I come help you?*

No, he thought back at the voice.

Gromph tried to flinch away, but the lichdrow touched him with a long, thin wand of gem-inlaid silver. The touch of it sent a wave of blinding agony ripping through the archmage's body. Every muscle tensed, joints popped, and the wizard clenched his teeth against the pain. His eyes watered more, and Gromph could feel tears streaming down his tingling black cheeks.

He turned away from the lich, rolling in the air, and faced down toward the gate. His eyes closed against the light, but he blinked them open and saw the briefest flash of a silhouette: Dyrr in shadow against the sunlight. The lichdrow was below him but had been above him. Gromph wasn't sure at that instant what he was seeing. Dyrr had fooled him, or he was disoriented . . . or he was dying.

Am I dying? Gromph thought.

"Am I?" he said aloud then clamped a hand over his face, closing his eyes and mouth.

No, Archmage, said the voice in his head. *You are under the effect of a powerful enchantment.*

In that moment, Gromph lost all memory of any plan, of any determination, of any purpose for the ruin of a life he'd been cursed with. He wanted to get away. He needed to run, but he was still the Archmage of Menzoberranzan, so he cast a spell that would get him away a little faster, a little farther. With a few words and gestures he'd repeated so many times that even in his confused, despairing state of mind he managed to get right, Gromph brought forth the magic to open a doorway through the dimensions—a break in space and time.

Gromph levitated toward it, but something hit him and hit him hard. It was Dyrr. The lichdrow had put away his wand. The slim magical weapon caused physical damage and pain, but it didn't cause an impact—not like that. The air was forced from Gromph's lungs again, and he found himself pinwheeling through the air.

The light from the gate grew brighter and brighter, and Gromph was only dimly aware that he was moving toward it. The pain was everywhere, still burning from the wand and joined by whatever it was that had hit him to send him falling toward the light. The pain turned to numbness in spots then was gone, and Gromph took a deep, shuddering breath.

The ring, he thought. I have a ring that will . . .

Yes, Archmage, the voice said, *the ring. The ring will keep you alive but not forever.*

Gromph closed his eyes tight again and let his body relax. The ring he'd slipped on at Sorcere before meeting Dyrr at the Clawrift would regenerate injuries: knit broken bones back together, seal cuts, even re-grow severed limbs. He remembered putting the ring on but couldn't for the life of him remember why. What could possibly have been the point? To live? To live in the shattered ruins of a Menzoberranzan ruled by the traitorous Dyrr and an army of stinking gray dwarves?

Gromph touched the ring, grabbed it with the opposite hand, and was about to rip it from his finger so it would let him die, when he saw the lichdrow swooping down at him, cackling. Laughing at him.

"Take it off," Dyrr chuckled. "It won't help with burns anyway."

Archmage! another voice shouted into his mind.

The lich blinked and jerked forward with his head and shoulders. From the grotesque crown on his head came a tiny ball of undulating orange light. It spiraled through the air, riding a sort of wave, and drew a long, curved trajectory directly at Gromph.

Your fireball, the voice in his head warned.

"My fireball . . ." the archmage whispered, as he instinctively tucked himself into a fetal position, wrapping his body around his staff and closing his eyes tightly.

Even with his eyes closed the flare of hot orange light burned his retinas. The fireball warmed his skin but didn't burn him. He and the other Masters of Sorcere had thought, of course, to protect him against fire.

"A little longer . . ." the archmage murmured.

"Gromph," the lichdrow spat back. "You live!"

"For now," was the archmage's shaking, muttered reply.

Dyrr didn't wait for Gromph to elaborate. He began to work another spell.

The fireball had broken Gromph's concentration on the levitation effect, and once again his stomach lurched up as he began to fall. Gravity was still upside down, and his fall took him away from the gate and toward the ceiling.

While Dyrr finished his spell, Gromph began to list in his own mind the many reasons he should simply let himself fall into the ceiling and die.

Before the troubled archmage could reach a conclusion, shards of jagged, half-molten rock burst into existence, flying with extraordinary speed toward the falling archmage. There were too many of them to count, and Gromph, mumbling to himself of his lost position and the bleak fate of his House, didn't bother trying.

When the meteors entered the area in which Gromph had affected gravity, their courses radically changed. They went everywhere, scattering, dipping, curving, colliding with each other, some even curving back at Dyrr.

One of the burning projectiles struck Gromph a glancing blow, sending him spinning as he fell. Pain blazed in his side, and without thinking he cast a spell. With only a few words and a quick gesture, Gromph's skin tightened, stretched—painfully—and took on the gleam, and the hardness, of cold black iron.

Very good, Master, the voice . . . it was Nauzhror . . . said.

Gromph watched one of the meteors come right at him. He might have twisted out of the way, but he didn't care. The rock hit him square in the chest, exploding in a shower of yellow-orange sparks and sending a deafening clang rippling away from him in the air. He started to spin in a different direction and began to wonder why he hadn't hit the ceiling. As he whirled around he saw Dyrr slip through a dark hole in the sky that was rimmed with purple light like faerie fire. The lichdrow was passing through a dimension door of his own to avoid the meteors that had come careening back at him.

Spinning, falling, Gromph saw the jagged, stalagmite-cluttered ceiling racing toward him, closer and closer—only inches from oblivion, from the sweet release of death—

—and the spell effect ended.

Gromph hadn't made it permanent after all. Gravity went back to its normal place, and once again Gromph hung in midair for a second—less than a second maybe—his stomach feeling as if it were rotating in his belly. He started to fall again but toward the floor—toward the Clawrift, toward the light, toward the gate, toward wherever it was that Dyrr was trying to send him.

Gromph didn't care. He'd go, then. He'd go anywhere as long as he could get out of Menzoberranzan, where every stone, every stalactite and stalagmite, every glow of faerie fire, reminded him of his failure and despair.

Archmage, Nauzhror said. *Gromph . . . no.*

Closing his eyes against the blinding sunlight, Gromph fell through the gate. Squinting, able only to see a vague play of shadow and light, he watched the gate close behind him. He was enveloped, enclosed in blinding light.

He hit the ground hard enough to break a leg, more than a few ribs, his left arm, and very nearly his neck. Quivering from pain and shock, blinded by the relentless sunlight, Gromph lay in a heap on a bed of what felt like some kind of moss. Blood roared in his ears, which were still ringing from the whine of the meteors and the rush of wind. Something in his chest popped, and his leg twitched out from under him, rolling him over onto his back.

Gromph put a hand over his face and realized that his broken arm was obeying his commands with only a little pain. His leg was numb and tingling, and he could actually feel his ribs popping back into place.

The ring, he thought again.

He almost wanted to laugh. It was his own fault after all, for insisting on wearing that cursed ring. He'd wanted to save his own life when he'd put it on, and it hadn't occurred to him then that all it would end up doing was keeping him alive in whatever blazing hell Dyrr had banished him to.

Gromph blinked his eyes open and found that he could actually see. The light was still uncomfortably bright, but something had moved between the brightest part of it and himself. The archmage blinked again, rubbed his eyes, and struggled to sit up. His face was still wet with tears, and he was breathing hard—panting like a slave at hard labor.

"Are you *keerjaan*?" a voice asked.

Gromph held out a hand, fending off the voice, and blinked some more.

It was all at once that he realized the thing that had come between him and the source of the light was a creature of some kind, and it was speaking to him.

"Am I . . . ?" the archmage started to answer.

He paused, rubbed his eyes, and found himself concentrating on a spell he'd long ago made permanent. It was a spell that allowed him to understand and be understood by anyone.

"Are you all right?" the strange creature asked, and Gromph understood.

He looked up and saw that he was surrounded by tiny, drowlike creatures—drowlike in that they were roughly the same shape, with two arms, two legs, and a head. There the similarity ended. The creatures that surrounded him had pale skin that was almost pink. Their hair was curly and an unsightly shade of brown-orange. Their skin was spattered with tiny brown spots. Plastered on their faces were the most childlike expressions of delighted curiosity. They hovered around him in a circle, several feet off the plant-covered ground, each of them borne aloft on a set of short feathered wings of the most garish colors. Most of them were naked, though some wore robes of flowing white silk, and a couple wore breeches and fine silk blouses. They were no more than three feet tall.

"By all the howling expanse of the Abyss, Dyrr," Gromph murmured, curling his legs under him and resting his face in his hands, "where have you dropped me?"

Words began to pop into his mind like soap bubbles bursting:

Halflings.

Spells.

Crushing . . .

Crushing despair.

"Damn you," Gromph breathed, his body relaxing, his eyes drying, his mood lifting as if by magic.

It wasn't magic that was lifting it, he realized. It was magic that sank it in the first pace.

"Well played, traitor," Gromph said, looking up into the bright blue sky of the . . . where was he? The World Above?

"Who are you talking to?" one of the winged halflings asked, tipping its head to one side like a confused pack lizard.

"Where am I?" Gromph asked the strange creature.

The archmage, not waiting for an answer, stood, brushing soot, dust, and pieces of the odd, needle-like plant life from his *piwafwi*. He leaned on his staff, but thanks to the ring he was feeling stronger with each breath.

"You don't know where you are?" one of the winged halflings—a female—asked.

"Tell me where I am, or I'll kill you and ask someone else," Gromph growled.

The halflings reacted, maybe with fear—Gromph couldn't be sure. They bobbed up and down and quivered.

"Are you a cambion?" one of them asked.

"I am a drow," Gromph replied, "and I asked you a question."

The winged halflings all looked at each other. Some smiled, some nodded—some smiled *and* nodded.

"How did you get here?" the female asked.

"I asked you a question," Gromph repeated.

The female smiled at him, and Gromph had to squint from the brightness of her perfect white teeth.

"How could you come here from . . . where did you come from?" one of the males said.

"I am from Menzoberranzan," replied Gromph.

"Where's that?" asked another of the males.

"The Underdark," Gromph said, his crushing despair gone, being replaced by burning impatience. "Faerûn . . . Toril?"

"Faerûn," one of the males gasped. The others looked at him and he said, "I was from there. From Luiren. Faerûn is a continent, and Toril is a world. On the Prime."

The other winged halflings nodded and shrugged.

"So," the one who'd asked the question before repeated, "how could you come here from Menzoberranzan, the Underdark, Faerûn, Toril, and not know where you are?"

"You're not even on the Prime anymore, drow," said the halfling who'd claimed to be from Faerûn. Gromph could see contempt starting to manifest in that halfling's beady brown eyes. "You've come to the Green Fields, and you don't belong here."

"That's all right," Gromph said. "I'm not staying."

Looking over the vast landscape of gently rolling hills covered in a blanket of the tiny green, needle-like plants and punctuated with a scattering of rainbow-colored blossoms like delicate, paper-thin mushrooms, Gromph almost sank into despair again.

Dyrr had sent him far—sent him to another plane of existence altogether.

"The Green Fields," Gromph repeated. "Halfling Heaven. . . ."

Nauzhror, he thought, sending the name out into the Weave. *Grendan? Can you hear me?*

Nothing.

Gromph sighed. It was going to take him a while to get home.

Chapter

FIFTEEN

"Oh, now, why the long face?" Aliisza purred.

Her hand slipped along Pharaun's waist, tickling him, but he didn't move. She smiled and wrapped her arm around him, sliding her hand onto his back and moving closer and closer until her body pressed against his. She was warm—almost hot, and she smelled good. She felt better.

"Your journey is barely beginning," the alu-fiend whispered into his ear. Her breath was so hot it nearly burned the side of his neck. "I almost envy you the sights you'll see, the things you'll experience. You will be in the presence of your goddess soon enough."

"Will I like what I see?" he asked. "Will the experience be a fulfilling one? Will my goddess speak to me?"

Aliisza stiffened, but just for a second, then she wrapped one leg around him and nestled in. The force of her embrace turned them slightly in the air. Pharaun glanced down at the ship of chaos and his companions, a hundred feet or more beneath them, oblivious to their presence there.

"Those are all things you'll have to discover on your own," she said.

"Then how can you be sure it'll be something to envy?" he asked, his voice playful but forced, his attention returning to her.

"I envy you the surprises," she replied with a wink.

"Have you been there?"

"To the Abyss?" she asked. "Not for a long time."

"The Demonweb Pits?"

The alu-fiend withdrew enough to look him in the eye, smiled, and said, "No, I've never been to the Demonweb Pits. Have you?"

Pharaun shook his head. He could answer her but not when she was looking at him. He leaned into her, and she squeezed him tighter.

"I was there twice, I think," he said into the soft warmth of her long neck.

"You think?"

"It was a long time ago," Pharaun replied, "and it might have been a dream. There was the last time, when we were all there in astral form, but I thought you might have been there once in the flesh. You're a demon. You can go there and . . ."

Pharaun stopped talking. He wasn't sure what he was trying to say.

"Have you been to Menzoberranzan?" he asked instead.

Aliisza stiffened again and for a little bit longer, and he knew that she had.

"Will there be a city for us to return to?" he asked.

Aliisza shrugged. Pharaun could feel the gesture against his body.

"Answer me," he pressed.

"Yes," she said, "or no. It all depends on what you find in the Abyss and how soon Kaanyr and his new friends can break your matron mothers' backs."

Pharaun found himself laughing. He was exhausted again. The Lake of Shadows had a way of sapping his strength.

"Honestly, Pharaun," she said, "you ask me questions as if I'm some sort of fortune teller or oracle . . . or goddess. I don't know what'll happen to you and your friends. No one, not even your Spider Queen I think, can predict what will happen from minute to minute in the mad chaos of the Abyss."

Pharaun looked her in the eye and decided not to say the first few things that came into his mind.

"Have you thought about my coming with you?" Aliisza asked.

"Why would you help me pilot the ship?" he asked her, gently pushing her away. "We enjoy each other, but I can't imagine you're asking me to simply trust you. I'll need an answer."

Aliisza resisted playfully and flicked the tip of her tongue against his cheek.

"You're pretty," she teased.

"Not as pretty as you," said Pharaun. "Answer me. Why would you help me find Lolth and help Vhok and the duergar lay siege to Menzoberranzan at the same time? You're the enemy—the consort of the enemy, at least—of the city I call home. One might be tempted to choose sides."

"Whatever for?" she asked. "When I'm with you, I like you best. When I'm with Kaanyr, he is everything to me. Either way, I'm amused."

Pharaun found himself laughing again.

"I'll assume that's the best answer I'll ever get from you," he said, "or any other tanar'ri."

Aliisza winked at him again.

As Pharaun let his hands explore her exquisite body, he said, "We should begin our lessons. Quenthel and the others are anxious to get underway."

Aliisza responded to his touch with a sigh, then replied, "As soon as you wish, love. You know how to get there from here?"

"Through the Shadow Deep," he said.

The alu-fiend nodded and said, "From there to the Plain of Infinite Portals—the gateway to the Abyss. There you'll need to find precisely the right entrance. The place you seek—the Demonweb Pits—is the sixty-sixth layer. There are guardians there and lost souls and things maybe even you can't imagine. You might actually like the Abyss, and you might not. Either way, it will change you."

Pharaun sighed. She was probably right.

He really didn't want to go.

❦ ❦ ❦

Who is responsible? Quenthel asked.

Oh, Mistress, Mistress, K'Sothra answered. Of the five vipers in her scourge, K'Sothra was the least intelligent, but Quenthel listened anyway. *Mistress, it was you. You are responsible. It's all your fault.*

Quenthel closed her eyes. The skin on her face felt tight, stretched too thin on her skull. Her head hurt. She touched the viper just below its head, and K'Sothra writhed playfully under her touch.

Was it really my fault? the high priestess asked. *Could it be?*

She drew her finger away from K'Sothra, found the next viper, and cupped her head in two fingers.

I came back when she sent me back, and I served her as best I could, Quenthel sent to all five snakes. *I became the Mistress of*

Arach-Tinilith, and the worship of Lolth was never stronger. Isn't that what she sent me back to do?

There was no answer.

What will become of us all? she asked Zinda.

The black-and-red-speckled snake twitched, flicked her tongue at Quenthel, and said, *That is also your responsibility, Mistress. What happens as a result of your having driven Lolth away from us will be washed away if only you can bring her back. If you can attract her good graces again, she will save us all. If not, we will be destroyed.*

Quenthel felt herself physically sag under the weight of that. Though she tried hard to muster all her training and natural fortitude, she wasn't able to sit up straight. What weighed most heavily on her was the feeling that the snakes were right. It was her fault, and she was the only one who could fix it.

When will Lolth answer? Quenthel asked, moving her fingers to Qorra.

The third viper had the most potent poison. Quenthel only let her strike when she wanted to kill, when she wanted to show no mercy at all.

Never, Qorra hissed into the high priestess's mind. *Lolth will never answer. Menzoberranzan, Arach-Tinilith, and your entire civilization are doomed without her, and she's never coming back.*

Quenthel's head spun. She was sitting on the deck of the ship of chaos but still felt as if she were about to fall over.

That isn't necessarily true, said Yngoth.

Quenthel had grown more and more dependent on Yngoth's limitless wisdom. It was his voice that tended to reassure her, and to Quenthel he sounded most like a drow.

Why was I sent back? she asked Yngoth. *Is this why? To find her?*

When you were sent back, the viper replied, *Lolth didn't need to be found. Haven't you thought all along that you were sent back to sit at the head of Arach-Tinilith? To hold that post for House Baenre and preserve Lolth's faith and Lolth's favorite in the power structure of Menzoberranzan?*

I'm not sure now, the Mistress of the Academy admitted.

You were sent back for this, Yngoth said. *Of course you were. You were sent back to become Mistress of Arach-Tinilith so that you would be the one they sent to find Lolth when the goddess chose to turn away. You were meant to be the savior of Menzoberranzan and perhaps even the savior of Lolth herself.*

Quenthel sagged a little further at that.

How can you be sure? she asked.

I'm not sure, replied Yngoth, *but it seems reasonable.*

Quenthel sighed.

It was Lolth's plan all along that I go back there, Quenthel asked, *to find her? How will I do that?*

Get to the Abyss first, replied Hsiv. The last of her vipers was never shy when it came to offering his mistress advice. *Go there first and you will be guided to Lolth by Lolth. You will know what to do.*

How do you know? Quenthel asked.

I don't, Hsiv replied, *but do you have any choice?*

Quenthel shook her head. She hadn't had any choice in a very long time.

$$\text{\Large ❈ \quad ❈ \quad ❈}$$

Valas looked around at the ragged drow who made up the expedition to the Abyss. They didn't look very good. Aside from Danifae, who had more energy than Valas had ever seen, who seemed transformed by their trip to Sschindylryn, they were tired, ragged, temperamental, and unfocused.

"May I ask a practical question?"

Only Danifae looked at him. Quenthel was in a world of her own, deep in her own obviously troubled thoughts. The draegloth was pacing, almost pouting if such a thing could be possible from a creature that was half drow, half demon. The wizard was nowhere to be found.

"Where has the wizard gone?" the scout asked.

Danifae pointed upward, and Valas followed her finger to see Pharaun slowly descending from the darkness above.

"Never fear, scout," the wizard said as he finally settled on the deck, "I wouldn't dream of abandoning this great expedition to rescue our mighty civilization from the brink of annihilation. We are nearly ready to begin, though there are a few more things I need to do."

Valas stopped himself from sighing. The never-ending string of delays was wearing on them all—especially when they came with little or no explanation.

"You're keeping us here," the draegloth said, giving voice to what Valas was thinking—and what the others were likely thinking as well. "You don't want to go."

The Master of Sorcere turned on the draegloth and lifted an eyebrow.

"Indeed?" said Pharaun. "Well, in that case perhaps *you* can attune the third resonant of the Blood Helm to the planar frequency of the Shadow Fringe."

There was a silence while the draegloth looked at him with narrowed eyes.

"No?" Pharaun went on. "I didn't think so. That means you're going to have to let me finish what I need to finish."

The wizard looked around at the rest of them, and Valas shrugged, casually meeting his eyes.

"This is not some mushroom-stem raft," Pharaun said to them all, "splashing about on Donigarten Lake. This vessel, if you haven't noticed, is alive. It is a being of pure chaos. It has a certain intelligence. It has the innate ability to shift between the planar walls from one reality to another. You don't simply paddle something like this. You have to make it a part of you and in turn make yourself a part of it."

He paused for effect then continued, "I am willing to do that—for the good of the expedition and for the pure curiosity of it. It's a unique opportunity to explore some fabulously outré magic. What you must all remember is that if I don't get it right, we could never make it out of this lake. Worse yet, we could find ourselves scuttled in the Shadow Deep or lost forever in the endless Abyss."

The Master of Sorcere looked around as if he was waiting for an argument. None came—even from Jeggred, but he went on anyway, "This time it will be different—the Abyss, the journey there, everything. Last time we were projected across the Astral. We were ghosts there. This time we'll actually *be* there. If we die in the Abyss, we don't snap back into our bodies. There will be no silver cord. We will be real there, and if we die . . ."

Valas wondered why the wizard stopped. Perhaps Pharaun didn't know what would happen if they died there. If you die in your own afterlife, is there an after-afterlife? Thinking about it gave Valas the beginnings of a nagging headache.

"Have any of you ever been to the Abyss before?" Pharaun asked. "Really been there, physically? Even you, Jeggred?"

The draegloth didn't answer, but his smoldering look was enough. None of them had been there, none of them knew—

"I've been there," Quenthel said. The sudden sound of her voice almost startled Valas. "I have been there as a ghost, as a visitor, and as a . . ."

Danifae took a few steps toward Quenthel then sank to her knees on the deck half a dozen paces away from her.

"What as, Mistress?" the battle-captive asked.

"I was killed," the high priestess said, her voice sounding as if it were coming from a great distance. Her vipers grew increasingly agitated as she went on. "My soul went to Lolth. I served the goddess herself for a decade, then she sent me back."

Valas's flesh ran cold, and he found himself stepping slowly away from the high priestess.

"Why?" Pharaun asked, a skeptical look on his face.

The Mistress of Arach-Tinilith turned and gave him a dark, cold stare.

"I think he means," Danifae continued for Pharaun, " why were you sent back?"

"I've never heard anything about this," the Master of Sorcere added.

"It was kept secret," said Quenthel, "for a number of reasons. There were circumstances concerning my death and the one who killed me that might have embarrassed my House. It's not a simple thing, attaining a position like the one I hold. Indeed there is no position like the one I hold . . . in Menzoberranzan, at least. It was not a position House Baenre was prepared to concede to any other House. For ten years I was simply 'away pursuing studies' or some other excuse alternating between ludicrous and clever. Eventually I returned, then things happened and I was elevated to Mistress of the Academy."

"And now you're on your way back," Danifae said in hushed, heavy tones.

"It's as if someone has a plan for you," said Pharaun.

No one said anything more. Valas walked back to the bags and finished sorting the supplies.

🤞 🤞 🤞

Danifae stood up slowly. Quenthel wasn't looking at her, but it was clear from her body language that the high priestess had finished speaking.

Danifae thought through the revelation quickly but thoroughly. It didn't matter. It didn't change anything.

She turned, scanning the deck as she did so. The others had gone back to what they were doing. Each of them was undoubtedly going over in his own mind what Quenthel had said. She turned her back to them and stared at Jeggred. When the draegloth finally looked at her, she signaled him in sign language, careful to keep her hands close to her so the others wouldn't see.

It is time, she told him.

The draegloth nodded and glanced meaningfully at the tattered sails of human skin that sagged listlessly in the still air. Danifae nodded and began to ease her way across the deck.

It took them both several minutes to maneuver themselves behind the sail without making it obvious they were hiding.

When they were safely out of sight, Jeggred signed, *Where are we going, Mistress?*

Danifae smiled and replied, *Hunting.*

The draegloth's lips twisted into a fierce smile. The half-demon looked hungry.

Danifae stepped closer to him. She could see him stiffen, stand straight—almost at attention. The former battle-captive stepped closer still and wrapped one arm around the half-demon's huge waist. Jeggred's gray fur was warm to the touch and a little bit oily. He was surprisingly soft.

Danifae concentrated on the ring she'd taken from Zinnirit, and in the blink of an eye they were in Sschindylryn.

Jeggred took a deep breath and looked around at the dark interior of the gatehouse.

"Where are we?" he asked.

Danifae took his hand and led him to one of the gates. Not answering his question, she busied herself with the gate itself, activating it first, then tuning the location to the agreed-on meeting place. The portal blazed to life in an almost blinding torrent of violet light. Still holding Jeggred's hand, she stepped through. The draegloth didn't hesitate to follow, and they stepped out into a dimly lit ruin.

Even if Danifae didn't know exactly where they were she would have known they were on the World Above. The lighting was strange, a different color than anything found in the Underdark. The walls were made of mud bricks—very old, crumbling. Vines and moss grew in the cracks between the bricks, twisting in and out of every crevice, crawling up every wall, and matting the floor, eating away at the structure the way plants did on the World Above.

"It smells strange here," Jeggred grumbled. "What is this place?"

Danifae looked around to get her bearings. The dull gray light seeped in through dozens if not hundreds of cracks and holes in the decaying walls. On one side of the room a set of uneven steps led up to a floor above. On the other side was a similar staircase leading down. Danifae started up the stairs to the higher room, and Jeggred followed her.

"This was once a temple to the orcs' foul, grunting pig-god," she explained. "Now it's just another piece of rotting garbage being eaten away by the World Above. A suitable place to do what we've come here to do, don't you think?"

"What have we come here to do?" asked the draegloth.

Danifae, disappointed but not surprised that the subtlety was lost on the draegloth, replied, "The traitors are coming."

They came out into a more brightly lit room, and both of them had to shade their eyes with their hands. Danifae moved to a wide crack in the ancient wall and looked out onto the World Above. The sun had set, but the light was still difficult to take. In time, though, her eyes began to adjust. Half a dozen yards below her was what surface dwellers called a swamp. It was a place where water covered the ground—in most places at least—but it wasn't a proper lake. The whole area around the temple was choked with alien vegetation. The sounds of the myriad creatures of the World Above were almost deafening. The swamp crawled with life. Beyond the edge of the swamp, miles to the west, was a wide expanse of water: the end of a long river.

Danifae let out a slow breath through her nose and heard the draegloth scuffle on the loose rocks behind her.

"I hate this," she whispered.

"What?" Jeggred asked.

"The surface."

Danifae scanned the ground below the ruined temple. Finally she drew from a pouch one of the rings she'd taken from Zinnirit and turned it over in her fingers. The fading light played against its polished surface and picked out a scattering of ruby chips.

Pressing the ring into one of the draegloth's four hands she said, "Use this ring to return at will to the ship of chaos."

Jeggred nodded, slipped the ring on, and stood patiently behind her, listening attentively as she explained the proper use of the ring's magic. Confident that the draegloth understood, Danifae let the minutes drag on—and finally she saw them.

"There they are," she said.

The draegloth moved closer behind her, and she suppressed a gag when his breath rolled over her. She waited while he searched for them, and when he finally saw them he growled low in his throat.

"They're together," he said.

"They lied," said Danifae. "She didn't go to Menzoberranzan. She went to the Velarswood—a forest where there's a temple to . . ." She feigned difficulty in articulating the word. "Eilistraee."

Jeggred growled again and said, "And the weapons master?"

"He's made a choice," she replied.

Jeggred began to growl with every exhale. He was ready to kill. Danifae could smell it on him.

"Take the male," she whispered to the draegloth. "Just him for now."

She pushed Jeggred back away from the crack but held him so he wouldn't leave. Stepping up onto the bottom of the wound in the wall, Danifae drew herself up into the dimming light. She waved a hand over her head to attract her former mistress's attention.

It took an infuriatingly long time, but eventually Halisstra stopped at the edge of the swamp and pointed up at Danifae. Ryld looked up as well, and Halisstra waved in answer.

Danifae made exaggerated, wide gestures, an unsubtle form of the drow sign language, sending the message: *Only you.*

Halisstra turned to Ryld, and they conversed. Even from so far away Danifae could tell that Ryld was reluctant to let her go alone. The weapons master might have been a traitor to his city, his goddess, and his race, but he was no fool. Still, Halisstra managed to convince him—or command him—to stay behind. He stood with his arms crossed as Halisstra stepped gingerly into the swamp.

Danifae stepped down from the crack in the wall and took the draegloth by the shoulders.

Doing her best to withstand the half-demon's foul breath, she said, "Go. Don't let her see you."

The draegloth smiled, and a thick, ropy strand of drool dropped from his lower lip. His fangs glimmered in the dim light, and so did his burning red eyes.

Danifae thought he was the most beautiful thing she'd ever seen.

Chapter

SIXTEEN

The swamplight lynx didn't smell prey. The scent that filled the great cat's nostrils was something different. The lynx had never come across anything like it, but whatever it was, it was a predator—the odor of a meat-eater was unmistakable.

Padding softly, silently through the cold, shallow water, the lynx tipped its head up and waved its nose from side to side, honing in on the scent. A charge of energy thrilled through the cat. Its flesh tingled, its fur stood on end—a familiar feeling for the lynx, comforting, foretelling of a kill ahead and food.

The lynx moved from shadow to shadow, still inside the treeline. It caught sight of the competing predator and recognized the shape of a man. Powerful and cunning hunters in their own right, men never respected another predator's stalking grounds. They ignored the scent markers, the scratches on trees, the most obvious signs.

Its eyesight was the least of the cat's senses even in daylight, and the creature could see and smell only that the intruder was a man. It had no way of discerning the man's black skin, pointed ears, crimson eyes, and white hair.

The swamplight lynx gathered the Weave energy in its body, bared its fangs, and tightened into a crouch, ready to spring—when another scent all but slammed into its nostrils.

Another predator was approaching. It was bigger, and it smelled bad. It smelled like a scavenger.

The swamplight lynx relaxed but only a little. It watched the man, occasionally scanning the swamp's edge for the scavenger, and waited.

❧   ❧   ❧

Ryld was surrounded.

There were noises everywhere. The place Halisstra had called a "swamp" was even more alive than the rest of the World Above, and the weapons master didn't like it at all. He could see things moving in the darkness around him. There were insects and spiders, all manner of flying creatures, and snakes . . . lots of snakes. The ground under his feet was spongy. He'd felt similar in some of the bigger fungal colonies in the Underdark, but down there it was at least quiet.

The ruined temple rose in black silhouette against the night sky in front of him. He'd watched Halisstra walk toward it through ever deepening water with an increasing certainty that she was walking toward her own demise. Going to meet Danifae was stupid, even if Halisstra had allowed him to come along, and Ryld wasn't sure why he'd let it happen. Could it be that she simply wished it and he was so accustomed to obeying priestesses that he'd obeyed her?

The weapons master took a deep breath, set his feet close together, and pressed his hands palm to palm in front of his chest. He steadied his breathing and cleared his mind as best he could, surrounded as he was by the unseen dangers of the swamp. He watched tiny yellow lights flicker in the air—some kind of bioluminescent insects moving slowly, sluggish in the cold night air. Pinpoints of light spattered across the black dome of the sky, not painful to look at and actually helping Ryld's natural darkvision. There was no other light except—

Except for a faint purple glow shimmering in chaotic waves over Ryld himself.

Faerie fire.

Ryld drew Splitter and stepped back, opening his stance, then he turned around once three hundred and sixty degrees looking for anything moving toward him—looking for Danifae. It was a dark elf who had picked him out from the dark background using the magical ability she, like all drow, was born with. Who else could it be?

She must have already killed Halisstra, Ryld thought.

The world exploded in agonizing light, and he could hear something big running at him.

Ryld had been trained to fight when unable to see, and as the foe that blinded him charged, he fell back on that training. The weapons master surprised himself with how well he'd adapted to the way sound traveled on the surface world. He timed Danifae's charge—and it had to be Danifae—so that when she was no more than three strides from him, he stepped to the side. The echoes were oddly spaced. It almost sounded as if Danifae had four legs.

That aside, Ryld had estimated correctly, and he stepped out of the way of the former battle-captive in time to feel her brush past him in a rush of cold air and an unpleasant, uncharacteristic strong musky smell.

Still blind, Ryld heard her scuffle to a stop in the ankle-deep, wet moss. She turned quickly and Ryld could feel her ready to come at him again.

Ryld heaved Splitter in front of him, again as he was trained to do. The blade never bit into flesh and bone, but the purpose of that attack wasn't so much to kill as it was to fend off. He had been blinded by some sort of conjured light, which meant that his eyesight would return in time. The first rule of fighting blind was keeping yourself alive until you weren't blind anymore.

It was exactly what he was supposed to do, but it didn't work. The moment Splitter passed to his left side, opening up his chest and face, she—it . . . something . . . dived on him. It was definitely not Danifae. It was no drow at all.

The thing that smashed Ryld to the ground was enormous and covered in thick, coarse fur. It had four strong legs each with a set of long, sharp claws that tugged at his armor but were unable to cut him through his dwarven mithral breastplate.

Ryld smelled hot, rank breath, and a name came to his mind: Jeggred.

Why would the draegloth be there with Danifae? Unless the former battle-captive had brought Quenthel with her, but would they all really waste their time running after him and Halisstra when there was still a goddess to awaken?

Ryld blinked, his sight returning in aching, cramping vibrations in his tired eyes. The claws worried at his armor and came dangerously close to his face as the creature—could it be the draegloth?—shifted in an effort to find some gap in his armor to exploit for the kill. Ryld pushed up with the flat of his blade and both his feet and rolled the heavy creature off him.

When it hit the cold, spongy ground, it wriggled on its side in an effort to get to its feet. The thing growled, and the sound was both higher in pitch and less intelligent than Jeggred's. Ryld blinked blotches of purple from his eyes and whirled around and up to his feet, Splitter in front of him to guard against the inevitable next pounce.

If it was Jeggred, the draegloth was down on all fours and attacking him only with fangs and one set of claws. Ryld batted away a rake from the thing with the flat of his blade but failed to slice off the paw. It bit at him, but he stepped back, leaning away from the attack so that the creature's fangs snapped down on thin air.

Ryld blinked again, and his eyesight returned to nearly normal. He wasn't fighting Danifae or Jeggred but some kind of furred surface animal. Ryld had seen similar animals: cats. The one that was trying to kill him was huge, ten feet from nose to tail. Mottled gray fur rippled over rolling muscles. Its tall, pointed ears twitched and moved independently of each other to track Ryld as it circled him, and the weapons master turned to keep the animal in sight at all times. Steam puffed from its nostrils into the cold air.

Ryld felt a chill run through the undersides of his arms. He had a strange feeling of relief that he was only being hunted— again—by a native surface animal. Danifae hadn't taken her revenge after all, certainly not with Jeggred as her second. The weapons master briefly entertained the idea that Halisstra was right about her former servant, but the reality of his situation intruded once again.

The animal leaped at him, and Ryld was ready for it. He had Splitter up and to the side and had just tensed his arms in preparation for a downward slice across his chest to dig at the animal's head when the thing stopped. The animal halted in midair for a heartbeat then fell. It made a sound that was halfway between a growl and a whimper when it hit the ground, already scrambling to regain its feet.

The weapons master hopped back, bringing Splitter quickly in front of him to guard against—

"Jeggred," Ryld said.

The draegloth held the huge cat by its tail, his eyes glowing red in the darkness. Even as the animal turned on him, Jeggred's lips pulled back over his teeth in a feral, hate-filled smile.

❁ ❁ ❁

Halisstra stepped off the stairs onto what she assumed was the highest floor of the slowly crumbling structure and there she saw Danifae. A gasp passed across her parted lips at the sight of her former servant. Danifae had always been beautiful—that was part of what made her such a desirable possession—but though it hardly seemed possible, the girl had grown even more attractive. The ample curves of her strong body made an alluring silhouette in the dark space, and her bright white hair framed her round, beautiful face in a way Halisstra had never seen on her normally pragmatic and simple battle-captive.

"What's wrong?" Danifae asked, her voice quiet. "Do I look different?"

Halisstra nodded and stepped away from the top of the stairs, careful to keep her back to the wall.

"Yes, you do. Freedom agrees with you, Danifae."

"Yes, Halisstra," Danifae replied. Halisstra did not fail to miss the fact that Danifae had called her by name. "Freedom does agree with me," she continued, "but there is much to discuss and precious little time."

Halisstra arced an eyebrow and let a hand slip to the hilt of the Crescent Blade.

"You are in danger here," Danifae warned, her eyes darting to Halisstra's weapon. "I was careless and was found out."

Halisstra's blood went cold, and she said, "Found out?"

"I was gone too long," said Danifae. "I was questioned by the high priestess and the mage, and they . . . did things to me to make me tell them about you, about Ryld, and all of it. All of it that I know."

Halisstra tried to take a deep breath but found her chest tight with anxiety.

"Where are they?" Halisstra asked.

"Far away," replied Danifae, "and well prepared for their journey to the Abyss, but they sent Jeggred back with me."

Halisstra's blood ran even colder, and she said, "The draegloth? Why?"

"To kill you both."

Halisstra looked madly around the ruin and found the crack in the wall she'd earlier seen Danifae standing in. Though it meant turning her back on Danifae, Halisstra ran to the crack and began wildly scanning the dark swamp below for any sign of Ryld. There was a pain in her chest she'd never felt before. She couldn't see either the weapons master or the draegloth.

"He's out there, I assure you," said Danifae.

"So you drew me here?" Halisstra asked, not turning from her fruitless search of the swamp below. "You drew us both into a trap?"

"Yes, I did," said the former battle-captive, "but I can save you. I can save you, but I can't save you both."

"How can you stop a draegloth that has been sent to kill?" Halisstra asked. She scowled, still scanning the swamp. There were spaces where the trees were tall and thick enough to hide the surface all together.

Ryld must have gone in there, Halisstra thought, perhaps lured in by Jeggred.

"I can't stop a draegloth," Danifae admitted. "If Jeggred means to kill you both, he will, or Ryld will kill him, or I will kill him. Either way, there will be deaths tonight."

Halisstra sighed, not sure what to do and afraid that Ryld was already dead.

"I don't have to stop Jeggred," Danifae continued, "*or* kill him. Just go, and leave the rest to Ryld and me. If the weapons master can best the draegloth, fine. If not, I can convince Jeggred that I killed you."

"Why would he trust you?" asked Halisstra. "He'll want to see my body . . . or part of it at least. And what of Ryld?"

"Let me get you out of here," the former battle-captive said. "Get enough distance between yourself and the draegloth while he's still engaged with the weapons master and we can come to some arrangement. We'll have time to sort something out."

Halisstra shook her head and stepped away from the crack in the wall.

"I won't leave Ryld."

Halisstra smiled at the finality of her statement and the feeling that went with it.

"I can get you out of here fast," Danifae said, "and I can move Ryld almost as easily, but it has to be one at a time. Come with me now, and I'll go back for the weapons master."

Halisstra studied her former servant's face and saw nothing. Danifae didn't seem to be lying, but at the same time she didn't seem to be telling the truth. It was as if all expression had been sanded from her face. She was blank, impenetrable. That scared Halisstra.

"You've trusted me this far, Mistress."

Halisstra registered the return of the traditional title.

Danifae held out a hand to her former mistress, and said, "Trust me, Halisstra."

Confused, the First Daughter of House Melarn shook her head.

The former servant said, "The longer we do this, the longer your weapons master fights the draegloth . . . alone."

There was a brief moment of silence. Halisstra sighed, stepped toward Danifae, and took her hand. Eilistraee had been pushing her along for some time. Halisstra knew that, and she felt pushed again. She tried to remind herself of what she'd told Ryld, that Eilistraee was guiding her but no goddess was guiding Danifae.

As the interior of the ruined temple faded in a wave of vertigo and purple light to be replaced by a strange place somewhere that smelled and felt like the Underdark, Halisstra tried so hard to trust in Eilistraee that her head started to hurt. She thought about Ryld and her eyes filled with tears.

🐚   🐚   🐚

The animal turned on Jeggred, and it was all claws and fangs.

The swamp creature ripped a deep furrow in Jeggred's abdomen with its foreclaws. Blood welled up in the wound. Jeggred didn't flinch or cry out. Only a subtle narrowing of the half-demon's blazing red eyes indicated he'd felt the cut at all. The draegloth stepped in, slashing with two of his four sets of claws, but the cat leaped to the side, avoiding the attack, and at the same time stepped in again, forcing Jeggred to defend himself.

The cat was making a good showing of it, and Ryld knew it was the best chance he would have to run. By the time Jeggred managed to dispatch the beast—if he was able to at all—Ryld could be long gone. Even if he could leave Halisstra, wherever he went Jeggred would follow. If the draegloth had been sent to kill him, that's what he would do.

The cat bit at Jeggred, and the draegloth moved his arm in and allowed the creature to fasten its powerful jaws on his upper right wrist. The fangs dented the draegloth's skin but didn't puncture

200

it. Smiling, steam pouring from his nostrils into the cold air, Jeggred drew the claws of both of his left hands along the cat's flanks. The animal opened its mouth to howl in pain, and the half-demon's arm came free.

Jeggred let the animal cut him. Four parallel lines of deep red blood traced behind the cat's raking claws. The animal was trying to hurt the draegloth in any way it could, but it was wounded and desperate and was making rash decisions. On the other hand, Jeggred only *appeared* feral. He was in control of himself. Ryld could see it in every twitch of the draegloth's eyes that anticipated the cat's attacks three or four moves ahead. Though the animal clawed him, Jeggred got in closer and wrapped one of his bigger, stronger arms around the animal's belly. The draegloth's claws made a popping sound when they punctured the cat's flesh, then a ripping sound as they opened its underside in three deep, ragged incisions.

Things started spilling out of the madly writhing animal. Long ropes of intestines, things that must have been its kidneys, and other organs rode a torrent of steaming blood onto the spongy moss. Jeggred held the animal close to him and squeezed until more came out and kept squeezing until the cat was dead.

Ryld stood a few paces away, watching, ready. He thought back on his training and the single overriding principal of defending against claws. Things with claws—any number of demons, trolls, and the like—stabbed then pulled down. Claw attacks always came high and ripped down. All he had to do was be ready for that. There was the fact that anything that attacked with claws would never parry. If Ryld set his blade against Jeggred's attack, the draegloth would avoid contact with the keen edge or risk dismemberment. Ryld could use that to his advantage simply by defending against the draegloth's arms as if they were swords. Jeggred would be put on the defensive by being unable to defend, and he wouldn't parry Ryld's attacks, but he would dodge.

The draegloth looked up from his still-quivering kill and bared his knifelike fangs at Ryld. The weapons master stood his ground. He wasn't as strong as Jeggred, and he might not be as fast, but he was smarter and better trained.

That might be enough.

"Why are you here?" Ryld asked the draegloth. "Surely you didn't come all this way just to save me from that cat."

The half-demon, covered in the animal's still-hot blood, was steaming.

"I was told things about you, weapons master," Jeggred growled. "Disturbing things."

Ryld held Splitter in both hands in front of him and said, "I can only imagine."

"The priestess I can understand," said the draegloth. He took a wide, slow step sideways, moving away from the dead animal. "They're feeling particularly betrayed by Lolth. They seek power and communion, so it seems only fitting that if one goddess turns her back on them, they might seek the embrace of another, but you?"

"I can't seek the embrace of a goddess?" asked Ryld, stalling as he examined the half-demon for wounds and weaknesses.

"Why would you," asked the draegloth, "when you can have the embrace of a flesh and blood female?"

"You have me all figured out," the weapons master said, surprised that the draegloth seemed to have done just that.

"My mistress has," Jeggred said with a shrug. He stepped to the side again, beginning to circle Ryld. "She even now stands over the corpse of your traitor priestess. I get the pleasure of ending your life."

"It'll be a particularly painful and violent death, no doubt," Ryld said, irony absent from his voice.

The draegloth smiled, coughed out a laugh, and charged.

The big claws came in first, high, aimed for his chest. Ryld whirled Splitter in front of him then abruptly stopped the blade's spin and sliced up to parry the draegloth's right arm. As he expected, Jeggred drew his arm back sharply in an effort to avoid the enchanted greatsword. Ryld quickly changed direction, tucking the blade in, stepping back, and stabbing at the dodging half-demon. The tip of Ryld's sword penetrated the draegloth's furred hide under his shoulder blade to a depth of an inch or two. The half-demon, bleeding, hopped back, sliding off the blade.

Ryld stepped back too, rolling the greatsword in both hands in a slow figure eight in front of him.

Soon, one of them would be dead.

Chapter

SEVENTEEN

"Where is he?" Quenthel asked, her red eyes wild with barely contained fury.

"He's gone to kill them," Danifae answered.

Pharaun watched the exchange from a distance. He had sat cross-legged in the exact center of the deck, right in front of the mainmast, precisely where Aliisza had told him to sit. He could feel the ship of chaos vibrating beneath him, reacting to the power he was exerting over it.

"On whose command?" the high priestess asked.

"On yours, Mistress," Danifae answered, "through me."

"Through you?" Quenthel repeated. "Through *you?*"

Pharaun pressed one of his hands against the deck and felt the pulse in a cluster of veins that was growing there.

The high priestess slapped Danifae across the face, but the

battle-captive stood her ground.

"Halisstra Melarn and Ryld Argith are traitors," Danifae said. "They are traitors to this expedition, traitors to Lolth, and traitors to drow civilization. You know that, I know that, and Jeggred knows that. That's why he's there."

"On *your* command," the Mistress of the Academy pressed, "not mine."

"He's doing what has to be done," Danifae replied, her voice finally showing some emotion: anger and impatience. "You weren't able to give him the order, so I did it for you."

Pharaun laughed at the exchange and at the thrill of the ship reacting to his thoughts and touch. He found Danifae's hijacking of the draegloth fascinating.

"We have the time, Mistress," Pharaun offered in Danifae's defense—if only for the sport of it. "Why not let the draegloth clean up some messes? If Mistress Melarn is indeed a traitor, and after watching her in the face of Lolth's temple that's hardly a surprise, consider it a favor from a loyal young priestess in your service. Master Argith, on the other hand, is likely not a traitor to the City of Spiders. He lacks the necessary spark for rebellion, I'm afraid. If you wish to be concerned with anything it should be that the weapons master might actually kill your nephew."

Quenthel looked over at Pharaun, who met her gaze for a moment then returned his attention to the ship. The high priestess glanced at Danifae, who stood tall and resolute, giving no ground. The Mistress of the Academy held her scourge in one hand, and the vipers curled around the fingers of her other. She looked down at the vipers then back at Danifae. Pharaun watched the whole thing while feeling the ship's pulse momentarily quicken.

Quenthel took a step away and turned her back on Danifae, who sighed. Pharaun thought the battle-captive might have been disappointed.

"That," Danifae said to Quenthel's back, "is why Jeggred serves me now."

§   §   §

They began to circle each other, testing their steps on the spongy, uneven moss. Jeggred looked down and considered the puncture wound. He lifted one eyebrow in a sort of grudging salute then let his tongue unroll from his mouth. The black, rough tongue slowly licked the wound. When he smiled next, Jeggred's own blood stained his razor-sharp fangs.

Just keep your distance, Ryld told himself. Keep your distance and go for the hands.

The draegloth charged again, and again his claws came in high at first. Ryld had the wide, heavy blade of Splitter parallel to the ground. All he had to do was bend his knees, step in, then stand, and he met the draegloth's descending rake.

The weapons master stepped into the attack and parried precisely as if the huge claw was a sword blade. Jeggred brought his smaller claws down fast and hard so that Ryld barely had to press the parry. The draegloth drove his own arm down onto the blade. Ryld felt a tug, then release. Blood sprayed. Jeggred's right, smaller hand tumbled through the air and bounced once when it hit the moss.

Ryld didn't allow himself the time to celebrate having cut off one of the draegloth's hands. He stepped back away from the blood that was spraying from the half-demon's stump. Jeggred screamed—an unsettling, ear-rattling sound—and he started backing quickly away.

Well aware that the half-demon could change direction very quickly, Ryld stepped back too, though not quite as far.

"You will pay for that with your hands and feet, whelp," Jeggred hissed around clenched teeth. "I was following orders when I came here to kill you, but now—" he held up the stump from which blood was still pumping—"it's personal."

❦　❦　❦

A refreshing cycle of darkness had passed during which Gromph alternated between brief periods of Reverie, infuriating sessions with the same handful of winged halflings, and the casting of powerful divinations.

The darkness was a welcome comfort to the archmage's light-ravaged eyes. He had spent nights under the open sky before—though not many—and he had seen stars. The stars in the Green Fields seemed a little brighter than those visible from Faerûn. Gromph wasn't familiar enough with either to sense any difference between the number and positions of the stars there and Faerûn's, but he knew they were different. The Green Fields was a separate reality all together.

The needle-like plant that covered the rolling hills was something he'd seen before as well. In the trade language of the World Above it was called "grass." The halflings of the Green Fields called it "ens." There were other things he'd seen before in the World Above: "flowers," "trees," and things like that. It made Gromph wonder if there was an Underdark of sorts somewhere beneath his feet—then he reminded himself that he wouldn't be there long enough to find out.

The halflings he'd first encountered had all but adopted him. A few of the little folk seemed genuinely happy to receive him. The one who called himself Dietr and who claimed to have been from Faerûn was suspicious but wanted something—something he wouldn't or couldn't ask for. However they approached Gromph, all of them were easy and casual with each other. They had a sense of hospitality and were determined to help him. They brought him food that fell into one of two categories: heavy and swimming in fragrant cream sauces or a confusing variety of sweet, fresh fruit. Neither appealed much to Gromph, but he ate enough to give him the energy he needed to prepare spells and collect himself for his return to Menzoberranzan.

Gromph hadn't moved far from the spot at which he'd first appeared. The Green Fields seemed to be exactly that: an endless open landscape of green grass and other plants. Gromph hadn't seen a building of any kind, and it appeared as if the halflings lived out in the open, slowly but constantly moving.

When the light returned, Gromph knew he would have to be on his way. He cast the last in a series of divinations that would help him not only return to the Prime Material Plane but go back to Toril, back to the Underdark below Faerûn, and back to Menzoberranzan herself. It was no mean feat, and certainly Dyrr hadn't expected him to be able to accomplish it, but then Dyrr hadn't expected him to break free of the imprisonment either. The lichdrow's insistence on underestimating him would, possibly, allow Gromph the luxury of beating him.

The archmage stood, shielding his eyes from the pervasive light and watched Dietr and one of the females approaching with another tray of fruit. Dietr held a waterskin.

"We thought you might want breakfast," Dietr said.

The halfling looked at Gromph with that same expression of vague hopefulness and fear. The female barely seemed to notice him at all.

"I've had enough of your food," the archmage said, "and I'm taking my leave of your pointless expanse."

"Pointless expanse?" the female repeated, her ambivalence all at once replaced by anger. "Who are you to dismiss the Green Fields?"

"Who are you to speak to me at all?" Gromph asked.

He waited for an answer, but all he got was a squinting sneer from the winged female. Dietr's eyes bounced back and forth between them, and his breathing grew shallow and expectant.

"Leave me in peace," Gromph commanded.

When the two halflings didn't immediately turn to leave, the archmage raised an eyebrow. The female did her best to stare him down, but her best wasn't anywhere near good enough.

"You were alive once," Gromph asked her, "weren't you?"

Neither of the halflings responded right away.

"This one"—Gromph indicated Dietr with a wave of his hand— "was a living, material being on Faerûn. Where did you live before you went to your Great Beyond?"

Again the female said nothing.

"I'll admit to being curious," Gromph went on. "If you died on whatever world you came from and your soul came here to rest in peace for all eternity, what happens when I kill you here? Does your soul go somewhere else, or are you consigned to oblivion? Will one of your weakling halfling godlings stop me? Even a halfling god on his home plane can be an inconvenience I'm sure, but it might be amusing to make the effort anyway."

"If you think you can kill me, interloper," the female sneered, "try it now or shut up."

Gromph smiled, and it must have been that expression that made Dietr finally step forward, his hands held out in a gesture of weak conciliation.

"Easy," he said. "Easy there, everybody."

Gromph laughed.

"That's better," said Dietr, a grin plastered across his cherubic face. "If the venerable drow would like to leave, then he's certainly free to go on his way."

"There will be no violence here," the female said, her voice even and strong. "If I have to blast you to pieces to ensure that . . ."

"We've all been blasted to pieces at least once, haven't we?" Dietr said. "No one wants to do that again, so let's all be friends."

Gromph took a deep breath and said, "I will be leaving, but there will be residual effects from the gate, and you won't want to go where I'm going. Back away or not, I'll leave that up to you."

The female continued to stare daggers at him, but still she drifted the slightest bit back from the archmage.

Gromph looked her up and down. She was half his size, and she looked ridiculous. The whole world looked ridiculous—the whole world *was* ridiculous. Dyrr had sent him there on purpose, and looking at the winged halfling in her grass-infested setting made Gromph angrier and angrier by the second. Dyrr was trying to get rid of him, was trying to dismiss him by sending him to that pastoral universe, and Gromph Baenre, Archmage of Menzoberranzan, would not be dismissed.

"Fine," Gromph said, and he began to cast his spell.

He was only vaguely aware of the female moving farther away, and he assumed that Dietr was doing the same thing. The words of the spell came easily enough, and the gestures went smoothly from one to another. There was a part of the spell that few of the experienced casters who'd ever done it knew could be manipulated, and Gromph began to maneuver it. He wove into the spell a subtle modification that would take him *precisely* where he wanted to go.

He finished and could feel himself falling backward out of the Green Fields—and he felt a hand on his arm.

There was light everywhere but it wasn't too bright.

There was sound coming from all around him but it wasn't too loud.

There were colors in the air but they weren't too vibrant.

They were moving in every direction at once but not too fast.

They appeared in Menzoberranzan, their feet on solid rock, their eyes comforted by the gloom lit by faerie fire.

Gromph turned and looked at the halfling. He was naked, shaking, his wings were gone, and he looked older, smaller, and weaker. His eyes were red, his skin dry and yellow. His face, twisted in a rictus of suffering, revealed gray, decaying teeth.

With a sigh, the archmage turned to survey his surroundings. It was Menzoberranzan—the Bazaar. He'd made it. There weren't many drow in the streets, and the few who were there recognized the archmage immediately. The smart ones scattered.

Nauzhror, Gromph thought, sending the name along the Weave to the Baenre wizard.

After a tense moment of silence a voice echoed in Gromph's mind: *Archmage. It is gratifying to hear you again. Welcome back to Menzoberranzan.*

It was Nauzhror.

Before he could reply, Gromph was distracted by a high-pitched whine. He looked down at the desiccated halfling.

"You are a fool," Gromph said to Dietr.

The halfling cowered from his gaze and quivered.

"I didn't ask you to come with me," Gromph added, "and you don't belong here any more than I belonged in the Green Fields."

"I wanted . . ." the halfling began then coughed. Dust puffed from his throat. "I wanted to live again."

"Why?" Gromph asked.

"My mother. She has been attending seances to contact me. She has no other family and needs me to support her."

Gromph laughed.

"It's not funny," Dietr said.

Gromph laughed more then cast a spell.

"An amusing diversion, traitor," he said into the air, "but a temporary one. We'll finish it in the Bazaar. Now."

He still had ten words left in the spell but had nothing more to say.

The lichdrow has been hiding in House Agrach Dyrr, Nauzhror sent. *The siege continues at a stalemate.*

"I don't understand," Dietr said.

Gromph turned to look down at the halfling again.

"Can you get me home?" Dietr asked. "Can you send me back to Luiren?"

Gromph raised an eyebrow at the little creature's audacity then slid his tongue around a quick divination. Obvious as it was by the halfling's appearance, it didn't hurt to be certain. The spell revealed a telltale glow around the slight humanoid.

Where have you been? Nauzhror asked.

Nowhere I'd like to visit again, he replied, *but someone's come back with me.*

I see, said Nauzhror. *The gate effect seems to have given him some kind of physical form.*

But he died on this plane, Gromph added, *so when he came back. . . .*

"Yes," the archmage finally answered the halfling. "I can take you anywhere you want to go. Of course, I won't."

The halfling shook, and Gromph thought he could actually hear the creature's bones rattle.

"Please . . . ?" the halfling whimpered.

"Your mother will not be happy to see you, Dietr," Gromph said. "You died. Remember? You came back to this world unbidden. You came back as a . . ."

It is a huecuva, Nauzhror provided.

"An undead creature," Gromph said to the halfling. "You're a huecuva. Do you know what that is?"

The halfling shook his head, terror plain in his bloodshot eyes.

Gromph, my young friend, the lichdrow's voice reverberated in the wizard's head, *welcome back. Of course I accept your gracious invitation. It will be my honor to attend you on your last day.*

Gromph nodded, mumbled through a simple necromancy, and directed it at the halfling. The archmage felt the undead creature come under his control.

"Stand up straight," Gromph commanded, and Dietr instantly complied, though it seemed to cause him some discomfort.

Gromph cast another spell on him, one that set a flicker of magical fire playing over the halfling's dead flesh.

"No . . ." the halfling muttered. "Please . . ."

Gromph tightened his grip on his staff and conjured a globe of protective force around himself.

"Please don't . . ." the huecuva pleaded.

Gromph looked around the Bazaar—abandoned tents and stalls, most with their wares secured under lock and key, and a few curious drow eyes watching from safe places in the surrounding stalactites.

"Won't you please just let me—?" Dietr begged.

"Silence," Gromph said, and the halfling was compelled to obey. "You decided to come through with me, Dietr, and now you're in Menzoberranzan, not Luiren. In Menzoberranzan, undead are property."

The huecuva's mouth worked in silence, and his skin crawled over his bones.

Gromph felt something, a presence, and quickly scanned the Bazaar again. At the far end of the wide thoroughfare was a splash of green light. The spell he'd cast on Dietr continued to give Gromph the ability to see a distinctive aura around undead, and the green light was just such an emanation, but all Gromph saw was the aura—a smudge of green light surrounding empty space.

Gromph rushed through another incantation, leaning his staff against his chest so he could use both hands to work the magic. Twisting tendrils of blue-hot flame leaped from his fingertips, growing as they made their way unerringly at the green shadow. The fire shuddered in the air and was drawn thin. It poured into a spot at the top of the shadow and disappeared into it.

The crown, Nauzhror sighed.

"Stand in front of me," Gromph said to the halfling.

The huecuva did precisely as he was told, even as the wave of blue fire shot back at Gromph. The flames hit the halfling full in the chest, and activated the protective spell Gromph had cast on him. The blue fire was replaced by a flash of red-orange that carried back along the path of the reflected spell. The green shadow was replaced by the fully revealed form of the lichdrow Dyrr, who was no longer invisible.

The fire from the huecuva's defensive aura burned the lich, making Gromph smile. He looked at the halfling and saw that Dietr was smoking, his dead flesh smoldering. His face was twisted with agony.

"Go," Gromph commanded. "Kill the lich."

Dyrr cast a spell on him, but Gromph's defenses proved capable of turning it away. It made the archmage a little dizzy, and that was all. Dietr staggered forward, reluctant but compelled to act. He wasn't moving fast enough.

"Kill the lich," Gromph called after him, "and I'll send you home to your mother."

Dietr believed the lie and broke into a run. Dyrr moved up to meet him and raked a clawed hand across the huecuva's face. Red-orange fire flared at the touch, blowing blistering heat into the lichdrow's masked face.

Dyrr threw up an arm, but the damage had been done. He roared, frustrated and angry.

Gromph was already working his next spell. Before Dyrr could strike again, it took effect, and the lichdrow's arm stopped in mid-swipe. Gromph hadn't quite expected the spell to work, but it had. Dyrr was frozen.

"Take me home!" the undead halfling shrieked.

He raked his own set of undead talons across Dyrr's sunken cheeks. The frozen lichdrow growled at the pain and humiliation of the wound and was able to move again.

Taking advantage of Dyrr's misdirected rage at the huecuva, Gromph channeled the energy of a minor divination into a blast of arcane fire. He sent the silvery light pouring over the lichdrow and had to close his own eyes against its brilliance.

Dyrr had been casting a spell—likely one that would have blasted Dietr to flinders—but the arcane fire took him full in the face. His spell was ruined, and the lichdrow was burned again.

You're hurting him, Grendan said into Gromph's mind.

Dietr struck again, digging a deep furrow into the lichdrow's forearm. Thick, dead blood oozed slowly from the wound.

The lichdrow looked at Gromph, and the archmage could see in his undead eyes that he was hurt, and hurt badly. Gromph smiled, and—

Dietr exploded in a shower of black fire, dead flesh, and yellowed bones.

What's happening? Nauzhror asked.

The sphere of magical energy that surrounded Gromph winked out—its magic spent—as the archmage realized that the black fire that had destroyed his huecuva hadn't come from Dyrr.

The lichdrow looked up into the air over the Bazaar, and Gromph followed his gaze.

Nimor Imphraezl hung suspended on batlike wings a dozen yards above the floor of the Bazaar.

Wings? Gromph thought.

I knew he was no true drow, said Nauzhror.

"Well," Nimor said to the lich, his voice deeper, weightier than Gromph remembered, "seems you need me after all."

E I G H T E E N

Ryld stood knee-deep in the freezing water of the cold swamp. Jeggred was nowhere to be seen. The constant noise made it hard to pick out the sound of the draegloth moving. The strange smells masked Jeggred's rancid breath. The pinpoint stars and the odd patch of bioluminescence made it impossible to see the draegloth in the cold water and thick vegetation. The faerie fire the strange swamp cat had cast on him had long since faded away.

He saw things moving in the water from time to time, mostly snakes, but no disturbances big enough to be the draegloth. Something slid past his leg, but there was no sign on the slime-covered surface that anything had passed by. It was definitely something alive, but it couldn't possibly be Jeggred. It didn't touch him again, whatever it was.

Careful with each step, Ryld made his way across the swamp

much more slowly than he'd hoped. The thin coating of bright green algae that covered the water made it impossible for the weapons master to see his feet. With each step his boot met some resistance: a rock, something soft, something that might have been alive, something that was solid and round like a quarterstaff—there were a lot of those—and something sharp like a dagger blade.

A bubble as big as Ryld's fist slowly expanded on the surface a few feet in front of him, sat there for a few seconds, then popped. Ryld stopped and watched it and winced when the smell of the air that had been trapped in the bubble finally wafted past his nose. The smell was reminiscent of the draegloth's horrid breath, but it was different enough that Ryld was sure that it wasn't Jeggred who'd sent up the bubble—and it wasn't the first such bubble he'd seen.

Ryld stepped forward, his foot again brushing past some hard object below the water. He used a Melee Magthere technique to slow his breathing and steady the shivering that threatened to slow his reaction time. He could see his breath condensing in the air in front of him in puffs of white steam when he exhaled, the air cold enough to make his teeth sting when he inhaled.

An explosion of water doused his face and made him close his eyes. The water was thick with slime and grainy bits of something—Ryld couldn't even guess what. His eyes blazed with flashes of yellow light and pain that made his jaw tense. Still, he brought his sword up in front of him and slashed twice at whatever it was that had splashed him. His blade met no resistance.

From much farther below, a set of claws grabbed at his left thigh, punctured, then pulled down. The claws dragged deep, ragged furrows in his skin, and Ryld could feel the heat of his own blood soaking his leg then cooling when it mixed with the cold water of the swamp.

Stepping back and stabbing down, Ryld tripped over something in the water that felt like a length of petrified rope. Though he did his best to judge where the draegloth must have been to have clawed him like that, Splitter sank into the spongy ground under the water, never touching Jeggred. Ryld fell backward until the water wrapped him in its freezing embrace.

The draegloth's next attack pushed one of Ryld's arms off the pommel of his greatsword and flipped it out to his side. Another set of deep cuts appeared on the underside of his left arm. Ryld wanted to scream, but he was under water, so he kept his mouth shut and brought his greatsword back under control. Even in the roar of swirling water that overwhelmed his hearing, the weapons master could sense the draegloth's jaws snap closed half an inch from his throat.

The draegloth was on top of him, and all the half-demon had to do was keep Ryld under water and eventually the weapons master would drown. The mistake the draegloth made was to reveal his position so clearly, though, and Ryld took full advantage of that mistake.

Pressing up with one leg, Ryld felt the heavy weight of the half-demon. The weapons master pressed harder, curling backward and straightening his leg—not an easy task since the draegloth outweighed Ryld by more than two hundred pounds. He almost had the draegloth rolled over his head, but—maybe due to resistance from the water, the cold, shivering, or exhaustion—Ryld's knees gave way, and the draegloth fell onto him.

Jeggred's claws found the underside of Ryld's breastplate and made some shallow but painful cuts in the weapons master's belly. The cold water slowed the flow of blood, though. Ryld almost subconsciously noted the irony in that. He would drown in the water that was keeping him from bleeding to death.

Ryld pressed again, using Splitter instead of his legs. Either the draegloth feared the greatsword or being totally submerged made him lighter, but Ryld managed to roll the half-demon off him. He made a few more blind jabs with Splitter to keep the draegloth at bay while he stood.

When Ryld's head finally cleared the water, he looked around for Jeggred even before he started to breathe again. The draegloth was nowhere to be seen. Ryld struggled to his feet, slipping twice on what felt like slime-covered rocks. Still he managed to get Splitter up in front of him in both hands and ready.

Ryld staggered through the water and across more odd obstructions under it, several paces from where he guessed that Jeggred should have been lying after the weapons master rolled him off.

He would have kept going but stopped when he heard another loud splash behind him.

Ryld spun, keeping his sword up and ready, and saw a disturbance on the water: what he thought looked like signs of a struggle. Puzzled that Jeggred would be so brazen after having effectively taken Ryld by surprise more than once in that cursed swamp, the weapons master took one step closer to the splashing with his sword in front of him and over his head in an effort to be ready for any eventuality.

The draegloth burst out of the swamp in a flurry of claws and legs. Water arced from his white mane as his head snapped back. He was wrapped in dark green ropes, some sort of plant he must have gotten himself tangled in. Ryld thought he saw the plants move, slithering against Jeggred's body like constricting snakes.

Jeggred had barely enough time to take a deep breath. As quickly as he came up, the draegloth disappeared into another swirling eddy that broke up the slime covering the water.

Ryld didn't have time to understand what he'd seen. Something wrapped itself around his ankle and pulled. The weapons master knew a hundred tricks to keep him on his feet even if someone really wanted to pull him down, but as much as he tried, whatever it was that had him was too strong.

So he cut it.

Splitter was still in his hands and still as sharp a sword as ever saw battle in the Underdark. Ryld brought the weapon stabbing down along the side of his body then in and through whatever had grabbed him.

It wasn't easy—the thing around his ankle was as sturdy as it was strong—but he severed it and stopped short of cutting off his own foot. Ryld struggled backward through the water then stopped and turned when he saw something moving in the corner of his eye.

Half a dozen of the green, ropy vines were sticking up out of the water like snakes scanning for their next meal. Ryld saw no eyes, no mouths, only green stalks as big around as one of the weapons master's sturdy wrists. They had no faces, but they were very much alive and appeared for all the world as if they were looking for him.

One of the vines burst toward him, unraveling itself from the water to snake quickly through the air at Ryld's throat.

The weapons master sliced fast and hard at chest level and took the first four inches off the end of the attacking vine. Greenish-yellow sap leaped from it like blood from a wound, and the vine quivered then fell into the roiling, slime-covered water.

Another vine tried to wrap itself around Ryld from behind, and he could feel even more of them worrying him from beneath the surface. Ryld kept Splitter moving in fast, fluid motions in front of him and to either side, cutting through the water, taking the ends off one animated vine after another.

Jeggred came back up, gasping for breath and ripping at a mass of the dark green vines. He was covered in the swamp slime, vine sap, and blood. One of the vines slipped around his face and into his mouth—a mistake. The draegloth bit down, and the bloodlike sap splashed over his cheeks. The vine quivered and went dead, but half a dozen more burst out of the water to take its place, and the draegloth was dragged under once again.

This swamp, Ryld thought as he chopped down two more attacking vines, will kill us both before we can kill each other.

Another reason to hate the World Above.

Jeggred came back up again for just long enough to take another breath, and Ryld got the feeling that the draegloth was finally getting the upper hand over the damnable vines. Ryld cut through another vine then sliced off one that had almost managed to get all the way around his wounded thigh. The vines were still coming at him one after another, and Ryld had no way of knowing how many there were or if, let alone when, they might finally give up or he might kill the last of them. That and the possibility that the draegloth might come at him again made up the weapons master's mind.

Ryld looked around, flicking his greatsword to his right to slice a vine then in front of him to cut through another, letting the movement of the vines in his peripheral vision chose his targets for him while he scanned for an escape route.

To his right—he had lost all sense of direction a long time before so had no idea if he was facing north, south, east, or west—the water gave way to slightly more solid if not entirely dry land. Larger trees with long, whiplike branches made a forest of thin lines. Behind those hanging branches Ryld saw a scattering of orange lights that must have been torches burning in the distance.

He knew there might be any number of sentient creatures that could have lit those torches, and surely none of them were drow. Still, he might be able to use any sort of habitation to his advantage. If Jeggred chased him there, and it was a human town, an orc town, or an elf town, they might not like dark elves, but they'd be terrified by the draegloth. That could buy Ryld time, if not allies.

Another vine managed to get around his ankle and tug. Ryld went down to one knee, his face almost falling under the slimy water before he managed to slice the vine off him. He left a cut in his boot that let in the water, and he shivered. Free of the vine, the weapons master ran. He didn't bother trying to be quiet but splashed headlong through the knee-deep water. Behind him, Jeggred surfaced again, tore at the vines still covering his midsection, roared, took a deep breath, and went back down.

Ryld stepped onto dry ground and hopped in an unseemly fashion as a set of vines worried at his heels. The ground was slippery and muddy, covered in patches with slick moss, but Ryld continued running, working past the occasional loss of footing. From behind him came the draegloth's peculiar growl and a flurry of splashes. As Ryld ran through the stinging, whiplike branches, dodging between the close-set trees while barely managing to keep on his feet, he could hear the half-demon panting, tearing, and growling behind him. Jeggred had surfaced again and was fighting his way free of the vines.

The weapons master ran on, and soon the sounds of the struggling draegloth were joined by the faint echo of voices ahead. He came out of the forest of whiplike branches, still at an all-out run. The clearing was wide and relatively dry. A collection of stumps replaced the trees, and Ryld jumped up onto one of them then hopped to another and another, making his way toward the settlement. The stumps provided more even footing and were less slippery than the muddy, mossy ground.

The torches burned from long poles stuck into the ground in a circle around a collection of a dozen small shacks and tattered tents. Even Ryld, who knew little of the World Above, could tell that the settlement was a temporary one and not an established village. The voices he heard echoing from one of the more permanent-looking buildings sounded human. The weapons master could pick out the occasional word in the human's common trade language. He'd learned the language at Melee Magthere but had few opportunities to use it, and many words were still unfamiliar to him.

Off to one side of the settlement was a huge pile of trees, cut down, stripped of their branches, and stacked carefully in a pyramid almost ten feet tall. In Menzoberranzan it would have been a king's ransom in wood.

Ryld made his way one stump at a time toward the bigger building but paused briefly to sheathe Splitter—and he was hit hard from behind. He fell forward off the stump, the greatsword still in his right hand, and pain blazed from his back. He fell onto a stump, pushed off, rolled forward, and saw the dark shape of Jeggred scrambling up behind him. The weapons master kicked out hard with both feet and smashed the draegloth between his legs. Jeggred grunted and backed off, long enough for Ryld to get to his feet.

Splitter in both hands, Ryld sent a feint at the draegloth's midsection. Jeggred fell for it, spinning to the side. The weapons master hopped back up onto one of the stumps and jumped backward again from stump to stump. The soaking-wet draegloth was covered in slime, sap, and blood. His crimson eyes blazed in the darkness, and steam poured from his mouth and nostrils.

Ryld tried to think of something to say, perhaps to taunt the draegloth, but his mind was a blank. Pharaun would have had a thousand irritating quips on the tip of his tongue, enough to drive his opponent to distraction, but Ryld could only keep his mouth closed and his mind on the fight. The two of them had gone well beyond conversation anyway.

The Master of Melee Magthere knew that the building was behind him. He could see the orange firelight from the windows growing brighter and could hear the voices growing louder. There didn't seem to be any change in the tone of the random bits of conversation that drifted out the window. No alarm had been raised.

Jeggred clawed at him with one of his larger hands, and Ryld stepped in to cut his arm but found out the hard way that the attack was a feint. The claws of the draegloth's remaining smaller hand ripped across Ryld's face. The weapons master stepped back, and there were suddenly no more stumps behind him. He slipped on the muddy ground and at the same time slashed across his opponent's midsection. The tip of his greatsword traced a line of red across Jeggred's thigh, and the draegloth drew away long enough to allow Ryld to get his footing and jump three long paces backward.

Orange firelight lit the battle-ravaged draegloth and glittered off his massive, daggerlike teeth. With a fang-lined sneer, the draegloth launched himself at Ryld. All the weapons master could do was bring up his hands—and his sword—to meet him.

Jeggred hit him hard enough to drive the air from Ryld's lungs and push his greatsword into him so hard it sliced into the side of his face, nearly cutting the weapons master's ear off. Ryld felt his feet leave the ground, his body completely at the mercy of the draegloth's inertia. They went through a window, glass shattering into millions of tiny knives that cut them both in a hundred places. Ryld could only close his eyes and grunt when he hit a wood floor so hard with the heavy draegloth on top of him that at least one of his ribs snapped like a twig.

The draegloth rolled, and Ryld pushed him off. Before he knew what was happening, they were both sitting on the floor of some kind of ramshackle tavern surrounded by a dozen very surprised humans.

❦ ❦ ❦

Let it in, Aliisza whispered into Pharaun's mind, *but not too far.*

Pharaun sat on the deck, his legs crossed, his eyes closed, and his palms pressed down against the pulsating surface of the living vessel. He tried to sort out the sensations that were coming at him. Some were physical, some were emotional, and some came in forms Pharaun had never imagined. He could smell something like algae cakes being grilled over an open fire. Flashes of light pulsed behind his eyelids and left trails and tendrils in their wake. The sound of the ship's pulse hummed in his ears. He grimaced when a horrid taste like rotting fish rolled across his tongue. That all happened at once then changed.

You will use your body to steer it, Aliisza continued, *as much as your mind.*

Pharaun could feel that she was right. A wave of hopelessness came from nowhere and made his flesh crawl. Almost at the same time he was charged with adrenaline and felt as if he could lift the ship physically over his head and throw it across the endless Astral and into the Abyss that way.

Like that, Aliisza whispered. *Yes . . .*

It wasn't wind or water that powered the ship of chaos but desire, entropy, malice, and confusion—those things and others like them.

You will have to gather the will to move, Aliisza went on, *which should be easy enough for you. Learn how to channel it through the ship and into the planar medium around you. There's no way to learn how to do that. You simply have to give yourself over to it, while keeping it at bay at the same time. Do you understand?*

Pharaun nodded, not wanting to speak.

Something entered his skin at the wrist—a thin tendril like

a length of string. The Master of Sorcere could feel it slip into a vein, tapping his blood. He tried to jerk his hand away, but his fingers were stuck to the deck.

Don't panic, Aliisza sent. *It won't take enough of your blood to weaken you, but it must have some or the connection will fail.*

You're asking me to trust it? Pharaun asked her. *To trust this construct of demonic chaos?*

He felt her touch his cheek, her fingers warm and dry, but he couldn't see her. She remained invisible, insisting that he not reveal her presence to the others. Pharaun was content to keep her a secret.

Another wave of conflicting emotions rolled through him, and he rode it out.

The ship will feel what you feel, Aliisza told him, *even as you feel what it feels. It will follow your commands now. When you're ready, will it into the Shadow Fringe and on from there.*

Will it? asked the mage.

The same way you would lift your arm or open your eyes, she answered.

That easy?

The alu-fiend laughed and said, *There are three sentient creatures out of a thousand that can do what you have done, my dear. Bonding with a ship of chaos is a dangerous proposition.*

How so?

If it hadn't accepted you, it would have killed you, she replied, *and in a very ugly, mean way.*

Pharaun sighed, interested but not surprised.

You would have let it kill me? he asked.

Aliisza thought about it for a long time then said, *You have to do this, one way or the other. I had faith in you.*

Pharaun caught the sarcasm in her tone and cracked a smile. She was an alu-fiend and by all rights on opposing sides of a bloody, ever-unfolding war. Why would she care if the ship of chaos killed him or drove him mad?

The tendrils slipped out of his wrists, and his palms came free of the deck.

Navigating the ship will require your full attention, Aliisza advised, *but if you're adrift or on a predetermined course, you will still be able to speak with your comrades and even cast spells.*

Convenient, the mage remarked.

The ship of chaos was a war ship, Pharaun, she replied. *It was created to fight, and the tanar'ri who built it had no interest in having the most powerful spellcaster among them bound to the deck, helpless and mute. The ship will require a lot of you but not everything. Don't give it any more than it needs.*

Cryptic, the mage shot back. *I like that.*

"Are you all right?" a voice asked, and Pharaun thought at first that it was Aliisza.

You know perfectly well, he thought to her, *that if I wasn't well I would simply—*"

He realized that it wasn't Aliisza who'd spoken but Quenthel.

"Master Mizzrym. . . ." the high priestess said.

Pharaun opened his eyes but had to blink several times before he could see clearly. The Mistress of Arach-Tinilith was standing over him, arms folded across her chest, her eyes stern and cold but distracted.

"I am well, thank you, Mistress," Pharaun replied. "I have reason to believe that I am fully in command of the vessel and that it is suitably powered."

He looked around at the others, who were standing behind Quenthel, also looking down at him. All he saw were Valas and Danifae.

"When the draegloth returns," Pharaun finished, "we can be on our way."

"We won't be waiting for Jeggred," Quenthel answered, eliciting a sharp look from Danifae and a lift of one eyebrow from the mercenary scout.

"Mistress—" Danifae began, but Quenthel held up a hand to silence her.

"Anyone who breaks off from this expedition," Quenthel said, "without my permission will be considered to have deserted it."

"Surely that wasn't the intent of your nephew," Pharaun replied. "I think it was hardly the intent of Master Argith either. Where we're going it seems to me that we'll need their str—"

"We won't," the high priestess interrupted. Looking off into the darkness she continued, "They are both strong, but where we're going there will be things around every stalactite that could rip them both to shreds. We're not going on a jaunt in the Dark Dominion. What we'll encounter will not be defeated by brute strength but with a clear and steady mind—the single-minded pursuit of one's own desires."

Pharaun frowned and waited for one of the others to say something.

Valas stood waiting for the females to sort it out.

"You seem to know what we'll see," Danifae said to the high priestess, "but you don't know, not for sure."

Pharaun, surprised by the way Danifae had pinned the high priestess down, looked at Quenthel, curious to hear her answer.

"I know that I can't stay here anymore," Quenthel answered. The vipers writhed slowly at her hip. "This place is killing me. We know what needs to be done. Live or die, we live or die in the Abyss at the side of the Spider Queen."

Pharaun lifted an eyebrow and smiled, glancing between the two females.

"We've not even begun," Danifae warned. "There will be much for Jeggred to do. We should wait."

"That, my plaything," the Mistress of Arach-Tinilith shot back, "is not for you to decide. You've presumed enough."

Pharaun recognized that it took considerable effort for Danifae to look down, letting her smoldering red eyes linger on the deck instead of boring into the high priestess. The battle-captive had come a long way, and Pharaun caught himself smiling at her.

"Master Mizzrym," Quenthel said, "take us to Lolth. Now."

"I will require a brief rest," the mage lied. Even as the words passed his tongue, he wondered why he was lying. He didn't look at Danifae. "One more period of Reverie for us all. We should face the goddess rested and at our best."

Quenthel didn't answer but turned and walked away. Danifae lingered.

What are you doing? Aliisza whispered into his consciousness, startling the mage. He'd forgotten she was there. *That's not true.*

The Mistress of the Academy, he told the alu-fiend, *isn't thinking clearly.*

Don't want to travel without your draegloth? Aliisza asked.

Would you?

Pharaun could feel her laugh in his mind.

"Thank you," Danifae said.

Pharaun looked up at her with a smile. Quenthel and Valas had both wandered off, but he used sign language to be sure they weren't overheard.

Why should I continue to help you? he asked. *What are you doing?*

She thought about it for a long time then signed back, *I want you to promise me that you won't leave without Jeggred.*

And if I do?

Danifae had no answer.

The Mistress irritates me, the mage went on. *I've made no effort to mask that. She's tried to kill me in the past. She has treated me with less respect than I deserve, but she is the Mistress of Arach-Tinilith, the most powerful priestess in Menzoberranzan if not in the whole of Lolth's faithful—the matron mothers included. This is her expedition, and her orders are law where I come from.*

Not where I come from, Danifae replied, *and I serve Lolth as well.*

"Perhaps," Pharaun replied aloud, confident that the high priestess had gone back to her quiet, oblivious sulking, "but in what way do you serve me?"

Danifae looked puzzled, her eyes inviting him to continue.

"You wish something of me," he explained. "You ask me to put my life at risk and my future in Menzoberranzan. You ask me to defy the sister of the archmage, my master, and the Matron Mother of the First House, his mistress."

"You want to know what I will give in return?" she asked.

It was his turn to let his eyes invite an answer.

"Answer this," she said. "Do you really want to travel through the Plane of Shadow, into the Astral, through the Plain of Infinite Portals, and to the sixty-sixth layer of the Abyss without Jeggred?"

"He would be of service to us all, I'm sure," said Pharaun, "as he has been, but he doesn't serve me. He doesn't really even like me, if that can be imagined. You, on the other hand, have made an important and powerful new ally to replace the one you've used up."

You think Quenthel is "used up"? Danifae asked silently.

"She's not herself," answered the mage. "That much is obvious, but the question remains: Why should I do anything for you?"

"What do you want?" she asked, and Pharaun got the feeling he could have asked her anything and she would have at least considered it.

"I would feel more comfortable if Ryld was here," he said, not caring if it made him sound weak.

Danifae nodded and said, "Even if he has gone over to Eilistraee?"

"I doubt that that's happened," replied the mage. "Master Argith isn't the religious type."

"His sword arm works for you, as Jeggred's claws work for me," she said.

Pharaun smiled, winked, and nodded.

"I suppose that's fair enough," she said, "but don't ask me to spare Halisstra."

"Who?" Pharaun joked.

That drew a smile from Danifae.

"Keep the draegloth away from Ryld," the mage said. "Bring the Master of Melee Magthere back here, kicking and screaming if you have to, but alive, and I'll take him from there."

"Agreed," Danifae said. She touched a ring on her right hand and disappeared.

That took Pharaun by surprise.

Interesting, Aliisza said from somewhere. *Who is she?*

A battle-captive, Pharaun replied, *or at least she used to be.*

Seems more like a priestess to me, said the alu-fiend.

Yes, Pharaun replied. *Yes, she does, doesn't she?*

NINETEEN

She spoke entirely in movement, in the subtle nuance of gesture and rhythm, and it all seemed like a glorious dream.

Halisstra felt her body moving. The air swirled around her, cool and invigorating. In the movement she sensed the presence of Danifae. The subtle curve of her former servant's hip turned in a way that suggested duplicity and with a grace that bespoke ambition. Danifae breathed discontentment and stepped into the Demonweb Pits.

Halisstra didn't watch, she danced. She was there, though she had no idea where "there" was. There was no space, only the movement within it—the movement that was the voice of Eilistraee.

Danifae and Halisstra both stepped in time to a different song. They moved toward the same endpoint but for different reasons and were surrounded by the same chilling stillness. In the sway of a shoulder, Eilistraee warned Halisstra not to trust Danifae but pushed her servant along the former battle-captive's path. Halisstra would lead some of the way, and Danifae would lead some too. Both goddesses would push and pull them from the edges, sending them toward a place and a time that no sane drow could possibly imagine except in a goddess-birthed nightmare.

Halisstra felt herself move through a still, empty space, and she knew that space was the Demonweb Pits—the home plane of Lolth, bereft of souls, an empty afterlife with no hope and no future. Halisstra felt Danifae whirl through that same dead space with her and look at Halisstra with the same dull fear. There would be no service, no reward but oblivion, and Danifae would arrive at the same conclusions, be dragged to the same realization.

Danifae can be turned, Halisstra danced.

Eilistraee hesitated.

It was with that wordless sense of uncertainty that the movement ceased. There was a solid, unmoving floor of sanded stone beneath her and dead gates all around. Halisstra rolled onto her back, wiped her face with her hands, and tried to steady her breathing. Sweat poured off her, and her body ached. She felt as if she'd been dancing for hours though she wasn't sure she'd actually been dancing at all.

Halisstra looked around at the interior of the gatehouse, searching for Danifae. The former servant was nowhere to be found. Even Halisstra's shouts went unanswered, so she wandered outside.

The cave's dull light revealed a large and complex structure. Halisstra knew she was in Sschindylryn but knew little else about the city. Not sure if she was coloring the world through her own filtered perceptions, she felt that the air in the City of Portals was heavy with dissent and nascent violence. She'd sensed the same thing before—in Ched Nasad.

An image of Ryld came to her mind—not so much an image

but the memory of the way he moved with her and the touch of his night-black skin. She'd led him to Danifae, who had led Jeggred to them on Quenthel's behalf. Quenthel knew that they—or at least Halisstra—had turned their backs on Lolth in favor of Eilistraee.

However, Ryld hadn't actually done that. A male, and not particularly religious, the weapons master served Lolth because everyone around him did. Ryld, like all drow in Menzoberranzan was raised with the words of Lolth never far from his ears. Halisstra had been raised the same way, but she had the sheer force of will to step back and examine the reality of the situation as it continued to unfold.

Danifae had a choice too, and the realization of it hit Halisstra the moment Danifae stepped out of the suddenly blazing-purple archway. The gate had burst into life, revealing Danifae and momentarily blurring Halisstra's vision.

Blinking, Halisstra stood and said, "Ryld?"

Danifae shrugged. It was a rude, dismissive gesture that set Halisstra's teeth on edge. The Melarn priestess's face flushed, her teeth clenched, but she did her best to swallow the anger at the same time pushing away memories of punishing her battle-captive, beating her, humiliating her, and breaking her.

"Where have you been?" Halisstra asked.

"With Mistress Quenthel," Danifae replied. "They're proceeding. I was sent back to retrieve Jeggred."

"You know where the draegloth is?" asked Halisstra. "If you do, then you must know where Ryld is."

"Jeggred was sent to kill him," replied Danifae. "I told you that."

"You did," Halisstra said, "but . . ."

"You want to know if the weapons master has prevailed," Danifae replied, "or if the draegloth is feeding even now."

Halisstra swallowed in a parched throat and said, "Does he live? Has Ryld won?"

Danifae shrugged again.

"You can get me back to him," Halisstra said. "Using these gates of yours, you can send me to his side."

"Where Jeggred would shred you as well and eat you both in alternating bites," said the former servant, "or, you can move forward as opposed to backward."

"Forward? Backward? What is that supposed to mean?"

"The way I see it, Mistress Halisstra," Danifae said, "you have two choices: Go to your lover's side and die there, or go back to the surface temple and your new sisters in Eilistraee."

Halisstra let out a breath and looked the ravishing dark elf up and down. Danifae smiled back, though the expression looked more like a sneer.

"They're leaving," Danifae pressed, "and they're leaving soon. If you go back to the temple where I first contacted you, if you tell them that Quenthel and her crew are on their way to the Demonweb Pits in search of Lolth herself, the Eilistraeeans might have enough time to help."

"To help? To help whom?" whispered Halisstra, then more loudly: "I should go back to the Eilistraeeans and tell them that we can follow Quenthel and the others to the Demonweb Pits. Would you stand by and watch that and not warn them . . . and not warn Lolth?"

"I'm still a servant," said Danifae. "I can't make the decision for you or ask you to trust me. I can give you no promises, no assurances, no guarantees about anything. For that, you'll have to look to your goddess. Either way, I can send you wherever you want to go."

She saw it. Only a flash, but there was the unmistakable look that had wrapped within it uncertainty, fear, embarrassment, and more.

Danifae was jealous in a very immature way that Halisstra was once again serving a deity who would answer the prayers of her faithful while Danifae still clung to the memory of a dead goddess.

"I have a choice?" Halisstra asked, slowly shaking her head.

"I can send you where you want to go," Danifae repeated. "Tell me if you want to go back to your temple to organize the priestesses there, or—"

"Organize?" Halisstra interrupted.

Danifae was irritated, and Halisstra was momentarily taken aback by the reaction.

"Surely Eilistraee grants them spells still," Danifae said. "They will be able to travel the planes without a ship of chaos. Eilistraee should be able to take you right to them."

Halisstra watched her former servant's face change again—saw that fear return.

"Or," Danifae said, her voice deep and even, "you can go try to help your weapons master against the draegloth and die."

Halisstra closed her eyes and thought, occasionally stopping to wonder at the fact that she was thinking about it at all.

"My heart," Halisstra confided in Danifae, "wants me to go to Ryld, but my head tells me that my new sisters will want to know what you've told me and that they'll want to go to the Demonweb Pits."

"The time you have to gather them," warned Danifae, "is drawing increasingly short."

Halisstra clamped her mouth shut while her throat tightened.

"Choose," Danifae pressed.

"The Velarswood," Halisstra blurted out. A tear glimmered in the faerie light and traced a path down her deep black cheek. "Take me to the priestesses."

Danifae smiled, nodded, and pointed toward a purple-glowing gate.

The two of them stared at each other while a few heartbeats went by. Danifae's eyes darted back and forth between Halisstra's as if they were reading something written across her pupils. Halisstra saw the hope in Danifae's eyes.

"How bad is it?" Halisstra asked, her voice almost a whisper. "What has she sunk to?"

"She?" Danifae asked. "Quenthel?"

Halisstra nodded.

"She can go lower," the former battle-captive said.

"Come with me," Halisstra said.

Danifae stood silently for a long time before she said, "You know I can't. They won't leave without Jeggred, and I have to bring him back."

Halisstra nodded and said, "After he's murdered Ryld."

Danifae nodded and looked at the floor.

"We'll see each other again, Danifae," Halisstra said. "Of that I'm certain."

"As am I, Mistress," Danifae replied. "We will meet again in the shadow of the Spider Queen."

"Eilistraee will be watching us both all the way," Halisstra said as she crossed to the waiting portal. "She will be watching us both."

Danifae nodded, and Halisstra stepped into the gate, abandoning Ryld to the draegloth, Danifae to the Mistress of Arach-Tinilith, and herself to the priestesses of the Velarswood.

"You seem as surprised as I am," Gromph said to the lichdrow, "that your friend Nimor has sprouted wings."

Dyrr didn't answer, but his ember-red eyes drifted slowly to the winged assassin.

"Duergar," Gromph went on, "a cambion and his tanarukks, and a drow assassin. Oh, but the drow assassin isn't even a drow. You've allied yourself with everything but another dark elf. Well, you haven't been a dark elf yourself for a very long time either, have you, Dyrr?"

If the lich was offended or affected in any way, he didn't show it.

"He could be allied with a drow, though," Nimor said. "We both could."

"You actually think I'm going to join you?" Gromph asked.

"No," Nimor answered, "of course not, but I have to ask."

"If I do," Gromph persisted, "will you kill the lich?"

Dyrr raised an eyebrow, obviously interested to hear Nimor's answer.

"To have the Archmage of Menzoberranzan himself turn on his own city," Nimor said, "betray his own House, and overthrow the matriarchy with a wave of his hand? Would I kill the lichdrow? Certainly. I would kill him without the slightest moment's hesitation."

That brought a smile to Dyrr's face, and Gromph couldn't help but share it.

Nimor looked at the lichdrow, bowed, and said, "I would try, at least."

The lich returned the bow.

"You're not going to do any of those things, are you?" Nimor asked Gromph. "You won't turn your back on Menzoberranzan, House Baenre, the matriarchy, or even Lolth, who has turned her back on you."

"That's all?" Gromph asked. "That's all you plan to say to try to turn me? Ask a question then answer it yourself? Why are you here?"

"Don't answer that, Nimor," the lichdrow commanded, his tone as imperious as ever. "He's drawing tales out of you. He wants time to try to get away or to plan his attack."

"Or," Gromph cut in, "he may simply be curious. I know why my old friend Dyrr wants to kill me, and I can guess at the motivations of the duergar, the tanarukks, the illithids, and whatever else crawls out of the crevices and slime pools of the Dark Dominion, drawn to the stench of weakness. You, though, Nimor, are half drow and half dragon, aren't you? Why you? Why here? Why me?"

"Why you?" Dyrr said, his voice dripping with scorn. "You have power, you simpleton. You have position. That makes you a target on a good day—and this isn't a good day for Menzoberranzan."

Gromph ignored the lich and said to Nimor, "My sister said the assassin she captured named you as an agent of the Jaezred Chaulssin."

Nimor nodded and said, "I am the Anointed Blade."

Gromph didn't know what that meant but gave no indication of that to Nimor or Dyrr.

"Ghost stories come true," Gromph said.

"Our reputation precedes us," replied Nimor.

"Chaulssin has been in ruin for a long time," said Gromph.

"Her assassins survive," Dyrr said.

His dragon half, Nauzhror said into Gromph's mind, *has been identified, Archmage. He is half-drow, half-shadow dragon. More than one generation, perhaps. An incipient species.*

"We have placed ourselves in city after city," Nimor said, "all across the Underdark. We've been waiting."

"And breeding," Gromph said, "with shadow dragons?"

Nimor's smile told Gromph how right Nauzhror had been.

"It's over," Dyrr said, and Gromph found it difficult to deny the finality in his voice. "All of it."

"Not yet," Gromph replied, and he started to cast a spell.

Nimor beat his batlike wings and shot up into the darkness. Dyrr followed, more slowly, wrapping himself in additional protective spells.

Gromph finished his spell and held his hands together. A line of blackness appeared between his palms and stretched to the length of a long sword blade. The line was perfectly two-dimensional, a rift in the structure of the planes.

Lifting into the air, the Archmage of Menzoberranzan threw his hands apart, and the blade followed him up. Using the force of his will, Gromph set the planar blade flying in front of him. Choosing a target was simple.

Nimor has to die first, Prath suggested, though it was unnecessary. *The extent of his true abilities is the only unknown.*

Gromph set the blade hurtling at the half-dragon assassin. Nimor flew as fast as anything Gromph had ever seen fly, but the blade moved faster. It cut into the assassin, and Nimor convulsed in pain. What makes a blade sharp is the thinness of its edge. The blade that Gromph conjured didn't actually have any thickness at all. Being *perfectly* thin, it was perfectly sharp. Anything that Nimor might have had on him to protect him from weapons would be of no consequence.

Blood pattered down over the floor of the Bazaar, and Nimor roared. The sound rattled Gromph's eardrums, though he didn't hesitate to send the black blade at the assassin again—but it disappeared.

Gromph whirled in midair to face the lichdrow. Dyrr held his staff in both hands. Gromph assumed he'd used some aspect of the weapon's magic to dispel the blade

Disappointing, Nauzhror commented. *That was an impressive spell. And effective.*

Nimor wasn't flying quite as fast, and he was still bleeding. Gromph had to keep his attention shifting back and forth between the assassin, the lich, and his own next spell, so he didn't actually see Nimor heal himself, but he did—enough to keep himself alive.

Gromph was nearly finished with his next incantation when Nimor blew darkness at him—it was the only way the wizard could think to describe it. The assassin drew in a breath and exhaled a cone-shaped wave of roiling blackness. Gromph tried to drop away from the darkness, but he couldn't. The twisting void washed over the archmage. It was as if all the warmth were drawn out of him. He shivered, and his breath stopped in his throat. His spell was ruined, cut off in mid-word, the Weave energy unraveling.

Part of the layers of defensive magic that he and the Masters of Sorcere had cloaked him in protected Gromph from the full extent of the freezing darkness's power. If not, Gromph would have shriveled to a dead husk.

"I was right," Gromph said to Nimor, trying not to gasp. "It was a shadow dragon, wasn't it?"

"More than one shadow dragon, Archmage," Nimor replied—and Gromph thought the assassin was trying not to gasp himself, "and more than one drow."

The half-dragon assassin drew a needle-thin rapier that glowed blue-white in the gloom of the abandoned Bazaar.

Caution, Archmage, Prath warned.

Gromph winced at the idiocy of his inexperienced nephew. The archmage was always ready for anything—though he wasn't fast enough to dodge out of the way of the rapier as it slashed across his chest.

Nimor had disappeared from where he'd been hovering, several paces away and appeared right next to Gromph and a little above—perfectly in a blind spot. All of that had happened in the precise same instant.

The assassin was gone again just as fast.

The slash in Gromph's chest burned, the wound crisp and jagged. He looked down at the cut. Frost lined the wound, and the blood that oozed from it was cold when it touched his skin. Gromph shivered.

Something hit Gromph from behind, and he grunted and doubled over when the air was smashed out of his lungs. It was a painful second or two before he was able to draw in another breath. Dyrr had hit him with something—a spell or a weapon—from behind.

The spell didn't pass through all of your defenses, Archmage, Nauzhror told him. *If it had, you would have been disintegrated.*

"Good for me," Gromph muttered under his breath, then he spoke the command word that brought the defensive globe from the staff.

Circled again in protective magic, Gromph turned in the air, trying to catch sight of at least one of his foes. He saw Nimor flying at him with that freezing rapier poised for another slash. Behind the assassin and off to one side, the lichdrow was moving his free hand through the air, his fingers leaving streaks of crackling white light behind them.

Pain blazing in his chest and back, Gromph twisted in the air when a cone of twinkling white light shot forth from the lichdrow's extended hands, threatening to engulf him in a blast of freezing air and cutting ice.

The archmage managed to twist out of the way of the spell, but he lost sight of the assassin in the process. Gromph braced himself for another icy slash from the rapier, but it didn't come.

The assassin had to dodge the cone of cold as well, Master, Prath said.

Gromph took advantage of the respite and drew two slim, platinum-bladed throwing daggers from a sheath in his right boot. Even as he drew the knives up along the length of his body, he spoke the words of a spell that would enchant the weapons to a greater keenness. The spell would make them fly truer as well, and farther, and he was sure they would pierce at least some of his target's magical defenses.

Gromph got his arm up to throw and finished the spell. When he turned to find his target, the pain was gone. The ring was working still, healing him almost as fast as the assassin and the lich could wound him.

A fraction of a heartbeat before Gromph could throw his ensorcelled daggers, Nimor appeared next to him again. The rapier made a shrill whistling sound as it whipped through the air, drawing a frosted white line across Gromph's right side. The pain was extraordinary, and Gromph's fingers twitched along with most of the other muscles of his body. He almost dropped the two daggers but didn't.

He's gone, said Prath.

Gromph had expected that.

I think it might be the ring, Nauzhror said.

The ring? Gromph sent back.

That allows him to slip from one place to another in an instant, Nauzhror explained.

Gromph had expected to fight Dyrr alone and had expected to fight him spell to spell. The archmage had to admit, at least to himself, that he was unprepared for hand-to-hand combat and that in that regard at least, Nimor was likely superior.

He put those thoughts out of his mind when he heard Dyrr casting another spell. He turned to look at the lich.

Dyrr had a strange look in his eyes, as if something was going to happen, but he wasn't sure exactly what. Gromph didn't like that look at all.

He's summoning something, Nauzhror said.

By the time the last syllable of Nauzhror's warning sounded in

Gromph's head, the lich's spell had done its work. Lurching out of thin air, a set of insectoid legs slammed down onto the rock floor of the Bazaar—then another set, and another and another and another. The insect's head was wider than Gromph was tall, maybe even twice as wide. On either side of its grotesque mouth was a curved, jagged-edged pincer. Two bulbous, multifaceted eyes scanned the abandoned expanse of the marketplace as the rest of the huge beast drew itself out of the Weave.

It was a centipede the size of a whole caravan of pack lizards, and behind it, Dyrr was laughing, and Nimor was flying at Gromph again.

One at a time, the archmage told himself.

He worked another spell on the pair of enchanted throwing daggers. The centipede lurched at Gromph, but it was moving slowly, still unsure of its surroundings and the extent of the lich's control over it. That gave Gromph time to finish the spell and throw the daggers. He didn't bother to aim. He tossed them in Nimor's general direction and let the spell do the rest. The daggers whirled through the air, their paths twisting around each other in a perfect beeline for the winged assassin.

With impressive agility, Nimor slipped sideways in the air in an attempt to avoid the daggers, but once set on their course, nothing so simple would deter them. The assassin had to twist in the air again, swatting at the blades with his rapier. The flash of steel—Nimor's thin blade and both daggers—became a whirling blur around the assassin.

Well played, Master, Prath commented. *That should keep him occupied.*

Again ignoring his nephew, Gromph called on the levitating power of his staff to launch himself straight up in the air. The centipede's hideous sideways jaws crashed together an inch below the soles of his boots, and it immediately drew back for a second lunging attack. Gromph, hoping he was well above the monstrous insect, twisted and rolled in the air, his eyes taking in every detail of the Bazaar and the surrounding stalagmites as he went.

The archmage stopped, hanging in the air between the confused centipede and the hovering lich.

"You don't like my new pet?" the lichdrow taunted. "All he wants is to give you a little kiss."

"I don't—" Gromph started, but the air was pushed from his chest once again when Dyrr, his staff held in front of him, used its power to thrust Gromph away.

The archmage could feel the giant insect behind him, looming like a stalactite fortress. Dyrr drew himself up higher in the air and the repulsion pushed Gromph down and away—directly into the centipede's greedy jaws.

The right spell came to Gromph's mind in an instant, and he wasted some extra energy to cast it quickly. The effect was one he'd felt hundreds of times, but he'd always hated it. His body felt as if it were drawing itself thin. He shivered despite himself and had to force himself to keep his eyes open when his vision blurred a little and the world around him became both distorted and somehow brighter, sharper.

He was surrounded by the inside of the gigantic insect. Muscles and rivers of green semiliquid that served it for blood, the odd line of sheets the thing seemed to be using as lungs, the husks of other too-big insects that it had recently eaten—then another thick layer of armorlike chitin, and he was through it. He had passed through the centipede, his body more a part of the Ethereal than the Prime Material Plane.

The centipede had no idea what was going on—how could it? Gromph knew the insect wouldn't have been able to feel him pass through it, but the tasty morsel of drow flesh it thought it was going to bite and swallow was somehow behind it.

Gromph caught a flash of movement out of the corner of his eye and turned fast to see Nimor coming at him again. The daggers were gone, and the assassin had a few new cuts, but he was no less deadly for the experience.

The centipede turned, moving its massive body—one that must have weighed several hundred tons—in a shockingly quick and agile twist. Gromph's ethereal body was still visible, though he appeared ghostly, oddly translucent. The centipede didn't seem to see him. Instead, its bulging eyes locked on Nimor.

Nimor slipped sideways in the air again and, fast as the insect was, the assassin slipped past its jaws in time to save his own life. The centipede would have bitten him cleanly in two.

Gromph levitated up past the reach of the centipede as his body faded back into its solid form.

"Dyrr," Nimor raged, "mind your pet, damn you."

Gromph smiled at that, but Dyrr's response was to begin another incantation. Nimor might have been angry at his undead ally, but they were far from turning on each other. The archmage knew that Dyrr's spell would be directed at him. Despite having spent a little time in ethereal form, the globe was still around him, so Gromph knew that Dyrr was going to be using powerful magic. The archmage turned in the air to face the lich, but all he could do in the seconds it took for Dyrr to cast the spell was hope the defenses he already had in place would be enough to save his life.

There was no visible effect when the lich finished his spell, no trail of light or clap of thunder, but Gromph could feel the magic wrap itself around him. The protective globe did nothing to keep the spell out, but other defenses came into play, and Gromph concentrated on those. Still, his body began to stiffen. The archmage could feel the moisture being drawn from his skin. He found it difficult to bend his elbows. It was as if he were being turned to stone.

He started to drop, and before he could take control of his levitation again, the centipede turned and bit at him. One of the insect's pincers caught the archmage on the thigh as he dropped past. It might have bitten his leg off, but it had the wrong angle, so instead it ripped his skin open and dragged its serrated edge deep into the muscle until it vibrated against Gromph's thighbone.

The archmage ground his teeth against the pain. Even with his muscles stiff and his breath coming in slow, shallow gulps, he used the staff to pull up into the air away from the centipede, which came at him again.

Blood oozed like thick mud out of the deep gash in his leg, and Gromph found it ironic that it was Dyrr's spell that seemed to be saving his life. The ring Gromph had been depending on didn't seem to be functioning.

Nimor hit him again, and the cold of the magic rapier made Gromph stiffen even more. A breath caught in his throat, and his stomach convulsed until he was wrapped in a ball in the air. He tried to blink, but he had to close his eyes, pause, then slowly open them again.

He tried to turn you to stone, Nauzhror said, his voice clear in Gromph's groggy mind. *You've resisted it thus far, Archmage. Don't let it in.*

Gromph turned his head slowly to the right—all he managed from an attempt to shake his head. The globe of protective magic that enveloped him disappeared, its energy spent. Gromph saw Dyrr draw himself up, only a few yards away. The lich cast a quick spell, and a flurry of green and red sparks, each as long as an arrow, streaked at him. Gromph managed to move his leg and extend his arm but couldn't get his jaw to open fast enough to utter the command word. The bolts of Weave energy smashed into him, burning him, shocking him, making him twitch, making his muscles extend then contract. The archmage's skin rippled, and his joints popped.

It was painful, and he was bleeding in wide, hot sheets across his thigh, which was open to the bone. He could move again but not fast enough to avoid the centipede.

The insect reared up, its massive pincers wide open, and closed on him in a lunge. Gromph hung in the air barely within its reach. The pincers came down and came together over his already wounded thigh.

Gromph felt himself tugged down by the centipede, then something gave and he bobbed back up. Before taking stock of his new wound, he levitated farther up, dimly aware that he was trailing something. He cast a spell even as Nauzhror and Prath shouted into his head. Something was wrong, but he needed to finish the spell before he could do anything else. He had to get rid of the centipede or it would eat him piece by piece while the damned lich stood by safely watching.

Gromph looked down and saw a spray of blood play across the centipede's wide, flat head, then fall through it as it faded. The spell took full effect, and the centipede was gone, but the blood still fell in a grisly rain onto the floor of the Bazaar far below.

Gromph reached down to his leg and felt something hard and jagged. He cut his finger on a sharp edge—the sharp edge of his own thigh bone. His leg was gone. The centipede had bitten it off. Gromph clenched his fists in anger and looked down. He could see his severed leg lying amid a shower of blood that still rained from his open wound.

Sparkles of light off to one side caught Gromph's attention. Nimor threw something, and Gromph instinctively blocked his face, fearing a spell. Instead, he saw the hilt of the winged assassin's enchanted rapier spinning to the ground far below. The trail of sparkling light was what was left of the freezing blade. Gromph's spell had done more than banish the centipede.

Nimor, to say the least, was not happy.

As the assassin launched a string of invectives his way, Gromph flexed his muscles and found that the stiffening effect was gone. He was in pain but not as much as he would have imagined. His ring was already starting to fight against the grievous wounds the archmage had suffered. Gromph knew that he'd survive, but there was still the matter of the leg.

Nimor swooped over him then disappeared into the darkness. Gromph couldn't see the lichdrow. He dropped slowly to the floor, coming to rest in a pool of his own blood. When weight started to return to him, he staggered and had to reactivate the staff's levitating power before he fell in a sprawl into the puddle of cooling gore. He hadn't thought about trying to stand on one foot. Instead, he let himself hover an inch off the ground, bent, and picked up his own leg.

It was a curious feeling, holding his leg in his hand, but the archmage brushed it off. The assassin and the lich were obviously regrouping after Gromph's powerful spell had disjoined the magic all around him—all the magic save his own—but they would be back.

Gromph felt the bone on his stump again and was pleased that the skin hadn't yet begun to grow over it. He turned the leg in his hand and—

A blast of cold air surrounded him, engulfed him, pushed him back and down, grinding him into the stone floor of the Bazaar and dragging him along. Gromph's head smashed into something that broke, splintered, and fell all around him.

He shook his head, and bits of giant mushroom stem and glass fell from his white hair. He was half buried in a shattered merchant's stall, but all Gromph could think about was how relieved he was to still be holding his leg. His body was covered in a thin layer of chilling frost that was already starting to melt in the cool damp air of the Bazaar.

The lich, Nauzhror said into Gromph's mind, *was outside the disjunction.*

I see that, the archmage answered, letting a wave of frustration follow the thought.

Gromph looked up and around. Dyrr was casting, while Nimor arrowed fast through the air at the archmage. He set another protective globe around himself, briefly worrying that the staff's power was being too quickly drained. It couldn't keep protecting him and levitating him forever.

The lich finished his spell, and Gromph smiled when a bolt of blinding yellow lighting crackled from Dyrr's hands, arcing through the air and splattering in a shower of sparks against Gromph's protective globe. Even as the lightning spent itself on his defenses, not even making Gromph's hair stand on end, the archmage cast another defensive spell on himself. Flames flickered almost invisibly along his body.

I see, Prath said. *It worked on the huecuva, but . . .*

Nimor was upon him, and Gromph tucked his body into a ball against the assassin's attack. The half-dragon's hands were bigger than they were in his drow guise, and each of this fingers ended in a thick, sharp talon of jet-black ivory. Nimor raked Gromph's shoulder with those formidable claws, but they skipped harmlessly along the sparking surface of the archmage's fire shield. Bright orange flames blazed up from Gromph's shoulder, covering the assassin's face. Nimor roared in pain and beat his wings once so hard that stinging shards of glass from the ruined merchant's stall whirled around the archmage. Each time one of the little shards of glass hit him, a spark of fire burst out in answer. The spell never burned Gromph, but for a few unnerving seconds he was surrounded in a cascade of roiling flame.

Nimor disappeared into the shadows in the cavern's vault.

The flurry of glass and fire subsided, and Gromph worked his way out of the wreckage of the merchant's stall. When his stump was clear, blood still oozing from it, the pain reduced by his ring to a dull, annoying throb, Gromph took a second to make sure his foot was pointing in the right direction and stuck his leg back on.

He held it in place and closed his eyes. His breath came in short, sharp gasps as the dull throb turned into a skin-quivering shiver. The feel of the bone reattaching, each fine blood vessel rejoining its severed end, nerves blazing back to life with a wild flurry of pain, itching, pleasure, then pain again, and his skin drawing itself together made Gromph gasp and shake.

The lich, Nauzhror warned.

Only then did Gromph become aware that Dyrr was casting another spell. The response that came to Gromph's mind was a powerful deterrent, one that would protect him where the staff's globe could not. Not pausing to consider any greater implications, Gromph drew together the required Weave energy, and the anti-magic field was up in time to block a huge explosion of searing heat and blinding fire.

It also suppressed the regenerative power of the ring.

No magic was working anywhere near Gromph Baenre, and his leg was only half repaired. He shuddered, clenching his jaw and eyes tightly shut as pain roared up from his leg to wrap his whole body in a spasm of agony.

"Well played, my young friend," the lich called down to him, "but that field will come down eventually. Meantime, you'll be bleeding—and I'll be waiting."

Gromph didn't bother to consider the lich's threat. He was in too much pain to think.

TWENTY

Piet squeezed the handle of his axe, hoping that his sweating palms would still be able to grip it when the fighting started—and the fighting would start soon. He glanced at his friend Ulo and could tell that Ulo was thinking the same thing. Piet could even see Ulo's fingers worrying at the handles of his two big knives, and he knew that Ulo's hands were sweating too.

They had come to the Flooded Forest to do some logging, make a couple of silvers, and mind their own business. Since they'd been there they'd seen ten of their comrades killed. Some had died in the inevitable accidents that one might expect at any logging camp, but most of them fell to the local wildlife. The swamp held all manner of arcane threats, from animated vines that dragged men down to a watery grave to lizardfolk who picked off stragglers at the edges of the clearing seemingly out of spite. Still, the ring of torches and the gods only knew what else—maybe even some sort of swamp etiquette—kept the really dangerous creatures out of their camp. The makeshift tavern where the men spent virtually all of their non-working time (and there wasn't much of that) seemed like a safe enough place.

Now a dark elf and some kind of huge demon-thing had smashed through the window, and all bets were off.

Piet and Ulo faced off against the dark elf. Of the two of them, he appeared merely lethal, where the demon-thing might have really done terrible things to someone. Piet's knees were shaking. So were his hands, and his jaw felt tense.

On the other side of the common room four of the other loggers, Ansen, Kinsky, Lint, and Arkam, were facing down the huge demon-thing. They were all armed—no one with half a brain went unarmed in the Flooded Forest—but their weapons looked puny against the massive creature. Ansen had grabbed a torch from a wall sconce, Kinsky had his axe with him, Lint was hoping to keep the monster at bay with the spear he used to fish in the swamp, and Arkam waved a broken axe handle in front of him. They all looked suitably terrified.

The dark elf had a huge sword—Piet had never seen a sword so big—but he was holding it in a loose grip, dangling to his right, the tip scraping the rough wood floor. The drow was wet and bleeding from his face, from his leg, and maybe other places as well. Piet had never seen a dark elf before. He'd actually always thought they were a myth, so it was impossible for him to get a read on the creature, but he seemed to be weak, exhausted, maybe even dying.

"Who are you?" Piet asked, not liking at all the terrified quaver he heard in his voice. "What are you doing here? What do you want?"

Difficult as it was for Piet to tell what the drow was thinking, the logger was convinced that the outsider understood him. The look he gave Piet in answer seemed haughty at first then wasn't so much haughty as . . . Piet didn't know what to call it. He thought he remembered a word: disdainful, but he wasn't sure he remembered what that meant.

The drow didn't answer. Instead, he started to bring his sword up, and Piet, afraid the drow was going to cut him, chopped down with his axe. Piet had spent his entire adult life—since he was eleven-and-a-half—chopping wood. He knew how to swing an axe, and he did it with speed, power, and precision. Still, he didn't come within an armslength of the dark elf.

Piet barely saw him move. He was a couple of feet to the right all of a sudden, standing between Piet and Ulo. The drow had his sword up, but it looked as if he was defending himself, not attacking. Ulo, surprised that the dark elf was suddenly standing so much closer to him, waved his knives in front of himself madly—cutting no one—and scrambled backward until he hit the wall.

"Stab him, Ulo!" Piet shouted, but it didn't look as if Ulo even heard him.

The dark elf came at Piet with his sword low, and Piet dodged out of the way instinctively. A rush of adrenaline coursed through him. He'd never moved so fast in his life.

He changed his grip on his axe and swung it sideways at the dark elf, who leaped back to let the axe head pass a few inches in front of his face. Piet reversed his grip at the end of the swing, twisted the axe around and swung again. He knew the dark elf would lean back again and was ready for it. He actually aimed at a point several inches behind the drow's head. The only thing he could see was the drow, and when the axe came at the dark elf's head, Piet closed his eyes, expecting a splash of blood.

The axe stopped, and hot, thick liquid splashed over Piet's face.

He closed his eyes tighter to keep the blood out of his eyes and tried to wrench the axe out of the dark elf's skull, but it was stuck. The falling body dragged Piet down with in and he slowly sank to his knees. Piet's forehead bumped the wall, which surprised him. He didn't think he was that far forward.

He wiped his eyes with one sleeve as he said, "I got him, Ulo! I split the black devil's sku—"

Piet stopped cold when he opened his eyes and saw exactly whose skull he'd split. Ulo's dead eyes stared back at him, glassy and vacant. Piet's axe head was jammed into the side of his friend's head, and blood was still oozing out from around it.

Piet's body shook, wracked by a spasm, but he kept himself from vomiting by pressing a hand tightly to his mouth, letting go of the axe that was still stuck in his friend's head, and rolling off onto the floor.

He looked up and saw the dark elf looking down at him, making no move to kill him, though the drow would have had an easy time of it. Piet met the black creature's gaze and got the sinking feeling that the drow was not only pleased with himself for getting Piet to kill Ulo but that he was thinking about trying something like it again.

"Men!" Piet barked, his voice cracking.

He wanted to warn them, but his throat was tight, and he had trouble forcing the words out. Looking up at the other four loggers, Piet saw the huge, gray-furred demon rip Arkam's throat out with one hand, as if he were digging a handful of shortening out of a pot. Blood poured out everywhere, and Arkam was dead before his gore-soaked body hit the floor.

Piet knew the second the two bizarre creatures burst in through the window that things were going to end badly for the logging crew, but there was something about the way matters were unfolding—the casual manner in which the gray demon ripped

Arkam's throat out and the conniving, almost mean-spirited way the dark elf made Piet kill his own friend—that made it seem too personal, as if they'd come there for that reason.

Piet's palms weren't sweating anymore. His jaw was still tight, but for a different reason. His blood pounded in his ears. The dark elf was watching the demon toy with Ansen, Kinsky, and Lint. He didn't even think Piet was dangerous enough to keep an eye on.

That, Piet thought, is your second and last mistake, drow.

Piet coughed back the bile that rose in his throat when he put his heavy-booted foot on his friend Ulo's split-open head and pushed while pulling on the axe handle. The axe head came loose with a nauseating sucking sound, but Piet managed to ignore it.

Axe in hand, Piet stood then lunged at the dark elf. The slippery drow dodged him again, quickly and easily enough that Piet thought he must have eyes on the back of his head. Undaunted, the logger swung again but sliced through nothing but air. The drow danced back, not even parrying with his huge greatsword, just stepping back, leaning to either side or backward as Piet swung again and again.

Piet finally gave up. His lungs were burning. He tried to speak but couldn't. He wanted to run but his legs felt like twigs ready to snap—he'd already spent a long day cutting down trees. All he could do was stand there and watch the dark elf watch the demon-thing kill the rest of the men in the room.

The demon had one of the heavy oak tables in his hands—the larger two of the thing's three hands—and was pressing Ansen, Kinsky, and Lint into the wall. Their weapons were caught between the tabletop and their own bodies. Ansen's torch burned his face, Kinsky's axe handle cracked his collarbone, and Lint's spear wagged impotently from behind the table, digging deep furrows into the roof beam above him.

The men were grunting and coughing. Ansen screamed. Smoke

billowed up from his hair, and the flesh around his right eye was crisping and beginning to flake away.

"Stop it," Piet gasped.

Neither the drow nor the demon even looked at him.

"Stop . . ." he moaned and was about to drop his axe when the door burst open, and five men all but crawled over each other to get into the common room.

Piet knew them all: Nedreg, the tall man from Sembia who was one of two men in the camp who'd brought a sword with him. Kem, the short guy from Cormyr who also had a sword and who hated Nedreg as much as Nedreg hated him. Raula, the only woman in the camp, had a spear she said was magical but no one believed her. Aynd, Raula's husband, had a spear that was so warped he didn't bother telling anyone it was anything but an old piece of Impilturan army garbage he'd found on the side of a road.

The first of the five to get into the room was the foreman of the camp: a big man named Rab who claimed to have been a sergeant in the Cormyrean army, who was on the battlefield the day King Azoun was killed. Everyone believed what Rab told them—whatever Rab told them—because everyone was afraid of him. Piet never liked Rab, but seeing him burst into the blood-soaked tavern with his greataxe at the ready was the most beautiful thing Piet had ever seen.

It was then, for no reason Piet could understand, that the dark elf finally attacked him. The greatsword moved so fast Piet could barely see it. Still, he managed to stagger back away from the blade. He tried to parry with his axe, but the dark elf never touched it. His greatsword whirled around it, flipped over it, pulled away from it.

Piet had taken maybe ten steps before he even realized he was walking. He was closer to the demon than he'd intended to go, but the monster was still pushing against the table behind which Ansen, Kinsky, and Lint were trapped. Ansen was still screaming. The tone of his voice had taken on a more desperate, almost girlish quality, and Piet found himself wishing the man would hurry up and die. It was the only humane thing.

The other two men looked as if they were trying to scream but couldn't. The demon-thing glanced up at the men who'd burst into the room but who were hesitating at the door still trying to understand the grim scene. The demon took advantage of their hesitation and pressed harder. Piet could see the thing's legs tense and the sharp claws on its feet dig into the floor. Kinsky's eyes popped out of his head, followed by a waterfall of blood. Lint coughed out a mouthful of blood, gurgled, and died. Kinsky tried to scream. The room filled with a series of loud cracking noises, and he went limp. Ansen finally stopped screaming, though he continued to burn.

Rab and the others charged at the demon. Piet wasn't even sure they noticed the dark elf.

"Why?" Piet asked the drow, who was watching the others charge the demon. "What are you doing here? Why are you doing this? What do you want?"

The dark elf turned to him and raised an eyebrow, looking down his nose at Piet—though the human was easily six inches taller.

"What do you want here?" Piet asked again.

"Nothing," the drow said in strangely accented Common.

Piet was aware of some motion below him—something that looked as if the dark elf had shrugged—then he felt something wet on his neck, warm liquid pouring down his chest. Piet put a hand to his throat and his fingers met a pulsing jet of hot red blood shooting in a four-foot stream from his throat. When he tried to speak, his lungs filled with blood, then his eyesight blurred.

The dark elf turned away from him, and as he died, Piet knew that the drow would never give him a second thought. He didn't live long enough to decide how he felt about that.

🦂　🦂　🦂

Ryld didn't give the dead human a second thought. Five more of them had come in, and though Jeggred had dispatched the first three humans he'd encountered with minimal effort, at least one of the newcomers looked like someone who could actually fight. Ryld didn't entertain for a second the thought that Jeggred might not be able to handle the five humans—even the one with the greataxe—but the five of them together might slow the draegloth down a bit, and that would have to do.

Ryld sheathed Splitter, and before the blade was entirely covered his feet were off the ground. He intended to jump through the window and almost made it when someone grabbed his foot. Ryld knew before he turned that it was Jeggred.

The draegloth pulled hard on Ryld's foot, and the weapons master twisted in his grip and kicked Jeggred in the face. The half-demon's head snapped back into one of the onrushing humans—one armed with a sword—who took the opportunity to slice at the back of the draegloth's head. The sword tangled in Jeggred's still-wet mane of thick white hair.

Two more of the humans came up on either side of the half-demon and jabbed their spearheads into Jeggred's back. The spearheads sank into the draegloth's flesh, and Jeggred let out a loud growl. He let go of Ryld, who landed on his feet, face to face with the draegloth. The humans withdrew their spears, and Jeggred and Ryld shared a look that said Jeggred wanted the human male and female with spears. The swordsman drew his weapon back to stab the draegloth from behind.

Jeggred spun away, sending the two humans with spears

scattering. The human with the sword was left facing Ryld.

"The draegloth will kill you all," Ryld said, reasonably certain he got the Common right.

The human seemed more frightened that Ryld could speak his language than he was of the dark elf himself. That was a mistake the man wouldn't make twice.

"Don't—" Ryld warned as the human pulled his sword up to hack down at the dark elf.

With an impatient sigh, Ryld flicked his sword in a fast arc in front of him and took the human's sword arm. The man staggered back, bulging eyes fixed on the blood pumping out of his stump. He looked at Ryld, made eye contact with him for the space of a heartbeat. The human seemed to be waiting for Ryld to say something, to explain why the drow had taken his arm. Humans were an odd lot.

Ryld shrugged. The man opened his mouth to speak then fell over dead.

The female human jabbed at Jeggred, and the draegloth grabbed the spear. He snapped it like a twig, and the woman backstepped away, her hands up in front of her face in a feeble attempt to fend off the half-demon.

Ryld suppressed the urge to laugh. Instead, he bent quickly and ripped the dead human's hand off the sword. He had to break a few of the man's fingers to get the weapon free, but it certainly didn't matter to the swordsman anymore.

The other spearman went for Jeggred with renewed fury, his hopelessly warped spear jabbing again and again at the draegloth, who danced out of its way, toying with the man. The woman had her hands on her mouth, apparently concerned with what might happen to the other spearman. There was something about the look on her face that Ryld recognized, and in response he tossed her the dead man's sword. She didn't notice the blade coming at her until it was halfway there, but she caught it just the same.

The woman met Ryld's gaze, and the weapons master nodded at the draegloth.

"Take the dark elf, girl!" the man with the greataxe yelled to the woman.

The man with the greataxe had been barking orders all along, but Ryld hadn't paid much attention. Hearing someone order his death wasn't an entirely alien experience for Ryld, but there was something about the circumstances that frustrated him. He'd just tossed her a weapon . . . so what if he'd taken it out of the severed limb of one of her comrades?

The woman hesitated, looked at the sword as if she wasn't sure what to do with it, then looked at Jeggred. The draegloth stepped into the man with the spear, deftly slipping past the spearhead, and grabbed the logger's head in one of his huge, clawed hands. With a twist of the draegloth's wrist and a bend of his elbow the human spearman's head came free of his shoulders in a shower of blood.

The woman screamed, and Ryld was taken aback by the sound. It was soaked with emotion—a sound Ryld hadn't heard often in Menzoberranzan. He looked at her and she met his gaze. Tears streamed down her face. She looked back at the draegloth, who was meeting the advance of the man with the greataxe.

The woman dropped the sword and ran, rushing past Jeggred and the man with the greataxe to stumble out the door. Ryld heard her footsteps recede into the night.

The weapons master longed to follow her.

🦂　🦂　🦂

Rab Shuoc was born in the Year of the Striking Hawk in the Cormyrean city of Arabel. He grew up there, the son of a city watchman, and spent his childhood hunting rats with his friends in the back alleys and occasionally following his father on his rounds in the wealthier sections of the city. It wasn't the slightest bit surprising to anyone who knew him when he joined the army. Rab was fiercely loyal to the kingdom of his birth and the king he admired more than anyone but his father.

He worked his way up the ranks, slowly, and was a sergeant when the ghazneths and goblins ravaged Cormyr and all but destroyed Arabel. He was nearly killed in the same battle that resulted in the death of the king, and he watched the city of his birth burned. His father was killed when part of a building fell on him. With the king and his father both dead, and no family of his own to tie him down, Rab simply walked away.

He went on to become alternately a sellsword, a tavern bouncer, an innkeeper, a weaponsmith, then a logger. He was strong and smart, so he soon became foreman. His employers paid Rab a considerable sum in gold to gather crews to go deep into some of the most dangerous places in Faerûn to find exotic woods. He quickly built a solid reputation among the lumber mill owners and loggers alike as a fair but tough leader who knew how to get the job done, and Rab always delivered.

During those hard forty-six years of life, Rab Shuoc had missed out on a lot. There had been women but never a wife and never any children. Since the war he hadn't even had a home. He rarely worked with the same men more than one season at a time and had no real friends to speak of.

He wasn't the kind of man who worried about his own happiness or even expected to be happy. He wanted to live, work, and be left alone.

When he stepped into his common room and saw some of his crew already dead at the hands of a dark elf and some kind of giant demon monster, he knew that if he wanted to live, he would have to fight harder than he ever had before. It was with that thought foremost in his mind that he stepped toward the two interlopers and got started with the last thirty seconds of his life.

Raula was smart enough to run, and Rab let her go. The dark elf watched her go too, and the demon ignored her. The huge, gray-furred creature locked its blazing red eyes on Rab and advanced on him. Rab hefted his greataxe and stepped into the demon's attack. He was aware of the drow facing him as well.

The drow came in faster than the demon, swinging his enormous greatsword in a wild, chaotic fashion. Rab was sure he could parry the uncontrolled assault with ease and he held the steel haft of his greataxe in both hands so the greatsword would bounce off it—but it didn't.

The tip of the greatsword wasn't where it was supposed to be. It didn't seem possible to Rab that someone could move such a huge, heavy weapon so quickly, but that strange dark elf had, and it was Rab who paid the price. The tip of the sword drew a deep cut across the logger's chest. Pain flared, and blood poured, and in that half-second of shock, the demon took his axe.

He'd been disarmed before but he'd never had an opponent actually reach out and take the weapon right out of his hand.

Rab was still puzzling over that when something even stranger happened: the dark elf drew his greatsword across the demon's back, cutting it deeply enough that blood sprayed from the wound and the creature roared. The drow said something in a language Rab didn't even recognize let alone understand. There didn't seem to be any anger, any emotion at all on the drow's face, but he was definitely trying to kill the demon.

The huge creature spun on the much-smaller dark elf, and Rab backed away. He only got one step back before the demon reached around and grabbed him by the shirt, taking some skin with it. The monster lifted Rab, who weighed well over two hundred pounds, right off the floor without any sign of strain.

Rab grabbed at the thing's massive clawed hand, but the demon's skin was like steel coated in coarse fur. There was nothing Rab could do but wonder at the monster's intentions. It whirled on the dark elf, who had his sword ready. The demon still held Rab's greataxe in one hand but almost seemed to have forgotten it.

The demon threw Rab at the dark elf. The human barked out an incoherent, scared sound that might have been a scream or a shout. He didn't even know. It was the sound a man makes when he knows he's got less than a second to live and there's nothing he can do about it.

Rab was impaled on the dark elf's greatsword. He could feel every inch of the cold steel as it slid through his chest. Strangely enough, it didn't hurt.

🕷 🕷 🕷

Ryld held the human up and looked past him at the draegloth. The man died trying to make eye contact with him—Ryld would never understand why humans insisted on doing that. Ryld tipped his sword down in hopes that the man would slide off but instead had to quickly jerk back to avoid the blade of the human's greataxe, wielded by Jeggred, as it chopped down.

The greataxe hit Splitter and sliced clean through. Ryld felt his eyes bulge and his blood at once boil and run cold. Splitter was broken. His greatsword. The weapon he'd practically lived for, had developed his skills around for years, was destroyed.

The human's axe must have been enchanted after all.

The man fell away on the remaining length of the greatsword blade, and the sudden loss of his weight made Ryld fall backward. He let go of the shattered sword, and it clattered to the floor next to him.

The weapons master reached for his short sword and almost had his fingers wrapped around the pommel when the axe blade came down again, split his dwarven mithral breastplate as if it were made of parchment, and buried itself into his chest. Ryld could feel the weight of it not only on him but in him. There was no pain, just a heavy, even pressure.

The draegloth stood over him, drool hanging from his exposed fangs in shimmering tendrils, his eyes aglow in the orange torchlight.

Ryld tried to breathe but he couldn't. No air was getting past his throat at all. He wanted to say something, but there was no way to form words. Besides, he didn't know what to say. He'd turned his back on everything he knew for a woman he didn't know at all, a woman who chose a path for herself that would inevitably lead to her own destruction as surely as it had led to his. Part of him wished he'd been killed by anyone but the filthy half-demon, but another part was satisfied that it took a draegloth to bring him down. He almost wanted to thank Jeggred for fighting him in the first place. It was more than he deserved.

Jeggred moved closer, and Ryld was thankful that he couldn't breathe. He couldn't smell the half-demon's breath.

Jeggred leaned on the axe blade and broke open Ryld's chest. The sensation was something beyond pain—a mind-twisting agony that only death could possibly cure.

He watched the draegloth reach into his chest. Ryld's body started to jerk, and he couldn't stop it. The draegloth grabbed and groped inside his chest, and Ryld's vision faded in and out.

When Jeggred pulled his hand away, Ryld's eyesight came back long enough for Ryld Argith, Master of Melee Magthere, to see that his heart was still beating when the draegloth began to eat it.

The weapons master's heart was strong, and Jeggred relished the texture as well as the taste of it. Ryld Argith was a worthy opponent, a good kill, and the draegloth wished he could stay and devour more of him. The drow was dead by the time Jeggred finished eating his heart, and he knew that Danifae and the others were waiting for him.

Not bothering to wipe any of the blood, slime, or sap off himself, the draegloth touched the ring that Danifae had given him and used its magic to return to Sschindylryn.

TWENTY-ONE

"Ryld Argith is dead," Danifae said to Quenthel, her eyes darting at Pharaun.

The mage sat quietly, legs folded, in front of the mainmast. He didn't look back at her, seemed to have no reaction at all. Danifae chewed her bottom lip, her eyes flickering back and forth between Pharaun and Quenthel.

"And?" the Mistress of Arach-Tinilith prompted.

"I killed him," Jeggred grumbled.

Danifae looked at the draegloth, whose eyes were locked on Pharaun. Still the mage made no move and never looked at either the draegloth or her. She'd promised to spare the weapons master but had lied. Danifae half expected the mage to burn her to ciders where she stood for the betrayal. Either he was too busy with his preparations for the journey, or he didn't care . . .

or he was planning something for later.

"And Halisstra Melarn?" Quenthel asked.

"I tore his body to shreds," Jeggred went on, oblivious to his aunt's question, "after I ate his heart. There's barely a piece bigger than a bite left of him, spread out over that freezing mud hole."

"Yes," Danifae said, smiling at the draegloth, who was still looking at Pharaun, "well, be that as it may, Halisstra has in fact done the unthinkable. She enjoys the protection of Eilistraee now, and there's no longer any doubt."

"You have evidence of that?" Pharaun asked, his voice quieter, weaker somehow, or maybe just bored.

"She told me," Danifae replied, still looking at Quenthel.

"It's true," the draegloth added.

Quenthel turned on Jeggred, her face tight, her eyes blazing. Still, she looked tiny in front of the hulking creature.

"How would you know, fool?" Quenthel spat. "You weren't brought here to think."

"No," the draegloth answered, not shrinking the slightest in the face of the high priestess's rage, "I was brought here to act. I was brought here to fight and to kill. How much of that have I done, my dear, dear aunt?"

"As much," Quenthel replied, her voice coming out almost as a growl, "or as little as I tell you. As *I* tell you, not Danifae."

Jeggred loomed over her, the muscles under his gray fur rippling with anticipation.

"Mistress Danifae," the draegloth said, "is at least trying. She's acting—"

"Without my direct orders," Quenthel finished for him.

Danifae was afraid that Jeggred would continue, so she said, "Only on your behalf, Mistress."

Quenthel lifted an eyebrow and stepped closer to Danifae.

"We talked about that, didn't we, battle-captive?"

"I am no one's captive now, Mistress," Danifae replied, "but still I serve Lolth."

"By turning my draegloth's head?" the high priestess said.

Danifae felt the skin on her arms and chest tingle.

"No," she said. "Jeggred helped me help you."

"Help me?" asked the high priestess.

The draegloth turned and skulked away. He found a spot near the bow and sat with his head bent downward. Quenthel was still looking at Danifae as if she expected an answer.

"Mistress," Danifae said, "I am without a home. You said you would bring me back to Menzoberranzan with you if I served you. That, and a host of other reasons, is precisely why I did what I did."

"*Did I ask?*" Quenthel roared. "Did I send you to do this?"

Danifae lifted an eyebrow herself and waited.

Quenthel took a deep breath and turned away from the former battle-captive to stare out at the black water, lost in thought.

"My loyalty is with Lolth," Danifae said, "and to the House of your birth."

"House *Baenre*," Quenthel said, her voice icy, "has no room for upstarts, traitors, or battle-captives."

"I think you'll find, Mistress," the former servant pressed on, "that I am neither an upstart, a traitor . . . or a battle-captive. It is not I who dances under the gaze of Eilistraee. I am here, and I am ready to serve you, to serve Lolth, to serve Arach-Tinilith, Menzoberranzan, and the entire dark elf—"

"All right," Quenthel snarled, "leave it out. I don't need my arse li—"

"Never, Mist—"

"Silence, child," the Mistress of Arach-Tinilith said. "Interrupt me again and taste venom."

Danifae got the distinct impression that it was a hollow threat, but she silenced herself just the same. It wasn't easy for her to do. There was much she burned to say to Quenthel Baenre, but she decided that she would say it to her corpse instead. Besides, the vipers at Quenthel's command were still dangerous, and all five of them stared at her, their cruel poison glistening on darting tongues.

"Everyone," Pharaun called from where he sat, his eyes closed. "Now that we're all here . . . what's left of us anyway . . . we'll be on our way.

"As the Mistress ordered," the mage added.

Danifae took a deep breath and a last look at the dreary Lake of Shadows and said, "We're ready, Master Pharaun."

Quenthel turned to look at her, but only out of the corner of her eye. A thrill raced through Danifae at the emotions plain in that look. The Mistress of Arach-Tinilith was terrified.

🕷 🕷 🕷

The ship began to move in response to Pharaun's will, and the wizard shuddered. Through his connection with the ship he could feel the cold of the water, the heat of his own body and the bodies of his comrades on the deck, and he could feel the lesser demons still being digested in the hellish transdimensional space that was the vessel's cargo hold. He found it an unusually pleasant mixture of sensations.

Still water rippled and tapped against the bone hull as the ship glided slowly across the surface of the lake. Other than that, nothing changed at first.

The walls are thin here, Aliisza whispered into his consciousness.

They are, he agreed.

The walls she referred to were the barriers between planes. In certain places and at certain times those barriers drew thinner

271

and thinner and often broke all together. The Lake of Shadows was very close to the Plane of Shadows. The barriers between the two planes were especially thin there.

It's good that you're starting slowly, Aliisza sent. *It won't take much before we slip into the Sha—*

They were there.

It took even Pharaun, who'd had quite a bit of experience in planar travel, by surprise. As they passed from the Lake of Shadows onto the Shadow Fringe Pharaun saw what little color there was drain from the dimly lit cavern.

The movement of the ship was smooth but disturbingly random. The deck rose gently, then fell gently, then rose a little farther, then fell not as far, then rose the same amount, then fell less far. Pharaun couldn't tell if, on aggregate, they were going up, down, or staying the same. Sometimes they slipped straight to one side or rolled gently to the other. His stomach rolled with the ship, and he felt increasingly nauseous.

Don't ride it, Aliisza advised. *Be it.*

Pharaun concentrated on the deck, on the palms of his hands pressing against the warm, living bone. He watched random memories from the devoured souls pass across his consciousness then looked deeper into the ship itself.

Though the vessel lived, it didn't think. He felt it react to stimulus, riding the cool water of the lake into the freezing water of the Fringe. It knew it had crossed into the Plane of Shadow by feel but had no way to form the word "shadow." The ship didn't like the Shadow Fringe, it didn't fear the Shadow Fringe, and it didn't hate the Shadow Fringe. All it did was ride the water from one universe to the next at the command of the Master of Sorcere.

Pharaun's stomach felt fine.

✿ ✿ ✿

Valas had traveled the Shadow Fringe before and was not impressed. It was a world devoid of color and warmth—two things the scout had little appreciation for anyway. Every turn in the caverns of the real Underdark had a requisite turn in the Shadow, but distance and time was distorted there, less predictable, less tangible.

The scout had been hired to guide the expedition through the Underdark, but they had left the Underdark. They were in a realm more suited to the wizard, on their way to a world only a priestess could appreciate. The time for Valas Hune to step aside was at hand.

Among the trinkets and talismans that adorned his vest was a cameo made of deep green jade that he wore upside down. He looked around, making sure that none of the others were looking at him. They were all too busy standing in awe of the difference in the air and water, obsessed with the feel of the ship moving across the shadow-water, to notice him. Touching the cameo with one finger, the scout whispered a single word and closed his eyes while a wave of dizziness passed through him.

Having sent his message back to his superiors at Bregan D'aerthe—a simple message they would easily interpret along the lines of "I'm no longer needed here"—Valas let go of the cameo and joined the others in marveling at the sometimes subtle, sometimes extreme differences in the world around them.

Bregan D'aerthe would answer in their own time.

✿ ✿ ✿

Danifae could barely contain herself. The feel of the deck rocking beneath her was thrilling. The draining of color from the world around her was exhilarating. The thought that they were on their way, and that thus far everything she'd planned had come to fruition excited her. The presence of the draegloth next to her reassured her.

Danifae had never felt better in her life.

"The wizard will avenge him," Jeggred grumbled in what sufficed for a whisper from the hulking half-demon.

"The wizard will do what is best for the wizard," Danifae replied.

"I don't know what you mean," said the draegloth.

Danifae could hear the frustration in his voice.

"You don't fear him," she said. "I know that. Forget the wizard. He won't put his own life at risk to defend Ryld Argith, who's dead anyway and no longer of use to anyone. Even now, if he isn't too busy piloting the ship, he's coming to the realization that the weapons master had abandoned us all—including him—anyway, so to the Hells with him."

"And to the Abyss with us," the draegloth said, "at Pharaun's mercy."

"Pharaun has no more mercy than you and I, Jeggred," said Danifae, "but he has his orders from his archmage and his own reasons for remaining with the expedition. If he puts anything at risk at any time in the Shadow Plane, the Astral, or the Abyss, he dies. Until then, I want you to leave him alone."

"But—"

"No, Jeggred," Danifae said, turning to face the draegloth and look him directly in the eyes. In the dull gloom of the Shadow Fringe, his eyes glowed an even more brilliant shade of crimson. "You will not touch him unless I tell you to, and even then only in the way I tell you to."

"But Mistress . . ."

"Enough," she said, her voice flat with finality.

There was a moment of silence intruded upon only by the creak of the rigging and the strangely echoing water splashing against the living bone of the ship of chaos.

"As you wish, Mistress," the draegloth said finally.

Danifae forced herself not to smile.

※ ※ ※

You will grow accustomed to the motion after a time, Mistress, Yngoth reassured her. *Eventually, you won't notice it at all.*

The vipers could speak to her, directly into her mind, but Quenthel didn't know they could sense what she was feeling. She hadn't articulated, aloud or telepathically, how uncomfortable she was with the motion of the undulating deck.

It's the water that's pushing us up and down, K'Sothra offered.

Quenthel ignored her, choosing instead to look out into the cold gloom of the Shadow Fringe.

"Care, all," Pharaun said, his voice distant and echoing in the strange environment. "We'll be crossing into the Shadow Deep. There are dangers there . . . creatures, intelligences . . . keep your arms and legs inside the rail at all times, please. Try not to make eye contact with anything we might pass. Be prepared for any manner of strange effects and all manner of strange creatures."

Only a wizard, Zinda hissed, *could offer such vague and meaningless warnings. Does he expect any of us to jump overboard in the Shadow Deep?*

He's right, Yngoth argued. *The Shadow Deep hides many dangers.*

"Hold onto something," the Master of Sorcere advised.

Perhaps the draegloth could keep you from falling, Mistress, Hsiv advised.

Quenthel's lip curled in a sneer, and she flicked the offending snake under his chin. She looked over at the draegloth. Danifae's hand absently stroked his mane, and the draegloth stood very close to her.

Quenthel looked away, trying her best to rid her mind of the image. She kneeled on the deck and wrapped her arms around the bone and sinew rail. No sooner had she tightened her grip than the world—or the water—dropped out from under the ship.

They fell, and Quenthel's stomach lurched up into her throat. Her jaw clenched, and all she could do was hold on, her body tense and ready for the inevitable deadly stop at the bottom of whatever they were falling into.

It took a terribly long time for that to happen. Finally Quenthel began to relax—at least a little—even though they were still falling and she continued to hold on to the rail for dear life. Quenthel gathered her wits enough to survey the rest of the expedition.

The ship's deck was elongated and twisted, as if it had been pulled at either end by a strong but careless giant. Pharaun seemed twice as far away, Valas twice as close, and Danifae and Jeggred appeared to be hanging upside down. The draegloth held the battle-captive in one arm and the rail in the other.

All around them black shapes flitted in and around the rigging, up and under the hull, and between the falling dark elves. The air was ribboned with black and gray, and there was a dull roar like wind but not wind that all but deafened her. The flying black shapes were either bats or the shadows of bats. In the Shadow Deep, Quenthel knew, the shadows would be the more dangerous of the two.

We're stopping, Qorra said, and Quenthel knew it to be true.

The sensation of falling had wafted away. It wasn't that they had slowed in their fall, and they certainly hadn't hit bottom, they simply weren't falling anymore.

"Sorry, all," Pharaun apologized, his voice cheerful and bright.

"A bit of a rough transition, that one, but you'll forgive my general inexperience with the whole piloting a ship of chaos thing, I'm sure."

Quenthel didn't forgive but also didn't bother to say anything. The ship was perfectly still, as if it had come up on solid ground, and the high priestess risked a glance over the rail.

They hadn't come to rest on the ground, she saw, but had stopped in midair above a rolling landscape of gray cluttered with vaguely translucent silhouettes of trees. The shadowy, batlike things still raced all around them.

"Oh, yes," Pharaun added suddenly, "and don't touch the bats."

Quenthel sighed but never touched a shadow-bat.

🕷 🕷 🕷

Pharaun extended his senses out into the Shadow Deep, using the properties of the ship of chaos in a way that felt natural to one who had become part of the demonic vessel. He did it the same way he would have strained to hear some distant sound.

The Shadow Deep is not unlike your Underdark after all, Aliisza said, *and like the Underdark it has its own rules.*

Pharaun nodded. He didn't pretend to understand those rules in any but the simplest way. He'd always been smart enough not to linger in the Shadow Deep.

We won't linger now, Aliisza said.

She touched his shoulder, and Pharaun took a deep breath. He was reassured by her touch, and not only for her help navigating and piloting the ship. With Ryld dead, he was alone with a group of drow who'd be as happy to see him dead as not. The alu-fiend might be more enemy than friend, but still Pharaun couldn't help thinking she was the only one he could trust.

Can you feel it? she asked.

Pharaun was momentarily taken aback. He thought she meant—

The gateway, she said. *Can you feel it?*

There was a lightness in his head and an itch on his right temple that made the ship turn and accelerate. His fingers curled, instinctively gripping the deck.

I feel it, he said. *The barrier is thinnest there. The ship will pass through.*

Yes, the alu-fiend breathed.

She wrapped an arm around him from behind and pressed into his back. Pharaun's heart beat a little faster, and the wizard was amused with himself. He couldn't see her, but he could feel her, he could smell her, and he could hear her voice echoing in his skull. He liked it.

At Pharaun's unspoken command the ship drifted across vast distances in insubstantial leaps. Like shadow walking, the ship slid across the Plane of Shadow faster than it should have, the distance compressing beneath it.

Will we fall again? Pharaun asked Aliisza as they neared the place where the Shadow Deep gave way directly to the endless expanse of the Astral.

No, she said, *it will be different.*

It was.

The ship was through in an instant. The darkness of the Shadow Deep with its sky of black and deep gray blazed into a blinding light. Pharaun's eyes clamped shut and were instantly soaked with tears. The ship shuddered. It felt as if the vessel were being battered on its side. Pharaun's breath caught in his chest, and there was a hard pressure there, a tightness. Fear?

Don't be afraid, Aliisza whispered.

Pharaun cringed at the word but had to admit to himself at least that he was afraid.

He blinked his burning eyes open, and his head reeled so he almost fainted. There was such an expanse of nothing on every side of them that he felt too out in the open, too vulnerable, too . . . outside to be anything but tense and jumpy.

The sky around them was gray, but it also held what Pharaun could only describe as the essence of light. There was no sun or any other single source of luminescence. The light was simply there, coming from everywhere at once, saturating everything.

Bright streaks of multicolored luminescence rippled across the backdrop of saturated light—brilliant and chaotic aurorae.

The ship rocked and shuddered, and Pharaun tensed again, fully prepared for the thing to shake itself apart. He held his teeth closed, then closed his eyes, and would have closed his ears if he could.

No, Aliisza advised, *don't close your eyes. Don't shut yourself off from it.*

Pharaun opened his eyes, mentally brushing off the resentment that boiled to the surface. He didn't like being told what to do, even when he knew he needed it.

She squeezed him tighter and whispered in his ear, "Think it. Think the name of it."

It? he thought to her.

Again she whispered with her real voice, her lips so close to his ear Pharaun could feel them brushing against the sensitive skin there: "The Abyss."

The Abyss, he thought. *The Abyss.*

There it was.

"What is that?" Quenthel asked.

"We're heading right for it," the draegloth said.

Pharaun laughed and moved the ship faster toward the disturbance.

That's it, Aliisza prodded.

They were moving toward a black whirlpool in the sky. It was as big as Sorcere itself, maybe bigger. It was huge. The closer they got to it, the bigger it became, and not only because they were moving closer to it. The thing was actually growing.

"We're not projections here," Valas said. "If we fly into that thing . . ."

"We'll end up where we meant to go," Pharaun said.

His own voice sounded strange in his ears, as if he hadn't spoken in ages.

Tell them to hold on again, Aliisza said. *They won't need to, but it'll reassure them.*

"Hold on," the wizard repeated. "Hold onto something, and hold on tight or you'll be tossed overboard and lost in the limitless expanse of the Astral Plane for all eternity, set adrift for all time to come, never to be seen or heard from again."

Aliisza giggled quietly in his ear, her breath tickling him.

They made straight for the whirlpool, and when the tip of the bow hit the trailing end of the disturbance, all Hell broke loose.

Literally.

Pharaun couldn't help but scream as the ship was whirled so madly around that his head snapped back and forth. His hands threatened to come away from the deck. Something hit him in the back of the head. Aliisza squeezed him, then let go, then squeezed him again. Pain flared in his legs and side, and he didn't know precisely why. The others were making noises as well: screaming, growling, calling out questions he couldn't understand, much less answer.

"This is it," Aliisza shouted into his ear. He still couldn't see her. "This is what you came for. This is where you're going. You brought yourself here, but now it's time for the Abyss to decide if you live to walk its burning expanse. The Abyss will decide if you get what you want."

"What?" Pharaun asked. "What do you mean?"

"The Abyss decides, Pharaun," the alu-demon said, her arms slipping away from him, "not you."

"We're almost there," the wizard said. "I feel it. It'll let us in."

Not me, Aliisza whispered into his mind. *I leave you here.*

"Why?" he asked, then thought to her, *Come with me.*

The alu-demon giggled then was gone, and Pharaun screamed again.

Until the roaring of the whirlpool dropped to nothing and his own screaming rattled his eardrums.

The ship stopped spinning but continued to fall, accelerating down and down while Pharaun struggled to regain control. Aliisza was gone, and the subtle help she provided, the extra consciousness at the helm, was gone with her. He tried to think of some spell to cast, but his mind, tied to the ship that was damaged in ways he was only dimly aware of, wouldn't form the list of spells.

The sky had gone red, and there was a sun, but it was huge and dull. The heat was stifling, and Pharaun had trouble drawing a deep breath. Sweat poured from him, stinging his eyes and soaking his forearms.

"Pharaun," Quenthel screamed, her voice shrill and reedy, "do something!"

Pharaun formed a number of replies as they continued to dive, faster and faster downward, but he didn't bother with any of them.

"Do something?" he repeated.

The wizard started to laugh, but the laugh turned into a scream when the ship rolled over upside down.

Below them was a level plain that went on and on forever in all directions with no horizon. Tinted red by the dull sun, the sand shimmered with heat. Scattered all over were deep black holes—thousand of them . . . millions of them.

He knew where they were. He had heard it described.

They had come to the Abyss. To the Plain of Infinite Portals.

They were falling and falling and screaming and screaming until they hit the ground.

The ship of chaos shattered into a thousand shards of bone and sinew, the human-skin sail ripping to shreds. The sound was a wild cacophony of snapping and booming and tearing and cracking. The four drow and the draegloth aboard the ship were sent spinning into the air, rolling and tumbling to a stop on the burning sand.

Chapter

TWENTY-TWO

It was raining souls.

All around Pharaun, one after another, transparent wraiths dropped from the burning sky onto the blasted sand of the Plain of Infinite Portals. He could pick out representatives of a thousand different races. Some he recognized, and some he didn't. There was everything from the lowliest kobold to enormous giants, humans by the hundreds, and no shortage of duergar. Pharaun could only hope that the latter were coming straight from the siege of Menzoberranzan.

Someone stepped close to him, and the Master of Sorcere turned to look. It was then that he realized he was lying on his back on the uncomfortably hot sand looking up. The wispy shade of a departed soul passed by him. The newly dead orc looked down but didn't seem to see Pharaun. Maybe the creature didn't care.

It was headed to some porcine hell to serve its grunting god or demon prince, probably as a light supper. So what if it passed a sleeping dark elf along the way?

Pharaun blinked, expecting the passing orc to at least kick sand in his face, but the thing's feet were as insubstantial as they looked, and it made no sign of its passing on the dead ground. The Master of Sorcere slowly rose to a sitting position under painful protest from a dozen muscles, at least three of which he hadn't realized he possessed.

Taking a deep breath, he looked around.

The wreckage of the ship of chaos seemed oddly suited to their surroundings. Jagged fingers of bleached-white bone stood up like a more substantial line of souls against the red sky. The parts of the ship that had been alive with blood and breath sat shriveled and gray on the unforgiving sand.

Jeggred stood slouched in the center of the wrecked ship, his wild mane of white hair blowing madly in the hot wind. The draegloth stared at Pharaun expectantly. He looked even more battered and bruised, and he was bleeding again from a number of small wounds.

Danifae stepped out from behind the enormous half-demon. She held a long shard of broken bone and was dusty and disheveled but otherwise looked no worse for wear. The battle-captive looked down at the bone fragment she carried then absently tossed it to the ground where it clattered to a stop amid a myriad of shards like it. Danifae followed Jeggred's eyes to Pharaun.

The sound of a sigh startled the mage, and he spun, still sitting, to see Valas crouched next to him. He hadn't seen or heard the scout approach.

"Are you injured?" the mercenary asked him.

The scout's voice rose and fell on the wind, sounding distant though it came from only the few inches between his lips to Pharaun's ear.

"No," Pharaun answered, hearing his own voice echo in the same way. "I'm quite fine, actually. Thank you for asking, Master Hune."

"I'm no one's master," Valas replied, not looking the mage in the eye.

He stood and began to wander slowly back in the direction of the debris field.

Pharaun asked of all three of them, "Has anyone seen Quenthel?"

"I will thank you," Quenthel said from behind him, "to refer to me as 'Mistress.' "

Pharaun didn't bother to turn. Quenthel walked past him, looking all around, apparently not giving the mage a second thought.

"My apologies, *Mistress*," he said. "I will extend Ma . . . Valas's question to the rest of you. Are you all all right?"

Quenthel, Danifae, and Jeggred variously shrugged, nodded, or ignored him, and Pharaun decided that was good enough.

"Frankly," Pharaun added, "I'm utterly shocked we survived that crash. That was impressive, even by my standards. What an entrance."

The others only sneered at him, except Valas, who shrugged and began to shift though the wreckage.

"Yes, quite an entrance, but I'm getting worried about our exit," Danifae said. "How do you plan to get us back?"

Pharaun opened his mouth to speak then clamped his teeth shut.

He didn't say anything to Danifae but assumed his silence was explanation enough. Pharaun had no idea how they were going to get back to their home plane, home world, and home city without the ship of chaos.

"Lolth," Quenthel said, "will provide."

No one looked at the high priestess or commented on how little faith was evident in her voice.

Danifae scanned around her and up into the air as the phantasms continued to drop from the sky, only to form columns then pitch themselves headlong into one of the endless array of black, puckered pits that looked like bottomless craters scattered around them as far as the eye could see in all directions. None of them were marked in any way that Pharaun recognized, and he hadn't the faintest clue which of the pits would take them to the Demonweb Pits, the sixty-sixth layer of that endless infernal plane.

"What are they?" Danifae asked, looking around at the falling apparitions.

"The dead," Quenthel answered, her voice barely audible through all the unnatural echoes that the air around them threw in and around her words.

"Departed souls from all over the Prime," Pharaun added. "Anyone who served one of the Abyssal gods in life will pass through here then jump into the appropriate portal and they're on their way. Each of these pits leads to a different layer, almost an entirely different world. There are an endless number of them. This plain literally goes on into infinity in all directions."

Jeggred snorted, stood, and shook blood, water, and sand from his fur.

"So?" the draegloth asked.

Pharaun shrugged and said, "Actually I was hoping you could tell us more, Jeggred. After all you were sired by a native of the Abyss, and even a half-blooded tanar'ri should have some sensitivity to—"

"Never been here," the draegloth grunted. "You've mentioned my sire for the last time, too, wizard."

Pharaun was interrupted before he could answer the draegloth's unsubtle threat.

"How do we find the right one?" Danifae asked. "The right portal, I mean."

Jeggred growled once and said, "There is only one entrance for each layer, but there are an infinite number of layers. We could be standing right next to the pit that will take us to the Demonweb Pits, or it could be a thousand miles or more in any direction . . . a million miles even."

"Not likely, actually," said Pharaun, "but thank you for the vote of confidence anyway, honored half-breed—" Danifae put a hand on Jeggred's arm when the draegloth lurched for Pharaun at the sound of that word—"but I was guiding the ship, at least up until the very end there, and I was willing it not simply to take us to the Plain of Infinite Portals but to the one portal that would take us where we wanted to go. Even though we crashed, we must be close by it. The ship was moving us at least in its general direction before things went astray."

"Well it's good to know that you're not entirely inept, Pharaun," Quenthel said, her voice louder and oddly more confident than it had been in a long while, "but I will take it . . . take *us*, from here."

Pharaun watched another ghostly orc step past him. It dropped into a deep back hole in the ground. There was no sound, nothing at all to signal that it had hit bottom or that anything had happened to it at all. It was gone.

"My first instinct," Valas said, "would be to pick out a column of drow and follow them."

"Do you see any drow?" Quenthel asked.

"No," Danifae whispered.

The sound of her voice made Pharaun's skin crawl.

"So what do we do?" the draegloth asked.

"Follow me," the high priestess replied. "I'll know the right pit when I see it."

"How?" Pharaun asked.

Quenthel said, "I've passed through it before."

The Mistress of Arach-Tinilith set out before any of them realized she meant to leave right away. Danifae and Jeggred watched her go then shared a look that made it obvious that neither of them believed the high priestess.

Valas followed her, as did Pharaun, albeit as reluctantly as Danifae and Jeggred.

$$\text{\small ✤ \quad ✤ \quad ✤}$$

Aliisza watched from a safe distance as the dark elves brushed themselves off and regrouped.

Have I underestimated you? she thought, watching Pharaun struggle to his feet.

She whispered, "Probably not," to herself and mulled over her next move.

Kaanyr Vhok's instructions were clear, even if they hadn't included helping the drow get to the Abyss in the first place. She was supposed to watch them, so she would do that at least until she got bored.

Aliisza looked out over the Plain of Infinite Portals, the gateway to the Abyss, and sighed. It had been a very long time since she'd been home, and at first it looked the same. She watched the ship of chaos fall through a red sky she used to fly through as a girl, then crash on sand she once sculpted into monsters from faraway universes—monsters like solars, ki-rin, and humans. It looked the same, but it wasn't—not quite.

Perhaps she had spent too much time with the goddess-obsessed dark elves, but Aliisza was sure there was something different about the Abyss, as if a piece of it were missing.

The feeling didn't make sense, and it confused the alu-fiend and made her uncomfortable, so she pushed it out of her mind.

Aliisza forced herself to smile even though she didn't feel like smiling, as she followed the drow from a safe distance and invisible.

❀　❀　❀

The alu-fiend wasn't the only demonic creature that watched the drow just then. Another looked on from a similar far vantage point, cloaked in invisibility and other defensive spells. The creature seethed with hatred.

Floating in the air high above the Plain of Infinite Portals, the glabrezu touched the ruined stump of its legs and growled, "Soon, drow. Soon . . ."

❀　❀　❀

Halisstra ran a finger along the warm, glowing edge of the Crescent Blade and marveled at its beauty. It was a magnificent weapon, and one she would never feel worthy of. Ryld should have drawn that blade, not her. Ryld would have known what to do with it.

The Melarn priestess felt the absence of her lover in a physically painful way. There was an emptiness in her chest that burned, that ached, that throbbed with uncertainty and longing, and a host of other emotions both alien and familiar.

"If you can't do it," Feliane whispered to her, "you need to tell me now. Now, before we go any farther."

Halisstra looked up at Feliane and her eyesight blurred with tears.

"Tell me," the Eilistraeen prodded.

Halisstra wiped her eyes and said, "I can do it."

The elf priestess stared at her, waiting for Halisstra to go on.

Halisstra looked down at her tear-soaked hand with blurred vision. Her eyes were hot, her throat so tight it was painful. She hadn't done much crying in her life and had certainly never cried over the fate of a male, a soldier . . . anyone.

I've changed, she thought. I am changing.

"He didn't want me to," Halisstra whispered.

"He wanted you to go back to the Underdark," said Uluyara, "if not to Lolth."

Halisstra looked up at the drow priestess. Uluyara stood in the doorway, framed by the blinding twilight behind her. She was dressed for battle, covered in tokens made of feathers, sticks, and shards of bone. Halisstra nodded, and Uluyara stepped in.

The drow priestess crossed to the bed that Halisstra had once shared with Ryld Argith and kneeled. She took Halisstra's chin in one rough-fingered hand, holding her gently and forcing their eyes to meet.

"If they killed him," Uluyara said, "it's but another reason to do what you've been doing, another reason to leave them behind at least and defeat them forever if possible."

"By killing Lolth?" asked Halisstra.

"Yes," answered Feliane, who still stood leaning against the weed-covered wall, also dressed for battle and for a long journey.

"I need you to tell me something," Halisstra asked, her eyes darting back and forth between the two women. "I need you to tell me that this is possible, I mean even remotely possible."

Uluyara smiled and shrugged, but Feliane said, "It's possible."

Both Halisstra and Uluyara looked over at her.

"Anything is possible," Feliane explained, "with the right tools and with a goddess on your side."

"Eilistraee can't go where we're going," Halisstra said, "not to the Demonweb Pits."

"No, she can't," Uluyara agreed. "That's why she's sending us."

"If we die there," Halisstra asked Uluyara, who dropped her hand from the priestess's chin, "what becomes of us?"

"We go to Eilistraee," Uluyara replied.

Halisstra could hear the certainty in the drow's reply and see it in her eyes.

"I don't know that for sure," Halisstra said.

"So," said Feliane, "what do you know for sure?"

Halisstra looked at her and the elf returned the gaze with almost perfect stillness.

"I know . . ." Halisstra began even as she was thinking it through. "I know that Lolth abandoned me and was a cruel mistress who let our city, our way of life fall into ruin, perhaps simply to satisfy some whim. I know that her temple on the sixty-sixth layer is sealed and there are no departed souls there. I know that eternity is closed off to me, thanks to her."

"What has changed?" asked Feliane.

Halisstra looked at Uluyara when she said, "Eilistraee."

"Eilistraee hasn't changed," Uluyara whispered.

"No," Halisstra agreed, "I have."

Uluyara smiled, and so did Halisstra, then the Melarn priestess began to cry.

"I miss him," she said through a sob.

Uluyara put a hand on Halisstra's neck and drew her closer until their foreheads touched.

"Would you have been able to miss him," asked Uluyara, "if you were still Halisstra Melarn, First Daughter of House Melarn of Ched Nasad, Priestess of Lolth? Would that ever have entered into your mind?"

"No," Halisstra replied without hesitation.

"Then Eilistraee has touched you," said Uluyara. "Eilistraee has blessed you."

Halisstra looked up at Feliane and asked, "Do you believe that too?"

Feliane looked at her for the span of a few heartbeats then said, "I do. You wield the Crescent Blade, if for no other reason . . . but there are other reasons. Yes, I think Eilistraee has blessed you, indeed, and blessed us all with your presence."

Halisstra nodded then looked to Uluyara. The other drow female nodded and hugged her. The embrace was a quick one, sisterly, warm, and reassuring.

"Well," Halisstra said when the embrace ended, "I think we should begin. There's a long road ahead for us and the most frightening opponent of all at the end of it: a goddess on her home plane."

Uluyara stood, helping Halisstra up with her. Halisstra dressed for travel and for fighting as the other two had, but when she was done she felt heavy and stiff.

Gromph's world had been reduced to a series of circles.

The antimagic field surrounded him in a circle of null space that would dissipate any spell that tried to pierce it and suppress any magical effect within it. The pain in his leg circled all the way around, where the interrupted regenerative effect of the ring had only partially reattached it, leaving a ragged, seeping wound all the way around the middle of his thigh. Past the outer edge of the antimagic field a tiny circle—a sphere really—of condensed magical fire orbited slowly around and around. It was Dyrr's next explosive blast of fire, held in check, circling, waiting for the field to drop. The lichdrow was circling him too, and like his fireball, waiting.

Gromph sat on the cool rock floor of the ruined Bazaar trying not to actually writhe in agony, concentrating on his breathing, and making himself think.

"How long can it last, Gromph?" the lichdrow taunted from well outside the antimagic field. "Not forever, I know. Not as long as my own would. Am I that frightening to you that you have to hide so, even in plain sight?"

Gromph didn't bother answering. He wasn't afraid of the lichdrow. In fact, he was more concerned with Nimor Imphraezl. The winged assassin had disappeared into the shadows, back into his natural element. He could be anywhere. Dyrr, a being literally held together by magic, would no more cross the threshold of the antimagic field than he would throw himself headlong into the Clawrift. Nimor, on the other hand, had likely lost most if not all of his magic in the disjunction anyway and needed no spell to cut with his claws.

The Weave was blocked by the field, but that was all. Gromph, weak and in pain from loss of blood and the morbid wound in his leg, was all but helpless against anything but spells. Nimor could walk right up—anyone could walk right up—and kill the Archmage of Menzoberranzan with a dagger across the throat.

At least, Gromph thought, I don't have to listen to Prath remind me of that.

The field blocked the telepathic link he'd established with the other Baenre mages. Gromph was entirely on his own, though he was sure Nauzhror and the others were still watching.

"Please tell me you aren't going to just sit there and die," Dyrr said. "I've come to expect so much more from you."

"Have you?" Gromph answered, every word coming with a painful effort. "What have you . . . come to expect . . . from Nimor?"

"Why, Archmage," the lich replied, "whatever do you mean?"

"Where is he?" Gromph said. "Where has your half-dragon

gone? He could kill me easily enough, and we both know that. Has he—" Gromph winced through a wave of pain—"abandoned you?"

"I never trusted Nimor Imphraezl," said the lich. "What's your excuse?"

Gromph puzzled over that last comment.

Still, some of what the lich said rang painfully true. If he didn't drop the antimagic field, the ring would never finish reattaching his leg. If he sat there he would succumb to shock, loss of blood, even infection soon enough. The only thing keeping Dyrr from killing him was killing him.

Gromph did nothing to alert Dyrr to his intentions. He didn't draw in any dramatic, shuddering breath. He didn't move his trembling, pain-ravaged body. He didn't even look at the lich or at the bead of compressed fire waiting for its chance to immolate him. Everything that was happening was occurring inside his mind.

Gromph mentally arranged spells, bringing the opening stanzas to mind, willing his fingers in advance to form the gestures. He kept one hand on his staff, knowing that its magic wasn't gone but was simply suppressed, waiting the same way Dyrr's fireball—and Dyrr himself—was waiting.

He dropped the antimagic field, and in that same instant the globe burst back around him and the spell tripped rapidly past his lips. The bead of fire dropped out of its lazy orbit and shot at him as fast as a bolt from a crossbow, but Gromph's spell was a split second faster. The spell enabled him to push the bead of fire away with a wave of invisible force. Using the power of his mind, Gromph seized control of the nascent fireball and sent it hurtling back at the lichdrow.

Dyrr backed quickly away from it then turned and flew fast. Gromph kept the fireball racing toward the lich, gaining on him.

The pain in his leg began to fade and was replaced once more by pulses of nettling as it drew itself together. Concentrating on chasing the fleeing lich with his own fireball, Gromph didn't see the blood that still surrounded him—his own blood—being soaked up by the skin of his leg. As it drew into his tissue, the blood itself warmed, and one by one the cells came back to life.

The bead of fire was within a handspan of the fleeing lich when Nimor stabbed Gromph in the back.

The archmage might have thought that he'd be accustomed to the odd blast of mind-ravaging agony by then, but the pain hit him full force. He could feel every fraction of an inch of the blade's path through his skin, into and through the muscles of his back. He could feel the cold steel pierce his heart.

Gromph gasped and lost control of the spell that held the fireball. He closed his eyes against the flare of it exploding—too far from Gromph to burn him but too far from the lich to damage him either.

That wasn't the only fire. The flickering shield of arcane flames that had surrounded him before he cast the antimagic field had returned to him as had the globe. Fire poured over the wound in Gromph's back even though it hadn't protected him from the dagger. Fire washed over Nimor, who released the knife and staggered back, waving off the flames that once again seared his shadow-black face.

The dagger was still in him, still in his heart, and Gromph lurched forward to sprawl on his stomach on the unforgiving floor of the Bazaar. The ring fought second by second to keep his heart intact, to keep it beating, to keep his blood flowing, but it did nothing for the pain. The archmage's vision blurred, and when he tried to reach behind him to pull the dagger out of his back he could only twitch his arm uselessly at his side.

The archmage was vaguely aware of heat, light, and the sound of crackling, a dull roar . . . fire.

He blinked. His vision cleared enough to see a row of burning merchant's stalls and a thick column of smoke rising into the still, warming air. Hovering in stark, spindly silhouette against the blinding orange flames was the figure of the lichdrow Dyrr.

Gromph coughed and felt something warm and thick trickle from his lips. The dagger twitched in his back, and Gromph was afraid that it was Nimor, turning the blade, driving it deeper, or withdrawing it only to plunge it home again.

No, Nauzhror said into Gromph's confused, slowing mind. *It's the ring. Don't move, Archmage. Try not to move for a few seconds more.*

Gromph looked up at the hovering lich and saw another black silhouette join him to hover far above the burning stalls. The second silhouette had huge, semi-transparent wings traced with veins.

The dagger twitched again, and Gromph coughed more blood as it came free of his heart, only to knick his lung.

A few more seconds, Master, Nauzhror said. *Patience.*

Gromph let that last word play in his mind. He had no choice but to be patient. To him, it felt as if the pain were actually pushing him down, driving him into the rock beneath him.

The two black figures started to grow against the roiling backdrop of uncontrolled fire. They were coming for him. They meant to end it.

The dagger slipped out of Gromph's back to clatter on the stone floor beside him. He shuddered through a last spasm of pain and clenched his chest when his heart skipped a beat then started up again, strong and regular. The archmage began to cast a spell.

Gromph rolled into a seated position as he cast, turning to face his enemies with fire reflected in his stolen eyes. Nimor was closer, coming at him with his shadow dragon's claws, so Gromph directed the spell at him. The archmage sent a rolling wave of blinding fire at the assassin, but Nimor stepped quickly to one side and was gone, sinking into the shadows like a rock slipping under the surface of Donigarten Lake.

The conjured fire flared past the spot where the assassin had been standing, burning nothing but empty air.

Gromph cringed.

It's all right, Archmage, Nauzhror said.

No it's not, Gromph shot back at him. *I'm using too much fire against Nimor.*

It's true— Prath began but stopped so abruptly Gromph was sure it was Nauzhror who silenced him—lucky for Prath.

The lichdrow stopped his advance and waved his hands in front of him. Gromph tightened his grip on his staff, sighing as the last of the grievous wounds were closed forever by the magic of the ring.

A faint mist coalesced in the air in front of Dyrr, adding to itself one mote at a time until a wide, flat cloud of churning mist rolled out away from the lich and toward Gromph.

The archmage got to his feet and uttered the single triggering command that activated another of his staff's array of powers. Gromph couldn't see it, but thanks to the magic of the staff he was keenly aware of the confines of the invisible wall he'd conjured in front of him.

The cloud of—Gromph assumed—poisonous gas that Dyrr had conjured mixed with the smoke from the burning stalls, slowing it but not stopping it. Gromph set the wall of magical force between himself and the cloud, and in a moment the mist began to spread along the flat surface of the wall, well away from the archmage.

Dyrr, obviously not surprised by Gromph's simple solution to the killing cloud, arced high into the air and flew over the wall of force. The lich drew a wand from the folds of his *piwafwi* and stared at Gromph with a face devoid of emotion.

Gromph began to cast, judging the time necessary by the lich's flying speed. Even when Dyrr accelerated, Gromph had the opportunity to finish the spell and step through the doorway he opened in the air next to him. Like passing through an ordinary door, Gromph stepped out the other side having traveled a dozen yards across the burning Bazaar. He watched the lich swoop down, swing his wand through the spot where Gromph had been standing, then come to rest on the ground growling in frustration.

Gromph dropped the wall of force and smiled.

The cloud of poisonous gas—Dyrr's own spell—burst through when the wall fell, and the lich only had time to look up before the mist engulfed him and he disappeared inside its black-and-green expanse.

Gromph took a deep breath and glanced down when the fire shield finally faded from him. The spell he cast next was one of his most difficult. He worked it carefully and reveled as its effects washed through him. All at once he got the distinct impression that someone was behind him, and he knew that the spell was warning him. No one was behind him yet, but someone would be.

Gromph spun in place then stepped back when Nimor appeared from the shadows, already bringing one black-taloned hand down at the archmage's face. The tips of the claws passed within a finger's breadth of the archmage's nose. Nimor let the surprise show in his eyes, and Gromph had to admit to himself at least that he was just as surprised.

The archmage skipped back several steps, and so did the assassin. Nimor looked at Gromph with narrowed eyes that glowed in the smoky shadows of the burning Bazaar. Gromph had a clear vision of Nimor stepping in then quickly to the left and slashing at his side—then Nimor did just that. Gromph managed to step away again, and again the assassin was taken aback by the archmage's newfound reflexes. What Nimor didn't know was that it wasn't reflexes but foresight.

Gromph reached into a pouch—an extradimensional space that held much more than it appeared capable of from the outside—and drew a weapon. The duergar's battle-axe was heavy, and the weight and heft of it was unfamiliar to Gromph. The archmage had been schooled in the use of a number of weapons, but the battle-axe was hardly his cup of tea. It was unwieldy and unsubtle, almost more a tool than a weapon. However, there was more to that particular axe than its blade and a handle.

He knew that Nimor was going to step back and give himself a chance to examine Gromph's weapon. The archmage also expected that Nimor would move a few steps to one side in order to turn Gromph around and place himself between the half-dragon and the cloud that still concealed the lichdrow. Gromph gave him the chance he wanted to study the axe but didn't oblige him with the superior position.

Archmage, Nauzhror said, *are you certain?*

Gromph assumed that the other mage was referring to the battle-axe, and the obvious fact that Gromph meant to actually fight the assassin with physical weapons.

Gromph sent back the answer, *I know what I'm doing*, at precisely the same moment that Nauzhror repeated, *Archmage, are you certain?*

Gromph realized he hadn't heard Nauzhror the first time. It was the spell, showing him the future.

I see, Nauzhror replied and Gromph could feel that the other Baenre mage understood that Gromph had armed himself with perhaps the most potent weapon imaginable: the ability to perfectly anticipate every move of your opponent.

The voice came to his head for real: *I see.*

Gromph knew that Nimor was going to rush him in an attempt to push him back toward the cloud of poison gas, so the archmage stepped quickly to the side and circled. Nimor took one step then stopped, eyeing Gromph.

The lich burst out of the cloud, trailing tendrils of toxic mist as he rose into the air. He turned and faced the archmage.

"Go ahead," said the lichdrow with a leering, evil smile, "try to fight him with your stolen axe. I'll enjoy watching Nimor shred you."

The half-dragon assassin smiled at that, and Gromph saw him coming in with one wild slash after another, a flurry of claws and kicks and head butts. Gromph had no idea what to do.

In the instant that Nimor started to run toward him, Gromph realized that knowing what your opponent intended to do might not be enough.

TWENTY-THREE

How could there be any sense to a world that existed in a universe made of chaos? In a place where the only rule was that there were no rules?

When they were there last, not very long ago, they walked enormous strands of spiderweb and saw nothing alive until they were beset upon by a horde of feral demons at the gates to a temple sealed by the face of Lolth herself. There, a god tried to break through but couldn't.

Though they had been away from the Demonweb Pits for only a short time, much had changed.

The smooth expanse of the gigantic webs was pitted and worn. Patches of what looked like rust went on for acres at a time. In spots they had to climb or levitate up and down cliffs of crumbling webbing and traverse craters big enough to hold all of Menzoberranzan in their uneven bowls.

All around them was the stench of decay, so intense at times Pharaun Mizzrym thought he would suffocate.

The wizard had been walking for hours in uncharacteristic silence. None of the drow or the draegloth commented aloud on the state of the Demonweb Pits. It was too difficult to voice the palpable sense of despair the ruined place imbued in them all. They stopped occasionally to rest, and minutes would go by where they didn't even look at each other.

Constantly on their guard for the plane's demonic inhabitants, at first they were all on a knife's edge, but as the hours dragged on and they saw nothing alive, let alone threatening, they soon began to relax. That was when the despair deepened even further.

They walked on and on and finally came to Lolth's temple. The once imposing, otherworldly structure stood in ruin, infected by the same decay as the universe-spanning web. The obsidian stone had turned brown and was crumbled away in spots. Huge columns of smoke rose from the interior. Many of the great buttresses stood like shattered stumps, amputated by some inconceivable power. The surrounding plazas were difficult to traverse, littered with boulders of carved stone and iron rusted and twisted out of shape. Bones lay everywhere—the bones of millions stacked in great piles or scattered as if by the cruel winds alone. The petrified spider-things they had marveled at before were gone, leaving holes in the floor of the plaza and along the buttresses as if they'd pulled up their feet from the stone and marched away.

The party traced the same path they had taken when in astral form and came once again to the entrance to the temple. The great stone face was itself shattered, revealing glimpses of the visage of Lolth but only in tiny, enigmatic fragments.

The doors swung wide.

"It was the gods," Valas whispered, his voice echoing in a million tiny pings across the ruined plaza.

Vhaeraun, who had come to kill Lolth because of their own rash decision to lead one of his priests there, had been confronted by Selvetarm—Lolth's protector—at the temple gates. Their duel was a sight that would be burned into Pharaun's memory if he lived to be ten thousand years old, and the contest had caused much damage, but. . . .

"Not this," the Master of Sorcere said, his own voice echoing, though in not quite the same way. "This is different. Older."

"Older?" the draegloth asked, his eyes darting from rock to rock.

"He's right," said Danifae, who was crouching, holding the skull of something that might have been half drow, half bat. "These bones are dried and bleached, almost petrified. The stone itself is crumbling to dust. The webs are rotten and brittle."

"This place was razed a century ago or more," Pharaun said.

"That's not possible," Valas argued, staring up at the open doors. "We were just here—*right* here, and the doors were sealed, and . . ."

The others didn't expect him to finish.

"Lolth has left this place," Quenthel said, her voice so quiet it barely managed to elicit an echo at all.

"She has left the Demonweb Pits?" Danifae asked. "How could that be?"

"She has left the Abyss," the Mistress of Arach-Tinilith said. "Can't you feel it?"

Danifae shook her head, but her eyes answered in the affirmative. The two females shared a long, knowing look that raised the hair on the back of Pharaun's neck. He sensed similar reactions from Jeggred and Valas.

"That's it then," said the Bregan D'aerthe scout. "We have come here to find the goddess but instead we have found nothing. Our mission is at an end."

Quenthel turned to glare at the scout, who returned it with a steady, even gaze. The vipers that made up the high priestess's scourge writhed and spat, but Valas paid them no mind.

"She isn't here," Quenthel said, "but that doesn't mean she isn't . . . somewhere."

The scout took a deep breath and let it out slowly, looking all around at the ruined temple.

"So where is she?" he asked. "How much farther do we go? Do we search the limitless multiverse for her, plane by plane, universe by universe? She's a creature of the Demonweb Pits, and here we stand on the sixty-sixth layer of the gods-cursed Abyss and she's gone. If you don't know where she's gone to—and she could be anywhere—and she won't tell you where she is, maybe we all have to accept the fact that she doesn't want to be found."

It was the most Pharaun had ever heard Valas say all at once, and the words made his heart sink.

"He's right," said the Master of Sorcere.

To his surprise, Quenthel nodded. Danifae's eyes widened, and Jeggred growled low in his throat. The draegloth moved slowly, in that fluid, stalking way of his, and went to stand next to the former battle-captive.

"This is sacrilege," Danifae whispered. "Heresy of the worst sort."

Quenthel turned to look at the other priestess and silently raised an eyebrow.

"You presume to allow some—" Danifae turned to briefly glare at Valas— "*male* to speak for Lolth? Does he decide the goddess's intentions now?"

"Do you?" Pharaun couldn't help but ask.

Surprisingly, Danifae smiled when she said, "Perhaps I do.

Certainly I have more claim to that right than Master Hune. Capable a scout as he is, this is the business of priestesses now."

Quenthel stood a little straighter, though her shoulders still hunched. Pharaun marveled at how old she looked. The high priestess had aged decades in the past tenday, and exhaustion was plain in her heavy-lidded eyes and blunt temper.

Pharaun couldn't look at her, so he looked down at the floor of the plaza. He scuffed his boot through brown-powdered stone.

"I was wrong," the Master of Sorcere said. He could feel the others looking at him, could sense their surprise, but he didn't look up. "This didn't happen a century ago. This place was destroyed . . . no, a battle was fought here, and it was fought a millennium past at least. At least."

"How can you say that, wizard?" asked the draegloth. "You were just here. Weren't you? Isn't this the same place Tzirik brought you?"

Pharaun nodded and said, "It is indeed, Jeggred, but the fact remains that what we see all around us is an ancient ruin, the corpse of a battlefield that's lain cold for a thousand years or more."

"We were only just here," said Valas.

"We aren't in the Underdark anymore, Master Hune," said Pharaun. "Time might move very differently here, in fits and starts like distance in the Shadow Deep. This could all be more illusion than real, the whim of Lolth or some other godly power. It could be that we simply see a ruin where there is nothing, see a ruin where there is in fact an intact temple, or everything we see is real and made a millennium old by a power so vast that it can manipulate time and matter and the æther itself."

"The Spider Queen isn't here," Valas added.

"If the priestesses say that she is not here," Pharaun replied, "then I'm content to believe that's true."

The Master of Sorcere looked up at the enormous open doorway, big enough for House Baenre to pass through it intact. The others followed his gaze.

"These doors were sealed shut before," Pharaun said, "but now they're open. Why?"

"Because Lolth wants us to step through them," Danifae said, her voice carrying a certainty that surprised Pharaun. "Who else could have opened them?"

Pharaun shrugged and looked at Quenthel, who was nodding slowly.

"We go on," the high priestess said.

Without a glance at the others, Quenthel walked toward the mammoth doorway. One by one the others followed: Danifae, then Jeggred, then Pharaun, and Valas at the rear. Each stepped more reluctantly than the last.

※　　※　　※

On the planes of chaos there were so many names for it, Aliisza didn't remember them all: temporal flux zones, slipped time layers, millennia sinks. . . . It had been a very long time since she'd seen one, and it took her almost as long to realize what was happening.

The sixty-sixth layer of the Abyss had been abandoned. The glue that held the planes together was the gods themselves, and in the planes of chaos, just as in the planes of law, when all the gods left a particular place, entropy progressed in fits and starts, and even chaos itself spiraled out of control.

In the case of the sixty-sixth layer, there was the rest of the Abyss to hold it together and to provide echoes of its past that were strong enough to keep its physical form—in that there still was a sixty-sixth layer. Time was moving forward faster at times, then slower, then it might reverse itself. It was impossible to pin down, even for a tanar'ri like Aliisza. Places like that were better left alone, better avoided, better forgotten.

She watched Pharaun and his companions walk through the massive temple gates with a heavy heart. She didn't know exactly what they would find in there, but she was sure that whatever it was it would be disappointing for them. They had traveled to the sixty-sixth layer to find Lolth, but Lolth wasn't there. It was a guess on her part, but an educated one: the plane had been abandoned for longer than anyone imagined—longer than Lolth had been silent.

"There's a lot you never told them," Aliisza whispered to the Spider Queen.

If the goddess could hear her—and Aliisza had no reason to believe she could—Lolth didn't answer.

The alu-fiend absently scratched a doodle in the brown dust on the underside of the massive web strand onto which she clung: a bit of graffiti no eyes would ever see. Her mind was racing; she had a lot to think about.

Aliisza had abandoned Pharaun and the others, leaving them to crash into the Plain of Infinite Portals simply on a whim. It pleased her that Pharaun survived, but she didn't give the others a second thought. Still, Aliisza had made her choice, and it was an obvious one. She chose Kaanyr Vhok.

Though she knew she would go back to him, she also knew that she had helped Pharaun and his expedition along a bit more effectively than Vhok would have approved of. He might not have asked her to stop them, but he certainly hadn't asked her to help them. Aliisza knew the cambion well enough, though, to know that the more she came back with, the more forgiving he would be.

Pharaun and the other drow disappeared into the abandoned ruin, and Aliisza closed her eyes.

She was a tanar'ri and as such could move about the planes

with a bit more ease than most. With a thought she was back in the Astral, floating free in the endless æther.

"You left the Abyss," Aliisza whispered to herself, though she addressed Lolth, "before you fell silent, so . . ."

She didn't bother finishing the thought, only concentrated on a name: Lolth.

She closed her eyes again and let the name roll over and over again in her mind, and after a time, her body began to move. Any god's name has power, if you know how to use it.

When she opened her eyes she was surrounded by ghosts.

Translucent gray shades floated all around her, all of them with similar features: the pointed ears, almond-shaped eyes, and thin, aristocratic faces of the dark elves. There were a lot of them—a war's worth—and they were all headed across the Astral Plane toward the same destination.

Aliisza drifted in front of one of them, a strong-looking male dressed for battle, regal in his armor and helm.

"Can you hear me?" she asked the spirit. "Can you see me?"

The dead drow looked right at her and lifted an eyebrow. He stood stock still, but his body continued to drift through the endless expanse, unerringly falling sideways toward its final destination.

"My name is Aliisza," she said. "Do you know where you are?"

Yes, the drow answered directly into her mind. His mouth was open, but his lips didn't move. *I can feel it. I'm dead. I died. I was killed.*

"What is your name?"

I was Vilto'sat Shobalar, the soldier answered, *but now I am nothing. My body rots away, my House forgets me, and I pass on. Are you here to torment me?*

"I'm sorry?" the alu-fiend asked, confused by the drow spirit's sudden change of subject.

You're a demon, he said. *Are you here to torment me? For my failure on the battlefield or simply to satisfy your cruel nature?*

Aliisza's hackles rose, and she couldn't help but sneer at the dead drow. He had obviously mistaken her for a different sort of tanar'ri altogether, and she didn't find it flattering in the least.

"If I was here to torment you," she said, "you'd know it, mushroom farm."

Vilto'sat Shobalar turned away from her with a look of haughty contempt that was the only thing, apparently, dark elves took to the grave.

Aliisza moved on along the line of dead drow, and as she progressed in the direction of their travel, moving faster than the wandering souls, the density of the ghosts increased, as if they had been stacking up, one after another, for a long time. Finally, her curiosity getting the better of her, she stopped another drow spirit: a female dressed in finery that made the alu-fiend momentarily jealous.

"Lady," she said, sketching an overwrought bow that the dead dark elf seemed to find insulting, "may I speak with you briefly as you complete your journey?"

There's nothing you can do to torment me, demon, the shade said into Aliisza's mind, *so move on and let me be dead in peace.*

Aliisza hissed and almost reached out to grab the female by her throat then realized that her hands would pass through the priestess. The dead female would have no physical form again until she arrived at her final destination. The Astral Plane was only a way to get from one universe to another. There, the dead drow were incorporeal ghosts.

"I'm not here to torment you, bitch," Aliisza said, "but I will if you don't answer a question or two."

Lolth has turned her back on us, the priestess replied. *What worse could you do?*

"I could leave you in the Astral forever," Aliisza replied—a hollow threat, but the ghost didn't need to know that.

What do you want? the drow replied.

"Who are you," she asked, "and how long have you been here, awaiting Lolth's grace?"

I am Greyanna Mizzrym, the ghost replied—and Aliisza thought something about the name was oddly familiar. *I have no idea how long I've been here, but I can feel myself moving. That only just started. Is Lolth ready to take us in? Has she sent you?*

"Can you feel her?" Aliisza asked, ignoring he dark elf's questions. "Does she call you?"

The priestess looked away, as if listening for something, then she shook her head.

I'm moving toward something, Greyanna said. *I can feel it, but I do not hear Lolth.*

Aliisza turned to look in the direction the line of drow souls were moving. At the end of the very long line was a whirlpool of red and black—a gateway to the outer planes that was drawing the souls in.

"That's not the Abyss," Aliisza said.

It's home, whispered the bodiless soul of Greyanna Mizzrym. *I can feel it. It is. It's the Demonweb Pits.*

Aliisza's heart raced.

"The Demonweb Pits," the alu-fiend repeated, "but not the Abyss."

Aliisza stopped herself and hung in the gray expanse off to one side of the procession of dead drow.

"Well," Aliisza whispered to an unhearing Lolth, "moving up in the world, aren't we?"

The alu-fiend closed her eyes and concentrated on Kaanyr Vhok. She let her consciousness travel through the Astral and back to the cold, hard Underdark. There she found her lover's mind and dropped a message into it.

Something is happening with the Demonweb Pits, she sent. *It's a plane unto itself now, and the gates are open. Lolth welcomes home the dead. She lives.*

That was all she could say, and she hoped it would be warning enough. Aliisza could have shifted back to the Underdark in an instant and been by her lover's side, but she didn't. She wanted to stay where she was, though she didn't know why.

🕷   🕷   🕷

Nimor had given up trying to claw Gromph. Instead, he started to work on forcing the archmage to attack him, but the drow wouldn't oblige. The feeling Nimor had that Gromph somehow knew what he was thinking—maybe before he even thought it—grew stronger and stronger and made Nimor start to second-guess himself. It was no way to fight.

Nimor stepped back and so did Gromph. The assassin could see Dyrr slowly circling them both from a safe—some would say cowardly—distance. The assassin was about to speak when a familiar nettling buzzed in his skull.

Aliisza is in the Demonweb Pits, the voice of Kaanyr Vhok sounded in his head. *Something is happening, and it will be bad for us all. I'm not waiting to find out how bad.*

For the first time in a very, very long time, Nimor's blood ran cold.

Gromph twitched, almost gasped, and Nimor couldn't help but look at him. Their eyes locked, and an instant of understanding passed between them. Nimor stepped back, and Gromph nodded. The archmage still kept the ghostly battle-axe in front of him but didn't advance. He breathed heavily, sweat running down the sides of his face and matting his snow-white hair to his forehead.

Again, Nimor was about to speak, and again he was interrupted.

"What are you doing?" the lichdrow demanded. "Kill him!"

Nimor let a long, steady breath hiss out through clenched teeth. It was bad enough that a key component of his alliance was abandoning the cause, worse still that Lolth was somehow, for some reason he might never understand, choosing that moment to finally return—or do something that scared Kaanyr Vhok, anyway, and the cambion wasn't the type to scare easily. All that, an opponent he should have been able to dispatch with nary a thought but who was able to outthink and outfight him at every turn, and the damned lich was barking orders at him.

Dyrr began shouting again, but Nimor didn't understand what he was saying.

"I can't—" the Anointed Blade started to say then stopped when he realized that the lich was casting a spell.

Gromph heard him too. With one hand still holding the axe in front of him, the archmage tapped his staff on the pockmarked floor of the smoldering Bazaar and was instantly enveloped in a globe of shimmering energy. No sooner did the globe appear than Dyrr finished his muttering, and the sound of the lich's voice was replaced by a low, echoing buzz.

Nimor, eyes still locked on Gromph's, blinked. The archmage glanced over at the lich, and one side of his mouth curled up into the beginning of a smile. Nimor had to look, and he knew that Gromph had no intention of attacking him anyway.

The buzzing sound grew louder, escalating to an almost deafening roar. Nimor saw what looked like a cloud of black smoke winding through the air at him, and it was a few seconds before he realized it wasn't smoke. The cloud wasn't a cloud at all, but a swarm of tiny insects—perhaps tens, even hundreds of millions of them.

The swarm descended over Gromph, but they didn't penetrate

the globe that surrounded the archmage. Nimor had to assume they were being directed by Dyrr, so when the insects turned on him, he took it personally.

Before the first of them could land on him, sting him, bite him, or do whatever they were meant to do to him, Nimor stepped into the Shadow Fringe. The act was second nature to him. He was there in the Bazaar, then he wasn't. The swarm became a shadow, the Bazaar a dull world, barely corporeal, drenched in blackness.

Nimor looked at his claws. His mind was strangely blank, his mood impossibly serene.

"Is that it?" he said aloud into the unhearing shadows. "Have I lost?"

He closed his eyes and thought of the lich . . . and stepped back into the solid world right behind him.

Nimor grabbed the spindly undead mage from behind and beat his wings hard to pull him up and away from the floor of the Bazaar. The lich stiffened and drew in a breath—perhaps to cast a spell—but was wise enough to stop when Nimor pressed one razor-sharp talon into the lich's desiccated throat.

"You might not bleed, lich," Nimor whispered into the lichdrow's ear, "but if your head comes away from your neck . . ."

"What are you doing?" Dyrr asked, his voice a thin, reedy hiss. "You could kill him. Our moment is at hand, and you turn on me? *Me?*"

"You?" Nimor sneered. "Yes, you. I should kill you now, but then you're already dead, aren't you, lich? All you did was waste my time, and now the Spider Queen is rattling in her cage, and our time together is spent."

"What?" Dyrr asked, honestly confused. "What are you saying?"

"Not that you deserve to know it before I let Gromph Baenre kill you," Nimor replied, "but it's over."

"No!" the lich shouted.

Nimor grunted when something pushed hard against his chest His hand came away from the lich's throat, and he was forced backward, driven through the air by some unfathomable force. Despite any attempt to fly, Nimor was repulsed.

The assassin spared a glance down at Gromph, who had put away his stolen duergar battle-axe and was looking up at them, laughing.

Nimor laughed too. Why not?

"We failed, lich," Nimor called to Dyrr, "but at least for me there will be another chance."

"*We* failed?" the lich wailed. "We? No, you wretched son of a wyrm, *you* failed. You'll go back to the Shadow with your dragon's tail between your legs, repeating your feeble excuses to yourself over and over again. Blame me if you wish, Nimor, but I'm still here. Live or die, I'll still be here, in Menzoberranzan, fighting."

"Perhaps," Nimor said, the first waves of a profound exhaustion beginning to soften his tired muscles, "but not for long."

The lich screamed his name, but Nimor didn't hear the first echo before he drifted into the Shadow Fringe and was gone from Menzoberranzan forever.

Inside the temple walls was a city twenty times the size of Menzoberranzan. Like the walls and the surrounding plazas, the city was a battered, war-ravaged ruin that looked to Pharaun as if it had been abandoned for a thousand years or more.

The architecture throughout mimicked all manner of dark elven dwellings, from the calcified webs of Ched Nasad to the hollowed-out stalagmites of Menzoberranzan. The only thing the structures had in common was that they were all at least partially collapsed and they were devoid of life.

Valas appeared behind the mage as he always did, as if by magic. Pharaun didn't bother trying to pretend the scout's sudden appearance hadn't startled him. The time for keeping up appearances and jockeying for position in the party had come and gone.

Valas nodded once to the Master of Sorcere and said, "There's more metal the deeper in we go."

Pharaun found himself shaking his head, unsure at first what the scout was trying to tell him. He looked around more closely and saw that Valas was right. Though they had seen jagged, twisted chunks of rusted iron and scorched steel in the plaza outside, the deeper into the temple they walked, the more they all had to step around larger and larger pieces.

Valas stopped and reached out to touch a gently curving wall of steel three times the scout's height.

"It looks like it was ripped off of a larger piece," the scout said. "I've never seen this much steel."

Pharaun nodded, examining the relic from a distance.

"It looks like a piece of a giant's suit of armor," the wizard commented, "a giant bigger than any you might find on the World Above, but this is the Abyss, Valas. There could be such a creature here."

"Or a god," the scout replied.

"Selvetarm was that big," Danifae said. Both the males turned to look at her, surprised that she'd stopped to join the conversation. The former battle-captive had been walking in silence with the draegloth never far from her side, apparently unfazed by her surroundings. "So was Vhaeraun."

Valas nodded and said, "There are other pieces, though, and there are things that don't look like armor."

"The mechanical bits," Pharaun interjected. "I've noticed those too."

"Mechanical bits?" the young priestess asked.

Pharaun continued walking as he said, "The odd moving part. I've seen hinges and things that seem to act almost like a joint, like a shoulder or knee joint in a drow's body but with wires or other contraptions in place of muscles."

"Now that you mention it," Valas said, "some of them did look like legs or arms."

"Who cares?" the draegloth grumbled. "Are you two really wasting your time examining the garbage? Do you have no understanding of what's happened here?"

"I think we have at least a rudimentary understanding of what's gone on here, Jeggred, yes," Pharaun said. "By 'examining the garbage,' as you so eloquently put it, we might gain some understanding beyond the point where it can still be described as rudimentary. Alas, that's not a state of mind with which you tend to be familiar with yourself, but those of us with higher—"

The air was forced out of Pharaun's lungs in a single painful grunt. The draegloth was on top of him, smashing him into a crumbling pile of bricks that had once been part of a soaring cathedral. The wizard brought to mind a spell that didn't require speech but stopped himself from casting it when Danifae's voice echoed across the temple grounds.

"Jeggred," she commanded, "leave it."

It was a command someone might give a pet rat distracted by a cave beetle. As the draegloth withdrew and Pharaun struggled to his feet, he wondered which was a greater insult, Jeggred smashing him to the ground or Danifae's rude remark. The Master of Sorcere brushed off his *piwafwi*, did his best with the wild mop his hair had become, and cleared his throat.

"Ah, Jeggred, my boy," the wizard said, letting the sarcasm drip freely, "was it something I said?"

"Next time you talk to me like that, mage," he draegloth growled, "your heart will follow Ryld Argith's through my bowels."

Pharaun tried not to laugh and said, "Charming as always."

"Come, Jeggred," Danifae said, waving the draegloth into step behind her.

Pharaun finished assembling himself, and as he was about to

move on he stopped and turned, having caught someone looking at him from the corner of his eye. Quenthel Baenre stood partially blocked by another huge, jagged hunk of steel. The look the wizard saw on her face was ice cold, and if they had been back in Menzoberranzan it would surely have presaged Danifae's death.

🕷 🕷 🕷

After the echoes from Dyrr's last, barely-coherent shout finally died away, came a moment of almost complete silence. The lich hung in the still air, trembling with rage. Gromph took a moment to survey the ruined Bazaar.

The fires had burned themselves out, and the smoke slowly dissipated. Dozens of stalls, tents, and carts were ruined—burned or shattered. Great cracks and pits had been dug into the stone floor, which was scorched in large swaths of dusty black.

A few whispered words drifted across the otherwise quiet space, and Gromph saw a few inquisitive—and unwise—drow beginning to wander into the edges of the ruined marketplace. They had sensed that the duel had come to an end, but Gromph knew how wrong they were. Something, and it wasn't only Gromph's ability to outthink him, had scared Nimor off, had given the Anointed Blade the impression that he had lost.

Why did Nimor abandon the fight, Archmage? Nauzhror asked. *What does he know?*

Find out, Gromph ordered then turned his attention to Dyrr.

"We can finish this now, if you like," Gromph said.

The lich took a deep, shuddering breath and shook his head.

"It's as it should be," the archmage added.

"I suppose it is, my young friend," the lich answered, his voice u, the highest ranking wizard in Menzoberranzan, and st powerful. It's only symmetrical that we eventually face each other. Power abhors that sort of imbalance."

"I don't know," Gromph answered with a shrug. "I don't consider balance. I worship a demon. I serve chaos."

Dyrr's answer was to begin casting a spell. Gromph stepped back and used his staff to levitate, hopping a dozen feet up into the air and hovering there. He looked down and could see a small group of drow—fifteen or twenty and mostly older males—begin sifting through the ruined stalls. They must have been the merchants themselves, finally unable to stay away, not knowing the fate of their livelihoods.

Gromph thought to warn them off but didn't. He didn't want to.

Dyrr finished his spell, and at first it looked as if the lich burst. He grew, ballooning up to twice, then three, then four times his normal size and bigger. He changed in every conceivable physical way and dropped from the air with a resounding crash that made the merchants scatter back past the edges of the Bazaar. Gromph watched the bystanders gape in awe and fear at what Dyrr had become.

It's a gigant, Nauzhror said. *A blackstone gigant.*

Gromph sighed. He knew what it was that Dyrr had turned himself into.

Under normal circumstances, a blackstone gigant was a construct, created by priestesses of any number of dark faiths to be used as servants, guardians, assassins, or instruments of war. Carved from solid blocks of stone, they were formidable creatures that could destroy a whole city if left unchecked. What Dyrr had done was change his form from his normally thin, aged drow frame to the form of a gigant. In the process he had become, for all intents and purposes, that new creature.

The gigant was easily forty feet long from the top of its massive, drowlike head to the tip of its curling, wormlike tail. It had four sets of long arms with drowlike hands big enough to close over Gromph entirely, though the hands were oddly twisted with three multi-jointed fingers ending in black talons not unlike Nimor's. The lich had opted to retain his black coloration, but the creature's eyes blazed a bright blue. Shafts of light extended from them, cutting through the haze of smoke that still hung in the air. It opened its mouth and revealed fangs the size of short swords, set in rows. Slime dripped from its twisted lower lip. It was in constant motion, twitching and squirming like a maggot. The weight of it dragged ragged scars in the floor, and the sound of grinding, cracking stone overwhelmed all other sounds.

The creature started to destroy everything it could reach, and it could reach a lot. What merchants' stalls were still intact and unburned were ground to splinters under the colossal beast's raw tonnage. The once curious merchants ran for their lives, but as the gigant writhed across the Bazaar, it rolled over one fleeing drow after another. When it rolled on to reveal them once again, instead of the mass of unrecognizable paste Gromph expected to see, there was left behind an array of what looked at first like statues. The petrified forms of a score of drow lay perfectly still, scattered across the ruined Bazaar. The touch of the gigant had turned them to stone.

Its fit of destructive rage finished, the gigant turned its attention to Gromph. The shafts of light from its eyes fell on the archmage, illuminating him where he hovered a dozen yards above the floor of the Bazaar.

Gromph cast a spell as the gigant came at him, gnashing its massive fangs and petrifying a handful more of the careless drow merchants. The spell made Gromph difficult to see. His form became cloudy, indistinct, and he dropped quickly to the ground. The boots he was wearing would help him run faster than any drow. Difficult to see and moving fast, Gromph managed to stay out of the raging gigant's way.

"Can you hear me, Dyrr?" Gromph called out.

The lich didn't answer. Gromph wasn't sure if he could in his current state. The gigant growled and gnashed its teeth and came at him again. Gromph literally ran in circles in an effort to contain the dangerous beast in the Bazaar. Any living thing it touched turned to stone, and too many Menzoberranyr had perished already. If the siege truly was coming to an end, it was time for the wasteful killing to stop too.

"Dyrr, answer me," Gromph tried again, but again there was no response.

Instead, the gigant glanced down at the petrified drow left in its wake. When the beam of light from its eyes played on their stone forms, the rock-hard drow lurched into motion. The petrified merchants drew themselves up, staggering slowly like zombies, and each one turned its head up to regard the gigant as if listening for orders. Dust fell from them in gently wafting clouds.

The gigant hissed at each of them, and as it did so one after another of the animated statues turned to face Gromph and began to stagger slowly toward him.

Gromph could move many times faster than the petrified drow, but there were a lot of them: a dozen, then more, and he knew that eventually he would have to do something about the blackstone gigant and its cadre of animated statues in the heart of Menzoberranzan.

The lich isn't answering you, Master, Nauzhror said. *Perhaps he can't. Perhaps he's more gigant now than lich.*

What does that mean? Prath asked.

It means, Gromph answered, *that what a lich might be normally capable of, normally resistant to, may no longer apply.*

Like what? Prath asked.

Gromph and Nauzhror projected the same word at precisely the same time: *Necromancy.*

❦   ❦   ❦

"That's impossible," Valas said. "It's the size of a castle."

Pharaun shrugged, nodding, looking up at the enormous wreck.

"Bigger," the Master of Sorcere replied, "but it walked."

The wreck was once a sphere of polished steel three hundred feet or more in diameter. It lay amid the ruins of half a dozen smaller stone and web buildings, one side of it gone completely. On the whole it resembled a discarded eggshell, but in fact it had once been a walking fortress. Pharaun tried to imagine the sight of the thing intact, standing on legs that were left bent and torn underneath its bulk.

"Some kind of clockwork contraption," Valas persisted, "that big . . . It would have to have been built by a . . ."

"A god?" Pharaun finished for him, when he sensed Valas hesitating to draw the same conclusion. "Or in this case a goddess. Why not?"

"What would you use something like that for?" asked Danifae.

"War," Jeggred offered, though there was enough of a lilt in his voice to make it almost sound like a question. "It's a war machine."

"It's a fortress," Quenthel said. There was a finality, a certainty in her voice that made the others turn to look at her. "It's . . . it *was* Lolth's own fortress. It once resembled a clockwork spider, and from within Lolth herself could traverse the Demonweb Pits, protected and armed with weapons the likes of which no drow has yet imagined."

"I think . . ." Danifae said. "I think I remember reading something about that but always thought it a fantasy, a bit of harmless heresy to thrill the uninitiated."

"You know this for sure?" Pharaun asked Quenthel, though

he could see in her face that she had no doubts.

The high priestess looked the Master of Sorcere in the eye and said, "I've been inside it. I've seen it move. It was inside that spider fortress that I first came before the Spider Queen herself."

Pharaun turned from Quenthel's gaze to look at the massive wreck again.

"She seldom left its confines," Quenthel went on, her voice growing softer and softer as if she were receding over a great distance. "I don't think I ever saw her leave it, in fact, in all the years I . . ."

Pharaun didn't turn back to look at the Mistress of Arach-Tinilith when he said, "We should go inside. If Lolth never left that fortress, perhaps she's still in there."

"She isn't there," Quenthel said.

"The mistress is right," said Danifae. "I can feel it—or, rather, I can't feel her."

"She might still be inside there," the wizard said, knowing that he was taking his life in his own hands again by suggesting the possibility—even though he was sure each one of them had at least briefly considered it. "Her body might be, anyway."

No one said anything in response, but they did follow when Pharaun began the long walk to the fallen spider fortress.

As minutes dragged, the walk grew increasingly difficult. Fatigue had long since made itself known, and though they occasionally stopped to eat and drink from the supplies that Valas had given each of them from his dimensional containers they were all hungry, thirsty, and ready to drop. That, coupled with an increasing denseness in debris and intervening walls of stone, web, bricks, or steel, reduced their speed to a quarter of what they hoped for.

Still, the draegloth managed to get close to Pharaun's side. The mage was reasonably confident that the defenses he already had running would prevent the half-demon from taking him down before he could defend himself, so he didn't stop and challenge the draegloth.

"You would like it," Jeggred whispered to Pharaun. The draegloth's whisper was as loud as a drow's normal volume, but still no one seemed to have heard him. "If Lolth is dead in there and all we find is a skeleton, you'd be happy. Admit it."

"I admit nothing," the Master of Sorcere replied. "As a matter of policy, actually. Still, in this case I truly hope we don't find Lolth dead in there. If I did, what would you care anyway, draegloth? Would you run and tell your mistress on me? Which of your two mistresses would you tell first? Or would you even tell Quenthel at all? Honestly, Jeggred, you're acting as if you expect never to see Menzoberranzan again."

"Am I?" the draegloth asked. He was fundamentally incapable of sarcasm. "How so?"

"You're ignoring the wishes of Quenthel *Baenre*—" the wizard stressed that House name—"in favor of the whims of a servant. Here, in the very heart of Lolth's power."

"Danifae is a servant no longer," the draegloth said. "I have seen many—"

Fire.

The word formed in Pharaun's mind even as his skin blistered and his clothing threatened to catch. The flames came at them in a wave, engulfing all five of them in blinding tongues of orange, red, and blue. Pharaun could hear his defensive spells crackling to hold out the heat, and though he was still burned, he survived it. Not all of the others were in as good shape, though, and Pharaun immediately searched his mind for a spell that would protect them all—and if not them all then Valas, Quenthel (she was the sister of the archmage, after all), Danifae, and Jeggred . . . in that order.

He didn't have a chance to bring any spell to mind, though,

before another wall of fire passed him, burning him even worse as it went.

Foul, coughing laughter echoed down from above, and Pharaun looked up to see a vicious tanar'ri hanging, by dint of at least some simple magic, in midair above them. The thing was like some kind of mad, twisted bull, and it lacked feet.

Pharaun recognized it at once, even as he was conjuring a sphere of Weave energy around himself to protect him from certain spells. The tanar'ri was a glabrezu, and it looked familiar.

"The ice . . ." Danifae suggested, her voice hissing through clenched teeth.

Danifae and Quenthel bore shiny patches on their black skin. They had been burned worse than Pharaun but not quite enough to raise blisters. Quenthel drew the healing wand and lost no time passing it over her own skin.

"I had it trapped in ice," said Pharaun, "and left it there."

The mage glanced quickly around for Valas, but the scout was nowhere to be seen.

"Typical demon," Quenthel mumbled. "Chewed its own legs off to get out of there."

Jeggred roared with rage. Smoke rose from his singed fur in black-gray wisps.

"You followed us all the way here, Belshazu?" the Mistress of Arach-Tinilith asked. "So we could kill you?"

"Quite the opposite," said Jeggred's father.

❦ ❦ ❦

Halisstra Melarn was flying.

Though that wasn't an entirely accurate description of what was happening to her, it was what all her senses told her. Below her stretched an eternity of gray nothing punctuated by swirling storms of color and distant chunks of drifting, turning rock as big around as a mile and as small as a single drow. Above her and to every side was precisely the same thing.

She had recently visited the Astral Plane with the party of Menzoberranyr and her former battle-captive, but that had been a very different experience. At that time, under the care of a priest of Vhaeraun, she'd felt like a ghost being pulled along by a chain. Through the power of Eilistraee, however, she was actually in the Astral, not projected there, and there was nothing anchoring her to the plane of her birth.

Halisstra Melarn felt more free than she'd ever felt before. Her lips turned up into an unashamed smile, and her heart raced. Her hair blew out behind her though there wasn't technically any wind. Her body responded to a mere thought in the æther medium of the Astral Plane, and she soared and swooped like a darkenbeast at play.

The only restraint she felt was the need to keep close to her companions, Uluyara and Feliane. Halisstra could see that the surface elf and the drow priestess were enjoying their flight through the Astral as much as she was, and both of them shared her smile. Still, the gravity of the mission that brought them there was never far from their minds.

Halisstra had risked everything and lost everything to be there. Ryld was surely dead, as dead as Ched Nasad, and any life she might ever have had in the Underdark was behind her. Ahead was uncertainty but acceptance. Ahead was risk but at least the potential for reward, where all she left behind was hopelessness.

"There!" Uluyara called to her fellow travelers, breaking into Halisstra's thoughts. "Do you see?"

Halisstra followed the other priestess's black-skinned finger, and found her body shifting in the "air" to begin flying in that

same direction. Uluyara was indicating a long line of dull black
shadows, and Halisstra had to blink several times before she began
to understand what she was seeing. It was as if she were looking
at a vast gray screen behind which, like actors in a shadow play, a
line of drow were slowly drifting toward a common goal.

"Approach them slowly," Feliane warned. "They may not even
be able to sense our presence, but we don't know for sure, and
there are so many of them."

"Who are they?" Halisstra asked, though even as the last word
left her mouth she realized what she was seeing.

"The damned," was Uluyara's whispered, heavy reply.

"So many . . ." Halisstra whispered in the same stunned
monotone.

"All the drow who died while Lolth was silent, I would suppose," said Feliane. "Where are they going?"

"Not to the Abyss," Uluyara replied.

As they came closer and closer Halisstra couldn't help but pick
out faces among the slowly drifting forms of the recently deceased.
All of the dark elves appeared uniformly gray, as if they were merely
charcoal renderings and not real drow. When she looked directly
at one of them, a female probably too young for the Blooding,
Halisstra could see right through her to the spinning rock that
was passing behind.

One of the shades noticed her and briefly made eye contact,
but the departed soul didn't slow in its progress or make any move
to speak to her.

"Where are they going?" Halisstra asked, seeing first one, then
another of the ghosts wearing a symbol of Lolth or other trinkets
and heraldry that showed them as devotees of the Spider Queen.
"If not the Abyss, if not to Lolth's domain, then where?"

Hope leaped in Halisstra's chest. If the dead among her loyal
followers weren't going to Lolth's side but were going *somewhere*,

perhaps there was some hope for a follower of the Spider Queen besides oblivion.

"Eilistraee's own spell," said Feliane, "was drawing us to the Abyss, and we weren't going this way."

"When I was in the Demonweb Pits with the Baenre sister and the others," Halisstra recounted, "we saw no souls such as these. Quenthel remarked on their absence. The sixty-sixth layer held only hordes of feral demons, two warring gods, and a sealed-off temple."

"Should we follow them?" Feliane asked Uluyara. "If they are Lolth's followers, they might be moving toward her, even if they aren't moving toward the Abyss."

"Could Lolth have abandoned the Abyss itself?" Halisstra asked.

Both Halisstra and Feliane looked to Uluyara for answers, but the drow priestess only shrugged.

Halisstra willed herself closer to the line of souls and watched them go by, waiting for an older priestess to pass, someone who looked as if she might have some insight. As the dead filed past her, Halisstra saw mostly males, warriors obviously, and a few driders in the mix. From their costumes and heraldry, Halisstra could tell that the drow came from a number of cities spread across the length and breadth of the Underdark.

Finally, a priestess approached whom she thought looked suitable, and Halisstra drifted closer still. She reached out her hand to touch the passing soul, when someone called to her.

Halisstra, the voice said, echoing directly into her mind.

Halisstra blinked and slapped her hands to her head. She was only dimly aware of Uluyara and Feliane asking after her condition.

The sound of the psychic voice echoed in her skull, the gravity of it pushing all other thoughts away.

"Ryld. . . ." she said through a jaw tight and quivering.

I'm here, the Master of Melee Magthere whispered into her consciousness.

Halisstra opened her eyes and was face to face with the ghostly shadow of Ryld Argith. The drow warrior stood tall and proud in his shadowy armor, his hands at once reaching out for her and pushing her away. Tears burst from her eyes, blurring her vision of her lover's disembodied soul.

I loved you, he said.

Halisstra had been trying not to cry, but with those three words she broke into body-racking sobs that sent her drifting slowly away from him in the Astral æther. She wanted to say a hundred things to him, but her throat closed, her jaw clenched, and her head throbbed.

I gave up everything for you, he said.

"Ryld," Halisstra managed finally to say. "I can bring you—"

He didn't so much say "no" as he imparted that feeling into her consciousness. Halisstra gasped for air.

I go to Lolth now, said Ryld. *I don't belong with Eilistraee, even if I belonged with you.*

"I didn't choose her over you, Ryld," Halisstra said, though she knew she was lying. "I would have turned away from her if you'd asked me to."

Again, the feeling of "no."

"I wanted you," she whispered.

You had me, he said, *for as long as you could.*

"Halisstra," Uluyara whispered into her ear. Halisstra realized that the other drow priestess was holding her arm. "Halisstra, ask him where he's going. Ask him where Lolth has gone."

"He's going to her," Halisstra said to Uluyara, then to Ryld: "I love you."

She blinked back her tears in time to see him smile and nod.

"To Lolth?" asked Uluyara. "Where is she?"

"That's why we're here now, isn't it?" Halisstra asked the slowly drifting soul of Ryld Argith. "Because we loved each other."

Because we left our world behind, he said. *Because we left our-selves there. You were able to create a new Halisstra, but I was not able to make a new Ryld. I'm here because I deserve to be. If not, the draegloth could never have beaten me.*

"And we would still be together," she said.

Tell your friends, he said, *that Lolth has taken the Demonweb Pits out of the Abyss. We have been waiting, some of us for months, to feel her pull us across the Astral to her, and only now are we compelled so.*

"Lolth," Halisstra said to the other priestesses, her voice tight with regret, anger, hate, and too much more to bear, "is bringing them home."

"The Demonweb Pits is no longer part of the Abyss," Uluyara guessed.

She's changing, Ryld said and his thoughts had the feel of a warning. *She's changing everything.*

Halisstra felt Uluyara's grip on her arm tighten, and the priest-ess whispered to her, "Let him go. There is only one way to serve him now."

"W-we can bring him . . . bring him back," Halisstra stuttered, watching Ryld turn from her and drift slowly away with the other uncaring shades.

"Not if he doesn't want to go back," Uluyara whispered, and the hand on her arm slipped into a snug embrace.

Halisstra wrapped her arms around Uluyara and wept as Ryld dwindled from sight farther and farther along the line of the damned.

TWENTY-FIVE

"Welcome to the Abyss, corpse," the glabrezu said. His voice was a low, rolling growl. "Welcome to my home."

"Belshazu," Quenthel said, her scourge in her hand, vipers writhing expectantly.

The demon didn't look at her. Instead, he kept his burning eyes locked on Pharaun.

"I'm going to rip your soul from your body, mage, and eat it raw then vomit it up so it drips all over your quivering corpse and soaks into your shriveling skin and runs into your gaping mouth so it knows that you're dead," the demon ranted.

"Well," Pharaun replied, "if you say so."

"You will die," Belshazu said to Pharaun, "in the shadow of your dead goddess's ruined fortress."

The Master of Sorcere saw Jeggred step up next to him from

the corner of his eye. The draegloth was growling almost as low and as thunderously as the glabrezu—the demon that happened to be his father.

The glabrezu, its severed legs dripping dark blood onto the ancient battlefield, turned slowly to the draegloth and said, "When I'm done with the drow, son, you can join me—have your freedom from the dark elves at last."

Jeggred drew in a breath, and Pharaun could tell he was ready to pounce, though the glabrezu was hovering well out of his reach.

"Jeggred . . ." Quenthel started but stopped when the draegloth whirled on her.

"It's meat to me," Jeggred growled. "Just another tanar'ri scum. That thing is no parent of mine." He turned to the glabrezu. "Call me 'son' again, demon, and it'll still be on your lips when I rip off your head."

"Fear not, draegloth," the demon replied with a feral grin. "Even if you were full-blood I wouldn't give you a second thought. For a half-breed I won't even bother killing you." Belshazu turned his attention back to Pharaun but spoke to the rest of them. "All I want is the summoner. Give me the wizard, and you can go on to meet your Spider Queen."

"Only him?" Quenthel asked.

Pharaun looked at her, and she tried to avoid his gaze, keeping her attention on the hovering glabrezu.

The demon glanced down at his severed legs and said, "The trick with the ice . . . I had to snip my own legs off." He held up one of his four arms, one of two that ended in a hideous, sharp pincer claw. "They won't grow back. At the very least, the whoreson owes me two legs. Give him to me now, and be on your way."

"Everyone," Quenthel said, her voice faraway and bored, "step aside."

The draegloth growled, and Valas appeared from behind a pile of broken bricks, shifting his feet in an uncharacteristically audible way. Pharaun looked at Quenthel, and she met his gaze evenly.

"Are you serious?" the wizard asked.

"Yes," Quenthel replied. "You summoned him, you bound him, you froze him in ice. The rest of this expedition is too important to waste fighting every monster we stumble across—not anymore anyway, and not to settle vendettas you bring upon yourself with your own simpleminded carelessness."

"Pharaun summoned that demon on your command, Mistress," Valas reminded her, but she didn't acknowledge the scout at all.

Pharaun looked at Belshazu, who was quietly laughing, obviously surprised that Pharaun's companions had so quickly and easily sold him out. The wizard scanned the glabrezu quickly and found that he was flying thanks to a thin platinum ring on the little finger of his left hand.

"It's all right," Pharaun said. "All we're talking about here is one legless glabrezu. Go on ahead, and I'll catch up in a minute or so."

The glabrezu roared and moved closer. Pharaun's first impulse was to run, his second to stand and swallow. He forced himself to do neither. Instead he prepared his first spell.

Something drifted past Pharaun's face. He leaned back a bit to avoid it, but something else tapped him under the chin. Dust rose up from the ground all around him—and pebbles, shards of petrified bone, and little bits of twisted, rusted iron. He looked at the glabrezu, who was holding up one of his two proper hands, a knowing grin on his canine face.

Pharaun's stomach lurched, and he felt himself being pulled upward. His boots came off the ground, and he was falling—but falling upward along with the debris around him. The others backed out of the area where gravity had been reversed. Quenthel watched with a look of irritation, as if she were disappointed that the demon was taking so long to kill him. Valas drew his kukris but seemed unsure if he should intercede. Jeggred looked at Danifae, who waved him off but watched expectantly.

With a sigh, Pharaun went to work.

He touched the Sorcere insignia and used its levitation power to counter the gravity reversal. It was disorienting, but he managed to hover at the same level as the glabrezu. He then touched his steel ring and brought forth the rapier held within it.

The weapon flew at the demon. As the blade flashed through the air, the glabrezu slashed at it with his claws and snipped at it with his pincers. The demon had the advantage of being able to fly with the enchanted blade, and they quickly matched speeds so that Belshazu and the rapier were evenly paired.

Pharaun took advantage of the stalemate to cast a spell. His stomach lurched again, and his levitation started to pull him up instead of down. The demon's upside-down gravity was gone.

Belshazu could parry the animated sword's attacks but couldn't hurt it. At the same time the rapier nicked the demon here, slashed him there, and blood started to drip onto the dead ground from half a dozen cuts.

"Unfortunate," Belshazu hissed, almost to himself, "but I would have liked to keep this one after I kill you."

The demon made a gesture difficult to define—a blink, a shrug, a shudder—and the blade shattered into a thousand glittering fragments of steel that rained down onto the ancient battlefield.

Pharaun felt his blood boil, his face flush, and his breath stop in his throat.

I should have remembered, he scolded himself. *I should have known he could do that.*

The Master of Sorcere wanted to hurl a string of invectives into the air, at Belshazu and the cold, uncaring multiverse, but he swallowed it. Still, he'd always liked that rapier.

"I'll take the value of that blade out of your guts, demon," Pharaun threatened.

The glabrezu's animal face twisted into a feral grin again as he rushed through the air toward Pharaun.

From behind him, the mage heard Valas say, "You'll leave a fellow drow to a filthy demon? You'll leave us without a mage?"

"Yes," Quenthel replied with an utter lack of regret that Pharaun actually found refreshing.

The tanar'ri approached quickly, and Pharaun pulled an old glove from a pocket of his *piwafwi*. He started the incantation even before the glove came out of the pocket, and by the time the glabrezu was in striking range, the spell was done.

A hand the size of a rothé appeared in the air between the wizard and the demon. Though Belshazu tried to avoid it, he couldn't. The hand opened and pushed him through the air, forcing him away from the wizard no matter how hard he resisted the conjured hand.

Pharaun turned to Quenthel, who looked at him blankly when he said, "What I'm about to do, I should do right here and let you all taste it, but I won't. I'll push him away first and keep you at a safe distance. Nonetheless, I want you to remember, Mistress, that I can do this again, and by all rights I *should* do it again."

He didn't bother to wait for a response—none came anyway—instead he turned back to the glabrezu who had been pushed by the spell several paces away in the air over the ruined temple grounds. Pharaun started to run over the uneven, debris-scattered ground, counting his paces as he went. Belshazu ripped and slashed at the conjured hand in a mad flurry of uncontrolled, frustrated attacks but to no effect. The magic held.

When Pharaun had gone twenty paces away from the rest of the expedition, he stopped. He held the hand in the air, no longer pushing the glabrezu, but keeping him at bay. As he ran he'd gone over in his mind again everything he'd learned about tanar'ri in general and glabrezu in particular. When he stopped he cast a spell—not a terribly complicated one—that would prevent another inconvenient manifestation of the tanar'ri's natural magic. A ray of green light leaped from Pharaun's outstretched hands and found its way unerringly to the floating demon. The spell would hold him to the sixty-sixth layer of the Abyss, preventing the glabrezu from teleporting even within the confines of the plane.

"Tell me the—" the wizard called out to the demon, stopping when Belsahzu's huge pincer burst through the conjured hand.

Solidified magic burned away from the surface of the black fist like blood clouding in water. The glabrezu grinned, grunted, and slashed at the hand. The great fingers twitched, their grip loosening.

The wizard had never seen anything tear through that spell in the same way. The glabrezu was more powerful, more uniquely talented than Pharaun had given him credit for. Even as those thoughts passed through his mind, the drow mage pulled another spell out of the Weave.

The demon's hideous pincer broke through one of the fingers. When it came away from the hand, the black magic burst like a bubble and the finger was gone. Belshazu pushed at the quivering, dissipating hand with one severed leg and his all-too-intact arms. As Pharaun's next spell began to form in the air above the demon, Belshazu fell out of the conjured hand and onto the wreckage-strewn ground.

The demon roared at him, and it was all Pharaun could do to force himself to appear unaffected by the deafening, terrifying sound. Belshazu stood but didn't look up—didn't see the slab of stone assembling itself bit by bit in the thin air above him.

"Tell me the truth." Pharaun slid a loose strand of hair away from his eyes and asked, "Can you tell I haven't washed my hair in over a tenday?"

The glabrezu growled, roared again, and leaped into the air—

—just as the wall of stone fell.

The demon disappeared under it, and the ground shook. The wall cracked as it came to rest on the uneven surface. Belshazu lifted the several-ton slab off him just enough to turn his head and reveal burning eyes sunk in a bleeding, animal's head.

The look of the battered creature made Pharaun smile. The spell he'd had to move so far away from the others to cast safely came to his lips as the tanar'ri continued to slowly dig itself out from under the stone slab. When he completed the incantation, Pharaun opened his mouth wide and screamed.

The sound came not from his lungs, throat, or mouth but from the Weave all around him and inside him. The sound rolled up, louder and louder, then shot out of him: a mad, keening shriek that smashed into the demon so hard it even blew the massive slab of stone into smoky vapor, then blew that smoke away into nothing. The sound crashed into the glabrezu, shaking him and spinning him into the air. Bruises exploded on Belshazu's tough red hide, and his bones cracked loudly one by one. The demon couldn't muster the breath necessary to scream, though Pharaun reveled in the obvious fact that he wanted to.

Especially when pieces of him started coming off.

Pharaun kept screaming, continued pushing air out of himself. The sound shredded the glabrezu, taking off skin, plates of exoskeleton, divots of fur, claws, fangs, eyes, then blood and entrails. The whole mess whirled in the air as if it were being stirred in a great invisible cooking pot, then all at once the spell—and the hideous shrieking scream—was gone, and the shredded remains of Belshazu fell in a heap on the battle-scarred ground. Blood continued to rain down in tapping spatters for a minute after the last big piece hit the ground.

Pharaun sighed, pushed away his errant hair again, and stepped gingerly into the mess. He kicked pieces this way and that with the toe of one boot until his eyes settled on the thin platinum band. He bent and retrieved the ring, making some effort not to touch the tanar'ri's blood.

"You owed me a ring," he said to the demon's mute remains then slipped the ring on a finger and turned back to rejoin the drow who had been more than happy to let him face the glabrezu alone.

❀   ❀   ❀

"It looked big from a distance," Pharaun said as he ran a hand along a cold, rusted metal rib. "It's even bigger from the inside."

The Master of Sorcere looked up along the line of the gently curving steel beam and tried to guess how far above his head it ended—a hundred feet, maybe a hundred and fifty?

"Why was this just left here for a thousand years?" asked Jeggred. The draegloth was sniffing the outer surface of the great spider fortress and seemed dissatisfied. "It should have been cleaned up. Wouldn't the goddess want it cleared away?"

"It hasn't been here a thousand years," Quenthel said. She was standing inside a huge tear in the side of the broken sphere, her arms crossed in front of her. "I told you all, I was here."

"How long ago?" asked Danifae.

The high priestess looked at her with open contempt but answered, "Ten years."

"Ten years ago," Pharaun asked, "was this thing intact and moving?"

The Mistress of Arach-Tinilith nodded.

"How were you here?" Danifae asked.

Quenthel turned to Pharaun and said, "If there is anyone alive in here, could you sense them?"

The wizard glanced at Danifae, who offered him a bored shrug.

"There are spells," he answered Quenthel, "that will do that, yes. Do you think we'll find someone alive in here? Lolth herself, perhaps?"

"If the Spider Queen is anywhere," said the Baenre priestess, "she'll be here. This is her palace. Still, I don't sense her presence. I still can't feel her here at all."

Pharaun nodded and looked around at the ruin again.

"Far be it from me to argue, Mistress," he said to Quenthel, "but I find it impossible to believe that this construct was in operation a mere ten years ago. I'll admit I've never seen materials like this—steel beams big enough to hold up a building, a magical construct as big as House Baenre—but I've seen steel both old and new, and this steel has been laying out here for somewhat longer than ten years. I will accept that you're reluctant to tell us how you came to be here a decade ago, but . . ."

"But what?" Quenthel snarled.

Pharaun stopped to think. The Mistress of Arach-Tinilith watched him the whole time, and finally he shrugged and shook his head. Quenthel turned and strode deeper into the wrecked spider fortress.

Pharaun could feel someone looking at him, and he turned to see Valas lurking at the edge of a shadow. The scout was standing outside the wreck. Following Valas's glances, Pharaun watched Danifae and Jeggred follow Quenthel into the ruin. When the three of them had disappeared into the maze of twisted metal, Valas stepped closer.

"Do you really think she's alive in there?" the scout asked.

Pharaun shrugged and said, "At this point, my dear Valas, I'm willing to accept nearly anything. Time seems to have no meaning here—a different meaning anyway. Everything Quenthel says may be true, but then here we are at the very heart of Lolth's domain, and where is she?"

"Where are the souls of the dead?" asked the scout.

"We should be swarmed by departed ancestors, shouldn't we?" Pharaun agreed. "There should be all manner of creatures here: demons, driders, draegloths . . ." Pharaun paused to chuckle. "All manner of things that start with 'd' . . . but all there is is wreckage and ruins, calcified bone and rotting stone. It's the stuff of an epic lament."

Valas stared into the darkness inside the spider fortress and sighed.

"I don't know my way around in there," the scout said, his voice barely above a whisper. "Why am I still here?"

"You were hired," Pharaun said. "House Baenre pays Bregan D'aerthe . . . everyone knows why you're here."

"No, I said, why am I *still* here?" the scout asked. "I was hired as a guide to get this expedition through the Dark Domain, and I have done that."

"You have indeed," Pharaun replied.

"I never said I knew . . ." Valas started, but ended with a sigh.

"You're out of your element," Pharaun said, "as are we all, but we could still certainly benefit from your skills."

"I could have helped you with the demon," said the scout.

"Quenthel wouldn't allow it," Pharaun replied.

"You got us here," Valas said, "and as far as I know, even with the ship destroyed, you're the only one who can get them home, yet she risks you to prove a point that no one needs proven? Does that make sense to you at all?"

Pharaun smiled and shook his head, sliding an errant strand of hair out of his face, then said, "I have been a thorn in the high priestess's side since we stepped out of Menzoberranzan. I've lost track of the various different reasons why she might want to kill me, as I've stopped counting the reasons I'd like to see her dead, too. Still, perhaps she was confident that I could handle the demon on my own. I did, after all."

"There might have been a time when I'd have thought that was good enough," Valas went on, "but after all this, I can't help thinking it's just stupid, and potentially wasteful. Her behavior is erratic."

"I think we're all a bit erratic," Pharaun admitted, "but I agree in principle with what you're saying. I think the snakes are whispering to her more and more. She's lost control of both the draegloth and Danifae, has never had control of me, and knows that you're only here because of House Baenre's gold. We finally get to the Demonweb Pits and this is what we find? An ancient ruin? She should be insane. We all should be."

Valas thought about that for a while, and Pharaun waited for him to respond.

"My contract is at an end," the scout finally said.

Pharaun nodded, shrugged, and said, "I will leave that for you to decide, but I have to admit I'd rather have you stay with us than leave. I can use spells, as the priestess asked, to find anything that might still live here, to find any latent sources of magic. If I'm the guide here, fine, but we could well need you again soon. Besides, can you even get back on your own?"

The scout tipped his head up, raised an eyebrow, and gave the hint of a smile that faded before it was completely recognizable.

"Well," Pharaun said, "perhaps you can then. I'm going inside anyway, and if you'd like to join us, so be it. We can discuss why, if you're capable of returning to Menzoberranzan on your own, you're concerned that I might be the only one who can get you back and Quenthel's tried again to kill me."

The scout bowed ever so slightly and held back a smile.

"Why do you care, anyway?" Valas asked.

"About what?"

"All of this," said the scout. "Lolth . . ."

The scout nodded and Pharaun replied, "I'm curious. It's a unique challenge for a spellcaster, and my hard-fought position in Menzoberranzan depends on the harder-fought position of my superior, who depends on the matriarchy for his power—his political power, anyway."

Valas nodded and Pharaun gestured toward the rip in the wall of the spider fortress.

"After you?" Pharaun said.

Valas walked past him, but his reluctance was plain in each forced step.

🕷 🕷 🕷

Halisstra couldn't move. She let herself hang in the æther, crying, holding her head in her hands, fending off both Uluyara and Feliane who were trying to comfort her. She could hear them repeating one reassurance after another and could feel them touching her, hugging her, wiping away her tears, but she didn't care. She didn't know what to do, and something was wrong with her.

We brought you along too fast, a voice hummed in her head. It was a female voice, quiet but strong. *I'm sorry.*

Halisstra blinked open her eyes and looked around for the source of the voice. Uluyara and Feliane had moved away from her—what would have been a few paces if they'd been standing on ground—and both of them stared with open mouths at an apparition floating only just within reach of Halisstra. It was the ghost of a drow female, resplendent in robes of flowing silk, all color drained from her, a wind that Halisstra couldn't feel carrying her long white hair in a halo around her head and brushing her robes out behind her.

"Seyll," Halisstra whispered, the name almost sticking on her tongue.

The shade, who was looking Halisstra directly in the eyes, nodded, and again the voice sounded in her head. *Eilistraee has many gifts to offer our sisters from the World Below. Pain, unfortunately, is one of those gifts.*

"You can keep it," Halisstra shot back, anger rising to replace the crushing remorse that the disembodied soul of Ryld Argith had left in its wake.

Feliane and Uluyara reacted to her reply with puzzled expressions, and Halisstra realized they couldn't hear Seyll.

I know, the dead priestess replied. *Believe me, I know what it's like to experience these emotions all at once and for the first time. Your mind has been trained not to recognize them, but they've been there all along, waiting for you to find them and set them free. Freedom isn't always easy. You've gone on a long journey within yourself to a place where the emotional consequences may be more painful, but the rewards will be greater than you've ever imagined.*

I don't care, Halisstra thought back. *I don't want it. Right now, I'd go back to the Underdark if I could.*

Would you?

In a second, Halisstra vowed. *There when I was being manipulated I knew it and knew the ends to which I was being pushed. There I was a priestess and a noblewoman.*

And here? Seyll asked. *What are you now?*

An assassin, Halisstra answered. *I'm an assassin in the service of Eilistraee.*

What do you suppose is the difference between an assassin and a liberator?

A liberator? Halisstra asked.

When you kill Lolth, Seyll said, *and you* will *kill her, you will set thousands free . . . millions.*

Dooming them to a life of despair and remorse?

And love, contentment, trust, and happiness, Seyll replied.

Halisstra paused to think about that, but her mind was blank. Her eyes burned, her jaw ached, and she felt heavy—so heavy she actually began to sink in the weightless æther of the Astral Plane.

Feliane and Uluyara appeared on either side of her, holding her gently by the arms. Halisstra didn't look at them or at the ghost of Seyll. Instead, she let her eyes wander up and down the long column of silent souls. The dead were returning to Lolth. Everything she had feared had not come to pass.

"I could go back to her," Halisstra said.

She could feel both Feliane and Uluyara stiffen. From Seyll she felt a wave of disappointment mixed with fear.

"If she would have you," Feliane whispered.

That stopped Halisstra. Had she passed a point of no return, one where Lolth would reject her or worse, punish her for the heresies she'd already committed? Would Eilistraee abandon her for even considering a return to the Spider Queen? Would she manage to work herself into a godless afterlife by her own indecision?

No, Seyll whispered into her mind, obviously having sensed her thoughts. *Eilistraee understands doubt and weakness and forgives both.*

"Do you understand, Halisstra," Feliane said, "what Seyll has given up by coming here?"

Halisstra shook her head in an effort to gently shake off the elf's words.

"She has abandoned Arvandor to come here," Feliane continued. "Seyll has doomed herself to an eternity in the wild Astral, and she's done it for you."

"Has she?" Halisstra asked, eyeing the ghost of Seyll, who floated there staring at her. "Or has she done that for Eilistraee? Did she come here on her own, or was she sent by a goddess who fears the loss of her assassin?"

Yes, Seyll said. *Yes to all those questions. I have come here on my own, for Eilistraee, to protect you from Lolth, to protect you from yourself, and to assure that you will do what you must do.*

"Why?" Halisstra asked. "Why now?"

Because something is going to happen, Seyll replied.

"Something is going to happen," Uluyara repeated.

Right now, Seyll asked, *this very moment, do you want to go back to Lolth? If she poured her "grace" over you right now, would you accept it, accept her, and turn your back on Eilistraee?*

"I don't know," Halisstra answered.

You must decide, said Seyll, *and you must decide now.*

The apparition gestured behind her at the long row of disembodied souls. Something was different, and it took Halisstra a few seconds to realize what was happening. The line of souls disappeared into the gray distance, what might have been miles away. The colorless ghosts were changing, one after another as if a wave was passing through them. Color and life, even substance returned to each soul in turn, but only for a brief moment, then the effect passed to the next dead drow in line. As the color passed in and out of them they convulsed, twisting in the air more from pleasure than from pain. The wave drew closer and closer, scattering the line of drow in its wake.

"She's back," Halisstra whispered.

Seyll came closer to her, wrapping her ghostly body around Halisstra, who stiffened but didn't push the apparition away.

She is back, Seyll whispered into her mind. *Soon her power will course though you. I can protect you, but you have to want me to. You have to want Eilistraee, not her. Not that demon. Please.*

"Please," Uluyara whispered.

Halisstra closed her eyes and tried to return Seyll's ghostly embrace, but her arms closed over nothing.

"Eilistraee," Halisstra called, her voice breaking, "help me!"

Seyll grew solid in her arms, and Halisstra felt the priestess's body quiver. Seyll screamed, and Halisstra heard it both in her rattling ears and in her tortured mind.

"Seyll," Uluyara shouted over the sound of pure agony that was ripped from Seyll's momentarily corporeal throat. "No . . ."

Seyll's body disappeared, and Halisstra's arms wrapped around only herself. The scream echoed in her mind but left her ringing ears to the silence of the Astral Plane. She opened her eyes and saw Seyll floating in the gray nothing in front of her. The priestess's body was twisted and broken, her face wracked with pain. She had grown more transparent, and was quickly fading away.

"Seyll . . ." Halisstra whispered.

The priestess looked her in the eyes one last time, and though it seemed to cause her a considerable amount of pain to do so, she smiled as she faded from sight.

Halisstra felt her body sag even as she was infused with an energy and confidence unlike anything she'd felt before.

"She's gone," Uluyara whispered.

"She didn't abandon only Arvandor," Feliane said, her eyes wide with horror. "She let the power of Lolth pass into her."

"To protect me," Halisstra whispered.

"It killed her," Feliane said. "She didn't choose the Astral, she chose oblivion."

"The thing that I most feared myself," said Halisstra. "It was oblivion that drove me to Eilistraee."

"She sacrificed herself," Uluyara said.

"For me?" asked Halisstra.

"And for Eilistraee," Feliane said.

Halisstra's mind reeled, but her eyes cleared of tears, and blood began to flow in her tired muscles. She felt alert, refreshed, even as she was overwhelmed.

"She sacrificed herself," Halisstra repeated, "so I could . . ."

"So you could serve Eilistraee," Uluyara finished for her. "So you could wield the Crescent Blade."

Halisstra put a hand on the hilt of the weapon that could kill a goddess and said, "I hesitated, but I hope not for too long."

"She's awake," Feliane warned, "or resurrected. She'll fight back."

Halisstra thought about that. She tried to imagine facing Lolth herself in battle, and for the life of her she couldn't.

"We'll follow the souls to Lolth," Halisstra said, moving in that direction even before she finished speaking.

Feliane and Uluyara fell in behind her.

"No," Pharaun muttered, "this way . . . ?"

He turned left when the corridor forked. He had cast a number of divinations and was doing his damnedest to follow them all.

"None of your spells are working," Quenthel asked, "are they?"

Pharaun didn't bother looking at her but continued along the corridor hoping he would stumble on something that might get them on the right track.

"I'm getting . . . contradictory information," he shot back, "but at least I'm doing something. You said you've been here before—why aren't you taking us right to her?"

Quenthel didn't answer, and they shared a look that served as an agreement not to continue bickering.

"It's as if the farther we go into this spider fortress, the stranger our surroundings become," Danifae said. "There were no right angles anywhere when we first walked in, but now there are. They seemed to appear the moment I got comfortable wandering the corridors without them. Still, we have seen nothing alive, haven't been harried by a single guardian, and for all intents and purposes we have the run of the place. What does it mean?"

"That Lolth wanted us to come," Quenthel replied, shooting a contemptuous glance at Danifae.

Pharaun and Valas exchanged a look that told each other they'd reached very different conclusions.

The wizard paused in a section of corridor that had widened out to well over twenty feet. The ceiling was low, the darkness comfortably dense, and the smell of rot fortunately not as overwhelming as it had been most of the time. He cast another spell and concentrated on his surroundings, searching for signs of life. He could sense dead spots through which his magic couldn't penetrate—walls perhaps lined with lead or some other particularly dense substance. Still, far at the edge of the limits of his perception, Pharaun could make out signs of life.

"A light wash," he whispered to himself, "but it's there."

"What?" Quenthel asked. "What's there?"

The wizard opened his eyes and smiled at Quenthel.

"There is something alive in here with us after all," he said, "but the sign is strange—diffuse and distant as if the creature is either very far away, only barely alive, cloaked in magic that protects it from divination, or some combination of those things. I can't get a . . . Mistress?"

Quenthel dropped to her knees, and Pharaun instinctively backed away. The air was charged, and the Master of Sorcere's skin tingled, but whatever was happening had a much more profound effect on the two females.

Quenthel dropped to her hands, her face coming dangerous

inches from smashing into the cold, rusted steel of the ruined spider fortress. Her muscles jerked and spasmed, and her face was twisted into either a rictus of agonized pain or a grin of some kind of feral pleasure—Pharaun couldn't tell which.

Danifae fell to the floor as well, but she was facing up. Her back arched, and soon she was touching the floor only from one tiny spot on her head and the tips of her toes. Pharaun couldn't help admiring the curve of her body, marred as it was by the same petty wounds—cuts, abrasions, welts, and bruises—that they'd all accumulated along the way. Not sure he wasn't seeing only what he wanted to see, Pharaun thought Danifae's expression was one of total pleasure, complete physical abandon.

Next it was Jeggred's turn to fall. The draegloth dropped to one knee, his three remaining hands reaching out to grab blindly at the walls. He ripped jagged rents in one steel partition. Brown dust covered his fur, clinging to it in clumps until it looked like the half-demon was rusting the same as the spider fortress. Jeggred screamed so loudly Pharaun had to clamp his hands over his ears.

Even as the draegloth's scream faded into panting—desperate gasps for air—Pharaun looked at Valas. The scout seemed entirely unaffected, and Pharaun himself felt no burning desire to writhe around on the floor.

"Whatever it is," Pharaun said to the scout, "it only seems to be affecting the—"

He thought at first that he was going to say "the females," then he realized that it was affecting the *priestesses* and the one creature among them born of Lolth's peculiar hell.

It ended as abruptly as it began.

Jeggred, who had been the one least affected by the sudden rapture, was the first to stand and begin to brush himself off. His face—normally difficult to read—gave Pharaun nothing.

"What happened?" the wizard asked, but the draegloth ignored him. "Jeggred?"

Quenthel sat back on her haunches and held her hands up to her face. Her eyes scoured her rust-dusted hands as if searching for something.

Danifae took longer to recover, rolling into a fetal position on the unforgiving rusted steel floor and making a noise Pharaun at first thought was crying.

"Mistress?" Valas asked, crouching to get to Quenthel's eye level but not stepping any closer than the half dozen paces that already separated them.

Quenthel didn't speak, didn't even give any indication that she had heard Valas. Pharaun didn't bother asking what happened. He was beginning to understand what he'd witnessed.

Quenthel began to speak.

At first she moved her lips in a mute pantomime, then she whispered at the edge of hearing, then she chanted a litany in an ancient tongue not even Pharaun recognized.

She continued for a minute or so then stopped. Pharaun's eyes played over her, and he watched as all the cuts and bruises, scrapes and welts faded away, leaving her skin a perfect, almost glowing black. She even seemed to gain back some of the weight she'd lost. Her hair appeared cleaner, softer, and even her *piwafwi* and armor shone with renewed life.

Quenthel Baenre stood and looked down at Danifae, who had uncurled herself to sit with her back to the wall, smiling as she whispered a prayer of her own that sealed her cuts, made her bruises disappear, and brought the twinkle back into her big, expressive eyes. A tear traced a path down one of her perfect ebony cheeks, and she didn't bother to wipe it away.

Pharaun looked back at the Mistress of Arach-Tinilith, who stood tall and still in the darkness of the spider fortress, seeming to glow. Her eyes were closed and her lips were moving.

In one fluid, graceful motion Danifae swept up to her feet, her perfect white teeth shining in the gloom as she grinned from ear to ear. Pharaun found himself returning that smile. Jeggred rolled up onto his feet but in the same movement sank down to his knees in front of Danifae and Quenthel. The draegloth was breathing hard.

"They are alive, and they're here," Quenthel whispered. She looked at Pharaun and more clearly said, "They are behind walls that shield them from your spells, and they are further protected from most divinations, but they are here."

"Who?" Valas asked.

"I sense them too," Danifae said. She put a hand on Jeggred's wild mane and absently stroked it back into place. "I think I could find them. I think they're actually waiting for us."

"Wait," Pharaun said, stepping closer to Danifae—until a fierce growl from Jeggred stopped him. The young priestess patted the half-demon's head. and he calmed quickly. "Did what I think happened actually happen? Did she . . . ?"

"Lolth has returned to us," Quenthel said.

"She has," Danifae agreed.

She appeared as if she wanted to say more.

"Is there something else?" Pharaun asked. "Is that it? Is our journey at an end?"

"Mistress?" Jeggred said, looking directly into Danifae's eyes. "What did the voice say? I couldn't quite . . . it was too far away to . . ."

Danifae ran her fingers through his fur and said, "The voice said—"

"*Yor'thae*," Quenthel finished for her.

"*Yor'thae*. . . ." Danifae whispered.

"High Drow?" Valas asked, correctly identifying the language.

"It means, 'Chosen One,' " Pharaun explained.

"One . . ." Quenthel whispered, shaking her head.

At the same time, Danifae mutely mouthed the word, "*Yor'thae.*"

Quenthel used her eyes to get Pharaun's attention then said, "Our journey is far from over, Master of Sorcere. Lolth has not only returned but she has asked me to come to her, has invited me to be her chosen vessel. This is why she brought me back, all those years ago. This is why she dragged me from the Abyss and back to Menzoberranzan. I was meant to come here, now, and to be her . . . to be *Yor'thae.*"

Deep in the heart of the First House, in a room protected from everything worth protecting a room from, Triel Baenre watched her brother fight for the life of Menzoberranzan.

He was losing.

She could see what was happening in the Bazaar, every detail of it, through a magic mirror, a crystal ball, a scrying pool, and half a dozen other similar items, most of which had been created by Gromph himself. She paced back and forth across the polished marble floor, looking from scene to scene, angle to angle, as the transformed lichdrow made a mess of the heart of her city.

Wilara Baenre stood in one corner, her eyes darting from one scrying device to another, her arms crossed in front of her, her fingers drumming against her shoulders with barely contained frustration.

"The archmage will prevail, Matron Mother," Wilara said, not for the first time that day.

"Will he?" Triel asked.

It was the first time she'd replied to one of Wilara's hollow reassurances, and it took the attending priestess by surprise.

"Of course he will," Wilara answered.

Triel waited for more, but it became obvious that Wilara had nothing else to say.

"I'm not entirely certain that this is a fight he can win," Triel said, as much to herself as to Wilara. "If we're all being tested and this is Gromph's test, he will pass or fail on his own. If he fails, he deserves to die."

"Is there nothing we can do to help him?" asked Wilara.

Triel shrugged.

"There are soldiers and other mages," the attending priestess went on.

"All of whom are required elsewhere. The duergar still press, even if the tanarukks are turning away," said Triel. "The siege of Agrach Dyrr goes on unabated . . . but, yes, there are always more soldiers, always more mages, and there is Bregan D'aerthe and other mercenaries. If the lich kills Gromph I certainly won't let him rampage through the rest of Menzoberranzan turning our citizens to stone and smashing the architecture."

"Why not send those forces in now?"

Triel shrugged again and considered the question. She had no answer.

"I don't know," Triel said finally. "Maybe I'm waiting for a sign from—"

She was back.

Triel fell to the floor, her body going limp, her head spinning, her mind exploding in a cacophony of sound and shadow, voices and screams. Tears welled up in her eyes so she could only barely see Wilara lying in a similar confused, twitching, limp state on the floor across the room.

The Matron Mother of House Baenre felt every emotion she'd ever known simultaneously and at their sharpest and most intense.

She hated and loved, feared and cherished, laughed and cried. She knew the endless expanse of the limitless multiverse and saw in crystal detail the square inch of marble floor right in front of her eye. She was in her scrying chamber and in the Demonweb Pits, in her mother's womb and in the smoldering Bazaar, in the deepest Underdark and flying through the blazing skies of the World Above.

She took a deep breath, and one feeling after another fell away, each a layer of confusion and insanity. Pieces of her mind began to function again, then pieces of her body. It took either a few minutes or a few years—Triel couldn't be sure how long—for her to realize what had happened and sort through the sensation that had been so familiar all her life, then was gone, then returned.

Lolth.

It was the fickle grace of the Queen of the Demonweb Pits.

Triel didn't try to stand at first but lay there and stretched, luxuriating in the wash of power, exulting in the return of Lolth.

Gromph knew of so many ways to kill someone, he'd forgotten more than most drow ever heard of. There were spells that would kill with a touch, kill with a word, kill with a thought, and Gromph searched his mind for precisely the right one as he ran to both avoid the rampaging gigant and keep it contained in the ruined Bazaar.

He wore the skull sapphire that gave him even more choices and afforded him protection from negative energy—like Nimor's enervating breath. In his memory he stored a few more, and in time Gromph settled on one spell, with some input from Nauzhror and the small circle of Sorcere necromancers. The archmage gathered the Weave energy within him and brought the words and gestures of the incantation to mind. However, in order to cast the spell—and it was a powerful spell indeed—the archmage would have to stop running.

It wasn't the first time that the battle with Dyrr came down to timing. Would he have enough time to cast the spell before the gigant rolled over him?

We can help you choose your moment, Nauzhror said.

I know, Gromph answered, *but there are always . . . variables.*

The archmage stopped running, turned, and began his casting.

The gigant looked down at him, bathing Gromph in the light from its mad blue eyes. Gromph was sure he had time. The animated, petrified drow were too far away and moving too slowly to be of any concern, and the gigant had been slapping its tail around the Bazaar at random, as if Dyrr had little control over his new body. Gromph trusted in that.

He was wrong.

One set of trigger words from completing the spell, the enormous black tail of the blackstone gigant rolled over him. Gromph felt the words stop in his throat and felt his joints stiffen then nothing.

❖   ❖   ❖

Triel stood and looked from scrying device to scrying device, trying to sort out what she was hearing. The magically transmitted voices of a hundred mages, priestesses, and warriors filled the air in an incoherent tangle of confusion and undisguised bliss. The doors of the scrying chamber burst open, and a priestess whom Triel recognized but whose name she couldn't instantly recall staggered into the room. Tears streamed down her black cheeks, and her mouth worked in silent, incoherent attempts to put into words what she, Triel, Wilara, and every other servant of the Queen of the Demonweb Pits all across the endless expanse of the multiverse had experienced.

The matron mother's attention fell on one image: Gromph, petrified.

He had lost. The lich, in its freakish monster form, had turned the Archmage of Menzoberranzan to stone.

Triel felt her jaw tighten then she stood for a moment, letting the anger wash through her.

"Is this a sign?" she asked the Spider Queen.

Lolth didn't answer, but Triel knew she could if she wanted to.

"It's a sign," the matron mother whispered.

Triel pressed her fingertips together, bent her neck in a slight bow, and willed herself to the Bazaar. There was a momentary feeling of upside down weightlessness, a black void, then she was standing in a deep crack in the stone floor of her city's market-place. The blackstone gigant reared up high above her, apparently having sensed her passage through the dimensions from House Baenre to the Bazaar. The creature opened its mouth to roar at her, but Triel spoke a few words, and it froze. The great, thrashing tail came to a sudden stop. It was as if time itself had taken a moment's pause. Smoke still rose around her, and the animated stone drow lumbered on.

"This has gone on long enough, lich," Triel said, "all of it. I will have no more dead drow, no more of my city ruined, no more challenges to my power or to the power of Lolth."

Triel doubted the lichdrow could understand her. He seemed to have been subsumed by his adopted form, but she said it to everyone she knew was listening in, from House Baenre, Arach-Tinilith, Sorcere, and perhaps beyond the city into the command tents of her enemies.

She called directly upon Lolth, beseeching the restored goddess for her most potent spell, asking for nothing less than a miracle.

Lolth didn't answer in a drow's voice as she had in the past. There were no words, only a feeling, a swelling of power, a rush of blood in the matron mother's ears.

Triel sank to her knees amid a scattering of rough gravel and broken glass and pressed her forehead to the cool ground. She didn't express her desires in words. She didn't have to. What she was working was a wave of emotion, of feeling, of pure fear.

The terror of Lolth herself blasted out in all directions at once, in an expanding circle of fear with Triel at its center. All across the City of Spiders, drow stopped in their tracks, fell to their knees, or lay prone. Some leaned against walls or collapsed on stairs, but all of them knew the purest fear, the fear of a goddess, the fear of the eternal, the fear of chaos, the fear of darkness, the fear of the unknown, the fear of the certain, the fear of treason, and a thousand other horrors that brought the city to a full stop.

The blackstone gigant trembled and broke apart. Triel, still kneeling below it, didn't dodge the falling black boulders, the pieces of the titanic construct, which disappeared before they hit the ground. Within seconds all that was left of the rampaging creature was the lichdrow, stunned, reeling, kneeling on the crumbling floor of the Bazaar a few paces in front of the matron mother. The animated statues stopped moving and stood frozen in place.

The wave of fear moved onward, past the walls of the city's vault and into the crowded approaches to the Underdark beyond. It passed through the duergar lines, overtook the retreating tanarukks, and blindsided the scattered illithid spies. It affected all of them in different ways, but it affected all of them. By the time it was done—and it didn't take long—there was no question, anywhere, that Lolth was back.

Triel stood and surveyed the damage. She looked down at Dyrr and knew she could simply step over to him and kill him with a thought—or at least a dagger blade across his undead throat—but she didn't. Killing the lich was someone else's job.

The matron mother stepped to the rigid, calcified form of her brother. The expression frozen on his face was one of anger. Triel smiled at that.

"Ah, Gromph," she said. "You couldn't do it alone after all, could you? There are limits to your power as there are limits to mine, but together . . ."

Triel embraced the petrified form of her brother, wrapping her arms around his back as she whispered a prayer to Lolth.

Warmth came first, then softness, then a breath, then movement, and Gromph's knees collapsed. Triel held him up, and he grasped her around the waist, his head lolling on her shoulder as he drew in a series of ragged, phlegmy breaths. When his legs came back under him, Triel released him and stepped back. Their eyes met, and Gromph opened his mouth to speak.

"No," Triel said, stopping him. She glanced at the quickly recovering Dyrr, and her brother's eyes followed hers. "Finish what you started."

He opened his mouth to speak again, but Triel turned her back on him. She could hear his feet shifting on the loose gravel and glass, and she knew he was facing his enemy.

Triel walked away.

TWENTY-SEVEN

Anger, hatred, and exhaustion passed between the archmage and the lichdrow. They were done with each other. Both only wanted to finish it. They stood a dozen paces apart, eyes locked. Dyrr began to cast a spell, and Gromph surrounded himself in another globe.

Gromph began to cast a spell too, and the lichdrow kept casting. He was doing something complex. He meant to finish it indeed.

Before Gromph could finish his spell—one meant to burn the already wounded lich once more—Dyrr whispered something the archmage couldn't quite hear, and the spell took effect. The skull sapphire burned red-hot against Gromph's forehead, and he reached up to throw it off him—but it disintegrated before he could touch it. The dust that fell over the archmage's face was dull gray and powerless. There would be no more protection from the skull sapphire and no more stored necromancies. Gromph knew it had taken a wish to destroy it.

His own spell ruined, Gromph brought another to mind and said, "Well, everyone's using the big spells today, aren't we?"

The lich ignored the jibe and started casting a spell the same time Gromph did. It was the archmage's that finished first: another minor divination spent to create a blast of arcane fire. The preternatural flames poured over the lich, who threw his arms over his face to block them but to no avail. Dyrr's dry flesh crisped and curled, and the lich staggered in pain.

When the fire burned out, the lich lurched forward, red eyes bulging, his ever-present mask burned away, his face twisted in hatred and agony. Gromph could feel that despite the arcane fire Dyrr had finished his own spell.

Cold coursed through Gromph's body, and he shook—and Gromph was getting painfully tired of shaking, shivering, and quivering—but the lich wasn't through with him yet. He could feel the warmth, the life itself, being drawn from him. He staggered backward, barely managing to stay on his feet.

"I'll drain you dry, Gromph," the lich grumbled, his voice raspy and haggard. "You'll die with me, with my House, and my cause."

The lich began to cast again, and Gromph recognized the peculiar cadence and structure that revealed the incantation as a powerful necromancy. Gromph knew many ways to kill, but he also knew that Dyrr probably knew more.

The archmage's hand tightened on his staff, and his arm jerked. A dull pain and a hard pressure settled in his chest, and when he tried to take a breath, no air came to him. His knees finally buckled, and he fell. Gromph forced air into his lungs, but barely a whisper made it in. Dark shadows began to coalesce at the edges of his vision, and his ears went numb with a roaring rush of blood as his body fought in vain to keep his brain alive. The ring was of no help. The lich wasn't wounding him, he was killing him soul-first.

Gromph tried to speak, to utter the words of a spell that might save him, but he couldn't. Dyrr stepped closer, moving to stand over him. Gromph barely managed to turn his head to look up at the gloating lich. The archmage had other means of escape but couldn't force himself to activate any of them. He could feel Nauzhror and Prath trying to speak into his head, but their words never fully formed. Gromph feared that his body was already dead.

He tightened his grip on the staff, and his arm jerked again—the staff.

Gromph forced every ounce of will he had left into pulling his other hand beneath him. He felt his fingers wrap around the staff.

"Fight it, Gromph," the lich growled at him. "Suffer before you die."

"Arrogant—" Gromph coughed out, surprising himself with his ability to speak, even if it was only that one word.

"What was that?" the lich asked, taunting him. "The last words of Gromph Baenre?"

"Not . . ." the archmage gasped.

Gromph's arms tensed, his hands tight around the staff of power—an item so prized hundreds had died just to possess it for a day.

". . . quite," Gromph finished, and he broke the staff.

The ancient wood snapped in response less to the force of Gromph's arms and hands than to his will. The staff broke because Gromph wanted it to break.

Dyrr had time to take in a breath, Gromph had time to smile, then the world around them both became a raging hell of fire, heat, pain, and death. Gromph couldn't see the lich blasted to pieces. He was too busy worrying that the same had happened to him. He closed his eyes, but the light still burned them. He felt his flesh peel away in parts, sizzle, and crisp.

It was over as fast as it started.

Gromph Baenre drew in a breath and laughed through waves of burning agony. The ring started to bring him back to life a cell at a time and he lay there, waiting.

"You've done it," Nauzhror said, and it took a few murmuring heartbeats for Gromph to realize he'd heard the Master of Sorcere's voice with his ears and not his mind. "The lichdrow is dead."

Gromph coughed and dragged himself up to a sitting position. Nauzhror squatted next to him. The rotund wizard began examining the archmage's wounds.

"Dead?" Gromph said then coughed again.

"The cost was high, and not only the staff of power," Nauzhror said, "but he's been utterly destroyed."

Gromph shook his head, disappointed with Nauzhror. The lich's physical form was blasted to flinders when the staff unleashed all its power in one final burst, but a lich was more than a body.

"Dead?" the archmage said. "Not quite yet."

🕷   🕷   🕷

Nimor Imphraezl stepped out of the Shadow Fringe and into the ruins of Ched Nasad. High above him, clinging to the remains of a calcified web street, was perched a massive shadow dragon, an ancient wyrm magnificent in the terror it inspired in all who gazed upon it.

It was a dragon Nimor recognized instantly. It was the dragon Nimor had gone there to see.

Stretching his own aching, exhausted, wounded wings—wings

that were puny in comparison to the great shadow wyrm's—Nimor lifted himself up off the rubble-strewn floor of the cavern and into the air below the dragon. If the wyrm took any notice of him, it gave no sign. Instead, it continued as it had been, directing the clearing of the rubble in the preparation for the rebuilding of Ched Nasad. It was a huge task, even for the dragon.

Nimor coasted to a slow, respectful stop on the web strand next to the dragon and bowed, holding the posture until the dragon acknowledged his presence. He was still bowing when the enormous shadow wyrm shrank into the form of an aging drow with thinning hair but a solid, muscular form, dressed in fine silks and linens from all corners of the World Above, every stitch as black as the assassin's heart.

"Stand," the transformed dragon said, "and heed me."

Nimor straightened, looked the drow-formed dragon in the eyes, and said, "I am less than satisfied with the results at Menzoberranzan, Revered Grandfather."

The dragon-drow returned Nimor's look and held it until Nimor had to look away. The assassin heard footsteps approaching but didn't turn around to look. Nimor knew whose they were.

"Nimor," someone said. "Welcome to Ched Nasad."

Nimor pretended to look around at the still smoldering ruins.

"Of course," the source of the second set of footsteps said, "it will look quite different when we're finished."

"I clearly remember your promise," the transformed dragon said. "Do you?"

"Of course, Revered Grandfather," Nimor replied, head held high, showing no outward sign of weakness.

Patron Grandfather Mauzzkyl drew a deep breath in through his nose then slowly said, "You promised to cleanse Menzoberranzan of the stench of Lolth. Have you done that? Is that why you're here?"

Nimor didn't nod, shake his head, or sigh—nothing to make it seem to the patron fathers that he was guilty of anything. The two patron fathers who had approached him from behind stepped around him on either side and stood before Nimor flanking the once majestic wyrm.

"No," Nimor said.

"I have come from the City of Wyrmshadows," the patron grandfather went on, "to aid Patron Father Zammzt in the reconstruction of Ched Nasad. Is that why you've come from Menzoberranzan? To aid in the cleanup?"

"No, Revered Grandfather," Nimor replied.

"Tell your tale to Patron Father Tomphael and Patron Father Zammzt," Mauzzkyl said, his voice cold and final.

Nimor closed his eyes and said, "I answer to—"

"Tomphael," Mauzzkyl said. "You will speak to me through Tomphael from this day until I order otherwise."

Nimor had no time to argue, but that was the last thing he intended to do. Instead he watched, barely breathing as Patron Grandfather Mauzzkyl turned his back then transformed again into a dragon. The great wyrm stepped off the edge of the shattered web and disappeared into the gloom of the ruined city.

"Tell me what you came here to say," Patron Father Tomphael said.

Nimor looked Tomphael in the face but saw no anger, pity, or contempt. Nimor had fallen in the ranks of the Jaezred Chaulssin, and he'd done it just like that.

"Something has changed," Nimor said.

"Lolth has returned," Tomphael finished.

Nimor nodded and said, "Or she will soon. Very soon. The lichdrow failed, and the tide is turning in Menzoberranzan. I thought we'd have more time."

"Dyrr is dead?" Tomphael asked.

Nimor nodded.

"And the cambion?"

"Alive," said Nimor, "but already withdrawing. He had an agent in the Abyss who gave a strange report. I still don't know what happened to the spider goddess, where she's been, or why she fell silent, but she has managed to pinch the Demonweb Pits off of the Abyss."

Tomphael raised an eyebrow, and he and Zammzt shared a glance.

"So," Tomphael said, "your tanarukks are deserting. What of the duergar?"

"Horgar still lives, and when I left him he was still fighting," Nimor said. "However, with the priestesses again able to commune with their goddess and the tanarukks marching home, the gray dwarves won't stand a chance."

"Menzoberranzan," Zammzt said, "is the greatest prize. It was always the one thing most out of reach. We have had successes in other cities. The Queen of the Demonweb Pits was gone long enough."

"Was she?" Nimor asked.

"Look around you," Zammzt replied. "Once this was a drow trade city, openly obedient to the priestesses. Now it is a blank slate, and even as we speak it is being transformed."

"The other patron fathers and I," Tomphael said, "under Patron Father Zammzt's expert guidance, will be concentrating our energies here."

"As you always intended?" Nimor concluded.

Tomphael sighed and said, "I know you've always considered me a coward, Nimor, but you were wrong. Only the fool misses the difference between the coward and the pragmatist."

"Only the young seek glory over success," said Zammzt.

"I could have won in Menzoberranzan," Nimor argued.

"Perhaps," said Tomphael. "If you had, this conversation would have taken a very different tone. It was your opportunity to surprise us, Nimor. That is what you failed to do—surprise us. Our plans did not depend on the City of Spiders being delivered to us on a silver platter, nor did they assume that Lolth was never going to return from wherever it is she's been. We had this one opportunity, and we took all there was to take. There will be other opportunities to take more."

"Other opportunities. . . ." Nimor repeated, rolling the words over on his tongue.

"You could be Anointed Blade again, Nimor," Tomphael said.

Nimor nodded, bowed, and said, "I will return to the City of Wyrmshadows . . . with your leave, Patron Father."

Tomphael nodded, and Nimor turned and stepped into Shadow.

※　※　※

Pharaun hadn't felt so good in so long, he'd almost forgotten what it was like to be healthy. The priestesses, perhaps reveling in the return of their spells, were almost continuously chanting healing prayers. They conjured a banquet and clean, cool water. They healed every wound and soothed aching muscles.

Stretching, feeling too good to bother with Reverie, Pharaun stood and watched Quenthel and Danifae work on Jeggred. Again, likely because they couldn't resist using the spells that had been denied them so long, the two females worked together. As they sat cross-legged on either side of a nervous, reclining Jeggred, Pharaun sensed flashes of the old physical relationship the two priestesses had shared not too long ago. There was the accidental touch that turned into a lingering caress, the heavy-lidded eye contact past the draegloth's wild white mane, and the occasional play of a tongue along parted lips as the words to a series of complex healings taxed even their spell-rejuvenated throats.

The result of all of it was that Jeggred's severed hand grew back. Pharaun found the sight of the thing slowly taking shape from the dead end of the stump even more fascinating than the exchange between the two females. The hand came together in layers: bone, sinew, muscle, blood vessels, skin, fur, claws.

When they were done, the draegloth stood, flexing his hand, jaw agape, body quivering.

The two priestesses stood with him, separating, their eyes once again going cold toward each other.

Jeggred looked first to Danifae and said, "My thanks, Mistress." Then to Quenthel, "Mistress Quenthel. . . ."

Anger poured over the high priestess's face like fog, and she turned away from her nephew, quickly gathering her pack.

"We've rolled around on the floor long enough," she said, already walking swiftly down the corridor. "This way."

Danifae motioned to Pharaun to proceed, and the wizard gladly went after Quenthel. Valas followed behind the wizard, and Danifae and the draegloth took up the rear. Any distance, any buffer between the two priestesses was a good thing, and Pharaun was happy to provide it as long as they got moving. The Master of Sorcere was all but overwhelmed with curiosity.

Quenthel led the way with a confident stride and such assurance that none of the rest of them argued or second-guessed her at all. They went from one corridor to another, passed through rooms, sometimes through doors that Jeggred had to force open by brute strength. All the while the interior of the spider fortress maintained its cold, dark, dead, rusted feeling. Though Lolth's power had definitely returned to the two priestesses, the construct was as dead as ever, and Pharaun got the distinct impression that wherever that power was coming from, it wasn't the sixty-sixth layer of the Abyss.

When they saw light at the end of one of the passageways they all stopped, clinging to the walls and the concealing shadows. As he ran through the spells still available to him and closed his fingers over a wand that would send bolts of lightning crashing through the air, the Master of Sorcere took stock of the rest of the expedition. Quenthel and Danifae both looked down the corridor with hopeful, excited expressions. Jeggred looked at Danifae in the same manner. Valas was nowhere to be seen—as was usual for the scout.

"What is it?" Jeggred asked, his voice as quiet as was possible for the massive half-demon.

Pharaun guessed, "A gate."

"It's where we have to go," Quenthel said.

"She's correct," said Danifae.

"Well, then," Pharaun replied, "we ought to proceed right away. Should we be prepared to fight our way through?"

Quenthel stepped away from the wall and started walking quickly, back tall and straight, toward the strange purple glow.

Pharaun shrugged and followed, still holding the wand in one hand and the list of spells in his mind. The high priestess hadn't actually answered his question after all.

By the time they got to the end of the corridor Pharaun's instincts were telling him to approach more slowly, more cautiously—but he'd also grown accustomed to following the lead of the highest ranking priestess in attendance, so he followed Quenthel into the chamber at the end of the corridor with a hesitation in his mind but not in his step.

The corridor opened into a huge, round, high-ceilinged chamber walled in the same rusted steel as the rest of the spider fortress. In the center of the otherwise empty space was a circle that appeared to be welded together from jagged, rusted pieces of the fortress construct itself. The circle stood up on its end, perhaps eighteen feet in diameter. The center of the ring was filled with opaque violet light, swirling and folding in on itself as if it came from a luminescent cloud of vapor trapped in the confines of the circle.

Pharaun heard footsteps and brought the wand out from under his *piwafwi*.

"You will not require that here, mage," a voice echoed in the chamber.

As the others filed into the room, Pharaun looked for the source of the voice. He sensed a figure lurking in a particularly dark shadow.

"There," Pharaun whispered to Quenthel. "See it?"

Quenthel nodded and said, "You will cast no spell; you will make no move toward it unless I order it. Do you understand?"

Pharaun said, "Of course, Mistress," but the others stood silent.

"I said," the high priestess reiterated, "do you understand?"

Danifae and Jeggred nodded, and Pharaun again said, "Of course, Mistress. Can you at least tell me what it is?"

"I prefer to be referred to as 'she'," the voice said, "being female."

The figure stepped out of the darkest part of the shadow and strode confidently into the purple light from the active but untuned portal. The sight of it took Pharaun's breath away.

The figure of a drow female slowly twisted and writhed a good ten feet in the air. The drow was perfectly formed and nude, her body more like Danifae's in its fullness than Quenthel's modest, strong frame. She dragged her hands over her body in long, slow caresses for which no part of her was forbidden.

From her sides grew two sets of long, segmented spider legs.

It was those four legs—and four more like it all together—that held the drow female up above the rusted floor.

Pharaun had seen too many driders to count, but what stepped out in front of him was no drider. Everything about the spider-drow creature demanded the wizard's full attention. The drow form was beautiful—beautiful in a way that Pharaun had no words to describe. Her long, spindly spider legs simply reminded him of where he was: the home plane of—

The Master of Sorcere shook his head slowly from side to side. It couldn't be.

"Lo—?" he whispered.

"I am not the Queen of the Demonweb Pits, Master of Sorcere," the spider-drow said in accented High Drow. "To even say it would be blasphemy."

"I've only read about you," Quenthel whispered.

A second spider-drow appeared, stepping lightly out of the gloom, and a third hung suspended from the ceiling, both their drow bodies those of a writhing naked drow female.

"Abyssal widows," Danifae said.

The name meant nothing to Pharaun.

"You are her handmaidens, and—" Quenthel started.

"And her midwives. We were only legend," the first abyssal widow purred. "We were only prophecy."

"Prophecy. . . ." Quenthel whispered.

"We exist now," the abyssal window said, "to guard the entrance to the Demonweb Pits."

"But," Pharaun said almost despite himself, "we're *in* the Demonweb Pits."

The beautiful drow female smiled, her teeth perfect and clean, the skin of her cheeks smooth and utterly devoid of blemish or imperfection.

"No," the creature replied, "not anymore."

"What's happened?" Quenthel asked. "Where is the goddess if not in the Abyss?"

"All your questions will be answered, Mistress," said the widow, "when you pass through the gate."

"It's a plane all its own now," Pharaun guessed.

The abyssal widows all nodded in unison and moved to stand on either side of the portal—guards along a procession route.

"You have come this far," one of the widows said.

"And so have proved you are worthy," continued another.

"To face Lolth and speed her into her new form," finished the third.

"Her new form?" asked Pharaun.

The abyssal widows all shared a coy look and gestured to the yawning violet portal.

"Did you . . ." the Master of Sorcere said, his throat dry, his hands shaking no matter how hard he tried to stop them. "Did you call yourself a midwife?"

"Pass," one of them said. "You are expected."

Quenthel stepped forward, Danifae close on her heels, and boldly walked into the roiling mass of purple light. She disappeared instantly, Danifae only steps behind her. Jeggred was a bit more reluctant, regarding the abyssal widows with blazing eyes as he passed them. Soon enough, he was gone as well.

Pharaun turned to Valas, whose eyes were darting from one widow to another. He had a hand on one of the many garish trinkets he wore pinned to his vest.

"So, Master Hune," Pharaun said, "here we are."

Valas looked at him and nodded.

"Where we're going . . ." the wizard said, pausing to gather his thoughts—not easy with the prospect of stepping through that particular portal looming so close. "It could be that your services are no longer required."

Valas locked his eyes on Pharaun's and said, "My services are no longer adequate."

Pharaun took a deep breath.

"Well," the wizard said, "as I said before, we would benefit from your skills and experience wherever we go, but here we've come to a point where you must make a decision."

"I have," said Valas, the look in his eye inviting no more conversation.

"Yes, well," Pharaun said, "there it is."

The wizard turned and without a backward glance stepped into the portal, leaving Valas Hune behind.

PHILIP ATHANS

The New York Times best-selling author of *Annihilation* and *Baldur's Gate* tells an epic tale of vision and heartbreak, of madness and ambition, that could change the map of Faerûn forever.

THE WATERCOURSE TRILOGY

BOOK I
WHISPER OF WAVES

The city-state of Innarlith sits on one edge of the Lake of Steam, just waiting for someone to drag it forward from obscurity. Will that someone be a Red Wizard of Thay, a street urchin who grew up to be the richest man in Innarlith, or a strange outsider who cares nothing for power but has grand ambitions all his own?

BOOK II
LIES OF LIGHT

A beautiful girl is haunted by spirits with dark intentions, an ambitious senator sells more than just his votes, and all the while construction proceeds on a canal that will alter the flow of trade in Faerûn.

BOOK III
SCREAM OF STONE

As the canal nears completion, scores will be settled, power will be bought and stolen, souls will be crushed and redeemed, and the power of one man's vision will be the only constant in a city-state gone mad.

"Once again it is Philip Athans moving the FORGOTTEN REALMS *to new ground and new vibrancy."*
—R.A. Salvatore

FORGOTTEN REALMS®

THE KNIGHTS OF MYTH DRANNOR

A brand new trilogy by master storyteller

ED GREENWOOD

Join the creator of the FORGOTTEN REALMS® world as he explores the early adventures of his original and most celebrated characters from the moment they earn the name "Swords of Eveningstar" to the day they prove themselves worthy of it.

BOOK I
SWORDS OF EVENINGSTAR

Florin Falconhand has always dreamed of adventure. When he saves the life of the king of Cormyr, his dream comes true and he earns an adventuring charter for himself and his friends. Unfortunately for Florin, he has also earned the enmity of several nobles and the attention of some of Cormyr's most dangerous denizens.
Now available in paperback!

BOOK II
SWORDS OF DRAGONFIRE

Victory never comes without sacrifice. Florin Falconhand and the Swords of Eveningstar have lost friends in their adventures, but in true heroic fashion, they press on. Unfortunately, there are those who would see the Swords of Eveningstar pay for lives lost and damage wrecked, regardless of where the true blame lies.

August 2007

BOOK III
THE SWORD NEVER SLEEPS

Fame has found the Swords of Eveningstar, but with fame comes danger. Nefarious forces have dark designs on these adventurers who seem to overturn the most clever of plots. And if the Swords will not be made into their tools, they will be destroyed.

August 2008

RICHARD A. KNAAK

THE OGRE TITANS

The Grand Lord Golgren has been savagely crushing
all opposition to his control of the harsh ogre lands of
Kern and Blöde, first sweeping away rival chieftains, then
rebuilding the capital in his image. For this he has had to
deal with the ogre titans, dark, sorcerous giants who have
contempt for his leadership.

VOLUME ONE
THE BLACK TALON

Among the ogres, where every ritual demands blood and every ally can
become a deadly foe, Golgren seeks whatever advantage he can obtain,
even if it means a possible alliance with the Knights of Solamnia, a
questionable pact with a mysterious wizard, and trusting an elven slave
who might wish him dead.

December 2007

VOLUME TWO
THE FIRE ROSE

With his other enemies beginning to converge on him from all sides,
Golgren, now Grand Khan of all his kind, must battle with the
Ogre Titans for mastery of a mysterious artifact capable of ultimate
transformation and power.

December 2008

VOLUME THREE
THE GARGOYLE KING

Forced from the throne he has so long coveted, Golgren makes a final
stand for control of the ogre lands against the Titans . . . against an
enemy as ancient and powerful as a god.

December 2009

A Certain Magical Index

7

KAZUMA KAMACHI

ILLUSTRATION BY
KIYOTAKA HAIMURA

"Hold on!! You weren't listening to a word I said! You were just smiling and nodding!!"

Academy City High School student **Touma Kamijou**

"What? No, I would never do anything like that."

Roman Orthodox sister **Orsola Aquinas**

"I have
nothing
to say
to that,
nor any
need to."

English
Puritan
Sorcerer from
Necessarius
Stiyl Magnus

"Coward!"

Nun managing the Index
of Prohibited Books **Index**

"Mgh......Papa..."

Roman Orthodox sister **Agnes Sanctis**

"Give it a rest,
Kaori Kanzaki.
You can't beat me."

Touma Kamijou's neighbor
Motoharu Tsuchimikado

"Have you come to stop me?"

English Puritan Sorcerer from
Necessarius **Kaori Kanzaki**

"But if you say so, then who am I to refuse?
It's your funeral."

Vicar pope of the Amakusa-Style Crossist Church **Saiji Tatemiya**

"Mm-hmm.
There are some other
things going on. Some
other things, you see."

Archbishop of the English
Puritan Church **Laura Stuart**

contents

VOLUME 7

KAZUMA KAMACHI
ILLUSTRATION BY: KIYOTAKA HAIMURA

NEW YORK

A CERTAIN MAGICAL INDEX, Volume 7
KAZUMA KAMACHI

Translation by Andrew Prowse
Cover art by Kiyotaka Haimura

TOARU MAJYUTSU NO INDEX
©KAZUMA KAMACHI 2005
All rights reserved.

Edited by ASCII MEDIA WORKS
First published in Japan in 2005 by KADOKAWA CORPORATION, Tokyo.
English translation rights arranged with KADOKAWA CORPORATION, Tokyo, through Tuttle-Mori Agency, Inc., Tokyo.

English translation © 2016 by Yen Press, LLC

Yen On
1290 Avenue of the Americas
New York, NY 10104

Visit us at yenpress.com
facebook.com/yenpress
twitter.com/yenpress
yenpress.tumblr.com

First Yen On Edition: June 2016

Yen On is an imprint of Yen Press, LLC.
The Yen On name and logo are trademarks of Yen Press, LLC.

Library of Congress Control Number: 2015046502

ISBNs: 978-0-316-27223-0 (paperback)
978-0-316-35984-9 (ebook)

10 9 8 7 6 5 4 3 2 1

RRD-C

Printed in the United States of America

PROLOGUE

The Opening Move

The_Page_is_Opened.

St. George's Cathedral.

Despite the moniker of "cathedral," it was just one of many churches located in inner London. It was a fairly large building, but compared to internationally popular sightseeing spots like Westminster Abbey and St Paul's Cathedral, it was exceptionally small. And, of course, it didn't come close to the Canterbury Cathedral, said to be where English Puritanism began.

Besides, there were many buildings in London named after Saint George. Churches were one thing, but there were also department stores, restaurants, boutiques, and schools sharing the name. There were likely dozens of St. Georges just within the city borders. And there may have even been more than ten St. George's Cathedrals in the first place—after all, the name was so famous it was even tied into the national flag.

Since its construction, St. George's Cathedral was the headquarters of Necessarius, the Church of Necessary Evils.

It wasn't a good connotation. Those who were a part of Necessarius were members of the Church, and yet they used tainted magic. Their duty was to aggressively destroy sorcerer's societies in England and annihilate the sorcerers belonging to them. They were considered boorish and uncouth by English Puritans, so they were moved out of Canterbury, the head church of English Puritanism, and relegated to St. George's Cathedral in what amounted to a demotion.

However…

Though it was once nothing more than a window-side post, Necessarius was silently but fervently bearing fruit.

And these actions granted them trust and privileges within the grand organization known as the Established Church. They did so well that while the heart of English Puritanism was still officially the Canterbury Cathedral, its mind had been entirely surrendered to St. George's Cathedral.

That was how this cathedral, just a stone's throw away from the center of London, had become the core of the largest religion in the country.

One morning, a red-haired priest named Stiyl Magnus was walking through London's streets, fretting to himself.

The city itself didn't look any different. Stone-built apartments constructed a little over three hundred years ago stood lining either side of the road as office workers hurried down it, their cell phones in their hands. At the same time traditional double-decker buses drove slowly by, the equally traditional red phone boxes were being steadily removed by construction workers. It was the same scenery as always—an amalgamation of the old and the new.

The weather hadn't changed, either. The skies over London this morning were clear enough for the sun to shine through, but the weather in this city was so hard to predict that nobody could really know what it would be like even four hours later, and many carried umbrellas with them. And it was hot and humid. London was known as the city of fog, but its volatile summertime weather was another problem entirely. Intermittent rain would bring nearby temperatures up, while the hot foehn wind and heat waves, growing more prevalent in recent years, led to extreme heat. Even snug little sightseeing spots had problems. Of course, Stiyl had chosen to live in this city in spite of its issues, so he didn't particularly mind.

The problem was the girl walking beside him.

"Archbishop!"

"Mm. I implore you, my good sir, do not call my name in such a grand manner. Today I have at last chosen a simple, plain outfit, you see," proclaimed a carefree voice in Japanese.

The voice belonged to a girl who looked about eighteen, clad in a simple beige habit. Incidentally, holy garb was supposed to be either white, red, black, green, or purple, and the embroidery could only be made with gold thread—so she may have been bending the rules a bit.

She was probably the only person who thought her outfit was blending in with the people in the city. Her skin was so fair it shone, and her eyes were a perfectly clear blue. Her hair, which looked like something that would be sold by a vendor of precious gems, utterly failed to fit in with the crowd.

Her hair was abnormally long, too. She wore it straight down—but at her ankles, it turned up and went back to her head. It was held there by a big silver barrette...and then it went all the way down to her waist again. Its length was roughly two and a half times her height.

London's morning rush hour—and Lambeth's in particular—was one of the most congested in the world, but nevertheless it seemed like the volume of nearby sounds was being lowered. Even the air around them felt akin to the silence called for in a cathedral.

She was the archbishop of the 0th parish of the English Puritan Church, Necessarius—the Church of Necessary Evils.

Laura Stuart.

The English Puritan Church's leader was the reigning king. And beside him was Laura...the highest archbishop, whose role it was to command the Church in place of the king, who was normally extremely busy.

The organization of English Puritanism was like an antique stringed instrument.

While the tool had an owner, a caretaker carried out the tool's maintenance and repairs. It didn't matter how excellent the violin was—if not used, its strings would slacken before you knew it, its sound box would be damaged, and the sounds it played would grow hoarse. Laura was the temporary performing musician who prevented that.

But this relationship, just like the one between Westminster Abbey and St. George's Cathedral, was now—both practically and on paper—turned on its head, and the ability to give commands rested in her hands now.

Despite her vast authority, the archbishop was now prancing along a morning street without any bodyguards to speak of.

The two of them were currently headed toward St. George's Cathedral. Laura was also the one who had instructed him in advance to come to the cathedral at this time, so she should have been waiting there...

"I, too, do have a location to which I must return home each day. I could never remain within the confines of such an antiquated cathedral for my whole life." Laura proceeded down the road, her footsteps not making a sound. "Let us talk whilst we walk, shall we? Lest we use our time poorly."

Most of the people passing by were company workers. After all, they were close to Waterloo Station, the largest in London. A nun and a priest wouldn't have been an unusual sight here. It was no Rome, but London still had as many churches as it did parks.

"Well, I suppose I don't mind. But if this was something you needed to call me out to the cathedral for, then you don't want to be overheard telling it to me, do you?"

"Pray tell, does it bother you? How small a man you are. Can you not possibly find any enjoyment in our constitutional? Priests listen to the confessions of the women as though they are playboys, after all. Haven't you even a modicum of desire for adventure?"

"..." Stiyl made a slightly displeased face, then said, "May I ask you a question?"

"Please, stay your formal language. What would you have of me?"

"Why are you talking like a complete idiot?"

"...?" The archbishop of English Puritanism reacted much like someone had just pointed out she'd buttoned up her shirt wrong—at first she was dumbfounded, then she froze in place, and finally her face went bright red.

"Huh? I— What? Do I sound odd to your ears? Verily, should I not be conversing in the Japanese language in the manner with which I am even now speaking?!"

"Umm, excuse me, but I can barely even understand what you're saying. Even your archaic Japanese seems messed up."

The people walking down the street in suits wouldn't have understood Japanese, but for some reason, the bustle around them had turned into whispering—and it felt like it was focused on Laura.

"A-argh...I did verily examine a great many things of literature, television, and all the rest...I even had a real-life Japanese person check my work, too..."

Stiyl sighed. "Who is this real-life Japanese person exactly?"

"A-a gentleman named Motoharu Tsuchimikado..."

"...He would dress his stepsister up in a maid outfit and then faint out of happiness. He's dangerous. Please don't consider him a standard Japanese person. Asia's culture isn't that strange."

"You have a point. I suppose then that I must mend my mistaken way of speaking lest I— Egads!" Laura's shout caused a flock of pigeons resting on the road to all fly up into the air.

"What's the matter?"

"It has become part of me! I'm never going to fix it *now*!"

"...Please don't tell me you spoke so idiotically during your conference with the Academy City representative."

Laura's shoulders gave a jolt. "N-no, it is nothing I must fret over. It's fine, everything is fine, entirely fine," she said, but her voice was trembling, there was an odd droplet of sweat dripping down her cheek, and her eyes were wandering.

Stiyl breathed a sigh that smelled of tobacco. "Anyway, we can talk about that once we arrive at the cathedral."

The two of them turned a corner, on which was situated a Japanese restaurant that Kaori Kanzaki frequented in secret, and continued.

"N-no! I have no need to feel such mortification. I declare that I have done nothing uncouth from the first."

"Give this nonsense a rest and get down to business, please. Oh, and if you're not confident in your Japanese, then can't you just switch to English?"

"N-nonsense...! Th-this has nothing to do with my not possessing confidence. Yes, that's right! It is simply that I am not well on this particular day," claimed Laura, acting extremely suspiciously. "As for work...Oh, but first—"

She took two pieces of paper that looked like sticky notes and a black Magic Marker out from the breast of her habit. Stiyl, who was familiar with using cards with runes on them, immediately understood what she would use them for.

"Squeak-squeak—♪"

While saying aloud the sound effect for the marker's scribbling, Laura began to draw some sort of pattern on the paper with the black marker. It was probably a talisman or circle. When the archbishop was in front of a large group of people for ceremonies and the like, she would act so solemn and majestic you would doubt she was even human—but right now she looked for all the world like a normal girl doodling in her notebook during class. He personally wished she would act that solemnly all the time.

Stiyl, a cigarette in his mouth, frowned a bit. He didn't like the sound this marker made very much.

"Squeak-squeak-squeaksqueak-squeak-squeak-squeaksqueak-squeak-squeak-squeaksqueak-squeak-squeak-squeaksqueak-squeak-squeak-squeaksqueak-squeak-squeak-squeaksqueak-squeak-squeak-squeak-squeak-squeaksqueak-squeaksqueak-squeak-squeak-squeaksqueak-squeak-squeak—♪"

"...Excuse me for asking, but what is it you're doing?" asked Stiyl, gritting his teeth and shaking all over. Veins were popping out of his temples, but he'd just have to endure that right now.

"Think of this as a token of my consideration. Here!" Finished drawing the same pattern on both pieces of paper, Laura pushed one of them into Stiyl's hands.

"Ahem! I ask of you—are you able to hear this sound?"

Stiyl heard what seemed like a voice speaking directly to his mind.

He glanced at her face to make sure, but as he thought, her small mouth wasn't moving. "A communication talisman?"

"It is by doing this that we may speak our minds with nary the need to converse aloud."

Hmm. Stiyl looked down at the card in his hand. She seemed to have gone out of her way to show consideration after his advice that others hearing them would be bad.

"Why does your mental voice sound as moronic as your real one?"

"What did you say? W-wait, Stiyl! I assert that I am speaking English in this moment!"

She fidgeted wildly yet silently, startling a cat curled up in front of a still-closed café. Stiyl sighed. Why couldn't she keep her cool now, despite all the gravitas she displayed as archbishop?

"Then it must be mistranslating you during the communication and conversion processes. How exhausting. I can understand you just fine, though, so let's proceed."

"W-we…Ahem! Then let us begin." Laura had been about to say something, but she swallowed it back down and changed the topic to something work-related. *"Stiyl, have you perchance heard the name* Book of the Law?*"*

"The name of the grimoire? If I recall correctly, it was penned by Edward Alexander."

Edward Alexander—also known as Crowley. He was at once called the greatest sorcerer of the twentieth century and the *worst* sorcerer of the twentieth century. He was a legendary figure, one whose aberrant, extremist, abnormal words and actions got him deported from many countries on many occasions, one who fueled the creative passions of many an artist…and one who made an enemy out of every single sorcerer in the world. Historical records stated that he died on December 1, 1947. He was such an utterly difficult and chaotic enemy that one could rightly say that his death loosened strings of tension across the planet.

Even after the great sorcerer's death, there was no shortage of those calling themselves his students or legitimate heirs. Even today, there was an investigation agency dedicated to countering Crowley's own brand of artificial magicks. And, as is usually the case with people of such legendary status, Stiyl had also heard rumors that the man was still alive.

"*What about it? The original copy is in the Roman Orthodox Church's Vatican Library right now, isn't it?*"

He had traveled across the world as bodyguard of the Index girl while they were cramming the 103,000 grimoires into her mind. It was an easy task to recall the owners and locations of a hundred or so of the most famous ones.

"*Yes, well...Crowley was active in Sicily from 1920 to 1923, meaning the* Book of the Law *was lost during that interval of time.*" Laura continued, as if she were flipping through a history textbook. "*Now, Stiyl, mayhaps you know of the* Book of the Law*'s unique characteristics?*"

"..."

Unique characteristics.

"*If I'm correct, and disregarding the reliability of Crowley actually having written it, there are several academic theories on the matter. One goes that the* Book of the Law *contains angelic techniques unusable by man that were revealed to him by Aiwass, the guardian angel he summoned. Another says that as soon as you open the book, it proclaims the end of the era of Crossism and the coming of an entirely new age...Sure, it's impossible that he heard all that from angels—they have no will of their own—but the second one is interesting. And—*"

Among the English Puritan Church's speculations were many explanations that said the grimoire described methods by which to use the vastly powerful sorcery it boasted.

But everyone who heard all this came to one crucial question.

Why did it stop at mere speculation?

The Index of Prohibited Books should have had knowledge regarding the *Book of the Law.*

"*—nobody can decipher it, right? Grimoires are by nature written in various codes, but I hear this one is another story entirely. The Index gave up on deciphering it as well, and even Sherry Cromwell, the leading expert in code-breaking, gave it up as hopeless.*"

Yes—nobody could read the *Book of the Law*. By the Index's explanation, it was no longer able to be decoded using present-day linguistic approaches. Because of that, the passages of the *Book of the Law* were stuck in her head still in encoded form.

Laura smiled, pleased. *"If I were to say that someone who is able to read the* Book of the Law *has appeared, what would you do?"*

"…What?" Stiyl looked at her again. She didn't look like she was joking.

"She is a nun of the Roman Orthodox Church, and her name is Orsola Aquinas. It would seem as though she only knows the method to decipher it—she has not laid eyes upon the book itself."

"How, then?"

"This Orsola was apparently hunting for the method of decoding it using but a portion of its manuscript to serve as a reference. She had only the table of contents and a few pages from the initial section at her disposal."

The original copy of the *Book of the Law* was under such strict watch that even she wouldn't easily have been able to view it. And since she wasn't the Index of Forbidden Books, even gaining access to the original copy without proper care would be dangerous.

"The Roman Orthodox Church…is lacking cards to play in our overarching power struggle at the moment. Are they attempting to use the Book of the Law *in a plot to recover from that setback? Do they not see it as anything more than the blueprints for a new weapon…?"*

The Roman Orthodox Church was said to be the largest of the religious factions of Crossism, but there were reports that their strength had waned. Their greatest power, the Gregorian Choir, made up of more than three thousand people, had been destroyed by a certain alchemist. Since that was the case, Stiyl didn't doubt that they'd jump at the opportunity to replenish their lost strength by using the knowledge in the *Book of the Law* to plan and create a new spell to replace the Gregorian Choir and protect their seat at the top.

"Well, 'twould seem impossible for them to use the Book of the Law *to bolster their military forces. At least, there is presently no threat of*

the Roman Orthodox Church using it immediately to assail a place, so you can rest easy."

"?"

"Mm-hmm. There are some other things going on. Some other things, you see."

Laura sounded awfully certain, but Stiyl frowned. What was her basis for saying that? He considered briefly that there was a pact between the English Puritan Church and the Roman Orthodox Church forbidding the book's use, but...

...Then why would the Roman Orthodox Church need Orsola to decode the Book of the Law in the first place?

"You're such a worrywart. It is written upon your face. I keep telling you, all is well! All is well."

"But..."

"Ahh, how vexing, how vexing indeed! Whatever in the world the Roman Orthodox Church is plotting on using the Book of the Law for, they cannot, at any rate, carry it out right this second."

Before Stiyl could ask her why, she answered him.

"The Book of the Law and Orsola Aquinas—these both do appear to have been stolen."

"What...By whom?!" Stiyl couldn't help but say aloud. His outburst caused the eyes of the company workers heading to the station to all gather on him.

"I have a good guess, so your job is to hear the details from me and then deal with it. Though I am sure of one thing—our opponent will be Japan's Amakusa-Style Crossist Church."

"Amakusa-Style..."

Stiyl's current partner was Kaori Kanzaki. Amakusa-Style was a Japanese branch of Crossism, which she used to be the leader of—their priestess.

But Stiyl didn't see them as a Crossist religion. There was too much Shinto and Buddhism mixed into it. It hadn't retained the original form of Crossism.

"As a church, Amakusa-Style is significantly smaller than the national religions of Rome, England, and Russia. That they continue to thrive in the world is because of the presence of an irregular: Kanzaki. Their central pillar has been lost, so it is not odd that they should seek out the Book of the Law *and replace her with it. After all, using the book could seriously upset the power balance of Crossism."*

If Orsola Aquinas and the *Book of the Law* had fallen into Amakusa-Style's hands, they could use it at any time. In fact, it would be stranger if they *didn't* use it.

"But still!" Stiyl's voice became ragged. *"Wasn't the* Book of the Law *safe in the deepest part of the Vatican Library? Right now, Amakusa-Style is small enough to desire power. A religion of that size would never be able to break in there. I know because I've actually been inside the Vatican Library as that Index's bodyguard. There are no gaps in their security or any back doors. It's a wall, plain and simple!"*

"I'm saying the Book of the Law *wasn't in the Vatican Library."*

"What?" Stiyl's expression froze.

He passed by what appeared to be a horse-drawn wagon meant for sightseeing, the horse's hooves making clopping noises as they pranced along the road. There was a license plate politely affixed to the rear of the wagon.

"The Roman Orthodox Church had moved the Book of the Law *into a museum in Japan to hold an international exhibition. I expect I do not need to tell you why the Holy Stairs in the Archbasilica of St. John Lateran in Rome, which the Son of God is said to have ascended as he bled, are open to the general public, yes?"*

The Church opened its historical and religious articles to the public once every few years.

The reason was simple—it was to attract guests so they could collect donations from many disciples as well as recruit new ones. Because the Roman Orthodox Church had lost its most powerful weapon, the three-thousand-strong Gregorian Choir, they wanted to put as much as possible into creating new spells and strengthening their numbers.

The most effective way to gain new disciples would be to plan these events in places there were none already. Japan was suitable for that purpose, but going there would simultaneously weaken its controlling power. Amakusa-Style must have pinpointed that weakness.

"*That's absurd...They put something that dangerous on display, then let it be swiped out from under them? How much must the Roman Orthodox Church embarrass itself before it learns?*"

She chuckled. "*They are the most cognizant of that fact, I believe. They may have gained a terrain advantage, but their pride is in shambles now that a small religion in the Far East has bested them.*"

"*Right. So they shamefully and scandalously came crawling to us to see if we'd cooperate, is that it?*"

"*Nay. 'Twould seem they wish to settle things by their own hand. Because of that, we went to some effort in acquiring this information. It may be their last bit of pride speaking, but in all honesty, at this those fools need to wake up and face reality.*"

"*We weren't helping rescue Aquinas and retrieve the* Book of the Law *at the Roman Orthodox Church's request?*"

"*They were hesitating. And if Orsola Aquinas truly is able to decode the* Book of the Law, *we would need to move in anyway.*"

"*...Then you plan on placing them in our debt? Do you think those religious nobles would pay us back for anything?*" asked Stiyl, as if the whole matter were idiotic.

Stiyl was aware the Roman Orthodox Church—the majority of disciples ignorant of sorcery aside—had a famously high level of pride and self-regard. Perhaps it was a remnant of once having controlled Europe. That went especially for those thickheaded priests and bishops who belonged to stricter groups. Not only would they look down on those who got in their way, but there were even some who would outright tell people cooperating with them that their very cooperation made them pathetic and detestable.

"*Not a hair on my head wishes to support the fools who are causing the old way, Catholicism, to rot—in fact, they are the ones to blame for it being called that. But hear me, Stiyl—we have a larger problem.*"

"*And what's that?*"

"We cannot contact Kaori Kanzaki."

Laura used only the minimum number of words, and Stiyl immediately knew what she meant.

Kanzaki used to be the leader of Amakusa-Style Crossism. Though she was separate from them now, she still thought of herself as part of them. If she found out that her people were causing problems and making an enemy of Roman Orthodoxy, the world's largest religion with more than two billion believers, what actions might she take?

She was one of less than twenty known saints in the world, and her very existence would balance a scale with nuclear weaponry. The English Puritans had let go of her reins, and if she were to kill someone from Roman Orthodoxy on top of that, what would happen…?

"With her personality, it is indeed quite possible that she would lend a hand without ceasing to think of the consequences. Were she of average or below average strength, that would be one thing. However, as this is Kanzaki we're speaking of…"

Laura heaved a sigh, unamused. *"I would like to settle things afore Kanzaki has time to make a mistake. That is our top priority. I care not what method you select. You may retrieve the Book of the Law and Orsola, force Amakusa-Style to surrender by negotiation, or eliminate them along with Kanzaki by force."*

"You're telling me to fight Kanzaki?"

"Verily, I am, depending on the situation," replied Laura simply. *"Our own personnel are scattered, and they prepare even now to make for the Roman Orthodox search party in Japan. But you will be with a separate unit, so I would like you to make contact with Academy City in advance of that."*

Stiyl blew white cigarette smoke from his mouth as if to voice his doubts.

Not regarding the part about him being in a separate team.

The sorcerer Stiyl Magnus was never meant for team play. His personality was one reason, of course, but since he specialized in the usage of flame sorcery, going all-out meant nearby allies would run the risk of getting caught in the fire and smoke.

His Witch-Hunter King, Innocentius, was partly unstable because its strength wildly fluctuated depending on how many cards Stiyl deployed, but it still boasted power enough to be true to its name. The sight of a 3,000-degree Celsius ball of flames dancing freely and easily burning through even iron walls to approach and attack an enemy must have been the very vision of a god of death to his opponents. After all, excluding a certain boy's right hand, there was no possible way to halt its advance. His exploits could be summed up as "magnificent," given how many sorcerers' societies he had burned to the ground by himself.

So that wasn't the issue here.

"*This is* our *problem. Why do we need* them *for anything?*"

"*The Index of Prohibited Books.*"

Laura spoke the name of a person...no, the name of a *tool*.

"*When grimoires appear, especially one as major as the* Book of the Law, *we require an expert's assistance, do we not? I have already explained everything to them, so you may feel free to put your strength on full display. One condition, though—that you work with the* management."

"*...*"

"*What say you? You do not seem very joyful at your first with that in a while.*"

"Not at all." Stiyl bit back a few choice words and erased his expression. "*...By* management, *you mean the destroyer of illusions, right?*"

"*Just so. You may use him as you will. Oh, but pray do not kill him. We're only borrowing him, after all.*"

"*Should we be getting a citizen of Academy City involved in a conflict among sorcerers?*"

"*As long as you make use of some tricks, everything will be fine. In either case, they will not let her go based on the conditions of our exchange. We don't have the luxury of drawing out the negotiations.*"

"*I...see.*"

He couldn't quite grasp what either the leader of Academy City or Laura, walking next to him, was thinking. There were probably some dealings going on behind the scenes, though, so it wasn't Stiyl's place as an underling to say anything, but...

"Also, Stiyl. Take this with you, if you would."

Laura took a necklace with a small cross on it out of the sleeve of her plain habit and casually tossed it to Stiyl. He caught the symbol of faith with one hand.

"Is this a kind of Soul Arm? Though at first glance, it doesn't seem to have anything like that inside."

"Think of it as a small gift for Orsola Aquinas. When you meet her, give it to her when you can."

He didn't really know what she meant by it, but she didn't seem to have any particular desire to explain in detail. She was basically saying, "It doesn't matter, so be quiet and do your job."

The two of them stopped walking.

In front of them stood a church—not so big you would think it was a cathedral, and about a ten-minute walk from one of the largest stations in London.

St. George's Cathedral.

It was a sanctuary of darkness, a condensed version of the dark ages of witch-hunting and the Inquisition, where France's legendary saint, Joan of Arc, was burned at the stake.

Laura took a step in front of Stiyl and touched the heavy doorknob softly.

"Now then…"

She opened the heavy double doors and turned around, gesturing to the priest.

She spoke in a clear voice now, without using the cards.

"Why don't we discuss the details within?"

CHAPTER 1

Academy City

Science_Worship.

1

"The second semester is always busy, you know! There's the Daihasei Festival, the Ichihanaran Festival, the field trip where we study far away for a few days, the Art Appreciation Festival, the Social Studies Festival, the Great Cleaning Festival, Finals Festival, the Follow-Up Festival, the Remedial Class Festival, the Crying Detention Festival...It's basically all festivals. Everyone's gonna be busy preparing for them all."

September 8.

That afternoon, in the hallway of a student dormitory, Maika Tsuchimikado spoke in a carefree voice. She was around the same age as Index, if not a bit younger, and she was wearing a strange maid uniform. Even more mysteriously, she was sitting *seiza* atop an oil drum–shaped cleaning robot. The robot's programming was trying to move it forward, but Maika had stuck her mop on the floor in front of it to stop it, so it was just shaking and rattling around.

"But I'm bored! I have nothing to do! Touma won't pay attention to me! He won't play with me!"

Index stood in front of Maika Tsuchimikado and argued. She was sneering and moving from left to right. Her locks of silver hair and her long white hood fluttered. The calico cat she held in her slender arms appeared to be interested in the sparkling of the gold embroidery decorating her hood—it was waving its forepaws around and swatting at it.

She knew how busy Touma Kamijou had gotten lately. But he was the only one in Academy City Index could talk to.

Of course, it wasn't like he was locking her up in the dorm or anything. He had given her a duplicate key, so she did actually take walks here and there while he was away at school. (Of course, it usually ended up in her running back home after coming up against machines she couldn't handle—like the ticket vending machines at the station or locks that required fingerprint, venous, or bioelectric field authentication.)

This city was just *strange*.

Built when the western areas of Tokyo were developed all at once, this city of science was 80 percent students. While Kamijou was at school, Himegami and Komoe were at school, too. So when Index had tried to go out and find someone new to talk to, she found the city eerily empty. For the past week, she'd been looking around the city in her own way. She did discover that the lady at the clothes store would talk to her cheerfully—except when she was replacing clothing on the racks—but Index didn't quite think that's what she was looking for.

Maika Tsuchimikado, though, was an exception among exceptions.

In this city, people came and went at very specific times of day, but this girl alone wasn't bound to any of time's rules. Index had seen her around the city both in the morning and in the afternoon, at the convenience store, the department store, the park, the bread store, the station building, the student dorm, on the roads, and near school—it didn't seem to matter when or where.

Maika insistently pounded the palm of her hand on the cleaning robot, dissuading it from moving forward, and continued.

"Touma Kamijou has his own issues to take care of, so you shouldn't get in his way. He's not locked up at school because he likes it, you know. There are a lot of difficult things about school!"

"Mgh. I know that, but…How come you're not locked up at school, then, Maika?"

"Hee-hee! I'm an exception. Basic maid training is all fieldwork!"

The home economics academy Maika Tsuchimikado attended wasn't just a strange, anachronistic school that pumped out maids. They produced specialists—people able to assist their masters in any location, from scraping gum off the sidewalk to aiding international summits. Thus, Maika carried out her "fieldwork" in a variety of locations. Of course, not all the students were out on fieldwork. This was a special step only for those elites who passed a standardized test and were judged to have the ability never to look disgraceful despite still being in training.

Index didn't know about all the sweat and tears that went into it. She cutely tilted her head to the side.

"So if I became a maid, I could go anywhere I wanted whenever I wanted? I wouldn't be locked up at school? Could I even do field-work in Touma's classroom?"

"Well, no, that's not what maids really—"

"Then I'm gonna become a maid, too! And then maybe I can go to Touma's class to play!"

"That sounds great, but becoming a maid is no easy task, you know. You have no household skills whatsoever. You'd have it tough needing to make lunch for boys day in and day out."

"Then I'll make Touma a maid! Maybe then I can get him to come play!"

"That sounds so great I'm practically crying over here, so maybe the nice thing to do would be to not tell Touma Kamijou you said that!"

The bored Index puffed out her cheeks, annoyed, and then quickly jolted to the left.

"She's right. Sorry, but there's no time for you to be a maid—nor to make him one, for that matter."

Suddenly, a voice came from behind the girl in white.

Huh? Index's mind went blank for a moment. Maika, in front of her, was probably looking at the person standing behind Index. The maid's face looked more scared than surprised.

Who is...?

Before the sister in white could turn around and speak up...

A large hand pressed down over her mouth, sealing it like masking tape.

2

Touma Kamijou, an average high school student of the sort that seemed ubiquitous, trudged down the road in the evening sun.

An oil drum–shaped cleaning robot passed by him, and the propellers of the wind turbines that stood in for telephone poles spun around and around as if trying to swat away the city crows. There were plenty of advertisement blimps floating along in the orange sky, but the curtains hanging beneath them weren't simple cloth signs, but rather the latest in super-thin screen technology. One display said, WELL-PREPARED MEANS NO WORRIES! DO YOUR BEST TO PREPARE FOR THE DAIHASEI FESTIVAL! —JUDGMENT, the text a marquee running from bottom to top like an electric signboard.

The Daihasei Festival was basically a big athletic meet. Academy City had millions of students, and it naturally turned into a big affair with every school in the city participating. Plus, all of the students were espers who had grown into some sort of special power or another. On top of *that*, because the Academy City General Board had originally proposed the festival so it could gather data on large amounts of espers interacting with one another, full usage of one's powers was recommended for that day only. That meant you could see clashes between espers that you wouldn't normally be able to see. For example, during a soccer or dodgeball game, the ball could become invisible, or light on fire, or be frozen in ice. Anything went.

During that week, Academy City would be opened to both the general public and television crews. As far as he could tell, the ridiculously over-the-top situations that sprang up during matches drew in large numbers of viewers, since you absolutely couldn't see anything like it at normal sporting events. That was the reason Judgment always went full throttle preparing for it. Another part of it was the fact they wanted to raise Academy City's public image during those few days it was open. As a precaution, the city would also place Anti-Skill officers at crucial ability development locations under the pretext of special antiterrorism forces in order to prevent the general populace from getting into places the city didn't want it to see.

"B-blech..."

At least, that was what he'd heard from voices around him this week.

Kamijou had lost his memories after a certain incident, so he didn't know anything about the Daihasei Festival. But based on what he'd heard, he could guess, though, it would be an extremely dangerous event for him in particular. The fundamental rule was that you could use your powers freely. In fact, not being assertive enough in using them would land you right in the loving arms of a medical squad. That was Daihasei. In other words, depending on the time and place, there could be balls of fire, lightning attacks, and vacuum blades flying every which way during simple events like mock cavalry battles.

He looked at his right hand. In it was a power called Imagine Breaker. It would erase any strange ability, whether magical or supernatural, at just a touch. He still didn't want to be charging into a fierce, chaotic battle filled with dozens of espers with just *that*, though.

...Why do I have to work my ass off to set up for an event that could end up as yet another *bloodbath for me...?*

Even his preparations weren't going smoothly. As soon as he pitched an observation tent in the schoolyard, a female gym teacher had smiled in chagrin, clapped her hands together in apology, and said, "Sorry! We didn't actually need a tent!" And then when he put it away again, a tiny female teacher got mad and said, "Ahh! What are you doing, Kami?! Didn't you get the message that we needed the tent after all?" Just saying *what rotten luck* wasn't going to cut it.

He dragged himself toward his dormitory, his body completely exhausted from all the futile labor.

"Ah. Now that I think of it, the fridge is totally empty, isn't it?"

He could see a supermarket right near him, but he would have to go back to the dorm to get money first. *Man, I have to go back out again?* he thought, limping onto his street.

His cheap sneakers had hard soles, so every time they touched the pavement, it exacerbated the pain in his feet.

Then, once he got close to the entrance of his dormitory, he suddenly heard a girl's voice from overhead.

"Ahhh! T-T-To, T-T-T-Touma Kamijou! Hey, Touma Kamijou!"

Hm? He looked up and saw Maika Tsuchimikado leaning over the metal railing on the seventh floor, waving her right arm. She was kneeling atop a cleaning robot as always, so her current position looked rather precarious. Her left hand held a mop, and she had it stuck on the floor. It seemed to be preventing the robot from moving forward like it was supposed to.

"S-s-s-something happened, something bad happened! Also your cell phone battery is dead!"

"Huh?" At that, he took his GPS-equipped cell phone out of his pocket. Its battery had indeed run dry. He pushed a button and looked at the screen to find a ton of text messages from one Maika Tsuchimikado.

Come to think of it, though she spoke in a long, drawn-out way, her face did look a little pale.

He was a little confused, but he hurried into the elevator.

When he arrived on the seventh floor where his room was, Maika released her mop, binding the cleaning robot, which proceeded to sluggishly wander over toward the elevator. The cat, which was normally always with Index, was sitting in the hallway for some reason, its ears down. It was unhappily holding Index's free-with-contract cell phone in its mouth.

The cleaning robot arrived before Kamijou, and Maika put the mop back down in front of it to hold it in place again. "It's an emergency, an emergency! The silver-haired sister got kidnapped!"

"Huh?" he grunted without thinking.

She continued, her face white. "A kidnapper! She's been taken away! He told me if I reported him he'd kill the hostage, so I couldn't do anything! I'm sorry, Touma Kamijou!"

The silver-haired sister—that must have been Index. The maid didn't look like she was joking. And there were plenty of reasons people would want to kidnap Index.

She was a library of grimoires—there were 103,000 of them recorded in her memories. Sorcerers throughout the world desired that knowledge. Once, on August 1, she'd been kidnapped for that very reason.

"Wait a second. What happened? Could you explain in order?" he asked.

Maika began to explain little by little.

She had come to the student dorm for her "fieldwork" two hours earlier. While she was making her rounds, she ran into the bored Index on the seventh floor and started to make conversation. Then, someone came up behind Index and put a hand over her mouth, interrupting the conversation, and made off with her.

"Before the kidnapper left, he gave me an envelope. He wrote a bunch of stuff in it…"

She handed him an envelope—a wide one, like the ones used for junk advertisement mail. Her voice was more than a little unsteady. It wasn't plain fear—it was probably also guilt at not having been able to do anything.

He glanced down at the envelope, then back up. "No, if you had been careless, things would have gotten much worse than they are now."

He intended those words to comfort her, but she grew more worried instead. The tension in the air could burn through skin. She was just a normal student here who had no connection to any of this, so she couldn't help it.

"Anyway, what did this asshole look like?"

She looked up slightly, thinking to herself. "Umm. Well, he was at least one hundred and eighty centimeters tall. And he looked Caucasian, too. But his Japanese was really good, and just by looking at him I couldn't tell what country he came from."

"Uh-huh, uh-huh."

"And he had on these clothes that looked kinda like a priest's."

"Uh-huh?"

"But even though he was a priest, he smelled like perfume. And his hair was shoulder length and dyed really red, and he had a silver ring on all ten fingers, and he had this tattoo of a bar code underneath his right eye, and he was smoking a cigarette, and he had tons of earrings!"

"...Wait, I know exactly who that is. It's that rotten English priest."

She tilted her head to the side with a confused look. He checked out the envelope again. Inside was one piece of letter paper.

The characters were written in pen and looked as though they'd been drawn using a ruler. It said:

Touma Kamijou
If you value the girl's life
Come to the abandoned Hakumeiza theater
Outside Academy City
At seven PM tonight
Come alone

"...Using a ruler to conceal your handwriting? That's so old-fashioned."

Was he seriously trying to conceal his identity just by hiding his handwriting using a ruler? How behind the times was he? There were methods of appraising handwriting that looked at the indentations of characters and measuring the slight finger tremble that varied from person to person. It used the same technology as the lasers for reading data off CDs. And anyway, there was no shortage of psychometers in Academy City.

I think he's serious about this. At this point? Is this his idea of a joke or something? thought Kamijou, a bit baffled. *What is that idiot thinking? Did he get a late summer vacation and decided to come out here to fool around?*

As far as he could gather from what Maika had told him, Index's kidnapper seemed to be her colleague, Stiyl Magnus. But he would never threaten her life. Quite the contrary—he wouldn't hesitate to protect her even if it meant charging into enemy territory or into a fortress.

That reduced his nervousness by a good deal.

At this point, he felt bad letting Maika stay so seriously depressed about it.

"Ah, it'll be fine, Maika. I think the culprit is someone Index and I know. So you don't need to worry."

"Huh? You two know him?! His motive—was it love gone wrong?"

"Uh, what? No, that's not it... Though that does seem pretty possible."

All that did was make Maika's face go white. Kamijou sighed.

He shook the envelope, and out came a few more folded-up pieces of paper. He unfolded them to find an exit permit and related documents. All the necessary fields had already been filled in. *Where did he even get this stuff?* he thought, mystified. *I mean, with these I should be able to just walk out the front door, but you're supposed to go through a whole bunch of other steps to get these...*

He was appalled at the absurd juxtaposition of the threat letter and the carefully prepared documents to help him.

What could that priest be thinking, anyway?

3

Hakumeiza, the abandoned theater whose name meant "twilight seats," was only about one kilometer outside Academy City.

It had gone under less than three year earlier, so there were no visible signs of disrepair inside it. The interior furnishings had all been disposed of, so the place was completely empty. There was dust piled up here and there, since it hadn't been cleaned, but it still didn't give the impression of a *ruin*. It seemed like it would immediately spring back to life if given a thorough cleaning and restored with all its old furnishings.

It was as though the building was only hibernating for the winter. Maybe they hadn't knocked the place down because they were still looking for its next owner.

Index and Stiyl were up on its empty stage. The large hall, about the size of a school gymnasium, came with a fixed stage and audience seats. All of the light fixtures had been removed as well, so the only illumination was the evening light shining through the five opened entrances.

The thin dusk settled upon the stage, on which Index was sitting on her knees, with her feet out at her sides. She pouted and puffed out her cheeks. "Coward!"

"I have nothing to say to that, nor any need to." Stiyl Magnus nearly flinched for a moment at her hostile stare, but he would never let it show. The flame that he touched to the end of the cigarette in his mouth slowly rose and fell in the dim light. The white smoke billowing from it combed past a sign on the wall that read No SMOKING and disappeared.

"I believe you understand the general situation. I won't ask you if you need me to go over it again. Given how powerful your memory is, there would be no point in repeating myself."

"...An official edict from the English Puritan Church."

Index played back the explanation he'd been given after he'd brought her here.

Someone had appeared who knew how to decipher the *Book of the Law*, which should have been impossible to decipher.

The name of that person was Orsola Aquinas.

If the *Book of the Law* were deciphered, one might gain angelic techniques that would destroy the Crossist power balance.

During a trip to Japan, someone had stolen both the *Book of the Law* and Orsola.

The culprits appeared to be the Amakusa-Style Crossist Church.

The Roman Orthodox Church was beginning to take action to get the *Book of the Law* and Orsola back.

Nobody could contact Kaori Kanzaki of the English Puritan Church, who used to be the leader of Amakusa-Style, and they predicted she would do something less than desirable.

On the surface, the English Puritan Church was involved in this incident, since they were cooperating with the Roman Orthodox Church, but their top priority was to deal with the problem before Kaori Kanzaki had time to make any needless moves.

"So you're going to get a normal person like Touma wrapped up in this official 'job' of yours?"

"Actually, I'm somewhat unconvinced about why we need to, myself. But it's an order from the powers that be, and all that." The cigarette in his mouth wiggled as he spoke. "And it still puts us in a difficult position. He's from Academy City. If we went directly to him and asked for his help, people might see it as the science faction sticking their neck into the magic faction's problems. If this issue had occurred solely within Academy City, we could use our lame self-defense excuse again, but it's different this time. We needed a way to give him a suitable motive for getting involved with this."

And that had been the reason for the kidnapping.

In other words, Kamijou would leave Academy City not because of the *Book of the Law* or Orsola—he'd leave just so he could rescue Index. Then he would *just happen* to run into people from Amakusa, and end up with no other choice but to fight them to save his friend. That would be the justification.

Index was from the magic side, of course, but Academy City and the English Puritans currently had a handful of deals with each other that placed her temporarily in the city's hands. She *had* been entrusted to the city, so it wouldn't be strange for a resident of that city (Touma Kamijou) to go help her.

"I understand most of what's happening, but I'm still not convinced."

"Is that so?"

"Yeah. You don't have to be so roundabout with him. If you just asked him to help you, he'd do it. Even if it led somewhere dangerous, he'd definitely come to help. I guess that's why it's hard to ask him to do it, though."

"...Is that so?" Stiyl gave a slight grin. It was the smile of a father listening to his young daughter talk about a boy she liked.

"So what happens from here? The *Book of the Law* and Orsola Aquinas have fallen into Amakusa's hands. Are you saying we're going all the way to their headquarters?"

There was now a note of seriousness in her voice—likely because with Touma Kamijou now involved, she wanted to collect every tidbit of information she could in order to decrease the danger.

"No, the situation has changed slightly." Stiyl bitterly exhaled smoke. "Eleven minutes ago, the Roman Orthodox people clashed with the fleeing Amakusa members. It's going to be a war to rescue Orsola."

Index narrowed her eyes in thought.

He was probably using the cigarette smoke to communicate. Index had seen mana clinging to the thin strands of smoke on a few occasions already, and each time, the white smoke fluttered unnaturally despite the lack of wind. Signal flares were a means of long-distance communication that were used all over the world during every time period. She knew of more than a few spells that used the concept originating in many different ages and countries.

"If they had succeeded, then I wouldn't have needed to be here, would I?"

"That's right. But they haven't clearly failed, either. There were no deaths on either side, but apparently it was a chaotic battle. I'm not sure about the *Book of the Law*, but it seems that Orsola slipped away during the confusion."

"She didn't go back to the Roman Orthodox Church?"

"That's what it would mean. And as she is currently missing, she may have even fallen back into Amakusa hands."

"...That wouldn't be good."

Kidnappers used force to silence resistant hostages. If she had been grabbed a second time after already having fled, then who knows what they would do to her to exhaust her rebellious attitude?

That meant they didn't have time to be waiting here. The scramble between the Roman Orthodox and the Amakusa for the runaway Orsola would be spreading as they spoke.

"I'd like Touma Kamijou to hurry up, too, but I can't change the command I left for him at this point. I had wanted to meet up with him before the Roman Orthodox contact arrived, but..."

As Stiyl spoke, a figure appeared in one of the opened entrances to the great hall.

"...unfortunately, it looks like we, too, don't have to wait for him before starting."

The figure was their contact from the Roman Orthodox Church.

4

"I feel like I've been leaving the city a lot lately...It'd be nice if I could just relax and do some sightseeing," muttered Kamijou as he walked down a road along the outer wall of Academy City. The outer wall was more than five meters high and three meters thick.

Still, I guess security's lax because we're in the middle of setting up for the Daihasei Festival.

He shot a glance over his shoulder at the entrance, now far behind him. The preparations were as large as the festival itself, with 2.3 million people participating, in addition to a lot of tradespeople from outside the city. Normally Academy City's security was tight, but with the current situation, they had no choice but to loosen it. He had exit papers, but he felt like they hadn't checked them as carefully as they usually did.

And so, with a little of this and a little of that, he left the cat with Maika Tsuchimikado and walked out of the city.

He checked his watch—it was past six. There was still almost an hour before the appointed time.

The Hakumeiza theater in question gave him a lot of trouble finding it. The names of abandoned buildings weren't included on his cell phone's GPS map. It made Kamijou think they were too quick to update. He had considered picking up a "slow-to-update," faded Tokyo sightseeing guidebook on a convenience store shelf, but when he checked his pocket, his wallet wasn't there. When he realized he must have forgotten it in his room because he'd left the city right after talking to Maika, he opened his eyes wide enough to cause the clerk to draw back a bit and decided to read it in the store.

Umm...So I take that street, then cross the big road over there... Ugh! I-I feel like I'm about to forget where it is. Man, Index has got some brain up there...

Lost in thought, he saw a bus stop nearby. The Hakumeiza building site he was going to meet them at was about one kilometer away. He would have liked to take a nice, air-conditioned bus, considering he was exhausted after school, but unfortunately, he had no money.

Damn it...! Ah, doesn't matter if it's a bus or not—I just want to get somewhere air-conditioned.

The bus stop was small, with only two benches and an overhang to keep out rain. It looked like it was deteriorating, though—the plastic roof had all kinds of cracks in it.

Then, he noticed someone at the bus stop.

She looked like a foreigner—a woman about the same height as him. She was staring at the timetable signboard from super close, like she was about to devour the whole thing. From the way she was completely frozen like that, he considered she might not know how to read it.

And her clothing—what was she thinking in this heat?—was a jet-black habit, including, of course, long sleeves and a long skirt. Upon closer inspection, he saw lines of silver fasteners both around her shoulders and twenty centimeters above her knees, so she must have been able to take off both her sleeves and long skirt—but like an idiot, she was in full sister garb. She had a thin white glove on each hand, and he couldn't see her hair. Her hood was different from the kind Index wore; it was a wimple that completely hid her hair and everything on her head but her face. By how easily the single piece of cloth concealed her hair, she probably had it cut short.

He gave her a sidelong glance and thought, *Hmm, it's a sister...It couldn't be some maniacal nun who Index knows, could it?*

This was a bias that nuns throughout the world probably vehemently objected to, but Kamijou had run into all sorts of crazy people during his summer break, like Stiyl and Tsuchimikado. For him, a girl wearing a weird habit was someone to be careful around.

But...

"Excuse me..."

...the sister addressed him instead, beginning to speak in extremely polite Japanese.

"I beg your pardon, but will this bus take me to Academy City?"

Not only was it polite—it was weird.

Kamijou stopped in his tracks and turned around to face her again. All her skin but her face was hidden, but she was strange—she had quite a rousing chest and a slender waist. (Though depending on how you looked at it, they could seem purposely accented.)

"No, there are no buses going to Academy City."

"I beg your pardon?"

"What I mean is, Academy City is cut off from outside transportation. So buses and trains don't go there. Licensed taxis could bring you in, but it would be cheaper just to walk there normally."

"I see. I understand. Is that why you came out of Academy City on foot, sir?"

The sister said that pretty smoothly, so Kamijou looked back, but he couldn't see the gate from here. He looked at her again to see her rustling around in a sleeve, and then she brought something out. It was a cheap-looking opera glass. "I saw you from here," she said with a smile.

Then, a rickety bus arrived at the equally rickety bus stop.

Its automatic doors opened with a *hiss* of air being released.

Kamijou didn't have any intention to use the bus, so he decided to walk away from the bus stop a bit. He looked back over his shoulder to the sister and said,

"Anyway, you can't get to Academy City just by going on a bus. If you have a permit, you can just walk to the gate. It should take about seven or eight minutes…"

"Well, well, I see. I am deeply grateful for your advice, despite how busy you must be."

The sister in black smiled at him, bowed her head…

…and got right onto the bus.

"Wa…Hey! I just said not to take the bus like five seconds ago!"

"Oh, yes. You did, didn't you?"

The sister swept up her long skirt in both hands and joyfully alighted from the stopped bus.

He continued. "Like I said, Academy City is cut off from all outside transportation. So buses and trains won't go there. If you want to get into the city, then go walk through the gate, understand?"

"Indeed I have. I apologize for making so much trouble for you."

The sister smiled painfully and bowed her head again to him, then turned, went up the steps, and began to disappear into the bus.

"Hold on!! You weren't listening to a word I said! You were just smiling and nodding!!"

"What? No, I would never do anything like that."

The sister once again joyfully got off the bus. The driver, looking annoyed, closed the bus's automatic doors and floored it.

Kamijou looked at the nun as she absently watched the bus leave, growing intensely worried. If he took his eyes off her for ten seconds, she'd probably get lost.

But the sister, entirely ignorant of his apprehensions, said, "Oh, it seems you are quite frustrated with something. Would you like a piece of candy, perhaps?"

"Look, I'm not really frustrated. Candy? What, is this orange flavored?"

He had taken the orange-colored candy without any hesitation and pretty much unconsciously. He couldn't throw it away at this point, though, so he tossed it into his mouth.

Then...

"Ack, it's bitter! What is this? It's clearly not orange!"

She sighed. "I believe it is sour persimmon candy. I am not familiar with the details, but I hear it is good for when your throat is dry."

"...Right, because it makes your mouth water. But that doesn't mean anything if my body is low on moisture in the first place from walking around in this heat."

"Oh, my. Are you lacking moisture? If you had but said something—I have some tea right here."

"What? Did you just pull a magic bottle out of your habit sleeve? You know what, never mind. I think I'd actually really like that. What's inside?"

"It is roasted barley tea."

"Oh, I'll have some!"

Kamijou was honestly delighted. *Ice-cold barley tea is perfect for the middle of summer,* he thought to himself idly as he took the cup lid of the magic bottle.

"—Ow, it's hot! Why is it boiling?!"

She sighed again. "If I recall correctly, the people of this country appreciate hot drinks during the warmer seasons, don't they?"

"What are you, my grandmother? You're an old lady, aren't you? I thought the way you were talking and acting was suspicious! You think exactly like an old lady, don't you?!" shouted Kamijou, but the sister just stood there with a well-intentioned smile on her face.

He couldn't throw away the cup she'd poured the tea into at this point, though. Trembling, he downed the magma-like liquid.

"…Thanks. Also, I've got a question for you. You said you wanted to go to Academy City, right?"

"Yes, yes."

"Umm, I mentioned this before, but do you have a city-issued permit?"

"A…passport?"

This startled her, as he expected. You needed a city-issued passport to pass through Academy City's gates. The reason didn't need to be explained at this point.

After he told her that, the sister placed a hand on her cheek, worried. "Where might I be able to go so that I can acquire a permit?"

"…I'm sorry, but they won't let a random person in no matter how hard you try. If you were a relative of a student in the city or a supplier bringing goods or materials, that would be one thing, but even they have to be investigated."

"I see. Then I guess my only option now is to give up."

The nun's shoulders drooped dejectedly. She didn't seem to want to back down, though—so perhaps Academy City wasn't necessarily where she needed to go.

Unfortunately, this is something I can't do anything about…

He was stricken with a tinge of guilt, but suddenly he realized that the sister had said "good-bye" and had begun to walk toward Academy City's gate.

"Get back here, you!! Didn't you hear me?! You can't go in without a permit!!"

The sister stopped and turned back as if the thought hadn't crossed her mind.

Despite having been smiling in such a heartwarming manner the whole time, her face was now rapidly clouding over.

She seemed very worried about something, and he found himself daunted. In reality, sorcerers could jump over the walls and stuff at will even if they didn't have permits, but it didn't seem like she had such skills.

Nevertheless, there was nothing he could do for her right now. To get into Academy City, you needed to have a permit first and foremost. And he had Index to worry about, so he didn't have the luxury of wasting too much time here, either. Missing the specified time at the specified place was something he absolutely wanted to avoid.

"Hey. Why do you want to go to Academy City?"

The sister sighed once more and tilted her head a bit in worry.

"I am actually on the run right now."

Kamijou felt the temperature around him decrease.

"On the run...?"

"Yes. There was a slight bit of trouble and I am currently in the midst of my great escape. I had heard Academy City was out of reach of the Church factions, so I wanted to flee there if possible."

"The Church...Hey, does this have anything to do with sorcerers?" asked Kamijou.

The sister, visibly surprised, asked, "How do you know of the existence of sorcerers?"

"Guess I hit a bull's-eye, judging by that look." Kamijou sighed. "Academy City, huh? You know, if you're seriously being chased, then going into the city won't make you completely safe. Illegal invaders come screaming into the place pretty much all the time."

He knew about everything revolving around the girl named Index, so he was all too aware that fleeing into the city wouldn't shake off the sorcerers' pursuit.

"Then what should I—?"

The sister's face was slowly getting to the point where she might cry. He was pretty sure he knew how dangerous these sorcerer people were, so he was hesitant to just leave her here, but...

"—Would you happen to be able to read the bus route map?"

"How many pages ago did we leave that topic?! And this time you added a new term, 'bus route map'! Where did the issue of whether you could get into Academy City or not go?!" Kamijou shouted. He was thoroughly exasperated at the surprised sister who had backed up to the topic of some minutes earlier.

If sorcerers were really chasing her, he didn't think it would be good to ignore her. But he had a situation on his hands and couldn't

afford to take anything lightly. He was worried about Index, who had been kidnapped (apparently). It was a deeply suspicious situation, but he still couldn't ignore it. *I don't want to discard either of them! Jeez, what should I do?!* wondered Kamijou, about to start frantically scratching his head, when he suddenly realized something.

Wait…Why don't I take this nun with me to Index?

He thought it was a splendid plan.

He did seem to recall something in the threat letter about coming alone, though.

5

Stiyl and Index left Hakumeiza's great hall and walked into the remains of a lobby that must have been where tickets were sold.

A girl wearing a jet-black habit led them a few steps ahead.

She was about one or two years younger than Index, and her hair was a reddish-brown—she was essentially a redhead. Her hair was braided into many strands, each about the thickness of a pencil. The sleeves on the habit she was wearing were long enough to cover her fingertips, but in contrast, her skirt was so short you could see her thighs. Looking closer revealed a fastener-like object on the skirt's edge. She must have taken off a detachable piece of the clothing. Her waist was more slender than Index's, who was still definitely on the skinny side.

She was as tall as Index. But when you followed the sound of her clopping, horse-like footsteps down to her feet, you would find them wearing cork platform sandals thirty centimeters high. They were called chopines, footwear popular in seventeenth-century Italy.

She was a nun of the Roman Orthodox faith, and she had introduced herself as Agnes Sanctis.

"The situation is already a mess. We're getting conflicting information, too, so we don't exactly know where Orsola went, I suppose? We don't rightly know if they secured the *Book of the Law*, either, so we're in a pile of trouble."

There were no Japanese people here, but Agnes spoke in fluent Japanese.

"For the moment, our raid against Amakusa-Style as they were transporting the kidnapped Orsola could be considered a success. Despite one of our people rescuing Orsola, Amakusa kidnapped her again before they could reunite with the main force. Then, when we took her back a second time, a separate Amakusa-Style group kidnapped her yet again... We've been going around in circles. We spread out our scouting operations too thin, and it came back to bite us. Even though we have more people than they do, each separate group has been losing people, and they've been capitalizing on that. So while we've been stealing and capturing Orsola over and over and over and over again, Orsola herself, whom we should have caught up to by now, has disappeared to who-knows-where."

Agnes's tone was both rough and polite. If she had learned the language on the job, it might have been from talking to Japanese detectives and investigators.

As Stiyl mulled that over, Agnes spun around. Her short skirt fluttered, revealing more of her pale thighs.

"What is it? Oh, I apologize. I can speak English as well, but I can't seem to get my Italian accent out of it. No one usually cares, unless they're from England, anyway. So if you wouldn't mind, I'd prefer to speak in the local language."

Stiyl smoked the cigarette in his mouth, not seeming particularly concerned.

"No, I don't mind much. In fact, I could speak Italian as well."

"Please, don't. If I heard my mother tongue spoken with an English accent, I would be laughing too hard to do my job. We should stick to a language that's foreign for all of us. We won't get into any fights as long as we both sound weird speaking it."

Clop-clop went Agnes's platform sandals like a horse's hooves.

She had a point, but Stiyl needlessly worried about what language she planned on using with *actual* Japanese people in this country. If those around her couldn't use it in the first place, then he wasn't sure why she needed to learn the country's language.

Index had been silent the whole time. She didn't say a word.

She just pouted. She shot an angry sidelong glance at Stiyl to show that she wasn't talking to him, then returned her gaze to Agnes.

"So this Amakusa-Style borrowed the *Book of the Law* and Orsola Aquinas from your home. Do they really threaten you that much?"

"You mean, why is Roman Orthodoxy, the largest religion in the world, having so much trouble, don't you? Well, I don't actually have anything to say to that. We have more in terms of numbers and armament, but they've been disrupting us by using the terrain to their advantage. Japan is their backyard, after all. It does make me pretty mad that we're taking damage from someone with a numbers disadvantage, though. I don't want to admit it, but they're strong."

"...So they won't give in easily, will they?" Stiyl's voice was just slightly bitter.

He'd thought the "walk softly and carry a big stick" idea would have been the fastest and most peaceful way of resolving things, but if the opponent had enough might not to capitulate to your negotiations, the only thing left to do would be a protracted fight.

The longer the battle went on with Amakusa, the higher the danger that Kanzaki would stick her neck into this. Now that things had come to this, the smoothest option might be to abandon any sense of mercy and take down Amakusa with one blitz before she noticed.

The Roman Orthodox Church's objective was to retake the *Book of the Law* and Orsola Aquinas, not to annihilate Amakusa. If they were to get what they actually wanted, they would likely pull back right away. After that, they just had to worry about ridding Amakusa of their will to fight.

"I don't know much about the history of Crossism in Japan, but do you know what sort of techniques Amakusa uses? You might be able to set up some amulets or warding circles for searching or defense based on that."

Stiyl had been partners with Kanzaki, former leader of Amakusa-Style, in the past, but he never bothered to try and analyze her techniques. After all, she was one of less than twenty saints in the world. Even if he did figure them out, a normal person like him would never be able to use them. No human would ever think to measure the distance between the sun and the earth with a fifty-centimeter-long ruler.

Agnes looked worried at the priest's question as well.

"Actually...We haven't been able to properly analyze Amakusa-Style's techniques. If they were based on Xavier's Society of Jesus, then that would mean they were a branch of Roman Orthodoxy, but you can't even *smell* Christianity anymore. There's too much influence from Oriental religions, like Chinese and Japanese ones, mixed in there."

Stiyl still didn't blame Agnes even after hearing that. Just them being able to determine from their skirmishes yesterday that Buddhism and Shinto were mixed into things might have spoken volumes for their analytical abilities.

He looked away from her and to Index, as if interested in her opinion.

She had at least ten thousand times the knowledge of a normal person, so at times like this, she was the unchallenged champion.

The sister all in white spoke in a matter-of-fact tone.

"Amakusa-Style is famous for their secrecy. They're Christians in hiding from the motherland, after all. They thoroughly conceal their Crossism using Buddhism and Shinto, and they hide their techniques and spells within greetings, meals, habits, and behaviors—they hide all traces that Amakusa-Style ever even existed. So Amakusa-Style doesn't use any obvious incantations or magic circles. Their dishes and bowls, their pots and knives, their bathtubs and beds, their whistling and humming... They use seemingly everyday, ubiquitous concepts for their sorcery. I don't think even professional sorcerers would be able to figure out Amakusa-Style's spells, even if they saw them. I mean, it wouldn't look like anything except a normal kitchen or bathroom."

Stiyl slowly moved the cigarette in his mouth up and down.

"Which means they're essentially idolatry specialists. Hmm. They seem more suited for long-range sniping combat than close-range melee combat. Though we can only pray they're not part of something like the Gregorian Choir."

"No, not at all. Even when Japan is in isolation, they aggressively absorb the cultures of other countries. They possess close-quarters combat techniques as well—original methods fused from all manner of sword arts both from the east and west. They could be swinging around anything from katana to zweihänders."

"…They're warriors and scholars both, huh? What a pain in the ass," spat Stiyl resentfully. Incidentally, Agnes, who had at some point been driven outside the ring of the conversation, was shyly kicking her toes lightly against the lobby floor. Her short skirt fluttered every time she kicked it. Her feet made clapping sounds, which sounded a little silly.

The cigarette-smoking priest turned back to Agnes.

"So how far out does your search go for the *Book of the Law* and Orsola? We probably shouldn't be standing around, either. Where should we look?"

"Ah, right. We're handling the search on our end, so it's fine."

With the conversation now back on track, Agnes straightened up a bit hastily.

"We practically have a patent on human wave tactics. Even now, we're doing it with a group of two hundred and fifty people. Nothing will change by adding one or two more, and you're under different command anyway, so it would actually run the risk of getting confusing."

"So then why did you call us out here?"

Stiyl frowned just a little, while the corners of Agnes's mouth curled into a smile.

"It's simple. We want you to investigate what we cannot."

"Like what? There's no church in Japan directly administrating English Puritanism. In terms of places you couldn't search if we refused to help, it's pretty much just the British Embassy."

"No, there's also Academy City." Agnes waved one hand in the air. "Considering the occasion, it's not impossible. If Orsola fled into Academy City, Amakusa wouldn't be able to get to her. Or, rather, it would be more difficult to follow her. So I want you two to get in contact with the city. The Roman Orthodox Church has no connection to it, so it would be a pain for us to do it."

"I see…However, you might have told us a little bit earlier. I sort of wish I could make my past self ask you sooner."

As could be understood from Index having been entrusted to Academy City, there was a slender thread connecting the city to the English Puritan Church. It was just barely significant enough to say there was diplomatic relations, but that was enough to make it far easier for them to contact the city than it would have been for the Roman Orthodox Church, who had no such connection.

"…But that would mean she's fled into quite the troublesome spot."

"This is just a possibility. Let's pray that Lady Orsola at least has that much discretion. Anyway, about how long would it take to get in touch with them and confirm?"

"Right, it wouldn't be just a phone call. I would have to contact St. George's Cathedral first, and then have them put me through to Academy City…Even if I told them it was an emergency, it would probably take anywhere from seven to ten minutes. Also, if we get permission to intrude upon the city, things will turn into a hassle. It's technically possible to sneak in, but realistically, I'd want to avoid that."

"Oh, you can just ask them for now, so if you could do that quickly that would be gre—"

Agnes suddenly paused in the middle of her sentence and froze.

He followed her gaze to the entrance of the building in the front of the lobby. It was a large entryway with five glass double doors.

"What is it? What's wr—"

Stiyl also stopped mid-question.

"?"

Finally, Index followed where they were looking.

On the other side of the glass entryway was an open square of asphalt that used to be a parking lot. Despite the size of the building, it was an extremely small space. There should have been nothing there at the moment but robust weeds growing through the hardened cracks in its surface…but in the former parking lot that should have been empty, there was something.

Or rather, there was some*body*.

"Oh, it's Touma!"

Index said the name of a familiar boy.

"Or...sola...Aquinas?"

Agnes spoke the name of the sister in black walking next to the boy.

The two whose names had been voiced didn't seem to have noticed the sorcerers inside Hakumeiza yet.

6

A little while earlier...

Though the evening sun was cooler than other times, Kamijou was cursing the heavy manual labor of walking three kilometers in the summertime.

C-come to think of it, I was already totally beat from gym class and that other stuff today...

He had left his wallet in his dorm, so obviously walking was his only method of transportation.

The sister in black walking beside him didn't have any money, either. He couldn't help but wonder how in the world she planned on actually taking the bus. Dripping with sweat from all that had happened, he had trekked three kilometers down the road in the harsh last heat wave of summer in September and had arrived at Hakumeiza, but...

"Umm...Miss Nun Lady? You're wearing black clothing in this blazing heat. How are you going along smiling and not sweating at all?"

"Well, the agony of the flesh is nothing compared to the agony of the soul."

"...You're a nun *and* a masochist?"

"Excuse me, but how much longer must we walk until we arrive at the bus stop?"

"Are you still on that whole bus joke?! I told you we were going to go see a guy from the English Puritan Church! Were you just ignoring every single thing I said back there or what?!"

"Oh, my. Please excuse my rudeness—you seem to be sweating quite a bit."

"Argh! You keep taking the conversation in totally different directions!!"

"Now, now. I will wipe your sweat for you, so please hold still for just a moment."

"Eh, what? Hey, wait, *brfgh*?!"

The sister suddenly took a handkerchief out of her sleeve and wiped his face. It was only a handkerchief, but it was made of expensive-looking lace, and was faintly warm, and smelled like roses. He tried to escape from it, but she was pressing it against his face unexpectedly hard, so he couldn't.

"There, there. All finished."

The sister smiled at him brightly enough to shoot sunbeams at him.

"…Well, thanks."

Exhausted, Kamijou stepped into the site of the Hakumeiza theater.

Though the building looked giant even from far away, the parking lot right out front was so small it must have been for employees only. It was probably because there was a train station nearby, as well as a parking garage next door. The property was enclosed with two meter-tall metal plates, but the entrance for workers to go in and out had been forcibly opened—a thick chain and padlock were lying on the ground.

There was no heavy construction equipment or anything of the sort in the tiny parking lot. Even the building itself had no trace of graffiti or broken glass. Perhaps they'd found a buyer for it and someone came to do periodic maintenance on it.

When he and Orsola approached, they could see that Hakumeiza was larger than a gymnasium and constructed in a perfect square. Maybe it resembled a famous theater somewhere, and maybe it was just that designing the building had been a pain.

All right, I guess they're inside. It's hot out here, after all.

He directed his gaze to Hakumeiza's entrance. It was large, with five glass double doors lined up. There were no boards or anything in the way. It was less of a ruin and more just closed for a while.

As he thought about this, one of the five doors in front of him opened up.

"Huh?" he grunted.

Out of the three that exited, he recognized two of them as Index and Stiyl.

The last one—he didn't know her. She was a foreigner who looked a little younger than Index. She was dressed in the same black habit as the nun he'd met at the bus stop. However, this girl's habit had been made into a pretty small miniskirt—she must have undone the fasteners on the skirt to remove that part. His eyes fell to her feet, and to his surprise, she was wearing wooden sandals with soles thirty centimeters high.

As soon as Index saw Kamijou, she burst out,

"Touma, where did you meet that sister?"

"... That didn't take long. Anyway—and this question is mainly for the evil priest next to you—but why did you bother with such an elaborate faked kidnapping again? And I would definitely like to know why you made me exhaust myself by walking three kilometers in this insane heat! Please, go ahead! Actually, no—you're gonna tell me whether you like it or not!!"

Stiyl turned a tired expression on the shouting Kamijou. "Ah, what? So you knew it was a trick. I wanted to call you out here to get you to help search for someone. I just used the Index of Prohibited Books as a decoy. By the way, this is the one in charge here. She's Agnes Sanctis, from the Roman Orthodox Church."

Stiyl pointed in her general direction with the tip of his cigarette, and the nun wearing the platform sandals bowed and said, "H-hi." It looked like she was aware already that Japanese people bowed their heads all the time, but her motion was exaggerated, making her look like a hotel worker.

Kamijou was a little embarrassed at someone he'd never seen before suddenly addressing him. He was currently at max anger, but he couldn't let himself vent it on someone he had no acquaintance with.

As if pressing him hard now that his pace had been broken, Stiyl said, "Sorry, but we don't have time to go along with your nonsense. Like I said before, I brought you here to have you help look for someone. Two hundred and fifty people are looking for her now, and yet they can't locate her. It's a race against time. Her life is on the line, so we need you to help us quickly."

"Nonsense...? Hey, that's no way to treat a guest you're asking for help! Damn it, what is this? What do you mean her life is on the line? Explain it to me! And besides, I'm an amateur! I have no skill at tracking people down! Don't leave such an important job to a high school student!"

"Oh, everything is all right. If you just hand over the nun next to you, that'll be fine."

"What?" Kamijou's eyes became pinpoints.

Stiyl, who seemed to think this was truly foolish, exhaled cigarette smoke. "That nun is the missing person we were looking for. Her name is Orsola Aquinas. All right, thank you very much. You did very well. You can go home now, Touma Kamijou."

"...Excuse me, but I was set up in all this, and in addition to having left the city with a suspiciously acquired Academy City exit permit in one hand, I walked three kilometers when it's almost forty degrees out. What's my position in all this?" Kamijou muttered, looking down. However...

"I already said you did well, didn't I? You want me to treat you to some shaved ice or something?"

Index's face turned blue and panicky at seeing Touma Kamijou looking down and grinding his teeth.

They heard a funny *grrkk* come from around Kamijou's temples.

"You know, until now, I know we're not what you could call *friends*, but we were getting along just fine otherwise. I'm serious. I seriously thought that, you know? Yeah, at least, until this moment!!"

"Enough of your jokes. Just hand Orsola over to Agnes already. What? You want me to pay more attention to you? Unfortunately, I can't take away your loneliness, and I wouldn't want to anyway because it would be creepy."

On top of getting seriously angry, having been ignored so briefly caused Kamijou to collapse where he stood, as if he had burned out. "Urgh, uuuuuuurrrrrgh. I don't even have the energy to make dinner tonight anymore. Index, we'll have to have commonplace takeout pork bowl for dinner tonight."

Kamijou ignored the always-hungry girl shouting, "What?! But Touma!!" and turned back to face the sister in all black, Orsola Aquinas. "...You did say someone was after you. Did this search have something to do with it? You should be fine now that your allies are here, right?"

When Kamijou addressed her, Orsola's shoulders gave a jerk for some reason. It was a small tremble, like she had tried to suppress it and failed.

He tilted his head. She seemed to be looking at Stiyl and the others, not at him.

Stiyl closed one eye, uninterested. "Hmm. There's no need to be anxious. We English Puritans are getting out of here as soon as our job is done. Well, I suppose you should at least have that much caution."

For an outsider like Kamijou, everyone looked lumped together as either "someone from the Church" or "someone belonging to the magic world."

He wondered, though, if they were viewing one another as hostile and subdividing them into Roman or English or whatever. But then…

"Oh, no. I can't give her to you so easily."

Suddenly, they heard a deep, male voice.

Unnaturally, it came to Kamijou from straight above. He looked up to the night sky and saw a paper balloon about the size of a softball floating around seven meters up in the air.

The thin paper making up the balloon was vibrating of its own accord, creating the man's voice he had just heard.

"Orsola Aquinas: You should know that best of all. You could live a much more meaningful life with us than you could going back to the Roman Orthodox Church."

That moment.

With a sharp *zip*, a single blade plunged out of the ground in between Kamijou and Orsola. It came close to being a surprise attack to the spots of Kamijou and the others, whose attention had been directed overhead.

And then two more came up around Orsola with a *zing* and a *ging*!!

The swords that leaped out at them slid in a straight line through the ground like a shark fin cutting across the surface of the water.

The three blades cut across the ground, carving out a triangle two meters on each side with Orsola at the center.

"Aahh!" As Orsola felt gravity give way, she gave a cry that sounded more bewildered than afraid. But before it could turn into a clear scream, Orsola's body began to plunge into the dark underground along with the entire triangular piece of asphalt.

"Amakusa!!" shouted Agnes, trying to reach her hand out, but she was too late. Orsola was already being swallowed up into the pit of darkness. Kamijou frantically ran to the edge of the hole and swore angrily.

"Shit, a sewer...?!"

The paper balloon overhead continued in an enthusiastic yet still focused voice.

"If we simply follow the Roman Orthodox commander, it did not matter where Orsola Aquinas flees or who she is captured by—she would eventually be brought here. I suppose running around underground waiting was well worth it!!"

Kamijou couldn't get even a marginal hold on this situation. Who was hiding in the sewers? For what reason had they suddenly taken Orsola away?

He knew one thing, though.

They came out suddenly and without warning with blades and had kidnapped someone. And from what it sounded like, it was not just a random occurrence, but something they had planned beforehand and had waited and waited for their chance to come.

"Damn it!!"

Kamijou peered into the triangular hole in the ground. As it was dark, his depth perception was a little off, but it didn't seem too steep to him. He faced the hole, about to jump in, when...

"Wait! Don't do it, Touma!!"

The very moment Index shouted...

Glitter—light glinted off dozens of blades in the darkness.

As if reflecting a little bit of light from the evening sun, the orange rays radiated and twisted inside the sewer. With the light from the

blades, only the faint outlines of those hidden underground came into view. The sight reminded him of bandits wielding rusted swords and axes, waiting with bated breath in the thickets beside a thin mountain trail for their sacrifices to pass by.

A ball of pure malice blew straight into his face like a burst of hot wind.

In an instant, Stiyl, beside Kamijou, whose movements had been locked down, pulled out cards with runes inscribed on them.

He threw the four cards on the ground, positioning them around himself.

"TIAFIMH (There is a fire in my hand), IHTSOAS (it has the shape of a sword), AIHTROC (and it has the role of conviction)!!" Stiyl shouted, flicking his cigarette directly upward. An orange trail followed it up, and in the next moment, a sword made of flames jumped into his hand along that line.

The newly created source of powerful light immediately wiped away the darkness in the sewer.

Stiyl brought the flame sword around in a large arc...but then stopped suddenly.

Inside the sewer illuminated by the flame sword, there was nobody. All those people had vanished into thin air along with the darkness that had been wiped away. All of those silhouettes in the hole holding swords, as well as Orsola, who should have fallen in, had disappeared in the blink of an eye—like a pack of sea lice attached to a riverbank all running away at once.

The paper balloon that had been lazily floating overhead slowly descended to them.

Nobody reached out a hand for it as it fell into the triangular carved hole in the ground.

"Shit! What the hell is going on here?" demanded Kamijou as if spitting something out. "Hey! You're gonna explain this to me in full, right?"

"Actually, I am the one who'd like an explanation for this," responded Stiyl Magnus, as if to crush the paper balloon under his foot.

INTERLUDE ONE

At last, the sun set on the shore, fortified with man-made objects, and the night was welcomed in.

It was a craggy area only a few hundred meters from a swimming beach. Just onshore was a cliff almost ten meters tall, and tetrapods were piled up high so that waves wouldn't erode it.

Now that the sun had completely set, the sea was covered in a deep black.

Then, as if awaiting the night's arrival, a hand appeared from the surface of the dark water.

It wasn't just a hand—it was a covered one. Heavily armored fingers, shining in silver, grabbed hold of one of the concrete tetrapods. Then, a person in Western-style full-plate armor broke the surface of the water and climbed up onto it. Clad in steel from head to toe, it was questionable whether there was even a person inside.

When the first one made it to land, twenty more of the "knights" emerged from the water's surface. One after another, they climbed atop the tetrapods, emulating the first. The lettering emblazoned on the arms of their armor read UNITED KINGDOM—letters that also represented the nation called England.

They had swum here.

That wasn't a figure of speech. They had begun in England,

rounded the Cape of Good Hope, passed through the Indian Ocean, and had at last infiltrated the water of faraway Japan.

It was sorcery for manipulating ocean currents using the legend of Saint Blaise as a framework. Simply put, this was a technique for high-speed sea travel that allowed one to go fast enough to circumnavigate the earth in three days. It was not a Soul Arm–like function attached to their armor—it was something activated purely by each individual knight's own body. The armor they currently wore had no such functionality. Because the knights themselves were so highly maneuverable, adding Soul Arm effects to the armor would have just slowed them down. With their tremendous strength, they could go on rampages more violent than effects produced by Soul Arms, so they would have run the risk of destroying their armor with their own power.

They were simply called the Order of the Knights.

They had once gone by names such as "Seventh Mace" and "Fifth Axe" in England but had abandoned such titles seven years ago. That was not because the current Order had lost its outstanding individuality, but because the Order had been reborn by each knight having acquired every skill.

The reason they needed to acquire such strength was related partly to circumstances particular to England and partly to the original objective of establishing the Order.

Right now, the United Kingdom operated under a complex three-sided chain of command.

The Queen Regnant and the Royal Family Faction, headed by Parliament.

The Knight Leader and the Knight Faction, commanding the knights.

The Archbishop and the Puritan Faction, led by the faithful.

Their power relation was as follows.

The Royal Family Faction issued royal commands to the Knight Faction, controlling them.

The Knight Faction used the Puritan Faction as convenient tools.

The Puritan Faction gave direction to the Royal Family Faction under the name of Church advice.

In this beautifully triangular system, if one attempted to carry out an agenda while even one of the others was not convinced of the policies therein, the other could present total opposition by taking the long way around the chain. However, there was another reason that the United Kingdom was said to have the world's most complex Crossist culture.

The United Kingdom was a combination of nations consisting of England, the northern part of Ireland, Scotland, and Wales. Reminders of this remained to this day—certain places even issued their own currency.

For example, there could be bad blood between the Puritan Faction's English and Welsh members, despite them belonging to the same group. Conversely, it wasn't unusual for separate factions within one nation, like the Puritan and Knight Factions of Scotland, having pipelines to each other. When Sherry Cromwell, the code-breaking expert, bared her fangs at the English Puritan Church—which she belonged to—she had this sort of backing in addition to her personal motive.

Three factions and four cultures.

This two-dimensional diagram where each affected the other led to the nation called England becoming more complex. In turn, the greatest mission given to the Knight Faction was to **make sure this complex combination of countries didn't break apart in midair.**

Thus, these particular knights hadn't been persuaded beforehand...

...that the English Puritans—the Puritan Faction—had gained the same power as the Knight Faction.

The English Puritan Church, also known as the Anglican Church, had originally been created to oppose Roman Orthodoxy, which had the entire world under its rule. They wanted to operate their own nation themselves, but if they didn't obey the Roman Orthodox Church, they would be attacked as a nation that disobeyed the teachings of the Crossist god. So by placing an independent church within

England, they could explain themselves by saying their actions were in line with the teachings of the god of Crossism—meaning English Puritanism—even if they weren't strictly following Roman Orthodox canon.

In other words, the English Puritan Church had been created as a political tool.

The Church was the oil they had created to lubricate the giant cogs of the royal family and the knights under its command.

But right now, the relationship between the Puritans and the royal family and knights was being undermined by the Puritan chain of command.

Nobody appreciated the fact that their actions were being restricted by something created to be a tool.

Actually, though, with the Knight Leader and Queen Regnant as their masters, the knights would not only cut corners when carrying out the Archbishop's orders—in severe cases, they'd outright spurn them.

Their answer to their current mandate, to support the rescue operation of the *Book of the Law* and Orsola Aquinas, had been simple: All members of Amakusa should be killed.

They had no obligation to put their lives on the line for an order from someone who didn't acknowledge them—the Archbishop.

They didn't take their religious and ethical relationships with the Roman Orthodox Church or Amakusa even slightly into consideration.

It wouldn't affect England's national interests in the least if Amakusa were to disappear.

It would be easy to kill them. The skills of the knights—the many works passed down through legend by the Murder Crusaders, who buried multitudes of heretics during the Crusades—were powerful enough to wipe a small island off the map.

A sect on a far eastern island nation, they could destroy within a day.

And they wouldn't care what happened to the possible hostage, Orsola, in the process.

The English Puritan Church didn't actually have any interest in the contents of the *Book of the Law.* They were already recorded in the prohibited Index's memories, so they just needed to leave it to her. Whether Orsola lived or died, it wouldn't damage English interests. The Roman Orthodoxy might cause a fuss about it, but the chore of suppressing that would fall to the Archbishop.

The Archbishop had warned them to be careful of what action Kaori Kanzaki, former leader of Amakusa, might take, but the knights were far from taking that piece of advice to heart. If Kaori Kanzaki came upon them, blinded with rage over Amakusa being annihilated, they would just make her into a bloodstain on the wall as well.

Or they **would have**.

But all those plans went awry in just three seconds.

Once the knights had broken the surface and climbed atop the tetrapods...

...*it* appeared from below and pierced through them.

Bang! Boom!! The many tetrapods, each weighing more than a ton, blew away like a volcano had erupted. The knights on them, having also been thrown upward, recovered their balance in midair and scanned the surface below to look for a landing point.

At ground zero—the center of where the twenty-one knights and vastly numerous tetrapods had gone flying—was a lone girl.

She had long black hair tied in the back, white skin covered in lithe muscles, a squeezed short-sleeved T-shirt, jeans with one leg cut off, western boots, and a katana more than two meters long called "Seven Heavens, Seven Blades" resting on the leather belt at her waist.

Kaori Kanzaki.

She didn't speak. She began her attack on the twenty-one airborne knights without a word.

It was a simple thing she was doing. She would attack each of the twenty-one knights, one at a time, who were floating without footing and unable to move. Not by using her sword to slash, either—but by politely bashing them with its sheath.

But she was so desperately fast. Too fast.

The knights hadn't actually been in the air for one second yet. But they all immediately felt like they had been frozen in midair. That was how fast Kanzaki's movements were. It was like time had stopped, and she alone was moving through it freely.

If someone had been observing time properly, it would have looked like an invisible storm erupting from ground zero.

Each knight that took a hit from the scabbard crashed into the ground, sank into the cliff face, or struck the road on the shore. Those launched into the sea skipped across it like a thrown pebble.

After mowing down twenty-one knights in all, Kanzaki quietly landed atop one of the tetrapods.

When the damp night wind lightly caressed her hair, the floating knights at last fell to the ground. A loud *wham* echoed across the dark seashore.

"I tried to hold back. This way, there would be no fatalities. Wearing sturdy armor made my job easier, and for that I thank you."

"You...bastard..."

The knights took her quiet voice as an insult and tried to stand. But they had been utterly shaken to their cores, and moving their fingers was all they could manage.

That's why the knights instead moved their mouths—the one thing they could still operate freely.

"Do you...understand? Who you just...attacked? You've just bitten the hand...of the three contracts and four lands...of the United Kingdom itself!"

"I, too, am a part of it. I'm sure those above me will take care of this, as it was trouble not between us and Roman Orthodoxy or Russian Catholicism, but within the English Puritan Church itself...Oh." She realized the knight who had spoken had lost consciousness, and she promptly stopped talking.

"There were some I tossed into the ocean...But it didn't look like they had disengaged their submersible technique yet, so I don't believe I must worry about them drowning," whispered Kanzaki to herself, glancing once at the dark surface of the sea.

*   *   *

"Your words lack punch when you say them with such worry on your face, you know."

"Hm?" Kaori Kanzaki finally stirred and turned around to the familiar voice. It was a young man with short, spiky blond hair, blue sunglasses, a Hawaiian shirt, and shorts.

Motoharu Tsuchimikado.

Kanzaki saw where he was standing and was surprised. Her honed senses wouldn't have missed someone's approach in the first place... Nevertheless, when she looked at Tsuchimikado, ten meters away, she still couldn't feel his presence.

"Have you come to stop me?"

When Kanzaki reached for the hilt of her katana, the eyes behind the sunglasses remained smiling.

"Give it a rest, Kaori Kanzaki. You can't beat me." Despite the situation, he showed no nervousness, held no weapon, and didn't even position himself for a fight. "No matter how strong *you* might be, you can't kill people. And an esper like me might die just from using magic to fight you. This battle...I would die whether I won or lost, but are you really prepared to kill Kamikaze Boy Tsuchimikado and keep moving forward? Eh?"

Kanzaki clenched her teeth.

She manipulated her techniques so that people wouldn't die. For Kanzaki, a fight in which someone would die whether they won or lost held no meaning. In fact, that was the worst outcome she could imagine.

She could feel her fingers trembling as they touched her katana's hilt.

Then Tsuchimikado pulled a one-eighty and switched to an innocent, childlike grin. "That's fine, you can keep glaring. I wasn't told to stop ya personally, Zaky. Though I was told to head you off and eliminate you if it looked like you were gonna cause an issue. And I've got my own job to do anyway."

"Your...own job?"

"Yeah. I got the cushy job of digging around for the original copy of the *Book of the Law* while the Roman Orthodox Church and Amakusa are preoccupied with their little firefight."

Kanzaki's eyes narrowed slightly. "On whose orders? The English Puritan Church's or Academy City's?"

"I wonder. Well, common sense will lead you to the answer. Which wants grimoires—the magical world or the scientific world, hmm? Well, considering which I'm the spy for, it's pretty easy to figure out."

Kanzaki fell mum at Tsuchimikado's words.

There was a terrible air dominating the area, one that could freeze even the tropical night wind flowing between them.

Seconds of silence ensued, and the first one to break eye contact was Kanzaki.

"…I need to go. If you want to report this to your superiors, feel free."

"Is that so? Ah, we'll handle rounding up all these groggy guys. It'd be a pain if the police picked 'em up, after all."

"I'm in your debt." Kanzaki bowed her head courteously, and Tsuchimikado said to her,

"By the way, what brought you so far from England anyway, Zaky?"

She left her head down and stopped moving.

After a good ten seconds had passed, she finally lifted her face.

"Who knows…?" she said, smiling mechanically, like she was angry and about to cry at the same time.

"…Honestly, what *do* I want to do?"

CHAPTER 2
Roman Orthodoxy
The_Roman_Orthodox_Church.

1

The sun set and night came.

But it didn't come quietly. Agnes, in her black nun's habit, was busy shouting to the other similarly dressed sisters in another language, giving commands and pointing every which way. She was also writing something in a small book with a quill pen at an incredible speed. Index told Kamijou it was like a telephone call: When she wrote in that book, the letters would apparently show up in a book somewhere else. He thought privately that it was more like a text message than a phone call.

A brigade in black—probably the regular sisters of the Roman Orthodox Church—was heading into the sewers via the triangular hole left by Orsola's kidnappers. Another group spread open a map and began to draw lines in red ink, also with feather pens. He couldn't tell whether they were designating escape routes or giving directions for the search or their security net.

On this busy, bustling night, Kamijou, Index, and Stiyl were stiffly standing apart from the others. Kamijou couldn't speak a foreign language (and no, he didn't even know *which* foreign language they were speaking in), so he couldn't participate in the conversation. Index and Stiyl were keeping quiet. If they said anything careless, it could spark chaos among the Roman Orthodox sisters—they were part of a different chain of command.

Remembering how hungry he was little by little, Kamijou spoke up. "Hey, why did Index and I get called out here, anyway? The Roman Orthodox people are doing everything that needs to be done. We're just sitting here bored—is there a reason we're still here?"

"...Well, our reinforcements should be arriving somewhat soon. What are those knights doing?" Stiyl said bitterly, blowing out some cigarette smoke. "Also, this incident requires our power. Well, more accurately, *her* power."

Her must have meant Index. "Hers?"

"Yeah. This all has to do with a grimoire. And not just any grimoire—the original copy of the *Book of the Law.*"

In place of Stiyl, who said so in a relatively self-absorbed fashion (meaning he had no desire to explain), Index summed it up in simple terms for him.

According to her, the *Book of the Law* was a grimoire written in a code that nobody in the world could decipher. Its contents were very valuable; anyone who could decipher it would gain vast power. And now a girl had appeared who had finally come up with a way to decode the supposedly indecipherable grimoire.

Because of that, both the *Book of the Law* and Orsola Aquinas, the girl who could decipher it, had been taken from the Roman Orthodox Church by the Amakusa-Style Crossist Church.

The one he had met already was Orsola, and it seemed that she had fled during the chaotic battles between Amakusa and Roman Orthodoxy, which involved her being kidnapped and rescued over and over. And they speculated the reason they didn't know where the *Book of the Law* was, was because it was in Amakusa's hands at the moment.

Amakusa-Style...Amakusa?

Kamijou tilted his head—he'd heard that name before.

But anyway.

"Nobody can decipher it, huh? Not even you, Index?"

"No! I've tried to, but it's not written in normal code."

"Hey. Is this *unreadable grimoire* really that valuable? I mean, nobody's read it, so couldn't it just be scribbles inside?"

"It could be," Index agreed simply. But the fact that she didn't get angry made her seem relaxed, like an adult admonishing a child—as though he were an ignorant amateur meddling in a professional's business.

Stiyl spat out his now-short cigarette and crushed it with his foot.

"The techniques written in the *Book of the Law* are simply too powerful—it's said that using them would declare the end of the entire Crossist-dominated world. It has a pretty interesting history. We don't even *want* to confirm whether it's truth or fiction—if it's sealed up, then obviously we'd rather leave it alone. After all, according to one theory, it lets you use angelic techniques beyond the comprehension of man."

Kamijou froze upon hearing those words.

"An...angelic?"

"Yes? Perhaps that's a little fanciful for an unbeliever like you to imagine."

Stiyl sounded like he was ridiculing him, but he was wrong.

Kamijou knew. He knew the meaning behind the word *angel*. He knew what the angel called Power of God had done. That spell it had used on one seashore that summer night—the one that had instantly covered the entire sky in a vortex of enormous magic circles. He knew of the "miracle" that could reduce half the world to ashes. And even that was probably nothing more than a fraction of the kind of techniques angels used.

Giving that to a person, to be used at will?

He gulped. "But...still, if nobody's ever decoded it before, then it might not even be real," he said.

Index's head bobbed up and down. "Yep. But when it comes to the *Book of the Law*, it probably *is*, Touma. The sorcerer who strove to pen it is legendary at this point. It's so high-level it could even appear in the New Testament. He was only active around seventy years ago, but it wouldn't be going too far to say he rewrote whole millennia of sorcerous history. About twenty percent of sorcerers in today's world are his followers and imitators. And something like *fifty* per-cent of them are affected by him in some way. He was the real deal." Her words were serious, and Kamijou found himself unable to care-lessly get a word in. "I think the *Book of the Law* is real. I wouldn't even be surprised if it was even crazier than the rumors, either."

A few sisters in black ran by them.

After a few seconds, Kamijou finally spoke up. "Umm…Who is *he*?"

"Edward Alexander. He's also known as Crowley. He's buried in a graveyard in the English countryside now." Stiyl lit a new cigarette. "In a word, he is recorded as the *worst* human in history. In one experiment during his travels, he used his wife, who had been trav-eling around the world with him, as a vessel so he could contact the guardian angel Aiwass. And when his daughter Lilith died, he used her to construct a theory of magic without twitching an eyebrow. And he apparently sacrificed girls the same age as his daughter in *that* experiment…However, his accomplishments *did* lead to new definitions of other worlds—overlapping planes in different layers than our world, such as the celestial and demonic planes—and revo-lutionized sorcery at the time."

Stiyl adjusted his position because the wind had changed direc-tion. It looked like he didn't want the smoke to go toward Index, but instead it ended up coming straight to Kamijou. He coughed hard, and Stiyl gave a truly evil smile, bellowing smoke out of his mouth like a fire-breathing monster. "Well, the many stories about him, good and bad, just and evil, big and small, are well-known to sorcerers. It's the same for the *Book of the Law*. When he lost his way, he would perform bibliomancy with the *Book of the Law* and choose his original path from its contents. In other words, it has the turning points of the world's greatest sorcerer—it is a grimoire holding the reins of modern western magic history as a whole. It would be wise to consider that it has quite a history attached, yes?" Stiyl clicked his tongue as if his own words tired him.

The Roman Orthodox sisters who had passed by them earlier

returned, going the other way. One held a giant cog one meter across as she ran—was it used as a weapon or for some other purpose?—and she made a slightly disgusted face at the smell of cigarette smoke.

"Wait, so if you're sure it's such a crazy book, why not just get rid of it? It's a book, right? Just burn it or something."

"You can't burn grimoires. Especially not original copies. The letters, phrases, and sentences written within use the flow of energy within the earth as a power source to convert to magical code and turn into an automatic magic circle. So just sealing one away is the best we can do." Index smiled vaguely. "But if I dug the original out of my memories and wrote a copy of it, it wouldn't do anything like that."

"You still need someone's mana, even if it's weak, to activate an automatic magical circle like that. The *writer's own mana* is used as the starter to rev up the engine, basically. Most sorcerers writing a grimoire don't even notice that their mana is being inscribed along with the characters they write. You wouldn't be able to avoid it even if you knew—it happens no matter what kind of writing utensils or paper you're using. But she doesn't have the power to temper her life force and create mana, so that wouldn't be a problem. Most suitable for one who manages a library, wouldn't you say?... Though the fact that this state of affairs was deliberate is *quite* displeasing."

"Hmm. Is that right, Index?"

"Uh, huh? Starter? What does *rev up* mean?"

Index was the one he was looking to for more explanation, but she looked the most confused of all.

Stiyl faithfully tried to explain what the words *rev up* and *starter* meant. (For some reason, he looked a little happy about it.) Kamijou watched him out of the corner of his eye and grimaced to himself.

He hadn't thought this was such a big deal at first. Until a few moments ago, he had figured that as long as they rescued Orsola, everything would work out.

But now that didn't seem to be the case.

He knew what an angel was. He knew about the technique used by

Misha Kreutzev, the Power of God, that could burn down half the planet.

He knew what a sorcerer was. Those he had met so far didn't show mercy or hold back. They would set to work achieving their goals using all the power at their disposal.

What if one of those sorcerers got ahold of the angel skills from the *Book of the Law*?

Shit...

Index said that original copies of grimoires couldn't be burned.

She said the reason was that the book itself would turn into an automatic magic circle.

But if Kamijou used his right hand...

If he used the Imagine Breaker inside it, then maybe...

This is the worst. It doesn't look like I can get off this ride while it's still going!

2

Finally finished giving orders in a foreign language, Agnes walked over to Kamijou and the others, her short skirt fluttering in the breeze. Her strangely high platform sandals made *clip-clop* noises when she stepped, like horse's hooves.

Kamijou winced to himself. She was a little younger than Index, but magic types didn't seem to care much about seniority. He could tell that much just by seeing the strange nuns from English Puritanism and Russian Catholicism (well, in the latter case, he only had Misha's outward appearance to go by). On top of that, until a few moments ago, she had been coolly flinging orders in some other language directly to dozens, and through indirect communication with hundreds more.

But *his* problem was less how self-important she seemed and more the foreign language part. His mental situation could be summed up in one sentence as "How to deal with foreign languages you can't speak: If she talks to you, your only choice is spirited, high-speed body language!!"

Agnes was on her way over, ready to attempt a culture exchange in a different language at any second. He held his head up straight and steeled himself for a beautiful interpretive dance, when…

"Ah, erm, I…If you don't mind, I now would like to start explaining the current situation, so are you all quite prepared, mayhap, pray tell?"

"…"

Bam! It was Japanese.

What the heck? he thought. *She may be unique, but this is…*

The Roman Orthodox sister was holding herself somewhat tightly. She wobbled uncertainly, and her face was bright red. *I see—it doesn't matter where you go, people are always nervous about foreigners fast-talking them.* He nodded to himself, oddly convinced. Agnes continued. "I-I'm sorry. I seem to be somewhat nervous speakin' Japanese poorly around actual Japanese people. Ah, could I use a different language? One apart from both of our cultural spheres, if you don't mind, like, preferably maybe Avar, or a Berber language…"

She spoke super fast. Index said something in a foreign language that was probably along the lines of "calm down and take deep breaths!" He glanced over to see Stiyl looking down darkly, saying, "Well, you're not the only one I know who uses strange Japanese," an explanation nobody was really asking for.

Agnes placed a hand on her flat chest and took a few deep breaths. She was forcibly trying to suppress her agitation. And despite probably being used to wearing the thirty-centimeter platform sandals, her feet wobbled like a drunk, helped along by her nervousness.

But she was still trying to carry out her duty, so she straightened right up and said, "I apologize. I shall start again. In terms of our current and future actions, we—Hyaa?!"

Before she could finish speaking, Agnes, who had forced herself to stand up straight despite her quivering feet, completely lost her balance and toppled over backward. "Wah, wah!" Her hands swam through the air as if she were grasping at straws, and then one latched on to Kamijou's hand.

"Whoa?!"

She fell to the ground, dragging him down with her. Unable to take the fall gracefully because of the suddenness, he slammed onto the asphalt. He attempted to writhe in pain (in relative seriousness) when he suddenly realized there was a piece of cloth fluttering above his head.

It was Agnes's skirt.

When he brought his face up, he saw a paradise spread out a few centimeters away from his nose.

Wha, whawhawhawhawhawhawhawhawhawhawhawhawhawha-whawha?!

The moment the scared Kamijou panicked and tried to pull his neck out, Agnes finally got a grip on the situation. She gave a shrill "Eek?!" and pushed her hands down onto her skirt with all her might to hold it down. It was an action that she'd taken in defense, of course, but she ended up slamming his head down so he couldn't pull it out of her skirt.

His entire field of vision had been blocked off by the skirt and her thighs, but Index's shout still reached his ears.

"T-To-To-To, Toumaaa! You think maybe that's going a little far for pranks?!!"

"No getting hot and bothered during work. Come on, get up already." Stiyl gave him a swift kick in the side, and with that Kamijou finally succeeded in removing himself from the prison of Agnes's skirt and thighs. The kick seemed less like it was Stiyl's own volition and more because he had to do something because Index was yelling.

Having been kicked in the gut, Kamijou coughed and shook his head.

Then his eyes met those of Agnes, who was plopped down on the asphalt. She was trembling, her face was bright red, and there were tears welling up in the corners of her eyes.

He blanched. "I-I'b sowwy…"

"N-no, you don't need to apologize. I was the one who fell over and caused it. It'd seem when I'm nervous, my balance goes a little haywire…Umm, can you stand?"

Agnes stood up adroitly in her twelve-inch-tall platform-sandal-clad feet and slowly extended a hand to the battered Kamijou. He made a face like it was a ray of light piercing dark clouds and reached out for it. Index watched and got a little mad.

Maybe Agnes had calmed down a little from that—her body was still tense and bunched up, but the nervousness was fading from her voice. "All right, then I would like to begin explaining the current trends of the *Book of the Law*, Orsola Aquinas, and Amakusa, and discuss our actions henceforth and so on." She was still wobbling nervously, and as if she was scared she'd fall again, she unthinkingly reached out to grab hold of Kamijou's clothing. Her hand stopped partway there, though. She was probably opposed to clinging to a man she'd just met—and besides that, he'd just dove into her skirt a few moments ago. After groping around, she latched on to Index's habit instead. "Orsola Aquinas has been confirmed to currently be in Amakusa hands. That goes for the *Book of the Law* as well, in all likelihood. We have a little less than fifty Amakusa members involved in this matter. It looks like they're using the sewers to get around, but it is also possible they have already gone aboveground."

"Does that mean you don't know anything?" asked Index, on whom Agnes was leaning, a little painfully.

"Yes. We're tracking Amakusa's movements using the lingering traces of their mana, but it's not going well. I suppose I expect nothing less from the Amakusa-Style Crossist Church, considering it's a sect specializing in secrecy and stuff." Still wobbly, Agnes pointed out the triangular hole in the ground. "We have another team drawing in a perimeter in conjunction with them, but it looks like they'll be the ones to nail the target first."

"A perimeter...How big is it?" Kamijou asked, tilting his head. Index was staring at him as if pleading him to do something about the heavy Agnes on her, but he decided to ignore her.

"It's about ten clicks in radius, centered here. One hundred thirty-two streets and forty-three sewer passages—you may consider us to have enough allies to cover the entire range." Agnes was practically hugging Index at this point. "Of course, if they try to take the *Book of the Law* and Orsola to their headquarters, they'll have to run into the perimeter somewhere. Our intel says their base's location is apparently somewhere in the Kyushu region...and, well, that *apparently* is another issue. Of course, things will change if they decided not to break through the perimeter and just force the decoding method out of Orsola."

"They probably won't. Even as she is now, Orsola probably readied the knowledge of how to resist mind-reading sorcery. On the other hand, there's no good place to drag it out of her physically, either." Stiyl gave a puff of cigarette smoke. "There are too many enemies around them for them to settle down. They need to torture Orsola, obtain the decoding method, and create a decoded copy of the *Book of the Law*. I think that's a bit more than one day's work. And if they want to get the information from her and break her spirit without letting her kill herself, the best forms of torture would be those that don't require them to directly touch her—forced menial labor, sleep disturbances, or the like. But they'd need around a week for those. One or two all-nighters isn't enough for torture; the human mind is set up so that it first starts to break at one hundred and twenty hours of sleep deprivation."

Kamijou was dumbfounded at Stiyl's detached words.

Those *were* the words of an expert specializing in witch-hunting and inquisitions, but that expert's point of view was that those who kidnapped Orsola were capable of doing such a thing. And from what Agnes had said, such a group was acting in tandem with almost fifty people.

The Amakusa-Style Crossist Church.

But something was bothering Kamijou—Oh, right. He'd heard the term *Amakusa* from Kaori Kanzaki and Motoharu Tsuchimi-kado in the past. He heard that Kanzaki used to be its leader, and that she had left the organization to protect her precious underlings.

Were those people she wanted so much to protect *low* enough to cause this incident out of greed?

Or...

Or had those Kaori Kanzaki wanted to defend...

...changed after she left them?

"What's wrong, Touma?" Index canted her head to the side, and the action caused her to collide with Agnes's, who was clinging to her.

"Nothing. What should we do at this point, anyway? Those Amakusa guys are gonna run into your perimeter soon, right?"

"Ah, y-yes." Agnes still seemed a little nervous. She was almost pressing herself against Index's cheek. "Basically, I want you to be rear support...The chances are low, but they *could* always use the *Book of the Law*. I think it'd be best if an expert in grimoires was there to—"

"Argh, you're being annoying! I can't breathe!" Index flapped her hands around. "But are we going to be able to catch Amakusa that easily? Huh, Touma?"

"Why are you asking *me*? Wouldn't it be? I would think if a group of forty or fifty people was walking around in suspicious nun's habits, they'd stand out no matter what."

"Amakusa doesn't have an official uniform, Touma. They specialize in secrecy, so if they were just walking around the city normally, you probably wouldn't be able to tell the difference."

"..."

"What is it, Touma? Why do you look like you don't believe me?"

"Don't worry about it," replied Kamijou. He didn't see a single person dressed normally anywhere around here, so he wasn't sure how universal her definition of *normal* was.

"Anyway, members of Amakusa are experts in hiding and fleeing. It would be stranger, I think, if they hadn't predicted what the Roman Orthodox Church would bring down on them after they seized the *Book of the Law* and Orsola Aquinas. And if this incident *was* planned out, then they would normally have countermeasures for it."

Agnes, now completely leaning on Index, looked a bit flurried. "B-but in reality, they have no way of busting through our perimeter—"

"Yes they do. There is such magic."

She sucked in her breath at the immediate response.

"It's a technique limited to Japan, though. In simple terms, there is a handful of special points throughout Japan called *eddies*, and there is a type of map sorcery that lets you move freely among them."

"The Great Coastal Map of Japan...Tadataka Inou. I see," Stiyl muttered bitterly, as if remembering something.

Kamijou had no idea what they were talking about, so he asked. "What's that? Tadataka Inou...Is he a legendary sorcerer or something?"

His question resulted in everybody there shooting him an ice-cold glare.

"Umm, Touma. The first person to survey and create a map of Japan can be found in timelines in the normal world, you know."

"You don't seem to be too knowledgeable about history, hm? You probably don't even remember five prime ministers back, do you?"

"...Even an Italian like me knew *that* much."

Touma Kamijou, the young man with failing marks, began to mope at their omnidirectional verbal assault.

"Anyway, there's a special thing planted in this Edo-period map of Japan. Everyone here knows of the Idol Theory, right?" Index paused. "Other than Touma, I mean."

Regular people normally didn't know any occult lingo, but everyone around him was treating it as obvious, common knowledge. He felt like they were leaving him alone in the dark.

"Study session time for Touma, then! Idol Theory is the fundamental theory describing how to effectively use the power of God and angels. Say you have a crucifix—a well-done one, replicating the one used to put the Son of God to death. If you applied the theory and put it onto the roof of a church, it would receive a portion of the actual crucifix's divine power. Of course, the replica would normally store less than 0.000000000001 percent of it. Even the legendary replica of the Holy Manger stops at just a few percent. Well, even with one percent of the original's power, it would have power rivaling the Twelve Apostles."

There were countless crucifixes spread throughout the world, from the ones perched atop churches to the ones nuns wore around their necks. Apparently, even with that power spread out across all of them, the power of the original wouldn't decline at all. Kamijou figured that it was like the relationship between the sun and solar panels.

"And this Idol Theory is a theory that says you can reverse it. In other words, not only does the real thing affect the idol—the idol also affects the real thing."

"A theory...So they don't know for sure?"

"There are a lot of exceptions it doesn't cover—that's why it's just a theory. But that's where getting punished for mishandling a Bible comes from. The Greeks persecuted Crossists long ago, and there are plenty of stories in the Bible of Greek idols getting struck by lightning and destroyed. And long ago in Japan, there were plates called *fumi-e* that had Crossist symbols on them, and you were supposed to stomp on them to prove you weren't Crossist. It's theorized that by harming such an idol, it would work in reverse, and it would cause harmful effects on the original." Index seemed a little dissatisfied as she spoke. She probably didn't like words like *apparently* or *hypothesis*, being a self-styled treasure trove of knowledge. "Tadataka Inou reversed this Idol Theory. If the real thing can influence the replica, then why not reverse it? He wrote in entrances and exits to teleportation points on his Great Coastal Map of Japan that weren't originally there and, in doing so, actually *created* forty-seven 'eddies' on the islands of Japan."

Kamijou desperately tried to mentally organize all this "common" information being rattled off to him.

The Japanese archipelago and the elaborate miniature map of Japan that this Tadataka Inou guy had made were linked in some way. He had scribbled in some warp points onto that map of Japan, and that led to actual warp points being created on the Japanese archipelago.

So then, whatever you happened to doodle on a map of Japan would become the truth? "Wait. That's absolutely nuts! What if someone erased part of the map? People and cities would just be wiped out!"

"That wouldn't happen. Listen, in order for something to be an idol, it needs to be a proper miniature. If there is even a slight magical disturbance between it and the real thing, it loses its function as an idol. That's why Idol Theory isn't all-powerful. If the original 'image' gets messed up, the theory itself no longer applies." Index told him in a serious tone that there used to be a branch of sorcery that tried to use likenesses of the Son of God in order to manipulate the Son of God in Heaven, but that all ended in failure. "On the other hand, it means Tadataka Inou was amazing. He added something that was clearly not right and bent the 'golden ratio' of his miniature by a tiny bit. I think he's the only one who's ever been able to do something like that in the whole history of sorcery. If he was a sculptor, he might have even been able to manipulate the Son of God and angels…Of course, just controlling the map of Japan is pretty shocking in its own right!"

"…Okay, so then Amakusa can use it freely?"

"Yep. Tadataka Inou had a strong interest in foreign countries during the Edo shogunate, and there was even one time his faction tried to sell the Great Coastal Map of Japan to Philipp Franz von Siebold. He would have known about the current ban on Crossism through his Dutch studies, so it would be appropriate to say that he had unofficial contact with Amakusa mainly out of academic interest."

Whatever the pesky details were, this was the conclusion: Amakusa had magic right now that would let them instantly warp to anywhere in Japan they wanted. So they wouldn't even need to break the perimeter.

Agnes had been listening to Index with a dumbstruck face.

As he continued arranging the information thus far in his head, Kamijou asked, "Then what do we do? They might have already warped, right? Since there's only a certain number of points, should we investigate them all?"

"We can't do that. Only twenty-three of the eddies from the Great Coastal Map of Japan have actually been discovered—even though when they tried to sell the map over to the black ships, the specifications said there were forty-seven of them."

More than half of the points were still a mystery. That meant they couldn't follow them or meet them where they were going.

"And in addition to this special movement method using the Great Coastal Map of Japan, Amakusa is famous because the location of their base is unknown... That's how it should be, though, since otherwise they could have their escape routes cut off. Agnes said earlier that it was *apparently* in Kyushu, but that's not certain, either. There are countless pieces of information saying where Amakusa's headquarters are, and it still isn't even close to being pinpointed. Either the information is false or they're using all of those places as bases. And we don't even know which of *those* it is."

Agnes paled. She grabbed Index's shoulder with both hands to support her body and shouted, "Th-then what do we do?! Wait, if you had information like that, why didn't you say anything until now?! We can't get the jump on them, and we can't pursue them to their base. If they make the jump, it's all over! If we had hurried to deal with them before that, we might have been able to do something! Why are you so relaxed about this?!"

"Because there's no need to hurry," said Index flatly, dumbfounding Agnes once again. "The Great Coastal Map of Japan was a map surveyed by using the stars in the night sky. The motion of the stars is a special quality permeating the map itself, and it has a big effect on using this method. Basically there's a time restriction. You can only use the method at certain times." She looked up into the sky, her silver hair swaying. "Right now...As far as I can tell from the stars, it's about seven thirty PM. The usage restriction will lift right after the date changes, so we still have about four and a half hours. Plus, the eddy point they need to warp from is in a fixed location. Out of the twenty-three known eddies, there's only one within the perimeter that they can use," Index declared confidently. "Of course, we can't discard the possibility that there's another one that hasn't been discovered yet."

Whenever she turned up in this kind of situation, it always reminded Kamijou that she lived in a different world. "So where's this point, then?"

"Touma, don't you have a blinky-blinky map? Give it to me for a minute!"

"You mean the GPS in my phone?" He handed his cell phone to her, but she scowled at it, so he decided to stand next to her and hold it sideways. She ordered him to go more to the right, a little farther down. After various other commands, she finally indicated one point with her slender, fair index finger.

"It's right there."

3

"Our recon team reported that they discovered two suspicious persons near the point in question. They're likely to be Amakusa, but we're leaving them alone for the moment."

They got results not fifteen minutes after Agnes had delivered the command upon hearing Index's advice. It really gave Kamijou a sense of how different things were when you had more people. He was all over the place during Angel Fall, despite it being a chaotic situation to begin with.

"But they say they couldn't locate the main Amakusa force, the *Book of the Law*, or Orsola."

"Makes sense. Going in with dozens of people at this hour would be sure to raise eyebrows. They're still **open for business** over there, after all."

Kamijou didn't know exactly when the stores would close up, but it still wasn't even eight yet.

If the Amakusa members planned to flee from here using the tricks in Tadataka Inou's map, then they would need to use a movement point called an "eddy." He and the others were planning to crush Amakusa when they got to it and rescue the *Book of the Law* and Orsola.

"It's possible there are other points we don't know about—and possible that they won't use the special movement method. Since we can't see the main force anywhere, it will be hard to split up all our personnel among the designated regions. Unless we funnel a lot of power into both the upkeep of our perimeter and searching those areas, their chances to escape will rise, so. It's just that it would still be real risky..."

Agnes sounded worried, but Index didn't let it get to her. "I think that's normal. It isn't like there's any definite evidence that what I'm saying is true."

Agnes continued. "Thus, we have seventy-four people to use, including myself. We're reorganizing our weapons and Soul Arms now, but we cannot promise victory should we encounter Amakusa's main force. I'm sorry, but I'll need to have you protect your own hides."

Until now, Amakusa had fought on equal terms with less than fifty people against the Roman Orthodox Church, which boasted more than two hundred fifty. Her remarks were understandable.

Stiyl lit a new cigarette. "We don't mind. I can't get in contact with those Knight idiots who promised to send us support anyway, and we can't have ourselves being luggage, either. How long will the reorganization take before you can move out?"

"Selecting weapons and armor...And including the application of holy water and each individual reading scripture aloud to gain protection..." Agnes thought for a moment. "Three hours, give or take...At the latest, we'll be done by eleven."

"And when we include transit time, we'll need to settle things in a little over half an hour. Well, it's fine—even if we were really early, we'd just be waiting in vain if the Amakusa main force didn't come to the point in question anyway."

With this and that, it was decided that mobilization would be at eleven PM.

Clap, clap!

Agnes clapped her hands together, fired off an order in a foreign language, and the sisters dressed in black all began moving at once. The seventy-four of them immediately formed two- to four-person teams and hastened their respective preparations.

For Kamijou, who had grown accustomed to seeing individualistic— or to put it more negatively, *self-centered*—sorcerers like Stiyl, Tsuchimikado, and Kanzaki, the perfect order with which this group operated was a little surprising.

The plan was that Agnes and the others would split into teams to rescue the *Book of the Law* and Orsola and prepare for combat individually. Those who were finished would switch out and grab a meal and a nap. But how could they catch any shut-eye just hours before a battle?

He was dubious, but according to Agnes, you wouldn't sleep too soundly in a bed if the battle dragged on. It seemed to be common sense for them that if they had any time at all, they should sleep in short bursts—even for just ten or twenty minutes—and recover their stamina. He figured the women in this group must be used to fighting under such conditions.

Of course, he, Index, and Stiyl didn't need to prepare anything anyway, so they ended up getting food right away and taking a nap. He wondered if maybe that was Agnes being considerate toward her guests. And incidentally, their meal and rest would both be outdoors.

Why was he camping out in the middle of Japan's capital, again? He couldn't help but find this odd, but then he considered it calmly—the sight of seventy-strong people dressed in strange clothing assembling at a restaurant or hotel and preparing for battle would be surreal, and akin to camping out anyway.

But if we're going to be starting at eleven...Am I going to make it to school tomorrow? Ah! Wait a sec, isn't the deadline for avoiding the summer homework penalty coming up?

Panicked, he turned his thoughts back to Academy City, but there was nothing he could do about it.

Due to various circumstances, he never finished his homework from summer break. Miss Komoe had given him a replacement assignment because of that (she had created handouts for him alone). The deadline, if he recalled correctly, was tomorrow...

Ahhhhh!

He blanched. He thought he'd have finished it for *sure*. The hard-working Touma Kamijou had been desperately racking his brains and desperately evading Index's desire to play and the cat's desire for snacks all day. In all honesty, there was a part he would never have been able to do on his own. But after Mikoto Misaka taught him the trick to solving those problems yesterday (she stuck with him for hours for some reason, despite getting angry at him constantly), he had sped up his pace, and he had just begun to catch a glimpse of a ray of hope that he'd finish within the day.

Crap, crap, she'll be so mad! What do I do, ahh...Miss Komoe will definitely get mad that Mikoto helped me, no doubt. Ahh...I haven't said this in a while. One, two—what rotten luck!

He began to tremble a little. He quietly looked up at the night sky—and decided to believe the shining, transparent drops coming from his eyelids were sweat.

His shoulders drooped. He trudged over to the camp in the corner and got himself some soup and bread that seemed Italian but he didn't really know the names. As he munched on it, he took a quick look at his surroundings. There were a number of dome-shaped tents all over the Hakumeiza parking lot. The parking lot was definitely not big enough to cover everyone, but some could sleep inside the building. Besides, more than half of the Roman Orthodox people here were urgently making preparations and didn't seem to have time to catch a nap anyway.

It all made Kamijou hesitant to go to sleep by himself without a care in the world, but Stiyl had said bored people wandering around would be much more of a nuisance.

No one's gonna call the police on all these people camping out in an abandoned building, are they? Or did they do that magic to keep people away so that wouldn't happen? Kamijou thought as he entered a tent in the campground and wrapped himself up in a blanket.

Stiyl was already lying down next to him, and Index was apparently in the next tent over. The sorcerer had wanted to be in the same tent so he could protect her, but that opinion didn't seem to go over well. *If only Kanzaki were here—she's a girl...*, he had muttered, grinding his teeth, while sticking rune cards all over the tent she was in. Kamijou looked at them. It seemed like Innocentius's power level varied based on how many cards Stiyl used, and the man had been lamenting how limited he was with such a small tent.

Kamijou lay in the tent for a little while, but he just couldn't seem to sleep. It wasn't that he didn't feel tired or that he was experiencing pre-battle excitement—he just felt awkward resting by himself when so many other people were working outside. And when he envisioned them in his mind's eye, he couldn't help but think of Orsola, dressed in the same habit.

"...I'm going to go help with something." Squirming, he crawled out from underneath his blanket.

Stiyl seemed annoyed. "I won't stop you, but please try not to break any of their Soul Arms with that strange right hand...And if you do, you're on your own. The English Puritans will have nothing to do with it."

Spurred on by the extremely unpleasant advice, Kamijou left the tent.

The night was sweltering. It was hot and humid outside, too. He saw a girl with a big bundle of silver candles in her hands, a sister carrying a good number of old Bibles, a lady hoisting a huge wooden wheel you might see on a horse-drawn carriage—all going to and fro in the crowd, busy as bees. He didn't know how to use any of that stuff.

All right. I wonder if there's something I can help with...Wait, huh?

He noticed something and stopped. Index's tent, the one right next to his, which was plastered with cards—the zipper for the entrance was open. It didn't look like there was anyone inside.

Where did she get off to—Wait, whoa?!

As he was looking over there and walking, he suddenly noticed that he had lost all sensation underfoot. He had unwittingly stepped into the equilateral triangular hole Amakusa had opened in the ground.

Eek, I'm falling!!

Just before his body slipped into the sewer without a sound, as he flailed about in midair, a sister in black hurriedly grabbed his hand. She pulled him up, then gave him an angry lecture in some foreign language. He didn't really understand what she was saying.

Aw, jeez, am I being a huge bother right now or what?

A heavy, dark aura coiled itself around the dejected Kamijou as he observed the triangular hole he was about to fall into.

Amakusa used the sewers as a route to directly attack the surface from underground. Until now, he had considered this place to be relatively safe to wander about, since it was essentially the Roman Orthodox base. Maybe, though, the line was a lot thinner than he thought. It was the command center of Amakusa's pursuers. He realized they must be concerned about the fleeing Amakusa coming to this base and wrecking it, since it would make it easier for them to run away.

Well, I doubt pulling an intricate surprise attack on an amateur like me would mean much. If there was an important point somewhere here, like an HQ, that could be in danger, though.

That said, he couldn't tell the difference between the tents that were important and the ones that weren't. For the time being, he saw a tent that was a size bigger than the others and got the detached impression that they'd probably go for something like that. But then...

All of a sudden, a loud *bam* exploded from the large tent.
A girl's shriek followed in its wake.

"...?!" Kamijou's mouth dried. His vague idea from a few seconds ago shot back across his mind.

Amakusa was able to directly attack the surface from underground.

And they would probably go after tents important to Agnes and the others.

But that means...really? Are you serious...?

"Damn it!"

The silver lining was that the tent was quite close to Kamijou. He tightened his right fist hard as a boulder and dashed for it. There were many sisters nearby, but they were standing there at a loss at the sudden situation. Kamijou ran through them to the entrance of the big tent and pulled the zipper on it down in one motion.

"Amakusa!!"

At the same time he shouted, there was something heavy in the opened entrance—and *bam*! It slammed right into Kamijou's gut. It was heavy and warm, and he thought he could feel watery moisture. *Gah...?!*

Kamijou got goose bumps everywhere at the strange sensation. He was about to swing his fist down when...

...he realized that the person with her arms around his stomach was a completely naked Agnes Sanctis.

"
....
...................Huh?"

Kamijou heard the sound of a huge bell ringing in his head as his mind went completely blank.

The stark-naked Agnes's hair was wet with water, and there was moisture on her skin, too. Her soft skin was tinged faintly in red, with white vapor rising from it. But his embracer was trembling all over, her eyes were firmly shut with her face buried in his stomach, and she was muttering things in another language—all these amounted to the fact that something was wrong.

He didn't understand what Agnes was saying, but as she clung to him, she pointed at something. He looked that way.

There was a small slug stuck to the corner of the big tent.

As she pointed, she said something in a foreign language.

"W-wait, Agnes. Just get off and put on some clothes. And I only understand Japanese!" Kamijou shouted, his face bright red. Her trembling stopped immediately.

With much trepidation, she looked up.

Her eyes locked with Touma Kamijou.

In the next moment...

Agnes passed out and fell straight backward.

Ugeh?!

The ground was made of rough asphalt. He hurried to gather her up right before she collapsed onto it. A strangely warm sensation came through his shirt, sending all the nerves in Kamijou's body into a frenzy. Agnes was more slender than Index overall, so she had a firmer feel—but that, in contrast, only seemed to emphasize her softness on a part-by-part basis.

Uh...?!

Then, when Kamijou directed his gaze straight up to get his eyes off of Agnes, now snug in his arms, he saw something else and quaked again.

There was a big metal basin in the middle of the tent. And there was a metal bucket hanging from the tent's ceiling, right above the basin. There was something like a watering can spout in the bottom of the bucket and a faucet attached to it. It looked like a simple shower, where you put hot water into the bucket and turned the faucet in order to get it to come out. And in reality, water *was* flowing from it at the moment.

And in the middle of the basin area...At the very center of the tent, still being blessed with a rain of hot water...

"...Touma?"

...was a nun with silvery hair and green eyes, speaking in a very low voice. She wasn't wearing anything, of course. Her slim chest, to which her hair soaked in hot water was sticking...Her belly button, to which just a few water droplets were gathered...He could see everything. She had pale skin to begin with, which ended up emphasizing the redness coming from her body warmth even further.

"N-no, please, wait, Mr. Kamijou totally thought Amakusa had attacked and he was worried so he ran over here so he hopes you take that into account, too, that would be nice and..."

"Ooh..."

"??? Ooh?"

Kamijou had been watching Index's each and every movement with fearful eyes, but...

"...nn, hic. Waah..."

Sh-she's cryiiiinnngg?!

Jolt!

Touma Kamijou's body gave a strange reaction to the unexpected

development. Meanwhile, big teardrops fell from Index's eyes, and she was rubbing them with her hands.

Suddenly, he noticed excessively cold stares collected on him from nearby.

More than one hundred nuns had directly labeled him as a man who makes completely naked young girls cry (not to mention their similarly naked, unconscious leader beside him). The color drained from his face.

"Huh, wait, c-calm down, please, Miss Index! This isn't your personality! Don't you usually do something more like this? See, Mr. Kamijou's head is right here! Just chomp it down as hard as you can already!! Wait, what? Stop, stop! Why do you look so unusually serious?! Th-that was just a figure of speech what are you doing with that saw you could slice up a huge cow with that thing wait a minute sto—Gyaaahhhh?!"

"Didn't I tell you not to make a nuisance of yourself? Hm? What are you clutching your head and crying for?" Stiyl, lying down, tiredly questioned the worn-out Kamijou upon seeing him return to their tent. The tent's opening had been shut—he may have known something had happened, but he didn't seem to realize it had to do with Index. If he found out, the crazy priest would end up chasing him all over the camp with a flaming sword in his hands.

He would rather avoid any further trouble—after all, Agnes had just plainly condemned him, saying, "...I need to look over our plans. Please leave me alone." So he crawled under his own blanket, still rubbing his stinging head. The sorcerer had said earlier that using even five or ten minutes of free time to get in a bit of sleep and rest your body was basic battlefield knowledge, but he didn't think he'd be able to sleep until the pain in his head went away.

"Hey, Stiyl?"

"What is it? I am very irritated right now, so if possible, I would like you to leave this for later."

"I want to ask something."

"Everyone here has such bad crisis management. So what if it's the

Book of the Law, anyway? They're running around like chickens with their fool heads cut off for *one* grimoire! Do they have any idea how many sorcerers are after the girl controlling 103,000 of them—?"

"Is there a girl you like?"

"Bwah?!" Stiyl's breath caught in his throat and he broke out into a full-body shiver.

Kamijou thought this was something you were *supposed* to ask at a sleepover. It seemed *that* was a Japanese-specific custom, however. "Hey, Stiyl. I want to ask something."

"I respect women like Elizabeth I, and St. Martha is a good example of the type I prefer. The anecdote where she exterminates an evil dragon using only prayers of love and charity mesmerizes me. Any other questions?"

"The Amakusa-Style Crossist Church... That's where Kanzaki used to be, isn't it?"

"..." Stiyl narrowed his eyes in thought and fell silent for a bit. He tried to take out a cigarette, but he must have figured that smoking in bed was bad, because his hands stopped halfway there. "Who did you hear that from? Kanzaki wouldn't have gone into her personal history very easily. Was it Tsuchimikado?"

"Yeah. He told me while you were busy being that guy at the beach." Stiyl's face basically became a question mark, but Kamijou left that aside and continued. "But, well...Aren't they Kanzaki's friends?" He paused, perplexed. "...Are we still doing this? Like the time with Misawa Cram School?"

There was one other time when Kamijou and Stiyl had formed a united front in the past.

That battle couldn't be called *pretty* even in flattery. A lot of people had been hurt, and some had even died. He got the picture—that's what clashes between sorcerers, or between groups or organizations of them, meant. Their professional world didn't permit weakness, and that was what created specialists like Index and Stiyl.

But...

As a professional who knew how strict it was, wouldn't he be extremely hesitant about this?

"We are." However, Stiyl Magnus gave a prompt decision, without even a second of hesitation. "Of course we are. Whether it's obeying orders from above—or even if they're trying to stop me, I already decided I'd do anything to protect her. I'll kill anyone I need to. I'll burn them alive. I'll burn even their corpses to nothing. Whether it's while she's watching or while she isn't." His own words seemed to pain him. "Don't get me wrong, Touma Kamijou. Everything I'm doing is for that girl. And if you did something to the contrary, I would turn your bones into ash at this very moment."

"..." Kamijou gulped.

When all was said and done, that was the whole reason for the things this man, Stiyl Magnus, did. The fact that he was an English Puritan, the fact that he gained power to fight as a sorcerer, the fact that he came on orders to save the *Book of the Law* and Orsola—anything and everything.

"I made an oath long ago—*Relax, and go to sleep. Even if you forget everything, I won't forget a thing. I will live and die for your sake.*"

His conclusion was enough to make him shudder.

At the same time, a deep sense of human kindness was in his voice.

Kamijou carefully chose his next words—he thought it would be rude if he didn't. "But then why did you get Index involved in something like this?"

"I'm not the one who planned this—if I had the choice, she wouldn't be anywhere near this place," answered Stiyl smoothly. "But I must not settle things on my own. They would judge her worthless then. If I cannot display value in using Index to my superiors, they might end up sending her back to London. Tearing her away from her life in Academy City would be the most unbearable thing that could happen to her right now." His voice was casual. Given that Stiyl Magnus was her English Puritan colleague, Kamijou would think he'd be happier if she came back—but Stiyl Magnus spoke in a casual voice. "Go to sleep. We only have two hours until the assault. We'll start to have nightmares if we talk for much longer."

Leaving it at that, the runic sorcerer shut his mouth and his eyes.

*　　*　　*

How am I supposed to get any sleep when people could start killing one another in a few hours? he wondered. But after wrapping himself in a blanket and closing his eyes, drowsiness must have overtaken his body at some point. In other words, he was asleep before he knew it. Maybe he was a lot more tired from Daihasei Festival preparations than he'd thought.

Mm...huh...?

Kamijou then opened his eyes for a simple reason—because he felt a weight pressing down on him.

Rustle—he perceived the weight of a grown person, saw some kind of swell in his blanket, and felt the soft, warm sensation of human skin.

He began to hear a soft sleeper's breathing from inside the blanket.

Hey, wait. Crap, could this be...?! Damn, I just remembered that you can't lock tents!

Normally, Kamijou spent his nights locked in his bathroom, sleeping in his drained bathtub. For a simple reason, too—to stop Index from climbing into his sleeping space no matter what. He was always so thankful he had a long bathtub he could stretch his legs out in.

Not only was the crime of invading someone's sleeping space already having a terrible effect on the healthy young man, but Stiyl was also sleeping next to him right now (and he had just said some serious stuff about oaths before going to sleep). Depending on how this turned out, he could be quite literally beheaded for his crimes.

And atop Kamijou's body as it exuded a cold sweat, a fairly young girl's body squirmed about. He came in contact with all kinds of defenseless parts of her—he thought his heart would stop.

"...(Wh-whoa?! Wait, wait a minute, Index! Hey, sleeping next to me would be one thing, but taking up a position right on top of me—isn't that going way too far?!)" protested Kamijou hurriedly in a low voice (though he thought he was practically yelling).

"Mm...What is it, Touma...?"

Then he heard a familiar voice from the entrance to the tent.

He looked to see Index, her eyes half-closed in sleepiness, opening the zipper on the tent and about to creep into his blanket.

Huh?

Kamijou looked at her, aghast.

"Mgh......Papa...*Lo non posso mangiare alcuno piu qualsiasi piu lungo......*"

The one who came out of the blanket was Agnes Sanctis.

She was probably half-asleep and so didn't realize, but there were less than three inches between their lips.

What?! Are you serious?! She has this sleepwalking-into-other-people's-futons habit, too?! Wait, didn't she just get done telling me at the shower to go away?! Eeeek!

He averted his face from the small lips verging on touching him, then hastily crawled out from under Agnes. As he rolled, he pulled the blanket off of her.

"Wha?!"

Kamijou was dumbfounded.

From out of the blanket appeared Agnes, wearing nothing but a white lace bra and panties with rope sides that were tied in bowknots.

And as if she normally did so before sleeping, her habit was neatly folded up in a corner of the tent.

Index, in a complete daze, looked at them both and spoke.

"...Papa?"

"Waaait! Index, I don't know what's going on, either! I absolutely did *not* force a young girl to call me such a particular name! I do *not* have a habit of wallowing in self-satisfaction like this!!" Kamijou attempted a vindication, trembling in fear from having gotten his head bitten in regards to Agnes just a little while ago.

Index observed his expression of fear.

"Ah-ha...Maybe this...is a dream?"

"Huh?"

"Yeah, even Touma would never be this unfaithful. So this is a dream." She yawned.

"Y-yeah, that's it! This is a dream! You're silly—Touma Kamijou is a woman-discarding bad-luck flag master who always runs away. He would never do something this shameless, would he?!"

He had been attempting to lead the sleepyhead Index on as if through hypnotism, but...

"Mmh. Okay, if this is a dream, then it's okay. I can bite Touma as much as I want and it's okay. Since this is a dream. And I can vent all my complaints from today on him and it's okay. Mmh."

"Huh? Ah, what?! W-wait, Index!! No, this is all definitely re—?!"

Kamijou frantically tried to correct himself, but he couldn't stop her—she bit down onto his head with all her might. At the healthy male high school student's shriek—no, scream—Agnes, still half-asleep in her underwear right next to him, jerked awake and sat up. Incidentally, when Stiyl Magnus, who had been sleeping in the same tent, had given one look to all the commotion, he had rolled over to face away from them and gone back to sleep.

4

Eleven o'clock PM.

The Amakusa vicar, Saiji Tatemiya, and his forty-seven subordinates assembled at the specified eddy point for the special movement method, Pilgrimage in Miniature.

It was no mystical forest or mountain, however. It was in the corner of a huge theme park specializing in confectionery, above which hung a signboard reading PARALLEL SWEETS PARK.

The result of a collaborative effort by four major confectionery companies, the power plant–sized site played host to seventy-five sweets shops representing thirty-eight countries from around the world. Several donut-shaped waterways overlapping one another like the Olympic rings formed the basis of its structure. The confectionery booths, which were small as food carts but clearly manned by skillful folk, lined the outer edge of each circular waterway. The spaces inside the waterways were open plazas and spaces for manufacturer exhibitions and events. At the moment, they appeared to be running a campaign involving chilled sweets and sherbets—perfect to battle the lingering heat of summer.

The eddy positions established by Tadataka Inou remained fixed, but the development situation of the town changed on a daily basis. This place was still relatively usable. On some eddies, however, there were apartment rooms or bank vaults constructed on them, making this method of movement completely unusable.

The members of Amakusa, already having infiltrated Parallel Sweets Park, immediately got to work preparing for their Pilgrimage in Miniature.

The method could only be used starting at midnight, but it was an established tactic to prepare beforehand. They would only have five minutes to actually utilize it, after all. Beginning the preparations when that window opened wouldn't give them enough time. And there was no rule saying they had to finish preparing at midnight exactly, either. They could finish up beforehand, then just flip the switch at midnight to activate it.

And though they were preparing sorcery, they weren't drawing suspicious magic circles or reciting spells or anything.

Aside from sneaking into a theme park after closing, the young adults weren't behaving particularly strangely. A group of four or five of them was having a chat. Some were opening up wrapped hamburgers or bags of potato chips and eating them. A few were pointing at the park map directions and arguing about them. Some were standing around and flipping through guidebooks. All of them were only doing very normal things.

Even their clothing looked quite a bit more natural than Index's or Stiyl's. One girl was wearing a white camisole and denim shorts. One boy was wearing layered shirts and big, baggy black pants. One woman had taken off her suit jacket and had it hanging on her arms. If there was anything a little weird, it was that ten of them, at most, were carrying things like sports bags, cases for instruments and surfboards, and canvas cases—as transport for weapons.

But those who were knowledgeable would understand.

Their clothing and casual actions all, without omission, held calculated, magical meaning.

The gender distribution. Their age variations. The combinations of clothing colors. The act of the four or five of them forming a circle. The details of their casual chat. The religious rites of eating. The ingredients and color of the hamburger and the ritualistic meaning of eating meat. The number of bites. The timing of taking drinks. The directions the men and women were walking. The positions they stopped at. The way they read their books. The total number of characters on each page.

Every one of these aspects was disassembled into "characters" and "symbols" as the wriggling flow of people would form a single spell or magic circle. They picked up the few remaining religious practices in everyday life and reassembled them. Amakusa's techniques wouldn't leave a single trace of magic having been used. They had inherited all their ancestors' history—of those who needed to always be on the run from the shogunate's cruel oppression.

Now then.

Saiji Tatemiya, standing on his own, scythed his own sword horizontally.

The metallic streetlight raining light below was sliced in half, and it fell to the ground.

We'll show you, Kaori Kanzaki—our priestess. We'll show you what the diversified religious fusion of Crossism, the Amakusa-Style Crossist Church, has become! he said quietly to himself, tilting his head up to see the night sky.

5

Historic ruins, under the veil of a dark night.

That's what Kamijou thought of Parallel Sweets Park, where the special movement method would be carried out, when he saw it from far away. The man-made amusement center about two hundred meters in front of him was devoid of light. The buildings, normally adorned with the myriad of vivid colors befitting a theme park, were now smothered in blackness. All of the facilities had been designed for fun and entertainment, of course, but it only made it feel even more out of place. An awful, damp breeze began to wipe the sweat on his cheek.

He looked away from Parallel Sweets Park. Dozens of sisters all clad in black had assembled in the big department store parking lot; that was a bizarre sight on its own.

His eyes casually met with Index's. She was writing something on her palm with her index finger—some kind of mental preparation, he guessed. She still didn't seem to want to get him involved in a clash between sorcerers, and she looked more on edge than she had earlier this evening. Maybe her tension was due to the elevated danger; there were significantly fewer Roman Orthodox personnel present now than before.

On the other hand, Stiyl, standing a few steps behind her, was smoking a cigarette like he always did. But he would have been coming up with all kinds of plans to protect her.

Agnes's platform sandals galloped over to Kamijou and the others.

As one would expect given her age, she was pretty depressed before, during the shower thing and the half-asleep crawling-into-his-blanket thing. Now, though, he couldn't see any of that on her face. She seemed to be the type who could forget about personal feelings for her job; he didn't see any of the nervous wobbling from when they first met, either.

"We've located Amakusa's main force in Parallel Sweets Park as we predicted. But we can't get a read on the *Book of the Law* or Orsola. I don't believe this to be the case, but this *could* all be a diversion. Therefore, we haven't loosened the perimeter our other units in the area are deployed in. Only those who are here will be doing combat." Agnes spoke as if this was already decided, and she was just making sure they knew.

Kamijou mulled over what she said for a moment. "Kinda sucks that we don't know *who* in Amakusa has the *Book of the Law*. Or whether Orsola's even in the park. Can we still save her? If it takes too long to find her, they could run away with her or take her hostage."

Actually, it would make more sense to use a hostage, since they're at a disadvantage, wouldn't it? he wondered.

He recalled Orsola's face. Ignorant of the ways of the world and ignoring the words of others—a girl he was pretty sure would wander off if you took your eyes off her for a second. He didn't want to see blades or guns to her throat or villains using her as a shield.

But Agnes wasn't about to spend time worrying. "If they escape Parallel Sweets Park, then that's what our perimeter's for. As for the hostage bit…meh, I don't think they'd use her as a shield."

Kamijou cocked his head to the side in confusion.

"Amakusa's number-one objective is to get Orsola to tell them how to decode the *Book of the Law*, right? If the worst happened and she died while they were using her as a shield, their whole plan would fall apart. If they're this attached to the book, then Orsola will be safe."

Stiyl spoke up, his cigarette moving around as he did so. "Amakusa's goal is probably to use the *Book of the Law* to fill the hole in their strength left by Kanzaki. The fact they're being so stubborn here means they're *that* desperate. If they fail to get their hands on the *Book of the Law*, it's all over for them. So they should be treating Orsola like an ice sculpture."

"…Then again, that means we'll need to find Orsola before Amakusa turns to self-abandonment," said Kamijou, feeling the scales tipped in an odd direction. If they drove Amakusa's backs against the wall before they found Orsola, they could self-destruct along with her. But if the Roman Orthodox Church went easy on them, they wouldn't have the leeway to search for Orsola; given the difference in their forces, there wasn't much room to hold back.

Agnes, too, seemed to understand how difficult it would be to show mercy. "So I want to split our forces. Eighty percent of the Roman Orthodox Church personnel will be the main force and act as a decoy, smashing into Amakusa from the front. Meanwhile, you three will do a search of Parallel Sweets Park as a commando unit.

If you locate the *Book of the Law* and Orsola, please secure them, got it?" She clapped one of her platform sandals on the ground. "If you can't find her before the special movement method expires at 12:05, then we'll have to treat her as not having been here. If that happens, please get yourselves out of Parallel Sweets Park. We'll do a thorough investigation of the park ourselves after neutralizing Amakusa."

If they didn't find Orsola before the time limit, and she also ended up being inside the park, that in itself would end up being dangerous for her. One had only to look at Parallel Sweets Park to realize it wasn't very good for a manhunt. After all, from what Agnes had said, there were seventy-five stalls sitting in the park.

Kamijou gulped audibly, and Index opened her mouth to speak. "There's also the eddy itself. If we don't destroy that, they might be able to run away with Orsola. Touma could easily get rid of it, but we'd need to wait until it opened at midnight in that case. To stop them before that, we could just break the physical items they used to set this up—but Amakusa would have camouflaged everything. Finding all that stuff would be hard."

"Searching for the book and Orsola, *and* destroying the point... Looks like our schedule's going to get a little busy," remarked Stiyl, spitting out his cigarette and crushing it underfoot.

Agnes, having determined that they were ready, raised a hand. All the nuns behind her—seventy strong—hoisted their weapons in the same way, sending the ring of cold steel through the night.

Their weapons weren't all the same. There were obvious ones like swords or spears in the crowd, then there were those that Kamijou supposed *could* be used, like silver staffs and giant crosses. And then there were some crazy things: a giant cogwheel as tall as him and a pine torch. He couldn't even take a stab at what they were for. Agnes herself had been given a silver staff by one of the sisters.

"...This can't be forgiven," she said odiously into the darkness, resting her staff against her shoulder. "When Crossism first spread, it was with the goal of saving everyone. And they're using that power for *this*? They wield their violence for something so stupid, and they're forcing us to use even more stupid violence against them. Why can't they realize such a simple chain of events?"

"..." The answer to that was simple—all you had to do was take a step back and think about it—but Kamijou felt like it was a very difficult problem for the people concerned. Of course, he agreed with her opinion as much as the next guy.

"Well, maybe this isn't the right way of putting it...But it's not only Amakusa—this is why I don't like sorcerers. It's people like this. Especially those modern western sorcerer societies that popped up at the start of the twentieth century. They all use Crossist techniques that are underhanded or split hairs with the ideology. I mean, they even typically use the names of the archangels for their magic circles, like the Likeness of God, Michael, and the Power of God, Gabriel.

"Even besides the twentieth century, like during the witch-hunting days, alchemists contracted to royalty would always make these declarations. 'This is a secret technique in Crossism, so it isn't actually witchcraft. I am no more than another one of God's faithful sheep,' they said." Agnes stomped her feet. They made a *clip-clop* noise. "They meticulously comb through the Bible from start to finish, scrutinizing every single word from the mouth of God. They plumb it for contradictions and holes while sipping their sweet honey. Their black magic goes against the will of God. That is the identity of our true enemies—not the terrible ones without, but the abominable ones within. Sorcerers are like the politicians who bring countries to ruin by exploiting loopholes in the law. People like us obey the rules and stand in a single-file line to receive our daily bread—and they cut in front of us in line, acting all innocent and stuff.

"That's why all this weird trouble keeps happening. I would not tell them not to partake of their bread—I'd tell 'em to get to the back of the line like they're supposed to, you know?"

Kamijou heard all this and was understandably a little dubious of what sounded like a policy of Crossist supremacy. But the important part was that she couldn't forgive Amakusa for breaking the rules when everyone else was obeying them (or so Agnes believed).

As a side note, Stiyl Magnus, a sorcerer by trade, was smirking and ignoring Agnes's indignation; Index looked slightly worried.

Well, Necessarius is full of sorcerers, so they probably feel offended, huh? But still, Agnes...Girls can really change their expressions a lot. She was all nervous and wobbling around before. What strange creatures.

When he glanced around him to change the subject, he only saw Roman Orthodox sisters in every direction.

"Still, though. For someone saying all those modest things about not being able to spare all her forces, you got this many people to gather up with a single word," he remarked in slightly shocked admiration.

Agnes smiled. "It is our privilege to outnumber all. We have comrades in 110 countries around the world, you know. Even in Japan there are plenty of churches. In fact, a new house of the lord is being constructed as we speak—the Church of Orsola. I think it was somewhere around here, actually. Right nearby. I think they were bragging that when it was finished, it would be the largest church in Japan. It was supposedly as big as a baseball stadium." Agnes's soles softly *clipped* and *clopped*.

"Orsola?"

"Yes. She has quite a record, you know. She spread the teachings of God to three heretic nations, earning her the special privilege to have a church built in her name. She was very good at speaking, wasn't she?"

Now that she mentioned it, Kamijou figured she might have been right. It was just that all the Japanese-speaking foreigners coming out of the woodwork tonight lessened that sense for him. He was grateful for it, of course—Japanese was the only language he could speak.

"Once the church is finished, we'll send you some invitations. But before that, we should settle the issue at hand. Let's pray for a splendid conclusion with a good aftertaste."

Agnes gave an intrepid grin, hoisted her heavy-looking silver staff on her shoulders, and clapped the heels of her feet twice on the ground. The twelve-inch-high platforms slid off and they turned into normal sandals. It seemed that they were made to come on and off at will, just like the fasteners on their habits.

"...Umm. I understand it's easier to move around like that. But why don't you keep those off normally?"

"Shut up. It's called fashion. I'm very particular about it."

6

11:27 PM.

Kamijou, Index, and Stiyl arrived at the chain-link fence near Parallel Sweets Park's employee entrance.

Though they had yet to set foot on the battlefield, Kamijou could feel electricity tingling his skin. Someone could have been watching them from the vast expanse of darkness beyond this fence, and they wouldn't know. Their enemies probably had to limit their hiding places to a single part of the park—but the whole thing was already looking like a giant enemy breadbasket.

And she's in the middle of it...

How hard must it have been for Orsola to be left behind, alone? He considered what he'd feel like if dozens of villains with swords and spears were surrounding *him*. *Like shit*, he thought bitterly. *If I knew this was gonna happen, I would have just forced Orsola into Academy City in the first place...*

"Hey, Stiyl."

"What?"

"Do you think we can really do everything we need to before time runs out? We have to destroy the point, search for the book, and rescue Orsola—all of those things."

Stiyl remained silent for a moment at his question. Index, too, looked between them nervously. After a pause, the sorcerer answered. "Honestly, it's going to be tough. We don't even know where in the park the *Book of the Law* or Orsola is. Plus, there's actually one piece of information I didn't tell the Roman Orthodox Church."

Kamijou tilted his head in confusion.

"Right before this incident occurred, Kaori Kanzaki, who should have been in England, disappeared. She's probably acting on behalf of her former subor—Her friends. If we try to deal major damage to Amakusa, the saint might attack."

Kamijou was taken by such surprise and nervousness that he thought his mouth would dry up like a desert.

Kaori Kanzaki was such a strong sorcerer that she could suppress a real angel, as she had during the Angel Fall incident. He hadn't personally seen her in battle, but he found it easy to imagine how dangerous she would be as their enemy.

And even *he* understood clearly that Stiyl's prediction could very probably end up as reality.

"So don't think about accomplishing all our jobs. The plan was bound to fail in the first place—and we've got enough danger on our plate right now. The worst thing that could happen is them deciphering the *Book of the Law*, so try to prevent that."

"Well, then..." Kamijou looked between Stiyl and Index before continuing. "Then can we make Orsola our top priority?"

"I don't care one way or the other. The book is a complete waste without the decoder. This girl here has all the knowledge of the book itself in her head, so we're not interested in the original copy, either. And the Roman Orthodox Church is the one that owns it, so even if it's lost, it's no skin off the English Puritans' back."

"I think it's a good idea, too. And if we told you no, you'd just go charging in there anyway! We're already short on people, so we all need to stay together."

Both Index and Stiyl, the English Puritan sorcerer, answered without much worry.

They probably had their own issues as professionals, but they still accepted the opinion of an entirely ignorant amateur.

"All right. Thanks!"

They both made rather bewildered faces. Index exaggerated her facial expressions from the start, so that was normal—but Stiyl, depending on your point of view, almost looked comical.

He clucked his tongue. "Don't go cramping my style before we go charging in. The diversion starts at eleven thirty. We'll be infiltrating when that happens, so we should—"

"Touma, don't relax once we're inside, okay? Make sure you hide behind me and listen to what I tell you to do, or you'll be in danger."

"Hah? What are you saying, you silly sister? When it comes to sorcerers, my right hand is like an iron wall. You should be the one hiding behind *me* and taking *my* advice."

"..." Kamijou and Index hushed up at their difference in opinion.

"—We should be going in soon, so I'd appreciate it if you focused on this. Seriously," said Stiyl calmly, feeling excluded from the conversation. And right that moment...

...there came a *bang* from the distant admission entrance.

"...Hey. Is that really the diversion?" murmured Kamijou, a little dazed at the sight of the giant, burning, roaring pillar of flame.

"It means they'll lose unless they use things like that, Touma. Don't let down your guard!" said Index.

"And it's not causing an issue. They're combining sorcery to keep people away and to interrupt. But I don't feel the mannerisms of Roman Orthodoxy in the technique—I don't feel that unique accent...It must have been Amakusa. Rather annoying that they have techniques this powerful."

Either way, the time had come.

Index pressed herself against the chain-link fence and focused on something past it. After confirming there were no magical traps set up, the three of them jumped the fence and snuck into the unlit park.

The park lights were off, making it a dark bubble within a bustling city. Kamijou even felt like the starlight here was stronger than it usually was. They had entered from outside the actual viewing course. Once they passed between a gelato stand and an almond jelly stand, neither of which was much bigger than a mobile home, they entered the course.

It was a giant circular path. Right in the middle, there was a waterway—actually, more like a moat—and the surface of the water was about three meters under the walkway. He couldn't tell how deep it went. There were tons of little stands along the outer edge of the course, on the outer circumference. All they had were counters like the ones on food carts—they weren't made so that people could eat inside them. The space on the inside part of the waterway had been made into a plaza. There were many tables and chairs there, so that must have been where people took their treats.

According to Agnes, there was more than one ring—there were several adjacent ones, forming a shape similar to the Olympic rings.

"..."

It would have been a whale of a time had they come in the afternoon, but Kamijou knew they were in a different world right now. Without any lights, all the tiny stalls with their rustic, closed shutters easily felt like they were refusing them. The place felt eerie, like a person's face lit up by a flashlight from below. Even the ravenous Index, normally the merriest of them all, was just looking into the darkness in tension.

"Touma, Touma. We don't have time. If we're gonna look for Orsola, we have to start."

"Right—we only have thirty minutes. We could also set up an ambush if we found the eddy, but given the situation I'd say the odds of that are pretty low," said Stiyl, who, unusually, wasn't smoking so that he could blend into the night.

They started to hear the sounds of angry roaring, shouting, things breaking, and explosions. It seemed the Roman Orthodox and Amakusa had clashed in earnest.

"R-right. Got it."

The moment the words left his mouth, they heard a metallic *thump.*

Huh? he thought, inadvertently turning his head upward toward the source of the noise, when...

...from the roof of the gelato specialty shop came four boys and girls leaping through the air.

* * *

All of them were gripping western-style swords.

"?!"

Kamijou pushed Index out of the way and Stiyl caught her neck and pulled her in to him. A moment later...

Slice!! came the blades swinging straight down, leaving vestiges of reflected moonlight in their wakes. Like a bolt of lightning, they struck at the point Index had just left.

One young man and three young women. All were about the same age as Kamijou. Instead of eccentric habits, they wore what you would if you were going for a walk through downtown. Their ordinary clothing, however, made the sinister glistening of the swords in their hands feel intensely out of place.

In an annoyed tone, Stiyl said, "A hand and a half sword, a bastard sword, a boar tuck, and a dress sword. Man, the people in this country really have a thing for *our* culture, don't they?!"

Kamijou thought to himself that those names were right out of a fantasy role-playing game. Their designs were diverse, their sizes ranging from a little more than a meter to a little less than two. And one of them, he had no idea what it was designed for—it looked like a rapier, except the very tip of it was a ball.

Damn...it. The diversion didn't pull them away one bit, did it?!

The four of them landed, separating him from the other two. Considering how narrow the path was, he couldn't just go around them and join back up with his comrades, either. Stiyl scattered a few rune cards and whipped out a flame sword, saying,

"Take this. Keep it close if you don't want to die!"

He removed something from inside his clothing and threw it to Kamijou. He frantically caught it—it was a silver cross on a necklace.

"This is..."

...What do I do with it?

As he brought his face up to ask, though, one of the Amakusa girls silently sent the tip of a slender, double-edged sword about the length of a deck brush (apparently called a "dress sword") roaring toward him.

"Whaa?!"

Panicking, Kamijou jumped backward to dodge it. But then the girl charged, and he couldn't deal with it. The only reason he was able to dodge the next horizontal stroke was because he tripped over his own feet and fell onto his back.

"Watch out, Touma!!"

A moment after hearing Index's shout, he saw the girl bringing the dress sword down like a guillotine. He didn't break his fall; instead, he continued his backward roll and managed to evade it.

She didn't look like she'd used any magic at all.

The Imagine Breaker in his right hand wouldn't help him at all in a situation like this. As soon as he tried to do anything with it, she'd cleave it right off.

"Index!" shouted Kamijou, but there were four weapon-wielding assassins in the way, so he couldn't leap in carelessly. Stiyl was standing in front of Index with his flame sword in order to protect her, but two of the assassins went charging at them, intent on piercing both the shielding Stiyl and Index's delicate body with their swords.

Then there was a dull *boom!!*

"—...?!"

Kamijou thought his heart was going to stop when he saw what was happening, but upon observing calmly, he saw that not a single drop of blood had been spilled. In fact, the two assassins who had rammed into Stiyl had gone straight through him.

A mirage.

The false image swayed, struck a sarcastic smile, and disappeared into the void. For some reason, the smile wasn't directed at the Amakusa assassins—it kind of seemed like his eyes were locked right on Kamijou's.

He no longer saw either of them anywhere.

The four assassins all turned their gazes to Kamijou.

Hey, wait...A-aren't you supposed to agree on a signal or a meeting place when we have to run?! Are they making me the decoy again?! Something like this happened before, too. Back during the whole alchemist thing!!

Dazed and confused and now on his own, Kamijou turned his back to the enemy and began to run as fast as he could. His sudden decision seemed to catch them off guard. He looked behind him as he ran to see that three of the assassins had spread out. Maybe they were searching for the disappeared Index and Stiyl.

And the last one…

Only the girl who had pointed her sword at him before was pursuing him. And she was fast. She was catching up to him, fast as a bird, despite holding such a heavy sword.

Agh…shit…! I won't get away from her by running straight!

In panic, he strayed from the circular viewing course and dove into a cramped space not seventy centimeters wide between two shops. It wasn't even an alleyway—it was just a gap.

He tried to run through the narrow gap, but he tripped over something and fell spectacularly to the ground. Apparently they had planned to renovate the shops, because there were signboards on the wall and a box of construction materials on the ground. That's what Kamijou had tripped over.

Gah…! Don't leave your crap lying out like this!

Even if he continued to run away, he'd find the girl's sword sticking through his back. He gave a quick glance at the contents of the scattered toolbox, looking for something that could serve as a weapon. But he quickly realized it was futile—he didn't think he'd be able to beat a real sword by swinging around a hammer. His assailant was quite capable of slicing in two anything he found to throw at her.

…Slicing them? In that case!!

Then, the girl holding the dress sword slid around the corner on her shoe soles and entered the gap as if she were a car drifting around it.

He grabbed a toothpaste-like bottle from the various tools littering the ground and immediately threw it behind him at her.

The girl, without realizing what was coming, swung her sword to cut it down and dove into the gap.

"!!"

He rose right away and crossed his arms in front of his head to protect it.

Her sword didn't stop. Her strike came roaring down perfectly vertically, cutting the wind itself, and closed in to slice both him and his upraised arms in two.

Thump.
There was a dull noise, but the sword that struck his arms didn't even make it past one layer of skin.

Inside the toothpaste-like tube had been grease used for construction.
The sticky substance had completely dulled the sword's sharpness like blood or animal fat stuck to a katana. If her weapon had been as heavy as a Japanese katana, then even with a dulled blade, it probably would have broken his arm. But he couldn't expect a dress sword—a rapier, extravagantly adorned with precious stones—to do that.
"?!"
The girl panicked and tried to ready her dress sword again...
"Too slow!!"
...but before she could, he waved both hands to get the sword off of him and tackled the girl right in the stomach, bringing his arms around her. His entire body weight was enough to send her falling to the ground on her back. Kamijou was too much of a softie, though, not to put his hands around her head to prevent it from slamming into the ground.
As they collided, the girl went *oof* as the air left her lungs, and she hadn't moved since then. She had essentially been hit with a judo throw without being able to take the fall, so there was really no helping it.
"...Goddamn it. That hurt."
After just checking to make sure the girl wasn't hurt, Kamijou sank to the ground. When he looked up, he saw a night sky, enclosed on four sides by building walls. It was a sight he was used to seeing in alleys.
Back-alley brawls in Academy City didn't obey general Japanese common sense—they were far different from the normal, the average, the standard references. There were people who flung around strange

powers that could be as dangerous as a handgun depending on how they used them. And there were also plenty of delinquents with special weapons meant to fight against such espers. Kamijou had still been able to move his body without being overtaken by fear when he saw the blade because it was just something else he'd gotten used to.

He stayed there for a few moments to catch his breath, but finally grabbed the dress sword the girl was carrying. It was slender but felt oddly heavy—maybe it had something to do with its center of gravity. He thought for a moment about whether or not he would be able to use it, but he gave up on that. He didn't even know how to hold a sword properly, so he didn't think he'd be able to deal an effective blow with one. And even if he did strike well with this real sword, just thinking about what it would do to the opponent made his spine freeze. It may have lost a lot of its sharpness, but he didn't want to go swinging it around.

Still, if he left the sword here, he'd have a problem when the Amakusa girl woke up. He decided to leave the area, dragging the sword behind him.

Damn, are Index and Stiyl all right? What about Orsola? Should I meet up with them first or go search for her by myself?

This was all definitely because they hadn't decided on how to contact one another or on a meeting point to get to later. But he had never even thought they might end up taking separate paths, so what was he supposed to do? As he mulled over what course to take, he left the gap between shops, sword dragging behind him, and returned to the circular viewing course—

—when just then, someone suddenly rammed into him from the side.

"?!"

It was the perfect sneak attack, launched from the shadow cast by the wall of a shop. He lost his balance, then immediately threw his sword to the side—he at least wanted to avoid impaling himself the instant he fell over.

Things had completely switched around from just a minute ago as he was tackled to the ground. He was able to take the fall, though, so he didn't suffer as heavy damage as the girl had. He clenched his fists to defend against being straddled and attacked further...

"...What?"

...but he opened them back up. If this were an enemy, something was odd. A black hood, a black habit, and not a single inch of skin exposed from finger to toe despite this heat...The sister's arms were behind her back, with her right hand and left elbow—and vice versa—stuck together, all wrapped up with white sticky tape. Her mouth had been sealed with the same tape, too. He looked closer to see that it was like cloth, and there were tons of strange symbols written all over it that looked kind of like slightly misshapen Japanese characters.

And, well, anyone could have looked to see it was Orsola Aquinas.

Slump. Kamijou could feel his whole body draining of strength at the overwhelming relief.

"Mgh! Mghh-mgh mhhff mggh mffh mgh mmmm mgh mmmmgh mgh ffffm mmmff!"

Orsola, her mouth covered by the strange-looking amulet thing, was looking at him, desperately trying to convey something to him.

"Huh? You came all the way to Japan, so you want to go see real-life sumo wrestlers, you say? You know, not every single person in this country does sumo wrestling. You really are an old lady, aren't you?"

"Mgghhh!!"

"What? Hey, wait, that was a joke!!"

Before he could defend himself, a fairly serious head-butt crashed into the pit of his stomach. He fell onto the ground with Orsola. At first he just coughed a few times, but then he noticed his hand on something soft. She didn't seem to realize it, but it was her large, warm, pulse-conveying chest.

Buh! Bghahh?!

His face turned bright red as he crawled out from underneath her, then ran his right index finger along the talisman thing covering her mouth. She looked surprised for a moment—he had touched her, though indirectly, on the lips—but a moment later, when she saw how the talisman thing had come off so naturally, her surprise was multiplied by a factor of ten.

"E-excuse me. You are the one who I met at the bus stop earlier, aren't you? But, why...?"

"I came to rescue you, obviously! Ah, shit, I'll explain what's going on later. Let's just get out of here!"

Kamijou looked to and fro, and after making sure nobody was around, he picked up the dress sword he had thrown to the ground before.

Orsola was gaping a little. She spoke—not to him but to herself. "Wh-what?

"Are you really...here to rescue me? And it has nothing to do with the *Book of the Law*...?"

"*Like I give a shit about something that stupid!* Do I look weird enough to you that I'd come all this way for one old book?!" He madly scratched at his head and shouted, causing Orsola's shoulders to quiver.

"I-I see. Umm, well... Thank you for taking care of me."

"...Sure. I don't really need thanks or anything. Anyway, what are you doing out here? What happened to Amakusa?"

"Th-they appear to be fighting with the Roman Orthodox Church. I managed to escape in the chaos...Amakusa does not seem to be familiar with this sort of restraining and confinement, however."

Dress sword in hand, he went behind her and destroyed the seals on her arms as well.

Orsola rubbed her now-freed hands and said, "Th-thank you very much. But, hmm...How did you...?"

"Hm? I just have that kind of ability...But it's complicated, so maybe I shouldn't bother with any weird explanations. You'd be stumped if I suddenly started rambling about scientific ability development, right? And by the way, you sure do seem calm in this situation. You'll need to be a little more serious than that if we're going to get away."

"Nevertheless, they have been fighting near the entrance, and I was unable to go over the fence because my hands were tied—what should I have done? I had no choice, so I was searching for another…ex—?"

Before Orsola could finish, he grabbed her arm and dove into the narrow space between the two shops again. She nearly screamed when she saw the Amakusa girl lying there, but…

"…Quiet!"

…he hissed a warning and covered her mouth with his right hand.

They ran through the space and pressed themselves against the back wall of one of the shops. The pitter-patter of multiple sets of footsteps echoed from the front of the circular viewing course, then went away. It felt to him like they had realized Orsola had escaped and were looking for her rather than trying to follow him or Index and Stiyl. Them gripping strange swords and axes and hurling orders every which way struck him as extremely ominous.

When he heard their footsteps grow distant, Kamijou slid down the wall onto the ground. Orsola did the same, sitting elegantly next to him.

7

The place where Kamijou and Orsola took a seat seemed to be in a blind spot for Amakusa. There was a handful of low-hanging trees in the area behind the shop, and if they kept themselves low, they wouldn't be seen from afar.

But on the other hand, now that they'd found themselves a little hiding place, they were now unable to make a move. They heard the footsteps of the young men and women of Amakusa running around the viewing course just nearby intermittently, so if they were to leave they would be spotted right away.

He was worried about Index and Stiyl. Now that he'd secured Orsola's safety, if they were stuck in the park unable to escape, they would be in needless danger. But there was no way for him to contact them, and it would be reckless to leave this place and look around the park for them.

"That special movement method thing can only be used from 12:00 to 12:05, so if we just stay put, it would ruin Amakusa's plan, but..."

He went to check the clock on his cell phone, but the liquid crystal display backlight would stand out in this darkness, so he decided against it. *It'd be real nice if I could use this to contact them, though,* he thought. Index's cheapo phone was in their cat's mouth, and there was no way for him to know Stiyl's number.

When he stretched his legs, still sitting, they met the hilt of the dress sword he'd put on the ground. The sound and feeling brought Kamijou's attention from the inside back to the outside.

And that made him finally notice how heavy his breathing was.

He wiped his forehead and his hand came back with a lot more sweat than normal. Perhaps it was because of the tension—but just moving his body a little had made him break out into a sweat like he'd just run a marathon.

Oh? noticed Orsola, who took the lace handkerchief out of her sleeve. Kamijou tried to back away from her on the ground—he had a bad feeling about this.

"N-no. Don't worry, it's not a problem and look it will get your handkerchief dirty and this happened at the bus stop too didn't it and *mgh*?!"

Before he could finish, he found the flower-scented handkerchief pressed against his face despite his argument.

"If you do not wipe it properly, you could come down with a summer cold. Now, then. Come to think of it, I get the feeling I did this sort of thing at the bus stop, too."

"I just said that same thing eight seconds ago, you know! You're just like an old lady—you never listen to people, and wait that hurts, that hurts!! Please, could you not stuff it in my mouth and no—*grgh*?!"

Kamijou, suffocating a little, desperately tried to repel this handkerchief assault, but he came up empty. Once Orsola had thoroughly deployed her handkerchief, she gave such a brilliant smile that he could almost see the nimbus behind her.

"Excuse me, but you were a citizen of Academy City, were you not?"

He coughed and groaned. "...Hm? Well, yeah."

"Then forgive me for asking, but what would someone from Academy City be doing in a place like this? It doesn't seem to be unrelated to the Roman Orthodox Church's movements, but I was of the impression there were no churches in Academy City." Her voice sounded mystified.

His answer, on the contrary, made it sound unimportant. "Well, it's a little special in my case. I know a couple English Puritans. I just got wrapped up all of a sudden in this, and now they're making me help them with God knows what."

Her shoulders twitched. Her action looked like she had heard something she couldn't ignore. "Umm, should I not have? You were part of Roman Orthodoxy, right? Do the Roman Orthodox and English Puritans not get along with each other?"

"No, that isn't it at all." She made a slow movement, as if she were thinking about something. "I would like to make certain—you are helping now because you were requested to cooperate by the English Puritan Church, yes?"

"That's right." Kamijou nodded along, and Orsola stopped for a moment in thought.

"Oh? You are sweating a bit, aren't you?"

"No, seriously, I'm fine already!"

"So then you are of English Puritan descent, not Roman Orthodox?"

"Urgh, *now* we're back on topic?! W-well, no, it's nothing crazy like that. Oh, and just so you know, I don't have any pull with them. I'm from Academy City, after all."

"I...see." For some reason, she smiled in relief. "Indeed you are. It is obvious that one like you is better off having no connection to our world of the church."

"...That right? Hmm. Then I guess there's really no point in my holding on to this," he said, looking at the cross Stiyl had given to him when they parted ways. He didn't know what kind of power it had, but he'd caught it with his right hand, so it probably didn't do anything anymore.

"Oh. Did you receive that from your English Puritan acquaintance?"

"You can tell?"

"Crossism may be one religion, but there are various forms and types of the cross—like the Latin cross, the Celtic cross, the Maltese cross, Saint Andrew's cross, the pectoral cross, and the papal cross."

"Huh, I see. But there's no point in my hanging on to this. I'd feel bad holding it as someone, er, outside the profession. So I'd like to give it to you, if that's okay."

He thought he'd said it casually, but Orsola nearly jumped off the ground. "Oh, my, is that all right?!"

"Um, yeah, sure. I don't know why Stiyl gave it to me at all, but it probably doesn't have much meaning. I mean, he knows I can't use magic...He likes being sarcastic, so he could have just given it to me as a prank. Also, I don't think this cross has any value anymore. I don't have a clue about sorcery, but my right hand already touched it, after all," said Kamijou, handing the cross necklace over to Orsola.

But then for some reason, she grabbed his hand like she was giving him a handshake. Then, she covered it with her other hand. "I have just one request to make of you."

"Eh, uh...what?" The blundering Kamijou's voice nearly cracked at the sensation—her hands were softer than he'd imagined.

"Would you be willing to put this around my neck yourself?"

"Huh? Well, sure, I don't care."

At his answer, Orsola closed her eyes and raised her chin to make it easier to put the necklace on her. It almost seemed kind of like she was looking for a kiss, and he dropped his gaze in a fluster. But that only brought into view her chest—which was ample already, now emphasized even further by her upturned chin.

Bgah?! He nearly exploded.

"? Is there something the matter?"

"N-no...Nothing's wrong! Seriously, nothing!"

"?" Orsola seemed confused, her eyes still closed. Flustered, he undid the thin necklace clasp. And then he brought it around Orsola's throat, which was covered by white cloth. After doing that, he realized he should have just gone behind her. When he did it from the front like this, it looked like he was trying to embrace her. It immediately set him on edge. His fingers touched the back of her neck. After his hands rattled a few times in nervousness, he finally managed to link the necklace chain back together.

Looking satisfied, she ran her fingers over the cross at her chest a few times. He watched them nonchalantly, and then realized his eyes were being sucked in by the swelling of her chest and quickly looked away. Even paying the least bit of attention to it would bring him to ruin. Unable to endure the silence, he groped around for any topic at all to talk about.

"By the way, you knew how to read the *Book of the Law*, didn't you?"

"The way to read it—well, it's more like the way to decode its encryption, but…" During the first part of her sentence she looked carefree, but then her body tensed up.

"Uhh, no, that's not it. I don't want you to tell me. I just kind of wanted to know why you were investigating that book in the first place. It's pretty dangerous, isn't it?"

Orsola stared at him for a little while but finally loosened up. "It would not be wrong to say that I desired power from it," she said, shaking her head. "Do you know about the original copies of grimoires? Or how they cannot be destroyed by any means?"

"Mm. Yeah. I only heard it from someone, though. What was it? The characters, phrases, and sentences in a grimoire are like magic circles or something?"

"Yes. A grimoire is like a blueprint. It means that grimoires that show how to control lightning will end up also having safety measures that create lightning. With ones as strong as the original copies, even if a person has no mana, it amplifies the minute energies flowing from the earth, becoming a self-defense magic circle that continues to work almost permanently." She briefly looked like she was thinking about something. "With current technology, it is impossible to get rid of grimoires that have reached this state. The most that can be done is to seal it so that nobody may ever read it.

"However," she continued, "that is with current technology. If the original text is a kind of magic circle, then by appending characters and phrases to certain places to break the magic circle, like using a lever to switch rails on a train track, one should be able to use the magic circle against itself—in other words, to force the original text to destroy itself." And at the end, she said clearly,

"The power of grimoires doesn't bring anyone happiness. The only thing they create is conflict. That's why I was investigating its inner workings—in order to destroy these kinds of grimoires."

Kamijou looked at Orsola again.

She had worked out a method to decode the *Book of the Law*, so he had thought her mind was swimming with eagerness to obtain the book's power—but it was actually the exact opposite. She wanted to rob the book of its dangerous powers—that's the only reason she researched grimoires.

He felt very slightly relieved at that, and then—

—there was a dull *bang*!

In front of the shop—near the viewing course, he thought. But before he could stand up in a hurry, something came into sight.

Whoosh—something was dancing in the night sky. It looked like a person.

It was a priest, with red hair and black clothing.

"St...Stiyl?!"

Before Kamijou could say anything, Stiyl Magnus fell quickly toward the ground.

He crashed straight into the ground on his back, ruining the low shrubbery that had been concealing them. There were cuts all over his clothing, made by a bladed object, and blood was dripping from his skin.

There was a loud noise in front of the shop, and he got blown all the way here—did he come over all that?!

As Kamijou imagined the unimaginable, Stiyl, on the ground, said, "Damn...it. Touma...Kamijou? What are you doing? Run away, now!!"

No sooner had he thought *Huh?* than the two side walls of the shop he had his back to began to swell outward like a living being.

"?!" In front of Kamijou, who couldn't understand what was happening, almost as if a killer whale were piercing the ocean surface and jumping, the shop walls smashed into a thousand pieces and someone jumped out. Behind the person, the building collapsed, its supports gone. Pieces of the building as thick as a human arm came clattering down right next to him—but he didn't move a muscle.

In fact, he was smiling.

The man had a slender build, and yet he was wearing a T-shirt and jeans that didn't fit him—they were so big a sumo wrestler could have worn them. He looked like he was in his mid-twenties. There were red crosses on his T-shirt's white fabric, centered on his right arm. His hair looked like it had been intentionally spiked up with gel or something, but the most striking feature was its color. It was overwhelmingly black. His hair, which was probably black already and then dyed black, had an odd, beetle-like luster. The laces on his basketball shoes were abnormally long—more than a meter. With laces that length, Kamijou didn't think you would trip over them even if you mistakenly stepped on them because of how much leeway you had. There was a necklace around his neck that looked like a leather strap, and four or five ten-centimeter-long battery-powered fans hung from it.

His fashion sense was strange, and Kamijou couldn't quite tell what he was going for. But of course, the most inexplicable thing about him was what he was holding in his right hand.

A flamberge.

A two-handed French sword from the seventeenth century more than 180 centimeters in length. The undulations on the surface of the blade were its main characteristic—the curves were made to make wounds larger. Originally they were metal, or, if they were being used ceremonially, made of beaten gold. But this blade was pure white. It was like a plastic model one step away from completion. Maybe he had shaved a dinosaur bone down to use for it, or maybe it was a unique cluster of carbon—or maybe an aerospace material.

Kamijou was a simple high school student, so he couldn't make the guess just by looking at it a little. At the very least, though, it didn't look like metal. The large sword didn't fit with modern society no matter how you looked at it, but this man was holding it lightly with one hand.

"Heh-heh. What are you doin', mister Puritan priest? Come on—where'd your pride as an English gentleman go? Show it to me—show it to Saiji Tatemiya. Man, you wouldn't even be able to protect one girl like this."

Stiyl swore bitterly under his breath and took out rune cards.

He wasn't looking at the danger in front of him, this man with the sword.

He was looking beyond that—at a single sister in white, standing ready on the viewing course on the other side of the destroyed shop. Her fate was his top priority.

"Did you fight this whole time while protecting her...?" muttered Kamijou absently.

Stiyl's sorcery was like a game where you had to secure control points. He could only use powerful magic in places he had his rune cards hung up. For someone like him, this battle was something to be avoided. If he had to fight while moving the whole time, he wouldn't have time for his control-point-securing game. And if he had to fight in that situation while protecting Index on top of that, he had no choice but to literally use anything, even his body, as a shield.

"Don't...waste time thinking about things you don't need to," said Stiyl in a voice like he was going to spit up blood. "...All right, we've got Orsola Aquinas secured. As always, I can't tell whether that luck of yours is good or bad...Anyway, now we just need to make an opening and escape. We don't need to defeat that guy—if we can get away, we'll win."

Stiyl tried to stand up on his trembling feet, but he didn't seem able to put much strength into them. Saiji Tatemiya watched him merrily for a moment, then switched his gaze to Orsola.

"And why do we have to butt heads with each other at a time like this, anyway? I explained this about a million times. Orsola Aquinas... We have no intention of harming you."

The one explaining spoke in a flimsy tone that didn't seem to have much in the way of persuasive power. It even sounded like he was implying disappointment at his own subordinates for having let Orsola escape.

Orsola looked at the destroyed shop, the wounded Stiyl, and then Tatemiya's flamberge, then said, "I am certainly aware that your words are filled with hope. However, I cannot have faith in peace gained through the use of weapons."

"That's a shame. I mean, it's not like it will do you any good to go back to the Roman Orthodox."

Tatemiya swung the sword in his right hand around a bit, as if checking his shoulders.

"..." Kamijou silently moved in front of Orsola to cover her.

He didn't have a weapon. He couldn't win against this opponent by swinging around something he was unfamiliar with. It would probably be better not to go with any weapon rather than a sword that was really heavy and he couldn't use.

Tatemiya first looked at Kamijou's face, then at the dress sword at his feet. "No martial arts stance, and no Soul Arm. And no magical symbols hidden in your clothes, either. Completely unarmed, in the purest sense of the word, eh? Hah, I didn't intend to cross swords with an **amateur**, but...well, we can't all have what we want. Did you steal that sword from Uragami?"

He was emitting a chilling, invisible pressure that seemed to be twisting and warping the outline of his body.

Kamijou didn't recall any name like that, but... "If you mean your lackey, she's sleeping over there. I made sure she didn't hit the back of her head, though, so she's alive."

"...What, and that makes it all right? You makin' fun of us or something?" Tatemiya's tone now sounded anything but lighthearted. Kamijou felt like it gave him a glimpse of the man's humanity.

His opponent wasn't just a monster—he was a person who would get angry over the safety of a friend.

"Then if you're still able to fight for someone else, could you please put that sword down? I don't want to fight someone like you if I don't have to."

"Oh, sure, I'd be all for it, but we've got our own problems, y'see. Our main enemy might be the Roman Orthodox, but if you English Puritans are connected to this, then we can't let you off the hook, either. Plus, we can't give Orsola to anyone like that."

Tatemiya swung his big, nearly six-foot sword lightly up in the air like a cheerleader baton before continuing. "That means you're already a target, too. 'Course, if you drop to your knees right now and surrender, you won't have to see any blood you don't want to." He was smiling, but his voice sounded apologetic. He probably predicted how Kamijou would answer before he even made the proposition.

Kamijou was scared, for sure. He knew what professional sorcerers were like. The ones who gave the most trouble were those who didn't overestimate magic.

People with absolute power, like Aureolus's alchemy, would only prepare one trump card. On the other hand, those without an excessive faith in trump cards, like Motoharu Tsuchimikado, would instead set up their hand with enough cards, countless cards, to make up for it.

Saiji clearly belonged to the second group. He could probably send Kamijou's head flying with one sweep of that flamberge, even without using magic.

One look at his ability to take down Stiyl without suffering a single wound (protecting Index though the sorcerer may have been) spoke volumes of the man's depth.

Kamijou shuddered—this wasn't someone he could beat squarely. It was like telling a relatively quick-footed child to race an Olympic track-and-field athlete. Would it be better...to obey and surrender?

He couldn't match the man's skill, nor had he set anything up beforehand to get around that.

Still...

What would happen to Stiyl?

The priest, still bent over, was glaring at Tatemiya, his breathing ragged.

Stiyl had his own goals—and he was here because he believed they would do Index good. For him, failure just wasn't an option. Neither the hopeless reality nor any words Kamijou could give would be enough to hold Stiyl Magnus down.

And if Kamijou couldn't stop him...

...then it was pretty evident what was waiting for him.

What would happen to Index?

Even now, the girl looked like she'd spring between Kamijou and Tatemiya given the slightest opportunity.

If Stiyl and Tatemiya clashed, if they exchanged blows even once, they wouldn't be able to play the surrender card anymore. If it came to that, she'd probably do anything to let Kamijou, a sorcery amateur, escape. No matter how little strength they had—no matter how clear the gap in their power was—no matter how much Kamijou hoped against it.

And finally...

What would happen to Orsola?

The Roman Orthodox sister was uneasily glancing back and forth between Kamijou and Tatemiya.

Saiji Tatemiya desired the knowledge, the technique, the *power* that the *Book of the Law* possessed. So long as that was true, then Orsola wouldn't be killed here. In fact, they would probably even make sure any stray bullets didn't strike her.

But if Orsola were taken away from here, she'd be brought to Amakusa's base. If she were to refuse to instruct them on the way to decode the *Book of the Law*, then it was pretty clear what would be in store for her.

Tatemiya and Amakusa weren't looking for Orsola Aquinas herself, but rather the way to decipher the *Book of the Law*. He didn't want to think about what would become of her after they got the information they needed.

"The way to read it—well, it's more like the way to decode its encryption, but..."

—And she never even *wanted* the book's power.

"It would not be wrong to say that I desired power from it."

—And she was trying her hardest *not* to cause this to happen.

"One should be able to use the magic circle against itself—in other words, to force the original text to destroy itself."

—These people smiling before him were scorning all her tireless efforts, ignoring her feelings, and trying to use her as a tool for their own greed.

"The power of grimoires doesn't bring anyone happiness. The only thing they create is conflict. That's why I was investigating its inner workings—in order to destroy these kinds of grimoires."

Kamijou pushed the dress sword aside with his foot and took a step forward.

Whether it be unsightly or comical, Kamijou was the only one here who could clench his fist and stand up to them.

Did he have a reason to loosen those five tightened fingers?

"...Don't look down on me," said Kamijou lowly, putting even more force into his tightly gripped right fist.

Saiji Tatemiya, who had been watching him, gave a sigh that sounded sincerely regretful. "Those're some eyes you've got there. Glaring at me like that's gonna make me feel sorry for you. No, no, I'm seriously sorry about this. I know what I gotta do, but that straightforward response—it's starting to make me not want to kill ya."

Tatemiya shook his undulating flamberge lightly.

"But if you say so, then who am I to refuse? It's your funeral."

Right as those words left his mouth...

Kamijou heard the loud *bang* of an explosion. The sound of Tatemiya's feet hitting the ground alone had explosive energy. Before Kamijou's body could even freeze in tension, his opponent took his first step forward. One more step until his blade would reach.

When he saw the light glinting off the sword blade, conveying the man's brute force, Kamijou's mind was stunned, like a frog in a snake's gaze.

He reflexively thought to cover his face with his hands, but that wouldn't be nearly enough to protect him.

Gh, gah...! Don't fear...just move!! Kamijou commanded his quivering body in desperation and finally took his first step of a run. Not backward but forward. Tatemiya saw Kamijou charge at him from a little bit to the right and actually gave a dubious expression. He probably couldn't figure out why an amateur was jumping straight into his attack range.

"Hah!!"

Exhaling, Tatemiya brought his sword straight down over him like a bolt of lightning.

There was a roaring *crack* as it split the quiet night air.

A single, decisive attack meant to split Kamijou, speeding at him like a bullet, in two.

"…!"

This time, it wasn't just a little bit—he devoted his entire body and jumped at a ninety-degree angle to the right. The giant blade cleaved through the droplets of sweat dancing in the air. Jumping in a way that completely ignored all of his momentum put a huge load on his ankles. Kamijou failed to land, lost his balance, and crashed into the back wall of a store beside them.

"Shh!!"

Then, Tatemiya, rotating his entire body, whipped his blade to the side in a straight horizontal sweep. But it seemed like he noticed it after he started the swing…that Kamijou, his back against the wall, was smiling fearlessly.

I can do this…!!

Kamijou crouched down as far as he possibly could.

He knew that if he fled to the side when his opponent brought the sword down, he'd normally follow up with a horizontal slash. Bringing the sword up again would have created an additional step.

With his body as low as he could get it, he charged Tatemiya, his face low enough that he could lick the ground. He didn't need to think about anything but a horizontal slashing attack. Even if Tatemiya had tried to unleash a top-to-bottom one, he'd be a beat too late. If he did that, then Kamijou's fist would reach him before he could swing his sword completely.

So Saiji Tatemiya had gone with a directly horizontal sweep, just as Kamijou had predicted from the beginning.

Kamijou let the sword graze right over his head, and though his heart was in the iron grip of terror…

"Woh…ohhhhhhhhhhhhhhhhhhh!!" he shouted, clenched his fist, and lunged right into Tatemiya.

Even Orsola, his ally, gulped at his drive.

Right after Tatemiya swung his powerful, two-handed stroke, he couldn't do anything about Kamijou's fist…

And then…Saiji Tatemiya vanished.

Tatemiya had been right in front of him, but now he was about one meter back. And his sword, which had completed a horizontal strike, was somehow already prepared over his head.

It was like he had turned back time and redone it.

No—as if he had used an illusion or something to lure Touma Kamijou out.

"Ah…?—?!" A chill came over him, and he rolled to the side, when…

Roar!! The vertical attack split the ground in two like a piece of paper being torn apart. Because of all the friction, the hollowed-out earth glowed orange like magma. No one could look at this and think it obeyed any physical laws.

Magic?—Then I'll…!

He put energy into his right hand. If that sword was a magical article, then he might be able to destroy it by touching it with his right hand. So he went to thrust his fist toward the blade coming at him.

"No…! Don't do it! Touma!!"

He just barely stopped his fist at Index's shout. Defenselessly, he spotted the young girl thoughtlessly running out to him out of the corner of his eye.

No way…You mean it's not magic?!

Tatemiya's behavior.

That downward swing, so fast he couldn't see it, and that powerful attack that had split the ground open.

Were all of those simply feats of strength? He shuddered.

"No, don't! Index, don't come over here!!" he shouted, but it didn't sway her. Tatemiya's blade severed even the sound as it swung down. Kamijou had figured an attack with his right hand would deal with this and hadn't thought of any alternatives. And he didn't have the time to anymore. His eyes ballooned as he watched the blade closing in on him.

"AOF, TMIL—ASTPGW, ATDSJ, TM! (An original flame, thy meaning is light—a sword to protect gentle warmth, and to deliver strict justice, to me!)"

At the same time as Stiyl's shout, there was a *boom!!* as a flame sucked in oxygen and exploded. The flame sword he gripped sliced through the dark of night, and Tatemiya was forced to divert his attention to it for a moment.

"Shit!"

Meanwhile, as Tatemiya was facing to the right, Kamijou jumped the other way, barely managing to get out of range.

Or at least, he tried to.

Tatemiya, looking in the wrong direction, slid in the same direction Kamijou was running. His legs weren't moving. It was an unnatural movement, as though he were slipping on ice.

Sor...cery...?!

Kamijou's spine froze, and just then...

Swoosh!! The sword whirled around like a tornado, going for a straight horizontal cut. Kamijou immediately ducked to try and avoid it...

...but *wham!!* came a heavy impact striking the evading Kamijou's flank.

He looked carefully and saw a soccer ball–like object made of clear ice buried in his body. The instant he realized it, the ice ball disappeared strangely, like it was being painted over. Kamijou was sent flying into the ground by the ice attack and began to roll over.

—Let's go back to when Kamijou had just clashed with Tatemiya.

The instant the young man looked like he would be killed, Index couldn't help but start running.

So that's...Amakusa... Index shivered as she ran.

And though she shivered, she found herself in admiration.

The techniques Amakusa used were, in and of themselves, quite commonplace. At the very least, they weren't flashy or unique and didn't possess vast attack power—like Stiyl's Innocentius or Aureolus's Ars Magna.

However, they used that fact against itself.

Kaori Kanzaki's wire technique, Seven Glints, stood out the most here. Amakusa's basic strategy could be summed up with one word: *deceit.* If you thought it was a magic attack, it would just be a simple trick—and if you thought it was a trick, then real magic meant to kill would come at you.

Index ran.

Kamijou and Tatemiya felt strangely far away.

Obviously you would take entirely different defensive measures based on whether something was magic or not. If you misread it, you'd end up taking quite a bit of damage.

Index had a way of preventing sorcery with her spell interception technique. Sorcery started from a person's thoughts—so by acting and speaking in such a way to disrupt the mind of someone casting a spell, you could cause it to go out of control. For example, whispering nonsensical words into the ear of a person trying to say tongue twisters to induce mistakes.

However, spell interception didn't work on Amakusa-Style techniques.

Generally speaking, their spells, charms, and magic circles were unique—hidden within casual, everyday actions and words. They picked out subtle religious rituals and built techniques out of them. And this Tatemiya person had performed actions with magical meaning in a split second and was activating magic ten or twenty techniques at a time in the middle of combat.

With Index's voice and skill, she couldn't slip spell interception into a single motion that took only a split second to complete. By the time she thought to do something, Tatemiya's single motion was already finished. If she wanted to obstruct his sorcery, she would need to keep up with his swordplay movements, which he'd built into his techniques' activation conditions. But Index obviously didn't have any way of using such masterful martial arts abilities.

As a result of all this, Index jumping in wouldn't be able to force Saiji Tatemiya to retreat. Index, being a magical professional herself, realized the difference in their strength—and not in terms of simple quantity, but also the fact that his kind of power was overwhelmingly mismatched with her.

Touma Kamijou took the magical ice-bullet attack and fell to the ground.

Saiji Tatemiya whipped his flamberge up into the air as though he were about to hit a nail with a hammer.

Index didn't have any way of stopping that attack. Her spell interception wouldn't do much against Amakusa-Style techniques, either.

"Touma!!"

But Index didn't stop running.

She didn't think any longer of what would happen afterward.

Stiyl Magnus thought his heart would stop when he saw the defenseless Index jump out. She had no fighting power. If she stood up to Tatemiya, she would be sliced in two within seconds.

"Gah…!!"

He had one flame sword in each hand. He didn't have enough time to place all the rune cards to activate Innocentius again.

If he jumped out now, Stiyl would get to Tatemiya before Index. He might be able to distract him by attacking with the flame swords and blowing them up the moment they clashed with the opponent's sword.

But Kamijou stood between Stiyl and Tatemiya.

If Stiyl pointed his sword at Tatemiya, it would pierce Kamijou's body as well.

For just a moment, the flame priest's face warped into a bitter expression.

For a few moments, he was conflicted. And when that ended, the light of determination was already in his eyes.

I made an oath long ago…

Stiyl Magnus desperately worked his bleeding mouth to steady his breathing.

...*"Relax, and go to sleep. Even if you forget everything, I won't forget a thing. I will live and die for your sake!!"*

In order to protect that which he held most dear, he focused on the young man's back and readied his flame swords.

All the air vented from his body, and his consciousness wavered. He looked at Tatemiya, bringing his sword up in front of Kamijou. He frantically restrained himself from passing out and tried to somehow get a handle on the situation.

His feet trembled. It would be impossible for him to avoid Tatemiya's next attack.

Index had already started running, and in a few seconds, when she ran into Tatemiya, she'd be killed instantly.

He glanced behind him—Stiyl had his flame swords up, but Kamijou was a wall in the way of him using them.

Touma Kamijou revved his mental engine to full before even a second had passed.

So that nobody would be missing. So that nothing would be lost.

So that everyone could go home smiling.

"...Do it."

He clenched his fist.

"Attack us both, Stiyl!!"

He rallied every last bit of strength in his body and charged for Saiji Tatemiya without hesitation.

Those few words confused Saiji Tatemiya.

The English Puritan sister was approaching him from behind, but he could easily slice her in two. The young man had jumped for him, his fist clenched, in order to stop that, but there was still more than enough time for him to cut the boy down and then deal with the sister.

But behind that young man...

The English Puritan priest had burst into a sprint, his flame swords at his hips.

"?!"

However one looked at it, if that priest kept charging, he would end up having to go through the young man with his swords. But there was no hesitation in the priest's eyes. They were sharp as a knife blade, and there was a savage smile on his lips, as if calculating how to defeat his enemy were the only thing on his mind.

Tatemiya tried to ready his flamberge to defend against the flame swords. But when he did, the young man brought his right arm behind him and went to deliver a rock-hard punch.

"Crap...?!"

He wouldn't have enough time to deal with his punch and then defend against the flame swords' attack afterward. Plus, those flame swords weren't for slashing—they were for exploding. If he screwed up on how he responded to them, he'd be in mortal danger. If he didn't prioritize them and inject an anti-fire technique into his flamberge, the sacrificial boy could be engulfed in the explosion.

It's just a punch from an amateur—no problem; I've had a basic shock-absorbing technique on me since this battle began. I only need to worry about those flame swords, so I'll compose a technique for them right now!

Tatemiya brought his sword down into a horizontal stance. The flamberge was flame aspected, given the origin of its name—a flame-like sword—and his horizontal leveling of it was the code for "suppress," giving him the impromptu technique that would suppress flames.

Fine, got you, finished! When your careless flames come to hit me, I'll counter them with everything I've got...!!

Saiji Tatemiya's tongue came out of his mouth. It wriggled around and licked his lips greedily.

The priest charged at the young man's back, as if to assault him. The flame swords in his hands were aiming straight through the boy's body and right at Tatemiya's center.

I win!!

—Or so he thought.

*   *   *

Tatemiya tried to use a flame-resistant technique to try and blow back the heat and flames that were supposed to come at him when the flame swords exploded, but contrary to his expectations, nothing happened.

The young man's right fist was all the way behind his body, like a hammer about to drive into him. And the priest's flame swords had stabbed right up to that fist and nearly into it.

Bang!

With a sound like a balloon popping, the flame swords in the priest's hands scattered into little embers and disappeared.

"Wha...? Nnh, gahh...?!"

Saiji Tatemiya, who had only been considering his counterattack timing after he'd used his flame-resistant technique to defend, didn't understand what had just happened.

Boom!! came the ear-splitting roar as the young man's fist plunged right into Saiji Tatemiya's face.

Ga, bah...!! Wh, ah, it went through...the shock-absorbing tech...?!

Tatemiya's body bent all the way backward. Before he could regain his lost balance, the young man and priest both rammed into his body at full speed. Their pressure and weight made Saiji Tatemiya feel like he'd been hit with a battering ram—he flew horizontally through the air and slammed into the ground hard.

That's when Tatemiya appeared to lose consciousness.

The flamberge flew from his hands and came down to the ground with a clatter.

CHAPTER 3

English Puritanism

The_English_Puritan_Church.

1

The battle was over.

Kamijou figured it was because Amakusa's command had crumbled all at once, since they lost their leader, Tatemiya. He basically understood because the sounds from afar had abruptly stopped, and the tingling, tense air had cleared. He hadn't been given a thorough explanation, since they hadn't met back up with Agnes and the sisters, but it seemed like victory had visited the Roman Orthodox Church. If that wasn't the case, then it was strange that Amakusa wasn't sending reinforcements to Kamijou's group, since they'd been acting so uncontrollable and crazy.

He was a little concerned about the welfare of the Roman Orthodox and Amakusa, but Stiyl had reported no deaths on either side, and that the Romans had placed the Amakusa members under arrest. He wondered for a moment where all the man's confidence came from, but it seemed like he was communicating by using his cigarette ember. The way the smoke billowed apparently conveyed his intent, but Kamijou obviously couldn't tell by looking at it.

Saiji Tatemiya had been seated nearby, and rune cards attached to his limbs, chest, back, and forehead. It was apparently a brutal technique—one that would immediately douse him in flames if he were to move too much.

And, since Stiyl had gone to bring Orsola to Agnes and the others, Kamijou, Index, and Tatemiya were the only three people here.

And...

"Touma, Touma! Are you okay? Are you hurt? Does it hurt anywhere?!"

...at the moment, a white-faced Index was trying to take off his clothes.

"Hey, would you quit that, Index?! I'm fine, nowhere hurts really— bwah? A-are you an idiot or something?! Watch where you're touching!"

"Then make absolutely sure of it yourself! Like if there's anywhere that hurts or that's hot or something!!" she shouted, nearly crying.

Kamijou finally realized how much he'd worried her. But making a direct comment along those lines would be incredibly embarrassing, so he listened to Index without saying anything and checked himself. "Okay. My side hurts a little, but that's about it. It's not like I can't move or anything."

"Really? It's really no big deal?"

"Yeah. And I mean, I think I'm pretty accustomed to this. Back-alley fights with espers everywhere are pretty dangerous in their own right. And I fought magicians a whole bunch of times over summer break, remember?"

"I see... That's good..." Index made a face he found difficult to judge whether it was smiling or crying. He grew vehemently embarrassed and couldn't help but look away, but...

"...So then I can bite your head all I want, Touma."

What?

He couldn't ignore that—and the moment he heard it, the wild-animal girl Index launched a vicious assault on his head with her teeth.

"B-byaah?! Wait a second, Index! One second you're worried about my health, and the next this?! What'll you do if you make another wou—gyaahhh?!"

"I'm biting you because I'm worried about you! What in God's name were you thinking, Touma?! You're crazy! Not only did that guy have a huge sword, he was also a sorcerer! And you went up against him with just a fist! Maybe you should have used that weapon on the ground! And the enemy actually said that if an amateur surrendered, he wouldn't take your life! What were you thinking getting all determined?! You're hopeless!"

"Wait, wait, you might kill me if you keep doing this, Miss Index, ow! I got it! I sincerely apologize on all fronts for my own actions today, so would you please lighten up with the biting...?!"

"And also, also! Did you actually think this through to the end? Did you even know that Amakusa guy would need time to build a fire-resistant defensive technique?! If you messed up on how long he was gonna take for it, you would have gotten cut right in half!!"

"No, no plan or anything. That was actually me going in for a real suicide attack, it's just that Stiyl is so considerate, I had no idea about flame-resistant or defenses or—wait owwww?! I'b sowwy I'm sorry Miss Index pleeeaaaasssseeeee?!"

Kamijou thoroughly delivered the kind of scream he would have never voiced in serious situations. Finally, Index seemed to feel better.

"...Hmph. You're stupid. And reckless," she murmured to herself as she put her small chin upon Kamijou's hair.

Uh, wha...?!

Index, tired of being angry, probably did it with the same feeling one would when they got bored and put their head on their desk, but Kamijou's heart immediately began beating twice as quickly. Aside from the sensation of a girl's chin on his head, her long, silvery hair was giving off a sweet fragrance that wafted refreshingly to his cheeks, and above all, since he and Index were facing each other, her chest was super close—not even two centimeters from the tip of his nose. Normally he wasn't aware of it, but this close, he was made to notice just a slight bit of a bulge.

Why are all her attacks changing speed like this? Oh, I get it. Now she's gonna realize I'm looking at her chest and end up biting me again, right?!

Kamijou edged into a defensive stance, but contrary to his expectations, Index simply pulled herself away.

She stared up at the night sky for a few moments, listening carefully. "It's so quiet. You wouldn't think that many people were fighting."

"Yeah." He nodded along with her.

But right now, this silence was welcome. At the very least, he didn't need to worry about swinging around swords and lances, or people yelling angrily, or the sounds of things breaking.

"Hey." And then, all of a sudden, Saiji Tatemiya, seated nearby, spoke up to Kamijou. There was an odd tinge of impatience in his voice. Before Kamijou looked over there, Index spread out her arms and went in front of him as a shield. Tatemiya glared at them and said, "Shit. Sorry, but could you take these off for me, man? Well, I mean, I know I'm askin' the impossible. But I can't just leave her alone like this."

Huh? Kamijou frowned. *Who does he mean by "her"?* he thought... but it hit him a moment later: Orsola Aquinas. "What are you saying, idiot? Why would we let the most dangerous person here out of our—"

"You're the idiot here! Come on, just hear me out, all right? Do you *actually* plan on handing her over to the Roman Orthodox Church, man? You probably have no idea what kind of treatment she'll be getting after this."

Huh...? Kamijou didn't know what to say.

"No, Touma." Index actually sounded calmer than him. "This person uses his words as a weapon. So don't listen to him. How would our enemy benefit from telling us the truth, anyway—"

"*She's going to be killed,*" said Saiji Tatemiya, cutting her off. "Listen, I'll just tell you the ending first. Don't hand her over to the Roman Orthodox. They *actually* want to kill her."

"And you're Orsola's ally, so you want us to untie you and let you escape? You've gotta be joking. That's way too convenient. You're the ones who kidnapped her in the first place! And you stole the *Book of the Law*, too! She knows how to decipher what's inside it, so you kidnapped her, gave all these people weapons, and fought, and now you're saying *we're* the bad guys? That's the dumbest fucking thing

I've ever heard!!" Kamijou was so mad that he yelled loud enough to hurt his throat.

Tatemiya, however, didn't care. "We didn't steal the *Book of the Law*."

What?

Kamijou's mind blanked for a moment.

"I mean, just think about it. What would we need it for? Roman Orthodoxy is the world's largest Crossist denomination. It's got more than two billion followers in all. Would we want the thing so badly we'd pick a fight with *that*? It's just the *Book of the Law*."

"Don't give him a serious reply, Touma!" Index tensed up and said flatly, "I heard Amakusa lost its priestess, and now it's gotten a lot weaker. So you tried to make up for that missing strength by getting your hands on the unknown grand magics in the *Book of the Law*. Am I wrong?"

"I just said—*why would we need power in the first place?*"

Saiji Tatemiya smiled. The expression, with a bead of sweat sliding down his face, looked like he could have been impatient because he was running out of time.

Kamijou was perplexed. "Because if you didn't have it, you'd lose to other factions!"

"Yeah—if they even *attacked* us, man. But you just have to remember this. Amakusa's been oppressed for an extremely long time. Do you think we don't have any countermeasures for it? Nobody has ever found our base, and there are still plenty of eddy points for our specialty, the Pilgrimage in Miniature, set up by Tadataka Inou, that no one knows about."

Kamijou suddenly felt like he'd been caught off guard by the man's words.

That was right—they only knew twenty-three of the points used for the special movement method.

"How would anyone attack our base when no one but us even knows where it is?"

He has a point, he thought.

Nobody knew where Amakusa's headquarters was, so if they fled there, Orsola wouldn't be able to be rescued again. Because of that, the point of this battle had been to settle things before they activated the special movement method.

No one would be able to attack their stronghold—so they never needed to prepare to defend it in the first place.

"Then..."

Did Amakusa have some other objective than defense? Could they have been going after the *Book of the Law* to expand their military might?

Or were they...

"Lemme ask you something, man. What kind of grimoire is the *Book of the Law*, exactly?"

Saiji had been talking to him, but since he was a total amateur when it came to magic, he meekly looked at Index.

She began explaining, her expression reluctant. "The *Book of the Law* is a grimoire written in an extremely complex code—and actually, its grammar is strange enough that it wouldn't be an overstatement to say that it was written in a completely different language all its own. It's said that the only one to ever decipher it properly was Edward Alexander, the one who wrote it, also known as Crowley. He stated that the most important part of the book was 'There is no law beyond Do what thou wilt,' but nobody knows what that means." She continued smoothly. "The *Book of the Law*'s contents contain instruction from an enigmatic being called Aiwass, who could be said to be his guardian angel or one who must not be forgiven. One theory states it lets you freely use techniques that angels can use. It has enormous power. They say that as soon as you open the book, it announces the end of the age of Crossism and the beginning of a new era."

"That's the thing." Saiji Tatemiya smiled meaningfully. "That's the most important part. The *Book of the Law* does have enormous power. If it really did allow anyone to use angelic techniques, the era of a Crossist-dominated world would be over before the day was up. After all, everyone would be able to use powers stronger than the pope himself. The entire pyramid structure of the Church would come toppling down, but..." He paused for a moment. "But I don't actually think everyone thinks everyone wants this power."

"Why not? I'm not a sorcerer, so I'm not involved in this. But don't you professional sorcerers want to use stronger magic so you can move up in status?"

"There's the question of *why* we would need to move up in status in the first place. We don't need that kind of power. In fact, neither should any true disciples of Crossism."

"But the Roman Orthodox Church manages the *Book of the Law* because they want its strength, don't they?" This mystified Kamijou, but Index seemed to understand what he was getting at, since she made a sour expression.

"Here's the thing." He smiled quietly and answered the young man's innocent question.

"Why would Roman Orthodoxy, the biggest Crossist denomination with the most disciples in the world—two billion—want to *end the era of Crossism?*"

Oh. Then it hit him.

People who were already satisfied at the current balance wouldn't have any reason to desire change. In fact, that went even more for those who reigned supreme in this day and age.

"The Roman Orthodox were never *looking* for a weapon as strong as the *Book of the Law*. What they need is a weapon to help them gain control of the world, not one that would smash the world to pieces."

Kamijou and Index both fell silent.

It felt like the darkness of the night had grown many times thicker all of a sudden.

"So they decided to secretly get rid of the one person who could draw out the book's power. But she realized that, too. She used all the power she had to get to somewhere the Roman Orthodox couldn't reach...In other words, she manipulated her schedule so she could come here to Japan. Ironically enough, the *Book of the Law* was set to be transported here already. And then she came looking for help from the local Crossist sect—Amakusa. When all's said and done, we were really just helping her make her great escape."

Tatemiya heaved a sigh. "The book being stolen was a big farce put up by Roman Orthodoxy. There's no way we would steal it. They were probably trying to connect her disappearance with the book. If they came as a set, then everyone would think the kidnapping was so we could get our hands on it. If she had been the only thing to disappear, people might put it down to some other possibility. Like that she defected in order to flee the Roman Orthodox Church, for example."

Good and evil, offense and defense, capturing and rescuing.

Kamijou witnessed the single moment all of these flipped around.

"So can you still say that the Roman Orthodox Church is in the right here? Can you say with one hundred percent certainty that returning Orsola Aquinas to them was the right move?"

"..."

"If you can, then let's hear your proof. If you can't, then stand up and face your own doubts! Who's the real enemy here? Anyone could understand that if they just thought about it calmly!!"

Kamijou took one deep breath at Saiji Tatemiya's angry shout.

He closed his eyes.

He neatly arranged all the information in his head and started to verify it piece by piece.

Think.

Whose points are correct—the Romans or Amakusa?

Where is the contradiction?

"I can't. I still don't trust you completely."

"...Why not?"

"Even if everything you say is true," began Kamijou slowly, "then why did Orsola run away from you? I first met Orsola walking around by herself near Academy City. Stiyl explained before that the Roman Orthodox Church and Amakusa would have been fighting at the time. I think she probably looked for an opening in the fighting and *ran from both parties*. But if that's the case, then why?"

"…"

"What you're saying could be a lie. And even if it's true, that doesn't mean the enemy of our enemy is our friend. So I'll ask you. Why did Orsola Aquinas run away from you?"

If they were truly Orsola's allies, then she wouldn't have had any reason to run away.

Tatemiya smiled quietly at Kamijou's implicit declaration. It was a very weak smile, like he was tired of life. "She was the same."

"The same?"

"Yeah. The same as you, man. She did come to us asking for help—but at the very end, she wasn't able to trust us completely. She probably thought this about us. 'They have no reason to help me at the cost of making the largest Crossist denomination, Roman Orthodoxy, their enemy. They must be after the method of deciphering the *Book of the Law*.'"

Kamijou fell mum.

Tatemiya's eyes appeared to both be watching him and gazing at something far in the distance.

"Man, barking up the wrong tree, that's for sure. Why would we need to get our hands on that book?"

"? Then what did you try and save her for?" asked Kamijou carefully.

"*We didn't have a reason*," answered Tatemiya without missing a beat. "And we never did, either. We've done it this way since the beginning. And our current generation is even more exceptional. Why on earth do you think our priestess, that girl, was ordained our leader at such a young age? She stood before an evil dragon that could swallow mountains whole, just to protect one young girl's dream. She defended a small village from a big military force so that she could hear the one person's dying request. And from behind, we watched her this whole time. It may only have been a little while, but for us, it feels like we've done so forever."

Saiji Tatemiya spoke as though he were chasing the illusions of bygone days.

And as if boasting about his own family.

"That is why we do not mistake our path, and why we do not mistake how we use our strength—and how we've led ourselves along the straight and narrow. Many things are easier said than done—but she would actually do them. Her example taught us that people could become this strong. That people could become this kind. That all of that was within our reach."

Quiet dominated the air.

Tatemiya gritted his teeth to break the silence.

"...And that path she lived her life walking—we destroyed all of it."

"What?"

"Our deaths—our inexperience—caused the priestess to suffer. She was always the last one standing, and she began to believe it was her fault that everyone around her was falling. That ain't a joke. Our minds and bodies were what caused everything—the fact that we wished to stand together with her on the battlefield, and the fact that we fell in the process. And now we're in this sorry state. The priestess didn't do anything wrong, but we forced her to leave the place she belonged by herself."

Tatemiya talked as if stabbing his own face with a sword.

His voice, wrung from deep in his throat, contained vivid emotion.

"We stole her home with our inexperience. That's why we need to offer her home to her again. One where nobody gets hurt, one where nobody must grieve, one where everyone fights to put smiles on others' faces. A home where we all stand as one without hesitation to protect someone's happiness."

"..."

"That's why we extended a helping hand to Orsola—because she wanted help.

"Because we thought our priestess's home should be a world in which people would do that normally."

In the end, they weren't actually fighting for advantage or disadvantage, as they assumed from interorganizational deals. They were just fighting because the circumstance dictated it—not because they were looking to gain anything from it. The circumstance in question was too deeply entwined with the history of their group, so they couldn't get Orsola to understand. It had just created a misunderstanding. Was that it?

That was only *if everything Tatemiya was saying were true*, though.

Kamijou had begun to want to believe his words. But there was still no proof for any of them. Even if he felt like he wanted to trust Tatemiya, he couldn't find any evidence that would let him do so absolutely. He gritted his teeth. Who should he believe? Who was telling the lies? Many thoughts spun round and round in his mind, when...

...suddenly, they heard an ear-splitting yell from far away.

No—it was nothing so lackluster as a yell.

A shriek. A scream. A screech. **And if he had to guess**, it had come from a woman. But did it really come from a person? Kamijou wasn't even confident enough to say that. The high-pitched whine, like fingernails scratching glass or a chalkboard, physically made people cringe. And yet within the loud reverberation was plenty of raw human emotion. Fear. Denial. Despair. Agony. It was like a mud-soaked sponge being wrung out—he could tell that the repressed sound, unbecoming of a human, was soaked in all-too-real *human*-ness.

Index looked at Kamijou. He didn't look back at her. "Or...sola?"

"I'll ask you one more time...Did you say you were entrusting her to the Roman Orthodox Church, man? I thought she trusted *you*—not the Roman Orthodox."

"..." Those words made Kamijou think back.

"I would like to make certain—you are helping now because you were requested to cooperate by the English Puritan Church, yes?"

—Why would Orsola Aquinas have been so reluctant to ask him that?

"That's right..."

—Why did she look so relieved at that short statement?

"So then you are of English Puritan descent, not Roman Orthodox?"

—And she asked again, to make absolutely sure...

"It's nothing crazy like that. Oh, and just so you know, I don't have any pull with them. I'm from Academy City, after all."

—And those words, which he hadn't thought about very hard, made her so relieved...

"I...see."

—Those two words—how much meaning had been packed into them?

She probably had faith until the very end.

Faith that Touma Kamijou was someone she could trust herself to as long as she needed.

"...Shit!"

Kamijou clenched his teeth in anger. He quickly turned in the direction he'd heard the shriek. In hindsight, he should have just gotten her into Academy City even if they risked danger. That was it—that was all he had to do to make her safe!

"Give me a goddamn break. Why the hell did it turn out like this?!"

"Don't panic. It's not like that scream was her dying. The Roman Orthodox Church has their own stuff going on—they wouldn't be able to kill Orsola Aquinas right here and now. Actually, I'm completely certain of that."

"What?"

"I mean that if you hurry, you can still save her. But if you misstep here, who knows what will happen? Given the situation, I'm not gonna ask you anymore whether or not you trust us, man. We have our own circumstances, but securing Orsola's safety is the most important thing. So I don't care if you and I remain enemies or not!"

His shout implied that they were in a race against time.

"But just promise me this! That you'll get back Orsola Aquinas from the Roman Orthodox and take her somewhere neither they nor we can get to her!!"

His eyes were serious.

Serious enough to make Kamijou falter.

And then.

Suddenly, *ker-click*—he heard a footstep. He took his eyes from

Tatemiya. He turned around to the noise to see two sisters in black approaching, as if parting the darkness in front of them. They must have been from the Roman Orthodox Church.

One was tall, and one was short. The taller one was hoisting a wheel, bigger than a small round table, that looked like it came off a carriage. The shorter one had four leather pouches hanging from the belt around her waist. Coins or something must have been inside, because they jingled every time she took a step. The pouches were about softball size, so if they were filled with coins, they would have been as heavy as shot puts.

The taller sister drew an old leather notebook from her sleeve pocket and flipped through its pages; then, after nodding about something, she came over to Kamijou. Perhaps there was a photograph in there.

"You are the outsiders assisting us, yes? We have come to take custody of the imprisoned heretic leader. The enemy of God...Is that him?"

As she spoke, the younger sister moved toward Saiji Tatemiya, seated with rune cards stuck on him, in anticipation of the answer.

The four coin pouches at her hips jingled.

"Hey, wait a second!" called Kamijou, but the short sister didn't seem to hear.

For a moment, she reached a hand toward Tatemiya but then hesitated, realizing something. She went around him, carefully observing the rune cards attached to him.

Instead, the taller sister stared at Kamijou's face. "What is it?"

"Before you guys pull out of here, can you let me see Orsola one more time?"

"Unfortunately, I must decline. Though we have secured Sister Orsola's safety, we cannot call the situation safe just yet, since we don't know the true state of the enemy forces. In cases such as these, our rules state we must give first priority to the safety of our own personnel. Once we have safely seen her back to Rome, we will send you an invitation."

A perfect answer—so perfect that he had to frown.

"No, no. I'm not convinced. What was that scream from before, anyway? Wasn't that Orsola's voice? Is that the kind of noise that someone who's made it to safety would make? Anyway, I want to see her again. You don't mind, right? I just want to see her for a bit, say a few words, and that's it. We won't be seeing each other for a while, so I have to at least say good-bye."

"But our rules state..."

"Ah, jeez! Why are you so annoying about rules? Is Agnes over there? I'll just go over and ask her myself!"

Kamijou grabbed the tall sister's shoulder and brusquely pushed her aside.

"..." She relaxed her shoulders, as if amazed at seeing how much of a worrywart he was.

Then she took the giant wheel against her back and placed it in front of her like a shield with a dull noise.

Index's face immediately warped with nervousness. "Stop, Touma—?!"

But before she could finish...

Boom!!
The wooden wheel exploded.

"...?!"

For an instant, Kamijou didn't know what happened. Like a shotgun, hundreds of sharp fragments came flying, but only toward him. Once his thought process caught up, he covered his face and chest with both hands. A moment later, the countless splinters hit him right in the hands, legs, and gut. By the time he had begun to feel pain, his feet had already left the ground. As the stupid-sounding *ka-boom* hit him, he found himself being blown five or six meters back.

Index's clipped shriek reached his ears.

Out of the corner of his eye he could see Tatemiya trying to stand, but he stopped abruptly when a few rune flames singed his hair. He bared his teeth like a chained wild dog. The shorter sister appeared a little shaken up. She looked at the taller sister and asked,

"S-Sister Lucia…Umm, well, i-is this okay…? Didn't…Didn't Sister Agnes tell us to avoid needless contact with our *guests*…?"

"Be quiet, Sister Angeline. Damn, Agnes, this is why we shouldn't have let these heathens slip so close to us—we should have chased them away sooner. We all listened to your optimistic command to leave them be, and this is what happens…," muttered the taller sister to herself as if to calm her own emotions, shooting a glare at the shorter sister to silence her.

Her eyes had changed color. It was an abstract change, but that's what Kamijou thought. The taller sister's eyes had heat enough in them to melt butter into a puddle as she looked at Kamijou.

He was speechless—was this the same kind of nun as the ones who had given him bread and soup at the campsite?

"If only you weren't so weirdly obsessed with a *scream*, then we would have had less to do…Damn, why—why, this heretic, with his hand, on my shoulder, my shoulder, my shoulder. Sister Angeline! Find me the soap—no, the detergent! This is terrible. I am in the worst of moods. They spoke to me. Would you say a few words to them? I simply cannot stand it—I need to wear a mudguard apron or something."

Blood silently rose to the tall sister's face.

Her face wavered to and fro as her mouth produced a monotone voice.

"This is all getting more and more and more complicated. What are we to do? Let us say that Amakusa member resisted and killed you both. Ah, yes, that seems like the easiest option. After that, we must only seal Amakusa's lips, and there will be no problems."

The line sounded like an ad-lib correction for a stage play whose scenario had gone awry.

It sounded like a threatening voice, but Kamijou couldn't find it in him to answer.

Quite a few wooden shards had struck him, but they weren't actual blades in the first place, so his wounds were shallow.

But right after that…the slender shards piercing his skin suddenly began twisting up and down by themselves.

"Gh…gaaaaahhhhhhhhhhhhh?!"

As Kamijou screamed, as though pulling out an ax wedged in a big tree, the fragments began falling out one after another. The blood-splattered fragments returned to the tall sister as if by magnetism, and like a jigsaw puzzle being assembled, they re-formed the original carriage wheel.

"Touma!!" shouted Index, just about to run over to him in a panic.

However, at the sight, the tall sister commanded, "Sister Angeline!"

"Y-yes ma'am!" stammered the short sister in reply, slicing the belt at her waist and throwing the four coin pouches overhead.

Right then, *flap!!* With the sound of air hitting a big piece of cloth, six sparrow-like wings came out of each of the pouch openings. The wings shone in different colors for each pouch—red, blue, yellow, and green.

"*Viene. Una persona dodici apostli. Lo schiavo basso che rovina rovina un mago mentre e quelli che raccolgono!*"

The short sister raised both hands overhead as if to embrace the night sky, and at that moment,

Brrmmm!! With the speed of a bullet, the green-winged coin pouch grazed across Index and stabbed into the ground at her feet.

Bkk-bshh, came a small sound as the hard ground began to form cracks like tree roots.

"This is...?"

Index hastily tried to leap backward, but her body came right back down. She looked to see the drawstring on the coin pouch stuck in the ground was undone. It had wrapped around her ankles and was holding her down. Right when Index cast her gaze down to her feet, the other three pouches fluttered high in the air, aiming right for that new blind spot.

Kamijou paled. *Oh, crap...! If she hits her with that...!!*

The coin pouches probably weighed more than shot puts. With her feet stuck to the ground, Index wouldn't be able to avoid them, and it would be too much to defend with her hands.

"Shit! Index!!" he shouted, getting ready to run over there. Fortunately, the coin pouch binding her legs seemed to work on magical principles. It would be easy to punch it with his right hand and undo it.

But then...

"Worry about yourself, child. So that you may avoid as much pain as you can!"

Before he realized it, the taller sister hoisting the giant wheel had jumped above him. Kamijou, unstable and trying to stand up, locked on to the wheel's center point like the muzzle on a gun.

—?!

He shuddered and he felt his throat dry up. Punching the wheel and having it be blasted to smithereens clearly presented poor odds for him.

"Heathen child, are you familiar with the Legend of the Wheel?"

The tall sister smiled vacantly.

"Countless saints have been martyred since long ago. Those foolish people, high in the government, thought to end their lives by execution, but in their history of torture and execution, the wheel appears many times."

Kamijou didn't feel like engaging in small talk, but the wheel before his eyes was preventing him from moving. And meanwhile, the three coin pouches, dozens of meters in the air, turned and dove straight down to Index.

"They were giant wheels, with innumerable nails and blades stabbing into them, made to rip saints apart. But there are many reports of the wheels exploding on their own when they touched saints. Yes—Saint George, who exterminated dragons, and even Saint Catherine of the Alexandria. Fragments from the exploding wheels were said to have killed more than four thousand people who were there to watch the execution. The teachings of the Legend of the Wheel are as follows."

Her calm tone fried his nerves even more. The three coin pouches aiming for Index shot like a bullet toward her to smash her head in.

The tall sister viewed Kamijou as he began to sweat in nervousness from the other side of the wheel. She smiled, pleased. "The sinless will not be punished, and the sinful will receive judgment—know this, heretic. There is no salvation for you. Sister Orsola, both our comrade and a fool who must die—we must follow *procedure* for her, but we have no need to hesitate when killing the two of you."

"Shit...!!"

Thinking he was going to go save Index, he turned and gave his full attention to the bound girl in white. Before his eyes, the wheel began to crack apart. Time slowed—and Kamijou saw the wheel, split into six equal parts at its center like a pizza, begin to expand from within.

"Ga, ahhhhhhhhhhh!!"

He clenched his right hand and howled, but he was too late. He wouldn't make it. Before he thrust out his fist, the giant wheel wielded by the tall sister made an ear-splitting noise...

...and with a *ger-slam* it *bounced sideways.*

Obviously, it wasn't the tall sister's intention, nor was it due to Kamijou's fist.

The coin pouches.

The coin pouch with six red wings, which had been going after Index's head, had struck the execution wheel from the side with amazing speed. The impact wrenched the wheel from the tall sister's hands. It bounced on the ground a few times and flew into the darkness. The coin pouch that hit it burst open from the impact, sending unidentifiable coins of all sizes into the air.

The tall sister, suddenly without a weapon, hastily jumped away to put distance between her and Kamijou, then turned a glare on the shorter sister.

"Sister Angeline, have you gone mad?!"

"N-no, no...It wasn't me!"

Her savagely angry shout made the shorter of them blanch and explain herself, when just then,

"CTRTTOP, ABO! (Collect the remaining three to one point, and become one!)"

Index's clear voice *interrupted them.*

That instant.

Ker-crash, came the roar of metal being pulverized. The green pouch's drawstring came off from Index's ankles. The blue and yellow pouches going for her head instead shot off toward the short sister's face with incredible speed.

The three pouches collided with one another two centimeters from her nose and stopped dead. The extreme force pounded the hundred-some coins into a single metal lump, and it made a dull sound as it fell to the short sister's feet.

Plop. The shorter sister fell over on her rear with, strangely enough, a smile.

"The apostle Matthew, who felled two fire-breathing dragons using only a cross and prayer. By passing telesma through his emblem, the money pouch, one can create a weapon that tracks a target when thrown...," Index criticized, very quietly. "How sloppy. The incantation is long, and its encryption is all over the place. You're so preoccupied with stabilizing your own technique and not paying attention to anything else. It's easy to muscle on into it!"

Kamijou didn't understand what had just happened. Index couldn't use magic, could she? Or was it some other kind of trick? Something to let her interrupt the short sister's sorcery and hijack it...

"...Self-destruction—friendly fire. A tactic to use the penalty of magical failure against itself."

The taller sister cast her gaze around, then clucked her tongue and readied herself again. Even without a weapon, her will to fight hadn't waned one bit. With gentle movements, she made the sign of the cross...

...but then they heard what sounded like a high-pitched flute tone from far away.

Fweeeeee, came the birdlike scream. The taller sister looked hatefully into the black sky.

"The command to retreat? Sister Angeline!!"

"Ah, uh? B-but we haven't yet dealt with—"

"We are retreating. We can put the Amakusa leftovers down to the English already having let them escape. Ruining the pace of things will badly affect our unit as a whole and could cause harm to befall the group escorting Orsola. That is the larger problem at hand."

The tall sister turned on her heel and disappeared into the darkness, and the short sister followed her in a fluster.

"You get it now, right?" said Saiji Tatemiya sourly, looking up at the night sky.

"That's how Roman Orthodoxy, the largest Crossist denomination in the world, operates behind the scenes."

2

"I see. So that's why she looked so stupefied the moment she saw Agnes Sanctis. They probably cut us off from the main Roman Orthodox force because they've been looking down on us from the start, too. Hmph... Their chain of command would be left in disarray with English Puritans there, eh? That's rich," said Stiyl at leisure as they left Parallel Sweets Park. He must have heard Orsola's scream, too, but he didn't seem to have asked Agnes about it when he left her. If he hadn't known the situation and asked her, it could have turned into a diplomatic issue between the two Church organizations. Kamijou understood that, but he wasn't satisfied with it.

After the little fight, he had run to where Agnes had been, only to find that she and all the others had already withdrawn. And no assassins came up to pursue Tatemiya, either. With so many of his friends captured, maybe they had judged Amakusa as having already been destroyed.

The fact that they'd had so many people, yet still withdrew cleanly enough to leave no trace of their existence, sent shivers down Kamijou's spine. The fact that they hadn't given the English Puritans any sort of debriefing—or even a good-bye—must have meant they really didn't trust them at all. Securing Orsola was their primary objective. Maybe they figured that they'd only deal with Tatemiya and the others if they had the time. Or perhaps they would summon their entire force from all over the city and press for a decisive victory.

With all of that, Kamijou, Index, Stiyl, and Tatemiya were busy exchanging information. Kamijou, having been stricken all over his body with those wheel fragments, was wrapped up in bandages in many places.

"Even if everything that man says is true, they're not going to kill Orsola Aquinas right away. They have their own circumstances to consider...So, Touma Kamijou, don't you dare go running off somewhere right this moment. If you stand out, things will get pretty complex."

Kamijou made a dissatisfied face at the warning. "...What do you mean, circumstances to consider?"

"Roman Orthodoxy is Crossism's largest denomination, Touma. Most don't know anything about the occult, but it still has more than two billion followers, the pope still leads 141 cardinals, and it's still expansive enough that it has churches in 113 countries. It's all well and good that it's big, but if it gets too big, they might start to have problems."

"?" Kamijou still didn't understand.

This time, Tatemiya spoke up. "Well, in other words, basically... If they have that much influence, they're obviously gonna have a lot of different factions. First off, the pope and the cardinals govern 142 parishes, and depending on the country and region, it's 207—then if you add in clashes between old and young and between male and female, it's 252."

Stiyl blew out a puff of smoke, vexed. "With so many factions, people say Roman Orthodoxy has more enemies within it than outside it. People join up with others over minute problems with their own brethren and poke and prod at them. With all that, the current situation has a *very* delicate aspect to it. The *Book of the Law* is definitely a threat to Roman Orthodoxy, but Orsola Aquinas herself is entirely innocent. If they kill her unreasonably, their brethren around the world would turn against Agnes."

"Is that right? But we didn't do anything wrong, either. And they still came at *us* without a second thought." Kamijou lightly stroked the bandage on his arm with a fingertip. It was already oppressively hot outside—the bandages on him were only making it worse.

"That's because they can use the excuse that we're heretics or pagans. Any idea how much atrocity has been justified by simply saying how it's okay to punish those who disobey God's teachings?"

"That's what the sisters who attacked us before are probably thinking. But I think that's exactly why they can't inadvertently lay a hand on Orsola. Since thou shalt not kill those who believe in the teachings of God."

"..."

Kamijou glanced away and thought about it, gazing at the trees on the roadside illuminated by the streetlights. Even if Roman Orthodoxy had a rule that stated they couldn't kill other members of the faith, then why did Amakusa act to prevent Orsola from being assassinated?

He asked the question, and Stiyl answered, not treating it as very important.

"It's easy. There're exceptions."

"Exceptions?"

"That's right. Thou shalt not kill those who believe in the teachings of God—if you subscribe to this rule, then that means it's okay to drive those who don't from the Church and kill them."

His giant sword on full display, Tatemiya continued for Stiyl. Not that it mattered, but Kamijou began to worry how he'd explain himself if the police saw him.

"Criminals, witches, traitors... They cut off all connections with those who break the rules. And at the same time, they label them enemies of God."

"The way they do it is simple. Just test them. Let's see—for example, say there's a metal pole that's so hot it's burning red. They'll make Orsola hold it. If she were innocent, her Lord would protect her, and she wouldn't be burned. But if she was burned, then she would be judged one not worth protecting. It's absurd, isn't it? In English Puritanism, testing the Lord is treated as a sin."

"But that's...!" Kamijou was dumbfounded. "But of course she'd get burned! It would be weirder if she didn't!"

"You're right. They could find fault with her even if she wasn't burned. They could say she's being protected by the devil. Whichever the result, the one being tested is sure to be labeled."

That's savage, he thought. It was absolutely wrong to decide Orsola's fate with such messed-up methods.

"But on the other hand, this inquisition—or trial by ordeal, should I say. Anyway, until they're finished preparing to exile her, they can't take her life without due caution. If they follow proper procedure, they will go back to Rome first, and then it would take two or three days to get it ready. Still, anything they do will probably be overlooked as long as they don't kill her."

The Roman Orthodox couldn't care less about what she was thinking or the feelings with which she was trying to stand up to the grimoire's original copy. Because it was a nuisance. Because it was inconvenient. Because it was a pain. Because it wouldn't go well. Because it would make trouble. That was all it took for them to go after Orsola's life.

Even though they should have been the same.

Even though Orsola and the Roman Orthodox must have had the same opinions deep down.

Even though both of them saw the *Book of the Law* as dangerous and were acting because they wanted to do something about it.

Even though she was looking for a breakthrough, a way to dispose of the original copies of grimoires, which were said to be indestructible by human hands, despite the fact that they could decipher them.

Even though she just wanted to be useful.

Even though she thought the book was dangerous and wanted to do something about it.

"Do you know about the original copies of grimoires? Or how they cannot be destroyed by any means?"

—Was that really such a bad thing?

"With current technology, it is impossible to get rid of grimoires that have reached this state. The most that can be done is to seal it so that nobody may ever read it."

—Had Orsola Aquinas done something so wrong…

"That is, with current technology."

—...that she needed to go through someone else's procedure, be labeled a heretic, remain silent instead of asking for someone's help, and be executed?

"One should be able to use the magic circle against itself—in other words, to force the original text to destroy itself."

—No.

"The power of grimoires doesn't bring anyone happiness. The only thing they create is conflict. That's why I was investigating its inner workings—in order to destroy these kinds of grimoires."

—No!

"Like hell I'll accept that..." Kamijou clenched his teeth so hard they might break. "Even if they had that kind of reason, no matter what circumstances they have, that shit isn't okay! Seriously, what the hell?! What do they think human life is? Taking away everything important to a person, bit by bit—what the hell do they think human life is?!"

Touma Kamijou had amnesia.

So there were very few things he thought were very important. He only had a month's worth of memories from summer vacation in the first place. Compared to high school students with normal lives, he had but a fraction of things important to him. And most of what he had were messy memories borne from lying about his amnesia.

But Kamijou still felt as though...Even he, with such a scant number of things he could call precious—if someone were to come and steal them away as simply as crossing something out in a document with red ink, he would be angry beyond description.

Maybe those in the Roman Orthodox Church really were fighting to protect something precious to them. But they shouldn't be doing it.

Like a flock of crows pecking at somebody—stripping away everything someone held dear, one by one, *robbing* them—that was something that should never be done.

Why didn't they look for another way?

Why did the cheap, foolish method of killing her satisfy them?

Kamijou clenched his fists so tightly he thought they might bleed. The lights on the street, dotting the dark residential area at night, coldly illuminated them.

"...Where are they right now? Do you know anything?"

"I've got a good idea. But what do you plan on doing once I tell you?" answered Stiyl in an aloof way—and it made Kamijou want to grab his collar.

How the hell can this guy stay so calm? he thought.

His face looked like he was going to devour Stiyl, but the priest didn't seem disturbed at all. The cigarette in the corner of his mouth wiggled. In fact, Index, whom he couldn't see, seemed to be the one who was scared.

"I understand how you feel." Stiyl quietly exhaled smoke. "But how about we calm down a bit first, hm? There are close to 250 of the ladies just in this one town, remember? Remind me—was your fist convenient enough to wipe them all out?"

"...!!"

Kamijou gripped his own fists.

Yes, he knew that. His skill was only good for fights in back alleys. He could only beat people one on one. One on two was pretty risky, and one on three would end up with him getting beaten to a pulp. And while it may have been a sneak attack, that sister had just over-whelmed him by attacking with that wheel.

Barehanded fights in real life weren't like in the movies—one person couldn't beat dozens of opponents by himself in a fair fight. No matter how strong the person was, there was a strict rule to the effect that you couldn't possibly win given a certain number of people surrounding you.

And that...

...was if you weren't the kind of real combat professional you saw in manga and dramas.

The sorcerer—who should have been one of those combat professionals—blew out a little smoke, grinning comfortably.

"If Amakusa's story is all true, then we don't have anything to do at this point in the first place. Unfortunately, this story is already over."

"What...was that?"

"Just think about it, all right? Orsola Aquinas broke the Roman Orthodox rules, and now they're after her life. Agnes Sanctis followed her to punish her for breaking the rules. That's really all this incident was, wasn't it? The *Book of the Law*'s original copy is apparently safe at home in the Vatican Library. Given their position, they can't allow it to be used for evil. Amakusa's saying they don't plan on using it for evil, either. In the end, nothing has happened that would change what we English Puritans have to do. I'm not happy we didn't get to say good-bye now that everything's over with, but it's nothing getting so red-faced over will do anything about, is it?"

This time for sure...

This time, Touma Kamijou grabbed Stiyl Magnus's collar without a second thought. Index covered her mouth and let out a yelp as Tatemiya looked at him and gave a whistle.

But still, the rune sorcerer wasn't disturbed in the slightest. In the deserted night streets, his words echoed, alone, and disappeared. The flickering streetlights intermittently cast their shine on the priest.

"This is no more than the Roman Orthodox Church judging an internal incident by its own rules. As long as it doesn't affect anyone else, if we English Puritans foolishly complained about it, then it would be seen as a political intervention—it could even do great harm to relations between the English and the Romans...Unfortunately, it's time to give up on this, Touma Kamijou. Or do you want to save her even if you start a war?"

"...That's..."

"Whether it's English Puritanism or Roman Orthodoxy, don't go thinking everyone who's part of them are combat personnel like we are. In fact, most of them are people just like you. They go to school, spend time with friends, eat hamburgers on the way home—that's their whole world to them. They don't know about the sorcerers lurking in the shadows, nor do they notice all the deals made among various groups to keep a magical war from occurring. They are truly virtuous, powerless lambs."

Then, the sorcerer, with Kamijou still holding on to his collar, asked coolly.

It was indeed as though he were a demon urging him to an agreement.

"Now this is the problem—can you wrap them up in this? Do you *want* to get people, ignorant of the truth, who are part of these religions involved in this, rob them, kill them, take everything they have, just so you can protect Orsola Aquinas?"

"..."

The strength in the hands Kamijou was grabbing Stiyl's collar with faded. Index tried to say something, but she didn't know what, so she just took a long breath.

This was the difference between amateurs and professionals.

This was the difference between individuals and organizations.

Stiyl spat out his cigarette tiredly, crushed it with his foot, and turned to look at Tatemiya. "I don't have the right to stop *you* from doing anything, though. You can fight all you want for Orsola, since she asked, or your subordinates, or whatever you want. But if you're going, then you're doing it alone. If you try to get English Puritanism involved in this, they will turn this entire island nation into scorched earth to uproot and massacre Amakusa," threatened Stiyl—but Tatemiya's expression didn't change.

"Man, I know that much. Oh, come on, kid. Don't get so down. The English Puritan Church might not have any reason to fight, but we've got a big one. I'm just gonna pay a visit to their little hideout, rescue my allies, and maybe give Orsola a lift while I'm at it. What? We're used to throwing a few talented people at stupidly huge groups. Our sect evolved by opposing the Tokugawa Shogunate, after all."

Kamijou brought his head up at what he said.

Index, next to him, looked at Tatemiya's face.

"You're going to call the rest of your friends from Amakusa's main base? But you'll have to wait another day to use the special movement method, and if you wait that long, the Romans might go back home."

"Yeah. Can't take the safe option in this situation," said Tatemiya, swinging his white sword a bit.

Stiyl said in an uninterested voice, "Are you saying you're going alone?"

"There's no other choice, so I need to. Fortunately though, those idiots may have gotten taken away, but they haven't been executed... If they wanted to kill us, they wouldn't have bothered capturing us—they would have just cut us down on the spot. It'd be more realistic for them to deliver a sentence to us with Orsola, saying that she conspired with Amakusa to steal the *Book of the Law.* So if I break 'em out and incite things the right way, we might actually have a chance of barely winning." Tatemiya concealed his tension with a jovial expression. "The best time to go at them is when they're on the move." He waved his giant sword around. "Amakusa's been pursued for a long time—we're pretty familiar with how scary and fragile groups can be. A large group of people is at its weakest when it's on the move. After all, the Romans captured more than three hundred Amakusa members, y'know? They can't move around properly with only the nuns they have. If hundreds of sisters dressed in black went on parade through the city together, they could end up on TV as a demonstration or a riot or somethin'.

"So they're gonna have some kind of camouflage for when they move, just in case. Like splitting into smaller groups and going by car. It's an established tactic—when they're camouflaging themselves, they can't use the full extent of their power, making it the best—and only—time to launch a surprise attack."

From what Tatemiya was saying, the Roman Orthodox Church wouldn't use magic to move like Amakusa did. And it was too late at night for them to charter a boat or plane. Their exodus would probably wait to begin until morning, when the harbors and airports opened up.

"..."

Their moving was the greatest opportunity.

But that also meant they couldn't do anything until they started moving, too. Stiyl said that in order for the Roman Orthodox Church to erase Orsola, they needed to follow a procedure called an inquisition.

But on top of that, it meant that until they killed her, they could do anything they wanted and it would be overlooked.

Violence, inflicted by a surrounding group of two hundred and fifty people. In a way, that could be more terrifying than a punishment based on proper rules. After all, it wasn't clearly defined in their laws—there wasn't a clear line between how much was okay and how much wasn't.

Could they do anything to her as long as she didn't die?

Would they say she was lucky, no matter what they did to her, just because she was breathing?

Kamijou's face clouded over, and Tatemiya seemed to suspect his apprehensions. "...Might be a bit cruel to tell you to understand. Even we've got things we know we can and can't do." His words were mixed with bitterness. A professional like him could probably imagine things more vividly than an amateur like Kamijou. About how the Romans treated captured enemies.

Touma Kamijou punched a nearby telephone pole with all his might.

Despite being able to visualize the worst possible situation, he couldn't take any action whatsoever—and he felt ashamed to no end for it.

Stiyl disinterestedly looked at Kamijou, who was unable to make any sort of reply, and said, "Looks like that settles it. We should split up and hide as well. Guess I'll give the higher-ups a ring and ask what to do next. Our problems with the Romans and Amakusa have been cleared up, but I'll need to do something about Kanzaki now. Touma Kamijou, you take Index back to Academy City. Right now, having gotten their hands on the most important person, Orsola, the Romans wouldn't consider attacking you two outsiders, since it would mean picking a fight with the scientific side of things."

He lit a new cigarette. "Well, if the English Puritan Church at least had a proper reason to rescue Orsola Aquinas, it would be a different story—but this is all we can do." He blew out smoke, sounding thoroughly uninterested. "Right. Also, Touma Kamijou. There was something I wanted to ask."

"...What?"

He turned around, exhausted. Stiyl continued, giving a cynical smile. "That cross I gave you before. You don't seem to have it on you—where'd you put it?"

"..." Kamijou thought for a moment, then remembered. "Sorry. I gave it to Orsola. She seemed really happy I put it around her neck, though. Was it really that valuable?"

"No, it was an entirely normal iron cross. They're probably souvenirs produced en masse by some factory. They're all over England—it's the cross of Saint George, which is also part of our nation's flag." Stiyl grinned for some reason, seeming a bit pleased. "That cross has no value as an ornament or an antique. The thing had value while you were carrying it...but whatever. You don't need it anymore anyway," said Stiyl cryptically, blowing out another puff of smoke.

Without knowing what he meant by that, Kamijou withdrew to the dark road.

And thus the curtains fell on a disappointing ending to a disappointing incident.

3

Saiji Tatemiya was gone.

Stiyl seemed to want to guard Index until she safely got into Academy City. She was next to Kamijou, who was trudging down the night road, but seemed to be at a loss for words.

This may have been the capital of Japan, but when you got away from the center, it was veiled in the dark of night. Checking the time revealed it was past one in the morning, and most of the city lights were out. A few apartment complexes had lights in their windows here and there like missing teeth, and sometimes a taxi with someone drunk in it would pass by. The streetlights kept on flickering unreliably, illuminating the many moths gathering to them.

Their unexpected day revolving around fighting was already over. In just a few hours, he would be going back to his normal life, centered around school. Kamijou would shake the lack of sleep from his head, go to school, take some boring classes, talk about dumb stuff to Tsuchimikado and Blue Hair on the way home, and be on the receiving end of Mikoto's *biribiri* for not completing his summer homework after all.

"...What should I have done?" he said suddenly.

Index looked up at him, but he was still looking down, dejected.

He wanted to save Orsola Aquinas.

But he couldn't think of any way to do that.

"I get that an amateur can't think of a way to beat a professional. But I still think maybe there was something even an amateur could have done. Like when I first met Orsola, if I had just taken her to Academy City like she asked—what would have happened then? And if we didn't help the Roman Orthodox Church, maybe she could have gotten away with Amakusa and their special movement method."

"Touma..."

"No, I get it. Those things only seem hopeful because I'm not looking at their end results. Even if Orsola got into Academy City, the Romans would have given chase and followed her in. Even if we didn't help them, they would have used their human wave tactics, searched every nook and cranny, and found where Amakusa was gathering. I get all that, but still..."

He thought back.

Back to when he first met Orsola. That uneasy voice asking him to tell her how to get into Academy City. Her smile when they were hiding out in the theme park.

Her words, spoken strangely readily, as though she thought she'd finally found someone she could trust.

And last of all—that shriek of despair they had heard from somewhere.

"But really...what should we have done?"

He knew that just thinking like this was the act of an amateur who didn't fully grasp the dangers. This incident had nothing to do with him. A simple high school student had chanced a glimpse at how harsh the world of professional sorcery was, and now he was going back to his own world. No one would blame him for it. Anyone who knew firsthand how terrifying the real world of sorcery was would probably breathe a sigh of relief upon seeing his safe return.

Stiyl must have thought he'd finished explaining everything he needed to, so he didn't say even a word despite hearing Kamijou's complaints.

On the other hand, Index looked up into Kamijou's face. "...Touma. This is a problem for sorcerers, so you don't need to get yourself involved. I can't say much, since I can't do anything anyway, but Saiji Tatemiya said he'd do it, so I think we just have to trust him..."

"...Right."

Index looked about to cry at Kamijou's unfocused response. "That's right! Touma, there's no rule saying you have to settle every problem sorcerers have! I think if anyone, you should blame me, the anti-sorcery expert, for not being able to do anything. But the problems that can be solved will be solved even if you're not there. Touma, I think you've gotten involved with a lot of sorcerers, for an outsider. But there are a whole lot of sorcerers in the world you don't know, and they all have their own problems, and they figure them out without needing to borrow your strength. This time is the same—it's just that this is the first time you've seen an incident you weren't involved in ending."

"Is that right?" Kamijou answered mechanically—but he was surprised on the inside.

She should be able to imagine what fate awaited Orsola, too—but she had firmly told him not to get involved with this incident anymore.

Or maybe it was backward. If she made a contradictory statement, then maybe Kamijou wouldn't praise her anymore.

"Yeah. Things have been weird until now. No one can solve every problem they see by themselves. Touma, you can ask people for help. You can trust other people with the endings. Just because you see a house on fire and there's a little kid still inside, there's no reason you have to jump in. Calling for help in that situation isn't shameful at all," Index said. "Touma, I think you should rely on other people more. We're from Necessarius—that's what it was made for. No one will blame you just because you couldn't solve a problem yourself that even an organization like ours is having trouble with."

"..." It just so happened that he didn't have a place in this, in the end. Maybe that's all it was. Just because his part was over didn't mean the incident suddenly ended there. Maybe Saiji Tatemiya would just take up the mantle of protagonist from here and settle things.

She was right—just because a random attacker incident happened right in front of him, there was no rule saying that witnesses needed to resolve it. Nobody would blame the witnesses for the police arresting the criminal.

"I wonder if Tatemiya can do it."

"I think he has a chance at winning. He's a real sorcerer, after all. Amakusa has a particularly harsh history of oppression—these sorts of odds we're facing are their specialty. They wouldn't take on an enemy they couldn't beat."

I see, nodded Kamijou.

He thought to himself—this was enough. He thought to himself—if they'd resolve this incident without him forcing himself to fight, then there was no need for an amateur to butt in. That was a normal idea. A clueless amateur doing as he pleased and throwing things into confusion could trigger everything going in an even worse direction—so not getting involved instead seemed like a good plan in its own right.

There was no rule saying he had to resolve every incident.

In fact, if he took a step back, there were plenty more incidents resolved without Kamijou's help.

He didn't need to worry about having gotten a glimpse of one of them.

Even without his involvement, someone would take it upon themselves to close the curtains on it.

He looked up into the night sky and slowly stretched both of his hands into the air. Suddenly growing aware of all his pent-up exhaustion, he finally started to yearn for the futon in his dorm.

"Guess we'll go home," said Kamijou aloud—as if to draw a clear line between his normal and abnormal lives. "Oh, right. Before we go back, I want to drop by a store. Supermarkets and department stores won't be open this late, so it'll have to be a convenience store. The fridge is empty, so I figured I'd go and buy a bunch of stuff...but whatever. I want to see what places outside Academy City have—maybe they've got bento they don't sell on the inside."

"...Touma. I think I'm suddenly really tired of domestic life."

"Well, sorry. I'm just a boring high school kid who thinks it's fun to have a household account book now, that's all."

"I want to eat luxurious meals without having to worry about your account book once in a while."

"If you don't like it, fine. But tomorrow's breakfast will be an empty plate with some water. You'll have to make up for the rest with that active imagination of yours."

"Touma?!" shouted Index, despite it being night.

Kamijou looked at the girl devourer as her face paled at such a simple thought and grinned. "Then why don't I go hit a convenience store and find some breakfast for tomorrow?"

"Huh? If you're going to the 'store,' then maybe we should all go."

"If I brought you, I wouldn't be able to shop—you'd throw everything within reach into the basket. All right, I won't be long. Stiyl, could you bring Index back to Academy City ahead of me? You brought us out, so you can sneak back in, I'm sure...Actually, er, if you did that might be a problem in its own right..."

"If you say so. Your suggestion benefits her—so I don't mind..."

Stiyl wiggled the cigarette in the corner of his mouth up and down. "By the way, you know where it is?"

"...No, but...Convenience stores are everywhere—I'll just run around here for a bit."

"Fine." Stiyl grinned sardonically, disappearing into the dark night escorting Index. Index wanted to stay with Kamijou, but he waved his arms and refused.

He waited until he could no longer see them, then turned right around.

Right around—to return straight along the road he'd come.

"That asshole. Did he know…?" said Kamijou to himself, annoyed.

My wallet's still in the dorm, after all. Wouldn't be able to do much in a convenience store.

As he walked, he took out his cell phone from his pants pocket. Its white backlight cast a dim light on his face. He pressed a few buttons and, using his GPS service, started searching around on a map. He wasn't, of course, looking for a nearby store.

Touma Kamijou remembered Agnes Sanctis's words.

"It is our privilege to outnumber all. We have comrades in 110 countries around the world, after all. There are many churches even in Japan. In fact, a new house of the lord is being constructed as we speak—the Church of Orsola. I think it was somewhere around here, actually. Right nearby. I think they were bragging that when it was finished, it would be the largest church in Japan. It was supposedly as big as a baseball stadium."

Academy City's GPS was extremely accurate and updated frequently. There were even rumors it was precise enough to be used for military purposes. It displayed the newest buildings, of course, but also every single planned construction. In contrast, that meant that places like the Hakumeiza site were quickly erased from the map.

Of course, the names of planned buildings weren't listed on GPS maps—all it said was "planned site." But he could tell just by looking at the picture. He could only find one planned construction site giant enough to rival a baseball stadium.

"Yes. She has quite a record, you know. She has spread the teachings of God to three heretic nations, earning her the special privilege to have a church built in her name. She was very good at speaking, wasn't she?"

He quickened his pace as he looked at his cell phone screen. Just as she said, the Church of Orsola—the base of the Roman Orthodox Church—was in this town. Moving around with lots of people was a weakness of group action. If they wanted to lessen the risk at all, making the Church of Orsola—which was right around the corner—into a fortress would be logical. And they'd use magic

Kamijou didn't know of, whether the building was under construction or not.

The Roman Orthodox members had to be there.

Including Agnes Sanctis—and Orsola Aquinas.

"Once the church is finished, we'll send you some invitations. But before that, we should settle the issue at hand. Let's pray for a splendid conclusion with a good aftertaste."

He recalled Agnes's joke and chuckled.

"They haven't even finished getting ready for the party or addressing the invitations…but let's go crash it anyway."

With his destination clearly in mind, he didn't need to stand around.

He began moving even faster—and when he next realized it, he was dashing along the night roads.

He didn't have any reason to fight.

He didn't have to fight to know that someone else would settle everything by themselves.

Just because there was a burning building in front of him with a young child trapped inside didn't mean there was a rule saying Kamijou had to jump in there—that's what Index had said.

Asking someone else for help and leaving it to them wasn't a bad thing, she said.

But still…

If that child in that burning house was waiting this whole time for Kamijou to come save her, then what?

The wisest choice, obviously, would be to get in touch with the fire department as soon as possible.

But Kamijou didn't want to show his back to that child even by accident. Even if that was the safest and easiest choice for him to make, he didn't want to betray that faith.

Did Orsola Aquinas still have faith in Touma Kamijou?

Despite all the foolish choices he'd made, did she still trust him like a child would?

Fortunately for him, he had no connections with any specific organizations like the English Puritans or Roman Orthodox. He was never anything more than a student and an amateur, so nothing bound him. He couldn't ask for the help of professionals like Index or Stiyl, but there was instead something only an amateur could do.

His one misgiving was that he could be seen as a member of the science faction of Academy City, but if things really got dangerous, said organization would probably just expel him, erase him from the register, and treat him as though he had never been a part of it.

But Kamijou didn't care about that.

In fact, he had to laugh at himself for feeling like he wanted to choose this path.

Without a reason to fight, the boy ran through the night.

In reality, there wasn't a single reason he had to make himself fight...

...but he had a reason he *wanted* to fight, all the same.

4

Despite it being called the Church of Orsola, you couldn't call the building a church yet. It was about as big as four or five average school gymnasiums put together. Once it was finished, it would be a genuine cathedral, the likes of which had never been seen before in Japan. And placing it a stone's throw away from Academy City also implied a diversion against the science faction. But right now, the construction site's size was all it had going for it—inside, it bore nothing but a sense of desolation.

The outer walls of the church had just been finished, but there were metal scaffolds and ladders left alone nearby. As for its interior design, nothing had been done yet—it actually looked like a barbaric band of mercenaries had taken over the place. The windows were gaping open, stained glass planned to be fitted into them. In the planned location for the giant pipe organ, too, only an unnatural space lurked. The marble flooring and walls shined, brand-new, but on the other hand, on the wall behind the pulpit, there was a big cross standing up casually against the wall, originally planned to be hung on it.

But those things couldn't create such an eerie environment on their own.

Inside the cathedral, without any man-made lights, lit up only by the faint moonlight shining through the black holes without any glass, hundreds of sisters all wearing black, as if drenched in darkness, stood silently. They formed a ring surrounding something—and that ring was many layers thick. In their hands were obvious weapons like swords and spears, as well as religious ritual instruments such as giant cogwheels and claws. They all sparkled when the faint moonlight struck them. There were no other people there. The captured Amakusa members were on the same site, but in a different location, bound and under guard by about ten people.

The sisters' attention was not directed outside the building.

Their eyes were focused on the circular space inside their ring.

They heard a punch.

They heard a stifled scream.

"Come on, don't make things difficult, yes? Unfortunately, everyone here is quite busy, myself included. We don't have time to go along with your little games. Just accept the death penalty already, will ya—hey, are you listening to me? I asked if you're fucking listening to me! Answer me!!"

The *thud* of heavy fabric being kicked.

And with it, an otherworldly scream cut through the dark.

"Hah!! That's a nice scream you got there. Don't you think it's disgraceful? Like you've abandoned your womanhood? Ah, shit, looks like we'll have to rename this church, won't we? Naming it after a pig or an ass would be simply laughable!"

Orsola Aquinas didn't answer.

She was on the floor, beaten to a pulp. Her clothing was torn, as though she'd been dragged around while tied to a horse. Its fasteners were broken as well, and large pieces of fabric had been ripped off.

Agnes and the others weren't using any special magic to make Orsola suffer. They were simply kicking her in the limbs and the gut—and, given enough blows, it would create intense pain. Violence performed by more than two hundred people, even going easy on her, had still driven Orsola to the brink of death. After all, even if each person struck her once, that was two hundred strikes. It was the same as water dripping from the roof creating a hole. Orsola's limbs, sprawled out on the floor, showed no sign of any movement.

Orsola's leg, sprawled out on the floor and unmoving—Agnes stepped on it casually. Her thick soles applied pressure like a vise. She yelped.

"I mean, it's not like I don't understand why you'd run away. I know your fate—and you might be happier dying here. Inquisitions, attended by all the cardinals...Do you know what they're like? Ah-ha-ha! They might try to be way serious, but they're monsters. With that, it still can't match where it came from—England. If you want my opinion, ours are like playing pretend compared to theirs, you know. Hah, ha-ha! That old man still can't stop playing house—what a wonderful fate you have, to be pulled along by them and die! Isn't it?!"

"—?!"

Because of the intense, grinding pain in her leg, Orsola couldn't manage a proper answer. She also felt like if she opened her mouth carelessly, she would bite her own tongue.

Why did things come to this? thought Orsola hazily.

The *Book of the Law*'s original copy was a hindrance and an evil to all. Everyone wanted to burn it. It led all who acquired it to a ruinous end—it was literally *li libro di un modo pericoloso*. But human hands could not dispose of the original. They could only take temporary measures, locking it tight with a seal.

Orsola Aquinas wanted to do something about that.

Both she and the Roman Orthodox Church must have had the same feelings regarding wanting to erase the infamous *Book of the Law*.

So then why?

What changed to part their paths so definitively?

Right up until the very end, she thought she could see salvation.

Why did that boy hand me over to Agnes?

"Still, it looks like you've got a lot less friends to rely on now, eh? To think you'd come here looking for help from Amakusa, of all people!"

Agnes Sanctis looked down at Orsola.

Her expression looked like it was enchanted by a suspicious grimoire as *thud, thud,* she kicked Orsola's calves. The storm of pain resounded in her bones and threatened to tear her mind apart.

"Driven to the brink of death, you finally clung to a bunch of Asians you didn't know in some filthy island nation. Ah-ha-ha-ha! You mustn't do that, you know. You can't hope for anything from piglets who don't even read scripture. Under our rules, marrying someone outside of a baptized Roman Orthodox is equivalent to sodomy—you know that. Did you think it would be fine just as long as they were still Crossists? Amakusa, the puritans of England—it's ridiculous they'd even call themselves Crossists. They are not human. They are pigs and asses. Look where trusting your precious life to people like them got you. Jeez, tricking beasts like them really is too easy. Just tame them a little, and they'll bring rats back to you in their mouths!"

"...Tr...tricked?"

Orsola's awareness, hazy with pain until then, slowly turned back outward.

"Those people...Did you...Did you trick...them...?"

The sticky blood falling from her torn lips hindered her speech.

But that didn't stop her from asking.

"They weren't...co...cooperating...with you...You tricked...them...?"

"What does it matter? Whichever it was, we got our hands' on you, didn't we? Heh-heh, a-ha-ha!! Man, it was great! Comedy gold! They were all like, 'We'll rescue Orsola Aquinas from the evil Amakusa for sure!!' How moronic, right?! They delivered someone they should've been protecting straight into the hands of their enemy! They're hopeless, that's what they are!!"

"..."

Is that so? thought Orsola, her face losing a little bit of its tension.

They hadn't intended to sell her out to the Roman Orthodox Church—that wasn't it at all. Their smiles, their words—none of them had been a lie. They earnestly worried about her and came all the way to such a dangerous battlefield just to rescue her.

Even though it had ended in failure...

Even though their efforts were for naught, and her life was threatened instead...

They stayed her allies until the very end. They never once betrayed her, forsook her. They had fought for her until the last moment—those kind, reliable allies.

"The hell are you smiling for?"

"I...see. I...am smiling...am I?" said Orsola in a slow, gentle voice. "I seem...to have realized it. Realized the true colors...of our Roman Orthodox Church..."

"Eh?"

"Those people... They act on faith... They believe in others, believe in their feelings, and would follow them anywhere...for others. And yet we...How ugly we are. We...can only act...on doubt. You fooled those helping you, to execute me...You'll fool the people with a fixed trial...and even fool yourself into thinking it's what God wishes you to do..."

"__"

"Although...I'm not in a position to argue with it...either. If I had but trusted Amakusa...from the start...things wouldn't have gotten this bad. If I had fled with them by their plan...then those in Amakusa wouldn't have faced danger, either...In the end, this unsightly form of ours...Is this what the Roman Orthodox Church...really is?"

Orsola smiled.

With her beaten-up face, and without a hint of humor.

"...I can no longer...escape from your clutches. And just as you planned...I will be judged a false sinner...and be buried in the dark. But I am fine with that now...—For I cannot lie to myself...! And what's more...I absolutely, absolutely cannot...trick those who lent me their strength without expecting anything in return, can I? Never again...do I want to be called the same kind of person as you..."

"The words of a martyr. You expect to be canonized or something?"

Whap—with the lightness of kicking an empty can, Agnes's sole came down on Orsola's leg.

"If you want to die that badly, then be my guest. It'll be easier for us if you don't resist, after all. Curse those fools for causing this to happen to you as much as you please, and then die!"

Although Agnes would have known there was no way for her to resist. More than two hundred sisters surrounded her, waiting. And there was a strong barrier put up around the church, so she definitely couldn't make a run for it.

Her consciousness wavering, even Agnes's words, spoken right next to her ears, only came in bits and pieces. But Orsola still managed to think with her near-disabled mind.

"What...on earth...should I curse?"

"Wh...what?"

"They never...had a reason to fight. I asked him, and he said he wasn't a Roman Orthodox...or an English Puritan...He was just a boy. And yet, without any power or reason, he came running to me, a complete stranger...See? Where else in the world...could you find a more attractive gift than that...? Those people...they gave me such a beautiful gift...so what are you saying I should curse about them?"

Yes—she wouldn't curse them.

She would never curse them.

Even if they hadn't rescued Orsola safely, what they did couldn't be condemned. Because they had no duty telling them they needed to rescue her. They weren't fighting just because someone told them to. They flung themselves into battle, not bothering to use their "rights" to save her.

Just fighting for her, just standing up for her, was worthy of much gratitude.

So Orsola would never curse them.

She felt proud to have been blessed with the chance to meet people who would do so much for a total stranger. She wanted to thank God for making her lucky enough to be with them at the end.

She was satisfied.

That was enough.

Orsola Aquinas thought she would never again embrace such happiness with her hands...

...and yet that happiness hadn't ended.

*　　*　　*

For the next moment…

Smash!! came a sound as the barrier around the church was destroyed.

Agnes reflexively took her eyes away from Orsola.

Something had happened that forced her to do so.

"It…broke…? Could it be…? Hey! Someone check on the Protection of Giles we put on that door! And scout for enemies! Shit, what group could this be? No one person could have possibly broken a barrier of that level. What enemy faction could be attacking us…?!"

Commands, issued in rapid succession.

But before any of them could be carried out, she got the answer she wanted.

"Ah…" Orsola Aquinas looked.

The oaken double doors at the entrance to the church were thrown open. And there someone stood, like a rough storybook scene where the prince comes to save his princess.

The one standing there was just a boy.

It was an ordinary young man—and yet he neither fled nor ran.

Who was he here for?

What was he here for?

The two-hundred-strong sisters surrounding Orsola turned their harsh glares on the boy but didn't make a sound. There were already hundreds of people to cause violence against him, and none of them was normal, either. He had to have felt fear. There was no way he didn't. He was no more than an utterly average young man—so he must have been scared.

And yet.

And yet, without hesitation, he took a step.

A step into the church veiled in darkness, in order to save Orsola Aquinas.

He took the step…for her.

As if to declare that everything would be all right.

5

Touma Kamijou set foot into the huge, unfinished church.

It was a terrible place.

Hundreds of people were gathered here with no air conditioner on this sultry night—it may have been huge, but it felt like a secret room, wrapped in a strange heat. The thick smell of sweat drifted from the darkness, giving it the impression of a deep, giant nesting hole.

Hundreds of sisters dressed in black, blending with the darkness, eddying about.

He saw one girl on the floor in the middle of them, and his eyes narrowed without a sound.

Then he heard a derisive laugh that seemed to know what he was feeling.

He looked toward its source to see Agnes Sanctis for what seemed like the first time.

"You know, I did think it was quite strange." She giggled and broke into a smile. "Why did some total amateur like you, not even a sorcerer, get brought out to the battlefield as a guest?...I don't know what logic went into that one, but I suppose you must hold some absolute power over barriers."

"..."

"Oh my, what's the matter? Did you lose something? Did you want a reward? Oh, well, if you're still attached to that *thing* over there, I can strip her bare for you if you want."

Her voice was tinged with irritation and enthusiasm. It was a joy not unlike having drunk bad alcohol.

"Just one question. You're not gonna lie anymore, are you?"

"Lie? About what?! Can't you tell what's happening here? Who is the greater, and who is the lesser? You can't possibly be stupid enough to think you can stand on the same stage as me, do you? Now, I want to hear your choice from you—what will you do when faced with this many people?"

Just one versus more than two hundred certainly didn't present very good odds. If Kamijou fought them all head-on, he stood no chance. Agnes knew that, too. She casually walked right up to him, without any caution, as if to provoke him.

She thought that Kamijou could never strike her. If he threw even one punch, that punch would mark the beginning of a hopeless battle.

"Sheesh. You're an idiot—and a big one, at that. I thought the English Puritans made the wise choice and ran home—but what about you? Hmm. Well, whatever. You can't do anything by yourself, so if you want to run away, I'll let you do so. See? I'm giving you one last chance. You know exactly what you need to do, don't you?"

Kamijou smiled feebly at Agnes Sanctis's relaxed words. "My last chance...I know exactly what I need to do, huh?" And then, in a voice that sounded somehow relieved, he replied:

"You're right. This is my last chance, that's for sure. I completely understand."

Wham!! Kamijou's right fist tore through the air.

Agnes immediately crossed her arms to defend her face, but her legs came off the floor.

Her entire body flung away despite her guard, and she glared at Kamijou with eyes like a mad dog.

Not even one second of hesitation.

Without even showing a moment of indecision, the young man showed his preparation to the enemy before him.

"You...little...What the fuck are you doing?!" Agnes Sanctis yelled angrily, but Touma Kamijou replied with an even louder roar.

"What I need to do! Don't take me so lightly! I'm here to save her! Why the hell else would I be here?!"

Their emotions clashed against each other at close range.

Though they were both, in a word, "heated," their properties and temperature were entirely different.

Her cheek muscles trembled oddly and she began muttering to herself. The sisters in black, who had been standing idly until now, all turned to face Touma Kamijou. The hundreds of weapons they held made an eerie, mechanical sound, like soldiers marching forward.

"You... That's...pretty...funny." Agnes's voice and body both trembled. "There are two hundred of us. How much can you do alone in this situation?! Come on, then, show me! Ha-ha—with the number difference, I think you'll be mincemeat in less than a minute, though!"

The sisters in black all readied their weapons at her assertion.

Meanwhile, Touma Kamijou had no weapons—only his own tightly clenched fist.

Just before the two sides clashed...

...suddenly, they heard a voice.

"Give me a break. Don't start without me. You managed to slip right through the barrier. You could have at least given me enough time to set up the runes we need."

"Eh...?"

The very moment Agnes turned around with a dumbfounded look, there was a roar of flames sucking in oxygen—and with it, the orange explosion instantly dissolved the darkness dominating the incomplete church.

In the back of the church, exactly opposite where Kamijou stood—

There was a big hole in one of the windows on the wall behind the pulpit, about two stories up, waiting for stained glass to be fitted inside. He'd probably used the scaffolding on the outer wall to get there. Standing in the window frame was an English Puritan priest, with a flame sword in his hand.

"...S...Stiyl?"

In a daze, Touma Kamijou whispered the name of the priest with the cigarette in the corner of his mouth.

"We sorcerers were all ready to finish things up, so we'd planned to have the *amateur* retire. All those fake explanations and fake persuasions—for nothing."

Agnes spoke before Kamijou could. "English...Puritans? Absurd... This is solely a Roman Orthodox issue! If you interfere, they'll see it as meddling in our internal affairs! Don't you know that?!"

"Yeah, well...Unfortunately, that doesn't apply here." Stiyl blew out some smoke, annoyed. "Take a look at Orsola Aquinas's chest. See that English Puritan cross hanging on her neck? Yeah—the very same cross our *amateur* accidentally gave her." He grinned teasingly. "Placing that around someone's neck places them under the protection of the English Puritan Church—which means she has been baptized and is now one of us. Our archbishop prepared that cross personally. And she ordered me to hang it around Orsola's neck myself…It was low on the priority list, so I had left it for later and given it to that man over there. I figured it would be a bit of insurance, to make you think the amateur was under English Puritanism's umbrella should you have captured him…but somehow or another, it ended up on Orsola, just as planned. That means Orsola Aquinas is not a member of the Roman Orthodox Church—but one of the puritans of England."

"I get it. So that's why…" Kamijou absently thought back.

When he casually said he'd give her the cross, Orsola seemed extremely happy…

So this is what it *really* meant.

Agnes's face grew bright red. After moving her mouth up and down a few times, she said, "Y-you think such sophistry will work?"

"No, I don't. It's not as though it was performed according to English Puritan ceremony, by an English Puritan priest, in an English Puritan church." Stiyl wiggled his cigarette. "But that doesn't mean Orsola *isn't* in a very delicate position right now, does it? A Roman Orthodox disciple received an English Puritan cross—plus, someone from Academy City, in the science faction, gave it to her. I think we should take some time now to deliberate on what faction she is technically a part of right now. If you put her to trial as just a Roman Orthodox, then the English Puritan Church won't sit idly by."

Tap. Stiyl jumped from the window and quietly landed in front of the pulpit. He pointed the tip of his flame sword at the distant Agnes's face. "And above all—*you were nice enough to point your blades at her.*" Stiyl bared his teeth. "Did you think I was that naïve? That I was kind enough to let that slip?"

"Damn! Just because there's one more of you now doesn't mean—?!" she began to shout hatefully, but once again, someone *else's* voice interrupted.

"Man, hope you're not thinking you'll get away with just two!"

"?!"

As Agnes turned to face the audacious male voice, this time, the wall to her side blasted apart and crumbled. From the dense clouds of dust walked a tall man with a large sword.

"Tatemiya..." Kamijou voiced the name of the tall man holding the pure white flamberge of unknown composition.

Saiji Tatemiya.

The vicar—representative—pope of the diversified religious fusion of Crossism, the Amakusa-Style Crossist Church.

And behind him were gathered the members of Amakusa, who should have been confined in a separate building. They numbered about fifty—it was probably everyone who had been locked up.

"No need to ask me why I'm fighting here, is there?"

Surprised, Kamijou said, "Y-you...But you said it would be best to hit them while they were on the move..."

"Because I thought you'd give up and go home if I said that. I talked it over with the English Puritans and we *tried* to set things up so that we'd finish things before you made a move. You're an even bigger idiot than I thought. But you're fun to watch, so I can't really hate ya," answered Tatemiya, amazed.

And last of all, with a *click clack* of footsteps, the familiar voice of a girl in white came to him from behind.

"That's why I told you not to worry, Touma—someone else would settle things!"

"In...dex..."

Pat—a small, yet reassuring hand was placed on his astounded shoulder. "But we can't help it now that it's come to this, I guess!—Let's save her, Touma. Let's save Orsola Aquinas with our own hands!"

Yeah, nodded Kamijou.

Agnes Sanctis, watching the whole thing, exploded. With a single order—*kill them!*—the hundreds of sisters in the dark leaped at them to attack.

The final battle had begun—the final battle of those gathered to settle the score of this ridiculous story.

INTERLUDE TWO

In the middle of the night, Kaori Kanzaki stood on the roof of a building.

The landscape before her eyes portrayed the under-construction Church of Orsola. Its impression was far from that of a church—not a speck of silence, filled with the sounds of violence and breaking.

She was standing far away from the church, but her keen ears could hear what they said. They heard the words of those who stood up for a single girl.

Kanzaki never planned on taking Amakusa's side or killing the enemy Roman Orthodox from the beginning. She had not absconded right after the incident so that she could exercise violence.

She just wanted to make her true intentions known.

She wanted Amakusa to know that even without her, they would still be Amakusa, and nothing would change.

And they had just shown that, just as she'd believed they would. She narrowed her eyes in a gentle, natural smile, as though gazing at an object of nostalgia.

A place she could never go home to again.

But now she would be able to treasure that place in her heart, forever and ever.

From behind her, she heard unconcealed footsteps.

"Nyaha! I see you're feeling totally grateful and moved, there,

Zaky. Ain't it a sight? Your old friends didn't kidnap Orsola so they could use the *Book of the Law* for their own greed after all!"

"Tsuchimikado..." Kanzaki hastily erased her expression and turned around—but she couldn't seem to accomplish that when she saw Tsuchimikado's broad grin.

She spoke in a strict tone to hide her abashment. "Are you finished on your end? You were talking about snatching up the *Book of the Law*'s original copy using this opportunity..."

"Hmm, who knows? Maybe I did, maybe I didn't."

"..."

"I'm kidding. Don't look at me like that! You basically know what's goin' on, right? Amakusa didn't steal the book. It was all the Roman Orthodox Church tryin' to frame 'em. That means they didn't need to bring the thing into Japan in the first place, yeah? The one they brought here was a forgery. The real thing is deep, deep in the Vatican Library as we speak."

Tsuchimikado was reporting on his failure, but his voice was awfully bright. Maybe he didn't have much passion for his work—or perhaps he had lied, and he actually managed to steal the *Book of the Law*. Kanzaki didn't quite know what to make of it.

He walked up next to her. He placed both hands on the metal railing to prevent falling, and as he quietly gazed at where Kanzaki was looking, asked, "So, you satisfied?"

"...Yes. More so than I thought." Kanzaki looked at the church again. "They'll be able to keep Amakusa on the correct path without me. They've become very strong."

"Mm, yes. They're probably having a hard time, though—not gonna help 'em?"

"I do not have the right to stand before them. And they no longer need my strength. I was as training wheels on a bicycle," said Kanzaki, sounding a little lonely but proud.

She hadn't hesitated even a moment to give her answer.

Tsuchimikado suppressed a grin at her seriousness.

"What is it, Tsuchimikado?"

"I mean, nothin' much...It don't matter, but ya probably didn't expect Kammy to get involved in this, did ya? You still haven't thanked him for the Angel Fall business and the Index struggle, either. Now you've gotten him mixed up in another one of your problems—you're totally afraid of having to make it up to him, aren't ya, nya?"

"N-not at all. Nothing you are imagining is going to happen!"

Kanzaki replied with a very serious look, but for some reason, Tsuchimikado burst out laughing. He laughed so hard and so loudly that it brought tears to his eyes and he started to worry it would reach the Church of Orsola below.

"By the way! What could those bandages in your hands be, hmm? You weren't gonna sneak up on your unconscious friends and do secret first aid on 'em, were ya? And then after you were done, stroke their heads softly with a hand, smile a little, and quietly retreat? Pfft, ku-ku! Man, Zaky, you're so simple and cliché, you! I can't believe you were thinking of something so embarrassing with a straight face!"

"......?!"

"Hm? What's up, Zaky? Your temples are all pulsing and...Hey, wait, wait stop stop stop! I'm unarmed! You can't seriously use the Seven Heavens, Seven Blades on me! Does this mean you're gonna bandage me up first, nyaaaa?!"

CHAPTER 4

Amakusa-Style

Amakusa_Style_Crossist_Church.

1

The Church of Orsola consisted of seven sanctuaries.

Each of them was charged with one of the seven sacraments of Crossism. They weren't all the same size, instead varying in size and money spent depending on the frequency and importance of the sacrament. Orsola and the others were currently in the Church of Matrimony, which concerned wedding ceremonies. It was planned to receive the most in the way of finances, so the building was gigantic as well. Second largest was the Church of Final Anointment, which related to funeral proceedings; others with important religious significance, such as the Church of Holy Orders and the Church of Confirmation, followed, but nevertheless they couldn't expect much patronage from general visitors such as Kamijou, and so were the smallest ones. These small buildings were artfully adorned with statues, paintings, and stained-glass windows—it looked like they were aiming for additional income as a halfway art exhibit or museum.

That was as much info as the mobile version of its homepage on his phone could tell him. It was rather strange to see a website built by those on the occult side for their own choice, but maybe they wanted it to function as a sightseeing guide as well—the maps of its planned completion and even of the inside being made public could have been a money grab...though of course, it was only the places they *could* show to visitors.

"Damn!!"

Kamijou swept up Orsola into his arms and dove out the Church of Matrimony's back door. Not a hint of plant life greeted them as he stepped onto the perfectly flat stone ground. Armed sisters appeared from the doorway soon after.

He had waited for the very moment the dozens of Amakusa members clashed face-first with the Roman sisters to take Orsola and flee the Church of Matrimony. He didn't want to be separated from Index and the others if he could help it, but they were now divided by a human wave, so there was nothing he could do.

As he ran, he looked at Orsola's face and said, "Sorry I was late! Are you all right?!"

"...Yes. This much is really nothing at all."

Her clothing was cut up badly; the fasteners and other metal parts of it were broken, looking like something had crushed them in its teeth. She barely moved at all—just swayed a little—and held on to him tightly, which was all he needed to deduce how badly hurt she was.

But although her face held exhaustion, *pain* was nowhere to be found.

She looked as though she were about to burst into tears. With her hands up around his neck, she looked up at him like a child who had finally found her parents.

Jeez, what the hell! It was so easy—I had a reason to fight right here.

Kamijou held on to her as he continued his run.

However large the Church of Matrimony may have been, fighting against so many people inside it would have been suicidal. Strength wasn't the issue—it would be the human flood washing over him. And he was just a high school kid in the first place. He could win a one-on-one fight; one-on-two was dubious. Any more than that and he wouldn't think twice about running. That was the extent of his ability.

But.

But just because he wouldn't think twice about running didn't mean he had been defeated.

"Hm...!!" Before the countless hands of his pursuers could reach his back, Amakusa men and women, swords in hand, leaped down from the church's roof. Their blades blocked the Roman Orthodox weaponry close to impaling his body, and the brutal follow-up kick sent the front line of black-garbed sisters flying.

With the *whoosh* of a wave retreating, a portion of the Roman Orthodox sisters moved as a single creature and surrounded the Amakusa members.

Thanks a bunch...!

He ran farther, kicking an empty can left by a construction worker with his heel into the air. Of course, the effects of launching something like that were far from mowing down the sisters in black.

But when something flew through the corner of their eyes, they'd look that way whether they wanted to or not.

"?!"

As soon as they noticed the sisters' attention waver, the Amakusa members cut through the encirclement. They gave Kamijou a quick bow, then each of them began to flee as well.

He didn't have time to see that through to the end. The weapons wielded by the sisters may have been heavy, but they couldn't have been heavier than a human body. To close the slight distance that formed between them, the Roman Orthodox killers ran after Kamijou again.

A sister closed in on him, swinging a lit torch. A softball-sized rock of ice came flying at him from behind her. He continued to dodge them, holding Orsola close. He soon spotted metal construction-pipe scaffolding surrounding the long and thin Church of Confirmation, which was behind the Church of Matrimony, and dashed up in bounds. He used the slanted rungs to run up to the second floor. The torch-holding sister carelessly came after him—he kicked her down to the ground with his right foot. A moment later, another sister somehow jumped from the ground up to where he was with a single leap; as she set foot on the unstable scaffolding, Kamijou swept her legs out and sent her tumbling back down.

"—"

The eyes of dozens of sisters on the ground stared up at him on the scaffolding, observing him mechanically.

They would have realized by now.

They could surround him with dozens of people and attack all at once—they wouldn't have anywhere to run then. But if he found a place where they needed to fight one-on-one, he could pick out an escape route.

The metal pipes making up the scaffolding he stood on were long, thin, and unstable, so the sisters couldn't deliver a unified attack from all directions. If they were to follow him up the narrow scaffolding, they would inevitably need to get in a neat single-file line. In fact, if that many people all ran onto the scaffolding, it would buckle under their weight and collapse. Unless they were prepared to die, they couldn't use their numbers to their advantage because of the sacrifice it might require.

The sisters in jet-black pondered on what that meant...

...and then without exchanging a single word, their opinions aligned, and they all readied their weapons, still on the ground.

From staffs, axes, crosses, and Bibles to a giant clock hand you might use on a clock tower—the tips of all these myriad weapons pointed straight over their heads to where Kamijou was. Their blades shone in all the colors of the rainbow—red, blue, yellow, green, purple, brown, white, gold.

Agh...shit...?!

Kamijou hoisted the unconscious Orsola's body again in his arms, then began a mad dash farther up the metal pipe scaffolding. As he did so, feathers of brilliantly colored light flew at him one after the other. The shining weapons were like feather pens with arrowheads on their tips. In the blink of an eye they were speeding toward where Kamijou was sprinting with Orsola, trying to shoot right through them. The storm of feathers of light destroyed the outer wall of the church and the scaffolding alike without mercy. As soon as he heard the huge *clank* and the scaffolding swung, he realized they hadn't been shooting at him—they'd been going after the base of the scaffolding.

They certainly didn't seem to care about Orsola's safety. They just knew they needed to keep her alive—as long as her brain and heart were working, they probably didn't care what state she was in.

The entire scaffolding they were running on tilted over like a sinking ship.

Of course, jumping to the ground would land him right in the middle of the dozens of sisters.

"Ugh, aaaaaahhhhhhhhhhhhhhhhhhhhhhhhhhhhhhhhhhhh?!"

He gave a meaningless shout. Because the scaffolding was tipping over, his path was getting steeper and steeper. It was getting closer to vertical with each passing moment. Kamijou ran through it. The two-story scaffolding, at some point, had reached up to the roof of the three-story church.

He tightened his arms around Orsola and jumped with all his might.

Just when his feet landed on the marble church roof, the coffin of metal pipes and parts clattered to the ground in a heap.

His spine chilled at the sight of the scaffolding he was just on having collapsed, then finally stopped in place, still holding Orsola, and took a deep breath.

"A-are you all right?" she asked anxiously up at him, perhaps feeling like a heavy burden to him.

"Yeah, no problem," he replied, waving it off, looking at how Orsola was doing again. Her habit was torn all over thanks to the countless violent acts, her clothing fasteners were broken, and her skirt fabric was in shambles. Under normal circumstances the sight might have been rather arousing, but her thighs were black and blue with bruises like a rotten fruit, the discoloration of internal bleeding pushing any trace of that thought out of his mind.

...*Damn it.* He gritted his teeth, not saying anything aloud but yelling inwardly. *Not even a grown man could have stood up against your numbers, and you all ganged up on Orsola and beat her up like this? Agnes Sanctis!!* He really wanted to charge into the enemy line right this instant, but Orsola worried him more. He needed to do some quick first aid and let her rest somewhere, he thought urgently.

But there wasn't any calming down in this place.

They moved away from the edge of the roof toward the middle to avoid as many projectiles as they could, coming to a spot where the building walls would block seeing him from any angle below.

"Which means…"

He let Orsola down out of his arms onto the under-construction roof, and then grabbed a nearby box of construction tools with his hands…

…and *bam!!*

The next moment, with a tremendous noise, three sisters came jumping up from the ground.

Kamijou swung the box of construction tools, heavy enough to make him feel like the one being swung around. It struck one of the three sisters, who lost her balance and fell to the ground.

The other two landed on the roof without a sound, one readying her giant hour hand and one her giant minute hand. Each had bandages around the base, maybe to let them grip it.

He heard the rest of them, who didn't have such jumping abilities, running up the stairs inside the building to get to the roof, right below him.

He felt like he was at a disadvantage, so he looked around with his eyes only, without moving his neck, for an escape route…and then he saw the girl wearing a white habit, running through the middle of the vast church site that could be viewed in its entirety from the rooftops.

Behind her were likewise dozens of sisters clad in jet-black.

But his bird's-eye view told him how hopeless her situation was. There was another group of sisters closing in farther along her escape path. She must not have realized there were enemies in that direction as well. If she kept going, she would have to run straight into them.

"Index!!" he shouted unthinkingly—and at that, the two sisters jumped at him from the left and right, giant clock hands at the ready.

His voice didn't reach the girl running along the ground.

2

Between the Church of Matrimony and the Church of Baptism, Saiji Tatemiya brandished his sword. Because the Church of Baptism was positioned diagonally from the Church of Matrimony, it created a triangular courtyard.

Until he was the last one there, he brandished his sword. After the members of Amakusa had bought time at first to let Orsola escape, now Tatemiya was buying time for the rest of Amakusa to escape the Church of Matrimony. Dozens of his peers were currently scattered around, fighting.

Here and there on the polished stone courtyard without a hint of greenery, there were pedestal-looking things for sculptures to go on top. Once the church was finished, there would probably be an orderly line of angels, famous religious figures, and saints, but right now they just radiated emptiness. It felt like ruins after heretics had attacked and destroyed every piece of religious art here.

Saiji Tatemiya didn't fight while running, like Touma Kamijou did.

That was because he was skillfully throwing off the timing of the enemies' attacks. He would never launch into a full assault, nor resign himself to complete defense—he maintained a position right in between.

As soon as the sisters came forward to attack, Tatemiya would take just one step forward.

The sisters would then back off and regroup, and in that moment, Tatemiya would take just one step back.

With their predictions gone wrong and the wind naturally taken out of the enemy group's sails, their pace would be thrown off for just a moment. Tatemiya aimed for that moment and mercilessly brandished his sword. When the sisters would panic and move to defend, his heavy sword would knock an enemy—and her defense—way back.

Tatemiya wouldn't follow up. After pulling out one attack, he would patiently move back. By neither attacking nor defending, but keeping a precarious balance between the two, he purposely erected an invisible wall—a state of deadlock—that shouldn't have been there originally.

Though I'm not gonna be able to rely on this tactic for very long..., Tatemiya thought, leaping from rooftop to rooftop, catching his comrades brandishing their own swords out of the corner of his eye.

He pretended to give a smile of superiority, but on the inside he was nervous. Right now, all he was doing was taking advantage of the fact that the sisters were able to analyze the situation, and that they had some leeway to work with. If they decided to fight to the death, lost their minds' balance, and came at him in a full-blown assault, prepared for friendly fire and mutual kills, Tatemiya's plan would come crumbling down.

Whether it was attack or defense, the moment the balance tipped toward either of those sides would be the moment his psychological wall would collapse and he'd be swallowed up in the giant wave.

It was like fishing, he thought as he brandished his sword. If he recklessly cast his line into the water, the fish would just tear apart the string and run away. If he wanted to fish well, he needed to go along with the fish's movements to a certain extent, let them play with it, and make them think they had a chance of winning.

And then he heard the scampering of footsteps.

"More of them?!"

Tatemiya was startled, but the footsteps weren't coming after him.

The courtyard he was fighting in was between the Church of Matrimony and the diagonally positioned Church of Baptism, so it was a triangular space. And at the top of the triangle, in the slight gap between the two churches, there was the English Puritan sister wearing the white habit.

She seemed to have managed to flee from the Roman Orthodox

sisters, but she must have run into a group coming from the other direction. Well over twice the number of enemies as Tatemiya was facing were surrounding her, blocking any movement.

"Shit. Don't go making me look bad, damn it!"

Tatemiya hurriedly tried to back her up, but the dozens of sisters surrounding her all moved like a single creature and formed a human wall. From their point of view, every time an enemy died, the people they split off to do so would move to reinforce the rest. They were fighting against a group of stragglers, which was why they probably wanted to finish this battle as quickly as possible.

Tatemiya glared at the sisters, and they glared back.

Behind them, Index was being swallowed by a wave of countless people, and she was getting harder and harder to see.

"Don't...underestimate—!!"

At the very moment Tatemiya caught his breath to resort to a bold move and swung his sword back into position...

...he suddenly heard a man's voice coming to him from overhead.

"Stop! You can't get close to her right now!!"

Right when Tatemiya looked up, a second-story window of the Church of Baptism exploded outward with flames. A Roman Orthodox sister came flying out of the broken window like a bullet. She barely managed to coil her feet to kill some of the impact from landing, but that was all she could do. She lost consciousness and rolled over onto the ground.

In the window, holding a sword of flame, was Stiyl Magnus.

He spoke.

"It depends on the situation, but right now she's strongest when she's alone. If we get close to her, it will sap her strength. You don't want to get caught in something like this, either, do you?"

"What?" said Tatemiya dubiously, when...

Boom!! came an explosion from near Index.

Dozens, if not *hundreds* of people were completely surrounding her, leaving not a single gap—and then he saw Index. Meaning a portion of their siege had fallen. One of the corners of the thick C-shaped crowd of people was struck by an unseen power and completely blown away. It seemed to have landed a direct hit on about ten of the sisters, but one of them rolled all the way to Tatemiya's feet, dozens of meters away. At the sight of their ally flying over their heads like a rag doll, even the sisters facing Tatemiya turned around to Index.

Thud!! came another invisible burst, sending a handful of sisters flying.

"...What the hell is that?"

Tatemiya looked at the sister at his feet. Her face was a portrait of despair; her body curled up, stuck in the fetal position. And though she was unconscious, she trembled violently as if experiencing a night terror. Closer inspection revealed that her leg muscles had snapped apart. Her explosive flight had been performed by her own feet—as though some survival or defense instinct had gone berserk in an attempt to flee from Index's side even at the cost of ignoring her body's physical limits.

Stiyl jumped down from the second story and landed right next to Tatemiya with a *clap*. "You are Crossist as well, so you should understand. Crossist ceremonies each have their own weaknesses—though perhaps I should call them contradictions. These weaknesses, or contradictions, are what caused so many Crossist sects to be created—and all of them have formed even more weaknesses and contradictions. It's basically what sets Crossism apart from the rest."

"...What does that have to do with this?" Tatemiya waved the tip of his giant sword a bit, measuring his distance to the sisters.

"Floating in that area is the wisdom of all the world—all the knowledge of the 103,000 grimoires. She's using it to denounce the contradictions in Crossism and its teachings. The voice of magic's bane—Sheol Fear. For those working under the Crossist operating system, the contradictions in their faith are like security holes. Sheol Fear, which pierces precisely through them, is truly their bane. It causes the hearer's personality to fall apart like a jigsaw puzzle."

However, it would have no effect on those unrelated to Crossism, and grimoire authors like Aureolus would construct unique barriers so that the original copy wouldn't corrupt their minds. Of course, there were *extremely* few people in the world who could write an original copy and not be physically destroyed by it.

"Grimoires don't exist solely to be read. She can draw out the full power of grimoires even without magic using things like spell interception or Sheol Fear. There is probably no better candidate to be a library of grimoires than her."

Before the dazed sisters could re-form their ranks, Stiyl and Tatemiya stormed in. Stiyl's flame sword exploded, and the sisters pressed flat to the ground by the waves were skillfully knocked unconscious one by one by Tatemiya. Meanwhile, a little farther away, Index's casual whisperings were blasting tons of the sisters surrounding her all over the place.

Tatemiya was half-impressed and half-amazed. "With a hidden ball trick like that, why didn't she use it right from the start? And if she'd used it against us, she could've mowed us all down!"

"It's a delicate attack, and there are frustrating limitations. Religious brainwashing is easier to pull off on a group all at once than on an individual basis. You understand that, right? Sheol Fear uses what they call group mentality in science to break through the barriers of their minds and use them as footholds."

Stiyl caused his flame sword to burst, repelling the sisters edging toward him. One of them who tried to time her attack came away with a scalding burn on her cheek and quickly jumped away.

"The problem with activating Sheol Fear is that it requires a certain level of *purity* in their group mentality. It's easy to cast on a homogenous group where everyone has the same thoughts, but it brings with it a difficulty to cast on muddled groups with different ideas. And during combat on an individual basis, it has no effect at all...In our battle with you, Touma Kamijou and I were in the way, so the 'purity' of the group fell, thus she couldn't effectively use it against you. It has exceptions—and that's why I'm here as a bodyguard.

"In other words, if you jump in there now, the conditions required for Sheol Fear will be ruined," Stiyl said, disinterested, putting an abrupt stop to their pointless talk.

Ssshhh! A new set of footsteps.

They turned their gazes skyward to see dozens of sisters standing on the roofs of each of the two buildings surrounding the courtyard.

3

Inside the darkness-enclosed Church of Matrimony, Agnes stood with her back against a marble pillar.

Around ten sisters were waiting nearby as bodyguards, but every time they heard an explosion or a clash, they shivered and looked back and forth busily. Agnes simply stood with her arms folded and eyes resting—you wouldn't be able to tell who was guarding whom if you saw.

"Quit making so much noise already. You all look like idiots. Especially you, Sister Angeline."

"B-but Lady Agnes…"

Her clear sarcasm was met by an overreaction by one of the sisters. She looked as though she had seen the messiah as her ship was sinking. She probably wanted to ward off some of her tension by talking to someone.

"It's been more than ten minutes since the battle started. Even if you count Orsola, there's still such a difference in our numbers! This isn't normal. S-see?! That explosion—which side did that come from? Maybe they're on the offensive now…!!"

"…"

"W-we should go as well. We could use everyone we can—"

"There wouldn't be a point, so don't bother," said Agnes, sounding very bored.

"Th-then what should we do? They took Orsola away, so if they run away again—"

"They cannot run away," interrupted Agnes. Then, as if so sure about it that she was too lazy to give an explanation, she said,

"There's no way they can escape. That's just how this shitty world of ours is made."

The balance crumbled suddenly.

Index brought it on. It happened while she was attacking with Sheol Fear, which she'd reassembled to only catch the Roman Orthodox sisters, and wreaking havoc on the Crossist believers' minds by using the 103,000 grimoires. Suddenly, one of the sisters—if she recalled correctly, she was Sister Lucia, who had attacked Kamijou at the theme park with the wheel—shouted.

"*Dia priorità di cima ad un attacco! Il nemico di Dio è ucciso comunque!!*"

The sisters all stopped abruptly.

Their expressions disappeared without a sound. They joined their breathing like a military force giving a salute and took something out of their clothing. In their right and left hands were expensive-looking ballpoint pens.

"...?" At that point, Index anticipated some kind of magic attack focus fire on her.

But her prediction was completely wrong.

The next moment...

...the sisters surrounding Index, nearly a hundred strong, smoothly took their ballpoint pens and shoved them through their own eardrums.

There was a *squelch* like of fingers crushing grapes.

Crimson-red blood dripped from the holes in their ears.

They all tossed aside the two ballpoint pens they'd stabbed their ears with and took up their weapons once again.

Their faces were colored with intense pain, and yet their desire to destroy put magnificent smiles on their faces. On the sharp ends of the pens on the ground were stuck white stringlike things soaked in blood. They were human eardrums.

Index felt an overwhelming urge to vomit coming from deep within her.

"Are they…doing that to avoid Sheol Fear…?"

If they couldn't hear her voice, Sheol Fear wouldn't work. As Index realized this shocking fact, the sisters surrounding her all came for her at once.

"Damn it…?!" Stiyl had been the first to realize it. He moved to go help Index in a hurry, for a moment throwing off the rhythm of his linked combat with Tatemiya that had been going well.

He burst one flame sword after another, toppling sisters with their impacts left and right and momentarily blinding them with their light. But reaching Index was as far as he could go—the sisters had gotten used to his series of identical attacks and had even found a counter for them.

"Over here!!"

Just then, the double doors of the nearby Church of Final Anointment flew open, and Touma Kamijou shouted from them. A wound-covered Orsola was behind him as well, and she was using a big clock hand wrapped in bandages as a cane. He must have run out of ways to fight on the run with the wounded girl and decided to hide out for a while.

Index, Stiyl, and Tatemiya all managed to dive into the church. Kamijou hurried and shut the doors, and not a moment too soon—one after another, blades came piercing through the black oak more than five centimeters thick.

They had successfully shut the Roman Orthodox sisters out for the time being.

However, who knew how many minutes the doors would last? It was like the three little piggies nestled in their house of straw.

Kamijou sank weakly to the cold marble floor. "Looks like everyone's safe for now…Hey, can you walk, Orsola?"

"You are…quite a worrywart. I haven't sustained…such bad wounds."

Orsola's hands and feet were entirely covered by her habit, so it was difficult to tell by looking, but she appeared to have taken quite a bit of pain. Nevertheless, she gave a smile, though weak. Kamijou felt a pang in his chest, but there wasn't anything he could do about it. So instead, he tried to force a change in the topic. "...So what do we do now?"

No one present answered his question. They'd been keeping up the precarious balance of the battle, but it had come toppling down all at once, and everyone here knew it.

The members of Amakusa fighting outside were also barely maintaining equilibrium through individual surprise attacks and great escapes. They had their hands full with their own problems, so it would be hard to ask them for help.

With the *gash*ing and *thwack*ing of iron nails being hammered into a tree, holes opened one by one in the church's door. Index's face went a little pale. "I-I don't think my Sheol Fear can, umm, a-affect them with their ears like...th-that at all." She blanched, remembering the sight of them piercing their eardrums. "And I can only use spell interception against one person at a time. I don't think I can interrupt hundreds of people casting hundreds of spells all at once!"

"???"

Index gave an analysis of her own combat potential as though it were the normal thing to do, but Kamijou had no idea what was going on. What had Index done, anyway, and how had it worked?

This time, Tatemiya spoke. "My guys're doin' their best, but it's gonna be tough. The scariest thing is when people attack you prepared to die. If that flood of people hits us, it won't matter how much skill we've got, man. It's like an army of ants devouring a wild beast."

Along with his bitter words came the sounds of blades stabbing and thrusting into the doors. From the other side of the shredded door peeked in many sets of eyes.

Kamijou felt his gut freeze over.

If that door came down, the armed sisters would flood inside like an avalanche. They only had a few minutes' reprieve. If they couldn't find a way out of this, they were dog food—but the more they discussed it, the more it felt like they'd been cornered in a dead-end street. Kamijou felt a panic beginning to burn up in the back of his mind, but he couldn't do anything about it.

"Well, maybe if...Maybe if we had the *Book of the Law* here, we could use my decoding method and discover a way out...," said Orsola Aquinas suddenly.

Everyone present looked at her.

The *Book of the Law.*

The thing everyone had forgotten about—the one grimoire that triggered this whole incident. Said to have been written by Edward Alexander...the world's strongest sorcerer, Crowley. Thought to be able to freely control angelic techniques. Rumored to declare the end of a Crossist-dominated age upon opening it. The ultimate forbidden tome, sealing away utterly vast knowledge.

If the book was really that dangerous, they might be able to use it for negotiations just by declaring they'd undone the seal.

"But the book being stolen was just a farce made to trap us, man. I doubt the real thing was even ever brought to Japan in the first place. If they brought in a fake and the original is still in the Vatican Library, that's it."

""That's it!!""

Kamijou and Index spoke at the same time.

They had the original copy of the *Book of the Law* right here.

"Even Index couldn't decipher the book, right? That means **she's gone through it to try and decipher it.** So it wouldn't be strange if you still had the whole book stored in your memories, right?"

"Yep. The encoded text has been collecting dust in the corner, though."

This time, Stiyl's facial expression worsened. "You can't! If you do that, she'll record the contents of the *Book of the Law.* If that happens, far more sorcerers would start going after her!"

"??? Are you worried about me?"

Index, "a complete stranger," tilted her head in confusion, while Stiyl, "who knew her well once," reddened as if he'd been caught unawares, then immediately erased it with a click of his tongue.

Index **thought that sorcerers chasing her was a natural event,** and

Stiyl was well aware nothing he could say would stop her—as well as the fact that he couldn't think of anything better.

Stiyl made a sour face, then suddenly shouted, "Touma Kamijou!!"

"Wh-what?!"

"Grow stronger! If she dies because of what happens here, I will burn your body and soul to a crisp until not even ashes remain!!" He swore under his breath and turned away. Index was still looking confused, looking like she couldn't tell why he felt the need to get mad over this. Tatemiya looked at Kamijou and Stiyl in turn with a complicated expression. Kamijou wished he wouldn't look at him like that.

Index, her head still crooked in bafflement, asked, "So what is the decoding method for the *Book of the Law* like?"

"Ah, yes. I'll give you an explanation now."

At her question, Orsola smoothly and steadfastly began their conversation again.

A bead of sweat broke out on Kamijou's forehead.

He had thought it a pipe dream this whole time, but now that it was becoming real right before his eyes, he sensed the risks he hadn't given much thought to come rushing to mind one after the other.

Kamijou alone (ironically enough) truly understood from personal experience how dangerous these angelic techniques, which were no more than rumors and speculations for sorcerers, could really be. The "purge" that one of the archangels, the Power of God, had tried to unleash would have burned half the planet to a crisp with billions of bullets of light.

If they could use those here, it would completely change the situation.

But...

Was it really all right for *anyone* to possess such immense power?

Orsola read Kamijou's expression. "We are not saying we will use the *Book of the Law*'s power. We simply need to display our intent and ability to decipher and use it. I would much rather not use such a power," she explained seriously.

That's right—her reason for originally studying the book was about the seal on the knowledge within. Orsola wouldn't have wanted things to turn out this way, and even if they broke out of here for the moment, sorcerers around the world who desired the book's knowledge might begin going after her.

She had made this decision having considered all that.

She would take action she didn't wish to take. She had considered the dangers therein and yet still she said she would lend her power to Kamijou and the others.

The method to decipher the *Book of the Law*, a method no one in history had ever broken.

The very moment they unlocked the forbidden tome that not even Index, who contained 103,000 of them, could read...

"It's based on Temurah—in other words, a character replacement method. However, the rules are abnormal in that they are strongly related to the line number. First, you arrange the twenty-two characters used in Hebrew into two lines, then note the line number above each—"

Kamijou had absolutely no clue what she was talking about, but it all probably meant a lot to Index. Her face was more serious than he'd ever seen it.

Right now, the knots in the grimoire nobody could read were coming undone in Index's head one by one, being rebuilt as the blueprints for an ultimate weapon. As he thought about how mysterious it was, he got a chill—had they done something they would never be able to take back?

"—in other words, the character conversion pattern changes based on which line number of the character's page it's written on, so while it may look quite intricate, you understand the rules for sentences on the same line number don't change even depending on the page number, right? In addition—"

"You would take the phrases," interrupted Index suddenly, "converted by using the line number character conversion pattern, then match it up with the page number and change their orders. Then, finally, you'd come out with a single sentence. The title would be *The End of Two Ages*, and its contents outline physical angelic techniques in Enochian." It was as though Index had anticipated what she knew, and Orsola blinked her eyes in surprise. "That's enough, I understand it now."

Orsola, whose explanation was cut off in the middle—she should have been the only one who knew of this—paused in puzzlement. "Excuse me, but what is it that you understand?"

"Right," grunted Index.

"This isn't the correct method. It's a dummy answer set up to trap people."

"Wha...," started Orsola, her entire body freezing for a moment.

Index, though, looked her in the face with a truly pained expression. "I'm sorry. I got this far, too. Actually, there are tons of other dummies, too. That's what's scary about the *Book of the Law*." She exhaled. "There are more than a hundred ways to decode it. And each of them gives you different sentences. They're all dummies. It isn't that nobody can read this grimoire—it's that everyone can actually read it, but everyone gets lured in to a false decoding method."

"B..."

But..., she squeaked.

"It's set up so that even incorrect decoding methods give you readable sentences. So even if you come up with an incorrect one, you'll think that it's the right one. It stinks, but maybe there was no way you could have realized it. There is a sentence in English written on the front cover of the book—do you remember it?" Index's face looked like she was struggling to convey the harsh truth. "*There is no law beyond Do what thou wilt.* In other words, the decoding 'laws' one thinks are correct will lead to an infinite number of *mistaken* correct answers. It's a terrifying grimoire."

All hope vanished from Orsola Aquinas's face.

It was only natural. She had risked her life to take on this challenge, believing that the knowledge she acquired would make everyone happy, and vowing that they would one day be able to destroy the original copies of grimoires—the root of all evil.

*   *   *

The decoding method, her greatest treasure, dear to her heart, could do nothing.

Not destroy the original grimoire and not rescue her allies from this terrible situation—nothing.

"Depending on how ya look at it, this may have saved us. Hey, think if we tell 'em we don't know how to decode the thing after all, they'd let us off the hook?"

As Tatemiya finished his question, there was a *boom* and the church doors shook.

"I...don't think so. They can't retreat now that we've seen so much of what's happening behind the scenes," answered Stiyl, giving a thin smile to the hopeless situation.

There was no longer anything to be done.

Their hope was lost to eternity, having never gotten it in the first place.

We need to run away, thought Kamijou, feeling an intense panic. He went to guide Index and Orsola to the back door, but then he ran into Stiyl, his flame sword at the ready. His "certain kill" rune cards scattered helplessly all over the floor.

Ba-bam!! With a much louder impact, the doors of the Church of Final Anointment were destroyed and slammed down into the floor. As Kamijou and the others exchanged two or three words, into the church that carried out the ceremonies concerning funerals came hundreds of sisters all in jet-black, hoisting their religious weapons, flooding in like an avalanche.

4

Ten more minutes had passed.

Only their leader, Agnes Sanctis, stood in the darkness-enclosed Church of Matrimony. The ten sisters assigned to her guard had looked about to be crushed by the tension, so she had relieved them of their duty and ordered them to join the fray. It would have been more dangerous to head out directly to the battle, but the girls all went to the battlefield with bright expressions. They would still have been bound by a considerable, unseen fear.

There's no need for them to be in a hurry. Why are they so tense?

Remembering the faces of her cowardly subordinates made her sigh. She could still hear explosions and clashing from outside the building, but her face harbored no unease. With experience, one could understand the situation by sound alone: the fact that unlike earlier, the enemy's unity was now in shambles and they were completely on the defensive.

What's this?

Suddenly, her ears caught an odd noise that didn't fit into the rhythm of the battle.

It was one set of footsteps, and their owner threw open the double doors of the church.

Bang!! came the loud sound.

There stood Touma Kamijou, but Agnes Sanctis's face didn't show a hint of change. In fact, she almost seemed to be smiling. Unlike how he'd done the same thing before, his face was plastered with exhaustion and his body covered with wounds.

"No matter how I think about it, though, with that many people against you, you shouldn't have been able to move freely around here," remarked Agnes, resting her back casually against a marble pillar.

Kamijou smiled, his breath ragged. "Well...we made a little plan."

"A plan? Oh." She closed one eye. "I get it, I see! Is that so? After all that acting cool when you came in here last time, you ended up using your allies as decoys, didn't you? It's true—our forces are spread evenly to attack all of you, so nobody should have been able to get here, hmm?"

"..." He remained silent at the meaningful end to her sentence.

Agnes smiled gleefully—she had hit the bull's-eye. "Ku-ku. Orsola Aquinas said something. That you act on faith rather than deceit, or something like that. A-ha-ha! What a laugh. In the end, you're only alive because you deceived your own allies and used them as decoys!"

"No." He answered her scornful voice with the direct opposite—a friendly smile. "I have faith in them—unlike you. There are things only they can do. I can't do them, so I got them to give me something else to do. That's all." He tightened his right fist. "Though I wish they could have a little more faith in me. I told them they didn't need to worry, and I could handle my own problems by myself."

"...So you told them you could stop the whole attack if you defeated me, their commander? Wow, I'm surprised you can still manage to remain so optimistic. Even though everyone thinks a flock of sheep without a shepherd will go batshit insane." She lifted her back from the cold marble pillar. She kicked her toes against her silver staff lying on the floor, then caught the flying weapon with one hand.

"Well, that's fine. I was just thinking I had some time to kill. Sloth is a sin, after all. I will destroy one of your illusions, one of your hopes—it will make a great diversion!"

Touma Kamijou checked around him.

There were about fifteen meters between him and Agnes. The building was under construction and thus empty, so there were no obstacles in the way. Despite all those people warring outside, only Kamijou and the girl were in this closed-off space.

She held a silver staff in her hand. The angel at the narrow staff's tip was designed like an angel curled up like Rodin's *The Thinker*, its six wings enclosing it like a cage.

Clack, clack, came the hard sounds.

Agnes Sanctis took off the thick soles on both her shoes and jumped backward.

"*Tutto il paragone. Il quinto dei cinque elementi, ordina la canna che mostra pace ed ordine!*"

She held the staff with both hands, and after intoning words of prayer, the angel on the end of the staff spread its wings, opening up like a flower. The six wings stopped at equal points of a circle, like a clock face.

"*Prima. Segua la legge di Dio ed una croce. Due cose diverse sono connesse!*"

She lightly swung her staff as she spoke.

Clack came the sound of its tip tapping against the marble pillar beside her.

…? Kamijou frowned to himself at the strike that had been made outside her range, when—

Whack!!

A moment later, Kamijou's vision had toppled ninety degrees to the side.

"Gah…! Agh?!"

By the time he'd realized something heavy and metal had hit him in the side of the head, he was already crumpled on the floor. He desperately shook his unsteady head and made sure he had a clear view; then Agnes, with the bottom of her twirling staff, hit the marble floor with a *takk*.

Right as Kamijou, shuddering with fear, rolled along the floor, an impact struck it where his head had just been a moment ago. The dull *wham* created depressions and fissures in the floor like a hammer had slammed into it.

A…coordinate attack? A skill that uses teleportation?

He didn't understand, but he figured he shouldn't be standing around. Meanwhile, Agnes removed a knife from her clothing. Then, as though plucking a guitar string, she began to hack away at her staff.

Grrk zzhh grrkk greee!! came the odd noises as Kamijou fled, something invisible slicing through the air behind him.

"That staff…?!"

"Ha-ha! I guess it *is* pretty obvious. It's a little *too* similar for my liking to the map magic Amakusa was gonna use. When I harm this, it harms something else in turn. And if I use it like *this*…!"

She pretended to draw the knife along it again, then flipped around the staff and struck the floor. A sudden impact came rushing at Kamijou from above, and with no way to fend it off, it landed unnaturally onto his left shoulder. *Bam!* came the heavy blow, echoing through the building.

"…?!"

He could probably nullify her attacks if he used the Imagine Breaker, but since he didn't know where these attacks were even *coming* from, he couldn't bring his right hand in line with them.

When he stopped, Agnes twirled the angel staff again and slammed it hard into the nearby marble pillar.

Oh…shit…!

He hastily jumped to the side. The only good thing about this was that her attacks lagged behind her command—albeit for less than a second—giving him some leeway. So he should have just needed to keep moving to dodge the attacks, but…

Ker-slam!!

The attack shouldn't have hit—but it sank into Kamijou's left arm and side all at once.

"Guh…!!"

The sideways blow sent Kamijou sliding down across the floor. In his sides, right from the core of his body, burst forth a stinging pain. His left arm had been between the point of impact and his sides, and yet the strike had slammed into both. Caught in the middle, a joint in his left arm might have been dislocated, since he couldn't seem to move it, and the sense of pain in it disappeared. It just felt a little sweaty and hot all over.

Agnes struck the tip of the staff against the floor.

Kamijou immediately rolled to the side, but the impact hit him straight in the chest anyway. He lurched, the oxygen in his lungs being forced out, and yet he still tried to scramble backward. Agnes took the chance to promptly slit her staff with the knife and deliver a diagonal cut to his back.

Rrrrrip came the sensation of strands of muscle being severed.

For some reason, there was a second before he felt the pain explode, like thunder after a lightning strike.

"Gah, bah…aaaaaaahhhhhhhhhhhhhhhhhhhhhh?!"

He writhed against the searing pain in his back—and Agnes

swung her staff across. As it collided with the marble pillar, it sent his body flying across the floor like a rock skipping across the surface of water.

"You're not gonna be able to keep making those dull dodges, you know." Agnes twirled her staff, disappointed. "Maybe there's a little gap between my command and its activation, but I just have to work that into where I attack to eliminate the possibility of error. If I consider how you'll dodge and *set up* my mine attacks in the air where you'll dodge, you'll run straight into them! It's no secret. Didn't you realize my misses earlier were just my feeling you out?"

Kamijou moved his head, burning with pain, and managed to listen to what she said. He wobbled to his feet, paying attention to his stinging back.

Agnes already seemed sure she'd win. She rested her cheek on the staff she was so proud of. "Modern western magic uses weapons symbolizing the five elements: fire, wind, water, earth, and aether. Did you know that? Fire is symbolized by the staff, wind by the short sword, water by the goblet, and earth by the discus. They're called *aspected weapons.*" She gave a smirk. "This Lotus Wand I'm holding is the symbolic weapon for aether. It has some interesting traits. It's special because while it can manipulate aether, it can also be used as a weapon for any of the other four elements."

Swish! She swung the staff diagonally down.

The moment it collided with the floor, Kamijou felt a chill and jumped directly backward. But even that had factored into her plans, as a strike from right over him impacted him in the head. His knees gave way under him. He had been shaken to his very core.

He could blindly swing his right hand around all he wanted—but every time, as if laughing at him, a hit would get him in the gut from a different direction. His vision slowly blinked on and off. His legs had already started to give way.

Gh...gah...Damn it, I could erase it if I touched it. If I could only touch it. What do I do? How do I see where Agnes's attacks are coming from? How they're angled? I can get the timing at least, but...

Kamijou's face becoming one of desperation, Agnes curled up her lips in enjoyment. "The five elements grant everything in creation its form. What do you think happens when you apply this concept to Idol Theory? That grimoire library said so before, didn't she? Tadataka Inou's map is the same. Though all that had was a connection between the *map* and the *terrain*. The Lotus Wand applies to everything. *I can apply those laws to anything.* I can use the space itself, for example!"

Agnes smacked the pillar with her staff like a stake. Kamijou was slow to react, and a dull impact got him in the gut, sending him rolling backward. He tried to sit back up and finally realized that blood was dripping from his mouth.

He spat it out. "Urgh...gah......Damn. For someone who hates... the *Book of the Law* and all this magic stuff...you sure do use it plenty..."

Despite the fact that if she kept prattling on, he could recover his stamina, she didn't seem to particularly mind. "Ah-ha-ha. Angry 'cause you got beaten? The crosier used by high-ranking clergy was developed from the mace, a weapon used to bash enemies' armor in. What's wrong with using a tool for its original purpose? Ha-ha. Still, a steel cudgel being the symbol of peace and order? Makes me laugh."

Agnes stuck out her tongue, her expression enraptured, and licked the side of the staff. The odd sensation spreading through his body made him hastily leap back. She giggled at his reaction.

"Besides," she continued casually, "modern western sorcery, whose fundamentals were developed in the twentieth century, has all sorts of underhanded Crossist tricks built in, remember? As an alchemist might put it, I'm only using the unspoken depths of Crossism is all!"

She brought the staff down.

Kamijou immediately tried to dodge it, but his feet were lagging behind his conscious thought. There was a *thud* as the heavy impact knocked him in the back of the head.

"Agh...! I don't really...care what you say...I'm not a sorcerer."

"It's the same thing! You don't pray to God yet still receive His blessing. Such a thing mustn't be allowed. Of course not! We act for our own benefit. Why should our taxes get spent on people like you who never work? England and Amakusa are equally heretic scum. Any teachings other than those of the Roman Orthodox Church are no teachings at all! Those things don't even count as work. Anyway, you're a huge pain. Now stop complaining and accept a death on the assembly line!"

*Here it comes…*Kamijou gritted his teeth.

Agnes's attacks weren't as flashy as Stiyl's flame swords or Tatemiya's slashes, but nonetheless, he couldn't keep getting hit by them over and over again. His feet were shaking, letting him know that his limit was near.

He knew the attacks' timing.

If Agnes's attacks were magical, then he could erase them with the touch of his right hand.

So now.

If he could just figure out the angle and direction they would come from.

If he could accurately align his right hand with her attacks.

Here it comes!!

Agnes's face cleared and she swung the angel staff around like a conductor. Once again, his feet couldn't avoid the attack she'd placed in anticipation, one step ahead. He was blown back without any time to bring his right hand up, and he rolled onto the floor but used the momentum to spring back to his feet.

Bam! He channeled strength into his feet and dashed forward with all his might so that he could gain even one step.

There were about seven meters between them.

Kamijou's feet could carry him within range in two or three steps, but there was no panic on Agnes's face. She must have judged that if he were coming straight at her, he would be easy to anticipate. She gripped her angelic staff tightly with both hands and slammed it into the floor as though she were splitting a watermelon.

There was the heavy *wham* of a collision.

If the impact came straight down, it would crack his skull to pieces without a doubt.

However.

That attack...

Kamijou skidded to a halt.

She had anticipated his movement, one step ahead of him—so if he didn't take another step forward, it wouldn't hit him.

...It's the one I've been waiting for!!

Then, he took his clenched right fist and thrust it straight into the space *one step ahead of him.*

Pop!! There was a roar, like a balloon popping. There was a sensation, like an invisible, giant soap bubble breaking, and the attack that would have hit him was instead blown away without a trace.

"Huh?!"

Agnes, a professional, would have understood the strange thing that just happened better than Kamijou, an amateur.

He ran straight through the now-empty space like a bullet.

She hurried to swing her angel staff around.

But she couldn't get as much power as she wanted due to the unforeseen situation...

...Kamijou dove into range...

...Agnes's staff finally hit the marble pillar...

...Kamijou's head bounced to the side with a high-pitched noise...

...but still...

...but still, he never once opened that fist of his.

Crash!! went a sharp impact.

Agnes Sanctis's back slammed into the marble pillar behind her.

Her consciousness wavered.

Her mind was blanking out, slowly calling forth pieces of memories that she thought she'd sealed away.

Gh...ah...Am...Am I...?

Agnes desperately tried to hold them back, but the urge to vomit billowed up from her stomach like magma gushing forth, preventing her from doing so.

...going...back?

She remembered a back alley in Milan. All of the sun's light was stolen by the outward tourist city, and on the brick ground crawled people, mice, flies, and slugs, all together. A little gathering of the hopeless.

Back...there again?

Her memories burst. Their fragments tore at her heart. Behind a restaurant. Inside a garbage can. Wiping off the slugs crawling on the discarded meat. Brushing off the hairs of mouse corpses. Pulling off the detached wings of cockroaches. *Squish, squish. Squish, squish.* She chewed. She chewed. She chewed for all her days.

No...no...

Her whitening vision was recovered by her own words.

The weapon she'd been holding began to fall away from her exhausted, powerless fingertips. It was the knife she'd used to damage the angel staff. The symbol of her battle, the weapon to defeat enemies, fell from her hands and clattered to the floor.

However.

However, even without the knife, she would never, ever let go of this staff.

No, no! Like hell...I'll never...go back...!!

Gkk. She filled her hands with power, squeezing the silver staff as if to break it.

Her consciousness returned.

She regained her will to fight.

"""!"""

Touma Kamijou and Agnes Sanctis glared at each other.

There were about five meters between them. The distance could be spanned in the blink of an eye with either a close-range fist or a long-range staff. Their stare down was reminiscent of a sword showdown in a period film or a quick-draw contest in a western.

Sweat slowly dripped down both their cheeks...

Both their nerves and minds were stinging with heat...
Both their breathing had suddenly stopped...
"Hmph."
Then, Agnes gave a dissatisfied snort and suddenly broke her fighting stance with her staff. Moreover, she looked away from Kamijou and around at their surroundings.

It was an opportunity, but Kamijou wouldn't move so easily. He was searching for the danger that could be hidden within that opportunity. Agnes rolled her eyes back to him without moving her neck.

"I'm terribly sorry—you seem to be trying your hardest and all—but it looks like things are already over."

For a moment, he didn't understand what she said.
A few seconds later, he did.
There was no sound. The Church of Matrimony was now silent. Every single noise had stopped in its entirety. It was like he was standing alone in the middle of a closed movie theater by himself—the silence was deafening, piercing into his chest.

And it wasn't only because he and Agnes had stopped moving.
Outside...

The Roman Orthodox sisters, a whopping two hundred and fifty women strong—and the mixed force of English Puritans and Amakusa, barely numbering more than fifty. There were supposed to be more than three hundred combined outside this Church of Matrimony, and yet the sounds and echoes surrounding them had altogether disappeared.

That fact meant that...
It meant...
"
....
......................."

Stinging pains burst forth over Kamijou's entire body.
As though to put an eternal end to that pain, Agnes Sanctis made another declaration. "It would seem that you all decided that they

would hold out as decoys while you defeated me, the leader...," she said—ridiculing him, berating him, and in the end a little sympathetic—"...but it looks like things have ended far more plainly than the illusion you were chasing after."

Kamijou heard those words.

He listened to them, forgetting even to breathe.

The energy left his tightened fist. His reason for fighting vanished. He stood there dazed, as though wanting to say he no longer even had a reason to be standing here.

People's faces edged their way across the back of his mind.

Then, as though crushing them with his teeth, he declared, "Yeah..."

Then, at the end, *with absolute conviction*, he declared,

"You're right. Your illusion is over now, Agnes Sanctis."

Her face creased into a confused frown.

Bang!! Behind Kamijou, the double doors to the Church of Matrimony flew wide open.

Agnes Sanctis, looking directly at him, saw it from over his shoulder.

Timidly, fearfully, she saw what was there.

The silhouettes entering through the Church of Matrimony's entrance—they were not the subordinates familiar to her but the Index of Prohibited Books and Stiyl Magnus from English Puritanism, along with Saiji Tatemiya from Amakusa-Style Crossism cradling Orsola Aquinas in his arms, and behind him his colleagues.

And there was one more.

Standing beside Stiyl, a humanoid monster cloaked in orange flame.

Agnes did not know the identity of the monster.

If one who did saw it, they would have called it by this name:

The Witch-Hunter King, Innocentius.

A behemoth of fires blazing more than three thousand degrees Celsius. It was the last thing one would ever see, housed in a cycle of explosion and rebirth. It melted and reduced to ash all attacks and obstacles to destroy its enemy. It was an attack spell of a battle-lover who held true to his belief that the best defense was a good offense.

However, even if one who knew of the technique had seen it, they still would have doubted their eyes.

It was no longer the ordinary Innocentius. Its flames were denser and its presence more intimidating. The waves of heat flooding from its body warped the air surrounding it, giving an illusion of countless transparent wings growing from the giant's back.

"Cards used—four thousand three hundred," said the red-haired priest lightly, as though singing. "Not so many, in terms of numbers...but still, Amakusa isn't anything to shake a stick at. They made an even larger diagram using the rune cards' positions, used the diagram to transform the magical meaning of the entire area, then converted the whole Church of Orsola into one enormous magic circle. Though we did exclude this building from its effective scope so his right hand wouldn't interfere...A magic circle constructed with multiple layers, using every object here—I doubt I could learn such cheap tricks." Stiyl gazed in satisfaction at the flames roaring mightily upward. "I had everyone help me place the cards. Well, it was already nearly completed—just needed them to fit the last pieces into the jigsaw puzzle, as it were. Oh, come to think of it, I haven't introduced myself yet, have I? I'm not as good at making assaults on one place after another—I'm much better at creating a single point of control and defending it. Certain circumstances led me to desiring such sorcery."

She could see outside through the wide-open doors. Magical flames littered the flat, flora-less, stone courtyard, and sisters in black habits were lying there as if to cover it up.

Their bodies didn't appear to have been carbonized or badly burned.

The explosions they'd heard probably came from the flame monster. It had unleashed shock waves at the sisters and mowed them down dozens at a time.

Everyone who had fallen seemed only to be passed out.

There would have been barely one-fifth of all of the sisters who had been beaten into incapacitation. But perhaps that evidenced the destructive power of Innocentius—the sisters still holding their weapons had distanced themselves and were grinding their teeth. They must have seen that if they drew near without due caution, the explosive winds and flames would eat them alive.

"What did I tell you? We had a plan." Kamijou smiled savagely. "They weren't running all over the place to be decoys. They just needed to set up Stiyl's secret weapon and put cards all over the church, that's all...I don't know how any of it works, though, since I'm no sorcerer myself."

With the Imagine Breaker in Kamijou's right hand, he couldn't help with the work of spreading the runic cards. That's why he shouldered the responsibility of going after Agnes alone. So that he wouldn't destroy the runes—their true goal—he made Agnes misunderstand that he had gone for her, prepared to die, and having used everyone as decoys.

Even without the detailed explanation, Agnes seemed to have guessed the particulars.

As well as what she needed to do now.

Without falter, still hoisting her staff, she shouted to the sisters outside.

"What are you all doing?! We still have a decisive numbers advantage! These pests are insignificant before a combined attack!!"

She was right.

No matter how they looked at it, the numbers difference between the Roman Orthodox and Kamijou's group was absolute. The only reason they were still alive was their scrambling to use all sorts of clever schemes. If they created an encirclement so they couldn't escape then attacked all at once, they would easily win. However many dozens of sisters were slain in the process, more than a hundred more would march over their corpses and crush Kamijou and the others.

Stiyl, a professional sorcerer, was *not* engaging in killing—but that, too, was only because if he was slaughtering them, it would cause the sisters to panic, thus creating the danger of all of them attacking, prepared for their own destruction...or that *should* have been why, anyway. Because with that kind of spell, it was more difficult *not* to kill the enemy.

And yet...

Despite the sisters having an overwhelming numerical advantage, they did not move.

"What are you...?!"

Agnes thought about yelling angrily at her subordinates for not understanding basic logic, but somewhere inside, she had realized it, too.

A doubt.

Though the sisters understood the logical thing to do, somewhere in their minds they couldn't have faith in it. Should they fight or should they flee—their minds looked fixedly at the swaying scales before them. If even one of them moved, their group psychology would cause an immediate change in the flow.

Agnes Sanctis recalled the words of Orsola.

—*Those people...they act on faith.*

—*How ugly the Roman Orthodox Church is compared to them.*

"...That's...pretty funny."

She looked down, tightening her jaw so firmly her molars might break.

If the scales were settled in a precarious equilibrium, then she just needed to force them to tip. She would only crush the one before her, Kamijou, and show her superiority to them.

Even if she used the sisters to defeat Kamijou, it would not display an overwhelming dominance. But this was the same for Kamijou as well. If he clung to his friends to take down Agnes, he would be displaying his panic, his tension, his fear—and his inferiority. If he did that, the sisters' minds would be freed from restraint and they would be upon them like an avalanche.

In other words, it was one on one.

Touma Kamijou in one corner, and Agnes Sanctis in the other.

More than three hundred people in all surrounded them, but they were exceedingly alone.

Five meters were between them.

He was, of course, within the angelic staff's range. But it would easily be within his fist's territory with a tiny bit of effort. It was fifty-fifty—in other words, the one whose attack reached first would gain the honor of delivering the final blow.

What…do I do…?

She edged back and forth, gauging the distance, but on her brow was a bead of sweat.

Would her attack hit first?

Don't panic, she told herself, swallowing those words down. A simple clenched fist was no match for the convenience of her Lotus Wand. If she read his next attack and made one full swing, she'd demolish this *civilian* in one fell swoop.

What do I do…What should…What…?

But was it all right for her to leave everything up to the safe way—the full swing? What if he dodged it? And worst of all, what if she misread him and put it in the wrong place? No, she should use many smaller, faster attacks as insurance, then make her swing once he had stopped. But what if those smaller attacks were insufficient to stop him—what if he just dove straight in anyway?

But, well, no—however, still…But nonetheless, that notwithstanding…

The negative sentences continued to pile up.

In the end, she couldn't decide on how best to play her many trump cards.

The method…the timing, the weapon…the steps…what the hell do I choose?!

And in contrast…

In contrast, Touma Kamijou would not falter in using his own trump card. He already had all his force in the fist at his right, entrusting to it his entire life and not an iota less.

He had faith.

Faith that however much he was hurt, however close to death he tread…

Faith in the weapon he had, faith that the way he used his weapon was correct, faith that he would doubtlessly see his weapon defeat the enemy, faith in that outlook, waiting for the beautiful, victorious future ahead.

Touma Kamijou had faith—and that's why he could act.

"It's over, Agnes," he said without falter. "You've figured it out yourself, haven't you? Your illusion of confidence—it was destroyed a long time ago."

Stiyl plucked the cigarette out of his mouth and flung it carelessly to the side.

The orange light arced through the air out of the corner of their eyes, and the moment it hit the ground, it marked the start of the battle.

Bam!! Fierce footsteps.

Touma Kamijou tightened his fist like a wrecking ball and launched toward Agnes without waver.

What...What should I...Ah, ahhhhhhhhhhhhhhhhhhhhhhhhhhhhhh?!

Something in Agnes Sanctis's mind burst open then.

The moment of their clash was nigh before her eyes now, and yet the swaying scales never, ever, ever, ever delivered a conclusion. Agnes, pressed to make a choice but without having a satisfying answer, swung her staff with all her might, her face almost looking like she was about to cry.

One who bet everything on one last attack—and one who hesitated at that moment about what to bet.

The superior of the two did not need to be said.

Ger-slam!! A fierce impact.

Agnes's body flew into the air, grazed the marble pillar behind her, and plunged to the floor.

The heavy impact tore the angelic staff from her hands. As her body bounced many meters away across the floor, the wind all came out of her and she finally stopped moving.

Then she lost consciousness.

With that, the balance between Index, Stiyl, and the others and the Roman Orthodox sisters surrounding them had tipped all the way to one side. One of the sisters, convinced they couldn't win, dropped her weapon to her feet—and then the sound of another, and yet another came, until finally it was like a torrent of noise.

The battle was over.

The fist of a single boy had laid low an enemy numbering more than two hundred.

EPILOGUE

The Closing Move

The_Page_is_Shut.

Kamijou hadn't sustained as much damage as he'd thought.

His spotty memory started to force hazy blurbs together.

He knew he had collapsed in the Church of Matrimony, and that Index had shouted and run over to him; he remembered being in an ambulance; he remembered there being a bunch of time with special response or documentation or something; he remembered being diverted and brought into Academy City instead. He had promptly passed out when the frog-faced doctor looked at him, and he had awakened from his sleep on a soft, fluffy bed.

Same hospital as usual, huh? Ugh, damn it, I can tell just by how the room smells..., he thought, eyes closed and mind foggy, before suddenly realizing someone was nearby. A quiet breathing and slight rubbing of clothing reached his ears. He felt a warm, soft hand lightly stroking his bangs.

"Tsuchimikado got a good laugh out of it..."

He heard someone's voice.

"...but I still think this is fine."

Her tone sounded a little reluctant, as though parting with him. The hand stroking his bangs stopped without a noise and retreated from his head. The warmth of her palm faded.

Kamijou managed to slowly open his profusely heavy eyelids.

"Hm...Kanzaki?"

"Oh, did I wake you? I was just about to get going."

Kanzaki pulled back just a little bit in surprise at hearing his voice. It seemed she'd been sitting in the pipe chair for visitors beside the bed until now, looking at him.

He sat up in the bed and shook his head to shake off his sleepiness.

It looked like it was dawn. The fluorescent lights in the dark hospital room were off, and the glow of the morning sky filtered in through his window like the sunlight through leaves. On the small table next to his bed was an expensive-looking box of candy and a note she must have planned on leaving for him. As Kamijou's eyes drifted around, Kanzaki slowly stood up from the chair. She must not have been planning to stay long.

"...Oh..."

Kamijou hazily started getting his mind's gears in motion. He looked at Kanzaki again—she was wearing her usual outfit, a short-sleeved T-shirt tied at her waist so you could see her navel and jeans with one leg cut off so you could see her thigh. Her shirt being tied like that accentuated her already large chest, and you could see dangerously far up her thigh, up to where it started—*sexy as usual*, he thought, but he knew he'd be punched in the face if he said it out loud. He turned his attention to something else, eyeing the note on the side table.

"For now, you left a note...?"

As soon as he said it, *bwshh!* Kanzaki's hand shot out at a terrible speed and snatched away the small scrap of paper. It was an impossible new record by sports engineering principles. Her face turned bright red and her eyes wandered to and fro, and she started to sweat as she crushed the note up with extreme speed.

"I-it was nothing much. Now that I have the chance to talk to you directly, leaving a note is unnecessary, right?"

"??? But—"

"It is fine already. It would have been embarrassing the moment I saw you read it."

Kanzaki went to throw the balled-up note into the trash can, but then changed her mind and stuffed it into her pocket instead. *She*

must really not want anyone to read that, he thought, baffled. She put a hand to her abundant chest, took a deep breath, and her expression returned to normal.

"What of the condition of your body?"

"Well… There's still some of the anesthetic left in my system, so I can't really tell where it hurts."

"I'm sorry. There are…less than scientific healing methods involving eating that Amakusa has, but it seems they don't work very well on you."

"… What are you apologizing for? You can heal wounds by eating sushi and hamburgers and stuff? Wow, Amakusa is awesome—it's just like healing items in RPGs."

"Huh…?" replied Kanzaki with an uncharacteristically vague and confused expression, not quite understanding his simile.

"By the way, where did Stiyl get to?"

"He has left the city already. He said something about not wanting to stay very long in a place he couldn't buy cigarettes. He complained about the age verification here being too strict for him to get any, too."

It's supposed to be like that everywhere, retorted Kamijou to himself. "Can't he just get you to buy some for him?"

"I am only eighteen as well, so I cannot buy cigarettes."

....
....

"Why do you look like you don't believe me? Why are you pretending to clean out your ears?"

"You're lying! You can only fake your age so much with that body! You've got to be past marriageable age at this pooiiii-eeeeeeee?!"

Before he could finish, a light-speed punch from Kanzaki shot toward his face and stopped. He trembled—he couldn't even prepare for that one.

In a calm voice, she said, "I'm eighteen."

"Eighteen, yes! A high school girl, and yet adulthood is within reach! *Miss* Kanzaki!!"

Kamijou desperately smiled, his teeth clattering loudly. Kanzaki gave a very tired sigh and pulled her fist back.

"...I feel like perhaps I should have let you have the note. Our conversation won't get to the important part at this rate."

"Important part?"

"Yes, a debriefing, or what have you...I came to notify you of what became of Orsola Aquinas, but should I not have bothered?"

"Tell me! Please!!" Kamijou replied instantly, leaning forward.

Kanzaki relaxed her shoulders a bit at how willing he was to discuss the topic. "It's been decided that both Orsola Aquinas and Amakusa's main force have been incorporated into the English Puritan Church. This is largely to prevent any revenge or assassination attempts by the Roman Orthodox Church."

Kamijou recalled Agnes and the sisters under her command. "So then Orsola will still be in danger?"

"No. Behind the scenes, they might make it look like they're after her, but behind *that* it probably wouldn't have much meaning to go after her. The English Puritans have announced to the world of magic that Orsola's decryption method was false. They believe Orsola won't have to worry about being pursued for the *Book of the Law* now that people know it was a mistranslation."

So if Orsola then really *had* broken the book's code, everyone in the world would be after her now. *Definitely a lucky break*, thought Kamijou with a cold sweat.

"Hm? Wait, Amakusa's gonna be under the English Puritan Church's umbrella now, right?"

"Yes. However well hidden their base is, there's nothing in it for them to directly oppose the Roman Orthodox Church. I swear—there's evidence that deep down, they *wanted* this to happen. For example...do you remember the T-shirt Saiji Tatemiya was wearing? It was white, and there was a distorted red cross on it."

"...Was there? I guess you're right, come to think of it."

"There was. The red cross is the symbol of Saint George—the symbol of English Puritanism. He was probably fighting while dressed in it to show his intention to come to me, the English Puritans, or something. I thought I'd given them strict orders not to follow me."

"I see...," said Kamijou, impressed. "You're part of English Puritanism, too."

Kanzaki said, "I swear," again under her breath. He wondered if she realized her face looked like a mother looking at a child who couldn't be without his parents.

"But are you, like, personally okay with that? Amakusa's pretty small, but they're an independent group, right? It seems like they're being merged into a big corporation."

"They may be affiliated now, but it's not as though we told them to abandon their Bible and teachings. It is more akin to a group of samurai being employed to a feudal lord. The framework of Amakusa will still be around. And Amakusa has always been a denomination that changes form to most suitably match the time period and hide from history. They don't need to worry about remaining in their current form, so as long as they can live in peace, it doesn't matter what happens."

In spite of that, Kanzaki had, without any hesitation, let go of the tiny society she had reigned over as leader before, for the sake of those she had to protect. Getting a glimpse of that side of her made Kamijou think how cool grown-ups were. She seemed eighteen, but from his point of view, eighteen was enough to be an adult all your own.

As he turned that over in his mind, Kanzaki lowered her head, her posture formal.

It wasn't a cute little bob of the head—she kept it down and said, "Umm, well, that is, I'm sorry for all this."

"Huh? Uh, about what? Why are you bowing? What are you sorry for?"

Kamijou's head wasn't working quite right, since he'd just woken up—so the sight of a girl bowing to him like this was extremely scary. The feeling that he'd done something really bad overtook him.

Then Kanzaki spoke. "Well, I mean, that i-is," she stammered, unusual for her, "I caused you a lot of trouble for, well, personal reasons, and..."

It seemed like she wasn't used to saying these words at all. Kamijou, in his daze, plucked out of the situation only the core fact that she seemed to be troubled by something. "Wait, sorry, Kanzaki. Did I cause you some kind of trouble? I'll apologize, so—"

"N-no, that's not it. If you were to apologize now, that would put me in a truly awkward situation. Umm, it isn't that—so getting back to the topic, what I mean is…"

Whatever it was, it must have been pretty hard for her to say. Kanzaki twirled a finger through her bangs, preventing her own words from coming out of her mouth.

Then, the moment she seemed to make up her mind and say something, the door to the hospital room flew open with a *bang*—despite it being daybreak—and without a knock.

It was a tall man with blue sunglasses and a Hawaiian shirt.

Motoharu Tsuchimikado was swinging around a plastic bag with something that must have been a get-well present. "Hmm, hmm, hmm!! Kaaammyyy, I came to play! I couldn't afford an entire melon, so you'll have to make do with a premium pudding dessert from the convenience store with melon slices on top."

Kamijou looked over, away from Kanzaki and toward Tsuchimikado. "Yo. Isn't school starting in a couple hours? Shouldn't you be sleeping—Oh, sorry, Kanzaki. What were you trying to say?"

Urk—she flinched at that. Then, giving a sidelong glance to Tsuchimikado, she emitted an aura implying she didn't want to have to say it in front of him—why must he have come at this exact time?

"Ohhh. What's wrong, Zaky? Did I come right when you were finally gonna beg forgiveness from Kammy? I bet you're gonna say somethin' real clichéd, like, *I'll repay you for all the trouble I've caused* or *I'll do anything you want*, yeah? Pfft—dah-ha-ha-ha!! Hey—it's the crane paying her debts with erotica!"

"Th-that's not it! Who would spout such nonsense to this ignorant child?!"

"…This…ignorant…child…"

Kamijou hung his head, almost hearing a gong ringing in the background, and Kanzaki twitched.

"Uh, no, that isn't what I wanted to…I only said that to make Tsuchimikado take back his rude words, but the part about repaying my debts was, well…"

"But Zaky, you're gonna end up stripping, right?"

"I-I will not strip! And what do you mean *end up*?!"

"Oh? Then you're going for the whole wearing-whatever-clothes-he-wants-as-an-apology thing? You sure do know how to treat your patrons right."

"Would you be quiet for a moment?! You're making this more and more and more annoying with all your messed-up interpretations!!"

Kamijou absently watched them from afar as they reveled (from his point of view) in their yelling match, but suddenly the gears in his mind all clicked in a weird place.

…Wear whatever clothes…as apology…?

N-no, I can't—Kanzaki looks like she's being pretty serious and stuff, so I can't fool around like that now, come on, you know what'll happen if you make her dress in a swimsuit like the dumb one Index was wearing at the beach this summer, it only takes five seconds to realize what a crazy delusion that is, go away, go away!!

"…You look like you're overheating over there."

"No, it's nothing, really! I mean really—if a man like me even brought something like that to the register, it would mean the end of my life as Touma Kamijou, so I wasn't thinking about anything like that at all!!"

"???" Kanzaki struggled to understand the ambiguity and tilted her head. Tsuchimikado, however, grinned. "Heh-heh-heh. Now, what is thy desire?! A full-on ear-cleaning from an older, motherly lady while resting your head on her lap?! Or a surprisingly cute little bento from an older sister–like figure?!"

"Stooop! Our dumb conversations are one thing, but don't go exposing all my weak spots in front of a girl like this!!"

"Tsuchimikado. I do not understand the situation, but it appears that you are only stimulating an injured person in a negative way, so I'll have to ask you to leave the room."

"A-and what are you gonna do when it's just the two of you? Wait, could it be?!" Tsuchimikado's eyes flashed. "Is this the scene where you gently feed him little apple slices cut to look like rabbits?! I'm sorry, I had no idea!"

"No, it isn't! Please don't arbitrarily get on my nerves with your arbitrary interpretations!"

"Wait, what, then you're gonna do it mouth-to-mouth? You know, when you do that in real life it's kinda gross."

"Please just shut up and get out of here!!"

After she shouted so loudly he couldn't even imagine what Saiji Tatemiya's face (or anyone like him) would look like, Tsuchimikado grinned and jumped out of the hospital room.

Suddenly the early morning silence covered the room again.

As Kamijou watched Kanzaki's shoulders moving up and down in heavy, angry breathing, he trembled and thought, *Tsuchimikado, oh Tsuchimikado. I think you said all that stuff because you were trying to lighten the situation a little, but you left things a bit unfinished here!*

"E-excuse me, Kanzaki? A-are you quite all right?"

"...What is it? Why are you speaking so formally?"

"I-I'm sure you know this, but all that stuff about repaying your debts and borrowing and lending, that was all just Tsuchimikado's dumb jokes, you know?"

Kamijou had braced himself to be yelled at the same way Tsuchimikado had been, but surprisingly, Kanzaki answered in a stammering voice. "B-but I...What else would you have me do...? You're a civilian, someone I should have been protecting from the beginning—but I caused you to suffer all these wounds. Even I understand that this is far past the realm of just bowing and saying sorry. So..."

Her voice got weaker and weaker as her sentence got longer, as though her own words were sticking into her. Once again, she started playing with her bangs with a fingertip—maybe it was an unexpected nervous habit of hers. After that, she violently rubbed her temples like she was exhausted and breathed a heavy sigh.

Kamijou thought her actions looked kind of like a writer crumpling up a failed work and throwing it in the garbage.

Personally, he would have preferred the post-incident stuff *not* to drag out very long, and for her to just say, "Nice job out there, see ya! ♪" like Tsuchimikado might, then leave. But it didn't look like Kanzaki's morals would allow her to do that.

There was no choice. Kamijou sighed.

He switched mental gears over to something a little more serious.

"Wait, so, was this the important part?"

"Yes. I have this predisposition to cause trouble for others, but I've been causing you one issue after another after another, putting so much weight on your shoulders. Every time I've shrunk away from it. And this time, it wasn't just me—I got you mixed up in our problems in Amakusa as a whole…"

"Hmm. But is there really any need to worry about it? We settled our problems just fine—everyone's safe. I don't think any of us really got any more hurt than anyone else."

Kanzaki looked surprised. She blinked a few times, then said, "Our…?"

"Huh? Yeah, mine and Amakusa's. Oh, uh, I guess English Puritanism's, too. And Orsola and Index and Stiyl, and you, too. That's what I meant by *our*."

"…" Kaori Kanzaki listened to those words, flustered.

It was like a difficult problem she could never have solved had been figured out right in front of her in the blink of an eye.

"What're you so surprised about? I'm an amateur, so England and Rome might have problems and stuff but I honestly don't see them as much different. What I want to say is that the opinion of this dumb, ignorant child is that groups of people don't matter."

In contrast, Kamijou continued to speak without thinking about it too hard—as if saying the problem was so easy it didn't need much deep thought.

"It's not like I'm taking sides with Index's church or anything. It just so happens that Index is part of English Puritanism, so I'm their ally for the moment."

He heard the pitter-patter of footsteps from down the hall.

That's probably Index, he thought absently, continuing—as though confirming whose side he should have taken.

"If Agnes asked me for help sometime, I'd probably go help her. She just happened to be the bad guy this time, but there's no rule saying she has to keep doing bad stuff," he declared, smiling.

Kanzaki made another surprised face, then smiled, a little worried.

The reason he had for acting was so immensely simple that it almost sounded absurd.

But because of that, Touma Kamijou would never stray from his path.

Never.

England didn't have a rainy season or a dry season—instead, the weather changed from one thing to the other fairly easily all year round. In this city, it was common knowledge that the weather could shift in just four hours, so there were plenty of people walking around in broad daylight with fold-up umbrellas.

For these reasons, a sudden shower was currently hitting the city of London after being clear not too long ago. Nevertheless, the people of the city didn't consider rain a reason to stay indoors. The road was already narrow, but it was packed to the brim with a rainbow of umbrellas.

As the rain, almost a faintly damp mist, came down, Stiyl Magnus and Laura Stuart walked along next to each other. His umbrella was black as a cockroach, while the one Laura held looked like a teacup, white with gold embroidery on it.

"If we're just going back to Lambeth Palace, we should have just called a taxi."

"Those who cannot take the rain cannot live in this conurbation," said Laura, gleefully spinning her umbrella around. There was no doubt, however, that he was biased. Stiyl wasn't currently enjoying this mist-like rain very much. He was getting wet despite having an umbrella, and it made his cigarette wet—it was nothing but bad things.

He glanced at the tip of the cigarette, which he was finding difficult to keep lit, and sighed.

At the moment, he was following Laura, who was on her way back to her residence, delivering his final report on a certain incident as they went. The great and powerful English Puritan archbishop was the freewheeling sort who went to the cathedral when she liked and went home when she liked. She didn't seem to like staying in one place very much, so it was quite often the case that reports and war councils would be held during these walks.

There was no helping that Stiyl thought it troublesome to set things up to prevent sudden attacks and monitoring. There was a little trick on their umbrellas even now, making the area around them function like a telephone booth. It caused the umbrellas' fabric to shake and converted those vibrations into voices, while at the same time making it so that the voices didn't leave the "frame" of the umbrellas.

"——That should give you a basic idea of the incident. They intend to settle by claiming this was an independent armed action conducted by Agnes Sanctis and two hundred fifty under her command. By making it something they did on their own, the Roman Orthodox Church seems to want to defend themselves by saying they never wanted to assassinate Orsola."

"If they cannot rein in their own subordinates, they cannot get away with nothing, however," said Laura, giving a wry grin and fingering her hair. Her beautiful hair could be called majestic, and with the raindrops forming spider thread–like patterns, it evoked fascination.

Stiyl gave a quick glance at her face next to him and said, "...Did you need to go that far?"

"Mm-hee-hee. Does it concern you, Stiyl? That I have welcomed into the English Puritan Church the esteemed Orsola Aquinas and the fellows in the Amakusa-Style Crossist Church?"

"We don't need to protect her—now that they're officially saying they had no intention of killing her, they can't recklessly bring harm to her now. If a sudden, unnatural death were to befall her in this situation, I believe it would escalate into an international Church problem."

"Then they needst only accomplish a natural death, I suppose." Laura gave a barbaric smirk like a pirate.

The difference between her face and her expression gave Stiyl pause. "Come to think of it, you knew the Roman Orthodox's true intention all along, didn't you? Why didn't you just order me to save Orsola Aquinas from the Roman Orthodox Church in the first place? What a pain."

"Not *everything*. I hadn't surmised so far as Orsola having mistaken the decoding method. But," she continued, "for me, either way would have been fine."

Stiyl looked at her.

She twirled her pure white umbrella. "Just hypothetically, Stiyl. If we had blundered in our deliverance of Orsola, would the situation have changed? If she had been returned to Rome, she would have been put to death. Whether we succeeded or failed, either way, the *Book of the Law* would not have been decoded.

"So it didn't matter which came to pass," she concluded.

Whether Orsola lived or died was a small problem and didn't concern her.

Stiyl exhaled, unsatisfied, and said, "Then why did you give me a personal order to give Orsola a cross? You gave me more to carry out in an already urgent situation. You can say what you want, but you intended to save her right from the beginning, didn't you?"

"Urk."

"The complete lack of reinforcements bothers me, too. You probably had a big Necessarius force positioned on the shoreline of the Sea of Japan, which is why you couldn't spare any personnel, right? You used the cross incident as an excuse and put them there to raid Agnes's forces while they were taking Orsola to Rome. You really are embarrassing, you know that?"

"Mmgh! Th-that is most certainly not factual! I interceded in this altercation purely for the English Puritan Church's benefit!!"

Laura spouted denials, looking like steam was going to come from her ears, but Stiyl didn't bother to argue. The fact that she was the only one who was angry must have really gotten to her, because her face rapidly reddened.

"So what are these benefits you're referring to?"

"...You're so quick to turn me aside. I mean Kaori Kanzaki," she moaned in a huff. "This incident served as a good example. Kanzaki has immense power, and because of her upstanding sense of justice, she could always take independent action. Despite naught having occurred this time, she was actually still in a fairly dangerous position. We needs must obtain a new set of shackles if we are to stop that from happening again."

The relaxation left Stiyl's face.

Laura's expression, too, had suddenly become more mature. "We canst not stop her with force, yes? Well, we could if we put our minds to it, but we would definitively sustain much damage as well. You have perused the report telling what fate befell those Knight fools, yes?"

Stiyl recalled the details of the report from the separate force.

Twenty-one fully equipped knights had planned on their own to kill the members of Amakusa, but somebody single-handedly drove them into submission.

"And that is why she needs shackles that don't involve force. She possesses an ample bond with Amakusa. Therefore, we cannot use negative shackles like threatening her harm if she does not listen, but rather positive ones, like offering her protection from the Roman Orthodox Church if she listens. If we emphasize such negativity involving Amakusa, she may rebel against us, but if we offer something positive, she wouldn't do so. Right? What a delicious benefit that is."

Laura smiled happily—and it gave Stiyl a cold shudder.

Though she might have seemed thoughtless at first, she was still the leader of English Puritanism, and the cruel administrator and constructor of the system of the Index of Prohibited Books.

She created the rule that they needed to erase her memories every year.

She created a body that required maintenance from the English Puritans.

She lied that it was beneficial to the Church to keep Index from turning traitor.

She lied that she would die if they didn't, thus keeping Stiyl and Kanzaki from rebelling as well.

No one was more used to tinkering with all of the scales deciding a person's sense of values—their emotions, their reason, their sense of profits and losses, their ethics—than she. It bolstered the caution Stiyl felt toward her once again, but he was well aware there was nothing he could do about it. If he were careless, Laura wouldn't flinch to give punishment—*not* to Stiyl, but to Index. That's the kind of person she was.

Thump—Stiyl's shoulder bumped into a passerby.

It was a student trying to worm his way in between the two of them.

Whoops. By the time Stiyl's body recoiled, Laura was nowhere to be found.

The communication spell connecting their umbrellas was already cut off.

He hurriedly looked around—what had she just done? He just barely spotted the white, teacup-like umbrella with gold embroidery far away. And the wave of people eventually swallowed up that, too, and it disappeared completely.

"…"

Stiyl, caught completely unawares by the whole business, gulped.

He got another chill at the sight of the enigmatic leader of all variety of suspicious sorcerers, and thought.

She had helped Amakusa to cleverly prevent Kaori Kanzaki from acting.

He understood that.

Then why, in the end, did she save Orsola Aquinas?

He didn't understand that.

The way Orsola came up with to decode the *Book of the Law* was just a mistake, so there was no need to go through with securing her anyway. And saving her didn't bind anyone to her like she was doing with Kanzaki. She may have been an accomplished missionary worker—great enough to have a church built in her name—but she didn't seem to have the sort of charismatic attitude that could bring together whole groups and organizations like Kanzaki did. If she had, they wouldn't have been able to easily plot to assassinate her out of fear of riots and secessions.

"...She's damn devious," said Stiyl spitefully.

If he were able to think of even *one* calculated reason she'd saved Orsola Aquinas, then he would have been able to assert positively that she was evil. But this was another thing about Laura that was difficult to deal with—there wasn't enough for him to go on to say whether she was a good person or a bad person. In fact, she practiced both good and evil equally—truly as though keeping them in perfect balance upon scales.

The scales, of course, wouldn't tip one way or the other. With such a precise equilibrium being maintained, one couldn't judge her to be good or evil—no matter how much weight rode on either tray.

Thus, Stiyl couldn't say one way or the other, so he ended up slinking along under the English Puritan Church.

Or maybe that was her plan, the runic sorcerer speculated briefly before disappearing into the drizzle on the city streets.

AFTERWORD

For those readers who can easily read seven books straight through—pleased to meet you. For those readers who have been sticking it out since volume one—it's nice to see you again.

This is Kazuma Kamachi.

I've just been going along, taking it easy, but before I knew it I'd come to the seventh volume. Today, on September 8, I'm going at a slow, steady pace as always. The series has been bringing you fights on an individual level, but this time there was a teeny bit of organized combat involved.

The occult keyword this time around was *grimoire*. Well, actually, I sort of felt like I should have brought the topic up before now, seeing as how the heroine is a whole library of them. In any case, I had grimoires show up in all sorts of ways and places here.

Other than that, I tried to greatly emphasize the unique traits each organization has. Please, mull over each one and the crazy attacks they use and thoughts, circumstances, and ideals they bear. It would make me happy.

Mr. Haimura, the illustrator, and Mr. Miki, the editor, you're always doing so much for me—I may not ever get anywhere, but please, I look forward to working with you in the future.

And to everyone who picked up this book to read—I may not ever, *ever* get anywhere, but please, I'd like it if you watched over me, humoring me, as I continue worming forward in my vain struggle.

Now then, as I thank you all for the good fortune I've had to publish seven whole volumes,

and as I hope I'll be able to continue writing more without stopping,

today, at this moment, I lay down my pen.

Whenever the subject is sorcery, Mikoto and Miss Komoe don't show up!

Kazuma Kamachi